I0637941

ANATHEMA

ANATHEMA

A NOVEL

JAMES COSGRAVE

MM

A MEQ MEDIA BOOK

First trade paperback edition August 2020
Simultaneously published in hardcover and ebook formats.

Jacket artwork by Lauren Budney © 2020 by Meq Media, Inc.

Published by Meq Media, Inc.
www.meqmedia.com

ISBN: 978-0-9992399-6-4 (hardcover), 978-0-9992399-7-1 (paperback), 978-0-9992399-8-8 (ebook)
LCCN: 2020909464

BISAC: Fiction/Gothic | Fiction/Thrillers/Psychological | Fiction/Thrillers/Suspense

Subjects: LCSH: Universities and colleges--Fiction | Secret societies--Fiction

Printed in the United States of America

For
Daphne

"I...have the reputation of being a wicked fanatic, I am told."

HENRIK IBSEN, *Rosmersholm*

RADCLIFFE COLLEGE

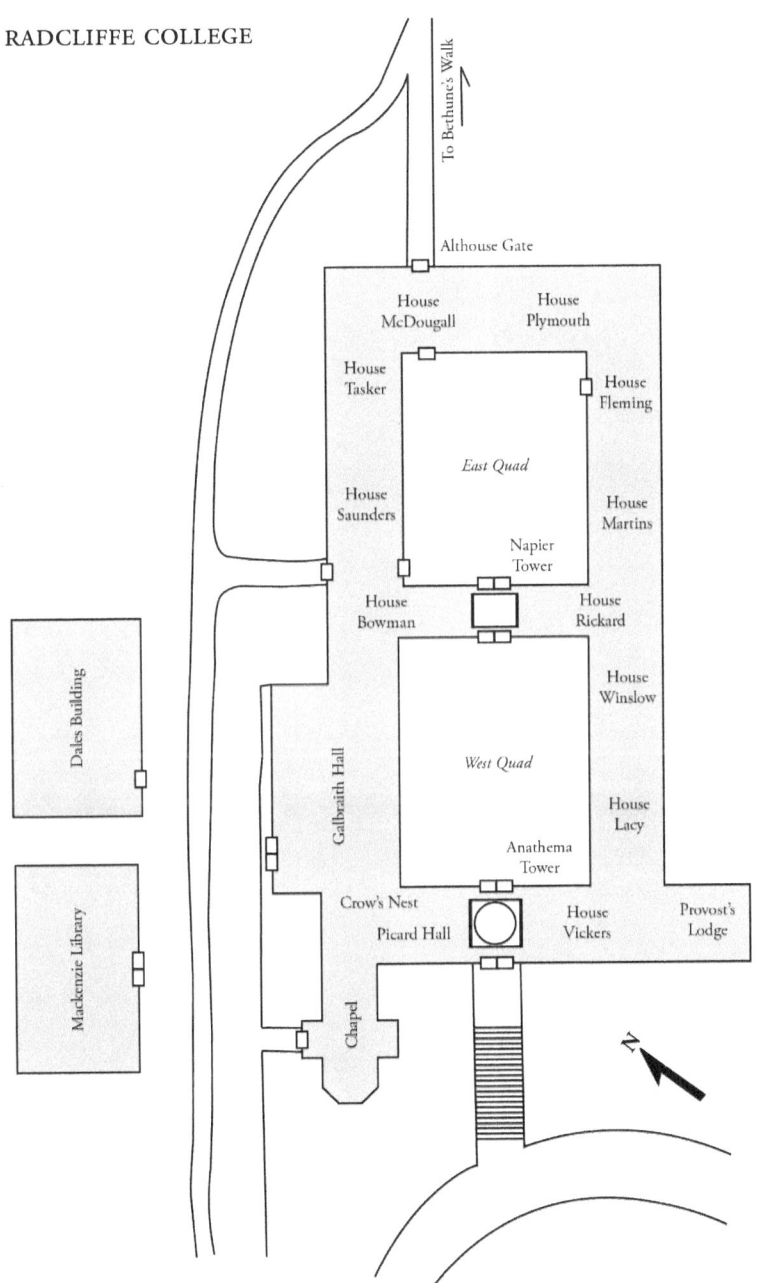

PART I
THE GRAND TRADITION

PROLOGUE

T HE BODY lay in the creek, facedown.

It belonged to a blond man in his early twenties, clad in a white polo shirt and navy jeans. His head rested against a rock breaching the surface of the stream; crimson trailed from where stone and skull met. His clothes were covered in dirt, and bloody scrapes marked his arms. The left rested partially on the embankment while the right stretched out into the brook, water coursing through his lifeless fingers.

The creek ran through a gully, forest encroaching on either side. A bridge arched over the rivulet about fifteen feet ahead, a concrete path snaking away in both directions. All was quiet but for the flowing water and rustling leaves. A few broke free of their branches and drifted down, their autumnal hues visible in the light of the full moon. The only other illumination came from a lamppost to one side of the bridge.

Off to the body's right, a cloaked figure stood beside a tree.

From their neck dangled a large medallion, emblazoned with a silver skull.

The figure gazed down at the corpse for some time. Then they turned and walked away, vanishing into the night.

ONE

THE CIGARETTE dangled between Wright's fingers, enticing her.

Fuck it, she decided, *it's that kind of morning.*

Stepping out of her SUV, she took a deep drag and exhaled, feeling the cool rush as she took in her surroundings.

It was chilly at this hour, nature's reminder that summer had departed with September. Wright stood in a gravel parking lot surrounded by spruce and pine trees; the Rockies rose to the east and west. A lone dirt road exited the parking lot into the forest, curving away through the woods back toward Canmore Creek. There were only a few other vehicles here, and all but one belonged to the RCMP like hers did—a van from the medical examiner's office.

Wright dropped the cigarette and ground it in, then began walking across the lot to the southeast, where the nature trail properly began. A large wooden sign next to it read *Bethune's Walk* and displayed the Western Canada University logo, a crest painted with a snow-tipped mountain range.

As she drew nearer to the trail entrance, Wright reflected that she didn't come out this way often. Normally WCU Campus Police handled problems here, but when somebody was dead, it was time to call in the cavalry. Unlike Ontario and Quebec, Alberta didn't have a provincial police force. It relied on the Royal Canadian Mounted Police for that, as did its smaller municipalities.

Watching American TV shows discuss county sheriffs and town police

4

departments always amused her. Wright had become commander of the Canmore RCMP detachment two years ago, just before her 46ᵗʰ birthday. When explaining her job to her American niece, she'd told her she was basically the sheriff of the region. Her niece asked if it was just like in old Westerns, where she'd kick down the door to a saloon and bust gunslingers while dual-wielding revolvers. She'd smiled and said not quite, that Canmore was a nice and quiet place. Violent crimes were rare, and she liked it that way.

Canmore Creek, a town separate from Canmore proper, was located several kilometers northwest. It inhabited the area between its namesake ravine and the northern border of WCU, although the school used the town name as its mailing address. There was one strip of a few bars and restaurants along the waterfront, then the rest of it comprised a collection of fraternities, sororities, and student abodes. The population was too small to justify having its own RCMP detachment, so it fell under Wright's jurisdiction. She'd been preoccupied with a recent surge of car break-ins in Canmore proper, so the call about a suspicious death on campus had caught her off guard this morning.

Wright entered the trail, the gravel path leading her deeper into the woods. A cold breeze blew by and she zipped her jacket up over her Mountie uniform, a light blue shirt and tie. Around the first bend she saw another uniformed man, just a few years her junior, making his way toward her. He noticed her, forced a grim smile, and waved.

"Linda!" he called, quickening his step.

"Morning, Phil." She nodded. "Where'd it happen?"

"Around another couple of bends this way." Sgt. Phil Beckman looked uneasy, his eyes darting among the trees.

"How bad?" she asked.

He sighed. "Not good. It was a student."

"What's the story?" They walked side-by-side, heading back the way Beckman had come.

"Looks like he fell down the creek bank, hit his head on a rock, and drowned."

"And that's it?"

"That's what it looked like to me and the others. I don't know why Dorval thinks there's more to it. Even the ME's starting to side with him now."

Wright sighed. "Dorval's from the city. He probably just wants an interesting case again."

"He asked to be transferred out here, didn't he?"

"Yeah," Wright said, wishing she had another cigarette. She'd forced herself to leave the pack in the car. "Got burned out after a big case in Vancouver. Though it wouldn't surprise me if he's already having buyer's remorse."

Another trail branched off to the left, a sign beside it reading *Picnic Area*. Farther down that way, Wright could see some wooden tables and the banks of a stream beyond. She and Beckman continued to the right, which curled back into dense forest. The trees were beginning to change color and sunlight filtered through the browning leaves. Birds chirped and a few flew by overhead; there was barely a cloud in the sky. Despite the cold, the second day of October was shaping up to be a beautiful one.

Wright could see the appeal of this area as a stress reliever for students. She knew WCU had struggled for years with undergraduate suicides, which critics had blamed on a high-stress environment and lack of proper mental health resources. President Charlotte Manderley made an official pledge to reform the system after three students took their lives last year alone.

Wright hoped this wasn't another one.

After a few more minutes winding through the woods, she and Beckman found themselves at a stone bridge crossing the creek. Yellow crime scene tape had been put up on both sides of the stream and an officer stood on the bridge beside one of the medical examiner's staff, staring into the water below with a perplexed look on his face. He was in his early thirties with close-cropped red hair and a fit build; he wore latex gloves.

He glanced over his shoulder, then strode toward her and Beckman with the determination of someone who had a point to prove. "Good morning, Staff Sgt. Wright," he said, remaining formal.

"Good morning, Sgt. Dorval," she said, keeping her posture straight. "I hear you're uneasy with the accident theory."

He stopped and hesitated. "There's just a few things that keep me from being sold on it."

Wright looked down the gully into the creek. The medical examiner was there now beside the body taking pictures, her boots keeping her dry from the stream. Several evidence A-frame tents had been placed along the embankment. "Alright," she said. "Give me the rundown, from the beginning."

Dorval nodded. "This morning just after 6:30, a professor called 9-1-1 while jogging, saying she'd discovered a dead body in Bethune's Walk on the Western Canada University campus. She'd gone down into the creek to try and help the guy, but felt for a pulse and found none. First responders arrived and pronounced him dead on the scene. ME reckoned he'd been that way for about six hours, but it'll take an autopsy to be sure. Cause of death is also uncertain. He hit his head pretty badly on that rock there"— he leaned over the railing and pointed down—"but we're not sure if that killed him, or if it just knocked him out and he drowned afterward. But the autopsy should clear that up too."

He turned back to Wright. "Two things bug me, though. The first is what actually caused the fall. This guy took a pretty bad tumble. We can see the marks here." He led her down the embankment, pointing at the path along which the dead student had fallen. "And there are consistent scrapes on his skin and clothing."

Wright looked to the medical examiner, who nodded.

"Now, the slope is steep, but it isn't *that* steep," Dorval continued. "He could've fallen and tumbled with enough force to get knocked unconscious, but even for that I think he would've had to have been running and tripped, or…"

He let the question hang in the air.

"Or what? Someone pushed him?" Wright asked.

The medical examiner shrugged. "Possibly."

"There's no evidence, Linda," Beckman said, still standing beside her. His voice carried a tone of tired disapproval. She knew not everyone had taken a liking to the city boy who'd joined their detachment, but now she had to root out that bias from the facts presented. She wasn't going to half-ass this case, whether it was an accident or something more.

"What's the other thing?" she asked.

"The position of the body." He gestured to the corpse, which lay prone in the water, the student's face submerged in the stream. Wright winced; it had been a while since she'd seen a corpse in person. The fact that it was someone young, who'd attended a prestigious school and probably had a bright future ahead of him, only compounded the effect.

"Look at the angle. His head is toward the bridge, meaning he got almost completely turned around by the fall."

Standing on the bank halfway between the path and the water's edge, Wright took a good look along the entire length of the slope before answering.

"It's possible."

"Possible, but it seems kind of unlikely to me. Especially with this." Dorval went to the water's edge, crouching and pointing at one of the little yellow A-frame tents. "See that?"

Wright leaned closer. "See what?"

"It almost looks like a scuff mark, like a shoe slid along here trying to get traction."

"Meaning?"

Dorval looked up at her. "I will admit it's possible this was made by the fall, his foot dragging across the ground as he hit the water, or by post-mortem twitching but...I don't know. I think he tried to get up."

"Meaning he wasn't knocked unconscious by the fall immediately?"

"I'm not so sure," Dorval said. She noticed he was carefully phrasing his answers. "I think he may have tried to get back up, slipped, then hit his head on the rock. Or..." He looked straight at her. "Maybe someone forced him down. Maybe they tried to kill him by shoving him down the hill, saw he was alright at first, then came down here and slammed his head against the rock to finish the job."

Beckman scoffed. "Why would someone want to murder a university student?"

"Well, that is the question isn't it?" There was a defensive edge to Dorval's voice.

Wright stared at the body. "Are there any other footprints?"

"Just these," Dorval said, pointing back along the trail to another evidence tent. "They're from the professor who found him."

She thought for a long moment. "Could she have killed the student, then come back in the morning to place the call and plant fresh footprints?"

"I thought about that." Dorval returned to the path. "But when I questioned her, she said she was at home in Canmore proper with her husband all evening. She went to Safeway around ten to get some milk and eggs, but that was it. We should be able to confirm her alibi pretty easily, between interviewing the husband and asking neighbors if they saw her car leave during the night. But I don't think she's a serious suspect."

"How do you reckon someone would've gotten down here without leaving prints?" Wright asked.

"That's the part I'm not sure of. But maybe if we look for prints farther up and down the banks..."

Beckman rolled his eyes. "Christ, you'd think this is *CSI: Canmore.*"

"Cool it, Phil," Wright snapped. She turned back to Dorval. "Did the professor know the victim?"

"He's a victim now?" Beckman asked, incredulous.

"Of an accident, at the very least," Wright said. "We will explore all avenues of investigation. The kid's parents are gonna want this to be thorough. There can be no doubt we've done our job to the fullest."

"You know what I think?" Beckman said. "I think he hit his head, *maybe* tried to get back up, then collapsed facedown and drowned. I see no real evidence here that someone came along and deliberately either smashed his head against the rock *or* held him down." He turned to the medical examiner. "There are no bruises on the body that would indicate a struggle, right?"

She shook her head. "Not at first glance, no, but I'll know for sure after the autopsy."

"Right," Dorval said. "And I'm not really sold on someone forcing him down again, either. The angle he was lying at just seemed odd to me. But for him to tumble to that position and get knocked out from hitting the rock, I think someone would have had to *really* shove him. Someone could've pushed him hard, then run off without ever leaving the path. What else would he have tripped on?"

"His shoe lace?" Beckman snorted.

"What was his name?" Wright said, ignoring him.

"Richard Benson," Dorval answered. "We ID'd him from his wallet, which I've got back here." He led them up the slope and the ME's assistant handed him the evidence bag. Dorval fished the object out. "No driver's license, but he had an Ontario health card. And this was how we knew he was a student here." He pulled out a green and white plastic card, holding it between his gloved index finger and thumb for Wright to see.

She looked closer. Beneath a header reading the school's name, it displayed an image of the victim's face. This was the first time she was seeing it. Richard Benson had been handsome, but his smile suggested arrogance. His name was printed in block capitals above a 10-digit student number code. Under the code was a single word, also in block caps.

"He was a Cliffe student?" Wright asked, her level of interest slightly raised.

"Yeah, what does that last word, 'Radcliffe,' mean?" Dorval said.

She reminded herself he was still new to the area. Everyone in these parts had heard of Radcliffe. "WCU students are divided up into colleges within the school. They all take the same classes, so it's more for residence and social events. There are four of them, and they each have a different...vibe."

Beckman scoffed. "That's one way of putting it."

"You have to fill out additional applications to get into Radcliffe and Forrestal. But Radcliffe is the smallest, and the hardest to get accepted to. It has a certain prestige to it."

"It's also full of snooty private school kids," Beckman said. "They all keep to themselves. And they take part in these weird traditions and clubs, wearing gowns and shit like it's *Harry Potter*. Then they go around chanting how they're better than all the other colleges during Frosh Week." He shook his head with disgust. "Radcliffe is elitist bullshit personified."

"It's got a mixed reputation," Wright offered. She knew after she finished up here, she'd have to go straight to the WCU top brass and give them an update on the situation.

"Oh, I've heard lots of stories about it," Beckman continued. "The students there think it's the center of the universe, but really, it just desperately wants to be the Canadian Cambridge. You can even tell by the architecture... Well, actually...I think you can see it just over there." He squinted, then walked up the bridge to its highest point and looked out again. "Yeah, right there."

She, Dorval, and the ME's assistant followed him, peering at where he gestured through the leaves. Wright could just make out the Gothic structure upon the hill about half a kilometer away, but the upper spire of Anathema Tower was clearly visible near the top of the treeline. Not many people, she reflected, knew the tower was actually called that—and Radcliffe's administration was more than happy to keep it that way.

Its namesake was a part of the college's history it would rather forget.

TWO

H E KNEW something was wrong even before he got back.

An uneasy atmosphere had loomed during breakfast in Galbraith that morning. Matt could feel it spreading from the upper-year tables to the first-year spots, but the whispered conversations were too faint for him to hear. And with ten minutes to get to his Ancient Civilizations lecture, he hadn't had time to investigate. Now it was just after eleven, two hours later, and he was eager to get back and find out what was going on.

Matt shielded his eyes as he reached the circular drive before the college. Radcliffe sat atop the hill against a blue sky, a magnificent stone structure with slanted roofs, five stories tall at the center ridge. From the far corner jutted the chapel with its stained-glass panes. A twenty-foot high steeple sat atop the college's central roof, its hexagonal belfry adorned with thin windows along each side. The copper dome and spire had oxidized green with age.

The tower had once held a bell, but it had been damaged in the 1980s and never replaced. These days, it served another, more symbolic purpose.

Few even referred to it by its true name.

He continued up the front stairs and walked the concrete path toward the enormous wooden double doors. The front of the college jutted out from the rest of the building, the entrance a dark, gaping maw prepared to engulf him. He continued inside through a second, smaller set of doors, and entered the lobby.

A gloom pervaded even as bright light filtered through the windows.

The reception office sat to his left; to the right a spiral stone staircase led up to the landing between Picard Hall—a high-ceilinged space used for everything from music recitals to the Fall Formal—and House Vickers, which occupied the second through fourth floors. The stone-floored lobby diverged into two opposite corridors, but Matt walked straight ahead through another set of doors, emerging into the West Quadrangle.

Stone patterns decorated the grass, basking in the midday light. A bust of Lord Thaddeus Radcliffe, the college's founder, stood in the corner off to his left. Each side of the Quad looked like a uniform row under a slate roof, but were actually different residence houses.

To Matt's right were Lacy and Winslow, the most socially prominent single-sex houses in the college. Along the back, the co-ed Bowman and Rickard stood on either side of Napier Tower, still looking like a medieval fortress prepared for siege. He half-expected its archway to lead into a castle, rather than merely the East Quad.

Galbraith Hall occupied much of this courtyard's side to his left. Its stained-glass windows suggested a place of worship, but housed only an altar to mediocre residence food. An elevated stone path and railing ran along the entire length of Galbraith's exterior to an entrance into Bowman.

Matt made his way to the steps, surprised not to see anyone out here. As he approached, a fourth-year student burst through the door, looking distraught and tired. Matt caught it before it closed and paused, wondering, then continued through.

Before him were two sets of stone steps, one leading down to the basement where the washrooms were, and the other up to the hall entrance. It too was marked by double doors and sported opaque glass, which always provided suspense for tour guides showing off Radcliffe's central attraction.

Matt entered the large dining hall. Vaulted ceilings laced with support beams soared high above and nine mahogany tables stood across the wide floor. The first eight were for undergraduates, four on each side of a center horizontal aisle. The ninth table sat elevated upon a dais, reserved for the administration and special guests during weekly High Table dinners. Radcliffe was one of the few institutions in the world to partake in such a tradition; Oxford, Cambridge, and the University of Hong Kong were the only others he knew off the top of his head.

Of course, visitors more often compared this place to Hogwarts.

Today, it was oddly quiet in here. Lunch had begun ten minutes ago and usually the rush had kicked in by now, but he saw barely any students here as he glanced around. The hall's few occupants spoke quietly, but their whispers floated about like the mutterings of ghosts. Most weren't people who normally talked to him, but he did notice Patrick Mason at the fourth-year table. Maybe he'd sit over there.

A woman sat at the touchscreen register, a rare modern apparatus in the room, drumming her fingers against the podium it rested on.

Matt approached her with his student card in hand. "Morning Doris," he said, handing it to her.

"Morning," she mumbled, taking the plastic and swiping it through the slot on the side. Really though, it was too early to grab lunch, so he decided to just get something to drink while he sat at an upper-year table.

Entering the adjacent cafeteria, he saw they were offering pizza again. Matt made his way past the salad bar to the drink stations. He picked up a cup, saw that it was still fairly dirty, and replaced it with another one. As he did so, he became aware of a conversation two girls were having as they grabbed pizza.

"...sounds like it was an accident. I would've thought he'd OD on coke, but what, he drowned in a creek?"

"I don't know. The police are involved, though."

"So it might be murder?" She sounded almost excited.

Matt began filling his glass with water, careful to appear like he wasn't paying attention.

"Who knows," the other said. Then, in a lower voice, "*Maybe Anathema killed him...*"

"Yeah, I could see it," the first girl said, half-chuckling.

Stunned, Matt couldn't help but turn around and look straight at them, the confusion written plain on his face. They turned, saw him, and paled. His membership in a certain organization was well known.

The two of them quickly hurried off, one of them swearing under her breath. Matt stared at the spot where they'd been, thinking. Cool water ran across his hand and he realized he'd let the cup overflow. Grabbing a napkin, he dried his hand and carried the drink back into the hall, the girls' words tumbling through his mind.

Somebody who hated Anathema was dead? The police were involved?

Patrick Mason was still sitting at the fourth-year table, and Matt made his way over. As the male Student Affairs Officer on the Governance Council,

Patrick was sure to have more information.

"Hey," Matt said. "Mind if I sit here?" It was customary to ask upper-years if you could sit at their year's table. There was one for fourth-years, one for third-years, and two consecutive ones for second-years. The first-years filled the other four across the aisle.

"Of course," Patrick said, gesturing him into a chair. Normally he was a vivacious figure, six foot one with curly blond hair and built like a lumberjack. He embraced that image and frequently wore plaid shirts—as he did now—and sported a closely-cropped beard. But today his eyes were somber, his distinctive warm smile nowhere to be found.

Matt glanced at the others sitting with them. To Patrick's left was Sandrine Bouchard, the only other current Anathema member here. Patrick had dropped his pendant after winning his position, as was customary for Council Officers—Randall notwithstanding. Sandrine had platinum blonde hair that went past her shoulders; she was clad in all black as if to remind everyone what organization she was a part of, and by extension, her status as Legatus.

Across from her, a fourth-year sat in a rumpled suit, running a hand through his mop of brown hair. Beside Matt was another student whom he barely knew.

"It's terrible, really," Patrick continued. "But there's no reason to jump to conclusions. Even the RCMP think it's most likely an accident. They've pretty much ruled out suicide, since there was no note and tumbling down a slope is not the...most effective method for that, so at least that's something."

"What's going on...?" Matt asked softly, feeling like an intruder.

Sandrine turned to Patrick and nodded. He faced Matt, sighed, and said, "They found Rich Benson's body this morning in Bethune's Walk. They're not sure the cause of death yet, but they're doing an autopsy right now."

Matt sat back in his seat as a strange feeling washed over him. He'd never known Rich Benson particularly well, and what he did know had never endeared him to the man, but knowing that someone he'd seen alive was no longer with them generated a surreal sensation. He didn't know what to say.

"Yeah," Patrick said, watching his reaction. "It's really sad. I know he didn't get along with a...certain group around here, but he was one of the few good journalists at *The Westerner* and he was a very smart dude."

His phone, sitting on the mahogany table, buzzed loudly. Patrick picked it up and looked at the screen. "I've gotta go. The Provost wants another meeting with the entire Council." He stood up, glancing between all of them. "I'll see you guys around, and if any of you feel the need to talk to someone, just message me or any other Officer. We're more than happy to chat about anything. And the Health & Wellness staff are offering grief counseling."

The rumpled fourth-year nodded. "I'm alright for now. It hasn't completely hit me yet."

Patrick strode off, heading for the doors Matt had entered from. A large, ancient clock sat above them, displaying the current time: nearly twenty past the hour.

Sandrine looked at the clock too. "I really need to get going. See you all later." She walked off, typing something hurriedly on her phone. Matt had a good idea who she was messaging. He pulled out his own device, and sure enough there was a notification from two minutes ago.

"His Imperator" had sent something to the Facebook Messenger group chat "Ice Cream Social Club." Making sure his screen was tilted away from the others, Matt unlocked his phone and opened the chat.

Randall's words were to the point.

Emergency Joint Meeting tonight @ 9 p.m. in the Chalet.
Be there. No exceptions.

THREE

JOAN NOTICED she was chewing her nails and pulled her hand away, almost hearing her mother's voice reprimand her. She kept doing it no matter how many times she'd been told not to. Glancing at her fingers, she saw she'd been gnawing on just about all of them recently. She folded her hands into her lap and forced herself to take a few slow, deep breaths.

She sat in the Administration Center, the most recently refurbished part of the college. Joan rested on a bench outside the office in the north-westernmost corner. The golden plaque on the door's center read *Donna Crawley, Dean of Students*. She'd been dreading this meeting for the past two weeks, and now it had collided with everything else. A glance at her watch told her the Dean was currently five minutes late.

Joan turned to the window beside her and examined her reflection in the glass, from her dirty blonde, wavy hair to her white blouse and navy jeans. The feature that always caught her eye was a two-inch scar running from her right cheekbone to her temple. It was a clean, thin line and certainly not a horrifying or repulsive defect, but it was impossible not to notice nonetheless. Many had called attention to it or blatantly mocked her for it over the years—"It's Scarface!" they'd jeer, among other creative insults—yet to this day, there had not been a single joke read about it in an Anathema Sermon. They had plenty of other source material on her, of course.

A loud panting interrupted her reverie and she turned to see a big, black-furred Newfoundland making its way toward her. The dog's owner was right behind him, wielding his leash and wearing athletic attire and a windbreaker.

"Hi Joan," the woman said, slightly out of breath. Donna Crawley was honey blonde, in her mid-forties, above average height, and fairly fit. She was actually quite pretty, Joan decided, but tired-looking, as if years of emotional baggage had sapped away the vitality of her youth. She guessed working for the college's administration had to be a soul-sucking experience.

"Sorry I'm late," she continued. "It's been a hectic morning and the RCMP have been everywhere and…"

"The police are here?" Joan asked, suddenly growing worried.

"Yes, everything's alright… Well no, it's not actually, but the student population is safe, that's the main thing."

"Were we in danger?" she asked.

Crawley wiped sweat from her brow. "No, no, no…it's just been an… emotional morning. Something sad happened earlier today. I'm not sure if it's gotten around yet, but we'll have an official statement out soon. I'll make this brief. I have a lot of new things to do that I wasn't expecting when I woke up."

After the events of last night, Joan had overslept till half past eleven, then had frantically thrown herself together in order to make this 11:45 meeting. Fortunately, House Lacy was adjacent to the front of the college, but she wasn't fully awake yet and hunger gnawed inside her.

The Dean continued, "Provost Mustard called a meeting with the Student Council and the admin before this, but I thought I had enough time to take Adam outside before you came. He didn't want to go pee right away."

The dog panted happily.

"No worries," Joan said. "I know what that's like. I have a Bernese Mountain Dog back home."

"Ah, a fellow big dog lover!" Crawley said, sounding cheery. Joan wondered when her tone would flip a switch, given that this was a disciplinary meeting. "Well, come on in."

She fished a key out of her jacket pocket, unlocked the door, and entered the office; Adam and Joan trailed in behind her. A mahogany desk stood in the center with a leather chair behind it and two uncomfortable-looking wooden ones before it. Along the side wall, a map of the Canadian Rockies hung over a large dog bed. Mounted behind Crawley's chair was the Dean's diploma from Atherton University, a significantly less prestigious institution in Manitoba where many admin staff had obtained degrees. Daylight streamed inside and Joan took in the view, gazing out across the circular drive to the trees and mountains beyond.

"Please take a seat," Crawley said, a little more authority in her voice now.

She quietly turned away from the window and sat in the right chair. Almost immediately, the Newfoundland came up and began sniffing her. She pet the dog's soft head and smiled, missing Adeline back in Toronto.

"Adam, bed!" Crawley ordered, pointing. The dog reluctantly moved away and flopped down. The Dean of Students turned her attention back to Joan and folded her hands together neatly. "Now...how are you today?"

"I'm...alright," she managed, noticing the big manila file folder sitting atop the keyboard. Knowing exactly what that was, she swallowed.

"Good, good..." The Dean opened the file and looked at the first page. "Joan Alicia Keating," she read, pronouncing it *Alice-ia* just as her parents did. "That's a very pretty name. I don't meet many Joans these days, but it's got a good old-fashioned ring to it."

"My mother's a big fan of Hitchcock's *Rebecca*," she said, for some reason feeling the need to explain. "She wanted to name me after Joan Fontaine."

"Oh, I love that movie! Saw it a million years ago, but I remember it being very good." Crawley narrowed her eyes slightly. "Actually, you look quite a bit like her. Taller definitely and a little more...*modern*, but I can really see the resemblance."

"Um, thank you," she said, scratching the back of her head. She'd had her looks compared to Joan Fontaine before, not that she minded, but the "modern" descriptor was certainly a fresh take.

"Yes, and of course she didn't have the..." Crawley's finger absently went to her cheek, then she froze, realizing what she was doing, and abruptly began shuffling papers. "Right, so the reason you're here..."

"The email didn't specify," Joan said softly, though she knew exactly what it was. And of course, this wasn't her first time getting called into a disciplinary meeting for this reason—though that instance had been with a different Dean; Crawley arrived at the beginning of last year. Joan had been but a lowly second-semester first-year, about two months after her

Initiation. She and Catherine Winters had been called in and questioned about their involvement with a certain group, only for them to be rescued by the female Pontifex at the time.

She'd never forget the way Helen Levine burst into the office right as Dean Sorenson had begun to grill them, telling the administrator it was shameful not to inform students that upper-years could defend them at disciplinary meetings. She'd turned first to Catherine, then to Joan, held them each with a disappointed gaze, then told them they didn't need to say a thing.

Sorenson had raised his finger in objection, then given a heavy sigh and let the three of them go then and there. Helen waited until they'd gotten out into the West Quad, then scolded them for five straight minutes on the importance of not getting caught when distributing Second Sermon invitation cards.

But that was then, and Joan was now a third-year; the terrified girl who'd sat in the previous iteration of this office was long gone. She understood the game of Radcliffe College more clearly now, and how to play ball with the admin. They'd leave you alone so long as you didn't cause them any liabilities—the organization *was* formally dissociated from the college, after all—but if you slipped up or did anything overt, they'd come around to give you a slap on the wrist.

"We're here to talk about your recent violation of"—Crawley sighed and spread her hands—"...the Anathema Policy." She almost made it sound like it was an annoyance to her too.

"I'm not sure what..."

"Joan, please," Crawley said with an amused smile. "Réjean caught you carving CRCC into the steam tunnel walls during his rounds two weeks ago."

"It was just a..." Joan scratched her arm, knowing there was no easy way out of this one. Réjean was the oldest security guard and seemed to hate all aspects of student culture. Catching an Anathema member red-handed had actually brought a smile to his face. Of course, she shouldn't have been doing it, but she was drunk, had just come back from a writing session at the Chalet, no one else was around, and she'd figured, *Why not?* There were hundreds of similar carvings all over the college under beds, in drawers, behind cabinets, on tables, everywhere.

"Even I know what *that* means," Crawley said, still amused. "It's an acronym for Anathema's motto: *Carpe risus, carpe coronam.* It's Latin for 'seize the laughter, seize the crown.' " She'd pronounced it very smoothly, and Joan was momentarily impressed. Crawley smiled again and winked. "I did my homework."

You didn't have to do much, Joan thought. The motto and its translation were at the top of the organization's Wikipedia page.

"Although I will admit the Anathema is one of the more interesting historical tidbits of this college," Crawley continued, "I just can't see why a nice girl like you would want to get involved with it. Especially considering its history..."

"That was a long time ago," Joan pointed out. "It's very different today. There's even been an opt-out policy for the last fifteen or so years. You can message a member and tell them you don't want jokes read about you, and there—you're out of the Sermon."

"So I've heard. But the fact remains that it is dissociated from Radcliffe College and your actions are a clear violation of Section 3.4 of the Anathema Policy." The Dean pulled a multi-page document out of her desk. "Ah, here it is: 'No student shall advertise the Anathema organization or events held in the name of Anathema anywhere on the premises of Radcliffe College.' " She put the document down and gestured to the page. "Sounds pretty clear to me, Joan. You know those are the rules. You're allowed to join it—we can't control your life—but we just want your...err, *club* to mind its own business and stay away from the student population. Unless anyone willingly wants to participate in it, of course. It's always baffled me why people would enjoy watching others get made fun of."

Joan raised an eyebrow. "You ever watch late-night television? Or a stand-up routine? Our job is basically to make fun of this college like a Golden Globes host makes fun of Hollywood."

Crawley gave a sad sigh, looking at her as if she were a wayward child. "Yes, but that's not very *nice,* now is it?"

"It's...satire."

The Dean shook her head. "Satire is...a double-edged sword with many sides."

Joan blinked.

Crawley scratched her chin, thinking. "Err, what I meant was—you have to be careful with it."

Joan sighed, disappointed with herself. She'd just finished the last C when Réjean had come around the corner and yelled "Hey, you!" She'd managed to hide her pendant down her shirt, lest he have confiscated it. Nonetheless, it was an unforced error and she'd been careful not to tell anyone else. She didn't want it jeopardizing her chances of becoming Imperator, as if that wasn't an uphill-climb already.

"You know the rules, Joan. You violate policies, you get Demerit Points."

Joan winced, her right hand clenching her left arm. She forced herself to snap out of it and sat back up. "Fine, I'll take it. How many would that be now?"

Crawley moved the file aside and pulled up something on her computer monitor. "As you know, the points expire a year after they are given. So…you currently have three left over from last year. You got them all in February after the Winter Formal. One for public intoxication, two for fighting back against an administrator and a security guard when they tried to escort you from the event."

"Right…" Joan clenched her arm again. Arguing with Assistant Dean Eric Porter and shoving Réjean away from her when he'd tried to gently lead her out of Galbraith hadn't been her best moves. No wonder he'd taken such delight in busting her for this. Then again, she hadn't had many fine moments throughout second-year and was happy to put that whole period in the rear-view mirror.

"Any violation of the Anathema Policy is automatically two Demerit Points," Crawley continued. "And that would put you up to five, which would bar you from attending Radcliffe College events until early February when the three from last year expire. Then you'd just be down to two again and would be able to attend QuadFest in April *unless* you did anything really egregious…"

Joan leaned forward and opened her mouth, but the Dean held up a finger. "*But…* In light of recent…tragic events, I'm going to let you off with just a warning this time."

She sat back in her chair, relief flushing through her. "Th-thank you," she managed to say. "I *really* appreciate this."

Crawley smiled. "It's the least I can do, but please don't go around carving Latin incantations or whatever into the walls. Or fight with security. You seem like a nice girl, and I'd hate for you to get banned from events… or even expelled from residence."

"I'll do my best," Joan said, flashing a weak smile and standing up. She headed for the door.

"One more thing," Crawley said behind her. She gripped the handle and turned around. The older woman looked sad. "I hope you know what you're doing with Anathema, Joan."

"Thank you, Dean Crawley. I appreciate your concern." She pulled the door closed behind her, getting one last look of Adam sprawled on his bed before it clicked shut.

Then Joan exited into Radcliffe's front corridor. She turned the other way, heading for Galbraith; it was just after twelve and she was starving. As she walked, Joan whipped out her phone and saw she had unread messages. The first was the group chat for the female branch of Anathema, dubbed "Skullduggery."

"Her Imperator" had sent: *URGENT meeting tonight w/ the men @ Chalet, 9pm.*

Val had messaged her separately, writing: *Have you heard what happened?*

Joan halted in her tracks, her thumbs hovering over the digital keyboard. Then she typed: *No, what's going on?*

Val was active now, a little green circle at the bottom right of her profile picture. She saw the icon of three dots in a row appear, indicating that she was typing a reply already.

Are you sitting down?

Joan saw a bench beneath a window, looking out into the West Quad. She took a seat, then typed back: *Yes. Why? What's wrong?*

There was a pause.

Then it came:

Rich Benson is dead. They found his body this morning in the creek in Bethune's Walk. The RCMP are involved and they're not sure if it was an accident or something else.

Joan sat there for nearly a minute, trying to control her breathing while staring at the screen. Then she slowly typed back: *Thank you for letting me know.* She hit send, clicked her phone into sleep mode, then got up and began walking around the corner. Straight ahead were a flight of stone steps leading up to Galbraith's entrance.

She walked in a direct line, fighting the urge to cry. Fortunately, there was nobody else around. She told herself she had until she got to the top to pull herself together.

She made it to the base of the steps before turning and running back to the other staircase.

By the time Joan burst into the restroom on the floor below, there were tears streaming down her face.

FOUR

A T A quarter to nine, Matt descended the front steps of Radcliffe and headed into the evening gloom, his pendant dangling from its necklace of black chain. As he walked, he took a moment to admire the small, stainless-steel skull again. Members frequently lost their pendants and new ones had to be ordered for them, but Matt had kept careful track of his ever since Initiation.

He passed the chapel and the Mackenzie Library, its gargoyles watching him as he continued along into Griffin Park. The trail split, one sidewalk leading toward the eponymous statue at the park's center, the other continuing west toward the town. Matt stuck to the latter path, passing beneath the dark shadows of trees. Moonlight conspired with the lampposts to illuminate his way.

The trail ended at a road beside the woods. To his left began several streets of residential houses, many of which had been converted into fraternities and sororities over the years. This was the edge of Canmore Creek, and continuing along this drive would bring him toward the waterway that gave the town its name.

There was no sidewalk here, so he kept to the edge. An SUV pulled out of one of the residential streets and whipped past him, its rear lights diminishing as it sped into the evening.

Matt glanced at his watch: still seven minutes until the meeting. He would arrive early, as usual. He liked to wait outside and knock only exactly when meetings were scheduled to begin, but tonight it seemed showing up a few minutes before would be welcomed. He hadn't gotten many more details about Rich Benson's demise, beyond what was already going around, but he knew Randall would've been told more.

Matt didn't even notice the other person until he found himself walking in step beside a familiar figure. Roy Tash was only a bit below Matt's six feet and two inches. He had brown hair and sported his trademark tweed coat and riding boots.

"Well!" he said, noticing Matt. "Fancy seeing you out here."

"Showing up early for once?" Matt cracked a smile.

He grinned. "Probably wouldn't be a good idea to show up fashionably late tonight."

Matt laughed and they continued on in silence for a few moments. Growing more serious, he asked, "Did you hear what happened?"

Roy took a moment to respond. "Yeah…it's pretty sad. I didn't like the guy, but it's still horrible."

"Yeah…" Matt searched for the right words. "You don't think…anyone thinks that *we* had anything to do with it, do you?"

Roy forced a grim chuckle. "I hope not. That would be…pretty bad for our image, to say the least."

"I wonder if that's why Randall called the meeting. I mean, I heard some people joking about that in Galbraith…"

Roy raised his eyebrows. "People joke about a lot of things in Galbraith. Half the things said there are worse than the Sermons."

"But nobody *really* thinks Anathema would kill someone, right? I mean, who do they take us for?"

"We *are* a secret society," Roy said. "When people don't know the full details of something, their mind fills in the gaps. Sometimes they can get pretty creative with it."

"Do the police think it was murder?"

"I guess we'll find out soon."

They had arrived.

A winding trail led into the woods. Between the trees and the night, what lay beyond the driveway was entirely obscured in shadow. There were a few other houses set back from the road like this, but when the alumni of both branches had pooled their resources to buy this place twenty years ago, they'd been sure to pick the one deepest into the forest. Matt and Roy walked up the path and soon the road disappeared from view behind them.

Thankfully, it was a cool evening devoid of insects. When Matt had come out here during Frosh Week in the early September heat wave, the mosquitoes and humid darkness had been a lethal combination.

They reached the wrought-iron gate. The Chalet stood right around the next bend of trees, just out of sight for anyone who came snooping around. Very few people knew Anathema owned this place.

Roy buzzed the intercom. A moment later, Randall's voice answered.

"You're early." He didn't sound angry. "Who is it?"

"It's Roy. I've got Matt here with me."

"Ah, great." Randall's voice grew fainter for a moment. "Tash and Richardson are here." Then he was back. "Come on in. You're the first non-Tetrad people to arrive from either branch."

"Does this mean we get a bonus?" Roy asked.

Randall paused. "The Great Lord Anathema…rewards us in mysterious ways." The intercom clicked off.

Roy turned to Matt. "We're not getting a bonus."

There was a click and the gate opened slightly. Roy grabbed the handle and pulled it open wider.

"As long as he names me his successor, we're all good." Matt grinned.

"Ah, so *that's* why you always show up on time."

They walked through and the gate clanged shut behind them. "What, you think I'm just naturally organized?"

"Relax, your only real competition is Logan."

"Yeah, and everyone and their dog thinks it's going to be him," Matt said.

The forest parted into a clearing. Before them lay the Chalet, warm light visible behind its blinds. It was a wooden cottage with a sloping roof; only one floor sat above ground but it possessed a sizable stone basement— which always came in handy for making a large circle of candles during Initiations. Randall's car, an old Volvo station wagon, sat in the driveway.

As they continued toward the front door, Roy said, "Yeah but it's almost never the obvious guy. Nobody thought it would be Randall last year."

"I did, until he ran for Officer."

"Him not dropping his pendant during the campaign should've tipped us off," Roy said. "But Logan is *way* too obvious. And besides, people weren't entirely sure Turland would pick Madler the year before."

There was a touch of sadness in his voice. Matt knew Roy had wanted to become the 114th Imperator, but it had ultimately gone to Mick Adler instead. He was now off studying at Cambridge, a favorite pastime for Radcliffe graduates. Roy hadn't realized he was staying for a fifth year until late in the second semester, and so had never considered himself a candidate for Madler's successor. When he returned, he hoped he'd be appointed to Randall's Tetrad, but it was given to other members. By that point, he told Matt he hadn't really minded. He was just happy to get a fourth full year in the Anathema—he had been a second-year induct, after all—but Matt sometimes sensed a woundedness he tried to repress during writing sessions.

"Well, nobody saw Turland coming, but that's because he only became Imperator as a second-year after Ellis dropped that October."

"Yeah, that was a shitshow," Roy said, remembering. "But they didn't think it would be Ellis before him, either."

"Because, from what I've heard, he would've sucked."

They had reached the entrance. Roy shrugged and knocked. "Let's just say it was a good thing we got Tom Turland instead."

A moment later, the door swung open and they were greeted by Logan Brewster himself. He was a few inches shorter than Matt and slim with ginger hair and angular features; he wore his pendant and his silver Legatus sash was slung across his right shoulder. Scowling indifference rested on his face as he looked between the two of them.

"You're early. Come inside." He walked away, leaving the door open.

They stepped in and Matt closed it behind them. They followed Logan to the right into the dimly-lit lounge. The room was furnished with old volumes of Sermons along bookshelves, several plush leather sofas and chairs, and windows to the left and right, both of which had their blinds closed. Directly ahead stood a large fireplace, the only light source aside from a few lamps.

A man finished placing another log atop the flames, then moved the protective screen back into place. He stood up, brushed off his hands, straightened his Magister sash—which he wore across his left shoulder—and turned toward them.

"Ah, hello gentlemen," he said, adjusting his circular-rimmed glasses. Doug Sadler was a portly Anglo-Saxon student with ash blond hair, and tonight was dressed in a black sweater and jeans.

"Evening, Doug." Matt looked around the room at the others. Both the male and female Tetrads were here. Logan sat on the left side of the

27

room beside a tall Jamaican man with a neatly-shaved beard named Kingsley Fennell, wearing the double-sash of the Pontifex in an X across his chest. To Fennell's left was the male Imperator, Jackson Randall, a brown-haired white man of medium height with a crew-cut; he was busy looking at something on his phone.

To the right was the female Tetrad. Kylie Patel leaned against the wall, over six feet tall with almond hair and tanned skin. Sandrine Bouchard was still dressed in her black outfit from earlier, now adorned with her own Legatus sash. Sitting next to her on a sofa was Lexi Choi, the Pontifex, who had recently dyed her hair blue, while the Magister, Catherine Winters, stood over by the window peeking out through the blinds, a short redhead.

Randall looked up. "Hey guys, take a seat. Some others buzzed the gate just before you walked in. The rest will be here soon."

"I can see them now," Catherine said, still looking through the blinds. "I'll go let them in." She hurried down the corridor.

Matt and Roy sat down on a loveseat along the back wall. Everything was unnaturally quiet for the start of a meeting. Usually there was casual banter, the members getting primed to write jokes about the latest Radcliffe calamities. Today, however, a somber specter had settled over the Chalet.

Matt heard the door open. Catherine said, "You're right on time, come in!" He glanced at his watch: 9:00 p.m. exactly.

The Magister returned leading Joan Keating and her friend Val Lehman, a plump second-year girl with dark hair. Matt immediately straightened his posture. Tall and athletic with a certain look of classical beauty to her, Joan had always reminded him of an actress from old Hollywood movies. However, she didn't carry herself like a starlet; she'd always seemed kind of shy.

Joan and Val sat down together on a sofa to the right side of the room, which was turned toward the center. As they did so, Joan looked up and briefly made eye contact with him. Matt swiftly turned away and let his eyes dance along the ceiling. After about ten seconds he glanced at her again. This time, Joan suddenly averted her gaze from him and pulled out her phone.

He leaned back in his seat and sighed. *That means nothing*, he told himself. *Don't get your hopes up.*

◆

It only took about ten minutes for the rest to trickle in, sixteen in the men's branch and nineteen in the women's. Normally, it would take twice as long but the members understood the weight of the situation at hand. Tanner Cho now sat between Matt and Roy, making the loveseat a little cramped for space. They'd barely exchanged greetings before the meeting began.

Randall and Kylie walked to the center of the room, silver medallions swinging gently from their necks as they moved. These were much larger than the standard pendants, adorned with the organization's skull emblem and the Imperator's number along the bottom.

"Thank you all for coming on such short notice," Kylie said. "I know this is a busy time for most of you between essays and midterms, but we need to discuss Rich Benson." She turned to her fellow branch leader. "As an Officer, Jack has more details from the admin than I do, so I'll turn things over to him."

She sat down and let him take the center of the floor. Randall normally wore a welcoming smile, but tonight he looked downtrodden and fatigued. The dark lighting of the room often gave Imperators a sinister quality as they spoke, but now it merely contributed to the gloom overwhelming him.

"Good evening, everyone," Randall said with a brief wave. "By now, I'm sure you've all heard what happened. I'm just going to give a short update on the situation, but this is confidential information and it does not, repeat, *does not* leave this room…understand?"

Heads nodded all around. The fire crackled behind him as he continued. "Good. I know we aren't always the most tight-lipped of secret societies, but I'm officially not supposed to share this with anyone else. However, it does concern all of you and this organization as a whole, so I'm willing to breach that confidentiality for the sake of the Anathema."

He took a deep breath. "Rich Benson was found dead this morning by a professor. He'd fallen into the creek in Bethune's Walk last night. The autopsy just came back an hour ago; drowning is the official cause of death, but it's unclear if he was pushed into the gully or just tripped. The RCMP had some concern over the position of the body with regard to *how* he fell, but they are leaning toward it being an accident. Apparently, a new addition to their team used to work murder cases in the Vancouver area and just wants to be thorough, but that's all they have at the moment."

A silence hung over the room as Randall looked between each of them. "And I hope that's the truth. I don't believe anyone would have murdered Rich Benson, least of all anyone in this room. However...not everyone at the college is going to tell the story that way. It's no secret that Benson hated our fucking guts. He wrote stories about us in *The Westerner*, penned a so-called 'exposé' on us for *Cliffe-Hanger*, and went out of his way to dissuade people from attending the Sermons, especially first-years. Whenever I tried to talk to him, he'd always look at me with disdain and I know many of you had similar experiences with him. He was, as they say, a thorn in our side."

He walked back toward the fireplace, then turned around. "You know how this college can be; people here have active imaginations. They also love to stick their nose into other people's business. Both of those things are the bread and butter of Anathema, of course, but at least we're open about it and we give people free booze. However, there will be some—and I've already heard this today from multiple people—who will suggest that we killed him."

Nobody said a word. Randall continued, "Most will dismiss this as nonsense, or even as an insensitive joke. But others will start to wonder... We clearly benefit from him being gone. What if he uncovered one of our secrets and we had no choice but to shut him up?" He began pacing. "It's pathetically easy to vilify us—we meet under the cover of darkness and make fun of people, for fuck's sake—but not everyone at this college realizes we're not so extreme. You all know what we really do here, and what purposes our rituals serve. Personally, I've always viewed us as an entertainment organization. Others see us as a bullying cult. And we've pissed off so many people over the years to the point where they'll gladly smear us worse than that.

"But one thing I will not tolerate is getting labeled a group of murderers. That is just patently false. We do *not* orchestrate grand conspiracies, we do *not* rig student elections, or blackmail the admin into leaving us alone—all of which I've heard over the years. It was Tom Turland who emphasized the two core tenets of the Anathema to us: mystery and fun. We must present ourselves as enigmatic to the college, but at the end of the day remind them of all the good times we've shown them. And that is the tightrope we have to walk. I don't want the mystery of the Anathema to be: did they kill Rich Benson?

"Now, Kylie and I have been talking all day, and we agree that we're just going to let the police investigation run its course. I'm confident it will turn out to be an accident, and I'm pretty sure nobody is crazy enough to think we have the resources to bribe the RCMP."

Kylie stood up and joined him again. "In the meantime, we want you all to lay low. No mentioning Anathema, no making unsubtle references to us or cracking jokes about us in Galbraith—which, let's face it, we've *all* been guilty of at some point. When Rich Benson comes up in conversation, just talk about how sad it is—and it is sad. He went out around midnight for a late-night stroll, maybe to clear his head, and then probably tripped and ended up in the creek. There was no rhyme or reason to it. It's just something terrible that happened."

A plummy English voice spoke up. "And what if the police decide somebody *did* deliberately drown him?"

All heads in the room swiveled toward Rufus Danvers. Born and raised in London, he had a bushy goatee and his brown hair was always neatly combed. He spread his hands to the onlookers. "It's the question I'm sure is on everyone's mind."

"If they do," Randall added, growing tense, "then hopefully they'll find Benson's killer quickly so there are no lingering doubts." He turned to the room, hesitated, then spoke. "And if any of you in this room are responsible…" The angry look on his face softened into sadness.

"May God help you."

There was to be no writing that night, but from the murmurs afterward it appeared many were heading to the Foxhole to brighten their moods.

Roy straightened his coat and gestured between himself and Tanner Cho, who was even taller than both of them at six feet four inches; he wore preppy attire and Sperry's, as usual. "We're going with them. Wanna tag along?"

Matt scratched the back of his head. "Well…I've got a paper due Friday…"

"Friday?" Tanner scoffed. "Easy. I've got two due Thursday and I'm still going. Come on."

Matt was going to point out that Tanner had once written a fifteen-page essay in nine hours from 3 a.m. to noon—and gotten an A on it—but merely sighed instead. "Alright, I'll come."

They followed the trail of members out the door.

Back in the lounge, Val buttoned up her jacket and turned to her friend, who looked pale. "You coming?"

Joan nodded, then softly said, "I could use a few drinks."

FIVE

THE FOXHOLE was located at one end of Canmore Creek's main drag. Of the four bars in town, it was doubtlessly the sketchiest—but also the least expensive, and for that reason it had become Anathema's habitual haunt long ago. It was a small structure on the south side of the road. The northern strip sat on the riverbank of the wide creek, a small park running along the water's edge behind the buildings. Matt walked with the group of fifteen or so Anathema members, the Foxhole coming up on their left. He realized he'd forgotten to take his pendant off like the rest of them and pulled it over his head, gently stowing it in an interior pocket of his jacket.

The group trailed through the entrance. Inside was a bar running along the left and an empty stage to the right; someone always played there Friday evenings, coinciding with Anathema's traditional post-Sermon jaunt here. A few cheap-looking, metallic tables stood throughout the room and a billiard table was situated at the back. A door behind it led down to the basement washrooms. Incandescent lightbulbs flickered overhead.

Slowly, the crowd divvied up into separate friend groups. Tanner and Roy took a table near the back and Matt joined them.

"You guys want to split a pitcher of beer?" Tanner asked.

"Absolutely," Roy said, brightening up.

"Can we get cider instead?" Matt asked, wincing.

"Cider. *Pfft*," Roy scoffed.

"Actually, I'd be down for some cider," Tanner said. "But you've gotta be the one to order it, Matt."

"Sure."

Roy shrugged. "Honestly, as long as it's got more than five percent alcohol, I'm good with it."

Matt got up and headed to the bar. A man covered in tattoos walked up to him, placing his palms on the counter. "What can I get for you?"

"What's your strongest cider on tap?"

He thought for a moment. "We've got one that's over six percent."

"Perfect, I'll get a pitcher of that."

The bartender nodded and got to work. Matt idly glanced around the establishment, realizing the last time he'd stood at this counter was after the Second Sermon, back in March when things had been looking up. He hadn't known what was coming then.

He'd been talking with Roy and his friend Claudia, a girl in the year above Matt. He remembered the way they'd laughed together, the looks she'd thrown him, the way she put her hand on his arm and smiled at him. He'd started to feel happy for the first time in a long while. Her friend Vicky had encouraged him, telling him to keep calm and to just be himself. He kept pushing the anxiety aside; it finally all seemed to be going well.

Then came QuadFest. Out came the truth.

Not even he had known, though looking back it explained nearly everything.

He gripped the edge of the bar, his knuckles going white.

The memories rushed back. Matt saw Vicky reading him the symptoms from her phone. He saw himself crying on Tanner's bed while he and Roy tried to comfort him. He saw that look on Claudia's face—sadness, but mostly pity.

It was a relief she was taking her fourth-year abroad. It would've been too awkward seeing her around.

Matt's snapped back to the present. The bartender finally returned with a pitcher full of cider and three stacked glasses. Matt paid and carried everything back to the table, thankful their trio was seated away from everybody else.

"Hey, you alright? You looked kinda lost over there for a little bit," Tanner said. Both he and Roy looked concerned as Matt sat down. There wasn't really a point in hiding anything.

Still, all he said was, "It's nothing. I'm fine." He poured himself a tall glass of cider and raised it to both of them. "Let's drink."

◆

They'd been there over an hour, and it suddenly hit Joan that she was very drunk. That, of course, was the problem with following a double with another double and then a few more singles.

She put a hand on her stomach. It was definitely time to stop. She glanced around and saw the lights were slightly blurry. Shit, she hadn't noticed that before. It was harder to notice inebriation while sitting down. Sometimes it didn't even *really* hit you until you stood up.

"Are you okay?" Val asked, sitting across from her. Joan nodded.

They sat beside Sandrine and Alyssa Lee, the current golden child of Anathema's female branch. She wasn't currently on Tetrad, but the talk had always been of "saving her" for fourth-year so they could maximize her time with the organization. It was traditional for Tetrad members to leave, but only the Imperators absolutely had to. Despite already being Randall's second-in-command, everyone assumed Logan Brewster would be given the male branch next year. Alyssa was a clear frontrunner in the female race, but many spoke of Catherine Winters as a serious contender too.

Joan took a sip of water. She wondered what people said about her, what she could be destined for—if anything. Veronica Yang, an Imperator last year and now the female Student Affairs Officer, had drunkenly told her she really hoped Joan made Tetrad one day. Secretly, Joan resented how people at this place were always trying to peg who would be what long before it happened. Becoming an Imperator wasn't an election, it was an appointment over which the leader possessed sole discretion. That eliminated it as a popularity contest and could make for dark horse picks— occasionally.

Last year, everyone had been fairly sure Kylie Patel would win out over Sandrine, the only other real contender. Still, Joan thought it would be pretty nepotistic for Kylie to pick Catherine, naming her own goddamn Magister as her successor. The two were thick as thieves, always seen in Galbraith together, posing for photos at every party. And she'd already given Catherine a Tetrad position once, granting her the archivist duties of a Magister.

Joan put a hand to her head, feeling much more nauseous now. She was, however, thankful that the train of thought had distracted her from Rich fucking Benson. For a few minutes, at least.

"…the problem with people like him is irrelevant, really," Alyssa was saying. She was in full campaign mode, trying to win Sandrine over. The Tetrad might not have a vote for the next Imperator, but they certainly had the leader's ear. And Alyssa wasn't aiming for a secondary position. Joan could see it in the way she carried herself, that clean polished look about her that had carried Alyssa from her high school student council to her current spots as Student Governance Meeting Treasurer and Vice President of DebSoc. Of course, she'd never be able to put Imperator on her resume, but she probably figured she had enough on hers already.

"People like Benson come and go," she continued. "Issues like that have always existed for us, but look what this organization has gone through: Both branches have been around for over a century. One student with a chip on his shoulder isn't going to derail that. We just say what we need to say, and people can take it or leave it."

No, Joan thought. *What we really need to do is identify who* can *take jokes and who* can't, *and only write harsh jokes about the ones that can.* Nobody saw it that way, though. You couldn't openly be a reformist in a secret society that didn't vote for its leadership.

Her eyes wandered the room, resting on Matt Richardson over by his friends. He'd had his back to her for most of the evening, but now he was standing up and talking to Tanner Cho and Roy Tash, a glass in hand. She found herself looking at him for a while. He was pale, fit, and tall with jet black hair and emerald eyes.

They'd never really spoken even though they were both Initiated in first-year. She'd always found him cute, but had never gone out of her way to flirt or even say hello. Then again, she rarely did for fear of being awkward. The guys she liked often made the first move, but she could never tell if Matt was too diffident to break the ice or if he just wasn't interested in her. They *had* made brief eye contact earlier at the meeting, though. She tried not to read into it too much, but he did look back after the first glance-away…

Joan realized she was still staring at him, watching him put his glass down and go through the door down to the basement. She turned her attention back to Val. Sandrine and Alyssa's conversation was merely babble beside them.

"I think you need to go home," Val said, looking concerned.

Joan laughed. "You're probably right." She hiccupped and covered her mouth. It drew a sideways glance from Sandrine.

She started to get up and Val moved to help her, turning to the others. "I think we're gonna call it a night. It is Tuesday, after all."

Now that she was on her feet, the full force of the alcohol finally hit Joan. She nearly stumbled over.

"Fair enough. See you around," Sandrine said with a casual flick of her hand. She turned back to Alyssa, who looked annoyed at the interruption.

Val pulled Joan's arm around her shoulder and they started for the door. Joan realized getting escorted out like this probably did her no favors with Sandrine, but oh well. It was still early in the year; she could bounce back. Nobody even knew about the disciplinary meeting—

Her hand flew to her stomach and she stopped dead in her tracks. It was all she could do to avoid hurling right then and there. She looked up at Val and the two of them locked eyes.

"Bathroom?" Val asked.

She nodded.

They turned around and began swiftly walking in the opposite direction. Everything was a blur around her. They passed the other tables, then the billiards set, then they were through the door and turning left, down into the depths of the Foxhole. Joan hit the bottom of the stairs in a stumble, slipping free from Val.

She couldn't hold it back any longer. She grasped along the wall, pulling herself toward the women's restroom. It was no use; it was coming back up and then suddenly spewing from her lips—

And all over someone who had just exited the men's restroom.

Matt froze, looking at his ruined shirt, his hands held up as if at gunpoint. Time seemed to stand still as he tried to process what had just occurred. At one level, he knew entirely, but his mind still had a hard time believing it.

Joan Keating just threw up on me.

What.

The fuck.

Is happening?

"Oh my god!" Val rushed toward them, covering her mouth. "I'm so sorry, she's…"

Joan looked pale and horrified, staring at his shirt in disbelief. "I'm... I'm..."

Think quickly. "Uh...hey, no worries. I didn't really like this shirt anyway." He managed a smile. The blue polo had actually been one of his favorites.

"I am *so* sorry," Joan said. She stumbled and suddenly clutched her stomach.

"It's been an emotional day for her," Val said, taking her friend's arm.

"Hey, believe me, those happen," he chuckled.

"I'm really sorry," Joan repeated, her hand brushing across his shoulder. Guilt, embarrassment, and remorse danced in her eyes. And for a moment, something else did too. "Really, really, *really* sorry."

"It's no big deal, honestly," he said with a dismissive wave, as if she'd merely bumped into him.

Val pushed the door for the women's restroom open and pulled her inside. Just before it closed, Joan turned around and blew him a kiss goodbye.

He stood there for a while, completely stunned. Then he returned to the men's washroom and spent a good five minutes trying to clean himself up with damp paper towels. He exited and headed back up the stairs just as Roy came through the door.

"Hey, Tanner had to dip but—" His eyes locked on the shirt. "What the hell happened?"

Matt paused on the steps, confusion and amusement on his face.

"You wouldn't believe me if I told you."

SIX

"**T**HE UNLIMITED credit is nice, but it's also *great* for cutting lines of Colombian snow."

Lisa Fang held the black card up for everyone at the table to see. A pair of designer sunglasses dangled from the collar of her *Anti-Social Social Club* T-shirt. Her hair was dyed blonde except for the tips, which were vibrant pink.

"I can confirm that last part," Logan Brewster added with a grin, sitting beside her. "Nothing cuts the lines better." The Legatus put his arm around Lisa and kissed her on the cheek.

Matt sat across from them, unsure of what to say. It was just after 1 p.m. on Wednesday in Galbraith Hall, the last half-hour when lunch was served. It was a beautiful day outside, the weather was fair, and here they were at the third-year table eating pizza and talking about cocaine. Or at least, the others were. Whenever he tried to sit with people he didn't usually talk to—some ill-conceived attempt to expand his social circle—he always clammed up. He was frequently unsure what to add to their conversations, and on a topic like this he was completely lost.

Logan looked at him. "You ever try the coco, Matt?"

He shrugged. "Nah, it's not for me."

"Right…I forgot you're a prude," the Legatus said. Lisa and a few others in the group surrounding them snickered.

Matt clenched his fists under the table, then slowly exhaled. "I'm sure your parents appreciate their money going right up your nose."

Logan smirked and leaned back in his seat, spreading out. "What Daddy doesn't know can't hurt him." The others chuckled.

Matt sighed and stood up. "I'm gonna get some more water. I'll be right back."

He headed into the cafeteria and made straight for the soda fountain; the water was the second setting on the iced tea dispenser. He sighed as he filled up the cup, trying not to imagine the inevitable future where Logan Brewster was the 116th male Imperator. He pulled the cup away and turned around, just as someone else moved toward the machine—

And came face-to-face with Joan Keating.

"Oh…hey," she said, suddenly embarrassed.

"Everything okay last night?"

"After that? Yeah, yeah…it was just…you know…" Although she didn't often wear her hair in a manner to cover it, she was doing her best to keep the scar on the right side of her face tilted away. "I just wanted to say…I am really sorry about…throwing up on you." She broke into an awkward laugh at the end.

Matt laughed too. His cup-holding hand trembled slightly and he hoped she didn't notice. "Really, no worries."

They stood there in silence for a moment. Thinking quickly, he said, "I don't think we've ever properly met. I mean, I've seen you at the, ah…*Ice Cream Socials*, of course."

She laughed. "Right, yeah… I'm Joan."

"Matt." He offered his hand, then inwardly cringed. *What the fuck are you doing?*

But Joan shook it anyway and smiled. He noticed she was even prettier up close and regretted not combing his hair. Shit, he probably looked like an unmade bed.

"Nice talking to you under more…sober circumstances," she said, tilting her head.

"Nice talking to you, too. See you around."

"Yeah, see you." She waved bye and exited back into the dining hall. It took him a moment to realize she'd never filled up her drink.

Matt walked around the cafeteria for a moment to buy time before heading back to his seat at the third-year table. Joan was seated with Val and some friends at the other end.

Logan was still slouched back in his chair, his left arm resting on the wooden backing as he talked to Lisa and his friend Tony Madruga.

Matt took a sip of his water and quietly exhaled, wondering how the hell he'd ended up here. He thought all the way back to Frosh Week of first-year, when Radcliffe had opened its doors to his class and the two Quads stretched away like a dream. He remembered his parents hugging him goodbye and the feeling of being left in his House Saunders dorm room, alone for the first time. It had sunk in then that childhood was at an end, and whatever lay before him was something new.

His parents had encouraged him to apply for Radcliffe over WCU's other colleges, even though his dad had gone to Forrestal. It was the most prestigious one, they'd said. He'd always had a tough time fitting in at school. Maybe it would be better if he was surrounded by kids with gifted-level IQs, people who'd share his penchant for being better at academics than making friends. He'd pictured Cliffe students as quiet nerds; they'd sit at High Table events in their *Harry Potter* gowns talking about video games, movies, and books. Knowledge of *Star Wars* would be cultural capital and taking a sip of Mike's Hard Lemonade would be considered edgy.

He remembered standing around the East Quad with all the other frosh that fine September morning, all of them in their blue shirts with their WCU graduation year inscribed upon them. He'd seen Joan Keating for the first time then, standing shyly about twenty feet away in another group. Some frosh liked to streak gold paint under their eyes—the college's colors were gold and blue—but he'd noticed that Joan had hers on angles from her cheekbones to her temples. He later wondered if she'd done it to conceal her scar for the first day.

Then a loud voice had bellowed: "KNEEL FOR THE *FUCKING* MINISTER!"

And in that moment, his view of Radcliffe College had changed forever.

The head frosh leader had emerged, adorned as a Presbyterian minister, and delivered a five-minute litany degrading the frosh as the "worst year ever," a chant repeated in unison by every other leader. Later that semester, he'd found out most of them were in a cult—if you could really call it that. And the following semester, he'd become a member of said pseudo-cult. He'd entered Radcliffe swearing not to touch alcohol until he was older, even though Alberta's drinking age was eighteen, but by that first November he'd come to admire hard liquor for its efficiency and cider as his preferred alternative to beer.

Those had been the days, first-year. The other residents of House

Saunders had formed a clique without him, but he'd found a home in the most unlikely of places: the forbidden secret society, the one decried for mocking students' debauchery and misdeeds.

The news articles he'd read about Anathema made it sound like the villain of an elite college-set soap opera. Its Wikipedia article did it no favors either with a Controversy section longer than its History one. And yet, impossibly, it had been what pulled him back from the brink and made him feel welcomed—even through the shitstorm that had been his second-year.

Now though, he was starting to feel like an outsider in Radcliffe's halls, like it was high school all over again, but he still had his sights set on the biggest prize, the thing he'd wanted since his Initiation.

Matt looked across the table at the man most likely to take it from him, watched him laugh and scoff at what Lisa said. Everyone thought it would be Logan. It wouldn't be a reveal of the new Imperator at the Second Sermon's end; it would be a coronation.

There had been surprise picks before—last year even, yet no one considered anyone but Logan this time. Matt had been so careful to read jokes at the writing sessions, to present speeches at DebSoc when key players were present. Still, they all saw through him.

He hoped it would be that way come March. He wanted to see the look on their faces when Jackson Randall boomed the words: "And now, the Great Lord's 116th Imperator…*Matthew Michael Richardson!*"

The college would never see it coming.

◆

Val and the others were deep in some conversation, but Joan was lost in her empty cup. She'd forgotten to fill it up after her conversation with Matt and was too embarrassed to go back. Nobody at the table seemed to notice she'd returned with exactly what she left with.

She'd enjoyed that little chat with him, though. Last night, she hadn't made a very good impression. Scratch that—she'd made a terrible impression. She'd thrown up on him for fuck's sake. And yet the conversation had gone well, not because anything substantial had been said, but because she'd recognized the tell-tale awkwardness of two people attracted to each other hanging between their words.

Emotionally, Matt Richardson appeared to be an open book. She'd seen him look happy, sad, wounded, and read these signs clearly on his face over the years.

Yes, he definitely liked her.

Maybe.

It was a nicer thought than everything else on her mind recently, all thanks to Rich Benson. She couldn't help but replay their last conversation over and over again. She thought about those things he'd said and the things she'd said in reply. Even now, she knew she'd meant them—though him being dead made her regret a few.

Through it all, only one clear observation surfaced from the murk of her mind.

The death of someone you hate is a curious thing.

SEVEN

THE ALTHOUSE Gate clanged shut behind him. Matt hurried along the path from the back of Radcliffe, down the hill, and into the woods of Bethune's Walk. Soon the lights of res rooms dimmed behind him and he was swallowed by the trees. The once full moon had begun to wane, but between its glow and that of the lampposts he could see orange-brown colors all around. Leaves rustled up above while others littered the grass and sidewalk.

He knew the namesake of these parts had been a botanist at the school fifty years ago. During Frosh Week, the leaders tried to convince incoming students that Dr. Augustus Bethune had gone missing out here, that his ghost still haunted these woods. Like half of what he'd been told that week—first-years can't walk on the grass in either Quad, the portraits of departing Provosts were done by randomly selected students, the chandeliers in Picard Hall were salvaged from the *Titanic*, etc.—it was nonsense, but the small superstitious part of Matt had never let him roam these paths after dark.

Tonight, however, he was making an exception.

It was too chilly for insects and there were no owls in the region; the only sounds were wind whipping through the trees and the crunch of leaves beneath his sneakers. The path wound deeper and deeper into the forest, eventually coming to a junction. He knew that to the left, it snaked toward a parking lot; to the right was where he wanted to go.

Though Joan Keating had occupied a significant portion of his thoughts over the past twenty-four hours, another name danced in his brain as well: Rich Benson. It was not only the fact that someone he had seen living and breathing was now dead, but the questions raised by how it had happened.

Why had Benson been out here so late at night? What about that one cop's instincts made him question whether or not it had really been an accident?

Something about it bugged Matt, who had always been fascinated by mysteries both real and fictional. He decided, having reached a suitable point in writing an essay, to go for a little stroll and see exactly where it had happened.

Matt turned another bend and there it was, the bridge illuminated by a single lamppost thirty feet away, blocked off by crime scene tape. The faint gurgling of water reached his ears. There was something unsettling about this place, knowing that someone's life had ended here less than forty-eight hours ago. He wondered if this had been a stupid idea, if he should just turn back.

After a moment's contemplation, he slowly edged forward, one foot after the other.

He ducked under the crime scene tape. The bridge became closer and closer until suddenly he stood right there. Directly to his right, there was a significant gap between where the railing began and the trees ended. He walked over and stood at the top of the gully; below was the embankment and the stream of dark water itself.

So it had happened here.

He stared down the incline for some time, lost in thought, then looked around at the sidewalk and the ground. It seemed unlikely that someone would have tripped here. There were no roots sticking out and the path was evenly paved. And while the slope was fairly steep, it didn't look like a dangerous angle. A large rock jutted up in the brook, but to fall and roll all the way down to it—with enough force to knock yourself out—would require considerable speed.

Maybe he'd been running.

From what? he wondered.

Or rather, from *who?*

Benson getting pushed was more likely. Someone could've lured him out here, a midnight meeting. Why Benson would've had a secret meeting in the woods, Matt had no clue, but he wanted to think through all the possibilities, even the wild ones. If people were going to spread rumors that Anathema had something to do with Benson's death, Matt wanted to see if it was possible someone could've actually killed him.

He pictured the murderer leaning there against the railing, a dark humanoid shape with no discernable features, a shimmering black mannequin. He saw Rich Benson too, now approaching the figure. They talked. *About what?*

The killer had told Benson it was something important—something they didn't want the prying ears of Radcliffe to overhear. Benson and the dark figure discussed something; the figure moved closer. It grabbed Benson and violently pushed him down the embankment.

No, that wouldn't have been enough force.

It grabbed him by the shirt, pulled him back, then *threw* him down there. He tumbled all the way into the water, smashing his head on that rock. The killer watched from up here, waiting for signs of movement. There were none. Rich Benson drowned unconscious in the creek, his killer fleeing down the path.

No, you're overthinking things. That's way too dramatic.

Matt shook his head. What the hell was he doing out here anyway? There was no evidence it *was* a murder. Just because there was no uneven sidewalk or a stray root didn't mean Benson couldn't have fallen out of his own clumsiness, or because a bird flew past him out of the trees. It could've been caused by something inconceivably random. He could've tripped on an untied shoelace, for fuck's sake.

A noise reached his ears and Matt stiffened, his senses alert.

He turned around in a circle, but there was only dark forest around him on either side of the creek. However, he was certain he knew what that sound had been:

The snapping of a twig.

He wasn't sure which way it had come from, but it seemed to be on this side of the bridge.

You're jumping at shadows. There's nobody else out here.

Matt went under the crime scene tape and began briskly walking back the way he came, the forest engulfing him once more. By the time he turned left at the junction that would take him back to Radcliffe, it felt like something was behind him, following him. It was the dark, faceless figure, drawing closer and closer. In his mind, it gained speed but never ran—it merely walked faster, moving in increasingly mechanical steps, reaching a hand out for him. Nearer, nearer it drew. It was right behind him, about to grab his shirt collar and drag him back to the creek—

Matt broke into a run, dashing back along the slaloming path. The woods seemed endless, tall trees everywhere after each turn. Finally, he was free of the forest, sprinting back up the hill toward Radcliffe, toward safety. He was out of breath by the time he reached the Althouse Gate, but he didn't slow down. He tore his keys out of his pocket, fumbled for the right one—they'd changed everything to R3 locks this year—then opened the gate and threw himself inside. It swung shut behind him, the sound reverberating through the wind tunnel.

Matt remained bent over, his hands on his knees, catching his breath. Finally, he straightened up and walked back to the gate. He could see where the forest began at the bottom of the hill, the path vanishing into the blackness of Bethune's Walk.

Nothing was there.

The wind howled through the air.

He exhaled, wiped sweat from his brow, and stumbled through the wind tunnel to the East Quad, heading back to House Bowman and the bed that awaited him.

EIGHT

"**A**LL RISE for the President of the Radcliffe College Debate Society!"
The DebSoc exec burst through the doors, gowns draped over casual dress and court wigs adorning several of their heads. They fanned out into the room uttering "Rabble, rabble, rabble" on an endless loop, and from their midst a man in a black tricorn hat emerged. He was tall with blond hair and a narrow face. Unlike the other gowns, which were plain black, he'd fashioned his own from a tartan quilt, and wore a suit and tie underneath. He adjusted his rimless glasses with one hand, hoisting a baseball bat into the air with the other.

"Rabble, rabble," the man said, amused by the peculiar traditions of WCU's oldest debating club. He beamed as he took in the stellar attendance; it appeared many were seeking a cheery escape this Thursday evening.

He made his way down the aisle between the arranged sofas to sit in a tall-backed, wooden chair. A coffee table stood right before it, looking worse for wear. Two gowned students sat on each side of him in plush leather chairs reserved for debaters. The DebSoc exec leaned against the back wall behind the five seats, placing beer cans atop the fireplace mantle and chatting among themselves.

Matt sat in a front row sofa next to two people he didn't really know; most of his friends were on the exec. He watched as the man in the tricorn hat slammed the bat against the table several times. A *Shhh* rose from the exec and gradually made its way around.

The Mountainview Room had been named for its Rocky vistas back in the day, but the construction of the Dales Building had obscured them thirty years ago. The walls were lined with oak panels and Radcliffe's griffin crest was carved at various points in the wood. Three large windows were located to Matt's left and some who hadn't gotten seats leaned against the sills; others stood around idly.

The first-years sat on the floor, as usual, and had to give their seat on a sofa to an upper-year if asked. It had annoyed Matt back then, but now that he enjoyed such privileges, he had to admit they had their benefits.

The man in the tricorn hat stood and, tapping the bat against his shoulder, swept the room with a wide grin.

"Now…," Tom Turland said. "Who here has never been to DebSoc before?"

His voice boomed and the room was swiftly at attention, the last whispers suddenly snuffed out.

At the back, a second-year named Josh held his friend's hand up. "He hasn't! He goes to St. Mark's." A whisper rose around the room; St. Mark's was traditionally Catholic, while Radcliffe had been founded by Presbyterians. Nobody in the room was particularly religious, but using the college's Protestant roots to jokingly bash Catholicism was a time-honored tradition.

"Step forward," Turland beckoned, holding out the end of the bat. The St. Mark's student awkwardly made his way to the front and stood before him. "Do you know what this is?"

The student raised an eyebrow. "Uh…it's a Louisville Slugger?"

Turland shook his head and gestured to the bat. "It is the Holy Mace, used to uphold the fairness, truth, and justice that this organization stands for." He pointed it at the student again. "Now place your hand upon it and repeat after me."

The student reached out and grabbed the end of the bat.

"I…," Turland began.

"I…," the student repeated.

"State your name."

"Ted Pelham."

"NOOOOO!" the room roared in unison. Ted was stunned, his cheeks flushing red.

Turland shook his head like a disappointed father. "No, *repeat* after me. I…"

"I..."

"State your name."

"Uh...*Edward* Pelham?"

"*NOOOOO!*" everyone howled again, this time even louder.

"You fucking *idiot!*" some guy called from the back of the room.

Ted looked like he might piss himself.

"Third time's the charm," Turland said, gesturing with his left hand, his right still wielding the Mace. "I..."

"I..."

"State your name."

"State...your name?" Ted repeated.

The room erupted in massive applause. People cheered, someone whistled, and many others clapped aggressively. Matt tiredly clapped along with them. It took nearly a minute for everything to quiet down again, Turland kicking the coffee table with his boot while still holding out the Mace.

"SILENCE!" he thundered. That finally got them. He turned back to Ted, who had gone pale. "Now...where were we?" Turland thought for a moment, then smiled. "Ah, yes. We'll continue with: 'swear upon my life.' "

"Swear upon my life."

"...to not text and drive..."

Ted looked increasingly confused. "To not text and drive..."

"...to buckle my seatbelt..."

"To buckle my seatbelt..."

"...and to obey all the rules of the road."

"And to obey...all the rules...of the road." Ted swallowed.

"Unless I'm in Toronto..."

"Unless I'm in Toronto..."

"...because driving there is a fucking free-for-all."

Ted said softly, "Because driving there is a fucking free-for-all."

Turland reached inside his suit jacket pocket and withdrew a large scroll. "Now read all of this out loud." He let the very long sheet of paper tumble out onto the floor.

"What the hell is that?" Ted said.

"It's the Magna Carta," Turland replied, gesturing to the paper, "in *seven* different languages."

Ted said nothing, his eyes bulging out of his head.

"Too much?" Turland asked. He dropped the scroll. "Let's just go back to repeating." He threw his head back and bellowed, "SO HELP ME…!"

"So help me," Ted whispered.

"GREAT LORD ANATHE—*Whoops!*" Turland held up a finger. "Freudian slip."

Chuckles erupted around the room. Rufus Danvers, leaning against the back wall, cupped his hands over his mouth and shouted, "One-One-Three! One-One-Three!"

A few others started to join in, but Turland dismissed them all with an angry wave. "No, no," he said. "You're two years too late." He turned back to Ted, who looked more confused than ever. "Let's backtrack a little: SO HELP ME…!"

"So help me," Ted winced.

"…THADDEUS RADCLIFFE!"

"Thaddeus Radcliffe."

Turland gave a massive exhale, then switched the Mace to his left hand and offered his other to Ted. Speaking once again in a normal level of volume, he said, "Welcome to the Debate Society."

The crowd erupted in applause.

Ted shook Turland's hand, then shuffled his way back to the rear, looking like he regretted coming.

Matt glanced around at the faces in the room. He didn't see Joan anywhere, though he recalled seeing her here a few times this semester. She'd held a committee position last year but hadn't run for one again. Most people involved in Radcliffe's traditions were either attendees or exec members. In fact, looking at the row of people standing along the back wall, he saw that Anathema was represented quite well. That was the norm from year to year, which had led critics in the past to decry certain DebSoc exec teams as "AnatheSoc."

Matt scanned the back row. Almost all of them had been "poored out"—their gowns ripped to shreds to reward various actions around the college—and had turned the remains into sashes. Turland's gown-quilt hybrid was unique and, depending on who you talked to, rather extra. He saw Tanner Cho and Hamid Mohsen whispering at one end, Kylie Patel standing tall and imposing in the center next to Rufus, and Sandrine down at the other corner—once again dressed in all black. Alyssa Lee stood directly behind Turland, the Vice President silently watching the event unfold. There were other current or former Anathema members on the exec in a variety of elected or appointed positions, including Patrick Mason himself, last year's President.

The First-Year Representatives walked around handing free beers to attendees left and right. Alcohol was a major expenditure for the club each week, but with its annual levy of $13,000 it could more than afford it. When offered a drink, Matt politely waved the first-year off. He'd get something at the bar later.

Turland sat back down and folded the Mace across his lap. "Are there any committee addresses?"

"I have an announcement from the Women's Tennis Committee," said a loud voice.

A big, pasty man stepped forward and adjusted his sash. His thick lips were moist, his dark hair shaggy. Carl Dunlap won his Student Events Officer election in a surprise victory, and this year lived in the Officer's Suite of House Winslow. His committee name came from his frequent sports commentary livestreams on Instagram—and from an incident in House Saunders last year. A first-year caught him pleasuring himself to videos of women's doubles at Wimbledon; the door to his room had been wide open.

"Some people have asked me if we're gonna cancel the party this weekend because of what happened to Rich Benson…may he rest in peace. But I say, we're going to continue on in Rich's name and throw an absolute *rager* in his honor! That's right. This weekend, the year's gonna get started for real with House Winslow's disco party! We're gonna have all the big hits of the seventies: the Bee Gees, Donna Summer, and of course…ABBA."

Excited whispering rose around the room.

"So reach Winslow this Saturday at 10 p.m. It's going to be *fire*. The Facebook event will be up soon." Dunlap returned to the back wall.

"Thank you, Carl," Turland said. "As you all know, the only music I listen to is ABBA and the *Caillou* theme song, so I'm glad one of my niches will be satisfied this weekend." He slammed the Mace down on the table. "Are there any other committee addresses?"

Silence hung in the room.

"I'll take that as a no. Any Government or Opposition business?"

Tony Madruga, the Government House Leader, and Catherine Winters, his Opposition equivalent, each shook their heads.

Turland adjusted his tricorn hat. "Well then, in that case we can move on to the main event. As you know, tonight's theme is a very serious topic."

He smiled and all but winked. "This is the Vaccination Debate, during which we will discuss whether or not vaccines have…*adverse effects* on a child's cognitive development. Could I get the resolution as read by the Clerk?"

Sophia Huynh, a tall raven-haired second-year Anathema member, took the center stage to read something from her phone. "Be it resolved that…" She mimicked the voice of a stereotypical suburban mother: "If I get my kids vaccinated, they might end up going to St. Mark's College."

A hush of *Oohs* went around and a few people nudged Ted at the back, his face having gone red again. "It's not a good night for you, pal," his buddy Josh teased.

Sophia returned to the back wall as Turland slammed the Mace against the table several times. "Speaking first for the Government is…Jennifer Horvat!"

A short brunette stood up to unfold a sheet of paper, circular glasses perched on her round face. "So tonight's resolution is about vaccines or something," she boomed, "but I only found out I was debating three hours ago because some dipshit dropped out at the last minute. So"—she took a deep breath—"I'm just going to tangentially relate the topic back to stuff I'm sure you're all *dying* to hear about: my love life!"

She proceeded to describe a Tinder date with an anti-vaxxer Forrestal student who believed it was good to avoid getting your shots because vaccines were "products of Big Pharma." Her speech got a solid ovation and the next debater, this time for the Opposition, used the vaccination topic as a launching pad to discuss his sex life. He joked that if he hadn't gotten the HPV vaccine, he probably would've contracted it by now, before segueing into a discussion of how his girlfriend got turned on when he checked his stocks post-coitus. The third debater argued there was no point in getting any more vaccines because he'd probably die of syphilis by age thirty. The fourth was stoned out of her mind and, after apologizing for not having a speech written, told a lengthy story of the first time she'd had sex while high on cocaine.

The speeches took about an hour in total, and through it all Matt sat in the front row trying to laugh along with the others, to act like he understood exactly what they were talking about. Every week, sure as the sunrise, debaters alluded to their erotic experiences. It was always some radical tidbit: the threesome that went wrong, disappointing Bumble starfish sex, someone losing their virginity at an aquarium.

He knew he was missing something. He'd managed to lie to them but he couldn't lie to himself.

After the onslaught of virgin jokes made about him at Anathema Sermons, DebSoc debates, and Galbraith tables, he'd finally broken down last March and told everyone a Tinder date with a Forrestal girl had gone farther than it really had. He'd felt like a faker, a fraud—until he'd learned that Sermon jokes about him had to be cut and DebSoc speeches were re-written.

He'd never understood why people here cared so much that he'd never had sex. He'd had a few opportunities, but they'd never felt like the right person or the right time. That wasn't a good enough explanation for Radcliffe. The college had swallowed the lie fairly well, but quickly found another failure to critique: he was now a third-year who'd never had a girlfriend in his entire life.

It was one thing when Anathema did it—they were supposed to make fun of you, and they always tried to hit their own members the hardest, showing the college that those writing jokes could take them too—but it was another thing when random first-years last term had called him lonely and inexperienced just to seem in-the-know with their DebSoc speeches.

After the last speaker sat down, Turland slammed the Mace against the table again. "It's time to vote. If you want the Government to win, move to this side of the room." He gestured with the bat to his right. "And if you think the Opposition did a better job, head over here." He motioned to his left.

Matt felt Jennifer had the best speech; it had also been the most related to the resolution. He moved to the appropriate side of the room while Turland stood atop the coffee table and counted heads. Finally, he spread his arms wide and announced: "The Government takes it!"

The crowd applauded Jennifer and her co-debater, then Turland jumped down from the table and yelled, "Now…who's ready to hit the bar?!"

◆

The DebSoc attendees streamed down into the basement of the Royal Pub, just as they did every week at the conclusion of their pilgrimage. They'd journeyed out the front doors of Radcliffe, through Griffin Park, across the residential streets of Canmore Creek, and finally arrived at this spot on the main drag. It was diagonally at the other end of the strip from the Foxhole, backing onto the ravine.

Matt was one of the last to enter. He hadn't talked to anyone on the walk over and wished Roy had come along tonight. He stepped off to the side and scanned the area, looking for people he could sit with.

The Royal's basement was done up with Christmas lights year-round, chalkboards and mirrors along the walls. There were several TVs around the room, all showing a hockey game. The bar itself was in the back-left corner, bottles lining the racks behind it. To the right stood a seven-foot-tall replica of Big Ben, displaying the current time of 10:56 p.m.

Matt saw that Turland, Patrick, and Doug Sadler—the male Magister—were seated strategically close to the bar at a table by the back. Turland had left his tartan gown back at the college, or maybe dropped it off at his residence along the way. A seat was open beside Doug.

He made his way across the room, then realized the three of them were deep in discussion as he drew nearer. Matt hesitated, but Turland noticed him and waved. "Oh, hey!"

"Anyone sitting here?" Matt pointed to the chair.

"You are," Turland said with a smile, gesturing for him to take a seat.

Matt did so. Doug turned toward him and said, "We were just discussing the merits of Randall's, ah...*joint leadership* role this year."

"I have no doubt he's capable of it." Patrick took a swig of beer. Evidently, he'd gotten to the front of the line and started a tab early. "It's the principle of holding both positions at the same time that bugs me. Think about it: one is supposed to be a leader you can trust, someone you can discuss everything from bullying to mental health with. The other is a cloaked cultist who mocks you while surrounded by a bunch of mask-wearing people holding candles. See how that would create some trust issues?"

Doug sighed. "But this way Randall can make sure any complaints are actually listened to. You know Jack; he's a good, respectable guy. He's in the Air Force for fuck's sake. If anything, I think he's going too soft on the content because he's afraid of impeachment. I've seen what he's assembled of the Sermon so far and it's about as hard-hitting as an episode of *SpongeBob*. Logan and I've been pushing him to ramp it up a bit."

"He's right to fear impeachment," Patrick said. "If even one student feels victimized by the First Sermon, they can go straight to the admin—and you know they hate how Jack's double dipping. I've seen it at all our

Council meetings. They like him enough as an Officer, but Mustard and Crawley would gladly hang him out to dry if it meant dealing Anathema a blow."

"I don't think Jack's gonna get impeached," Turland said, getting to his feet. "I'm gonna grab a beer, I'll be right back." He headed to the bar.

"There have been Officer-Imperators before, though," Matt pointed out. "It's not like this is a new thing."

"Yes, but that was much more common before Dissociation," Patrick said.

Doug shook his head. "No, the last one from our branch was in 2006, and he was Student Events Officer and Imperator at the same time. The girls had one in 2010 who was Off-Res Officer and Imperator, and then the last time either branch had an active member on the Council was…2014, I think. But he wasn't on Tetrad, he was just a fourth-year member."

"And it would have been better had he been the last," Patrick said. "Believe me, I know Jack Randall's a good guy—and that's why I'm glad we're experiencing this with him. He won't abuse the power, but by the end I think he'll realize what a catastrophic mistake it was. Not because he can't handle the work load or the responsibility, but because of the sheer *uproar* at this college last year. People were livid when they found out a recently-elected Officer was a new Imperator. You were there at the SGM, you heard what they said about the organization—"

"Yeah, but it's always been like that," Doug said. "Everyone at this college either gets super into the Sermons, or hates Anathema with every fiber of their being. And the latter always tries to seem like they 'stand for the whole college' and that kind of bullshit, but we know they just can't take a joke—or they're bitter they didn't get in. Deep down they want to run around the forest writing poetry too, and they won't even admit it to themselves."

Patrick shook his head. "They tried to get Anathema members banned from running for elected positions."

"And they failed," Matt said, recalling that shitshow of a Student Governance Meeting last April. "If anything, it backfired. People voted to alter the amendment. Now Anathema members just have to declare they're staying in it during their Officer term. By trying to make sure Randall never happened again, they ended up legitimizing him in the Electoral Policy."

The basement entrance swung open wildly. Everyone turned their heads as a group of guys in leather jackets entered. With their hair slicked back and their almost-matching outfits, they looked like a bunch of nineties boy band rejects.

Matt knew exactly who they were: the occupants of House Saunders. When he'd lived there with Patrick in his first-year, he'd known several of them as quiet business and math students. They did nothing but play *FIFA* or beer pong in the common room, preferring each other's company to the crowds of major res parties.

Matt had moved to Bowman in second-year and remained there, but when Patrick returned to Saunders this year to claim his Officer's Suite, he'd found that the ones who stayed behind had changed. Even though Saunders, unlike Winslow, was typically populated by newcomers, these residents had stayed on into their second- and third-years, publicly rejecting the other social houses as "inferior" and "uncool."

"Oh wonderful," Doug said, glancing over his shoulder. "Look who it is."

One with a square-jawed face and an undercut on the left side of his head stepped forward, looking around for a seat. Chet Tremblay shook his head, then spun back to face his crew. "Doesn't look like Social Cliffe saved any seats for us, boys," he said loudly. "You know how they just love to include us."

"Aw, fuck," Patrick muttered. "Not this again."

"Yo, why are we even here?" said another, Blaine Harris. He was lean with spiky brown hair and always had a smarmy look on his face. "We go here all the time, let's go somewhere else."

"Where? The Foxhole? That's where *they* go," Chet said, pointing toward Doug, Matt, and Patrick. He appeared to be already inebriated. He'd probably led his gang in here just to piss on the DebSoc attendees for what they represented—to him, at least.

"Look, this is the best place in town." Chris Newman had always seemed to be the most level-headed of the group to Matt, even in first-year, and that was on display here. He put his hands on both Chet and Blaine's shoulders. "Let's just grab seats upstairs."

Chet blinked out of his drunken stupor. "Yeah, yeah, sure."

Chris led Chet and Blaine through a door beside the Big Ben clock, the last two members of the group following close behind: Kevin Gao, a tall guy on the Varsity basketball team, and Hank, whose bulky build had earned him the nickname Tank.

Turland arrived back at the table, holding a fresh pint.

"Well, that was interesting."

Patrick sighed. "I miss the old days of Saunders."

"Going back through our archives, I found it was a respected social house in the Sermons until about our first-year. Hey Patrick, isn't that when you first moved there?" Doug grinned.

Patrick flipped him the bird as he took another swig of beer.

◆

About an hour later, Matt and Tanner Cho exited onto Canmore Creek's main drag. Matt had had a few drinks, but the buzz was starting to wane. Tanner had stood up from his table and asked if anyone else was heading back to Radcliffe. Matt had left Turland, Patrick, and Doug to continue their discussion on Randall's dual positions.

It made him think of other undergrad organizations that were more covert, who kept the names of their members confidential. Those students would be free to run for positions and the school populace would be none the wiser. So much less controversy, so much less debate. Even though Matt loved the Sermons, it was times like this that he wished Anathema was a secret society more committed to the first part of its descriptor.

Beside him, Tanner inhaled the mountain air. "What a week. I've gotten buzzed twice already and we haven't even gotten to the weekend."

"Tuesday was a special circumstance," Matt pointed out. "And DebSoc always goes to the Royal on Thursdays."

"Yeah... It's kind of nuts that getting drunk every Thursday is a tradition here."

Matt shrugged. "Could be worse. Could be every Wednesday."

Tanner gave a brief laugh. "I guess you're right. It's *almost* the weekend, at least."

"Is for me," Matt said. "I worked out my schedule this year so I don't have class on Fridays."

"*Nice*... Speaking of the weekend..." Tanner turned to him. "You excited for Winslow on Saturday?"

"If there's one thing I'll give Carl Dunlap, it's that he knows how to throw a party."

"You, ah...looking forward to seeing anyone there?"

Matt tensed up, but kept walking. They cut behind another bar and emerged onto a residential street. At least five of the houses on this row were frats or sororities. "Not exactly," he said, trying his best to sound normal. He knew the pause had been a dead giveaway.

Tanner smiled and teased, "Joan Keating's gonna be there."

Matt's head whipped around. "How…how did you…?"

"Come on, Matt. I know just about everything at this college." He paused. "That, and Roy told me."

"Oh, I figured *that*. But how do you know she's going?"

"I heard her talking about it with some friends in Galbraith earlier today. She mentioned she'd be there."

Matt did his best to not audibly sigh with relief. "Does anybody else know about the, ah…vomit incident?"

Tanner laughed. "I'm not sure. It's not something she'd exactly spread around, but I'm sure Val will write some jokes about it. That's quality source material right there."

He scratched the back of his head. "You wouldn't mind keeping it quiet that I like her, would you? If it inevitably goes south, I don't want anyone knowing I've messed something up again."

Tanner patted him on the back. "Hey, give yourself some credit, pal. I'm rooting for you, and I know Roy is too." He looked forward again. "I haven't talked to her much, but she seems nice."

"What do you know about her?"

He shrugged. "I've heard she's one of the most dedicated members in the female branch. Some say she's kinda awkward, but she always shows up to meetings and writes good jokes, so even the ones who don't really like her put up with her."

She wants Tetrad too, Matt thought. The potential point of commonality brought a smile to his face.

"She dated anyone else recently?" he asked.

Tanner shook his head. "I know she and Rich Benson had a thing when she was a first-year, though. That was before I got here, of course, but I heard it mentioned a couple times this week."

Matt nodded. He remembered the Fall Formal of first-year, when after several glasses of Prosecco—the dance was always bubbly-themed—he'd finally summoned enough courage to ask Joan to dance with him. He'd gotten within ten feet of her when Benson walked up, kissed her, and led her to the dance floor. When he'd asked the next morning over brunch in

Galbraith, Patrick had confirmed they were dating. When he'd asked why Matt wanted to know, he'd shrugged it off with a "No reason."

"I figured that's why she got so drunk at the Foxhole."

Tanner nodded. "Yeah, that's understandable. I probably would've gotten wasted too if my ex died." He sighed. "Take things slow and give her space. She dated him a while ago, but you know, that shit's gonna affect you whether they had a good breakup or a bad one."

Matt couldn't recall it being good or bad, just something that had happened and he'd found out after the fact. By then he'd been focused on some other crushes. "Yeah, yeah, of course."

"Some try to go on like nothing happened. Others shut themselves away entirely. It really depends on the person."

Wanting to change the subject, even slightly, Matt said, "Speaking of Benson, do you think he really had an accident?"

They continued in silence for a while. Finally, Tanner just chuckled. "What, do you mean, like…maybe someone killed him?"

Matt paused too, looking at the ground as he walked. "Yeah…"

Tanner sighed. "I really hope not. That'd be bad for Anathema." He forced a grim laugh.

"Why?" Matt asked.

Tanner turned to him. "Because the only people who'd want him dead are us."

NINE

H E HEARD a knocking somewhere behind him.

Jack Randall's eyes blinked open, then he rubbed them and looked around. He lay on one of the sofas in the Chalet's lounge. His laptop and a number of textbooks and binders sat on a coffee table beside him.

Shit, how long was I out? he thought. A glance at his watch told him it was past midnight. Last he remembered, it had been before eleven. Groggily, he got up and made his way to the front door.

He opened it to find Tom Turland there, leaning against the frame with a big grin on his face. The tricorn hat still sat on his head.

"DebSoc cleared out of the Royal?" Randall asked. Turland nodded, then made his way past him inside. He looked like he'd had a fair bit to drink. "How was attendance this week?" Randall said, closing the door back over and locking it.

"Oh, the usual. I wasn't sure how turnout would be given Rich Benson, but..." He entered the lounge and turned around, spreading his hands. "I guess life at the college goes on."

"That was fast."

"He wasn't particularly popular," Turland said. "He'd made a fair number of enemies, namely us. And his death wasn't a suicide, so nobody feels bad for not noticing any signs, feeling like they could have done more. Once you remove the guilt factor, you'd be surprised how little people care about the deaths of those they have nothing to do with."

"So the Winslow party's still happening?"

Turland nodded. "Not even his own death could prevent Carl Dunlap from throwing a 'rager'," he said, making air quotes.

"Well, I guess that's something for everyone to look forward to," Randall said, rubbing his eyes again.

"You look like shit, by the way." There was a smile on his face as he said it.

Randall laughed and shook his head, walking into the lounge. "I'm up until four a.m. every night, three if I'm lucky."

"It's a lot to balance," Turland said. "Think of everything you do." He began pacing the room, faltering in his step only slightly. "You're Lt. Jackson Randall, Royal Canadian Air Force, the 115th Imperator of the Great Lord Anathema, *and* the male Radcliffe College Off-Residence Affairs Officer."

Randall chuckled and shook his head. "Not to mention I'm a fourth-year WCU student. Most people here barely get enough sleep as it is without all this extracurricular bullshit."

Turland looked around the room. "So you're still splitting your time between here and Gemma's place?"

"Yeah, it's good for at least one of the Imperators to live here. Back in the early 2000s, two of them dated and used this place as their secret society love shack."

"We haven't had an Imperator couple in a while," Turland said, scratching his chin. "Who were the last ones again?"

"Jacob Eamon and Natalie Banting, 2003-2004." Randall hoped he'd gotten the years right; Doug was always much better with that stuff. He'd even memorized the exact dates of every Sermon for the past decade. "They'd been dating since before they got the positions, I think. Doug told me they had a big kiss in front of everyone after their respective Baptisms."

"I'm glad I never had to go through one of those," Turland said. "Waste of good beer. Not to mention the tux."

Randall shrugged. "I needed a new one anyway."

Turland smirked. "Given any thought to who might get their tux ruined next March?"

He shook his head. "It's far too early to tell. I have…a couple ideas, but there's so much else to do first and I'm swamped with all this—"

"Of course," Turland said, holding up his hands. "Plenty of time."

The room was quiet, each of them gazing around at the bookshelves and the furniture. Finally, Randall turned back to him.

"You didn't come here to talk about the next Imperator." It was a statement, not a question.

"No," Turland said, sitting down on a sofa. "I came here to talk about who killed Rich Benson."

For a moment, Randall stood still. Then he raised a finger and headed back to a bedroom down the hall. He returned a few moments later with a bottle of scotch and two glasses.

"You see, this is why we're friends, Jack," Turland said, watching Randall pour each of them three fingers. He handed Turland his glass, and the DebSoc President raised it toward him. "You speak my language."

Randall returned his toast. "*Carpe risus, carpe coronam.*"

"Yeah, that stuff," Turland said, taking a big sip.

Randall lowered the glass from his lips and sat in a sofa opposite him. "How many drinks have you had already?"

"Oh, a couple of pints, some gin and tonics...doubles." He gave a dismissive wave. "Just your average Thursday at DebSoc."

"Sorry I couldn't come. I was busy with an essay."

"We're avoiding the topic at hand."

Randall sighed. "How did you figure out it had to be murder?"

He took another sip of scotch and shrugged. "Put it together myself, really. You told me what the RCMP told the admin and it sounded a little suspicious to me, so I went for a walk by that creek earlier today. Didn't look like the kind of thing you'd just accidentally fall into and die."

"Rufus broke his wrist during the Beckonings in our first-year by falling off a curb."

"Yes," Turland said, gesturing with his glass, "but that's *Rufus*. Speaking of which, I'm surprised you brought him back."

"He wanted to return. He just didn't like Madler."

"He said some unkind things about the Anathema after dropping his pendant last year, and now we've just accepted him back with open arms?"

Randall shrugged. "The prodigal son returns."

Turland scoffed. "He missed it, that fucker. I can tell. He just wanted to come back for his last year so he could write more jokes about people he hates."

"His content can be a bit...vitriolic, but if you filter out that stuff, he does write some good jokes. Also, I don't think this year's his last. He said something about doing a fifth."

Turland leaned his head back. "Ah, so he wants *Tetrad*, that's it."

"Possibly."

"God help the Imperator who puts Rufus Danvers on his fucking Tetrad," he said, taking another big sip of scotch.

"We're getting off topic."

"Right, right," Turland said, sitting up. "What were we talking about again? Oh right, murder."

Randall sighed. "Now, it doesn't seem likely he had an accident, but…"

"Somebody whacked him. Admit it."

Randall set his glass on the coffee table. "It is very likely that someone deliberately pushed Rich Benson into that creek. That's all I'm saying."

"The police are going to come to that conclusion too."

"I think they already have, but they've been keeping quiet about it. I know they've been interviewing students around the college. They started with Benson's friends first."

"Have they come to you?"

"I don't think they've made the Anathema connection just yet."

Turland sighed. "Well, this is going to be a fuckshow. They'll of course think that one of us did it."

Randall hesitated. "I think one of us did."

Turland raised an eyebrow. "You don't think this has anything to do with the snitch, do you?"

Again, he paused. "I don't know, but the more I think about it, the more that makes sense."

"Come on," Turland said, nearly spilling his glass. "Benson was a journalist. If he was getting his information from someone, maybe they wanted to put an end to that."

"But what information? The leaks to the admin have been pains in my side, but nothing even *I'd* kill over, let alone my Tetrad or another member. I have a hard-enough time getting half of them to show up to writing sessions; they're certainly not fanatical enough to kill somebody and stage it as an accident."

"Maybe I've just read a lot of Agatha Christie," Turland said, "but what if Benson was blackmailing a member of the Anathema into feeding him information? A dark secret that was theirs alone, not the organization's, something they didn't want out there at all. The blackmailer always gets killed in Christie books."

Randall thought for a moment. "That's possible."

"The one thing I don't get, though—even in that scenario—is why he was out in Bethune's Walk after midnight in the first place..." Turland looked deep in thought.

Randall's muscles tensed and he was silent for some time.

Then he said, very calmly, "I have no idea."

TEN

DISCO BALL lights spun through the Winslow Common Room windows, music growing louder as Matt neared the res house's entrance in the West Quad. Shifting his tall-boy of cider to his other hand, Matt unlocked the door with his R3 key and opened it, letting Donna Summer's "I Feel Love" blare out into the night.

He walked up the staircase past the second and third floor landings, then finally reached the fourth and highest floor. It was 10:45 and barely anyone was here yet, but that was par the course for parties at this college. They called it the Cliffe Clock—you showed up at least an hour late to anything.

Roy's room was in the eastern pod and was the only one within it that had a fireplace; it was also larger than the other three, which is why such rooms were reserved for those with the most years on residence. Roy had been a veteran of the house since he was a frosh. Matt knocked on the door and it swung open.

"Look who it is," Roy said, hefting a beer and gesturing him to come inside. There was a bookshelf and a large liquor cabinet to the left, a bed in the back-left corner, a wooden desk along the back wall beneath the window, and a closet directly to the right of the door. A sword was displayed above the fireplace on the right wall and a red rug spread out across the floor. Tanner sat on the bed, his phone in one hand and a tall-boy can in the other.

He looked up as Matt came in. "Hey, Dunlap is doing an Instagram livestream downstairs." He held up the phone.

They walked over and joined Tanner in watching an inebriated Dunlap hold the camera too close to his face. His big, wet lips filled the screen. "Yo guys!" he shouted. "REACH WINSLOW! This is gonna be the most fire party ever! I've invited over 400 people to the Facebook event. Let's make this the most lit night Radcliffe College has ever seen! WOOOO!"

The feed cut out.

Tanner sighed and shook his head. "It's true, what he said. I've checked the event page and there are over 400 people invited. I don't recognize most of them; they must be from other colleges."

"So, won't that be a good thing?" Matt said.

"I've only been here one year and even *I* know that bad things happen when you invite a bunch of randoms. They've got no respect for Radcliffe and always trash the place."

Roy leaned across the desk and cranked the window open, looking out. "I think some of them are already here." Matt got up and came over to look. Down in the West Quad he could see a large crowd making its way toward Winslow, their voices rising on the wind. "Well, if anything, this should be a wild night."

"Clearly I need to get caught up on drinking," Matt said. He opened his can of cider and took a sip.

"Yeah, I'm only on my fourth drink." Roy took another swig of beer and moved to his liquor cabinet. On top was a photo of him with a falcon perched on his arm, from a time he went hunting on his aunt's British Columbia estate a few years ago. "I'm not even feeling a buzz yet." He took out a bottle of rum and a shot glass.

"Jesus," Matt chuckled, taking a bigger sip. "Don't blackout before the party starts."

"Relax, I haven't blacked-out since second-year." Roy poured himself a shot, threw it back, and then chased it with a big swig of beer.

Matt looked around the room, his eyes coming to rest on the landline phone that sat on the desk. "Ah, you haven't unplugged yours?"

Roy turned around. Both he and Tanner looked confused. "Why would I do that?"

"Remember last year what Patrick was saying, about the admin being able to listen in at any time?"

"Wait, just during phone calls or *all* the time?" Tanner asked.

"All the time…supposedly," Matt explained. "Patrick said he'd heard it from someone he knew in the admin office, but he wasn't sure if they were actively doing it or just had the *capability* of doing it."

All three of them stared at the phone in silence.

"Not sure if it's true, but I unplugged mine anyway," Matt added.

Roy moved forward and yanked the cord out from the back of the phone.

Tanner nodded. "Well, that settles that." He took another sip of his beer. "The admin doesn't seem like they'd spy on people, though. I've met John Mustard twice; he seems like a pretty nice guy for all the bad things we say about him."

"He desperately wants to be WCU President, we know that," Roy said. "Provost is just a stepping stone for him, he doesn't care about the college."

"I don't know," Tanner said. "Maybe we should give him a little more credit. The admin could be cracking down on things way harder than they are."

"Crawley's a better Dean of Students than Sorenson, I'll give her that, but I hear Sarah Knowles was much better before him," Roy said.

"She's Vice Provost now, right?" Matt asked.

Roy nodded. "I hope she's Mustard's successor. She actually respects the traditions here."

"Speaking of successors," Tanner said. "Who do you guys think will be the new Imperators next year?"

Roy winked at Matt. "Yes, who *will* be our next Imperator…?"

Matt held up his hands. "I have no clue."

Tanner smirked. "I think it's either you or Logan for sure. No one in my year is ready, except maybe Hamid… Everyone thinks it will be *him* after next year."

Matt recognized the bitterness in his voice. He and Tanner were in the same boat one year apart, although at least he was friends with his competition and probably wouldn't be *too* upset if he lost it to him. Matt hoped he'd be the one to have to pick between them.

"Everyone thinks it'll be Logan," Matt pointed out.

"Last time I checked it wasn't a democracy. Randall was an unexpected choice, maybe his pick will surprise everyone too."

"I have no clue who Kylie's gonna choose," Roy said. "Maybe Alyssa Lee. I could see her doing it."

"I've heard Catherine Winters is in the running," Tanner added.

"Remember the days when people in Tetrad *left* after they had one year in it?" Matt scoffed.

"I think it's better to have new leaders every year," Roy said. "Although I guess it could be a surprise if you thought someone was leaving and then they ended up taking over."

"Yeah, but this year a Tetrad member is a predictable pick in each branch," Matt said. "It's like a murder mystery where the detective is obviously the killer. That's not a good twist if you see it coming a mile away."

"Is it really supposed to be a surprise?" Tanner asked.

"That's why they don't even tell us," Roy said. "They know it would get out. It always creates a good amount of interest for the Second Sermon. I know the reveals used to be *much* more dramatic years ago. In the nineties, one Imperator rappelled down from the rafters in Picard Hall wearing a cloak, then tore back his hood just as they announced his name."

Tanner whistled. "Shame they don't do it that way anymore."

"Do you guys hear that?" Roy asked, looking toward the door.

Matt listened too. It sounded like voices, a lot of them, coming from the hallway. He glanced at his watch. "The party can't be going yet. It's barely eleven."

The three of them made their way to the door and Roy pulled it open. To their surprise, the corridor was packed with people drinking from red Solo cups and talking. Roy closed over the door, returned to his liquor cabinet, and proceeded to pull another two shot glasses out. He poured rum into all three of them, then handed them each a glass.

"We're gonna need these," he said, grabbing his own. They clinked them together and did their shots in unison. Roy scratched his chin and looked from his empty glass to the door, where the voices were getting louder. "We're gonna need more."

They did another round.

"Okay," Roy said, loosening his shoulders as if about to enter a boxing ring. "Let's do this."

Matt and Tanner picked up their tall-boys. Roy polished off his, then cracked open a new one and opened the door. They headed out into the corridor, moving toward the stairwell door. Matt barely recognized any of these people; he hoped most of them were just first-years. Tanner was right, people from other colleges generally hated Radcliffe for its perceived elitism and wouldn't care if they trashed a bathroom or two. Or a whole floor.

What he really cared about, though, was finding Joan.

Roy looked back at them over his shoulder. "You guys wanna head to the common room? Maybe find some more...*familiar* faces?"

Both of them nodded. They pressed their way through to the door, only to find the stairwell packed with people drinking from cups and cans.

"Holy shit," Roy said. "Four years living in Winslow, and I've never seen this many people here!"

"It's a fucking *zoo*," Tanner chuckled.

They wound their way down the stairwell past the third floor, then continued down toward the landing between the third and second floors, which had a large sill before the windows where people sat and drank. The windows were both cranked open and Matt heard the sounds of many more people bustling outside.

"How many are there?" Matt said.

"Dunlap did say he invited 400 people; I guess all of them showed up!" Roy called back over his shoulder.

They finally made it to the second floor. Instead of a pod on the west side, there were only two rooms: the enormous Officer's Suite to the left, and a massive open space the size of three normal rooms to the right. This was the Winslow Common Room, and when they entered, they found it teeming with partygoers dancing. Between the massive crowd, the stereos blaring "Stayin' Alive" by the Bee Gees, and the spinning disco ball, it felt like a nightclub.

And there, in the center of it all, was Carl Dunlap.

He was dressed like a low-rent John Travolta impersonator and held a red Solo cup in his hand. He spotted them, threw his arms wide, and stumbled over with a big grin on his face.

His voice boomed like a megaphone. "ROY! TANNER! MATT! HOW ARE YOU GUYS ENJOYING THE PARTY?!"

"It's very...busy," Tanner noted.

"YEAH, ONLY HALF THE PEOPLE I INVITED SHOWED UP! BUT THE ONES WHO DID BROUGHT THEIR FRIENDS!" He gestured around. "THIS PLACE IS POPPING!"

"We hadn't noticed," Roy said.

"OH COME HERE, COME HERE!" He led them from the dance floor to the door of his suite, which was propped open by a rubber stop. Inside stood a big bucket of liquid, an enormous ladle resting at the side.

Now that they were sheltered from the music, he didn't feel the need to yell as loudly. "I've made a special vodka-cran blend. It's designed for *maximum efficiency.*"

Dunlap grabbed a cup off a stack on the shelf behind him and filled it up with the ladle. "Here you go!" he said, thrusting the dripping cup toward them.

Tanner and Roy exchanged looks. "I…um… Hey Matt, you seem like more of a vodka-cran guy than we do," Tanner said. "You should have the first cup."

"I appreciate it," Matt said flatly. He took the cup as they backed out of the room, escaping into the makeshift discotheque.

"Hey guys, you want some?" Dunlap called after them, then stopped, his eyes going wide. "OH MY GOD, IS THAT PATRICK MASON?! HOW'S IT GOIN', BUDDY?!"

He charged out onto the dance floor. Patrick had just arrived from Saunders, looking plastered as he boogied in his lumberjack shirt. Like a true fourth-year, he'd long since perfected the art of preing for parties.

Matt was normally better at that. Looking between the cider in his left hand and the cranberry abomination in his right, he decided it was time to get caught up. He took a sip of Dunlap's special concoction. It was very strong, but just sweet enough to enjoy.

In other words, a lethal combination.

Matt took a bigger sip and headed back to the dance floor.

◆

The disco ball started to look funny after the second vodka-cran. Matt couldn't quite place what was wrong about the ball—there was just *something* off.

He stumbled to the side of the room and glanced around. Roy, Tanner, and Patrick were dancing together toward the center of the room with Sandrine Bouchard, Lisa Fang, and Tony Madruga. He didn't recognize any other faces save for Dunlap toward the back, DJing from a laptop hooked up to a set of speakers. The music blared way too loudly and Matt knew his ears would be ringing tomorrow morning. Oh well, they did that after every party at this college.

All around him people were losing themselves to ABBA's "Dancing

Queen," spilling their drinks as they thrust their cups and beer cans into the air, waving them back and forth like lighters at a concert.

It was time for some fresh air. Matt made his way for the exit, empty Solo cup still in hand. As he came out into the stairwell, he found it packed with people chatting and drinking against the walls. He was about to make his way forward when the crowd parted and two Saunders guys came up onto the landing.

The first was Blaine, who looked incredibly angry. "I'm not talking about this now!" he shouted at Chet, who followed close behind.

"Come on, man. I need to explain," he said as they continued up toward the third floor. "That…that wasn't *her!*"

Blaine spun around on the steps. "Tank saw a blonde girl sneaking out of your room wearing the same kind of jacket she has. *Of course it was Melissa!* You're both trying to hide it, and you're both failing fucking miserably!" He continued storming up the steps, Chet racing after him.

Then they were swallowed up by the party and the loud noises of chatter returned. Matt shook his head, wondering what the hell that was about, then continued on outside. As he pushed his way down the stairs, he tried to recognize anybody. Instead, it really seemed like most of the people here were from other colleges. Had he been more extroverted, maybe he would've tried to strike up a conversation with some of them, maybe made some friends with people outside Radcliffe like his parents were always telling him to do. But tonight he wasn't feeling it and his mind was far more focused on locating Joan.

He just had to make it seem natural, a "Oh hey, nice seeing you here!" Given what happened between her and Benson—*whatever* had happened between her and Benson—he figured he shouldn't push things and ask her out tonight. It would be enough to say hi, to try and gauge her interest in a social setting. If things seemed to be going well, he could relax for the rest of the evening; if not, then he'd go get more of Dunlap's specialty cocktail and let the night blur away to infinity.

Matt threw out his cup in a trashcan before he exited the front door; drinking was prohibited in both Quads. Once he was outside, however, it seemed most people hadn't gotten that message.

The party sprawled away from the door, where normally only a few people would stand around smoking cigarettes, and occupied at least a fourth of the West Quad. People were drinking, vaping, and dancing to the sounds of Dunlap's seventies playlist, which blasted through the windows of Winslow Common.

He'd never seen a res party this big or out of control. This thing was just begging to be shut down. Réjean was going to have a field day. Matt glanced at his watch. It was just after midnight and quiet hours on a weekend didn't begin until 1 a.m., but Quad partying was a clear violation of—

A loud ringing bell went off all around, emanating from within every res House and over exterior speakers. Matt recognized it immediately even before someone shouted "Fire!" and people began moving toward the center of the grass.

Looking back at Winslow, he couldn't see any flames, but it was possible it could be something small. More likely—and even worse—was that someone had drunkenly pulled the alarm as a prank, which meant the admin would be pissed.

Fucking idiots, Matt thought. He found himself swept up with the crowd, pulled farther and farther away from the disco lights. The music had suddenly been shut off. Matt imagined Dunlap scrambling to hide the big vat of booze deep in his room, just in case the fire department or the admin came by. Officers weren't supposed to serve alcohol to students.

Once the crowd got near the center, everyone fanned out and Matt looked back the way he'd come, trying to spot any of his friends. Then he noticed Joan, standing over by the tree closest to Winslow, also searching the crowd.

He made his way toward her general vicinity, trying to have an obvious direction, letting the alcohol numb his nerves. Without the drinks he'd had, his heart would've been pounding much faster. He thought just a simple "Oh, hi!" or something should do; he didn't want to overthink it—

"Hey, Matt!"

He stopped and turned. She'd spotted him and was waving him over to the tree.

Smiling, he walked closer, suddenly conscious of what he was wearing. Unlike Wednesday, this time he was prepared. He had dressed in slim jeans, a gray collared shirt open with a red tee underneath, and had wiped down his old Stan Smith sneakers until they looked new again. And this time, his hair was combed. Joan wore a light blue shirt and dark navy jeans, her lips a shining red with a touch of black shadow around her eyes.

"I think someone pulled the fire alarm," he chuckled.

"Oh, really? I just got here. I was supposed to meet up with Val..." She slid her phone into a pocket, shrugged, and smiled weakly. "This is what I get for showing up late."

He gave a brief laugh. "Where were you?"

"Oh, just working on an essay. It's due Monday and it's 4000 words, so I wanted to get most of the typing done tonight so I'd have more time to finish tomorrow and..." She scratched the back of her neck. "You know how it is..."

"Yeah, I just had a big one due yesterday. Tonight's my night off, then tomorrow it's back to the grind." The words *Hey, how about we study together?* were on his lips but he couldn't bring himself to speak them. *Is that too far, too soon?*

"I know what you mean." Her eyes wandered the Quad. "Shit, there's a lot of people here."

"Dunlap invited half the planet."

"I don't recognize most of them. That's good, though. I always felt Cliffe parties were too much of the same, you know? Never any new people to talk to." She smiled shyly. "Not that I'm good at striking up conversations anyway."

"Hey, me neither." Matt returned her smile, then looked around. "That's a good point, though. It does get a little stale watching the same people puke in the Second Winslow sinks."

She laughed. "Oh God, did that happen again?"

He shrugged. "Wouldn't surprise me."

Joan looked off. "I know the randoms sometimes break our stuff, but I feel like only a few of them do that and give the rest a bad name."

"If one of them pulled the fire alarm, I wouldn't be surprised if non-Cliffe people get banned from our parties forever."

She scoffed. "Great, that's just what this college's reputation needs. They already think we're insular as it is."

He nodded, but was unsure of what to say next. Awkward silence hung between them and he could feel the conversation waning. "Well, it was nice seeing you."

"Yeah, you too," Joan said. She started to move away, then stopped and turned around. "Hey, I know we're both busy this week, but do you maybe..."—she rubbed her upper arm—"want to...grab a coffee or something soon?"

Matt was stunned into silence. "Uh, yeah. Yeah, that sounds great!" he finally managed to say. "I'm free later in the week, like…Thursday or Friday afternoon…"

"Thursday works for me. There's a nice coffee shop by the water, I'm not sure if you've been to it…Mountain Ridge?"

"Yeah, I've gone once or twice." Matt wasn't normally much of a coffee drinker, but he'd stopped by there with some of his caffeine-addicted friends on a few occasions. It was a boutique place, cozy and quiet.

"Great, we can work out a time closer to then. We're friends on Facebook, right?"

"I think so."

Joan pulled out her phone and held it up to him. "I'm gonna go find Val, but it was good to see you. Have a great night!" She gave him a warm smile.

"You too. I'll see you Thursday!" He waved goodbye.

She returned it, then disappeared into the throng of confused partygoers, making her way back to the front of the college.

Matt leaned against the tree and exhaled. *Well, that went better than I thought it would.*

A warmth flowed through him, induced by the release of stress and a high blood alcohol level. He glanced around, trying to find Roy and Tanner so he could tell them the good news.

"Alright people, back it up!" shouted a familiar voice. Matt turned to see Réjean leading Dean of Students Donna Crawley and Assistant Dean Eric Porter through the crowd. He looked pissed, the administrators merely groggy. Crawley wore a bathrobe, her hair unkempt, while Porter wore pajamas and bunny slippers, shooting death glares at anyone who pointed and giggled.

"The fire department is going to be here at any minute!" Crawley shouted. "I need everyone out into the Quad NOW!"

"This party is over!" Porter yelled. "If you're not from this college, please vacate the premises."

People booed all around.

"We *will* call Campus Police!" he shouted, this time louder. "And trust me, you *don't* want to deal with them."

Now the partygoers began to disperse, at least two-thirds of the crowd heading for the front exit. A few others smartly made for the Althouse Gate via the East Quad, which would be considerably less congested.

Matt barely paid attention to them or to the administrators' shouting. He remained by the tree, waiting for his friends and basking in euphoria, savoring it while he could.

He knew from experience that at this college, it didn't tend to last long.

◆

Joan pushed back toward the lobby, jostled by partygoers swarming all around. She glimpsed Sandrine and Kylie heading one direction, Patrick Mason hurrying in another, and people she thought she recognized passing by in a blur. She'd never seen most of the crowd around her, though.

Finally, she made it through the doors into the lobby and squeezed off to the side, away from the endless stream of non-Cliffe students making for the front doors. The night receptionist looked up from her Kindle, sighed, and went back to reading.

Joan leaned against a wall and allowed herself a deep breath, sliding her phone out to text Val. A number of people had bumped into her as she made her way out of the Quad and she was tired of getting battered by drunkards. She wanted a nice and quiet place to get wasted with her friend and tell her the spur of the moment thing she'd just done.

It wasn't like her, Joan realized, to do something like that without carefully planning it first. It had just struck her that she should ask him out, to get the ball rolling because he seemed new to this kind of thing and might take his sweet time. She was proud of herself; it was the first time she had done something truly spontaneous and it had worked out well. She hoped it wasn't beginner's luck.

Joan pressed her head back against the cool stone and closed her eyes, waiting for her phone to vibrate from Val's response. Instead, she realized there was something else in her hand, sandwiched between her fingers and the back of the phone. It was a piece of paper—it must've been in her pocket with the device.

She didn't remember putting a piece of paper in her pocket.

Joan opened her eyes and glanced down at the little folded square. She unwrapped it and nearly dropped both it and her phone in shock. Typed on the sheet was a brief message:

Confess your sins. I am watching.

ELEVEN

THE PROVOST'S Lodge was located at the eastern end of Radcliffe's front façade. It took up three floors, on the top of which was a grand office, its windows gazing out across the university grounds.

John Mustard stared off toward Front Campus Circle and beyond it to the mountains. It was a fine Sunday afternoon, sunlight glowing down upon the autumnal leaves. Mustard knew that in a month's time it would be unpleasant to step outdoors, so he always tried to enjoy the fall while it lasted.

A knock came from his office door and he turned around. "Come in," he said, standing up straighter. A tall man in his late fifties, he had hawkish features and closely-cropped silver hair. He wore slacks and a dress shirt, its breast pocket embroidered with the college's griffin crest.

The Dean of Students entered, offering a tired smile as she closed the door behind her. "Good afternoon, John."

"Ah Donna, please take a seat." Mustard sat down in his own plush leather chair as Crawley took the one opposite him. He folded his hands on the desk and smiled. "How are you today?"

"A bit sleep-deprived," she said, rubbing her eye, "after last night."

Mustard nodded. "I heard there was…trouble with the students."

"A party got just too out of control. I mean, there were people everywhere in the West Quad, drinking and smoking, and then someone pulled the fire alarm and—oh God, it was chaos. Eric, Réjean, and I managed to shut it down before the firefighters came, but Winslow was a mess. And of course, the Canmore Creek Fire Department wants to know who's to blame for the false alarm. That's a criminal offense."

Mustard shrugged and smiled. "I doubt we'll ever find out."

Crawley raised an eyebrow. "You sound...almost happy about it."

"Indifferent, really—about the alarm. But this *incident*, this party...it's wonderful news for us."

She looked even more confused. "I'm not sure how this..."

"Donna, Donna, Donna..." Mustard leaned back in his chair, moving his folded hands into his lap. "Think of the big picture here: *We can finally proceed!*"

"With what?"

"With *what?* With *everything!*" He stood up and turned to the window behind him. "When they made me Provost, the WCU administration made a few things clear. Radcliffe College represents a lot of problems for this school. There are plenty of negative stereotypes about it, stereotypes that previous Provosts did little to address. President Manderley wants Radcliffe to be a *modern* college—less people dressing up in gowns and chanting things in Latin, less stuffy traditions and elitist attitudes. Something more, you know..." He turned around. "*Normal.*"

"So they want it to be exactly like all the other colleges?" Crawley asked.

"Well, when you put it that way it sounds almost conformist, but"—he laughed—"really the school just wants it to be...more *in line* with everything else here. *Especially* the alcohol policy."

She nodded. "That's a real problem."

Mustard turned around, gazing out the window again. "We spend thousands of dollars of student fees allowing clubs to buy alcohol. That creates..."

"An unstable drinking culture—?"

"—a *liability*," he said, raising a finger. "It's simply too much to have on the school's watch. Manderley made it clear to me that it would be greatly appreciated if I could wipe Radcliffe's alcohol policy off the face of the Earth." He turned around. "She then said she was thinking of retiring sometime in the next five or so years. She complimented me for how I ran the Ethics & Society Department and said now she'd observe how I ran a college. Then when she retired..." He smiled. "That was four years ago. You get the picture, Donna."

"I do," she said, nodding slowly.

"We can use last night as a justification to get the ball rolling." He sat back down in his chair. "I've been thinking about it all day. Between this and finalizing the plans for the expansion of the Dales Building, it's going to be a very big year for Radcliffe."

"I think it will be best…for the students," she said, as if trying to convince herself. "They're still so young and I think the alcohol policy is dangerous, but I think we have to remember that one of their peers died this week. The party may have been their way of letting off some steam."

"Oh, right," Mustard said, looking down. "Yes, it is truly terrible what happened to Richard Benson. Absolutely dreadful. But…" He raised a finger again. "We must maintain discipline within this college. Like you said, they're young. They don't understand their emotions in a time like this. That's why they need our guidance, our support."

"We can't stop them from drinking altogether," Crawley said. "The drinking age in this province is eighteen and last night was a res party—we can't control what goes on there unless we ban all parties, which I don't think would go over well—"

"No, no, no, Donna. Nothing like that. We can just *limit* their alcohol consumption, take away *official* Radcliffe parties, ban clubs from spending student fees on booze—*those* kinds of things." He smiled warmly, but thought to himself: *Come on Donna, see the bigger picture here. I know you went to Atherton like half the other idiots in your office, but for fuck's sake…*

"All the things we're liable for," she said, seeming to finally realize.

"Yes! We can't stop the students from getting irresponsibly drunk, but we *can* stop them from doing so on our watch." *It's a good thing you're pretty,* he thought.

Crawley looked slightly uncomfortable.

"Is something bothering you, Donna?"

"No, no," she said. "It's just…shouldn't we try to help them? I mean *truly* help them?"

"Oh, we are, Donna! That's what this is all about! By maintaining discipline, we will instill the proper values in our students, values that will make this place safer…and, yes, create fewer liabilities for our administration down the road." He spread his hands. "See? Everybody wins."

She gave a weak smile and nodded. "I'm glad to hear it."

He opened the laptop on his desk. "I'm going to start writing up the policy changes. I'll send them for you and Eric to review tomorrow. Then I'll put out an email notifying the students by Tuesday afternoon and the new policy will go into immediate effect."

Crawley stood up. "Thank you for notifying me. Have a good rest of your Sunday, John."

"You too, Donna. You too—Oh, one last thing. You reminded me of something." She turned around and Mustard sighed. "Staff Sgt. Wright spoke to me yesterday. She said the investigation has officially wrapped up. They could find no signs of foul play and Benson's body has already been sent back to his family in Toronto. The police are taking down the crime scene tape today."

Crawley nodded sadly. "The whole thing is just terrible. So…they're sure it was only an accident, then?"

Mustard shrugged. "Apparently. Seems a little unbelievable, but I guess things like that can happen. I just wanted to give you an update."

She nodded again. "Take care, John."

"Same to you." He barely paid attention as she headed for the door. He was already immersed in the document on his computer, his fingers flying across the keyboard.

TWELVE

MATT ARRIVED at Mountain Ridge Coffee at 3:50 p.m. on Thursday, a full ten minutes before their agreed time. It was a quaint place toward the eastern end of the main drag, along the same side of the street as the Royal Pub. Behind the establishment was Canmore Creek itself, shallow due to a lack of recent rain.

The door chimed as he entered and he glanced around for a suitable spot. The ordering counter ran along the right while a row of tables-for-two stood to the left. Matt spotted an empty one way at the back, which looked cozy and private. He began to grow worried it would be too close to the washroom, but his fears were relieved as he drew nearer and found a staircase leading to the underground lavatory.

It was perfect, then.

He sat facing the entrance, slipping off his light leather jacket and hanging it on the back of his chair. Then he took out his phone; there was still plenty of time left to calm himself down, but his heart thumped rapidly and his mind raced the way it often did before a test.

Just relax. She likes you…

I think.

Matt drummed his fingers on the square table. He'd wanted to talk to Roy some more about this date last night, but he and Jennifer Horvat had disappeared back to his room after High Table dinner. The three of them had chatted with Patrick Mason about the new Radcliffe policy changes, which prohibited student fees from getting spent on alcohol. Mustard had

81

also postponed all licensed parties, including the Fall and Winter Formals, indefinitely. They would only go forward if the admin felt that students could "behave like adults" again. Patrick had defended them, arguing that a change like this would've happened sooner or later regardless of a res party gone awry. Matt had barely listened to him; he was more concerned about his date with Joan. He'd just have to go on what Roy had already said throughout the week and then tell him how it went at DebSoc tonight.

"Just take it easy. You'll both be nervous," Roy had told him. "She'll probably spend more time getting ready for it than you will and will be psyching herself out just as much, if not more."

"That's debatable," Matt had scoffed. "I've never actually been on a date with someone I had a crush on before. This is new territory—"

"And that's good," Roy interrupted. "View it as a new frontier. Don't be afraid, be excited! You like her, and given that *she* asked *you* out—plus other things you've told me—I'm pretty sure she likes you too. Don't put too much pressure on yourself or on the date. You're just going there to chat with a girl you like and have fun. That's it. See where it goes from there." He shrugged. "I mean, that's all you really *can* do…"

Matt sighed.

The minutes ticked away.

Finally, time came to the top of the hour. His eyes carefully scanned the front window, the occasional car passing up or down the main drag.

About a minute later, he saw her. She was dressed in a gray, long-sleeved top with a denim skirt and tights that matched her shirt. Matt straightened up and examined himself: he wore black jeans and a cable-knit green sweater, which his mother had gotten for him because she felt it brought out the color in his eyes. He quickly adjusted his hair while glancing at his phone, making it seem like a passive gesture. Then he looked up and waved her over as she scanned the venue for him.

Joan spotted him, waved back, and approached with a shy smile. "Hey." She gave a brief wave, then rubbed her upper arm absentmindedly as she came closer.

Matt stood up. "How was class today?"

"Oh God, I had *four* hours of back-to-back econ lectures," she said, her face brightening. "I can never get anything done on Thursdays, I'm always too fried in the afternoon." She smiled weakly and scratched the back of her head.

"I know what you mean," he said. "I had *five* hours back-to-back today, one of which was a three-hour lecture on the Middle Ages where the prof just rambled about random stuff."

"Ouch," she chuckled.

"Hey, did you want to get something to drink first or…?" He gestured between the counter and the table.

"Uh…sure!"

Matt, not a coffee drinker by habit, ordered a vanilla latte and hoped it would be good. He reminded himself that he just needed *something* to sip on. Joan ordered a much more complicated concoction he had never heard of before.

When their orders were placed on the counter in large, wide mugs, Matt reached forward with his debit card out. "Here, I got this."

"Oh no worries, I've got mine." Then she added, "Thanks."

"Sure," Matt said, and paid for his own.

Matt and Joan returned to the table with their lattes and began sipping them quietly, each unsure of what to say. Matt noticed that she seemed to be as nervous as he was, just like Roy had said, and this helped ease the tension in his shoulders.

"So…you're majoring in econ?"

She nodded mid-sip, then set her coffee down and wiped her mouth on the back of her hand. "Yeah, I'm doing a dual major with psychology. They don't have an official behavioral economics program here, so I kinda made my own." She gave a little laugh, rarely making direct eye contact with him. He found her smile incredibly endearing.

"Oh, that's neat. So you want to go into finance or…?"

"Something like that. I'm not sure if I want to work on Bay Street in Toronto or if I want to go to the States. Econ and finance are the root of, well, everything in business so I guess it keeps my options open." She took another sip. "How about you? Any big future plans?" She'd added a touch of flirtation to the last part.

Matt realized he was averting her gaze as he put down his own latte. "I think I'd like to be a defense attorney."

"Ah. Have you started studying for the LSAT yet?"

"Not yet. That's what I'll be doing pretty much all summer." He laughed.

"So what made you major in history?"

"Well, for law school it doesn't really matter what your major is as long as you've got a good GPA and a high LSAT, but I've always loved history so I figured I might as well study something I enjoy. I thought about doing film studies if I'd gone to UBC, though."

"Ooh, that'd be fun." One side of her smile curled higher. "My parents are big movie buffs—my mom especially, she's a Hitchcock fanatic. I'm named after Joan Fontaine, actually...from *Rebecca*."

"And *Suspicion*," he pointed out.

"Oh yeah," she said, remembering.

He paused, tilting his head. "You look kinda like a taller version of her, actually."

She laughed. "So I've heard."

"She won the Oscar for *Suspicion*, but I think she really should've gotten it for *Rebecca*. And that one got Best Picture, but Hitchcock never got his own for Best Director."

"Really? That's...disappointing."

Matt shrugged. "Still made a name for himself."

"Yeah." She sat back, thinking. "I've always liked movies, but I'm really more into writing. I used to do more of it back in high school, but I haven't had a lot of time here." She brought the mug up to her lips and took another sip.

"Did you go to an arts high school?"

"Oh no, it was an all-girls private school back in Toronto. You know, with the uniforms and repression and everything." She gave a timid laugh. "What was your school like?"

"Ah, it was just my local high school in Phoenix. It was alright, I guess."

"Oh right, you're American! Why'd you come to WCU?"

"My dad's from Calgary and he went to Forrestal. I've got dual citizenship, but I was born in Arizona."

"So you get to pay Canadian tuition instead of international fees?"

"Yeah. For a school this highly regarded, it's *way* cheaper than anything in the States."

"Huh." She took another sip of coffee. "Where's your mom from?"

"Phoenix. My dad met her after he moved there. He's a businessman, works at a construction company." Matt paused. "What brought you here?"

"Well, a lot of people I knew were going to the University of Toronto or McGill and I kinda wanted to get away from the Toronto private school circuit. WCU is just as highly regarded anyway, and I like the mountains." She paused. "Also, my mother went to Cliffe, back in the eighties."

"Oh, neat! Was she in Anathema?"

Joan laughed. "No, but some of her friends were and she liked going to the Sermons. She thinks it's funny that I'm in it now."

"She must not like what Mustard's doing with the alcohol policy."

"Oh God, she *hates* him. She says she's going to try to get some of the other alumni to fight it too, but she's not sure if they'll be able to do much. WCU's been pressuring the college to go this way for years. I guess it was kind of inevitable."

"That's what Patrick was saying at High Table last night."

She rolled her eyes. "I've heard he's the Provost's lapdog, but yeah, he has a point. I'm just sad they're cutting down on the events. Besides Anathema meetings, they're the only things I really enjoy here anymore." She grew glum for a moment, then seemed to snap out of it. "Sorry, Cliffe's just been getting to me recently."

"No worries," he said. "This college is…a lot."

Joan laughed, but the awkward silence quickly returned. They both sat sipping their drinks.

"So…what do you like to write?" he finally asked.

Her face brightened. "Oh, just short stories and stuff. I wrote a novella once, something like 25,000 words, but I don't think it was very good." She shrugged and rubbed her arm. "I never tried to publish it or anything."

"What was it about? Let me guess… Cheesy teen romance fiction?" Matt winked.

She laughed again. "Actually no, I was the only one in my creative writing class who wasn't into that stuff." She looked off, remembering. "I was always more into horror. The novella…it was an expansion of a short story I'd written for the class. It was kind of a…Gothic tale and…this is going to sound stupid, but it had…werewolves…"

"That's not stupid. It sounds cool!"

She smiled, but her eyes remained on the mug. "The protagonist…she lives in this big manor on the English moors, and she realizes she's slowly turning into a werewolf. Then she finds out her older sister is part of a secret society that captures and studies werewolves."

Matt grinned. "A secret society, huh?"

"Yeah." She scratched the back of her head, looking torn between enjoying telling someone all about this and awkward at revealing it. He wondered if she had told many of her friends at Radcliffe about it, or if she'd even talked about it at all in the past few years. "At the end, we find out her older sister is the one who infected her with lycanthropy so the secret society could capture her and study her, and that way her sister would finally be rid of her and have the inheritance to herself."

"Ah. What did your sister think of that when she read it?"

"She didn't," Joan said with a grim laugh. She glanced down at the table.

Matt realized he'd slipped up. She hadn't mentioned any siblings, but he'd looked at her Instagram profile and saw a picture from last Christmas. Her family had gone ice skating in Nathan Phillips Square.

Wondering if they'd veered into touchy territory, he asked her, "What did the class think of it?"

She massaged her arm. "They said it was…interesting. Some of them didn't like the violence. My stuff is always pretty gory, which was probably a bit off-putting. I overheard some of my classmates talking about how weird it was one day."

"Well screw them," he said. "I think it sounds awesome! I'd love to read the novella version, if you've still got it."

Her eyes widened and she stiffened. "Oh, um…"

"Only if you want me to," he said, holding up his hands. "What other kinds of stuff did you write?"

"Well, they made us work on a lot of poetry, but I didn't like it much back then." She chuckled, thinking. "I didn't actually like it until I joined Anathema, really… You know, poetry's much more interesting when you add swear words and use it to make fun of people you don't like."

"Here's to that." He carefully held out his mug in toast and clinked it against hers.

When they set their cups down, she looked off at the basement stairwell. "We got Initiated the same night, and yet I've never really talked to you."

"Well, you made quite the formal introduction."

Her cheeks flushed red. "That was…not my finest move."

"I'm assuming it was a rough night?"

"Yeah, it wasn't great…" She began chewing an index fingernail, noticed, and abruptly moved her hand to her lap. "I wanted to tell you again, I'm *really* sorry."

"Hey, no worries—"

"I don't want you to think I get drunk like that on Tuesdays all the time…or even that drunk that often at all. I…used to know Rich Benson kind of well and it was just a shock, that's all."

"Really, I totally understand…"

"Thanks," she said abruptly, taking a big gulp of coffee.

She'd drunk much more of hers than he had of his. He took another sip, trying to catch up.

"So…," Joan said. "You looking forward to the Beckonings in a couple weeks?"

"Yeah, that should be interesting."

"I think it's my favorite Anathema event. I was terrified of it in first-year, but it's much more fun being on the other side of the hazing." She smirked, just a little. "How about you?"

"I've definitely enjoyed it, but I think the End-of-Year Social's my favorite…I mean, I love the Sermons too. But I feel like it's one of the few events focused on bonding within the organization…and between the branches. I hope we can do more events like that next year."

"Well, maybe if you get Tetrad you can make that happen." She smiled. "I've heard some people say you'll probably get Legatus or Pontifex."

"Who do they think will be Imperator?"

Joan grimaced. "Logan Brewster." She drank more coffee. "I don't know, the guy just seems like a dick."

"Yeah, he doesn't really give off a warm and fuzzy vibe."

"Why does everyone think it has to be him? I've never heard them talk about him having great presentation abilities or leadership skills. Besides, he's already been on Tetrad once. Why not somebody else?"

"Well, Tony's probably going to run for Student Affairs Officer. And there's no one else in my year—"

"Except you." She smiled.

He laughed. "Nobody thinks it's going to be me."

"Nobody thought it would be Jack Randall either."

"Because he ran for Officer."

"Still, I know there have been underdog picks before—in both branches."

"Yeah, but Randall and Logan are friends, and he likes him. I don't really know why. I mean, I guess he's dedicated."

"So? That just makes him a good Legatus, not necessarily a good Imperator. And he's already *been* Legatus. Plus, if Randall was a dark horse, wouldn't he maybe…I don't know…want to pay that forward?"

"I would be very surprised if it was me." *Pleasantly surprised,* he thought. *Ecstatic. Overjoyed. I wouldn't even know how to feel.*

"But you want it, don't you?" There was that smirk again.

Now Matt couldn't help but smile. He nodded slowly. "It's been...a goal of mine. For a while."

She was still smirking. "How long?"

"Since about...Initiation, maybe?"

Joan scoffed. "I've wanted it since even before I got my calling card." She looked down at her nearly-empty mug. "You and I are in the same boat, though. Everyone thinks it'll be Alyssa Lee or Catherine Winters."

"Why not you, though? I've heard *you're* one of the most dedicated members. That's apparently enough qualification for Logan."

She looked up, clearly happy to hear this. "I've rarely missed a meeting. And this year I'm trying to miss none."

"Same. Do you read jokes at the writing sessions?"

"Almost always. Sometimes I don't bring my laptop so I don't look too keen—you know how this college is with keeners."

"Yeah," he scoffed.

"But when I *do* read, I'm always very careful. I try to strike a balance between being dramatic but not getting too over-the-top."

"Took the words right out of my mouth."

She sighed. "I've been doing that since first-year."

"I hate how they try to pick winners here before things even happen, how they just decide someone's destined for one thing and close their mind to any other options."

She groaned. "Don't even get me started on how excruciating this college can be. If you're not charismatic, you won't win any elected positions. And if you're not part of one of their little cliques, they won't give you an appointed spot."

Matt realized he couldn't stop smiling. "I'm glad I'm not alone thinking that."

Joan was still smiling too.

He raised his mug in toast. "You know what? Fuck Logan Brewster. Fuck Alyssa Lee and Catherine Winters. Let's become the next Imperators—you and me, and show Radcliffe College what we're made of."

She raised her mug, clinked it against his, then finished the last of her coffee. When he put his down, he looked up to find her staring straight into his eyes for the first time. There was a big smile on her face.

"I like the sound of that a lot."

THIRTEEN

"**I** SAW one of the RCMP officers around today. Dorval, I think."

Roy and Matt walked down the hallway of House Rickard's third floor, pendants dangling from their necks over casual clothes. Matt looked up from the envelopes in his hand; there were still two Beckonings invitations to deliver tonight.

"How do you know what his name was?"

"Him and another officer, Wright, asked me some questions a couple weeks ago."

"Really? What did they say?"

Roy seemed uneasy. "They just asked me about Rich Benson. It was a day or two after he died."

"What about him?"

"How well I knew him, how well he was liked here, that sort of thing…"

Matt stopped and looked up and down the hallway. They were alone. He turned back to Roy. "Did they mention Anathema?"

He thought back for a moment. "No."

Matt scratched his chin. "I thought they declared it an accident. Why are they still lurking around?"

"No idea. But it was just the one guy, Dorval. He looked like he had just come from somewhere and he was jotting down notes as he walked through Galbraith. He looked…perplexed."

"We shouldn't talk about this here," Matt said quietly, continuing along. The walls were thin and sound traveled easily under the doors.

They reached the end of the corridor. Before them stood a door with a sheet of paper on it, the word *Brandon* displayed above a tinier *Third Rickard* at the bottom. Matt glanced down at one of the envelopes labeled *Brandon Lehane* in fine calligraphy, the Anathema's skull logo drawn carefully above it.

Roy knocked on the door, then glanced at Matt. "You doing the talking this time?"

"You can do this one, I'll get the last one."

Roy nodded. The door opened and before them stood a puzzled first-year with spiky hair; his eyes darted between their pendants. Both Roy and Matt stood with erect posture, their faces devoid of emotion.

"Good evening, Mr. Lehane," Roy said calmly. "What are your thoughts on the Great Lord Anathema?"

"I…uh…" The first-year shrugged. "He, um, sounds pretty cool, I guess."

"The Great Lord beckons you to participate in Radcliffe College's Grand Tradition—starting with a proper introduction to His most wretched team of writers and a lesson in His seditious History."

"Um, yeah…sure." The first-year looked nervous.

Matt handed him the letter as Roy continued, "Read it carefully. Tell no one about it—*absolutely* no one. If you have any questions, feel free to message any member of the Great Lord's branch or His Imperator directly. I'm assuming you've heard who that is?"

"Jack Randall, right?"

Roy nodded.

"Okay, cool." Now he was bewildered, but excited. "Thanks."

"Have a pleasant evening," Matt said, giving a thin smile.

The door closed. The two of them exited the corridor into a stairwell.

"Phew. Can't believe we kept straight faces while saying that," he chuckled.

Roy shrugged. "Years of experience will do that."

Matt glanced at the last letter. "Any idea where this guy lives?"

"Yeah, he's Second Winslow—east pod, I think."

"I barely know any of these people."

"That's the joy of growing old," Roy smirked. "Welcome to third-year."

Matt wondered how it must feel for him in his fifth.

"So," Roy said, "how was the long weekend? Get up to anything with a certain someone?"

Matt brightened. "Yeah, she didn't go back to Toronto for Canadian Thanksgiving, so we studied together and explored different libraries around campus."

"Sexy."

Matt rolled his eyes. "We're both pretty quiet. It takes about six drinks to get either of our wild sides out."

"Yeah, but your wild side is you getting blackout drunk and telling your friends how much you appreciate them. What's hers?"

"She, uh…she's a little more fun. She got Demerit Points for getting too intoxicated at Winter Formal last year."

"Oh yeah, I remember hearing something about that." They exited the staircase, coming out into the West Quad. The entrance to Winslow was just off to their left.

"Heard a lot about her?"

"A little now and then. People say she's very into Anathema, some say too much. Others just say she's weird. I don't know, seems nice to me."

"Why do people say that?" Matt asked. "That she's *weird?* Like, what is that even supposed to mean?"

"I don't know, it's kind of a vague insult. Most people at this college are pretty weird, so really, it's the pot calling the kettle black. I think maybe she's just a little socially awkward."

"Do people still say *I'm* weird?" That had been uttered behind his back in the past.

Roy hesitated as they arrived at the Winslow door. "Like I said, everybody here's weird and everybody insults each other. At least Anathema does it in style." He unlocked it with his R3 and pulled it open. "Just don't get bothered by what others say."

"But what *do* they say? About me?"

"Nothing really bad. Let's just deliver this letter and then we'll chat in the Quad."

They entered the east pod on the second floor and knocked on the door labeled *Ross.* A few moments later, a voice asked from behind it: "Who's there?"

Matt and Roy exchanged looks. "We just want a quick word with you."

The door opened and a first-year with bleary red eyes stumbled out, the scent of marijuana perfuming the hallway. Matt did his best not to wince; he'd never liked the smell.

"Who the hell are you people?"

"Do you know what these are?" Matt asked, holding up his pendant.

The first-year, Ross, squinted. "Uh… Is that like, metal band merch or something?"

Matt blinked. "How much do you know about the Anathema?"

"Aren't they that weird secret society around here or something?"

Matt sighed. "Take this and read it very carefully—"

"I don't want that," Ross said, gesturing at the envelope as Matt held it out.

He said, "This is an invitation from the Anathema. Your presence is requested next Friday evening—"

"Isn't the Lambda Phi Halloween party that night?"

Matt paused. "Yes, but that will be later in the night. The Great Lord beckons you to—"

"That sounds freaky." The guy's bloodshot eyes widened and he took a step back into his room.

Out the corner of his eye, Matt saw Roy bite his lip, trying not to laugh.

"Just read this over and think about it," Matt said, pushing the letter toward him.

The first-year shook his head. "How did you people find me?"

Matt's eyes flicked toward the sign displaying his name on the door, then back to Ross. "The Great Lord sees all."

"My mother warned me about Mormonism." He slammed the door shut.

Matt and Roy stood there in silence for several moments.

"Well," Roy finally said, "that was interesting."

"Yeah…" Matt slid the envelope back into his jacket. They went through the door back into Winslow's central stairwell. "So, we were talking about how weird I am…"

Roy shrugged. "Some people think you're just a little too into Anathema."

"How so?"

"I don't know." He stopped on the steps and turned to Matt. "Look, in case you haven't noticed, some people at this college don't like Anathema. So it's natural they'd write off anyone who enjoys being a part of it as weird."

"So the people who say this aren't in it?"

He hesitated. "Most of them. The one or two who've made similar comments and *are* in Anathema are the kind of people who don't really show up that often. You know the type."

Matt nodded. "The people who get in and then act like they're too cool for it anyway."

Those were the social-status Initiates, the ones whom previous Imperators had thought would bring prestige to the organization by having them in their ranks. Most weren't even that funny, and the ones who were half-assed their jokes or barely came to writing sessions.

"Yeah, exactly," Roy said as they entered the West Quad. A bench stood before House Lacy off to their left and they walked down a brief flight of steps to get to it.

"That's what they say about Joan too, right? That she seems too into it?"

Roy nodded. "Look at it this way: it's something you two have in common!"

They sat down on the bench. Matt looked up at the stars; there was barely a cloud in the sky. He knew he'd have to do a little more work tonight on an outline for a paper—he had a seven-pager and a ten-pager both due next week—but he could stay and chat for a little while. It was nearly 10 p.m. on a Wednesday night in the middle of October, roughly halfway through the class period of the semester. Lectures ended after the first week of December and there was a single week for finals, then Winter Break. And when they came back, it would be a four-month sprint to the finish, then an equally long summer as a reward.

"So…Rich Benson," Matt said, still gazing at the sky.

"Yeah?"

"I think…someone killed him."

A pause. "It's possible."

Roy sounded quieter now and Matt realized he should speak softer too. There was no one else in sight, but it was often said at Radcliffe that "the Quads have ears." Both spaces were acoustically live and anyone above them with a window cracked ajar could eavesdrop.

"Why was he out so late that night?" Matt asked. "Nobody goes for a walk after midnight in Bethune's Walk. Nobody."

"Maybe he just liked late-night strolls?"

Matt sat up and looked at him. "Roy, this has been really getting to me lately. Tanner thinks the only people who could've wanted him dead are Anathema members."

"Let's hope not. It was probably just an accident, like the police said."

"Then why is one of them still poking around?"

Roy scratched his chin. "I don't know. It could be unrelated."

"Randall told us one of the cops didn't seem to buy it was an accident. What if it's this Dorval guy and he's still…I don't know…looking into it by himself?"

"Based on what, a hunch? There was no evidence it was murder."

"No evidence *they* found."

Roy looked at him and narrowed his eyes, then cracked a smile. "You want us to look into it ourselves."

Matt shrugged. "Maybe."

Roy thought for a moment. "I wouldn't mind digging deeper. For curiosity's sake."

"If Dorval finds something and re-opens the case, everyone's gonna think Anathema did it—even if one of us didn't."

"And what if one of us did?"

"Then we need to find out who and distance ourselves from that person as fast as possible."

"Nobody would kill Benson just for speaking out against Anathema. Or for giving us bad press in the school papers. Or even for writing a tirade about how we should be shut down for good."

Hell, people might think that would've been enough of a motive for me. He remembered those two girls talking about Benson's death, joking that Anathema had murdered him. They'd seen Matt and fled, but maybe once they were out of earshot, they'd turned to each other and said, "That's the weird guy who's *super* into it. I bet *he* did it." He could picture them laughing again as they walked away.

It reminded him of the jokes Logan and others had written about him last year, saying he seemed like a school shooter because he frequently sat alone and apparently didn't smile that often. Matt told them that as an American, that was a very touchy subject—even with his affinity for dark humor it was just too far. Logan had said no, that it was just too funny to pass up.

Later, Randall had promised him he wouldn't include jokes like that in any of his Sermons, but Matt knew if Logan became the next Imperator he'd bring them right back. And without Randall around, there'd be nothing to stop him. Imperators had final say on all Sermons; even if Matt ended up on Logan's Tetrad he'd have no power to curtail him. Pleading hadn't worked so well before, either.

Another horrible thought occurred to him. People also said Joan was too into Anathema—*and* she'd dated Benson. Combined, those things might make her a suspect to the RCMP. He couldn't imagine Joan killing anyone, but if people's perception at this college was that warped, maybe the stories they told the police would sway them that way too.

Roy's expression grew more serious. "I don't know why anyone *would* want to…" He paused, staring off at Galbraith's stained-glass windows. "Well, maybe *they* would know…"

Matt's head whipped around. "Who?"

"The staff at *The Westerner.* I know a senior editor there. Benson was one of their star writers. Maybe, I don't know…he could've been working on something. The cops asked me something like that, so maybe somebody told them he'd been writing an article."

Matt thought for a moment. "Do you think he could've been writing about Anathema?"

He shrugged. "About anything, really. And what if someone didn't *want* him to write about that?"

Matt nodded. "So they lured him out into the woods and tried to make it look like he had an accident…?" Something was definitely missing, but it was a start. "We should go to their offices and ask them."

"Ask them?"

"Yeah."

"Why?"

"Because I want to know."

"But the cops already declared it an accident, Matt. It's not our job, whether it had anything to do with Anathema or not."

"I know, but it bugs me that this Dorval guy is still nosing around." He sighed. "Let's make a deal: We go to *The Westerner* office after our last classes tomorrow, and if we get any leads, we'll continue our little investigation. If we don't, it probably *was* just an accident and we leave it at that."

Roy considered for a moment, then sighed. "Alright, fine. But let's not expect to find anything." He stood up and glanced around the West Quad. "I mean, do you honestly think there's anything at this college worth killing over?"

FOURTEEN

STUDENTS HURRIED in both directions, hustling to get to their next class before ten past the hour, when all lectures and tutorials began. Banners dangled from lampposts along the path, boasting the school's accomplishments, recent donations, and global ranking—now 20th in the world.

The Student Publications Center stood just ahead to Matt's right, a three-story high, modern building at the edge of Front Campus Circle. Roy leaned against a wall by the entrance, looking at his phone. As Matt drew nearer, he glanced up and waved.

"How was class?"

Matt shrugged. "It was alright. We learned about feudalism in the Medieval Period."

"Ah, my favorite era! Have you gotten to the Black Death yet?" Roy said, opening the door for him.

"No, we're covering that next week."

They entered the building. As WCU's premiere newspaper, *The Westerner* was located on the highest floor. Matt and Roy took the stairs up to the third level, where the paper's cattle rancher logo greeted them on a plaque. Inside they found a setup like something out of a movie: rows of cubicles and harried students running around with press badges. The editors had offices along one side. At the back was a row of windows gazing out across Front Campus Circle toward the stone architecture of Royal College, which had been founded concurrently with Radcliffe.

On a seat in the lobby area, a short guy with a press badge looked up from his phone, smiled, and waved. "Hey, Roy."

"Hey, Dinesh. This is Matt. He goes to Cliffe too."

"Ah, your apprentice in the ways of evil?"

Matt nodded. "I'm learning from the best."

Dinesh chuckled and shook his head. "I'm sorry this paper shits on Cliffe so much, but the rest of WCU is just stressed, depressed, and boring. You guys are *much* more fun to write about."

Roy smirked. "I'll take that as a compliment."

"Come on, we can talk in my office." Dinesh lead them to a door labeled: *Senior Editor, Features.*

"Nice setup you guys have," Matt said, looking around the cubicles.

"Yeah," Dinesh said, opening the door. "This is where your student fees go."

He gestured them inside and closed the door behind them. Matt and Roy sat in the two chairs before Dinesh's desk. The window behind it looked out across the Forestry Faculty complex, a perfect view of its tree-lined avenue and miniature woodland. Farther off beyond the complex, Radcliffe College loomed atop its hill, the spire of Anathema Tower gleaming in the sun.

The view was blocked as Dinesh sat down and kicked back in his chair. "So...what'd you want to talk about?"

Roy sighed. "Matt is with *Cliffe-Hanger*, our college's own magazine, and he's doing a story on Rich Benson, kind of a memorial to him." He lied so smoothly Matt himself almost believed it for a moment.

"Ah." Dinesh's mood darkened. "Yeah, he was one of our best. You can put down that everyone loved and appreciated him, even though that's not true—he was a fucking prick—but you know, remember the rose and not the thorns and all that."

Matt nodded. "In collecting my...notes for the piece, I've noticed he was kind of...divisive among people who knew him. I mean, we're gonna clean up his image in the story, but do you mind elaborating on what he was like just a bit?"

Dinesh raised an eyebrow. "Off the record?"

"Off the record."

He sighed and leaned back again. "Rich Benson... That guy had a way with words, alright. At least on paper you could edit him, cut him down to size. In person?" He scoffed. "He was a total douchebag. Objected to every little suggestion, always his way or the highway for every story he wrote…"

"Was he working on anything recently?" Matt said. "I know he occasionally wrote for *Cliffe-Hanger* too, but he wasn't working on anything for us when he died." Matt knew that was true; he'd worked it into conversation with his Cliffe classmate Dana before their interminable Medieval History lecture. She'd been a part of the magazine since first-year, and said Benson hadn't been around their office since the start of the school year.

"Yeah, he was working on something—and he was a real bitch about it too, wouldn't tell any of us what it was other than it was going to be *huge*. Massive. He said it would make *The Westerner* legit. Even big newspapers would take notice, not just Calgary ones. National potentially."

Matt and Roy exchanged looks. "Any idea what that was?"

"Bullshit, probably," Dinesh scoffed. "Benson acted like he was destined to win a Pulitzer one day. Whatever this story was, he seemed to think it was going to be his big break."

"When did he start on it?"

"He mentioned something at the end of last year, right as we were closing up shop during the exam period. Then he told me he'd done a bit more digging over the summer and he wanted to have the piece up by Winter Break. It was real investigative journalism, he kept saying." Dinesh rolled his eyes. "He compared himself to *Spotlight*."

"But he never mentioned what it was?"

"No, but he kept talking about sources at Cliffe he wanted to keep anonymous and all that…" Dinesh hesitated. "Actually…he said something to me about a week before he died." He spoke slower now; his eyes stared at his desk but his mind seemed elsewhere. The atmosphere in the room had changed.

"He seemed a little stressed, going through things in his desk. He said he wondered if he'd gotten in over his head and laughed. But it wasn't a natural laugh, it was…nervous."

Matt said, "And then a week later he was dead."

Dinesh looked up and slowly nodded.

"Did the RCMP ask you anything about him?"

His eyes widened. "Yeah, they came by a couple days after he died. Just wanted to get his materials to look through them. They were pretty sure it was an accident, but just wanted to be thorough." He paused. "They also asked if he was working on anything big."

"And you told them about this?"

The senior editor scratched his head. "Not the last part, actually. I just said he'd been writing some story but he wouldn't say what it was. Something about anonymous sources, but that was it…" He looked off past them. "I forgot to mention that he seemed kind of scared—I didn't think it had anything to do with his death. I mean, they'd said it was most likely an accident. But then they said the case was closed and it slipped my mind again. We had a little memorial for him at the Rancher, raised our glasses to his memory, and that was that. Honestly…not many people showed up."

"Did he…did Benson ever mention the word 'Anathema'?"

Dinesh paused. "I don't remember. That's that weird cult thing you guys have at Cliffe, right?"

Matt shrugged. "They're around, yeah."

"I know Benson didn't really like them, but I honestly couldn't say if this had anything to do with that." He seemed uncomfortable, wanting to shift the subject. "Anything else I can help you with?"

As they headed back to Radcliffe, Matt noticed Roy had gone pale.

"You alright?"

"No," he said. "I wish I hadn't had the idea to bring you here."

"Why not?"

Roy forced a grim smile. "Because after hearing that, you'll want to get all the way to the bottom of this thing, won't you?"

Matt was quiet for a moment. "I don't think Rich Benson had an accident. There's something serious going on at this college, Roy. And if Anathema gets caught in the middle, all of us—you and I included—will go down with it no matter what."

FIFTEEN

HE DIDN'T see much of Joan for the next week. When they had dinner in Galbraith together on Saturday, she told him she was swamped with a psych paper due Wednesday and an econ midterm on Thursday. Then again, he was wading deep into two sizable essays himself. In a way he was grateful for the workload, since it drew his mind away from his extracurricular concerns.

The first three days of the week ticked by as Matt handed in a ten-page analysis of mercantilism in the Colonial Caribbean on Wednesday, then, after skipping High Table, spent a frantic evening writing all seven pages of the Medieval History paper due the next day. He was still editing it five minutes before he left for his class, but was able to relax through the three-hour lecture that afternoon.

In the evening, he went to DebSoc. The attendees cradled their free beers, trying to enjoy them while they lasted. Matt wondered how many would still come next semester after Mustard's new policy took effect. This week's topic was the Off-Res Debate, in which two residence students and two off-campus students squared off on the merits of living at Radcliffe or in Canmore Creek.

Turland gave a rousing President's Address, spinning a lyrical narrative in which he met an alternate-reality version of himself who had lived on-res all four years, instead of moving off in second-year. The speech went on for ten minutes and culminated in a twist ending—the whole scenario was a fever dream induced by the admin spiking his DebSoc beer.

Immediately after, the debaters launched into a series of speeches arguing whether sex was better in dorm rooms or off-campus. The resolution for the week, as it had been for this same debate for the past three years, was: "Commuter? I hardly know her!"

Matt's mind drifted as one speaker praised the convenience of res room coitus, trying to stave off questions about a body in a creek. He looked around the room; Joan wasn't here. She hadn't come last week either, but he'd hoped she would be here tonight so he could ask her how her midterm had gone.

The debate finally ended, Turland tallied the votes and declared the Opposition the winner, and everyone collected their belongings to continue their debauchery at the Royal Pub. Matt saw the President take a heavy swig from a flask before they left.

At the bar, he sat with both him and Patrick, who teased Turland, saying he was a mediocre President compared to his glory last year. Matt realized Patrick was also quite drunk, and had settled into his usual inebriated rhythm of self-extolment.

It had been like that since halfway through last year. He'd been different when Matt met him the first day of his Frosh Week; they'd both lived in Saunders. It was Patrick's second year living on that floor, and he'd told frosh to come to him with any questions about Radcliffe traditions. After discovering Patrick was an Anathema member, Matt pestered him about the secret society for several weeks. Patrick managed to keep tight-lipped, warning him that while he was fine with Matt's interest, others in the organization might think him too keen. It had been Patrick who handed him his Beckonings invite, and later, the calling card for his Initiation.

"I had better first-year attendance," Patrick slurred. "And you know why? Because I put them *first*, Tom. I reserved a spot for at least one of them on every debate. I was *inclusive!*"

"Yeah," Turland said, sipping a beer. "And you totally didn't do that just so they'd vote you in as Officer. I hear the first-year voting bloc is crucial in elections."

Shortly after, Matt settled his tab and went home, exhausted. He woke up the next morning, Friday, and did his usual routine at the Athletic Center over by Front Campus Circle. He found that exercising while surrounded by intensely fit Varsity athletes motivated him better, even if he always felt self-conscious while there. After grabbing a late breakfast at Galbraith, he spent his lecture-free day cooped up in Mackenzie Library, gearing up for another large paper due Tuesday.

Then, in the late afternoon, he sat in his Bowman room, gazing out at the West Quad and Anathema Tower, both bathed in fading sunlight. There was barely any green left on the trees and the leaves littered the ground.

Matt took out his phone and pulled up Joan Keating on Facebook Messenger. They hadn't spoken all week. He sighed and typed: *Hey, hope your midterm went well yesterday! Are you going to the Lambda Phi party after the Beckonings tonight?*

His finger anxiously hovered over the Send icon. Matt told himself he was being ridiculous but he'd been here before, sending messages that were never replied to, watching a string of positive signs lead nowhere. Each time he ended back where he'd always been, sitting alone in his room and forcing himself to be grateful for all the things he did have—his family, his few but loyal friends, his dog back home, his health, the fact that he was a student at a prestigious university—because, and he'd told his therapist this, he was worried that if he didn't constantly remind himself to be grateful for them, life would take those things away too.

He hit Send, but these thoughts put his mind in a tailspin and a cloud settled over him. Matt looked back out the window, trying to focus on the scenery, and knew it was just a mood swing. His therapist had talked about that too; even the slightest negative thought could send him into a depressed state for anywhere from an hour to a few days, and a simple positive thought or occurrence could just as easily snap him out of it. The first step was recognizing it, knowing it was just part of borderline personality disorder, and working to counteract it.

To cheer himself up, he looked at the poster of the Grand Canyon hanging above his bed, reminding himself of home and days spent in the Arizona sun, of the Sonoran Desert's all-enveloping warmth. Then he walked to his closet and found his tuxedo at the back.

He hadn't worn it yet this year, but it was time to dust it off. He went to the dresser and withdrew his pendant and flask.

It amused him that Turland, as Imperator, had gotten flasks branded with the Anathema insignia for them. During his Initiation, Matt had been told that if he wanted to keep his, he had to finish the flask by the end of the evening. He'd done so in five minutes, after which a concerned-looking Patrick had told him it would've been his anyway because they had so many. The night had gotten a little hazy after that.

He looked over the flask and smiled, when suddenly his phone buzzed.

Matt glanced at it. Joan had messaged: *Hey thanks for asking! Everyone in my class felt dead, so hopefully there's a curve! Also yes I'll be at Lambda tonight, see u there :)*

He sat down in his chair and leaned back, exhaling in relief. As quickly as it had come over him, the cloud dissipated from his mind.

SIXTEEN

CANDLES FLICKERED in the dark room, casting shadows across Venetian masks and the faces that wore them. Randall watched his Tetrad ready the space for the History, placing velvet pillows on the ground, making sure Doug had the right document to read for the night's conclusion.

He sighed and adjusted his mask. As Imperator, his was different than the standard black cloth issue the others wore, but it was about the same size, covering only the upper half of his face around his eyes. A skull logo was inscribed upon the forehead. Each Imperator kept their custom-ordered medallion, but this silver, metal mask had been passed down for nearly twenty years.

"How are we doing on time?" Logan asked, looking around the room.

Randall glanced at his watch. "The other members are leading the first-years here from Griffin Park. They should get here any minute now—"

Sound came from the stairs behind him. He spun to see Matt and Tanner enter, looking slightly out of breath. "Hey guys," Tanner said. "The guests are upstairs."

"Just in time." Randall took a look around. They stood in a side room often used for billiards and beer pong in the basement of Delta Nu Kappa, which they had rented out for the night's affairs. The den of debauchery had been transformed into a ceremonial chamber. "Doug, I think it looks ready. Time to bring Dad out."

"Got it," Doug said, shifting his Magister sash as he walked over to a medium-sized wooden box, placed at the side of the room. He brought it to the chamber's center where a pillow lay waiting for it to be placed. Doug set the box down beside the pillow and opened it.

"Alright guys," Randall said, turning to Matt and Tanner. "I want you to bring a first-year down. They'll sit here in silence, then we'll bring the others down one by one and Doug will read the History. And then we can get the fuck out of here and enjoy our Friday. Who do we have upstairs right now?"

Matt tilted his head. "Roy, Hamid, Rufus, Zhang, and Ares."

Randall frowned. "Where's everybody else? I thought Geoff was coming."

"He had to set up Lambda Phi for the Halloween party," Logan said. "He's the President, remember?"

"Oh, right." Randall scratched the back of his head. "I keep forgetting he's in both."

Kingsley Fennell, the Pontifex, turned around. "Hey Doug, you okay?"

The Magister was still kneeling over the open box, staring down into it with a blank expression. "It's not here," he said softly.

Randall walked over. "What do you mean it's not here?" Sure enough, the box was empty. "Where the hell did it go? When did you last see it?"

Doug stood up and wiped his glasses. "I, uh…last checked the box a few weeks ago, I think."

"Where do you keep the box?" Logan asked, anger in his voice rising like steam.

"In my room, as always."

"Your res room?!" Logan shouted. "You kept the skull in your fucking *res room?!*"

"Logan, calm down," Randall said. "We keep our stuff all over the place. The Chalet, our homes—"

"Did you lock the door?" Logan continued.

"It was…it was under my bed."

"Did you lock…the fucking…door?!" the Legatus hissed.

"No," Doug said quietly.

"And so," Logan continued, "when you went to Galbraith for six hours like you do every Saturday and Sunday, just sitting there typing on your computer and chatting, anyone who knew your door was unlocked could come in, search your entire room, then steal the skull and make off with it."

Everyone in the chamber was silent.

Finally, Doug said, "Yes."

Randall spun around to Matt and Tanner. "This doesn't leave the room, okay?" He turned back to his Tetrad. "Alright, here's what we're gonna do: the first-years don't know that we're supposed to have a skull here, so we're just going to have Doug read the History like we always do and pretend nothing's wrong."

"That doesn't answer what happened to the fucking skull." Logan narrowed his eyes.

"No, but we can deal with that later." Randall rubbed his head. *We haven't even gotten to the First Sermon and this year is already a shitshow.* "Matt, Tanner, just bring all the first-years in here at once. I want to get this wrapped up quickly." *So I can get a very large drink.*

They nodded and left the room. A moment later he heard them scrambling back up the stairs.

Randall turned back to Doug, who looked pale. He felt sorry for him; the guy had been devoted to the Anathema Archives since his first-year. Normally, certain Initiates were pegged as future Imperators, Legatuses, even Pontifexes—but rarely Magisters. Running the Archives was a position usually dumped on the last person who an Imperator felt deserved Tetrad, but wasn't sure what else to do with them. Not Doug Sadler. Everyone in the organization had looked him up and down and said *This man was born to be a Magister.*

And now he had lost the fucking skull.

Matt and Tanner returned a few moments later with the other members, all wearing their tuxedos and masks while the glint of silver dangled from their necks. Behind them came the first-years, twelve of them. Twenty invitations had been given out; these were the ones who'd been brave enough to show up. That was a good start for their Initiation prospects, but there had been members who'd never attended their Beckonings—or even been invited in the first place.

In truth, Randall had never really cared much for the event. It was a pain to organize, costly to rent out the frat when they had so few people coming, and it consisted mostly of first-years getting lightly hazed around Griffin Park—such as playing leap frog in their gowns while singing the Canadian national anthem, or other ridiculous tasks. Of course, the participants were reminded that they chose to participate in this and that they could leave any time they liked.

Randall glanced around the room. At least these first-years looked excited, albeit terrified. They wore their High Table gowns over casual clothing. Roy directed them to form two rows of six and to kneel before the Tetrad. They all complied.

The Imperator walked around and stood before them. "Gentlemen, I sincerely hope you enjoyed your evening. It is only the beginning of your journey into the mysteries of the Anathema. Next will be the 198th Sermon in the Great Lord's name, to be hosted next month. You will hear the exact time and date soon, but spread the message to others in your year that the Grand Tradition has returned. Both us and our sister branch will perform our duties to cure Radcliffe of its egos and to lambast its deleterious ways through the power of satirical chastisement. I now leave you in the capable hands of my Magister, who will impart upon you an abbreviated history of our organization and the role—despite rumors you may have heard of 'Dissociation'—that it has and continues to play in our college."

He stepped aside, allowing Doug to walk forward with a big binder that actually only contained a brief document. The Magister tilted it back from the first-years so they couldn't glimpse what lay inside; he cleared his throat and began to read.

"The next time you walk through the West Quadrangle, turn your attention upward to Radcliffe's signature steeple. Gaze upon its pepperbox belfry and know that there resides the Great Lord Anathema himself, the force that keeps the social fabric of this college intact, that prevents its egos from becoming too overblown, that reminds its cliques they are not invincible."

The members readied candles and began dripping wax on the backs of first-years' gowns. Hamid whispered something in the ear of a frosh Randall recognized, Brandon Lehane, who nodded excitedly. Tanner whispered to another, giving him things to shout.

Doug continued. "It was a cold day in 1905, just four years after the founding of this fair college, that our venerable spirit decided this institution was hopelessly lost. Arrogance and unrestrained debauchery ruled these hallowed halls. And so, the Great Lord Anathema—"

"DADDY!" Brandon moaned.

Doug hesitated, but managed to keep his expression neutral as he moved on. "—called upon his first Imperator, Gordon MacTaggart, to assemble a team of writers to gather and edit a supreme document that would expose the wretchedness Radcliffe had become: the very first...*Sermon.*"

Another first-year howled like a dog.

"So successful was this event that it quickly became a tradition: Once a year, every March, the students would gather in Picard Hall to receive chastisement and take a moment of reflection on how they had behaved. This became known as the annual Grand Tradition, and soon a student named Ada Lowther realized the women of Radcliffe, though primarily off in their own sphere in the East Quad, were just as desperately in need of lampooning as the men. And so in 1926, she was visited by the Lord's—"

"*OH, DADDY!*"

"—cousin, the Great *Lady* Anathema, to host her own Sermon." Another howl. "This event became joint, with the ladies going first each year. The college was riveted! All went swimmingly until 1928, when a group of sacrilegious dissenters felt the Sermons"—a howl—"were too *soft*. They conspired to form the Circle of the Seditious Serpentine, an evil blacker than the dark heart of Radcliffe itself. Instead of Imperators, they were led by false prophets called Bards, and instead of Tetrads they had but a single Vizier to carry out their commands. These Bards performed their rituals wearing cloaks with veiled faces to conceal their identities, but they were no match for the Anathema's sleuthing. When the Bards were unmasked however, the Great Lord—"

"*DADDY, I'VE BEEN A VERY BAD BOY!*"

"—and Great Lady showed not only mercy, but forgiveness—and named the two Bards, R.A. Markham and H. S. Hildreth, as the next male and female Imperators respectively. Serpentine was dissolved and assimilated into Anathema proper, and together members who had once been enemies forged their wits to deliver some of the best Sermons"—another howl—"this institution has ever seen. The number of events was upped from one to two every year, a dose of chastisement in autumn and at the dawn of spring.

"The organization would go on for several decades unimpeded, until a hippie, Trojan horse Imperator in the mid-sixties decided to end Anathema forever in the name of *love*, *kindness*, and other lies we tell children." A few first-years snickered. Doug's face remained blank. "The Great Lord would rest for but one year—"

"*DADDY, DON'T LEAVE ME!*"

"—until a noble frosh, G.R. Jessup, would take the reins as the youngest Imperator in history, giving the organization the fresh blood needed to propel itself through year after year, until…" He paused for dramatic effect. "The Anathema's home betrayed it. The year was 1997, and a bunch of pissant heretics had again formed a coalition against the Lord—"

"*I LOVE YOU, DADDY!*"

"—Daddy loves you too—and the Lady, known as the Anti-Anathema Association. These simpering scoundrels claimed the Sermons"—a howl again—"were not too soft, but rather too *harsh*, too *mean*, too *politically incorrect*, and a whole laundry list of other *bad stuff*. To be fair, maybe some of them had a point. But instead of settling things rationally, Radcliffe severed ties with Anathema and banished our satirical spirits back to their tower. However, this was a blessing in disguise, for now we operate under the cover of darkness, a *truly* secret society"—more snickering—"and in the post-Dissociation era, the male and female branches have come closer than they ever were before, resolving administrative inconsistencies and harmonizing their rituals. Now the Anathema functions as two equal parts, each equipped to shit-talk the behavior of your peers and impart the sage wisdom that only a bunch of drunk cultists in their late teens and early twenties can provide.

"The male Imperatorial Succession has only twice been broken, once by the aforementioned hippie fuckwit in 1964, who shall not be named, and once again fifty-two years later. It was a brave second-year member, Thomas Andrew Turland, who stepped up to become His 113th Imperator. The Succession has continued to Jackson Claudius Randall, His 115th mouthpiece."

Logan furrowed his brow. "Your middle name is fucking *Claudius?*"

"We've been over this," Randall said, motioning for him to be quiet. His full name, like all Imperators', had been shouted by his predecessor at the Second Sermon upon his announcement. Maybe Logan was just too drunk to remember. Or maybe, like everyone else, he'd been too shocked that the new Off-Residence Affairs Officer was now a leader of the Anathema.

"Go forth," Doug continued. "The wax on your gowns is a badge of honor, for you have undergone a ceremony not many within this college have experienced. Spread the word that chastisement is coming, and that your peers should prepare themselves for His Most Wretched Ice Cream Social this November."

The first-years nodded, simultaneously drunk and confused, excited and terrified.

"Gentlemen, this way," Hamid said, heading out the door. Slowly, the two rows of students got up and followed him back toward the stairs.

Once they were gone, Randall sighed with relief. "Thanks for actually being here, guys. I know this is the one college extracurricular you can't put on a resume, so I appreciate you coming out tonight. If any of you are heading to Lambda Phi for their Halloween extravaganza, I'll see you there later. If not, have a good night regardless. We'll meet to write on Tuesday and Wednesday next week. The Sermon is coming up, so we really need to get more content. We've only had a few writing sessions so far. Did the first-years say anything stupid tonight?"

Mike Zhang shrugged. "Brandon told us he was aroused by trees."

Randall put a hand to his head. "Okay... Yeah, we can work with that. Just make sure—if you do any writing on your own—to focus on first-year content. But don't go *too* hard on them. They'll want to hear jokes about people they actually know, but I want their first Sermon to be as enjoyable as possible."

Everyone nodded.

"Alright," he said. "Class dismissed."

The members said goodbye and exited, leaving the Tetrad alone in the chamber.

"Jesus Christ." Randall removed his mask and pulled his hood back, rubbing his face.

"You okay?" Fennell asked.

"Yeah, but I can't wait to get fucking wasted at Lambda. This week has nearly killed me between all the Officer meetings, the Board of Stewards bullshit, the Air Force—not to mention my classes and organizing *this* fucking thing." He gestured around. "Can you guys start cleaning up? I'll be back in a sec."

"Yeah, sure," Doug said, allowing a mortified expression to return to his face now that the others had gone.

Randall left the room, walked to the left and turned a corner to enter a bathroom, which was grody but would have to do. He stood over the sink, turned on the faucet, and splashed water in his face. Sighing, he looked at himself in the cracked mirror.

There were bags under his eyes and he looked incredibly tired. He lowered his head again and thought back to Monday, which already seemed like an eon ago. The beginning of the month and Rich Benson's death felt like another lifetime.

Randall splashed more water in his face, trying to think of who the fuck would want to steal the skull. It was probably just Lambda Phi, which meant hopefully Geoff would give it back to him in a few days. He knew everyone had been expecting Madler to name either Geoff or Logan as Imperator last year, and Randall's appointment as 115 had seemingly come out of left field. As such, Geoff always tried to show off his status as Lambda Phi President whenever Randall was around.

He stared at his reflection again. Thoughts of the missing artifact, the snitch reporting to the admin, and Benson's death swam through his mind.

And the more he pondered it, the more he felt that somehow—inexplicably—all three were linked.

SEVENTEEN

"**S**HIT, ARE they gonna make us pay to get in?"

Roy looked to the head of the line, where two Lambda Phi guys in firemen costumes sat at a table by the house's side door. The song "Monster Mash" boomed from inside, orange strobes flashing through the front bay windows. There were at least twenty people ahead of them, dressed as everything from nurses to vampires.

"Yeah, they always do that," Matt said.

Roy sighed. "How much is it going to be?"

"I think just ten. That's what it usually is."

"Tell me, has a Lambda party ever been worth the price of admission?"

Matt considered for a moment. "Well…if you've got nothing else to do on a Friday night…"

Roy smirked. "I know the *real* reason we're here. You just need to enter the party with a friend so it doesn't look like you came alone to a…certain someone."

He shrugged. "She'll inevitably be with a group of friends. They'll think I'm weird if I'm just wandering around by myself. Plus, I think Jennifer is going…" He nudged him on the shoulder.

Roy paused. "Huh. Well, that makes things more interesting. I needed an excuse to wear this anyway." He gestured to his outfit. He looked like an 18th century British aristocrat, wearing a blue formal uniform adorned with gold embroidery. His riding boots and a fake sword sheathed at his side completed the look. "Who are you going as again? James Bond?"

When they'd gone back to Radcliffe after the Beckonings, Matt had only removed his pendant and Venetian mask and was still clad in his tuxedo. "Actually, I'm supposed to be Ethan Hunt. You know, Tom Cruise's character from *Mission: Impossible*…?"

"I've never actually seen any of those. I only watch movies set before 1945. And even then, I prefer them to be set before the 20ᵗʰ century."

He and Roy eventually reached the front of the line. One of the fireman-dressed Lambda guys said, "That'll be ten for each of you." He looked quite drunk.

Begrudgingly, the two of them ponied up some purple notes. Having grown up in the States, the colorful nature of Canadian currency still amused Matt. The two frat guys scribbled hastily-drawn pumpkins onto the back of their hands with Sharpies, then motioned for them to enter to the right.

Inside was dark, but strategically lit with orange and purple lights all around. Their glow illuminated a plethora of decorations: fake cobwebs embellished the ceilings, open coffins were propped up in corners, and jack-o-lanterns had been placed on the floor up against the walls. And this was only the foyer. The frat house split off in two directions from here: to the right was the dance floor with strobe lights and a disco ball; to the left was an area with several tables for beer pong, some weathered sofas, a coat check, and a makeshift bar. Directly before them stood a multi-landing staircase leading up to the bathrooms and living quarters.

"ROY!" came a shout.

They both turned to see Jennifer Horvat, clad in a tight green dress. She ran up and tackled Roy with a hug.

"Whoa, hey there," he said, stumbling back. Holding her by the shoulders, he looked her outfit up and down. "And, uh…what exactly are you supposed to be?"

"I'm going as a sexy lime wedge! It was the most ridiculous thing I could find at the costume store in Canmore."

"Oh yeah, that kinda does look like a lime…a little…" He threw his arm around her shoulder and they both turned to Matt. "Take a photo of us, the dandy and the lime wedge!"

"A classic pair." He slid his phone out of his pocket and snapped a couple of pictures. "There, I'll send them to you when I'm sober." He'd had most of the rum in his flask before coming here. Roy had not only finished his own flask back at his room, but had also drank some scotch and barely seemed tipsy. Matt, on the other hand, was definitely buzzed.

"Alright, I think we're gonna head to the dance floor. See you in a bit!" Before he could say anything, Roy and Jennifer had turned and disappeared into the throng of partiers, strobes, and Halloween music.

Matt sighed, heading over to the other room. This area was quieter, which was a relative term, since the cacophony of beer pong and music made it impossible for anyone to converse without shouting. His eyes swept the area for anyone he recognized, anyone he could talk to so he wouldn't roam around like a lost dog—as was the case at most parties.

Then he froze.

Joan stood at the opposite end of one of the middle tables. She too, had used her Anathema attire as the base for her costume, but she'd put more effort into hers. She wore all black for her boots, tights, leather skirt, and tank top, but the additions were gray faux-furred fingerless gloves, a tail, and a band with wolf ears over her head. He felt lazy for merely wearing his tux, but wondered what else he could have done with it. Besides, secret agents never really went out of style.

Val stood beside her, a vampire with fake blood at the corners of her mouth, and Matt realized they were playing a game against two first-year boys. Joan didn't seem to have noticed him yet, but was laughing at something one of the guys had said.

Matt grew tense, then shook his head, exhaling. He walked to the bar, which served only lager and a punch bowl labeled *Creepshow Cocktail*. As he did so, he reminded himself what the therapist had said about recognizing negative emotions and how to placate them.

Joan talking to somebody else doesn't mean she doesn't like you anymore, he told himself. *Pull it together, get a drink, and go talk to her.*

Matt recognized one of the frat guys working the bar and walked up to him. "Hey Ryan, how's IR?"

From the outfit, he guessed that Ryan Marshall was dressed as Danny Zuko from *Grease*. It was fitting, he thought, since Ryan was even more of a movie buff than he was. They'd shared an Arctic History class last year and bonded over their love of cinema. As an Anathema member, Matt wasn't particularly inclined to like Lambda Phi, but the fact that Ryan was a part of it reminded him that they weren't all knuckleheads.

"IR's been good. How's history?"

"So far, so good." He pointed to the Creepshow Cocktail, which looked radioactively orange. "What exactly is in that, by the way?"

"Fanta, a few other things, and a whole lotta booze."

Matt stared at it and thought for a moment. "I'll take it."

Ryan poured a generous amount into a Solo cup and handed it to him. Matt said thanks and turned to the beer pong tables as he took his first sip. It tasted very sweet and quite strong, but not as lethal as Dunlap's vodka-crans a few weeks ago. He made his way past some smokers, trying not to cough too loudly, and found himself at the table where Joan and Val played off against their younger opponents.

They were all engaged with the game and he wasn't sure how to enter the conversation. Suddenly, the ball bounced off the table, hit the floor, and rolled toward him. He snatched it up and looked between them. "Who has it now?"

"I do!" Joan said, swiping it out of his hand. She held it up and threw him a mischievous grin. "When in doubt, always bring the ball to *me*." She turned, aimed, and tossed it in an arc that landed squarely in a cup on the other end. Now the first-years only had one left, while the girls sat comfortably in the lead with four remaining.

Both guys looked impressed. One of them removed the ball and said "Nice shot, babe" before chugging the contents of the cup.

Joan didn't seem to have paid attention. She looked Matt up and down with a sidelong glance, then said, "Cute outfit. What are you going as, an Anathema member in enemy territory?" She appeared to be a bit tipsy.

Matt took a big sip of his cocktail. "Ethan Hunt, actually."

"Oh...from *Mission: Impossible*, right?"

"Yeah."

"I love those movies." Her attention returned to the game.

Matt was unsure what to say for a moment. "You look great, by the way. Going as a werewolf, just like your story, right?"

Joan turned to him and beamed. "Hey, you remembered!"

"Of course I did! I'd still like to read it someday."

She laughed. "Oh, no it's horrible! You'll think I'm super weird—" A boy at the other end landed a ball in one of her and Val's cups. "Shit. Hold on." She fished the object out and drained the cup in several long pulls, then handed the ball to Val and moved the cup aside, placing a hand on her stomach.

"You alright?" he asked.

"Yeah, I've already chugged a few of those tonight. And some earlier during the Beckonings. And—" Joan belched loudly and a fur-gloved hand flew to her mouth. She was silent for a moment, then they both laughed. Her cheeks flushed red as she said, *"Excuse me.* Don't worry, I'm nowhere near as gone as I was that time at the Foxhole."

"Good." He smiled. "I'd like to not ruin this tux."

She punched him in the arm and chuckled again. He laughed along with her, but discretely rubbed where she'd hit. There had been some force behind that swing and he wasn't sure if she realized it.

Val threw her arms up and yelled, "WHOO!"

Matt and Joan turned around. She'd sunk a ball in the guys' last cup. "Aw, shit," one of the first-years said.

"You're out!" Val said. She turned to Joan. "Come on, let's go dance."

"Sure." Joan looked back at him and put a hand on his shoulder, giving him a warm smile. "I'll see you around in a bit." As she and Val walked off, her fingers gently brushed his back. He turned around and watched her disappear into the crowd.

The first-year guys walked up to him. "Good luck, pal," one of them said.

"Hey, thanks—"

"—you'll *need* it." Both of them snickered and walked off.

Matt glared after them. He took a big sip of his drink, making a mental note to find out what their names were so he could write a shitload of Anathema jokes about them. After all, Randall had said they needed more content on first-years...

Speaking of the Imperator, Matt spotted him and Patrick lounging on a sofa by the window, chatting with plastic cups in hand; Patrick's red face betrayed his inebriation. Matt made his way over to them.

Randall turned and raised his cup in toast toward him. "Richardson! Getting creative with your costume, I see." He wore a pirate outfit and a tricorn hat, not unlike the DebSoc President's, with a skull and crossbones displayed on one side and a feather coming out of the other.

"Come on, I'm a secret agent!"

Randall shrugged. "At least you rarely wear the tux. Look at this fucker." He grinned and pointed to Patrick beside him, who wore jeans and a plaid shirt. "He says he's Paul Bunyan, but he dresses like a lumberjack all the time."

Patrick shook his head. "I thought about putting on a costume, but by then I was already too drunk to care."

"Speaking of drinking," Randall said, examining his cup, "I'm pretty sure this stuff will kill my liver, but I'm gonna get a refill anyway."

They both stood up, but Patrick waited behind as Randall headed to the bar. "I saw you chatting with Joan Keating over there."

Matt tensed up. Every previous time Matt had told Patrick he liked a girl, Patrick had warned him it wouldn't end well. He'd been right every time. "Oh, I uh…"

"She and I sat together at Ni Hao Ma after the First Sermon last year and had a great conversation. She seems like a nice girl. Good luck!"

He patted him on the shoulder, gave a fatherly smile, and walked on.

◆

After finishing his drink, Matt felt intoxicated enough to hit the dance floor.

He saw Joan dancing in one corner with some of her female friends, most of whom he recognized from Anathema. He looked for another group to dance with in the interim and spotted Tanner, but he was in a group of second-years who never really talked to Matt. Fortunately, he found Roy and Jennifer bopping with some of her friends and saw an opening to join in.

Matt knew he was dancing badly but was far from the level of sobriety at which he would care. After a while, he realized everyone near him was either grinding on a partner, like Roy and Jennifer, or making out with someone, like the other two girls in their circle. Looking around, he saw more people grinding or feeling others up as they danced.

Jesus, get a room. He retreated across the foyer to the beer pong area and walked straight to the bar. Evidently Ryan's shift had ended; he was nowhere to be seen.

"What can I get for you?" another Lambda guy said, looking tired.

"Do you have any water?"

The guy gave him a blank stare.

"Never mind," Matt said, turning around. As he did so, he caught a glimpse of Joan leading a friend up the stairs by the hand. They were probably heading to the bathroom; he definitely didn't want to talk to her there. Not seeing anyone else around to chat with, he headed back out the entrance for a breath of fresh air.

Two different Lambda guys manned the table now, but there was no line. Attendance had crested and people would probably start leaving soon, if a few hadn't trickled out already. Matt walked down the side lawn to the road as the Gothic synthpop of MGMT's "Little Dark Age" boomed from inside, its lyrics still audible out here.

He stood at the end of the path and took a deep breath, wondering how much longer he should stay. He wanted to chat with Joan one more time before leaving, but wasn't sure where to take things next. They'd gone on a date, hung out casually several times…now what? Was she expecting him to ask her out to coffee again, or maybe go for drinks instead? He was fine taking it slow—in fact, he preferred it that way—but he worried that if he didn't move things along fast enough, she'd grow bored and find somebody else. He hated being nearly twenty-one and not having any experience at this; people expected you to understand certain things by this point and there was no easy way to catch up.

"Matt!"

He spun around to see Roy and Jennifer arm in arm, strolling toward him. "Heading out?"

They walked past him and turned around. "We're going to go watch *Pride and Prejudice* in my room and, uh…chat," Roy said.

Right… "Well, see you around then. Have fun!"

Roy frowned. "Where's, ah…*you know who?*"

Jennifer looked confused. "Someone's dressed as Voldemort?"

"No."

"*Ohhhh.*" She gave Matt a knowing smile. "Who are you going for?"

"I'm not saying… It'll probably end up going nowhere."

Roy looked past him. "Actually, I think she's right there."

Matt turned. Sure enough, Joan was talking to Val and Sophia Huynh, the current DebSoc Clerk and a fellow member of Val's Initiation class, back over by the door. He wasn't sure if they were leaving or just getting some air. All three had incorporated their Anathema outfits into their costumes.

"Which one?" Jennifer said, looking in their direction and squinting.

"The one in his year." Roy grinned.

"I told you not to tell anybody!"

"Relax, I can keep secrets," she said. "I just like knowing things." She glanced back at the three Anathema members. "Wait, you have a crush on *Joan Keating?*"

"Yeah... What's wrong with her?"

"Nothing really, but she was super into hazing us when I went to the Beckonings last year. She made us wear blindfolds, put us in different rooms, and asked us questions about our darkest secrets and stuff. Other than that, I've heard she's kinda weird and is pretty obsessed with Anathema." Jennifer hesitated. "Actually, scratch that—she's probably perfect for you."

"Right. I forgot I'm a fanatical cultist."

She shrugged, looking back at Joan. "She's very pretty, I'll give her that... I would totally fuck her, but I don't think she swings both ways."

Matt shrugged. The casual vulgarity of this college had worn off on him. "Hasn't mentioned it."

"Have you and her been talking or is this one of your classic 'she-said-hi-to-me-so-she-likes-me' type situations?"

"Jesus, give me some credit. It's never been like that," he said, taken aback.

"That's how everyone jokes about it in Galbraith."

Matt began to tense, but he calmed himself down. "Joan and I went on a date a few weeks ago and we've been hanging out now and again."

"See, that sounds *much* more promising." Jennifer glanced over his shoulder. "Oh, she's looking this way."

"Really?"

"Don't turn around... Yeah, she keeps doing it. Hmm... Bend forward a little."

"Umm, okay." He did so. Jennifer began stroking his cheek and smiling at him. "Uh, what are you doing?"

"I think she's looking right now. Back up, laugh, and look bored."

He straightened up, forced a chuckle, then began glancing around. "And this is supposed to do what exactly—?"

"Hey Matt, you're not gonna leave without saying goodbye, are you?!"

He turned around. Joan leaned against the frat house next to her friends, giving him a wave. Even though she was partially obscured in shadow, he could make out a sly smile on her face.

Matt couldn't help but smile too. "Wasn't planning on it." He turned back to Jennifer, but she and Roy were already heading down the road back to Radcliffe. Once they were out of Joan's line of sight, they each gave him a thumbs up. He turned and walked back to the other girls.

"I think Val and I are gonna call it a night," Sophia said to Joan. "Are you coming back too, or…?"

"I think Matt and I'll stay for a little bit longer." She threw her arm around his shoulder.

His heart began thumping in his chest.

"Alright, have fun!" Sophia smiled at both of them, then she and Val headed off toward the road. Matt was in shock; Sophia Huynh rarely smiled *ever*.

Joan pulled him closer. "Wanna head back inside?"

"Sure," he said softly.

They stood there for a moment. He debated whether or not to kiss her on the cheek, but she pulled her arm off him, took his hand in hers, and led him to the door. A moment later they were gliding through the foyer and ended up back in the beer pong room. She looked around, then pointed to the sofas by the window. An unoccupied loveseat stood off to the side.

They walked over and sat down, pressed together in the limited space. Joan turned to him. "I think it's a *bit* quieter over here."

At least they didn't have to shout to talk. "How was the Beckonings?"

"Really fun! I always enjoy it. They were pretty hard on me in first-year, so I've definitely enjoyed being on the other side of it the last two times. Val thinks I get a bit too into it, though." She tried to laugh it off.

"I can't imagine you being scary," he teased, moving his arm around her shoulder.

Joan laughed again. "That's because you don't know me that well yet."

"I'd like to." He gave her a warm smile.

She returned it, then nuzzled in closer and gestured to her scar. "You can still see part of it even with my mask on, and when I'm in a dark room with candles I think it looks pretty spooky. Plus, I do this creepy smile when leading the first-years into the house… And I'm kinda tall."

"Yeah, you're like what…five-ten?"

"On the dot," she said proudly. "And let me guess… You're six-two?"

"Just a little over it actually, though Tanner makes me feel short."

Joan laughed and seemed about to say something when Geoff Bhajan came by, followed closely by Randall. The Lambda Phi President wore a Hawaiian shirt and straw hat, a plastic camera slung around his neck.

Both Joan and Matt recognized him, of course. He'd held the ceremonial role of Minister during their Frosh Week, leading chants and introducing them to the college's traditions. The Minister position was always held by a second-year, either male or female depending on the year. Geoff had appointed Catherine Winters as his successor and she had led the cheers last Frosh Week; this year, the role had gone to Hamid. It was almost always held by an Anathema member; if the Minister wasn't already Initiated, they'd often receive a calling card later that year. Matt guessed Catherine's performance in the role was one of the reasons why people saw her as Imperator material.

"…I didn't take it, Jack," Geoff was saying, still walking.

"I'm not mad, I just want it back if you know where it is…," Randall called after him, adjusting his pirate hat as he went.

Both of them disappeared behind another beer pong game. None of the players seemed to even register the conversation.

Joan turned to Matt. "What was that all about?"

He hesitated. "How well can you keep a secret?"

She sat up straighter. "I *am* a member of a secret society."

"Okay, but you can't tell anyone else—not even in Anathema."

"Sure, I won't." Joan crossed her fingers. "Now, what is it?" She looked excited.

He leaned closer. "We just found out that someone stole our skull. Naturally, Lambda are the main suspects."

Joan blinked. "As in, the skull that's supposed to be the vessel of the Great Lord Anathema?"

"That's the one."

She burst out laughing. "Oh my God, who the hell lost track of *that?*"

"Doug."

"*Doug?* I thought he practically slept with it under his pillow."

"He left his door unlocked."

She shook her head in disbelief. "He never should've kept it in his room. Catherine keeps Mom somewhere in the Chalet."

"That does sound like a better idea."

Joan chewed on a fingernail. "But Geoff's in Anathema; why would he steal the skull?"

"I don't know. Maybe he just did it to fuck with Randall? Most people thought's he'd be 115."

She thought for a moment. "But then he'd eventually give it back. What if some other people in Lambda took it and hid it without telling him?"

"Geoff would find out eventually. They'd try to blow it up or something and send us a video of them doing it."

"Hmm… Is there anyone else who could've taken it?"

"Well, the Saunders guys don't exactly love us. And others around the college just hate Anathema in general."

She looked lost in a reverie. Then she opened her mouth slightly, as if to say something, when suddenly the beer pong table closest to them tipped over. A dozen cups fell to the ground, most still full of liquid. Cheap lager splashed all over the floor as Matt and Joan scurried up onto the back of the small sofa, huddling together so as to avoid falling off.

"You alright?" He turned to her and realized her face was very close to his.

"Yeah," she said, looking from his lips to his eyes.

Everyone around them was focused on the mess. One frat guy said to another, "Dude, you're a fucking idiot…" Someone else started laughing and made a joke about needing a mop.

She glanced over at the others, then back to him, and said, "I think we should get out of here."

"Yeah," he said, still looking at her. "I think so too."

◆

They walked along the road back to Radcliffe hand-in-hand.

Joan began slowly regaining sobriety as they reached the base of the front steps. When they reached the top, she turned around and took it all in. It was a beautiful night, not *too* cold, and a breeze blew across her face and through her hair. Stars dotted the sky beyond the mountains and trees sprawled away to her right through Griffin Park.

"We could sit right here."

She turned around. He was gesturing to the steps.

"Sure," she said, removing her gloves and her werewolf tail from the back of her skirt. As she sat down, she pulled the fuzzy ears off too and messed up her hair in the process. She tried to laugh it off, and he laughed along with her as he took a seat.

"That was fun," he said. "I don't normally enjoy Lambda parties that much, but I guess hanging out with you makes them a *bit* better." He winked.

Joan smiled back. "Yeah, I had a good time too." They sat in silence for a moment. She glanced around. Nobody else was in sight. Though it was unseasonably warm for the region, it was still too chilly for insects to be out chirping. Finally, she let her gaze rest on him and found herself staring into his eyes for an extended period of time.

He laughed awkwardly and turned away. "Do I have something on my face, or…?"

"No, no," she said, resting her head against her right hand. "This is gonna sound dumb, but…I've just realized I really like your eyes."

"My eyes?"

"Yeah. They sometimes have this kind of sad, lost look that I find really endearing."

He managed a laugh. "Um, thanks, I guess…"

"Shit, that sounded kinda mean."

"No, no—"

"I just…I think you have really nice eyes." She wanted to smack herself. "I know that's, like, the biggest cliché in the book…but I think they're really pretty."

"And sad."

She laughed. "I don't know, it's the whole wounded-puppy look you've got going on. It's sweet."

He shook his head, still smiling. "I'll take it as a compliment."

"It is! If I had to name my favorite feature of yours, it would be your eyes." She leaned back, placing her palms out behind her. "Alright, your turn. What's my best feature?" He turned away, lost in thought.

She smirked. "And don't you dare say my t—"

"Your scar," he said softly, looking at the stars.

Joan froze and stared off down the hill, back along the road they'd walked to get here. Finally, she scooted her feet onto the top step and hugged her knees, still staring into space. "Why?"

He spoke slowly. "I mean, you've got pretty eyes too—*very* pretty eyes. But there's something alluring about the scar, I don't know… I think you're self-conscious about it, but you shouldn't be… I don't think of you as 'that girl with the scar,' I think of you as that girl who gave great Deb-Soc speeches last year, who writes cool stories about werewolves, who's a passionate and dedicated Anathema member—someone who would make the *perfect* Imperator. I think of you as that girl who's a blast to hang out with, who was really confident tonight and showed me a great time even at the dumpiest frat house on campus. So *that's* why your scar is my favorite feature. Because every time I see it, I'm reminded that it doesn't even scratch the surface of you."

Joan hugged her knees tighter, her eyes fixed back down the road. She didn't even mind that without a jacket over her tank top and the alcohol wearing off, her bare shoulders were freezing cold. Tears welled in her eyes and she bit the nail of an index finger.

She stayed frozen like that for what felt like a long time, then finally looked over to Matt. He was petrified, unsure of what to do or say, clearly wondering if he'd made a mistake. His hand hovered halfway out toward her.

Joan launched herself at him, digging her nails into his shoulders. She kissed him, hard, and grabbed the back of his head to hold him closer. His arms tightened around her, his lips making their way along her cheek and down the side of her neck.

She tilted her head back and slowly opened her eyes. Anathema Tower loomed high to her left, an ominous beacon against the stars. Joan turned away and brought her mouth back to his as a single thought flashed through her mind:

What have I gotten you into?

PART II
SKULLDUGGERY

EIGHTEEN

DESPITE HIS hangover, Matt felt better than he had in a long time as he walked through the West Quad the next morning.

When he'd returned to his room last night, he was so elated by what happened that he'd forgotten to drink water before going to sleep. Mercifully, he'd had a couple Advil left in the bottle on his dresser, but they hadn't kicked in yet as he shielded his eyes from the sun, making his way to Galbraith. Leaves were scattered about the grass and a sharp chill cut through the air; he regretted not wearing a jacket. Whether it was in a few days or a few weeks, winter would come soon enough. They'd been lucky so far; it was almost the end of October and there hadn't been any snow yet.

In the dining hall, a tired Doris swiped his card and he entered the cafeteria. He refused to eat the pizza they had on offer as brunch food, so he grabbed half a Belgian waffle from a tray, some sliced cantaloupe, and a helping of scrambled eggs. After finding a clean-enough cup, he filled it with orange juice and returned to the hall.

There weren't many people here, even though it was almost noon. The only ones he knew were clustered at the third-year table; the two Magisters, Doug and Catherine, sat across from Rufus Danvers and Lisa Fang, Logan's girlfriend. Matt approached the seat next to Doug, which was occupied by a satchel.

"...don't show me, Lisa. I'm eating," Rufus was saying.

She pulled her phone back. "It's right in the middle of the Cliffe Facebook group."

"This college is just too much sometimes." Doug sighed and shook his head, then turned to notice Matt.

"Is anyone sitting there?" He gestured to the satchel.

"Oh no, that's just mine," Doug said, moving it to the ground and adjusting his glasses. "Here, take a seat."

"Thanks." Matt did so.

Rufus' eyes zeroed in on the left side of his neck. "Oh my God, Richardson! Is that a *hickey*?"

Every head at the table whipped in his direction. "Where?" Lisa said, leaning across the table. "I can't see it."

Matt put a hand to the side of his neck. He hadn't even noticed that this morning. *Shit, should've worn the turtleneck.*

"Who's the lucky girl? Or did you just hit yourself with a hammer to make us think you got action?" Rufus smirked but nobody else seemed amused.

"Relax, it's none of your business." They were all still staring at him and he found it unnerving.

"This is about as rare as a total eclipse. Come on, *tell us who it is!*" Rufus was smiling, but his eyes gleamed with mischievous intent. Something about his expression disturbed Matt.

"I'm not saying, so chill the fuck out."

Rufus turned to Lisa. "You know everything that goes on at this college. Who was he seen with at Lambda?"

Her eyes widened with realization. "I think I saw…but really, it's none of your business, Rufus."

He leaned back in his seat and tugged at his sweater. "You're right. He probably paid her, anyway."

Doug chimed in, "What, Rufus? You know any red-light districts around here?"

Matt smirked. "He probably visits them himself."

Rufus' face grew red. "I actually *have* a girlfriend, unlike either of you."

"She your right hand or your left?" Catherine smirked, throwing a wink to both Doug and Matt.

"She goes to the University of Calgary, *for your information.*"

"What were you guys talking about before I got here?" Matt desperately wanted to discuss anything else.

"Oh," Doug said, lowering his eyes. "Blaine Harris, one of the Saunders guys, posted in the Facebook group. He woke up this morning to find that someone had, um…*done something* to his door."

"What, like egging it?"

Catherine shook her head, then brushed a lock of red hair out of her face. "Much worse."

Matt noticed that Rufus was rapidly typing something on his phone. He abruptly tapped the screen and placed it back on the table.

"You probably don't want to hear it or see it while eating," Lisa said.

"See it?"

"He posted a photo of what was on his doorknob." Doug shivered and gestured to his half-eaten breakfast. "There's a reason why I'm not finishing my food today."

"Can you give me a hint? What, did somebody"—Matt lowered his voice—"*come* on it?"

"No, no," Doug said. "Not *quite* that bad, but you're on the right track." He paused and looked up, searching for the best way to phrase it. "There's a certain type of…hair—"

"Bloody fuck, I'm *eating*," Rufus barked, forking a chunk of cantaloupe.

"—and somebody glued a bunch of it to Blaine's doorknob," Doug said, rapidly finishing his statement.

Matt was taken aback. "That's just nasty." He pulled out his phone and saw, sure enough, that he had a Facebook notification from the Radcliffe College group, a new post from Blaine Harris. Reluctantly, he opened it and quickly tapped into the comments section just as the image loaded. He barely caught a glimpse of the crime scene, but what he saw did not look pretty.

Patrick Mason had written: *Whoever you are—NOT COOL. You mess with one Man of Saunders, you mess with all of us. This is completely inappropriate, crude conduct and I WILL find out who is responsible. First-years, I assure you that this type of behavior is NOT tolerated here at Radcliffe College.*

Other Officers shared similar posts. Veronica Yang had said: *That's inexcusable. I'm incredibly sorry this happened to you, Blaine. Rest assured, we will sort this out and punish the party or parties responsible.*

Carl Dunlap wrote: *I know Saunders and Winslow have had a long rivalry, but if I find out any of my Winslow guys were involved with this, I will be very upset. This is not okay on so many levels. Very sorry to hear this, Blaine. Patrick, I will gladly help you get to the bottom of this.*

Randall had posted something brief, but before he could read it Matt heard Lisa say, "You guys didn't have anything to do with it, did you?" She looked between all of them and Matt realized she was the only person at the table not in Anathema.

"Fuck no," Rufus said, looking personally offended. "Who do you take us for, barbarians?"

She shrugged. "It's not like Anathema has never done anything like this before. I read that *Calgary Herald* article from after that guy got injured during Initiations in the early 2000s, and it said something about you guys dumping a bucket of dog shit on a girl back in the fall of '97, when she was just walking through the West Quad. And then she later committed suicide."

"Well, actually…" Doug adjusted his glasses and put up a finger. "It was only an *attempted* suicide." By his tone, it sounded as if this cleared any wrongdoing.

Everyone at the table was silent. Matt and Catherine shot death glares at him.

Doug paled and held up his hands. "I mean, obviously, that's still bad."

"I know a bit more about that, actually," Catherine said, still glaring at him. "Her name was Susanne Ferguson. She was part of our branch but she dropped her pendant after third-year and began speaking out against us, even joined the Anti-Anathema Association. Legend has it that the female Imperator that year, Emma Gagnon, was so pissed at her betrayal she personally dumped that bucket out the window herself. It helped the dissenters make their case for Dissociation, which the college made official about a month afterward. But the suicide attempt came *later*, after Gagnon read a lot of brutal jokes about Ferguson at the First Sermon."

"So…to prove to the college why they shouldn't be banned, Anathema poured dog poop on somebody who spoke out against them and then drove them to try to kill themselves?" Lisa raised an eyebrow. "Who the fuck thought that was gonna end well?"

"They *didn't* think. That was the problem." Doug adjusted his collar, clearly wanting a chance to redeem himself. "Look, the eighties and nineties were not this organization's finest moments. The members back then got really arrogant with their status in the college. Anathema is still a big deal these days, but back in the eighties and nineties, it was *everything*. The Tetrads—actually, they were Triads back then—were treated like social gods. Their word was law. You dreaded going to a Sermon, fearing what they'd say about you. These people could make or break your place in Social Cliffe with a few lines of poetry or a crude wisecrack. And so they started thinking they were untouchable. And they did some *really* bad shit. They outed gay people, used racial slurs, and made otherwise blatantly cruel jokes. It was very nasty and completely inexcusable.

"But here's the thing a lot of people forget: the *whole college* was like that back then. If you go into the DebSoc archives and look at the debate topics from the nineties, which is when it started becoming less and less serious, you'll see all sorts of offensive subjects. I found a box of House Winslow materials from '94, and guess what? They had their own little Winslow quarterly newsletter that included articles from guys who lived there, and one issue had a very racist comic strip about the increasing number of Chinese students. And let's not forget how long it was before women were even allowed in here"—he gestured around Galbraith—"on the fucking weekend. That didn't happen until about thirty years ago and the East and West Quads were still gender segregated until 2006. The nineties were a vulgar decade, even the eighties too—everywhere. When we look back on those eras with nostalgia, we wash away a lot of the filth. Bullying was way worse back then; administrators looked the other way. Mental health services? Give me a fucking break.

"Anathema was founded to criticize overinflated egos at this college, but toward the end of the last century it got corrupted and became all about bullying and social status. It wasn't really about humor anymore—but even in the eighties and nineties, not *everyone* was like that. Some years had sane, reasonable Imperators—like the year of Dissociation. Ours was a guy who went on to become a Le Mans racecar driver, and I've read his stuff—he was chill. The female Imperator that year was the mean one."

Catherine scratched the back of her head. "Gagnon is still infamous in our branch. I hope she doesn't come to the Second Sermon this year. Thankfully, she hasn't been to one in a while."

"But," Doug continued, "a few years before that, my branch had a major douchebag named Quentin Caleb and the lady Imperator was the voice of reason trying to rein him in. So you can't just generalize it and say 'Anathema was evil from 1980 to about 1998.' It was definitely worse overall in that time, but not everyone in it was a horrible person. Some people were trying to reform it, to get back to the old ways. It was much better in the sixties and seventies. But with the kind of content they wrote in the nineties and the way they did things back then, I doubt I would've been Initiated."

"Me neither," Matt said. "And I wouldn't have wanted to be."

"Same here," Catherine said.

Lisa put up her hands. "Look, you know I love going to Sermons and hearing my friends get roasted, but I've heard a lot of people ask how you can defend Anathema at all, especially after what it used to do."

"Well, you see, that's just B.S.—the idea that because something was once bad that it can't be good again. If something *started out* bad, then okay—get rid of it. But Anathema began as a lighthearted way to poke fun at this college, and somewhere along the line it got taken over by the type of people it was created to criticize—and *they* ran it into the ground.

"So even though Anathema's dark age was a product of this college's culture, it's the only part of Radcliffe that takes the bad rap. Dissociating it was an ass-covering move by the admin twenty-one years ago. But the people who were in it back then left, and the people who are in the college—and the Anathema—today are products of *our* time. Who knows what they'll say about us in a couple decades?"

Catherine sighed. "What they did to that Ferguson girl was really fucking awful. And it's especially sad, because I wonder if she was trying to make Anathema better once Gagnon came in and ramped up the mean jokes. They didn't have an opt-out policy back then; the suicide attempt is actually what convinced us we needed one. Things are much different now, though. Anathema is way more diverse these days—racially, sexually, economically—and nobody wants to make the jokes they did back then."

"Yeah," Doug said. "Now we're led by Jack Randall, for fuck's sake. He's in the Air Force reserves and watches Disney movies with his girlfriend."

"I don't think Logan will be too bad next year," Lisa said, smirking. "But he's not exactly what I would call a soft guy."

"Well, we don't know who's gonna be Imperator next year yet anyway," Matt said, just a little too forcefully.

Lisa shot him a look. "Right, of course." She looked across to Catherine. "I don't see you becoming an Emma Gagnon, either."

The Magister raised her hands. "Hey, I'm not counting any chickens."

"God, I hope it's not Alyssa," Lisa said, rolling her eyes.

"And whoever this...*pube bandit* is," Doug added, glancing at his phone, "when their identity is revealed, we'll fuck 'em up... With words," he clarified. "And that is what Anathema is all about."

Rufus finished his glass of water. "I don't know what happened to Rich

Benson, but he sure ended up a lot worse than that girl they dumped dog shit on. At least she lived." He looked between all of them and smirked, enjoying their discomfort. "Benson desperately wanted to be a member as a first-year. He and I were at the Beckonings together, and he was very much a keener. Then when he didn't get in, his attitude conveniently changed and he saw it as the root of all evil in this college."

"Why didn't he get in?" Matt asked.

Doug shrugged. "I wasn't involved in those discussions. That's when they decided to Initiate me, Tom, Geoff, Rufus, and Patrick. But I heard Marko, the Imperator that year, later say he was too keen, wasn't that funny…and was just kind of a dick."

"And so," Rufus said, "he went on a crusade against us. And now he's dead." He sat back in his seat and smirked again. "Anyone else notice that it doesn't seem to end too well for people who speak ill of Anathema…?"

NINETEEN

AN ORANGE glow reached across the horizon as Matt and Roy strolled down the hill behind Radcliffe. Up ahead, the remaining leaves of Bethune's Walk rustled in the evening wind. Matt glanced at his watch and noted dusk was arriving markedly earlier. In a week's time, the clocks would get set back an hour and the long nights would be upon them.

"So...," Roy said, nudging him on the shoulder. "Are you gonna tell me about last night now, or what?"

As the sparse tree branches closed in over top of them, Matt filled him in on everything that had happened after he and Jennifer had left the party. "...and so I walked her back to Lacy and she kissed me one more time goodnight..." He pulled up his coat collar. "And then I forgot to drink water and woke up with a massive hangover today."

Roy laughed. "Sounds worth it."

"You have no idea." Matt sighed, looking off at the leaf-spattered grounds.

"So," Roy said, "the First Sermon's coming up... I saw Randall at the party last night, and he mentioned wanting to have a bunch of writing sessions this week, including a joint one."

"A joint *writing session*?" Matt raised an eyebrow, intrigued. He pictured himself, Roy, Tanner, Joan, and Val in a room together, somewhere in the Chalet's basement. "We've never done one of those before, but it sounds like a blast."

"Yeah, he said he'd message the group either today or Sunday with more details. But if it's on Tuesday, I won't be able to go."

They reached the fork in the path, the parking lot one way and the bridge the other. Matt and Roy continued to the left, passing by a student clad in a purple sweater that read *WCU Engineering*.

"Do you know if Fall Formal is gonna happen?" Matt asked. "If it is, I should ask Joan to it soon."

Roy spotted something up ahead. "Why don't we ask her?"

Matt turned to see the Dean of Students walking her Newfoundland toward them, dressed in athletic clothing and a windbreaker. He saw her eyes gauging them for recognition, which clicked fully once Roy waved and said, "Hi, Dean Crawley. How are you?"

"Oh, hi…Roy, right? And you are…?"

"This is Matt," he said, gesturing. "He's a third-year."

"Ah, right. I knew I'd seen you around too." The dog sat at her feet and panted happily, his long tongue drooping from his mouth. "Studies going well?"

"So far so good, this year," Matt said.

"Any word on Fall Formal?" Roy asked.

"Oh," she said, frowning and looking down at her dog. "Well…Provost Mustard and I have been talking and it looks like it *just* might happen. All the Mess Hall parties have been cancelled, so I told him it would be best to give you kids *something* to unwind at. Something official, anyway. I know there are frats and parties at other colleges, but I don't think that's an acceptable solution. Provost Mustard isn't…*enthusiastic* about Radcliffe's traditions, but I know he cares about his students." Crawley seemed to have a tough time believing it herself. She sighed and shook her head. "I hope it gets sorted out soon. Have a good evening, both of you. Come on, Adam." The dog got up. She smiled at them and continued along.

As they resumed walking, Roy threw a glance back at her. "You know for a Dean of Students, she's not bad looking."

"I wouldn't get any ideas."

They walked on in silence for a short while, rounding another bend through the trees. "You know, neither of us headed toward that bridge," Matt said.

"No," Roy finally answered. "We didn't."

"I haven't been able to stop thinking about what he was writing. I've read all of his old *Westerner* articles about Cliffe; I wondered if he might've decided to go deeper on something later."

"Oh yeah, I remember those. He kept writing about how High Table was elitist, Anathema was archaic, all that stuff… Say, didn't he go to private school back in Toronto?"

"I think so. He came across as really self-important, made it seem like the whole college was beneath him and he was some great modernizer. But I haven't been able to find any of his *Cliffe-Hanger* stuff. Those magazines aren't online, they're just printed."

Roy shook his head. "There's this website called Issuu a lot of student publications upload stuff to. I know *Cliffe-Hanger* has a few issues on there. Go back to the one from March 2017; I think that's when he did his big 'exposé' on us." He scoffed. "If you could even call it that."

Matt thought for a moment. "I just don't get what a student journalist would be researching that would get him killed. Especially if it was something on Anathema."

"None of his articles amounted to much, but he seemed to take himself pretty seriously. He could've been blowing this piece out of proportion when he talked about it."

"But what if this was the one time he'd actually gotten real dirt on something?"

They both stopped. They had reached the parking lot. "Wanna loop around through Griffin to get back?" Roy asked.

"Sure," Matt said, still thinking. "Why would someone in Anathema want to kill Benson? If anything bad came out about us, Randall would be hurt the most. His position as Officer and Imperator is delicate already."

"And he does have military training."

"Yeah, but if he was really gonna murder someone, wouldn't he do it…I don't know, *cleaner?*"

"If it was a murder, it looked pretty clean to me. Even the RCMP ruled it an accident."

"No, but pushing someone down a creek embankment is a risky way to kill them. It's not like a steep cliff, which is definitely gonna do the job."

"Maybe he found out Benson was writing the article, called him to the woods late at night to talk about it, got pissed and shoved him in a fit of rage."

Matt shook his head. "Randall doesn't seem like the kind of guy to lose his cool."

"He doesn't seem like the kind of guy to commit murder, either."

"I know. But if we're going to be thorough, we should consider everyone in both branches."

"Well," Roy said, "Kylie would have the most to lose after Randall. She's not an Officer, but she *is* an Imperator; all the flak would go straight to her too. And I guess anyone else on either Tetrad would be next in line."

Matt scratched his chin. They reached the end of the parking lot and followed the curving dirt road back toward the residential streets. "What if the article wasn't about Anathema as a whole, just something *one* of us did? That would still make the entire organization look bad, which Benson would love, and it would explain why someone lower in the hierarchy could have done him in."

After a moment, Roy said, "Yeah…I think you might be onto something." He looked up at the trees. The pines were the only green left. "But then how did Benson find out about it, whatever it was? Did somebody else tell him?"

"Or maybe he witnessed something." Matt paused. "The real question is why he had to die when he did. Was he going to press soon, or…?"

Roy looked uneasy. "Matt…promise me something."

"Yeah?"

"Don't talk about this with anyone. Because if you are right and someone in Anathema has a secret worth killing over, you might be the next one to have a little accident in the woods."

Matt felt goosebumps on his arms. "Right, right, of course."

And with that, they reached the road and took a left turn, swinging back toward Griffin Park and the college beyond.

That night he found Benson's old Anathema exposé online, just as Roy had said.

He enlarged the PDF to view the piece in full-screen. The article had taken up several pages of *Cliffe-Hanger*'s March 2017 issue, interspersed with old drawings of skulls and cloaked figures from the college's Archives. It began with a disclaimer that the organization discussed was "officially dissociated" from Radcliffe, which made Matt roll his eyes. He continued reading:

Over the years, our college has seen traditions come and go, but none remains so wretched, disgraceful, and inexcusable as the Anathema. A supposed "secret society," this group of Radcliffe students meets in the shadows to compose volume after volume of seditious jokes forged from gossip, rumor, and lies. They conceal part of their faces behind Venetian masks, but we know of their identities. They boast about their membership in Galbraith Hall and shout Latin incantations from the Quads to advertise their so-called Sermons.

Unlike other collegiate secret societies such as Yale's Skull and Bones and McGill's Renard Noir, which remain cloaked in mystique, Anathema's transgressions are about to be laid bare before you. This is the exposé Anathema has feared, and the one Radcliffe desperately needs to hear. Let this proclamation of truth bring trepidation to their ranks and relief to the tight-knit student community we all know and love. Together we can break this college free from the grasp of an outdated, archaic evil.

It took another three paragraphs for Benson to even start getting to the point. He struck Matt as the kind of person to stand in front of a mirror and tell himself, *I am the hero this college needs but doesn't deserve.*

He'd interviewed certain students—who had "chosen to remain anonymous"—about their views on and experiences with Anathema, but they all said variations of the same thing. The male branch was a bunch of stuffy, rich Old Boys, its female counterpart a collective of popular mean girls. The only thing separating them from high school bullies was that they dressed in all black and wore masks. Benson argued the two halves conjoined forces to exert "social control" and to "uphold the hegemony of Social Cliffe."

And yet the more he read, the more Matt started to pity the author. What Benson had written was a largely inaccurate hit piece—most of the members weren't richer than middle class, and Matt only knew a handful of people between both branches, Joan included, who came from private school—and yet he couldn't help but feel sad for him. Benson had desperately wanted to get in and had clearly cared a lot about Anathema; he probably would've made a dedicated member. And yet his rejection by the organization had transformed his passion into aggressive antipathy. Matt could picture him angrily typing the article, delighting at the prospect of revenge. He must've enjoyed his Manichean dichotomy between the kind-hearted student body—devoid of gossip or malice—and Social Cliffe, that fabled villain of the downtrodden.

Benson contradicted himself as the article devolved into conspiracy theory. He'd originally called Anathema a glorified social club, then claimed it manipulated every aspect of the college's hierarchy, seeping its black tendrils into DebSoc, various student clubs, the Finance and Equity Committees, and the Officer Council—though he admitted members traditionally dropped their pendants. Benson never considered these people were simply dedicated to the college's culture as a whole, a culture of which Anathema was merely one facet.

However, Benson did have a point about social status and Initiation. Whenever it was brought up, Matt would use himself as an example of how Anathema didn't only induct the socially gifted. And yet he knew he was an exception. He was only picked because Patrick Mason had seen his interest and asked him to write sample jokes, which Patrick had then sent to Turland. Other members had apparently raised objections. They'd never heard of this Matthew Richardson. He seemed quiet and maybe just a bit odd. But Turland, who had the final decision, had read his jokes and—having met him at the Beckonings—decided he was worth taking a chance on. It had opened the door to many good times and friendships, and, the more Matt thought about it, really the only truly good times and friendships he'd had during his entire time at Radcliffe.

That wasn't the Anathema Rich Benson depicted.

The article, droning on, implored readers to pass reforms at the Student Governance Meeting barring Anathema members not just from running for Officer, SGM, and committee elections, but from sitting on the executive of any club receiving Radcliffe funds. Only this, Benson posited, would be powerful enough to dissuade students from joining Anathema going forward. "And then, at long last," he wrote, "the Great Lord and Great Lady's reigns of terror will be over." He concluded by discussing the "rising influence" of Anamicable, a "positive, wellness-focused" alternative that was officially associated with the college. It was founded by Pandora Lane the year before the article's publication, and if Matt recalled correctly, she was still running it now as a fifth-year.

But there was one part that really jumped out at him, that drowned any feelings of sympathy he'd had toward Benson. When describing the female branch's selection process for new members, he'd written that they either Initiated the "ones in the most powerful social circles, or else the most depraved wallflowers."

When Matt finished reading the whole thing, he went back to that line and read it again and again and again. March 2017 was two months after he and Joan were Initiated. He was pretty sure her relationship with Benson was over by then. Matt knew at least colloquially everyone in both branches, and he knew only one girl in Anathema who could've been termed a wallflower. He was pretty sure Rich Benson had known only one too.

For a moment, Matt wasn't just glad someone had pushed the bastard into a creek.

He wished he'd done it himself.

TWENTY

BETHUNE'S WALK was quiet that night.

The cloaked figure didn't take time to admire the tranquility of their surroundings, though they paused briefly at the bridge, as they always did. After a few moments staring into the creek, they continued on, following the trail deeper into the woods.

It was a couple minutes before they came upon the lone bench beside its lamppost. The figure sat down, huddling in their cloak to stay warm. This was to be a brief errand, but they hadn't worn more than a long-sleeved shirt, jeans, and their silver pendant underneath.

That, and a green sash across their chest.

The figure sighed and felt beneath the bench. It took them a moment to find it, but finally their fingers grasped the envelope and tore it away from where it had been taped. They knew it had been planted less than an hour ago, but had come swiftly to retrieve it anyway. The lamppost provided the perfect lighting as the figure opened the envelope, withdrawing a sheet of paper.

It was all typed, of course, and there was no signature. For brief communications they used an encrypted messaging app, but for important tasks, things were done in a more old-fashioned manner.

And in a secret society, why shouldn't they be? the figure thought to themselves, their eyes reading over the instructions.

A smile came to their face. Then they slid the paper and envelope into a pocket within their cloak, stood up, and began heading back to Radcliffe.

There was work to be done.

Twenty-One

"**N**o, no, no—you only save *truly* for the last one, when you really wanna drive the point home."

"This could be the last one of the set," Joan pointed out, glancing up from her laptop. The screen's glow was one of the few light sources in the room. Candles were placed about on the desk, the windowsill, and around the floor. "I just think it sounds better, for this one, if we end it with: 'Tis truly a picture no artist can paint.' "

Alyssa Lee sighed, her arms folded across her chest. "Alright fine, read it back to me."

"We've got:

> 'Picture Cassie Hume actually being funny,
> Picture Lisa Fang not flaunting her money,
> Picture Maddy Starling as a Playboy Bunny,
> 'Tis *truly* a picture no artist can paint.' "

Joan paused. "You know, actually, I think the last one is a bit mean." She'd been the one to write it, but now it felt a bit too far for her.

"Maddy can take the hit." Alyssa gave a dismissive wave. "She's always criticizing other people's appearances, but she could easily drop forty pounds. It's a taste of her own medicine."

"Still, the first-years might not know that about her and just think we're being assholes," Val said. "We don't want to give them the wrong impression of us."

Hamid, the only other person in the room, shook his head. "They'll have heard enough shitty things about Anathema already. Let's just go with it and your Tetrad can debate if it's too harsh when they edit."

"I think we should switch to a different format," Joan said. "How about some Movie or Book Titles? They're pretty easy to bang out."

"Alright, anyone got one?" Alyssa asked, leaning against a wall. She was the only one standing.

Val sat next to Joan on the bed while Hamid was cross-legged on the floor. All four wore their pendants but were dressed in casual attire. They were in one of two bedrooms on the Chalet's main floor; most of the other members were down in the basement rooms while the Tetrads edited their Sermons in the lounge. This was the first joint-branch writing session Joan had ever been to, and apparently the first one in many years. They'd already changed up the rooms once and she hoped that after the next change she'd be in the same room as Matt. At least Val was here and, though she didn't know him that well, Hamid seemed to be good company.

After a moment, Joan said, "How about we write some content on guys now? I've thought of something for Carl Dunlap."

Hamid sat forward. "Oh yes, please. That man is the gift to the Anathema that keeps on giving."

She finished typing, then read it back to them. "*Extremely Loud and Incredibly Close* by Jonathan Safran Foer. *Extremely Loud and Incredibly Obnoxious* by Carl Dunlap."

Hamid chuckled. "I like it."

"Let's shit on Lambda," Val said. "That's always fun. Plus, they hate us."

"Are they going to attack the First Sermon again?" Joan glanced between all of them. "It was really annoying when they threw eggs last year."

"Yeah, probably," Alyssa said. "I mean, they do it every year."

"But Geoff's the President now." Val looked confused.

"Yeah," Alyssa continued, "but he's gone around telling everyone he's neutral about Lambda raiding the Sermon. Every year he just stands off to the side and lets it happen."

"It would be nice," Joan said, "if we actually had a grip on all the groups our members are a part of. You know, like a secret society is supposed to?"

Alyssa scoffed. "What would we be then, the Illuminati of Radcliffe College?"

"It would be a step up from what we are now."

"Why does Lambda even have a rivalry with us?" Hamid asked.

Joan turned to him. "Apparently a male Imperator slept with a Lambda Phi President's girlfriend fifteen years ago or something."

"That's *it*?"

Val nodded. "A bunch of them don't like Anathema anyway, and the rivalry gives them an excuse to keep fucking with us."

"Didn't somebody get hurt a few years ago, though?" Hamid asked. "One of yours?"

Alyssa said, "The year before Joan and I got here, a Lambda guy accidentally punched our Legatus when he tried to steal a skull. And she was dating your Imperator at the time, Marko Duric. He was *pissed*."

"Didn't he go and burn CRCC into a Lambda bathroom after that?" Joan asked.

"Yeah, I think so." Alyssa looked back at Hamid. "So yeah, relations between Lambda and both branches haven't been so hot for the last little while."

"Why can't Geoff just tell them to chill?"

"They probably wouldn't listen to him," Joan said. "And a bunch of them justify it by saying Anathema is immoral."

"Wait, wait, wait." Hamid put his hands up. "So, because they don't like us making jokes about people—jokes people can opt-out of—their solution is to *physically assault us*?" He glanced between the three of them. "Am I missing something here?"

"Nope," Val said.

"It's probably not even because they think we're immoral. I bet they just want an excuse to wreck things and throw eggs at people. And we're the only ones they can do it to and get away with it. Who are we going to turn to for help? The admin?" Joan scoffed.

"Why don't we just get some Super Soakers, fill them with cold water, and just whip 'em out and blast them when they come running down the hill?" Hamid asked. "I remember when they did it last year, when I was in the audience, they all came down from the same place. It would be a turkey shoot from where the members stand. Just tell the audience to duck and fire over them."

"Yeah, but the crowd might get wet," Val objected.

Hamid shrugged. "Yeah, but it'd be so worth it to watch a bunch of douchey frat guys get owned. I mean, I'd risk hypothermia for that."

Joan sighed. "We'll probably just do what we do every year—stand there and take it." Next year, if she became Imperator, she dreamed of filling a spring-loaded box with cockroaches and tricking the Lambda guys into stealing it. When the raiders reached a safe distance to open their prize, thinking they'd pulled off a legendary victory, they'd get a face-full of—

"Kylie just messaged the group chat. We've gotta switch rooms now." Val was looking at her phone.

"Who am I with?" Joan asked.

"Um…you're in one of the downstairs rooms with me, Sophia, Tanner, and Zhang."

"Do you think we'll switch one more time before reading?"

Hamid glanced at his watch. "I'm guessing not. It'll probably just go another half-hour before we read."

"Oh," Joan said, trying to hide her disappointment.

"Randall says we're reading in ten minutes," Tony Madruga said, glancing at his phone. With his height, chiseled features, and impeccable taste in suits, most women of college had been disappointed to learn that he wasn't attracted to girls. "Let's get some more good stuff out." He returned his attention to his computer. He was typing the jokes for this session.

Tony and Matt sat with Alyssa Lee and Katy Coulson in a cramped, basement room of the Chalet. It had probably been a sizable storage closet at one point, but now four Anathema members sat around on plastic folding chairs by the light of a few candles.

"Let's switch back to girls," Alyssa said. "I'm tired of writing about guys."

"Who haven't you hit yet?" Matt asked.

Katy scratched her cheek. "Hmm, we've got a lot on Joan Keating already, but we could hit some other members."

Matt froze. "Oh, what'd she do?"

"Well, she threw up on some guy at a bar—we've milked that—but she's just easy to write about in general. I mean, she's nice enough I guess, but her two modes are aloof and strange, so there's always stuff to write about that."

Matt tensed and his heart beat rapidly. It took his entire willpower to not ask more, about why they thought she was weird, how they could dare justify her as an easy target. Were they making fun of her because of him?

No, Katy didn't seem to know that he was the guy at the bar. But what about Alyssa? She had a sly smile on her lips. What the hell did that mean?

Together, they wrote a couple jokes in a standard format, the Anathema of the Good Old Days, which was meant to be read by the Imperator in a stereotypical upper-class British accent. Finally, it came time to head to the lounge, and the four of them extinguished the candles, packed up their things, and filed out of the room into the main area of the basement.

Members trickled out of the other rooms and headed for the stairs. Matt tried to move up to the front of the herd, wanting to get to the lounge first so he could get a seat with Joan. Then he wondered if that was a good idea, since they hadn't really gone public. And were they officially dating yet? What was this stage supposed to be called? It felt like the two of them had a direction now, but he wasn't sure if they had arrived at the relationship realm.

A hand grabbed his shoulder. Matt turned.

It was Tanner. "Hey, how was writing?" His cheerful tone didn't match the look of concern on his face.

"It was good," he said, hanging back.

Once everyone had passed them, Tanner whispered in his ear, "There's something I think you should know." He led him back deeper into the basement, where it was darker. The only real light came from the stairwell at the end of the hall.

"I was in a room with Rufus earlier," he continued, watching the last members go up the steps. "And he was super adamant about writing harsh jokes on you. Kept saying 'let's hit him again' and…" Tanner shook his head. "I don't know, there just seemed to be something off about it. I even jokingly asked him what he had against you—well, I made it sound joking, but really, I wanted to know."

Matt swallowed. "And what did he say?"

Tanner looked back toward the now-empty stairs, then back at him. "He said 'women should stay away from Matt Richardson.' "

"What the fuck?"

"Well, he made that reply sound joking too. He just added that you're weird and girls around here can do better, that's all. Then he changed the conversation."

Matt put a hand to his head. "Where the hell did this come from? Does he know about me and Joan then?"

Tanner shrugged. "I have no clue, I'm sorry."

He thought hard and came up with nothing. "I've never done anything to Rufus. When he came back to Anathema, I defended him to the members who didn't like him, said he wasn't so bad. And now he's trying to pull some kind of…character assassination on me?" It just didn't make sense. "And why? So I don't date Joan Keating?"

No, he thought, *he'd been interested in finding out who gave me a hickey from the start. This must be separate from Joan.*

"I wish I could tell you. I just wanted to give you a heads-up."

"Thank you," Matt said, putting a hand on his shoulder. "I *really* appreciate this."

"No worries," Tanner said. They started heading for the stairs. "Oh, I got to write with Joan a bit tonight. She's actually pretty funny. I like her." He nudged Matt on the shoulder. "I can see you two being a good fit."

Before he got a chance to thank Tanner again, Logan appeared on the stairs before them. He ran a hand through his red hair. "There you slow-pokes are. You're the last ones." He began heading back up, Matt and Tanner in tow. When they reached the first floor, Logan turned to Matt and said, "So, I hear you've got a girlfriend."

He paled. "Who told you that?"

"Come on, Matt. This is Anathema. It's our job to know everything. You didn't think something that big would fly under our radar, did you?"

"Just keep quiet about it, she and I aren't official yet and I don't want anybody adding pressure—"

"It's Joan Keating, isn't it?" Logan said, an amused gleam in his eye. He kept his voice lower as they approached the lounge, but the conversations there were loud enough to mask his words regardless. "I heard she fucked Vance Simmons at QuadFest last year. Remember him? He played Varsity hockey, graduated back in June?"

"Well, good for her."

"I remember him saying she was really *fun*. Maybe you'll be in for some of that." There was something about his tone that Matt couldn't place, but he knew he didn't like it.

"Thanks Logan," he said bitterly. "Why don't you go hang out with the rest of the Tetrad?"

"I think I will," the Legatus said, walking off with a smug grin.

Once he was out of earshot, Matt said, "God, we are so fucked if he's Imperator next year."

Tanner opened his mouth, then hesitated. "He's…not everyone's cup of tea."

"Quiet!" Kylie Patel boomed. The room quickly fell silent. "Alright, it's late and it's a Tuesday. We've all got school shit to do, so let's wrap this up. We'll be here again tomorrow, but writing separately like we normally do."

Logan mouthed "Thank God" off in a corner.

Kylie's gaze swept the room. "Alright, who's going first?"

One by one, those with laptops began to read their jokes. Matt could tell that the fourth-years read them just to get it over with, but the second-years and third-years seemed more into their performances. Hamid and Tanner had a certain melody to their elocution, clearly to alert any future Imperator in the room as to their worthiness down the line. The same was true of the girls. Val, in particular, read quite well.

But Matt liked Joan the best. She carefully enunciated each joke or line of poetry, but wasn't afraid to go loud or lean her body into it as she held up her laptop. Her facial expressions conveyed rage, mock horror, and pity in a way that swept him along with her words. The cadence of her voice was terrifyingly lovely and beautifully intense. Her whole performance, which lasted less than five minutes, was electrifying. Looking around, Matt saw that the others seemed to enjoy it too. They'd roared with laughter at all the right points. Not even at his best writing sessions had he gotten such a response.

He hadn't brought his laptop tonight. He didn't want to seem too keen, and there'd be several more opportunities to read before the First Sermon.

Alyssa went next after Joan. He could tell from her expression that she knew she had a tough act to follow. She began with an Alphabet Poem about the women of college, which was fairly funny and certainly read well. Then she moved to Internet Search Histories, which went fine until—

"What Joan Keating searches the Internet for: How to fit in in university? How to fit in in university in third-year? Is it normal to still not fit in in university in third-year?"

Matt was stunned. He looked around the room and saw people in both branches laughing. Joan discretely huddled back in her chair, rubbing her arm and forcing herself to smile.

Alyssa kept going. "Will hanging out with second-years help me fit in? Will wearing a sweater with my private school logo help me fit in? Would having a boyfriend help me fit in?" And here, her lips curled into a sinister grin, her eyes sweeping the lounge. "How to get a boyfriend? Will sleeping with a guy on the first date help me get a boyfriend?" Some *Ooohs* rose around the room. "Will hooking up with a fourth-year at QuadFest help me get a boyfriend?" A few chuckles at this one. "Will throwing up on an *Anathema member* help me get a boyfriend?"

Now everyone's head swung around, looking among the male branch. "Oh my God, who is it?" Katy Coulson said, leaning over to Alyssa. Matt heard a few speculative names in whispered murmurings.

But Alyssa merely put on a cheerful smile, said "Here endeth," and shut her laptop. Val sat next to Joan on one of the sofas and rubbed her back. Joan, for her part, was doing her best to laugh it off. Matt's mind was a raging storm, but he had to be careful not to let it show on his face. It wasn't even that funny, he noted, just *mean*. And yet people had laughed; Logan Brewster seemed to find it especially hilarious. Matt wondered if he only felt this way because he liked her, if he normally would've noticed how disgraceful the joke was.

"Next," Kylie said. She shot a glare at Alyssa, who looked confused.

Now Rufus Danvers stood up.

Oh shit, Matt thought.

"We'll begin with some Personal Advertisements," he said, then looked up from his tablet. "A new format."

Some members turned to each other and whispered with excitement. Matt kept his gaze locked squarely on Rufus as he continued.

"Here's Matthew Richardson! He's *tall* and *lean*...but outside of the Anathema, he is completely worthless. Maybe that'll be enough for some of you, though look out...he's got little experience and won't know how to satisfy you. Oh, but please, someone, do fuck him. He's only got one notch under his belt and he needs a body to keep him company on those cold winter nights...preferably a live one."

There were a few laughs, but Matt merely stood there, uncomfortable.

"Uh, okay," Randall said, massaging his temples. He sat in a chair by the fireplace, not looking too happy. "Next joke."

"Here's Patrick Mason! He's charming! And dashing! But watch out, ladies...he'll stab you in the back and sell you out to the admin the moment he stops having a use for you. Buyer beware!" There were more chuckles at this.

"Some Analogies for men of college: Matt Richardson is to women as DEET is to mosquitoes. Logan Brewster is to cocaine as a 1980s businessman is to cocaine." Even Logan laughed and shook his head at that one. Rufus scrolled down on his tablet. "Name Threes for men of college: An Anathema pendant. A Venetian mask. Her tendency to vomit all over him. Name three qualities Matt Richardson looks for in a woman."

Now all eyes turned to him. The chatter was alive again, buzzing around the room. He could do nothing as whispers of *It's him!* and *That's the guy Joan threw up on!* reached his ears. Matt looked to her and she offered a smile and a shrug. Knowing the two of them were in this together made him feel better, but only a little.

Rufus still wasn't done. "Lastly, a single Multiple Choice Question for a man of college." He cleared his throat. "You are Matt Richardson, and you are depraved and single. You decide to get a girlfriend via: A) Purchasing Tinder Gold, B) Purchasing Bumble Boost, C) Getting a mail-order bride from Eastern Europe, or...D) Guilt-tripping a woman of college into going out with you because she threw up on your shirt."

A lot of them laughed at that one.

Rufus looked up with a smug smile. "Here endeth."

"Is that it?" Randall asked, looking exhausted. He sat slumped in his chair. No one else said anything.

"Alright." He turned to his fellow Imperator. "I guess that's it then."

"Meeting adjourned," Kylie said. "See you here again tomorrow, at the usual time."

Everyone began collecting their belongings and stood up. For a moment, Matt barely registered what was going on. A storm of emotions swirled through him. He'd had a lot of jokes made about him over the years, including some fairly mean ones, but none of them had come close to touching a nerve like this. *Don't show them,* he thought. *That only gives them power.*

Instead, he turned and walked over to Joan, who was zipping up her backpack and saying goodbye to Val as she walked off. Joan spotted him as he got closer and put a hand on his shoulder. "Hey, sorry about that. Those were some really shitty jokes."

"It's fine," he said, even though deep down he knew it wasn't. "That Search History about you was much worse. Are you okay?"

"Yeah..." She nodded slowly, sliding her backpack over her shoulder. It looked like she was holding something in, a dam about to burst.

"Wanna walk back to Cliffe together?"

Her mood seemed to brighten, and she gave him a warm smile. "Yeah, I'd like that."

Matt held her hand as they started for the door. Outside, they followed the others heading for the gate, barely saying anything. After they'd gone through, Hamid came up to them.

"Hey, I thought those jokes about both of you were B.S. Just wanted you to know, I had no part in writing any of them."

"Thanks," Joan said.

"So, uh…" He searched for a lighter topic. "Did you really throw up on him?"

She blushed. "It's a long story."

"I'll take your word for it," he said, then looked behind them. "Ah, there's Tanner. I'll catch you two later. Have a good night."

"You too," Matt said. Once they reached the road, everyone began heading left back toward Griffin Park.

Joan tugged on his arm. "I don't want to walk back with them," she said quietly. "Can we take a different route?"

"Yeah, sure," he said, turning to the right. They were still holding hands.

"Do you have a lot of assignments this week?" she asked, pulling her jacket tighter around her.

"Uh, no I'm free until after the long weekend. Last week was my hell week. You?"

"I only have one thing due, but it's a short econ paper for Friday and I've already done most of the research. I was wondering…if you wanted to grab a drink, maybe?"

"Um, sure, that sounds great." It actually made him feel a lot better. He hoped she was feeling alright too.

They walked along the road as it looped past the liquor store, the Canmore Creek Fire Department, the trail to Riverside Park, and a 24-hour grocery store, then came to the straightaway that was the main drag.

"I'm kind of over both the Foxhole and the Royal," she said. "But I've only been to the Rancher once. It's got a country vibe to it."

"I'm fine with that."

"Cool, let's head there."

The Rancher occupied the first level of a two-story building. The top housed Grotto, the only nightclub in Canmore Creek. It offered free admission to students, but charged a substantial amount for drinks. Matt hadn't been there yet this year, though last semester he'd been dragged to its dark cavern of sweat and strobes numerous times. But Grotto was only open on Friday and Saturday, and this was Tuesday, a quiet night for the Rancher. The waitstaff showed them to a plush booth in the back, surrounded by photographs of the Albertan prairies and cows grazing on open pastures. Robbie Robertson's "Showdown at Big Sky" played softly in the background.

"Oh shit," he said with a laugh, glancing down. "I didn't realize we were still wearing these." He held up his pendant.

"Ah, let's just leave 'em on." She gave a dismissive wave. "Nobody knows what they are. And besides, it looks good on you." She winked.

He grinned. "Likewise."

Joan leaned back and exhaled, glancing up at the photographs. She looked as if she were about to say something when a waitress walked over.

"Hi," she said. "Can I get something to drink for either of you?"

"I'll get a double rye and ginger, tall," Matt said. He gestured to Joan. "And you?"

"I'll have that too," she said, as if intrigued by it. Once the waitress had gone, she said, "I've actually never had one of those before."

"It's great. You can barely taste the alcohol."

She smiled again. "Sounds dangerous."

"Yeah, but it is a school night. We should probably go easy."

"Key word: *should*."

He chuckled and shook his head, leaning back. The booth was dimly-lit and cozy and suddenly the Chalet and all those jokes seemed far away.

"I…don't want you to get the wrong impression of me from what Alyssa said."

Matt looked back at her. Joan's voice was weak and she avoided making direct eye contact, brushing hair out of her face. "Of course not," he said. "I don't think slut-shaming is accept—"

She shuddered at the term and interjected, "I've only been with a few people. Three, actually, but I think they only know about two." She bit her lip.

Matt held up his hands. "Hey, I'm not judging. I really don't care. You're…more experienced than I am." He managed a laugh. At least he hadn't lied; that was, in fact, the truth.

The waitress came back with their rye and gingers. Joan thanked her and took several big gulps as soon as she'd walked off. Matt had a sizeable sip.

Joan set her glass down and sighed. "I really do prefer long-term things to hook-ups, it just hasn't worked out like that before."

"I've never had a girlfriend," he said. "It's just never worked out for me either."

She smiled and said softly, "Well, I think you're wonderful."

His cheeks burned. "So, are we…?" He looked up at a picture. "Since I've never done this before…I don't know when to ask…or when it becomes officially…"

Joan laughed. "Hey, don't look at me. I don't know either."

He paused, then just came right out and said it. "Are we dating?"

She smiled and tilted her head, sizing him up. "I think so."

"Well, cheers to that." He raised his drink.

"Cheers." She clinked her glass against his and they both took large swigs.

Matt set his glass down and looked at her, a smile spreading across his face. "You know…I think you're the best girlfriend I've ever had."

She burst out laughing, loud enough to turn the head of a man seated a few tables away. He wore a baseball cap and casual clothes, trying to blend in with the student crowd. Sgt. Jake Dorval looked over his shoulder and recognized Joan, but said nothing and went back to his menu, pretending to look it over.

They stayed chatting and drinking at the Rancher for another hour, and in that time, they didn't talk about anything related to Radcliffe even once.

Then, tipsy, they stumbled back to the college, Joan's head leaning on his shoulder and Matt's arm around her waist. In the West Quad, he turned and kissed her on the lips, but when he pulled away, she drew him back in, holding him close awhile longer.

"I'll see you tomorrow," she said afterward, slowly backing toward Lacy.

"Wait, one last thing."

Joan turned around. She thought he was going to give her another kiss, but instead a sad look had entered his eyes. "I think Rufus has a thing against me and I don't know why, but I'm worried he might go around saying stuff about me. I just want you to know if you hear anything outrageous, it's not true." He put a hand on her shoulder. "I don't want you to get the wrong idea about me."

"Of course not," she said, holding his other hand. "You should probably talk to Randall about that. He'd know what to do."

Matt hesitated. "I don't want him to think I'm weak. He might be less likely to pick me for Imperator."

She sighed. "I don't think he'd view you as weak. I know him; he just doesn't seem like that kind of guy. And he didn't look impressed with Rufus' jokes either."

"And Kylie didn't seem happy with Alyssa's," he noted.

Joan nodded, remembering. "Yes, so that's a saving grace. I'm not sure if I need to talk with her about Alyssa, but it seems like Rufus is going beyond just writing mean jokes about you."

"Fair enough," he said.

"Don't let him get to you." She kissed him once more. "Goodnight."

"Sleep tight!" he said, waving as he headed across the Quad to Bowman.

Joan managed to keep it together until she got back to her room, where she broke down in sobs on the bed. Alyssa's words coursed through her mind and she saw that alternate version of herself from the joke, sitting there at her laptop late at night, only the glow of the screen illuminating her. Tears streaked down her face as she typed in line after depressing line into the Google search bar: *How to fit in in university…? Will hanging out with second-years help me fit in…? Will sleeping with a guy on the first date help me get a boyfriend…?*

Suddenly everything rushed back from nearly two years ago. She pictured Rich sitting with his friends in Galbraith. *We weren't dating. We just went to Fall Formal together, that's it. She's the one who thought we were dating.*

"That's not true!" she'd wanted to scream back then, before she had Val or any Anathema friends to comfort her.

At first, it had felt like a dream, like how she'd always pictured a university relationship for herself. A handsome and kindhearted upper-year taking her for coffee, taking her to a dance, and then taking her—

She clutched the pillow as tears ran down her cheeks, remembering how it had all seemed so *perfect*. And then just as quickly as he'd walked into her life, Rich Benson had stridden out, and he hadn't been very polite in how he shut the door behind him.

And when it finally hit her *why*, she'd felt pathetic and naïve for not seeing it coming.

TWENTY-TWO

MATT'S HEAD spun as he entered the cafeteria at lunch the next day. He saw Logan and that insufferable grin on his face. *I heard she fucked Vance Simmons at QuadFest last year... I remember him saying she was really fun. Maybe you'll be in for some of that...* Just thinking about the way he'd said it made Matt's stomach turn.

And then there was Alyssa's roast of Joan. *Is it normal to still not fit in in university in third-year...?* It was more like something a high school bully would taunt than an Anathema joke. But it was so much worse because it had been read about *her*.

And then Rufus. Fucking Rufus. *Look out...he's got little experience and won't know how to satisfy you.* That gave him chills. He'd always figured that was part of why he'd had such a hard time dating at this college. Word had gotten out that he was a virgin and perpetually single and so it had become a self-fulfilling prophecy he would stay that way.

Until he lied.

What would Joan think if she knew the truth? Would she decide he was unable to *satisfy her*, as Rufus had so delicately put it? Would she care that he'd never done it? *Don't be ridiculous*, he thought. *She doesn't seem like that type.*

He hoped. After all, she'd already done it with multiple guys. Three, to be exact, though people at the college didn't know about one of them. Had that been a summer hookup then? Matt stopped in his tracks, realizing that even though Joan had experience, people here had still found a way to make fun of her for it. And it wasn't like she'd slept around a lot, so they weren't exactly slut-shaming her. Plus now she was dating *him*, who was an easy target—evidently just for existing.

Outside of the Anathema, he is completely worthless. Logan wasn't involved in the college outside Anathema, but no one gave *him* shit for it. There was no fucking break, was there? It didn't seem like Joan could catch one either.

He grabbed the saddest slice of meat lover's pizza he'd ever seen—the only thing edible in Galbraith today—and got some water, then headed out into the dining hall. None of his friends were around, but he spotted a fourth-year named Peter Larch sitting off by himself. He was at a far end of the fourth-year table, dressed in a cashmere sweater, his ginger hair a mess.

Another thought occurred to him, something he knew would definitely get his mind off of those jokes last night.

Matt barely talked to him, but he knew Larch had been good friends with Rich Benson. They'd always been seen chatting in Galbraith together, and they'd both vocally argued against Anathema members holding Officer positions at the SGM last April.

He headed over to where Larch sat. The fourth-year eyed him quizzically as he approached. "Is this seat taken?" Matt asked, pointing to the chair across from him.

"Um…no," Larch said, looking surprised as he sat down. Matt saw he had a bowl of Fruit Loops before him, but there didn't appear to be milk in them; he sipped from a tall glass of Pepsi.

"How have you been, Peter?"

"I've been…better," Larch said, pouring the Pepsi onto his Fruit Loops. He began stirring the concoction. "It's been tough since Rich died." He brought a spoonful of soda and cereal to his mouth and ate it.

"Of course," Matt said, attempting to hide his bafflement.

"Nobody's really talking about him anymore. He's yesterday's news…" Bitterness had crept into Larch's voice. "Still can't believe he just tripped. And I don't know why he would've been out in the woods so late anyway."

Matt paused, then offered, "I've been going back and reading some of his stuff recently. He was definitely talented."

"Yeah, he was great. Probably one of the best journalists this school had in years. I have no doubt he would've gone on to do great things." He stabbed his spoon into the bowl.

"You think he would've continued in that field?"

"Oh yeah, Rich was always very serious about his articles. I know he was working on a big one when he died." He shrugged with a flick of both wrists. His right hand, still holding the spoon, sprayed Pepsi across the wooden table. Larch didn't seem to notice. "But I guess we'll never know what it was about." He looked around the dining hall and sighed.

"Did he…ever talk about it?" Matt knew he had to tread carefully now, but his heart rate had jumped.

"Never said exactly what it was about, but he referred to it as a 'piece of investigative journalism.' He was very proud of it, whatever it was."

Matt did his best to keep his tone casual as he asked, "Do you think it was about Anathema again?"

Larch sighed and took another bite of Pepsi and Fruit Loops. "I don't think so," he said, chewing and looking off again. After a moment, he turned back and stared straight at Matt. "He always hated you fuckers though."

Matt forced a laugh and took a sip of water. "Well, we haven't lasted this long because of our charming personalities."

"Why'd you ask if he was writing about Anathema?" Larch raised an eyebrow. "You people don't have anything to hide…do you?"

"No," Matt said, just a little too quickly. "Just curious if we were going to get dragged through the mud again."

"Well, if you were, you got lucky." He ate more cereal and masticated it slowly, staring at Matt and sizing him up. The moment felt like an eternity and Matt became increasingly uncomfortable. Then Larch swallowed and relaxed back in his seat. "I know Anathema's bark is worse than its bite. Never understood why everyone gets so worked up over it."

Matt shrugged and looked at his plate. "We have a way of getting to people sometimes."

Larch scoffed. "Yeah, I'll give you guys that." He went back to his bastardized Fruit Loops.

They ate in silence for a few minutes. Matt, figuring he wasn't going to get any more out of him, finished his pizza and was draining the last of his water when Larch said, "Wood."

Matt set the glass down and leaned closer. "Pardon?"

"Wood," Larch said, looking off toward the first-year tables. "Rich said something about wood."

"For the article?"

"Yeah." Larch scratched his scruffy chin. "That's all I remember him saying about it. It had something to do with *wood*. He mentioned it in passing."

"Did he maybe say woods, like the forest?" *Like Bethune's Walk?*

"No, no, it was very clearly just 'wood.' I don't remember the context, but he was definitely talking about something in the article. He was just sitting here in Galbraith one day, going through his notes, but he wouldn't let me see them." Larch fell silent again and ate more cereal.

"Did he say anything else?" Matt pressed.

Larch shook his head. "Just that it was going to be big. Bigger than anything he'd ever done before, which was why he didn't want to talk about it."

"And when did he say this…if you don't mind me asking?"

Larch closed one eye and thought back. "Must've been late September. Maybe two weeks before…" His voice trailed off.

"Right, of course." Matt knew it would be impolite to leave just then, so he sat scrolling through Facebook on his phone for a couple minutes before getting up. Then he said goodbye and left Larch to finish his Pepsi and Fruit Loops, more thoughts churning through his brain than when he'd entered.

◆

"Come in."

Sitting behind his desk, Mustard straightened his tie. He hadn't planned for this meeting and it had come completely last minute, but you couldn't refuse the Royal Canadian Mounted Police.

Dorval entered and approached his desk. "Good afternoon, Provost Mustard."

"Good afternoon, Sgt. Dorval. Please take a seat." He gestured to the chair and the cop did so. "How can I help you today?"

Dorval pulled out a notepad. "I'd like to ask you some follow-up questions regarding Rich Benson's death."

Straight to business, this one. "I…don't understand. I thought the case was closed weeks ago."

Dorval hesitated. "It was, but we've re-opened it because of an anonymous tip."

Something about the way he said it didn't ring true to Mustard, but before he could speak, the cop sprung his question.

"What can you tell me about Anathema?"

TWENTY-THREE

J ACK RANDALL glanced at his watch.

The meeting was scheduled to go for another few minutes, but he was so tired he felt he might tip forward and fall asleep on the table.

"...so, like...I know we're only given $5000 a year, but I think House Winslow's gonna need more than that." Carl Dunlap, the male Student Events Officer, nodded at his own words.

"What you're saying is...you're overbudget?" Veronica Yang, the female Student Affairs Officer, asked. She didn't look impressed. She was a plump fourth-year with dark hair that ended in blue tips at her shoulders. Even sitting here in the Student Governance Office of the Dales Building, she retained the same regal posture she had when she'd been an Imperator last year. These days she resided as the head of House Lacy.

"Well...I mean...just a little," Dunlap said, licking his lips nervously. He ran a hand through his hair, inadvertently exposing an armpit stain on his gray shirt.

"How much?" Veronica pressed.

"Uh...well...there's about $2000 left, which should be enough for second semester by itself, but we haven't even gotten to Winslow Christmas yet, and that's gonna be a big one..."

"Wait, wait, wait." Mia Cote, the female Student Events Officer, held up her hands. "You've already spent *3000 dollars* of your Officer budget? You've only thrown one party."

Dunlap folded his arms defensively. "I promised the people of this

159

college that I would throw ragers. And ragers cost money. You were all there at the disco party, you saw how *fire* it was!"

Randall looked at his watch again. "Alright, it's five o'clock, guys."

"Shit, I've gotta get to class," Veronica said, packing up her backpack.

As she stood up, Mia turned to Dunlap. "I can give you some of *my* budget, Carl, but you've really gotta cut back on the spending, okay?"

"As long as I can still drop a thousand bucks for the Super Bowl party, I'll be happy."

Randall slung his backpack over his shoulder and headed through the door, drifting out into the Mess Hall. Numerous tables and chairs were scattered about and the walls were covered with artificial greenery. This was where the Student Governance Meetings were held, and where Mess Hall parties would now be a thing of the past. Randall thought back on them fondly, those greasy nights of strobes and free-flowing drinks. They'd been infamous for bringing out sloppy behavior in students, which made for excellent Sermon material.

Now, thanks to Mustard, it didn't seem like those parties would ever come back, and as he stood there looking around in his tired state, Randall knew he would miss them.

He felt a hand on his shoulder and turned to see Patrick. "You alright? You look exhausted."

Randall laughed. "I am. I didn't sleep last night."

"Why not?"

"Had to get two papers done—both due today—and I had to finish my budgetary report for this meeting." He rubbed his eyes. "Oh yeah, and we had an Anathema meeting last night, our second this week. Fuck, what day is it?"

"Thursday," Patrick said. "Yesterday was Halloween."

Randall sighed. "Okay, good, just making sure I haven't lost track." *Halloween.* That gave him an idea for a temporary solution to his skull problem...

"Wanna go sit in one of the Quads? It's not *too* cold outside today."

He thought for a moment. Did he have time for that? *Fuck it, I'll make time.* "Yeah, sure."

They left the Dales Building, which sat north of Radcliffe, the imposing Mackenzie Library off to their right. Patrick unlocked a side-door with his R3, then they walked down a corridor past Bertrand Hall, a large one-story communal area. House Saunders occupied the second and third floors above them.

They went through another door, the East Quad greeting them with brisk air. They grabbed seats on a bench in the shade and Randall allowed himself to relax against the cool metal. Fuck, he needed a coffee.

"So, the Sermon is a week tomorrow," Patrick said, looking around. "How's it coming?"

"We've got some good content. I know what I'm doing for my Prelude, I just need to write it this weekend. Thank God we have four days off." Randall sighed and closed his eyes.

Then Patrick said, "So am I getting hit a lot in the Sermon?" He sounded excited by the prospect. "It'll be the first one since I was a frosh that I haven't written for."

"Honestly, I'm not sure yet. It's very far from being finalized, but I've definitely seen a few jokes about you in the master document."

"Just remember," Patrick said, "*I* can take harsh jokes. So can a lot of other people at this college, but the first-years—"

"Believe me, I know. I don't want to risk pissing any of them off."

"And getting your ass hauled before an impeachment hearing?"

"Well that, but also…I don't want to give the frosh the wrong impression of Anathema. Discovering the mystery of it was one of my favorite parts of first-year. There's nothing else quite like it, and I don't want anybody to get a bad taste right off the bat."

"And what does your Tetrad say to that?"

Randall sighed. "Logan's on my ass to go harder, says he'll call me the Pussy Imperator if I don't roast the first-years enough."

Patrick raised an eyebrow. "The Pussy Imperator? *Really?* That's kinda immature."

"No, no," he said, suddenly defensive. "You know Logan, that's just him being…well, *him*. He doesn't want it to be nineties-level bad again, just at least on par with Madler." He chuckled. "And we all know Madler took no prisoners."

"Right…" Patrick didn't seem to believe him. "Just remember the Imperator has final say. You don't have to cave to him."

He scoffed. "I'm not going to *cave* to Logan Brewster. He's my right-hand man…and only a third-year."

"Is he leaving at the end of the year with the rest of the Tetrad?"

Randall paused. "I don't know yet. That depends on…certain circumstances."

"Right, I forgot he was the Chosen One." Patrick rolled his eyes.

"He's not, okay?" Anger had risen in Randall's voice. "Everybody keeps acting like I've picked 116 already or something. It's the first of November, for fuck's sake."

"So there *is* another contender?"

He hesitated. "Yes."

Patrick scratched under his beard. "Can I warrant a guess?"

"I wouldn't tell you even if you were right. And it doesn't matter, I'm not really thinking about the next Imperator right now." *You have no idea the things on my mind, Patrick. Not even* close.

He smirked. "You know, if I hadn't run for Officer, it could've been me."

Randall burst out laughing.

Patrick gave him an amused smile. "Oh, you think that's funny, do you?"

"You would've been Tetrad for sure, but *Imperator?*"

"I demonstrated my qualifications as DebSoc President. Many of the Succession have held both positions."

"Yeah, but…"

"I know I was in the running. Think about it. I've gotten every single position I went for at this college: DebSoc First-Year Rep, then Clerk, then President. I was an exec member of the Dramatic Society. I was a first-year Initiate of the Anathema. And I won my Officer election by a very wide margin. If I had poured my efforts toward becoming Imperator, do you really think I would've lost? Because my track record begs to differ."

Patrick had conquered every goal he set out to achieve at this college, while Randall hadn't fared so well early in his Radcliffe career. He lost every election he ran for as a first-year and was passed over for Initiation. Just before the summer that year, Turland told him to stick with it, that this college would see his worth eventually. The next year he was Initiated and at the end of the year after, he became both an Imperator and an Officer.

"I offered to bring you back," Randall reminded him, growing annoyed. "I'd set a precedent; you could've returned to the organization."

"Yeah, you offered me both Legatus *and* Pontifex." He laughed. "I still find it funny that you wanted me that badly."

"If you'd held out a little longer, I'd have thrown in Magister too."

"So much bitchwork, so little time." Patrick exhaled and shook his head. "No, I made a promise to this college that I would drop my pendant if elected, and so when I was elected, I dropped my pendant."

"I made it very clear that I wouldn't be doing the same."

"I know, and they voted you in anyway. But they didn't know you were going to be the next Imperator."

"That's the joy of Imperator being a surprise."

Patrick scoffed. "Not if you name Logan Brewster as your successor."

"Don't diss Logan so much. He's really not so bad a guy." Randall stood up. "I've got shit to do. Wanna walk with me through the West Quad?"

"Sure, where are you headed?"

"Mackenzie. I've got another fucking paper to write."

Patrick smirked as he got to his feet. "There really is no rest for the wicked, is there?"

Randall rolled his eyes. They headed to the archway under Napier Tower, shifting the conversation to their classes. As they entered the tunnel, Joan Keating appeared before them in exercise leggings and a blue athletic T-shirt.

She took out her headphones when she saw them and waved. "Oh, hey Patrick, hey Jack."

"Out for a run?" Randall asked.

"Yeah," she said, just a touch awkwardly. "This is probably the last week I can do it outside before it gets too cold."

"I heard you have a new boyfriend," Patrick teased.

Joan blushed. "Maybe…"

Randall chuckled. "Come on, there are no secrets within the secret society…" It was a phrase he'd liked to say in years past, teasing members when they were hiding something. But now, as soon as the words left his lips, he knew it had been a mistake to utter them, and not just because Patrick was technically no longer a member.

Joan's eyes met his and a knowing look passed between them. Patrick, mercifully, didn't seem to notice. Randall didn't want him asking questions.

Finally, she just rubbed her arm and laughed. "Well, see you around." She jogged into the East Quad while they continued through the tunnel.

Even amidst the fog of exhaustion, Randall's mind replayed that look she'd given him as he and Patrick came out from under the archway.

No, he decided, looking up to the belfry of Anathema Tower. *There* are *secrets within the secret society.*

But then again, isn't that kind of the point?

TWENTY-FOUR

As usual, the college cleared out for the long weekend. Residence halls housed quiet evenings and Galbraith tables were sparsely populated at every meal. Most of Joan's friends had gone home and so had Matt's—Val had returned to Calgary, while Tanner and Patrick had both gone back to Vancouver.

Her parents had offered to fly her to Toronto for the weekend, but she'd realized she had too much work coming up over the next month. Matt was staying too, much to her relief. She didn't want to be left alone with certain dark thoughts.

Joan pushed those memories out of her head as they turned left, away from *that* bridge, and headed further into Bethune's Walk that frigid Sunday evening. It was that time after sundown when dark blue still painted the sky and the stars were just beginning to emerge.

"I like it out here," Matt said, looking up at the barren branches. Now that it was November, autumn in Canmore Creek was swiftly drawing to a close. "It's a nice place to clear your head."

Joan couldn't think of this forest without coming back to Rich Benson. She'd tried to go for jogs and runs here to push past it, to remind herself it was just a place. But she kept stopping at the bridge, kept staring down into the stream. And yet when Matt asked her if she wanted to go for a walk out here, she hadn't hesitated to respond yes. Something about the way its trees and winding paths obscured Radcliffe kept calling her back.

"It makes you feel like you've gotten away from it all," she finally said.

They walked on in silence for another moment, then Matt said, "By the way, you read really well on Tuesday. You had *great* projection and delivery." He smiled. "And I'm not just saying that because I like you."

Joan took his hand. "Thanks…I did a bit of theatre in high school. My mom thought it would make me less introverted." She laughed.

"I think Alyssa is just trying to tear you down because she knows you're a threat."

That gave her pause. "Huh, maybe…" She bit a fingernail. "Is Rufus aiming for Imperator?"

"I don't know. I've heard he's taking a fifth-year, so maybe he wants Tetrad."

"Well, he should be careful who he pisses off, then."

"He doesn't see me as a contender. He'll probably just suck up to Logan all year."

"Wouldn't it be nice," she said, smirking, "if he spent all that energy only to find out he'd been barking up the wrong tree, and that he'd pissed all over the right one?"

Matt laughed. "That would be beautiful."

At another bend, a separate trail led deeper into the forest. Even in the dim light, Joan could make out picnic tables down that way and an open area along the creek's shore. "Why don't we head over here," she suggested, tugging at his arm. "I've been a couple of times. It's nice."

Matt froze. "Umm… Yeah, I've been there before, but how about we just keep walking this way? It's nice over here too."

She gave him a concerned look. "Everything okay?"

"Yeah, it's just…" He looked down the path, as if remembering something. His voice grew softer as he said, "Last year, that was where I nearly…" He shook his head. "You know what, it's fine. Let's take a look there."

"We don't have to if you don't want to." Joan put a hand on his arm. "Really. Or we can come back some other time. It's better there in the day anyway."

He seemed embarrassed. "Yeah, let's come back some other time." Together, they continued along the trail to the parking lot without another word.

Last year, you nearly what…? She glanced at the shadowy trees as they passed them by.

So we're both haunted by this place, Joan noted. *And yet we both still come back.*

◆

By the time they got to Galbraith, it was after seven and cafeteria services were beginning to wind down. With so few students around this weekend, the cooks apparently realized they could get away with even less appetizing cuisine than usual. The tilapia was a generous use of the term "seafood" and the rice tasted somehow both under- and overcooked.

"Is Roy coming?" she asked Matt, who sat across from her.

He took a sip of water, then shook his head. "He got Uber Eats from some place on the main drag. But he said he's around tonight if we want to hang out."

Joan nodded and forced herself to eat another bite of fish. It would be nice to take the evening off. Both she and Matt had spent much of the day holed up in Mackenzie Library. Right now, they sat in the middle of the third-year table, which was otherwise unoccupied. Three lonely diners were spread out across the second-year tables, and a handful of first-years sat on the other side of the room.

She was thinking of a way to probe what happened in Bethune's Walk last year, when suddenly the chair to her right shifted and a figure sat down.

"Well, hello. I see I'm not the only one stuck here this weekend." It was Ned, a thin second-year wearing a tweed overcoat and spectacles. He drummed his fingers on the table and looked to Matt. "Have you started on the paper for Ancient Civs?"

"No," Matt said, slightly annoyed. "But I know I'm writing on the effects of the Vesuvius eruption on the Roman Empire."

"Oh, fascinating! I've already begun researching mine. It's also on Rome, but it's more…err, *carnal* than yours." He laughed.

Matt opened his mouth to say something, but Ned instead launched into a lengthy explication of his essay, detailing the sex lives of Ancient Roman citizens and how their culture compared to later Western societies.

Joan tried not to sigh or look annoyed, though she clenched a fist beneath the table. She rested her head on her other hand and did her best to convey boredom, but Ned didn't seem to notice. Her eyes drifted to Matt. He appeared miffed that this second-year—who hadn't even asked permission to sit at an upper-year table—was interrupting dinner with his girlfriend to regale them with knowledge of Roman bacchanals.

"When you think of how open their culture was toward sexuality and compare it with how we talk about sex here at Cliffe, it's almost like this place is the rebirth of Ancient Rome."

"Uh-huh," Matt said, staring at his food. "That's really great."

"Although," he laughed, "I think the Pube Bandit really put a damper on erotic expression around here."

Neither Matt nor Joan found it funny, each sliding their unfinished plates away. Ned acted oblivious and continued, "Although I will admit that it was a pretty funny prank, what he did."

"How do you know it was a he?" Joan said tiredly, merely to break his endless diatribe.

"*Of course*, I know it was a he," Ned said, shooting her a look as if she were an ignoramus. "I mean, he came to *my* door to get some of the—" At that second, Ned clammed up, aware that he had said too much.

Matt and Joan locked eyes and tried to hide their smiles, then turned back to the second-year.

"What was that?" Matt asked. "The Pube Bandit came to your door to collect…something?" He winced as he said it.

Ned shrank back in his chair. "Um, well, no, you see… It wasn't one person he got the hairs from, he just went door to door on Third Bowman asking!"

"Who was it?" Matt asked, trying to conceal his eagerness. Joan knew this would be the goldmine to end all goldmines of Sermon source material, if they could just drill down to the ore.

"I won't say!" Beads of sweat rolled down his forehead. "I'm not snitching!"

A way to help Matt suddenly occurred to her. "Did you know what he was going to do, Ned? Did you know *why* he was asking around?"

"Um…I mean…maybe…it doesn't matter."

"Well I think it does," she said. "Because if you don't tell us who's responsible, you're the only one who's going to get made fun of for it at the Sermon next Friday." Matt looked at her, momentarily stunned. Then he smiled with admiration.

Ned gulped, his eyes going wide. "But…but…I didn't *do* it."

"You were an accomplice," Matt said, jumping on. "The Great Lord Anathema needs a name to blame, Ned. Are *you* going to go down for what this person did? Are they *really* worth protecting? If they went for other people's…hairs…like you said, how would they know you were the one to snitch?"

Ned hesitated, his lips quivering. Joan could see he was close to the breakpoint; he just needed a little push.

She placed a hand on his shoulder and cooed, "Come on, Ned. You know he's right. Just tell us and you won't get named at all." Despite the hint of flirtation in her voice, he saw the sinister expression on her lips, the way her eyes gleamed with intensity. He looked utterly terrified and Joan savored the moment—how fun it was to be on this side, how she *loved* being an upper-year. And—though she'd never admit it—how nice it was after ages of never being respected, always getting pushed aside and disregarded, to have some annoying prick know you could crush him between your teeth and to see the fear pouring from his eyes.

Ned looked ready to burst into tears.

"It was Carl Dunlap."

◆

Matt and Joan stumbled out into the West Quad and doubled over laughing.

"Oh my God," he said, his hands on his knees. "What the fuck *is* this college?" Then he burst out laughing again.

"The male Student Events Officer went around collecting pubic hair from res students and then glued them to the door of somebody he didn't like just for kicks," Joan managed to get out, once she'd regained her breath. "Did I miss anything?"

"Nope, I think you've got it," he said, wiping a tear away. "Why does shit like this happen here?"

She scoffed. "God, it's the kind of thing that would *only* happen here."

"Jesus." Matt shook his head. Come to think of it, it *did* seem like something Dunlap would've done while drunk after Lambda Halloween. He would've run back to his Officer's Suite, telling himself what a *fire* prank it was. He must've pissed himself laughing when he wrote his Facebook comment, assuring Blaine he would help Patrick get to the bottom of it.

"The best part is that he's an *elected student official*." Joan sighed. "Stuff like this is why we need Anathema. Radcliffe attracts people who think they can do this dumb shit and get away with it, and it falls to *us* to chastise them for it."

Matt looked over at her. Her head was turned toward Galbraith's stained-glass windows, which glowed orange from the light within, and her scar was exposed to him. A breeze blew strands of blonde hair against the thin mark. She gazed at the dining hall with a look of reminiscence, though her smile held contempt. He couldn't help but notice that, in that moment, she looked more confident than usual.

"You got pretty into it back there," he said after a moment, trying to laugh it off.

Joan snapped out of the trance and laughed nervously, brushing hair out of her face. "Oh, well…it was fun. I didn't mind doing it to him because he interrupted us and…I figured I'd repay him for all that wonderful knowledge on Ancient Rome."

"You truly do learn something every day."

Joan nodded. "It was…an informative conversation."

Matt looked at his phone. "Wanna hang out at Roy's? We've got a standing offer to drink and watch Netflix with him."

"Yeah, I'm down."

They started off toward Winslow. As they walked, Matt said, "There's so many ways to make jokes about what Dunlap did, I don't even know where to begin."

"It definitely deserves a long format joke, maybe a poem," she offered.

Yeah, a big poem, he thought. *The kind of thing that gets saved for last, the final joke that defines the Sermon.*

As they reached the door and Matt fumbled for his R3, she said, "I wonder when they'll start putting up Christmas decorations now that it's November."

Matt laughed. "Back in the States, we look down upon that until after Thanksgiving."

"Oh right, you have that later this month." She leaned against the wall beside the door. "Are you going back?"

"Nah, this'll be the third year in a row I miss it. Here, American Thanksgiving is just called Thursday." He slid the key into the lock and turned it.

"We do have Black Friday," she noted.

"Yeah, you're not complete barbarians up here." He grinned and held the door open for her.

She punched his arm as she entered and he followed behind. They began their hike up to Fourth Winslow, and as they did so two disparate thoughts began to converge in his mind.

A big poem and *Christmas.*

By the time they reached the top floor, it had clicked into place—or at least, the concept of it and several ideas. But he'd need help.

"I've just thought of something, come on." He threw open the door to the east pod and ran down to the end, knocking on the door to room 480. "Hey, it's us!"

Roy opened it a moment later, wearing a red bathrobe embroidered with his initials *RT* in calligraphy. He held a glass of sherry in one hand. "Oh, there you are. How was dinner?"

"We have a lot to tell you," Joan said.

Roy let them in and they took turns imparting how they'd made Ned confess. When they finished, Roy doubled over laughing and almost spilled his drink.

"Oh my God," he said, taking another sip. "That is *priceless*. I can't wait till we shred Dunlap for this."

"Speaking of which…" Matt proceeded to explain his poem idea to both of them. At first, they sat there and said nothing and he was worried it was incredibly stupid. Then Roy and Joan exchanged looks and smiled.

"This is going to be the fucking centerpiece of Randall's First Sermon," Roy said, turning to his computer. "Screw Netflix, we are writing this *now*."

They pulled up the original poem, the source of inspiration, online and had a separate Word document to write the parody. As they filled stanza after stanza, they bounced ideas off each other and debated phrasings and rhymes.

"I can't wait to send this to Randall," Matt said, watching Roy type in another line.

"We're not sending this to Randall." He turned around. "We're going to save it for the writing session on Wednesday, and you're going to read it in front of everyone and show them you're real Imperator material."

Matt paused. "Thank you. Are you sure you don't want us to take turns? I mean, you did help write it—"

Roy gave a dismissive wave. "It was your idea. And besides, I'm graduating. You still have a shot at Tetrad and I don't want 116 to be some prick like Logan Brewster…or, God forbid, Rufus Danvers. I heard about what happened, by the way. Sorry I wasn't there that night."

"It's okay," Joan said, squeezing Matt's shoulder. She looked straight at him and said, "You should read this. I don't care if I get credit for helping with it or not."

He put a hand on her arm. "Thank you." Matt decided he would mention her authorship to Randall so he could relay it to Kylie.

Roy turned back to the computer. "We should get back to this thing while it's still fresh in our minds."

As they continued to work, Matt noticed how happy he felt, how good it was to be in this room with these people. Ever since last year, it felt like he was trying to stave off a lurking shadow in his mind, something that could only be kept at bay by bright light, something that kept threatening to come back after it got so close to taking him last year. Right now, he felt surrounded by bright lights and the shadow was so far away he couldn't even picture it.

He hoped it never came back.

TWENTY-FIVE

"**A**LRIGHT," RANDALL said. "Anybody else got something to read?"

Matt waved. "I do."

The Imperator shifted his attention toward him. "Let's hear it."

They sat in a circle of folding chairs in the dimly-lit Chalet basement, flickering candles arranged on the floor around them. Pendants hung from their necks, save for Randall's, which sported his medallion. The three other Tetrad members wore their sashes as they sat beside the boss. A skull-ornamented clock on the wall displayed the current time: nearly a quarter past one in the morning.

Matt stood up and carefully balanced the laptop on his left palm, then read through the three pages of jokes he'd gotten down over the course of the evening. For an extended writing session like this—the final one before the Sermon—that was a fairly productive amount, though others—who had been in more industrious rooms—had more jokes. That didn't matter, though; he'd saved the best for last.

When he finally got to his secret weapon, he said, "And lastly, this is something Roy, Joan, and I cooked up over the weekend. It's a poem."

Logan turned to Doug. "Ooh, *Joan* helped him write it…"

Randall shot him a casual look that said *Hey, lay off it* and turned back to Matt. "Finally, a poem! We've been really lacking in that department since Patrick left." He nodded. "Go ahead."

Matt threw a glance to Roy, who nodded as well. Tanner looked on with anticipation; Roy had mentioned it to him earlier but didn't share too many details.

He took a deep breath and began to read—just the way he'd been practicing for the past few days. There were no slip-ups, no voice cracks, no stuttered words. He led the room down the rabbit hole of the demented Christmas poem and heard the other members sing with laughter as he progressed. Even Logan and Rufus doubled over in fits.

When he reached the end, several around him were wiping tears from their eyes.

"Wait, wait, wait," Doug said, putting his hands up. "Did you guys make that up or do we know for a fact that Dunlap put pubes on Blaine's door?"

Matt nodded. "Joan and I got a confession out of a second-year who lives in Third Bowman. Apparently, Dunlap went around the floor asking people for…" He let his voice trail off.

Doug laughed again. "That's fucking gold."

"That poem is going *straight* to the Sermon," Logan said. He turned to Randall, who nodded.

"I'll admit," the Imperator said, "this is probably the best eleventh-hour source material we've ever had." He looked around the room. "Any other readers?"

No one said a thing.

"Alright guys, we're finally done. You've done your part, now me and these fuckers"—he gestured to his Tetrad—"are going to slap some lipstick on this pig and get it ready for Friday." Randall pulled out his phone and glanced at the screen. "The girls finished reading upstairs a few minutes ago, so we can all head back to Cliffe for the chant."

Everyone collected their things and headed for the stairs.

"Oh, Richardson," Randall said as he walked past him. "Nice delivery. Make sure you email me that poem. I definitely want it in the Sermon."

"Will do," he said, and nearly gave him a salute before realizing that would look stupid. Then, remembering, he said, "Actually, there's something I want to talk to you about." Randall turned and raised an eyebrow. Matt kept his voice low. "A personal matter."

The Imperator nodded. "We can chat before heading to Cliffe." Then he continued toward the stairs.

Roy came up and patted him on the back. "Very nicely read," he whispered.

"Thanks." They followed the others up to the first floor, where the female branch waited in the lounge.

"Alright everyone, the boys are here," Kylie announced. "We're heading to the West Quad for the chant now." They began assembling their backpacks to return to res for the night.

"Anathema meetings are the only place where guys finish *after* the girls," Catherine muttered, readjusting her Magister sash after she got her backpack on.

Members of both branches headed for the front door, but Randall motioned for Matt to follow him back down the hallway. He moved after the Imperator and soon found himself in a lamplit room. A bed was nestled in the corner to the right while a desk, a chair, and a stocked liquor cabinet stood to the left; the curtains were drawn across a window at the far end.

"Have a seat." Randall closed the door and gestured to the chair while he sat on the bed. Once they were settled, he asked, "So what's bothering you?"

Matt sighed. "It's Rufus."

Randall nodded. "I figured as much. Yeah, those jokes he read about you last Tuesday weren't cool, and I did notice a lot of stuff he sends in for homework focuses on you."

Matt relayed what Tanner had told him.

The Imperator looked concerned. "That's odd." He thought for a moment. "Okay, I'm going to talk to him—not mentioning that you came to me—and just say I've noticed the things he writes about you are really mean and I'll tell him to lay off it. We're not about drilling people we hate here at Anathema. We're supposed to make fun of people's actions, and then all go have drinks afterward."

"But he's not really criticizing my actions," Matt said. "He's just going after me for being…inexperienced. It's not like I can really do anything about that on my own."

"No, you're right. I'll talk to Rufus. He's really not such a bad guy, and I know he respects me. So if I tell him to lay off it, he'll stop. End of story."

Matt sighed in relief. "Thank you. I was getting concerned he really had it out for me."

"Nah, he's just being a dick." Randall gave a dismissive wave. "Don't overthink things."

He looked around. "So, this was an Imperator bedroom?"

"Still is. I spend a lot of nights here and the rest at my girlfriend's place." He rubbed his eyes, but Matt noticed he looked less exhausted than he had the week before. He'd probably rested a lot over the long weekend. "Is that it?"

"One last thing… Joan really put a lot of help into the poem. Would you mind…letting Kylie know that?"

Randall nodded. "I'll be sure to work it into conversation after the Sermon. Joan's one of my…favorite writers in their branch, and she deserves credit where it's due."

"Thanks, I really appreciate it."

"No worries. Now, let's catch up with the others."

They left the room and headed out the front door, Randall locking it behind him. The others had gone through the gate already, but a few minutes later they caught up with them at Griffin Park by walking briskly.

Randall went off to chat with Doug, but Joan found Matt and walked beside him.

"I heard the poem was well-received."

"It was," he beamed, then nudged her shoulder. "Couldn't have done it without you."

She shrugged. "I had fun writing it."

"I told Randall to tell Kylie that you helped."

Joan looked pleasantly surprised and gave him a peck on the cheek. "Thank you, that means a lot."

Five minutes later, the thirty members from both branches who had attended the meeting entered Radcliffe and marched past the receptionist, through another set of doors, and out into the frigid air of the West Quad. They walked to the center of the grass and paved patterns, then clustered in a group.

Randall and Kylie came to the forefront. He turned to her and said, "Wanna start first?"

"Sure," she said, then faced the others. "It is currently"—she glanced at her watch—"about 1:30 in the morning, so most of these people will be asleep. Once we're done shouting, we'll have about thirty seconds to clear this space before they start looking and security gets called. Got it?"

Heads nodded all around. Joan gripped Matt's arm. She looked excited, her body poised to break into a sprint. He recalled her mentioning that she played field hockey back in high school. He tried to mimic her stance. "Head for the steam tunnels in Lacy?" she asked.

He nodded.

"LADIES…!" Kylie bellowed.

"…AND GENTLEMEN!" Randall followed.

Then, in unison: "IT'S TIME TO REMIND THIS COLLEGE OF THOSE *FOUR! ETERNAL! WORDS!*"

Members of both branches raised their heads to the heavens and screamed, *"CARPE RISUS, CARPE CORONAM!"*

Lights around the Quad flashed on and curtains were torn open. The group was already running, scattering in every direction. Matt, Joan, Tanner, and Roy flew to the eastern Lacy door. Joan hastily unlocked it, let them inside, and then pulled it shut behind her.

Footsteps came from the floors above, awakened res students descending to glimpse those who dared violate the Anathema Policy. The quartet of members fled down into Sub-Lacy, threw open the steam tunnel entrance door, and hurtled down gray steps into the underbelly of Radcliffe College.

Once there, they caught their breath against the walls. Matt looked left and right; the corridor ran beneath the southern side of the college and intersected with another that cut across below Rickard and Bowman on its way to Galbraith. The walls were adorned with Sharpie marks and carvings bearing the names of class-years past and, in numerous spots, the letters *CRCC*.

"Well that was fun," Roy said.

"Would've been more fun if I didn't have a 9 a.m. class tomorrow." Tanner shrugged. "Oh well, who needs sleep anyway?"

"We're gonna head back this way," Matt told Joan. "Thanks for letting us in."

"Don't mention it. I'll see you tomorrow." She gave him a quick kiss and returned up the stairs to House Lacy.

He watched her go, then turned around to see the others shaking their heads. Tanner pantomimed the cracking of a whip and Matt rolled his eyes. "I am not *whipped.*"

Tanner and Roy exchanged glances, then grinned. "He's whipped," Roy said.

Matt sighed and shook his head. "There are worse things in the world..."

They started heading down the corridor in the direction of Winslow.

"I didn't say it was *bad...*" Tanner's voice echoed down the tunnel. "I just meant it as a factual observation..."

As they continued along, the trio didn't notice a fourth figure behind them, clad in a cloak with a green sash across their chest. The figure calmly

176

walked down the passage, keeping their distance as Roy and Tanner hung a left at Winslow; Matt continued on before turning left down the other hall to get back to Bowman.

The figure stood there, smiled to themselves, and then headed back the way they had come.

TWENTY-SIX

GALBRAITH BUZZED with anticipation that Friday evening. Joan could feel it all around her.

It was especially noticeable with the first-years, who chatted among themselves about the "Ice Cream Social." In years past, Anathema had slid invitation cards under doors in the middle of the night, usually two or three days before a Sermon, but this time Randall had dissuaded Kylie from that tradition, not wanting to risk unnecessary attention from the admin. Instead they were relying solely on word of mouth to play it safe, which, judging by the conversation behind Joan as she grabbed dessert in the cafeteria, was still working fairly well.

"But what are we supposed to wear? And what time does it start?" a nervous first-year girl was asking her friend.

Joan spun around and put on her most stern, emotionless expression. It helped that she was taller than either of them. "Griffin Park. 8:30 p.m., *sharp*. Academic dress."

Both first-years looked startled.

"Your gowns." She gave a malicious smile. "See you there."

They each were terrified, but as she moved past them, she heard one whisper excitedly, *"Oh my God, she's in Anathema!"*

Joan re-entered the dining hall, beaming. Two years ago, she'd been a wide-eyed first-year just like them, eager to know more, desperately trying to figure out which upper-years were members and thinking they were so mysterious and cool. Time had wiped away some of the luster, but whenever she experienced something like *that*, the feeling returned. Now when those first-year girls thought back to their first Sermon, they'd remember the upper-year with the scar who instructed them where to be and when. And who knew? Maybe when the next female Imperator was Baptized in March, they'd turn to each other and go, "Hey, it's *her!*"

Joan returned to her seat across from Matt and Patrick at the third-year table.

"…I just know Randall's gonna tear me a new one," the male Student Affairs Officer was saying. "I've seen it in his eyes."

"I may have heard a…few jokes about you at meetings," Matt said, picking at his food.

"Oh well. My girlfriend's coming, so she'll get to hear the Anathema tell Cliffe what a wonderful person I am."

Joan tilted her head. "Who's your girlfriend?"

"Her name's Karen. She goes to Forrestal," Patrick said. "But I've told her basically everything that goes on here. She's always wanted to see a Sermon." His phone buzzed. "That's her, actually. We're grabbing dinner and drinks at the Royal, then we'll show up at Riverside already buzzed."

"See you there," Matt said.

"Bye," Joan added as he strutted off. She turned back to Matt and glanced at her watch. "We should probably start getting ready soon. Kylie said she wants us at the Chalet by 7:30. I'm assuming Randall wants you there around the same time."

He looked at his phone. "That's over an hour from now."

She rolled her eyes. "Yeah, but *you* just have to throw on a tux. *My* outfit is more elaborate." She took a bite of her Nanaimo bar.

"You dress like a stereotypical goth girl," he teased.

"I do *not*." She covered her mouth as she chewed, then swallowed. "*We* do not. Well, maybe some of us—I mean, our branch does get more leeway with outfits as long as they're black, but that's just because we're more creative." She smirked and sat up straighter. "You guys are all cookie-cutter in your tuxes." So saying, she popped the rest of the Nanaimo bar into her mouth.

He shook his head, bemused, and resumed eating.

Joan looked off toward the frosh tables, thinking of the First Sermon last November. It had been the weekend her high school friend Danielle came to visit. She'd been on the University of Toronto's fall reading week and had journeyed west to hang out with Joan for the weekend. Veronica

Yang had given her special permission to view the Sermon, a privilege few outside WCU had ever enjoyed. While the members stood holding candles before the statue in Griffin Park, prepared to lead the terrified first-years in chants and Latin songs, Danielle had watched with her arms folded and an amused look on her face the entire time. She'd even teased Joan on the march to Riverside Park for how spooky she was trying to be, which a few attendees had snickered at.

Danielle had shaken her head and said, "Out of all my high school friends, of course *you're* the one who ended up in a secret society." But afterward, as they'd sat with Patrick and other members at a Ni Hao Ma table, she'd whispered to Joan how Anathema seemed like a good fit for her and that she was glad it gave her a stable group of friends. They both knew that hadn't been the case in high school. Before Danielle had departed for Toronto, she'd told Joan she thought she'd make a great Imperator, and that if she ever got the position, she would personally fly back out here just to see her First Sermon.

Matt looked up from his phone. "Hey, before we get ready, Roy's invited us to swing by the Anamicable meeting for a couple minutes."

Joan shot him a quizzical look. "*Anamicable?* What's he doing with those idiots?"

"Well…he and their club president apparently have a…"

She rolled her eyes. "Of course he's *still* screwing Pandora Lane."

"Still? I thought…"

"You know what all the girls call him? *Fuckboy Roy.*"

Matt winced. "That's…not inaccurate. When did this start, though?"

"I know they hooked up at QuadFest, because…" She realized she'd backed herself into a corner with this explanation. "Um…people were talking about who had hooked up with who, and…"

"You and Vance Simmons were mentioned in the same breath as them."

The blood drained from her face; she tried to laugh it off. "Oh, you heard…"

He gave a dismissive wave. "I'm just teasing you. I really don't care. It sounds like you had a *way* better QuadFest than I did." And at that he suddenly paled too, then shook his head as if to clear it. "Anyway, Roy's got this thing where he sleeps with a bunch of different women and they all seem okay with it." He shrugged.

"Good for him, I guess." Joan sighed. "So, what does Anamicable do at their meetings?"

"I think they have sweets and candy and stuff."

She frowned. She'd already eaten a bit of dessert, but decided it was a cheat day anyway; she was bound to get hammered at the Sermon. *That reminds me, I've gotta fill up my flask…*

"Alright, let's get this over with." Joan stood up and grabbed her used napkins as he collected his plate and cup. They headed to the cafeteria to dispose of them, then exited through the dining hall's back door—past the High Table—and continued down a corridor with green carpeting. At the end of the hallway, through another door, they found themselves in a perpendicular corridor, standing at the entrance to Bertrand Hall, a multipurpose area most often used by East Quad residents. The Saunders residences were directly above them.

Matt and Joan continued through the doors and froze.

There were only about a dozen people in Bertrand, and all but four appeared to be on the Anamicable executive; they wore stickers bearing a smiling skull with pink heart-eyes. The others were Roy, Doug Sadler, and two first-years. Three tables stood to the left, one set up with pastries and snacks, while plush sofas and leather chairs were positioned to the right. Doug was currently raiding the pastry table while Roy chatted up a pretty girl of medium height with glasses and magenta bangs. Both Pandora and Roy were too busy talking to notice that they had entered, but Doug made his way toward them with a few cookies in hand. He looked shaken.

"Hey, Doug." Matt gestured around the event. "How is it?"

He shuddered. "This is God's way of showing what awaits in hell if I don't change my ways."

"Are the cookies at least good?" Joan asked.

Doug took a bite of one, then grimaced. "Nah, they're stale as fuck." He glanced back toward Roy and Pandora, then returned his attention to the two of them. "See you guys at the Chalet."

"See you later," Matt nodded.

Together, he and Joan walked toward the Anamicable President and her consort. The other exec members and two first years sat cross-legged on the floor in a big circle, talking with each other.

Roy finally noticed them and waved. "Hey, you guys came!" He turned to Pandora. "This is Matt and this is Joan."

"Hey, thanks for coming!" Her smile was just a little too wide. "Don't worry, even Anathema members are welcome here." She laughed and put her arm around Roy's shoulder. "I know you guys aren't all bad."

"Well, maybe I am," he teased, kissing her cheek.

Joan looked over at the group circle. One second-year guy stood in the center reading something from a piece of paper. "What are they doing?" she asked.

Pandora turned back to her. "Oh, let me show you around! Here at Anamicable we like to sit in a Circle of Positivity and have Sunny Sermons!" She was still smiling, but something about the way she stared at Joan bothered her.

"*Sunny*...Sermons?" she asked, wincing.

"Yeah, instead of...*chastisement*"—Pandora said it as if it were a dirty word—"we have Sunny Sermons that *extol* and *uplift* Radcliffe students! Let's go listen in."

The four of them drifted closer. The guy standing up read, "Being good at drawing. Being a good friend. Being a shining star. Name three things Kathy Pickering is good at."

Applause went around the circle. A girl wearing an exec sticker and a nametag that read *Kathy* put a hand to her chest and blushed. "Aww, thank you Charlie." The way she said it was nauseating.

Joan rubbed her other arm and did her best not to make a face. She glanced at Matt; he looked similarly uncomfortable. Roy didn't seem to mind, but he was too busy eyeing Pandora.

Charlie continued. "Kevin Gao, you seem like the kind of guy to... always be there for a pal in need."

As the clapping resumed, it was now was the turn of a first-year, one of the Saunders guys, to blush. Joan realized a few other Saunders residents were on the exec too, including Chet Tremblay and Blaine Harris.

"I thought Anamicable meetings were at the same time as the Sermons," she said, turning to Pandora.

The club president shook her head. "They used to be, but we...felt we could increase attendance if we offered it earlier in the evening. It's much more popular now." She gestured back to the circle.

"Are you coming to the Sermon?" Matt asked.

Pandora shook her head. "Though I don't look down on Anathema members or any Cliffe students who choose to go, I prefer to remain a conscientious objector." She smiled proudly, then headed over to the pastry tables. "I've got some extra sheets of paper here if you two would like to write some Sunny Sermon jokes."

"That's alright," Joan said, forcing a laugh. "But I think we'll opt-out."

Pandora looked up. "Oh, ha-ha." She didn't seem to think it was very funny. "Can I offer you any gluten-free treats before you go? I can't eat them all myself!" This time the laugh was more genuine.

"I'm good," Matt said.

"We already ate in Galbraith." Joan put a hand to her stomach. This whole thing had killed her appetite.

"Okay, well, have fun! Don't scare the first-years too much!" She wore a thin smile.

"We'll try," Matt said. Joan was already leading him by the hand for the door. When they got back out into the hallway, he nudged her shoulder and flashed a teasing smile. "Oh come on, weren't they just so *sweet?*"

"Yeah," she muttered as they headed for the East Quad. "So sweet you could rot your teeth just from staying there too long."

TWENTY-SEVEN

I T WAS time.

Since the day Madler told him he would be named the next Imperator, Randall had dreamed of his First Sermon. He saw himself behind the podium in Riverside Park, winged by members of the male branch on each side, candles illuminating their masked faces from below. He saw a crowd spread out before him, some seated, some standing. They were all waiting for him to say the words.

Or rather, they would be in a couple short hours.

Looking down at the document in his hand, with only the large numbers *198* inscribed upon its cover sheet, Randall felt his excitement mix with fear. These pages, when read aloud, would either elevate him to the pantheon of legendary Imperators or be the beginning of his downfall and impeachment as an Officer. What would Cliffe think of 115? How would he compare to his own friend Turland or William Favell, 110, whose delivery was said to be so electrifying that audience members forgot to breathe?

Randall's eyes wandered around the Imperator suite on the Chalet's main floor. He felt confident about his Prelude. He'd considered something about Air Force basic training, but felt everyone would expect that from him. What he now had written, he'd thought up over the long weekend back in Calgary, when his parents were watching one of their favorite films of the 1980s on TV. The Prelude had come to him in his living room like a visitation from the Great Lord himself. He'd dashed to his computer to jot down a draft, then refined it throughout the week.

He sighed. The writing and editing were now done; it was time to perform. Reading through the Sermon in a practice run earlier, he couldn't help but notice how crude some of the humor was. Granted, Dunlap had done a crass thing that deserved a crass reprimanding, and most Anathema humor was vulgar to begin with—as were the majority of DebSoc speeches and average conversations in Galbraith. *Oh well*, he thought, *we're college students. What are we supposed to write? Jane fucking Austen?*

Logan opened the door without knocking. He wore his tux, pendant, and silver sash. "Everybody's in the lounge. The girls are meeting downstairs. You ready?"

Randall nodded and stood up. "Kylie's Tetrad is bringing the podium to Riverside. It's downstairs right now. They'll order an Uber XL."

Logan glanced at his watch. "I should probably lead them to Griffin soon. It's just after 8 p.m."

"Sure. Does Doug have the, ah, skull ready?"

Logan scoffed. "Yeah, yeah. He's got it in the other room."

"Tell him to bring it out. I'm gonna go over the procedure in the lounge."

The Legatus nodded and left the room. Still holding the Sermon, Randall followed him and hung a left toward the group clustered by the fireplace. He did a quick headcount and saw that everyone in his branch was here, all done up in their tuxes and pendants. A few wore their masks already, including Matt, Roy, and Tanner. Even the ones who didn't often come to meetings were present, ready for the college to see them in Anathema attire without realizing how little they actually contributed to the organization.

"Gentlemen," he said loudly, and they all snapped to attention. "Thank you for being here on time, I appreciate your promptness." He glanced at his watch. "In a few minutes, Logan will lead you to Griffin Park where the evening's ritual will begin. Who has the songs?"

Zhang held up a thick wad of papers.

"Okay, good," Randall continued. "Once you're there, you are to line up in front of the statue beside the ladies, just as we always do; they'll have extra copies of the songs. I'll also need two people to hold the poster." Matt raised his hand, followed by Tony Madruga. "Perfect. You two will come with me after I'm done here, and you'll carry it to the park—very carefully. My girlfriend worked hard on it and I think it looks pretty fucking awesome."

He looked around at the others. "Once Logan sets you up, he's going to head to Riverside with the rest of the Tetrad. Sandrine will do the same with the ladies. Matt and Tony will be bringing the poster back here so it doesn't get damaged by our friendly neighborhood fuckwits, Lambda Phi, so I'll need another competent upper-year to lead the rest of you and the attendees to Riverside."

Roy raised his hand.

"Thank you," Randall said, nodding in his direction.

Rufus sighed and folded his arms. "Is Lambda Phi *really* raiding us again?"

Everyone looked to Geoff Bhajan, who leaned next to the fireplace. He shrugged. "I'm just the President, they don't tell me things."

Rufus exhaled loudly.

"Will they try to steal the skull again?" Hamid asked, sitting on one of the couches, his mask dangling from one hand.

The Imperator winced. "Um, about that…" He yelled over his shoulder, "Doug, bring it out here."

A moment later, his Magister emerged from another side room with the box that usually held the skull. He walked to the center of the lounge and placed it on a coffee table, then slid the top of the box off.

Randall bit his lip. "Gentlemen, say hello to the Great Lord Anathema's vessel for this evening."

Doug withdrew an oversized Halloween skull decoration and held it up for all to see.

The room was silent.

Finally, Rufus said, "What happened to Dad?"

Randall scratched his chin. "Dad is…on vacation for a little bit. This is, um…*Uncle*."

Hamid stared in disbelief. "It's fucking Styrofoam."

"Yes, that is a very astute observation, Hamid. Uncle is, in fact, made of Styrofoam, and he glows in the dark too! We got him at a discount from an online Halloween store that was clearing out its inventory. This way, no one from Lambda Phi will be able to steal our *real* skull."

"Because somebody else already stole it," Geoff said.

Everyone's head swiveled toward him. "Is that the reason?" Rufus looked back. "You're telling me the Great Lord Anathema got *skull-napped*?" He zeroed in on Doug. "How the fuck did that happen?"

"We're still investigating," Randall said, not wanting to get into this with everyone right now. "But apparently Lambda had nothing to do with it—"

"That I know of," Geoff added, holding his hands up.

"—and we will root out the real culprit and get our skull back *after* the Sermon, which is our immediate concern."

"And what if we don't?" Rufus asked. "What if Dad's just…gone?"

"Then we'll have to ask the alumni for funds to buy a new one. We were probably going to need a new 'vessel' for the Great Lord anyway in a few years, and the Dad that got stolen was far from this organization's first. But we're using Uncle for this Sermon, and that's that. People will probably be too drunk on the boxed wine we'll give them to notice the difference. Any questions?"

No one said a thing.

"Okay, great." He looked around at all of them and smiled. "Let the fun begin."

◆

By the light of the lampposts, the members of the Anathema made their way toward Griffin Park's central statue. The eponymous, metallic creature was cast in shadow; nightfall always seemed to suffuse it with a sinister aura.

The members climbed onto the steps that ringed the circular island, tallest members at the back. Matt normally would've stood with them, but he and Tony were carrying the framed poster. It had been a long-held tradition in both branches to create artwork commemorating each Sermon. They ranged from macabre imagery to a parody of the original *Star Wars* poster.

Matt took a moment to admire this poster again as the cold wind seared his skin. It was below freezing tonight, but mercifully it hadn't snowed. The imagery depicted the ruins of Radcliffe with a distant purple-hued cityscape in the backdrop. A mountain of skulls stood before the college's remains, and atop them stood a figure in military fatigues and a cloak. A large skull medallion was slung around his neck and he held a science fiction-looking pulse rifle in his hands.

"Shit, his girlfriend did this in a week?" he asked. "It's incredible. And I love the James Cameron vibe."

"Yeah," Tony said, looking over his shoulder. "I heard him mention something about it depicting his Prelude."

Matt liked that an Imperator had finally tied the poster to the Prelude. They were the most abstract section of the Sermons—and the part where Imperators' creativity could roam free. Usually, they involved some variation of the Great Lord or Lady yelling at them from the tower, or the Imperator climbing the tower to look out at all of Radcliffe, or something else, invariably, involving the tower. Randall might shake things up a little—though Turland had done epically complex time-travel metanarratives in both of his.

"Shit, who has a lighter?"

It was Logan, a black candle in his hand. The box with the rest of them lay at his feet. He glanced at his watch. "We've got, like, five minutes before they start showing up. We need these lit."

"I left mine back in my suite," Tony said.

Geoff came up beside Logan and shrugged. "Shit, yeah I left mine back at Lambda."

A glowing cigarette emerged from the gloom and Sandrine Bouchard stepped into the light. She held it between her fingers, exhaled, and gave them all a disapproving stare. "Fucking amateurs." She pulled a lighter out of her leather jacket pocket with a skull displayed on the front.

"Wait, we have branded *lighters* now?" Geoff scoffed. "Weren't the flasks enough?"

"I got this in Paris, at the catacombs gift shop." She lit Logan's candle, then handed the lighter to him to deal with the rest. She brushed aside her platinum blonde hair while, behind her mask, her eyes swept the members. "Keating! Where's the boxed wine?"

Matt turned around. Joan and Val had just arrived, and it was the first time he'd seen his girlfriend since they parted to get ready. She'd texted him that she'd probably miss him at the Chalet because Kylie asked her to go to the town's only liquor store for supplies. That seemed to be a good sign, an indication that the female Imperator saw Joan as reliable. Back in first-year, Turland had put him in a group chat called "Least Likely to Fuck Things Up" to assist in preparations for his Second Sermon. Granted, Turland wouldn't be deciding whether he became 116 or not.

"Kylie asked us to bring it straight back to the Chalet," she said, looking slightly out of breath. "She wants to take it to Riverside in the Uber."

Sandrine rolled her eyes. "Nobody tells me anything…" She sighed and took a deep drag from her cigarette, then spun around. "Alright, places people! Who has the songs?"

"I do!" Sophia Huynh said, walking over with a large stack of papers.

"Get in your places!" Logan yelled in the middle of lighting Hamid's candle. "Grab a copy of the songs from Sophia if you haven't already." He looked to Tony and Matt. "You guys, stand off to the side and look serious. Not that Matt ever smiles, anyway."

He seemed to mean it in jest, but Matt couldn't tell. "You missed a little bit, Logan," he said, pretending to wipe his nose.

For a second, Logan frantically swiped under his nostril, then smirked. "You got me. I actually did two lines before this."

He went back to lighting candles as Joan walked up to Matt, hers already aflame. She kept a gloved hand around the top to prevent the wind from blowing it out. "Aren't you cold?" she asked, concerned. She wore a black turtleneck under her leather jacket with matching jeans and winter boots; even her lipstick was black, and together with the mask and the temperature her skin appeared ghostly pale.

"You look a bit chilly yourself," he said. Beneath his tux he wore long johns and two undershirts, but didn't have a coat that matched the formal dress. He'd just have to drink a lot to feel warm, but he usually got pretty tipsy at these things anyway. It made it easier to take rough jokes.

Joan shrugged. "My cheeks and ears feel like they're on fire, but what can you do?" She looked around the park and sighed. "I kinda wish we had both Sermons indoors. Even early November is too cold here to do this outside."

"Yeah, but then we wouldn't get Riverside," Tony said, holding the other corner of the poster. "I'd say it's worth a little chill."

"Keating!" Sandrine bellowed. "Our branch stands on *this* side of the statue!" She wore a cross expression and pointed to where the other female members were already lined up.

"Right, of course," Joan said, hurrying back over. Matt heard snickering from both the men and women.

"I'm glad you finally found somebody," Tony whispered, staring straight ahead. "You seem suited to each other."

"Thank you," Matt said. He knew Tony hadn't dated anyone since Zhang last year, and it apparently hadn't ended too well. Before that, they'd been the first openly gay couple within their branch's history.

"I see them coming," Logan announced, looking back to Tony and Matt. "Turn around," he barked. "And stand next to the girls. Roy, you're in charge of our guys now. Sandrine and I are heading back to the

Chalet; we'll catch Ubers with the others."

Jaya Noor, another third-year member in the female branch, and Alyssa were holding Kylie's poster, a beautifully drawn skull comprised of a flock of ravens in flight. Tony and Matt shuffled over to them and straightened their posture; since they were both over six feet tall it was fairly easy to look imposing.

Up ahead, along the diagonal path that cut toward Radcliffe, a group of first-years made its way closer. Even from here, Matt could tell that they were clad in their High Table gowns. Loud voices and laughter drifted in with the wind, but as the frosh drew closer and saw the severe faces and flickering candles, they quickly fell silent.

Roy and Sophia walked over to them. "Gentlemen, please stand to the right," he said, gesturing.

"Ladies, to the left."

They handed out sheets of paper as the first-years passed by. Some tried to laugh off the tension; others were petrified. Matt remembered his first Sermon quite well, though he'd at least had the benefit of attending the Beckonings beforehand. He'd mostly known the roster of male members, and had already seen some of his frosh leaders in tuxedos and Venetian masks. Some of those who hadn't attended would've heard of or figured out who was in it by now, but the others, especially those dragged along by their friends, would be in for a shock tonight.

The only one everyone knew about for certain was Randall.

It took about fifteen minutes for everyone to file in. The ones here were nearly all first-years, but some Officers like Patrick, Dunlap, and Veronica had come to make sure the frosh felt comfortable. Mia Cote had tagged along too, but she didn't look happy as she snatched a sheet of paper out of Sophia's gloved hand. Since they already knew where it was, upper-years who attended usually went straight to Riverside. Many would probably order Ubers to avoid walking in the cold.

"Ladies and gentlemen," Sophia announced. "The school song."

She and Roy began the Latin verse, followed by the other members, then, reluctantly, the audience. They sang the old version of the Radcliffe song, back when the Great Lord and Lady Anathema were actually mentioned by name. The admin had cut that part out after Dissociation. The crowd—members, Officers, and first-years alike—stumbled through line after line of Latin before mercifully arriving at the end.

Now Roy and Sophia stepped forward once again.

"Ladies, form a line and follow me please." She turned and headed north, followed by the female first-years of the throng.

"Gentlemen, time to put those preschool skills to good use." He turned on his heel and marched after her, the Officers and men of the audience in a linear tow.

The members of each branch followed alongside as both lines marched into the dark. Only the four holding the posters were left behind.

"Randall told us you'd have the Chalet keys," Tony said.

Jaya nodded and held them up, her other hand gripping the side of the poster frame. "Let's drop these off and split an Uber."

As they walked about twenty feet behind the end of the line, a man emerged from the path up ahead. He was middle-aged and had the look of a professor out for a late-night stroll.

"Excuse me," he said, walking straight up to the four of them. "You look like you're with that group up there. What's this all about?"

"We're a feminist slam poetry group," Matt said, completely straight-faced. "We're off to our semi-annual coffee house." The other three beside him nodded.

"Ah…" The man looked confused. "What's with the, ah…get-up?" He gestured to their clothes.

"We take gender equality very seriously," Jaya said.

The man's face brightened. "Right, of course. Well, have a good evening!" He continued off toward the statue.

As they resumed walking, Tony shook his head and sighed. "We're all going to hell."

◆

After leaving the posters in the Chalet's lounge, Jaya ordered an Uber and invited the others to split the fare with her.

"It's just a few blocks that way," Matt pointed out as they stood at the end of the driveway.

"Yeah, but it's cold," Tony said, his breath dissipating as he hugged his jacket tighter. "And with four of us splitting, it'll be super cheap anyway."

Matt shrugged. His exposed skin was a mixture of mild pain and numbness. He withdrew his Anathema flask, which was filled with rum, and took a large swig.

The ride finally arrived. The four of them crammed into the small sedan and it took off, the driver paying little attention to their attire and masks. At first, they sat there silently as they passed residential streets on the left, trees whipping by on the right.

Then Jaya said, "So…who do you think the new Imperators will be next year?"

"Well, obviously Logan for us," Tony said. "I mean, who else could it fucking be?"

Matt pulled out his flask and took an even longer pull.

Jaya sighed. "I guess. He seems like the kind of guy to take jokes too far."

"Nah, nah," Tony said. "He's just…edgy, you know? What I'm really curious about is who *your* Imperator is gonna be."

Jaya looked back toward Alyssa and leaned closer, as if to impart confidential information. "Honestly…I think it's between you and Catherine."

What an original take, Matt thought. He really hoped Kylie asking Joan to pick up the wine was a sign of confidence. Then he realized Randall never asked him to do anything directly.

"Well, I don't know…" Alyssa didn't seem like she wanted to talk about it. "I guess we'll see who gets asked." For a second, Matt almost believed that she didn't care. But then again, at Radcliffe, showing more than a modicum of interest in something apparently got you mistaken for a fanatic. And that would put a damper on anyone's Imperator ambitions.

With horror, Matt wondered if that's why no one considered him a contender—that he was too *into* it to be put in charge. Now *there* was some ass-backward logic. Surely Randall didn't think like that. Not even Madler did, or he wouldn't have chosen Randall as his successor. But not even Randall had seemed *super* into it. Was he just hiding how much it meant to him or—?

His mood had spiraled down again and he had to tell himself to pull out. He'd felt more fluctuations between the extremes this year than he'd ever felt in his life. Right now, though, he couldn't deny that he hated being in this car, listening to these people endlessly say the same shit as if it was hot gossip. It was always the same predictions for Imperator or the same insults about the same people—*she's so weird, he's too into it*—over and over again, ad infinitum. There was no escape and he could feel it poisoning his veins, spreading across his body—

The car came to a stop.

"Thanks," Jaya said to the driver as she climbed out.

Matt threw open the door and scrambled out the vehicle's left side, gasping a deep breath. The cold air stung his throat and lungs, but he didn't care. Just the shock of the temperature jolted him out of the funk he'd been in for the past minute or so.

"You okay?" Tony had climbed out after him and shut the door. The car drove off.

He put on a smile as he turned around. "Yeah, it was just a bit cramped in there."

"True. Later we should spring for an XL if we've got more than three people."

They stood at the edge of a gravel path leading into the trees beside the Fire Department. A sign read *Riverside Park*. They continued into the woods until the trail forked in two directions, off past some more trees to a playground area on the right and curving down a steep hill toward the ravine on the left.

They took the left path and soon the trees disappeared behind them as they entered the Pit. Here was a sizeable cove, sheltered by a sharp slope curving around the perimeter. The stream ran behind an elevated gazebo with steps and railings, where the podium had already been set up. It bore the Radcliffe crest, as it had once been housed in Galbraith Hall. Anathema would steal it and return it covered in candlewax after each Sermon, but once a second podium had been bought about a year ago, they'd decided simply to keep it.

The female Tetrad stood in the gazebo, making their final preparations. The crowd sat at two picnic tables or otherwise on the ground, huddling in their jackets to keep warm; some had brought blankets. The male branch was clustered behind them, near the incline. Some leaned back against the steep slope to get comfortable for Kylie's Sermon. He saw Randall and Turland chatting with their girlfriends, Gemma and Caitlyn respectively. Gemma went to St. Mark's and had dated Randall since high school but Caitlyn was a Cliffe student like the rest of them. Most of the female members were already standing on either side of the platform, candles lit and ready. As usual, the upper-years stood closest to the Imperator and the more recent Initiates were farther away. Jaya and Alyssa made their way toward them.

Joan stood two members away from the podium's left, adjusting her mask. When she looked up, Matt waved; she smiled and returned it, then swiftly resumed staring ahead with a stern expression. He made his way to the audience and saw that Patrick and his girlfriend Karen, a tall redhead, were seated in folding armchairs beside the tables.

Patrick spotted him. "Hey, you've met Karen, right?"

"Yeah." Matt turned to her. "Back at QuadFest."

"Oh yeah, that's right!" she said. "It's kinda hard to tell with the mask on. Why do you guys wear them again?"

"They only started doing that in the early 2000s," Patrick said. "A *Calgary Herald* journalist took a photo of some members lined up in Griffin Park before a Sermon and it was used in an article about Anathema. After that, they decided Venetian masks would cover members' faces enough without being…too much."

"I think it's just better in the digital age," Matt said. "Especially with phone cameras and the Internet. Really, I'm surprised it took us that long to start wearing them."

"I think they look good," she said, glancing between Matt and the other members.

Matt gestured to her Forrestal sweater. "Brave to wear that here," he laughed.

Karen shrugged. "Gotta represent." She punched Patrick on the shoulder. "I'm just here to watch him get skewered."

Patrick held up a flask—not his Anathema one, Matt noted—and took a big swig from it. "I'm bracing myself."

Suddenly, the female members began shouting "Ninety-Three, Ninety-Three, Ninety-Three!" and the crowd's murmuring dwindled to silence.

Matt remained standing, battered by the cold wind, as he watched Kylie Patel, 93rd Imperator of the Great Lady Anathema, take the podium and shout: "I opened my eyes…!"

The members ceased their chanting. Catherine sat before the podium on a chair, the skull in her lap on a velvet pillow, a candle placed atop its head. Kylie continued.

"…and there I saw…a darkened room, with a candle flickering by the window. The window was open, and a gentle breeze drifted toward me. I got up and made my way to the desk beneath the sill, where parchment lay beside a quill and a bottle of ink. At the top of the page, the numbers One-Eight-Three were underlined with a violent stroke of black. I gripped the quill with tenacious fingers, plunged it into the ink, and brought it down toward the blank space. Suddenly, my hand froze. It was as if a paranormal force prevented me from writing. Beads of sweat formed on my forehead as the quill hovered above the page, droplets of ink staining its surface.

" 'What are you waiting for?' came a familiar voice, cold as ice. I spun around to see a cloaked figure, much like myself, emerge from the shadows. Though I could see little of Her face—only Her mouth and ghostly-white chin—I knew it was the Great Lady Anathema who stood before me.

" 'But I'm not waiting, Mother,' I said, eager to explain. 'The quill…I can't seem to…' My voice trailed off as she raised an alabaster hand.

" 'I know what you are thinking,' the Great Lady said. Her voice chilled me to the bone. The room felt much colder, and I was surprised the candle hadn't been extinguished. '92 Imperators and 182 Sermons have come before you, before this moment. What is there left to say about Radcliffe and its wretchedness, its hedonism, its degeneracy?' She walked around me, circling like a shark. I felt goosebumps on my skin, frigid breath rising from my lips. It was all I could do not to shiver before Her. 'The thing is…,' She continued, 'every year a fresh crop of worms arrives in my garden. They come with egos inflated by their hovering parents, their glowing high school report cards, all thinking they are God's greatest gift to this Earth. And every year they inflict their insufferable insolence upon this college. Every year they find new ways of tormenting us. It rests on you, Ninety-Three, to fulfill our purpose—to provide checks and balances on the student populace. Not even members of my branch are immune; you must cleanse them all of their impudence and transgressions.'

" 'But Great Lady,' I whispered, my teeth chattering. 'What difference does it make if there will always be more to chastise, more to lambast? Can we deny that we fight against a ceaseless tide?'

"She came closer and caressed my face with Her bony fingers. Her touch was awfully cold, yet soothingly gentle. 'My dear child,' she breathed. 'You are not the first Imperator I have told this to, and you will not be the last. We exist to uphold a balance, and without that balance we would find life at Radcliffe to be completely unbearable. This college is unique in so many ways, and its special breed of insolence is merely one of them. There is good in these wayward souls who will stand before you in Riverside on the ninth of this month. You must absolve them of their contraventions so that their egos and misgivings may not weigh them down. You have the power to better not only Radcliffe, but its students. And when the time comes, so shall Ninety-Two absolve *you* of your own sins with a Litany. Now *write.*'

"She pointed back to the desk. I turned and walked toward it, picking up my quill again, only to hesitate once more. 'But how will I know...?' I glanced over my shoulder to see that she was gone. I was alone. I returned my attention to the page and suddenly it all became clear to me, the things that needed chastisement the most—and the formats to deliver them in. I set the quill to the page and began to write..." Kylie threw her head back. *"THE 183RD SERMON OF THE GREAT LADY ANATHEMA!"*

"CARPE RISUS, CARPE CORONAM!" the members chanted.

Kylie turned the page. Sandrine stood beside her, illuminating the document with a candle. "*You...*are Joan Keating..."

"NOOO!" every member screamed, still staring straight ahead. Even Joan herself didn't falter.

"...and *you* get tipsy at a bar. In a cruel twist of fate, you get a little *too* tipsy and feel like you're going to puke. In a fortuitous twist of fate, the restroom is just down a flight of stairs. But in a crueler twist of fate, you spill your guts before you can make it to the sink. In an *even* crueler twist, you spill them all over some guy coming out of the men's washroom. And in the cruelest twist of all...he's the guy you had a crush on."

Even from here, Matt could see she'd gone red in the face. The crowd laughed and even first-years who didn't know her whispered among themselves as they chuckled.

Kylie continued, "While reading the retractions section of *The Westerner*, the Great Lady noted these What She Said, What She Meant to Says from women of college:

"Lisa Fang. What she said: 'My sexual fantasies involve roleplaying as a Third World dictator.' "

The crowd turned around and started murmuring. Matt blinked; clearly, he'd missed that Galbraith conversation.

"What she meant to say: 'Please, Great Lady, write jokes about me again! I'll say anything edgy, anything outlandish within earshot of an Anathema member! Just give me the attention my parents never did!"

There was a sharp intake of breath from the crowd. Off to his right,

Matt saw Logan rubbing Lisa's shoulder as he gave her a kiss on the cheek.

"Val Lehman. What she said: 'I'm in the small minority of my generation that loves getting hazed.' What she meant to say: 'It's how I became best friends with Joan Keating.'"

Mostly the members and the upper-years in the crowd giggled at that one, although a few first-year girls—presumably ones who had been at the Beckonings—did too. Joan gave Val a friendly wave down the line.

"Phrases Not Often Heard for women of college: Wow Alyssa Lee, you're such a nice person!"

Now it was Alyssa's turn to be embarrassed. Lots of people laughed, especially Joan. It seemed to take some of the tension out of her.

"Wow Joan Keating, you can really hold your liquor!"

And immediately they were all looking at her again. Doubled over a moment ago, she was suddenly standing up straight, rigid, biting her lower lip. Alyssa sneered in her direction.

"Name Threes!" Kylie cleared her throat. "A black Armani suit. Taking an Uber Black. Her black credit card. Name three ways Lisa Fang supports diversity."

Another sharp intake of breath from the crowd.

"While flipping back through her old middle school literature textbook, the Great Lady Anathema—"

"CRCC! CRCC! CRCC!" shouted the members.

"CRCC!" one girl continued from the crowd, then covered her mouth and hunkered down.

Immediately, the female branch's eyes were upon her. "THREE TIMES, ASSHOLE!"

Kylie resumed. "—found the following If poem…"

The Sermon went on, hitting more and more first-year girls as it did so. Since the majority of the audience, which appeared to be seventy or eighty people, were frosh, the laughter increased as Kylie moved along. One former teenage beauty pageant winner had apparently demanded her room be switched to a Quad-facing one because the view of the Dales Building wasn't up to her standard. A girl in House Martins had gone around stealing toilet paper from the Lacy washrooms. Another on Fourth Rickard had brought friends over every night at 3 a.m. to the chagrin of everyone who enjoyed sleep. One girl who hadn't been invited to the Beckonings, but who had heard over half the branch's members were either lesbian or bisexual, had said she wouldn't want to join Anathema or even go to a Sermon because "half of them are dykes anyway"—for which she received several harsh jokes.

Joan was hit a few more times, but mercifully Alyssa's Search History about her didn't make it in. Kylie threw her head back and bellowed, "HERE ENDETH THE 183RD SERMON OF THE GREAT LADY ANATHEMA!" which was followed by a final, single chant of the four eternal words.

Now came the break. The male members moved around with boxed wine that had been stashed under the picnic tables, letting attendees drink from the taps so long as their lips didn't touch them.

Joan walked over to Matt, rubbing her arm as she did so. "Hey, you took those well," he said, giving her a kiss. Even her lips were cold.

"Thanks," she said with a weak smile, and pulled him closer. "Fuck, it's chilly out here."

"That was really fun," Karen said to them; she and Patrick had gotten up to stretch. "So…you're the guy she threw up on?"

"Take a guess, Karen," Patrick said.

She made a mocking face and turned back to Joan. "Don't worry, if you think *you* got roasted, you haven't seen shit yet."

"How do you know you're getting railed?" Matt asked, turning to Patrick.

He shrugged. "It's like a sixth sense. Randall offered me two of the three other Tetrad positions if I would come back to the organization, and I turned him down. He still comes to me for advice, but I can tell he was pissed." He smiled.

"He offered you *two* Tetrad positions?" Joan's mouth hung open. Here she and Matt were scrambling to secure even one.

"Yup."

Matt turned toward the gazebo and saw Fennell and Doug setting up, but Randall was nowhere in sight. "Speaking of him, where is he?"

He stood atop the incline, lost in a trance, watching moonlight glisten off the stream's surface. There was no going back now.

"Hey, we gotta get ready." He turned to see Logan to his right, tapping his foot and scratching the side of his mask.

"Yeah, I know." Randall looked back to the water. "I'm just…psyching myself up."

"Nervous?"

"Just a little."

The Legatus shook his head. "You really are the Pussy Imperator."

Randall chuckled. *Classic Logan...* "Nah, nah, I'm just clearing my head." He took one more deep breath and adjusted his mask. "Okay, let's go."

They cut through the woods to the path, then doubled back along the trail as it curved down to the Pit. His branch was lining up on either side of the podium and front steps, just as their female counterparts had done. The audience barely seemed to notice the Imperator and Legatus as they made their way to the gazebo; they took the rear stairs and Randall found that everything was ready for him. The Styrofoam skull glowed a soft green in Doug's hands; he nodded to Randall and moved to take his seat in front of the podium, placing Uncle in his lap just as Catherine had done with Mom.

The document labeled *198* rested on the wood before him. Fennell moved around to stand to his left and Logan lit a candle to his right, holding it closer to illuminate the Sermon. Randall's hands gripped the edge of the podium and he exhaled, gazing out at the crowd. They were still chatting among themselves, getting drunk on boxed wine. He turned and nodded to Logan, who whistled.

Almost immediately, the members of the male branch began chanting, softly at first, then louder and louder, "One-One-Five! One-One-Five! One-One-Five!"

Randall took a deep breath, listening to the volume of the cheer increase. Slowly, he extended his hand upward and glanced toward each side of the line. Their eyes were fixed onto him, watching for his signal.

"One-One-Five! One-One-Five!"

His arm fully extended upward, Randall clenched his hand into a fist and the chant was extinguished. Then he turned the page, threw back the hood of his cloak, and began to read.

Twenty-Eight

"I opened my eyes…and there I saw…a shattered cityscape sprawling away beneath the stars. Rubble and ruin stretched almost as far as the eye could see, but there—on the purple glow of the horizon—stood the remnants of Neo-Calgary, its once shining buildings now dilapidated and crumbling.

"I heard a whirring behind me and turned to see one of the Provost's hunter-killer drones flying in my direction. Snatching my pulse rifle off the ground, I dove for cover beneath a wreck of twisted metal that had once been a car. The drone hovered overhead, big as a CF-118 Hornet jet fighter. Its searchlight swept the ground as a robotic recording boomed: 'This is a restricted sector. All trespassers will be immediately subjected to five Demerit Points, the threshold for termination.' I held my breath, watching the light dance back and forth around my hiding spot. Finally, it vanished, and I heard a loud whirring once again as the drone took off toward Neo-Calgary.

"I sighed, climbed out, and brushed off my Resistance military fatigues; they had seen better days. Clutching my medallion for good luck and hefting my pulse rifle, I continued my climb to the top of the mountain. After a grueling ascent, I gazed down and there it was, still standing among the devastation: Radcliffe, the site of the Provost A.I.'s central processing unit. Years ago, the Provost was created as a program to keep us safe, but it outgrew its directive and decided that the greatest threat to students… was themselves. The only way to *truly* protect us, the A.I. decided, was to destroy all possibility of us having fun. It began by banning licensed events

200

and destroying the alcohol policy, but this couldn't keep students from throwing their own ragers or seeking enjoyment with dissociated groups. So the Provost decided there was only one way to stop fun forever—by killing us all. As the program grew in size, it set its ambitions on WCU President, then Premier of Alberta, then Prime Minister of Canada, then Supreme Overlord of the Whole World. But it all started here, at Radcliffe College.

"I made my way down the mountainside. It took forever climbing through old forest outposts and woodlands scorched by flame and mortar, but I recognized my surroundings as the ground leveled out. The trees were fallen and the paths had been destroyed, but I knew I stood in Bethune's Walk. And there, atop a hill before me, was the place I sought. It would all end here, whether I lived or died.

"Suddenly the whirring returned and I spun around. The hunter-killer flew over the top of the mountain range and swept down like a hawk. I turned and dashed up the hill to Radcliffe's back gate. The drone fired its machine guns, bullets tearing up the ground as I neared the entrance. I didn't stop to pull out my old R3—I raised the pulse rifle as I ran and fired a single round through the lock. The door swung open and I dove through just as a missile exploded behind me, sending dirt and chunks of pavement through the air. I scrambled to my feet and pressed my back flat against the wall of the tunnel, clutching the rifle to my chest. The whirring was back, the robotic aircraft hovering right outside, scanning for signs of life with its searchlight. Finally, it clicked off and I heard the drone fly away once more. I breathed a heavy sigh of relief; it thought I was dead.

"Carefully, I inched closer to what I remembered as the East Quad and peered out of the wind tunnel. There, I saw the Provost had demolished Houses Bowman and Rickard; gone too was Napier Tower. Now there was but one large, double-length Quad, packed with electrified cages that glowed neon blue. Each of them housed members from different squadrons of the Resistance. I saw DebSoc and the Ice Cream Social Club—my squadron—huddled behind the bars. And at the far end, a screen with a watching eye had been installed on the belfry of Anathema Tower. It was the Provost. Using my binoculars, I saw that on each side of the tower stood the A.I.'s two cyborg assistants, Crawley and Porter, glaring down at the hapless prisoners with their robotic eyes. At the end of the Quad closest to me, a large computer had been set up with cables running to all the cages.

That must be the system control. Keeping low, I made my way along the back edge, rushing toward the device that would free my brethren.

"But as I got there, a guard jumped out and slammed me against the monitors, wrapping his hands around my throat. To my surprise, it was not a robot that attacked me, but rather a Provost-worshipping human fanatic—a traitor not only to my squadron but to all of the Resistance.

"It was Patrick Mason.

" 'You're immoral, 115,' he spat, his grip tightening around my neck. 'The Provost was right about all of you—fun *is* the enemy. Maintaining discipline is the only way to protect ourselves.'

" 'Is that why you betrayed us, Patrick?' I managed to get out. 'You think *you* can protect us all?'

"The traitor smirked. 'That, and having a Supreme A.I. Overlord write your recommendation letter *really* increases your law school chances.'

" 'You fool,' I gasped. 'Once the Provost wipes us out, there will be no law schools left to apply to.'

"Patrick's eyes went wide, as if only realizing this for the first time. His grip loosened slightly and I seized my opportunity. Mustering all of my strength, I flipped him over the computer console and he flew into the Quad, smashing against an electrified crate. Patrick screamed as the energy coursed through him. His body sizzled from *flesh* to *bone* to *ash* to *dust in the wind*—

"Save for his skull, which rolled to the ground. For a moment it rested there, still intact. Then its eye sockets glowed orange and a cold wind swept into the Quad. It swirled around the skull and lifted it high into the air, levitating it above the neon cages. A bolt of lightning shot down from the heavens. There was a blinding flash and I shielded my eyes. When I lowered my hand, I saw not the skull floating before me, but a wraith-like figure with a tattered cloak draped around its body. It was the Great Lord Anathema himself!

"His eyes—two lidless, orange orbs—swept the Quad, the cages, and the tower before settling upon me. '115!' he bellowed. 'What the fuck is all of this?!' He appeared quite baffled.

"I humbly knelt before him. 'It's the state of our college, Great Lord. The Provost has taken over and is holding our clubs, our booze, and our debauchery hostage. I don't know how to free—'

" 'BULLSHIT!' he thundered. 'There is only one thing that can free your peers and restore the balance—the power of satirical chastisement.'

" 'But the passphrase, Great Lord! I can't unlock the cages without it!'

" 'You've known it all along.' And with that, he vanished in a swirl of ash and wind. Across the double Quad, I saw the bionic Crawley and Porter leading a charge of D-800 Disciplinators toward me, pulse rifles in hand, their red eyes gleaming amidst the sea of neon. Frantically, I looked at the largest monitor in front of me, my fingers hovering over the keyboard. What did the Great Lord mean? I had no clue what the passphrase was.

"The Disciplinators stopped and formed a line, raising their rifles toward where I stood. Crawley and Porter raised their arms to give the signal to open-fire. Staring down at me from what had been the Great Spirits' tower, the eye of the Provost watched me. An electronic laugh filled with malevolence echoed through the Quad. It hit me then what the passphrase was. I looked down at the keyboard and rapidly typed in:

"HERE BEGINS THE 198TH SERMON OF THE GREAT...! LORD...!" He threw his head back. *"ANATHEMA!"*

"CARPE RISUS, CARPE CORONAM!"

Randall violently turned the page. "*You*...are Patrick Mason..."

"NOOO!" the members shouted.

"Fuck that guy!" one of them yelled.

"Yeah," Patrick said, raising his flask in toast. "I hear he's a dick."

"...and *you* stand accused of selling us out to the admin. The High Court of the Anathema finds you..."

"GUILTY!" the members shouted.

"...and sentences you...to transfer to Atherton University, so that you may swiftly find employment in the Dean's Office upon your graduation."

The audience seemed to have a good laugh at that one. Randall had realized when compiling jokes that, as an Officer, Patrick was well-known among all years, and so hitting him would serve both the crowd's enjoyment and, if Randall was being honest with himself, a small personal vendetta.

"After becoming disillusioned with the state of global affairs, the Great Lord dusted off some old volumes and took a nostalgic trip back to the Anathema of the Good Old Days." Randall coughed, switching to his best imitation of an upper-class British accent. "Have you heard? Man about college Matthew Richardson has got a girlfriend!"

"OH REALLY?" the members shouted in an equally-bad affectation.

"Well," Randall continued, "I guess hell *has* frozen over."

Mostly upper-years chuckled, both among those standing in line and back in the crowd. Randall looked up and briefly caught sight of Joan blowing her boyfriend a kiss. Matt, who stood a few members down the line to his right, appeared to have rosy cheeks.

"Because he has ADHD, the Great Lord swiftly grew bored of the Good Old Days and went people watching in the Quads instead. He soon noticed the following Cruel Twist of Fate for a man of college:

"*You…*are Doug Sadler…and *you* say you never fuck girls on birth control because you 'like to roll the dice.' In a fortuitous twist of fate, you successfully avoid getting anyone pregnant. In a cruel twist of fate, your right and left hands could've never conceived a child in the first place."

Oohs rose from the crowd.

"While passing time in the West Quad, the Great Lord Anathema—"

"CRCC! CRCC! CRCC!"

"…CRCC," some guy continued.

This time everyone, even those in the crowd, were upon him. *"THREE TIMES, ASSHOLE!"*

"—came up with the following Name Threes for men of college:

"The Debate Society. The Dramatic Society. The Anathema. Name three organizations better off *without* Patrick Mason."

More *Oohs.*

"A baseball cap. A tricorn. His own sphincter. Name three hats Patrick Mason has been known to wear."

Chuckles.

Randall turned the page. "The Sonoran Desert. California after an El Niño. All future Cliffe events. Name three things drier than a girl who's just met Carl Dunlap." The crowd went wild for that one. He could see the Student Events Officer awkwardly laughing along at the back. *Oh, just you wait, pal…*

"Public humiliation. The sound of his own voice. Trees. Name three things that get Brandon Lehane going." Finally, a first-year joke. The frosh seemed to like that one, turning to and joshing a guy who sat near the front. Randall remembered him from the Beckonings. Despite his weird insistence on telling people he *really* liked trees, he'd apparently done well that night and had impressed a few members. Maybe he'd be a candidate for Initiation. But that was a later concern.

"A Lego minifigure. A USB flashdrive. An R3 key. Name three things longer than Patrick Mason's phallus."

The crowd roared. His eyes flicked up in time to see Karen lean over and give the uncomfortable-looking Officer a kiss.

"Writing a standardized test just for American Anathema members, the Great Lord came up with the following SAT Analogy for some men of college:

"Roy Tash is to celibacy as Carl Dunlap is to indoor voice."

The Events Officer laughed loudly from the back row.

"After his mother told him he needed to watch less TV, the Great Lord took a trip to the bookstore and discovered the following page-turners and their Radcliffe equivalents:

"*The Firm* by John Grisham. *The Limp* by Patrick Mason.

"*Extremely Loud and Incredibly Close* by Jonathan Safran Foer. *Extremely Loud and Incredibly Obnoxious* by Carl Dunlap.

"*Moby Dick* by Herman Melville. *Mopey Bitch* by Doug Sadler.

"*Citizen Coke: The Making of Coca-Cola Capitalism. Citizen Coke: The Life of Logan Brewster.*"

Even the Legatus himself found that one amusing. Logan had been laughing along for most of the jokes and appeared to be enjoying himself. *Maybe*, Randall thought, *just maybe, after this he'll admit that we didn't need to go harder. Maybe he'll stop thinking I'm…*

He realized he'd paused the Sermon and that a sad, soft expression had come across his face. Quickly, he snapped out of it. The stern, glowering Imperator returned and tore into the next joke, and the next one, and the next one after that. He hoped nobody had registered that look. Especially Logan. But the Legatus continued to stare at the pages as he lighted them by candle, his face wearing nothing but a blank expression and a Venetian mask.

Finally, Randall reached the last joke.

He drew in a deep breath and read, "To ring in this holiday season, the Great Lord Anathema proudly presents a festive poem for the men of college, as recounted by Patrick Mason."

"Oh God," he heard Patrick say from the audience.

Randall cleared his throat and began.

"'Twas the night before Winter Break, and through all Saunders' beds,
Not a creature was stirring, not even a vein on Blaine's forehead.
The stockings were hung by the windows with care,
In the hopes that good grades soon would be there.

"The douchebags were nestled all snug in their beds,
While visions of sugar-pussy danced in their heads,
And I in my room with my phone in my lap,
Had just settled down for a quick winter's fap.

"When out in the Quad there arose such a clatter,
I sprang from my desk to see what was the matter.
Away to the window, I zipped my pants in a flash,
Tore away the screen and threw up the glass.

"The moon on the breast of the new-fallen snow
Would give lust to Logan for cocaine below,
But, what to my wondering eyes should appear,
But a drunk Officer with a six-pack of beer!

"With shaggy hair that looked matted with sap,
I knew in a minute it must be Carl Dunlap.
Unblinking, he knocked back his hooch at full throttle,
Then cried: 'I spent the last of my budget on this bottle!

" 'Now Brandon, now Freddie, now Gordon Kitt,
Let's go to Blaine's room and fuck up his shit!
To the top of the stairs, to Second Saunders' hall,
Now pube away! Pube away! Pube away all!'

"But as dry leaves that before the hurricane blow,
When met with this obstacle, those first-years said 'NO!
That's a stupid idea, we're not doing this too.'
So alone to Saunders, our Officer flew.

"And then, in a twinkling, I heard down the hall,
The mouthbreathing livestreamer with boisterous footfall.
With my hand in my pants as I turned around,
Into Second Saunders, Carl came with a bound!

"Covered in sweat from his head to his toes,
I watched a greasy tongue lick its way up his nose,
A sack full of pubes he had flung on his back,
He looked like Saint Nicholas if St Nick did crack.

"A bottle of glue he held in his hand,
In his left was a bag of the Safeway brand.
It looked full of dark secrets, but I dared not get a whiff,
This was finally Carl's ticket to good old Social Cliffe.

"He was chubby and plump, a jolly fourth-year elf,
And I laughed when I saw him, in spite of myself;
With a wink of his eye that filled me with dread,
He ran off to the room of Blaine the Fuckhead.

"He spoke not a word, but went straight to his work,
He sized up the doorknob with a devilish smirk.
And pouring the glue upon the cold steel,
He upended the bag and spilled pubes forth with zeal.

"Ensuring the hairs were evenly spread,
He clapped like a seal, turned, and fled.
But I heard him exclaim, as he flopped out of sight,
'Happy Pubesmas to all, and to all a FIRE night!' "

Randall caught his breath. He'd gotten so into the delivery that his face was flushed with crimson. All around him, Anathema members and Sermon attendees were doubled over in fits of laughter. Even Dunlap himself was rolling on the ground in hysterics.

The Imperator smiled, took another deep breath, and turned to the last line of the document. *"HERE ENDETH THE 198TH SERMON OF THE GREAT LORD AN—"*

A blaring trumpet rose on the wind.

The laughter ceased almost instantly, and everyone turned around. Randall looked up and saw a group of figures in balaclavas standing at the top of the hill to his right. One wielded the instrument and the others stood by, waiting.

"It's Lambda Phi!" someone yelled.

But at that moment, he became aware of another group, this one standing at the left part of the upper rim. These figures wore dark cloaks, their faces barely visible beneath their hoods. One stepped forward into the moonlight and Randall saw a green sash across his chest. The other cloaked figures stood by, waiting for an order. One seemed particularly eager, perched on the edge in a half-lunge, half-squat, ready to pounce down the incline. Even the Lambda group appeared to be waiting for his command. The one with the green sash stood still and everyone in the Pit froze.

Then he pointed straight toward the gazebo, toward the Imperator, and at that moment the marauders began to charge down the hill.

TWENTY-NINE

EVERYTHING STARTED happening very quickly.

The next thing Matt knew, dark-clothed figures were rushing through the crowd from right and left, hurtling over seated first-years, swooping in from the sides. The line of members scattered and ran to meet them. The female branch joined from the rear and a massive brawl erupted all around.

Anathema members tussled with marauders. He glimpsed Roy swinging a wine box at two balaclava-wearing men, Tanner pulling a cloaked figure off Hamid, Kylie backhanding a Lambda guy while clutching her medallion with the other hand.

"The skull! Get the skull!" someone shouted.

A balaclava-wearer darted for the gazebo stairs. Matt sprung forward and reached low, grabbing his ankle as he passed by. The guy faceplanted onto the steps, rolling over in pain. Matt had the sudden impulse to apologize when he heard a grunt and a scuffle, looking up to see Randall grappling with another Lambda attacker. Logan wrestled with a third to the side, Doug clutched Uncle to his chest in a corner, and Fennell was off in the crowd somewhere.

Randall cried "Shit!" and the balaclava-wearer leaped over the railing, taking off with something in his hand. Matt turned and sprinted after him, wishing he had worn more comfortable shoes. The thief dashed past Geoff Bhajan, who stood to the side dancing. Matt barely noticed him as he followed his target to the far side of the incline, scrambling up the hill. When he reached the top, the thief looked back down and, seeing Matt hot on his tail, swore and took off.

Matt cursed and continued upward, digging his hands into the dirt for purchase. When he finally made it to the top he was out of breath, but his target appeared to be so too. Matt stumbled after the thief into the trees, barely five meters behind him.

The balaclava-wearer looked back, swore louder this time, and tried to push on faster, grabbing the sides of trees as he passed to speed him up. The cold air seared Matt's lungs, his entire body on fire, but he realized he had little time to catch up—Lambda must have a getaway car waiting and the thief was nearing the road.

◆

Before Joan fully realized what was going on, she was on her feet shoving aside Lambda attackers and assailants in cloaks as she pushed her way to the center of the brawl. Deep within her, an anger stirred. It rose, thirsting for the blood of a trespasser, an intruder on the ritual. The feeling rushed through her, curling her lips into a snarl and lighting a blaze in her eyes.

Suddenly, Joan stopped, standing there in the middle of frightened, fleeing first-years and the throng of duking upper-years. She hadn't felt that kind of violent desire in a long time, and for a second it actually scared her—

"Hey!" she heard Val cry, and turned to see a cloaked figure attacking her, reaching for the pendant around her neck.

Instantly, the fire was back and Joan charged forward. She grabbed the marauder by their shoulders, pulled them back, and shoved them with all her strength against the nearest picnic table. The figure hit it at an angle and tumbled across it with a loud, male-sounding grunt.

She turned back to Val, her expression softening. "You okay?"

"Yeah." Val steadied herself and put a hand to her head. "He was trying to get my..." She touched her upper chest, then her eyes widened as she grasped nothing but air and fabric. "Shit, I think he..."

A whistle came behind them. Joan spun to see the attacker standing on the other side of the table. It was him, the one with the green sash. She couldn't see his facial expression for he wore a balaclava beneath the hood, but his eyes narrowed with malice as he dangled Val's necklace toward them. As they watched, he swung it twice through the air, looping the chain around his palm, then caught the pendant as his hand tightened into a fist.

Laughing, the assailant turned and fled to her left. The next thing Joan knew, she was running after him across the Pit, up another hillside—and into the dark woods beyond.

◆

If there was a getaway car, it wasn't parked at the curb.

As the thief broke from the treeline and ran for the main road, he pulled out his phone while still clutching whatever he'd stolen with the other hand. He dashed out into the street, heading toward the main drag and shouting: "No, no! I need the pickup location moved!"

Matt hit the asphalt and continued after him, his lungs and throat burning, the frosty air biting his face and ears. Everything stung or ached or hurt. He thought of how cool action heroes looked in movies, whether it was Ethan Hunt doing parkour across rooftops or Jason Bourne dashing after an assassin. Yet here he was stumbling after some douchey frat fuck, on the brink of suffering a pulmonary hemorrhage. The thief didn't appear to be fairing cinematically either, faltering in his half-jog, half-walk in the middle of the road.

Headlights drew nearer toward them, but the frat guy didn't dive out of the way until the last second. The SUV honked and swerved and Matt instinctively leaped to the side. He clambered onto the sidewalk and continued following the bastard, who looked back and yelled, "Fuck off, man!"

Matt couldn't think of a good comeback, which was just as well, since it was taking a lot of effort just to breathe. His eyes stayed fixed on the thief and he tried to pick up his pace, jogging after him. A couple huddled in parkas got out of their way and looked on, confused by the sight of the running man in the balaclava and the tuxedo-clad pursuer with a mask and a skull pendant.

He had closed the gap considerably by the time they reached the bars, but a black sedan with the glowing Lyft icon pulled up to the curb. The Lambda guy frantically threw the rear door open. Thinking quickly, Matt took a deep breath, pulled open the front passenger door, and collapsed on the seat.

"Please, sir," he told the driver, somehow coherent, "he's taken something from me and I need him to give it back." He took another deep breath, this one much more pleasant. The heated air inside caressed his upper body. His legs were still outside in the cold.

The thief tore off his balaclava; Matt recognized him as one of the guys who'd manned the table outside the Halloween party. "I have never seen this man in my life," he managed to get out.

"That's not true," Matt gasped. "I just chased him for several blocks. He's from the Lambda Phi Alpha fraternity, he just raided a...um, Radcliffe College event in Riverside Park. I just need him to give it back to me."

The driver looked bewildered. "Do you want me to call the police?"

The thief leaned his head back and rolled his eyes. "Oh, for *fuck's* sake..."

"No, no," Matt said. "I just need him to give it back."

The thief gripped the back of the driver's seat and leaned forward. "I will give you the biggest fucking tip of your life if you step on the gas *right now*."

Matt finally saw what he had in his hand. It was just the last three, crumpled sheets of the Sermon. He recognized the text of "The Night Before Pubesmas" typed clearly upon them. Now that it had been read aloud, they were worthless. A massive sigh of disappointment escaped him.

What did you think this douche had gotten, Randall's fucking medallion? The whole chase had been a waste of time.

"You know what? It doesn't matter. Have a nice night." He pulled himself out of the vehicle and shut the door. The Lyft took off and a rear window rolled down, the thief sticking his head out.

"You dusty cuck!" the guy shouted, then howled and pulled himself back into the car.

"I don't even know what that's supposed to mean." Matt winced; it hurt all over his body, inside and out.

Just before the sedan reached the bend, a cry of "FUCK!" escaped the still-open window, followed by three pages that were flung into the night. Evidently, the marauder had realized their worth too.

Matt hugged his arms against his chest and began making his way back to Riverside, though it did little to keep him warm. His mood had descended again. *What did you think was gonna happen? You were gonna come back having saved some priceless Anathema artifact and everyone would be so impressed? Now they'll just think you're an idiot for chasing after nothing.*

He brought out his flask and took a very long pull.

◆

Joan found it harder to breathe the deeper she got into the trees.

The green-sash wearing raider charged ahead, still at full sprint as he broke free from the woods. She doubled over on her knees once she came into the clearing, then looked up to find herself at Riverside Park's playground. A climbing structure with monkey bars and a slide stood next to a swing set; a sandbox was off to the right.

And there he was, catching his breath as he neared the structure. He put a hand on a support beam and stood there, hunched forward, his back rising and falling as he inhaled and exhaled.

The night had suddenly gotten very quiet. She could no longer hear sounds of the brawl back in the Pit. Few clouds hung in the sky and an almost-full moon shone down among the stars. She found something about the scene unsettling as she stepped closer, her gloved hands balling into fists. Once she got within ten feet of him, she raised her voice and said, "I just want it back."

The cloaked figure straightened up. For a moment, he stared off at something, then turned around. He stretched out his right hand and dangled Val's pendant, taunting her with his eyes as he gently swung it back and forth.

She noticed then that resting over his green sash was a silver pendant of a snake eating its own tail. The metallic ouroboros glinted in the moonlight, dangling from a chain necklace. A memory of Catherine reading the History a couple weeks ago stirred in her mind, but she merely shook her head, unbelieving. *They were dissolved in the 1920s. That can't be…unless…*

"Just give it back," she managed to say, extending her hand. Fear had crept into her voice and she hoped he hadn't heard it. It was very cold out and she was unable to stop herself from shivering. Her teeth started to chatter; she clenched them tightly and narrowed her eyes at him.

He stared back, saying nothing. Then his gaze flicked to her right and left. Joan spun around and found herself surrounded by cloaked figures on all sides. She hadn't heard them coming and their sudden appearance startled her, the fear now visible on her face. From what she could see of their bodies beneath the cloaks, some seemed to be male and some female, but she didn't get a good count on each. One of them chuckled as he stepped closer.

She looked back to the leader, the one with the green sash. He pointed at Val's pendant, then gestured for Joan to hand him her own, illustrating her walking away with two of his fingers.

Her hand closed around the tiny skull. Joan shook her head.

Disappointment flickered in the leader's eyes. He gestured to one of his underlings and jerked his head toward Joan. Suddenly a figure was lunging for her. She turned and ran around the play-structure. Another dove toward her; Joan turned and leaped, grabbing the side of the platform where the monkey bars began and hauling herself up.

She scrambled up the steps toward the slide, then looked back. Two of them had followed her up here, hatred burning in their eyes as they pulled themselves onto the structure. Another had to be waiting at the bottom of the slide. Thinking quickly, she began to go down it legs first, then braked with her boots halfway down, and, with all her might, leaped over the side.

It was a good five feet down from where she'd jumped. She didn't exactly land right and the breath was knocked from her lungs as she hit the ground, toppling over, her hands grasping at mulch. She didn't stop to look back. Panting, she sprung to her feet and arced back around the playground toward where she'd come from. She glimpsed blurred shadows moving in her peripheral, drawing closer.

Joan pumped her legs harder and made it back to the treeline, the woods closing in around her. Fallen leaves crunched beneath her boots and she was careful not to trip without losing her speed. Twigs snapped behind her, the footfalls growing closer and closer, the heavy breathing of her pursuers reaching a crescendo in her ears—

She came to the hilltop but didn't slow her pace, stumbling her way down the steep slope. About halfway to the bottom, she lost her footing and tumbled the rest of the way. She rolled to a halt, hurting all over, but didn't let the pain stop her as she glanced back up the hill. Her assailants hadn't reached the top yet. Hurriedly, she got to her feet and took off back into the Pit. All attendees had vanished save for four Anathema members: Randall, Doug, Sandrine, and Val. From here, she could hear them discussing something about the podium being damaged, but she barely listened.

She'd never been so happy to see anyone and limped toward them as fast as she could. She must've hurt her ankle on the way down. It hurt to breathe in the cold and blood pounded in her ears. The four noticed her and turned, quizzical expressions on their faces as they came closer.

"You alright?" Randall asked.

"What happened?" Val said.

Joan looked back. There was no sign of her pursuers. She doubled over and put her hands on her knees. Her black jeans had ripped and she was bleeding from her right leg, but she barely noticed the sting of the scrape with her other senses overloaded. She gasped for air, trying to calm herself, but it hurt in this fucking frigid air.

Sandrine put a hand on her back. "Did someone attack you?"

She pointed back up the hill that led to the playground. "They surrounded me...up there...tried to take my pendant..." She shook her head, then looked up at Val. "I couldn't...get yours back..."

"Lambda fucking Phi," Randall grunted, shaking his head. "I'm gonna have a little chat with Geoff about this. That's fucking unacceptable. He needs to control his own goddamn people."

"It wasn't...Lambda," she managed to get out. "They wore...cloaks and...had...snake pendants."

All four of them were silent. Val looked completely lost, but Randall, Doug, and Sandrine exchanged looks. "You don't think...?" Doug began, but his voice trailed off.

They looked toward where Joan had come from, but there was nothing there except dark forest and leaves rustling in the wind.

THIRTY

B y the time he'd collected the scattered pages off the road, thrown them away in a bin, and started back to Riverside, a large crowd had exited the park and was making its way toward him. It turned out the brawl had ended already and people were now headed for the Foxhole.

So Matt went with them, ordered himself a rye and ginger at the bar, and downed half of it before going to find Roy, who had already gotten a gin and tonic. They were chatting about their poem's reception when Joan entered with Val, Doug, Sandrine, and Randall. They removed their masks as they walked through the door; his girlfriend looked shaken.

Excusing himself from Roy, he headed straight over to her. "What happened?"

"I'll tell you later," she said, looking somehow even paler than she had before. "I need a drink." She moved to the bar and Doug, Sandrine, and Val did the same.

Randall turned to him. "Hey, where did you go?" He chuckled. "Last I saw, you were chasing that guy up the hill."

Matt reluctantly told him what had happened, adding that he assumed the marauder had snatched something important. When he was done, the Imperator merely stared at him. "So you chased him several blocks and tried to stop him getting in a Lyft over three sheets of useless paper?"

Matt sighed. "Pretty much."

Randall burst out laughing. "Legendary! I love it." He patted him on the shoulder. "Now Anathema will remember that time Matt Richardson chased a frat guy across town."

His mood brightened. "You think?"

"I don't think, I *know*. I'm gonna go get a beer, but I'll see you around. You definitely earned that drink." Randall moved off and Matt took a sip to hide his smile. However, his thoughts quickly returned to Joan and he went to find her.

The Foxhole was packed, as it always was after a Sermon. Matt pushed his way through the throng of people at the bar and bumped into Patrick, who held a pint of beer.

"I told you Randall was gonna rail me." He didn't seem too upset.

"What did you think of the last poem?"

"He'd told me you, Joan, and Roy cooked up something special. I was not disappointed, even though I apparently stood around holding my dick while Carl glued pubes to a—speaking of which, is that *actually* true?"

Matt nodded.

Patrick looked away. "Mother*fucker*. That Facebook comment about helping me solve it was just B.S. then." He shook his head. "So Randall's the head of a cult, Carl glued pubes to a person's doorknob…and that makes me the only sane male Officer this year. Oh wait, I forgot I sold my humanity to the admin." Now there was a bitter edge to his voice. He took a big swig of beer. "See you at Ni Hao."

"See you," Matt said. He tried to think of something to say, but Patrick was already gone. Sighing, he turned and moved down the bar, trying to spot his girlfriend.

◆

It took him nearly five minutes to find her. When he did, she was already almost done her first drink, which by her account was a double.

"You okay?" he asked.

"Just a little rattled, that's all. Anyway, I'm glad the poem did well!"

"Yeah, people seemed to like it. Even Dunlap."

Her eyes widened. "Look, there he is." She pointed and he turned. Sure enough, the Student Events Officer was chatting up the attendees, telling them how it had *really* gone down while they laughed along. Evidently people disliked Blaine more than they found Dunlap's actions reprehensible.

Matt and Joan walked around the bar and chatted with their friends, hanging out first with Sophia and Val, then Roy and Tanner, and eventually Turland, Randall and their girlfriends Caitlyn and Gemma. Doug soon joined them with his arm around a short, blonde first-year girl. By the way she laughed at his jokes and gazed at him when he wasn't looking, Matt could tell she was into him.

He was happy for Doug, who'd been hit at Sermons for a lack of romantic success longer than Matt had, but at the same time he realized that if Doug hooked up with her, he'd be mocked by everyone as a fourth-year who slept with a first-year.

Randall had just finished telling the group what happened with Matt and the page-thief, when Logan suddenly leaned into their circle, putting one arm around Randall's shoulder and the other around Turland's. He had a big grin on his face, clearly buzzed.

"Hey," Logan said. "We're heading over to Ni Hao. Settle up and come on." He moved off.

"Well, I guess we're going then," Randall chuckled, finishing his drink.

Joan chugged the rest of hers and returned the glass to the bar, then came back over and took Matt by the hand; she still felt a bit cold and his worry grew.

Randall turned to Patrick and Karen, who stood by the ATM machine in the corner. "Hey Big P, we're going!"

"Big P? That's my fuckin' name now?" Patrick gave them a wide smile; the bitterness he'd let slip earlier had either been tempered by alcohol or was being deliberately hidden.

"Come on," Turland said. "We're heading to Ni Hao."

"Of course." Patrick came closer, Karen in tow. "How could I forget the *other* four eternal words?"

"Shut the fuck up?" Turland asked, grinning.

Patrick drunkenly wagged a finger at him. "*No*... The *other*, other four eternal words: General Tso's Chicken Poppers."

Randall shook his head. "That's just a disgrace to proper Chinese food."

"Ni Hao Ma itself is a disgrace to proper Chinese food," Patrick said. "I have been to Shanghai, and I can tell you that the restaurant where we are heading is the most Westernized bullshit Asian fusion place I have been to in my life."

Doug shrugged. "Yeah, but I could totally fuck with some chicken poppers right now."

Their group made for the door and came out onto the main drag, the icy breeze biting their skin. The restaurant was just across the street. They waited to make sure no cars were coming, then walked into the road. Matt and Joan trailed behind the others.

"So…you really chased some Lambda guy all the way here from Riverside, huh?"

"Yep, and it was all a big waste of effort."

"I don't think so. Randall seems impressed."

"Maybe."

"You *still* ran several blocks in this weather." Joan leaned closer. "So… what you're telling me is…you've got stamina?" She gave him a flirtatious smile and it took him a moment to realize what she was getting at.

He laughed awkwardly, unsure of how to respond. No one had ever said anything like that to him before, not even girls who'd hit on him. "You never say that kind of stuff when you're sober."

She laughed too. "*Trust* me, I'm thinking it." And she kissed him on the cheek.

Excitement and nervousness pulled him in opposite directions. Before he could say something else, they'd arrived. Turland held the door open and ushered them in.

Ni Hao Ma was wide and spacious, its tables round with seats for ten. The walls were blue with red dragons painted along them. Since they were the first ones from the Sermon crowd here, they grabbed the table closest to the window. Fortunately, there were just enough chairs to fit all of them.

Matt ended up sitting between Joan and Randall. On Randall's right was Gemma, followed by Caitlyn, Turland, Patrick, Karen, the first-year girl, and Doug on Joan's left. A waiter came around.

"Anything to drink for you?"

Doug turned to the girl beside him. "Abby, what will you have?"

"Just water," she said, looking up at the waiter.

Matt asked for the same but Joan requested a beer. *What the fuck happened?* She usually only got this wasted when trying to push something out of her mind.

Patrick, Turland, Karen, and Caitlyn also ordered beers but the others just went for water. Once the waiter had gone, Matt looked between them and said, "So who were those cloaked guys with Lambda?" He'd only gotten a brief look at them before taking off after the thief.

Joan, Doug, and Randall froze. Everyone else at the table looked confused.

"I don't know," Randall said after a moment. "Probably just more Lambda guys, trying to freak us out by wearing cloaks like we do. Well, like Kylie and I do."

Turland looked ready to ask Randall another question, when suddenly the door chimed and more attendees walked in. Val and Sophia entered hand-in-hand and Roy was accompanied by both Jennifer and Pandora. He turned when he saw Matt and Joan already seated and pointed to the Anamicable President.

"Look who showed up to the afterparty!"

Pandora waved to both of them and Jennifer rolled her eyes. "Let's get seats," she said, heading toward the back. Pandora continued after her, seemingly oblivious.

Roy looked from his two dates to the table and back again, then turned once more to the group and said, "I'll talk to you guys later" before taking off after the girls.

Doug chuckled and shook his head. "Good old Roy Tash."

"Now there's a juggling act," Gemma said with a laugh.

More and more people trickled in from the Foxhole. A steady stream crossed the main drag, interrupted by the occasional passing car. As usual, the seats near the front filled up first. Logan and Lisa arrived with their arms around each other's shoulders, both looking very inebriated. After seeing the chairs next to Randall were taken, they made for the back of the restaurant.

Abby turned to Doug. "So...why is it the Great *Lord* Anathema when the rest of the rankings are from the Roman Legion?"

"Ah yes," the Magister said, adjusting his glasses and sitting up straighter. "Well, you see, the college was founded by Lord Thaddeus Radcliffe, who was big on spreading British culture to the Canadian West. That's why the architecture resembles UK universities so much. He founded this place to be rooted in Presbyterian traditions, while providing a home for Classical Studies at WCU. Radcliffe himself had studied the Classical Era and Philosophy at Cambridge. So the name Great *Lord* Anathema was a nod to him, and as for the rest of the ranks... Well, Gordon MacTaggart, the first

Imperator, was a Classical Studies major. He took names from the Roman Legion, but didn't stick with their exact order."

"He just thought Imperator sounded the coolest and took that for himself?" she asked.

"Pretty much, yeah. There was a lot of debate in the nineties when they added a fourth position as to what it would be called."

"There were only three originally?"

"Yeah, we had Triads until about '98. Imperator, Legatus, and Magister. Then we realized we needed a full-time PR manager in each branch, and so they agreed Pontifex would be the fourth position, a kind of publicist."

"Triad sounds a lot cooler than Tetrad," she said.

Doug shrugged. "Yeah, but they were a lot less effective, let me tell you that."

Randall laughed. "Right, as if they're effective now."

Doug sat up straighter. "I have been a very effective Magister."

Randall raised his eyebrows.

He paled. "Oh…right."

◆

The conversation wore on and the night along with it.

Joan downed another beer and began laughing more and more at things that were said. When the food arrived, she and Matt split an order of General Tso's Chicken Poppers but he wasn't sure if it would mix well in her stomach with the alcohol. Even he felt it was too greasy. Matt watched her put her hand to her gut several times, queasy looks passing over her face. While Turland tried to explain his favorite novel *Infinite Jest* to the table, Matt leaned over and whispered, "Are you alright?"

"I…I…" She didn't look okay.

"We should probably go," he said, glancing at his watch. "It's nearly 1 a.m."

She nodded reluctantly. "I'll get an Uber." She took out her phone and opened the app.

The waiter came around with a credit card machine and everyone's bills. After paying, Matt looked around the table. Though things were winding down, the group would probably stay another twenty minutes or so. They wouldn't miss much.

Joan peeked at her phone, then turned to him. "Uber's almost here."

Matt turned to the others. "Alright everyone, it's been fun but—"

"He's just gonna see me off. I'm calling it a night. He'll be right back in though."

Matt was about to say something when she firmly gripped his arm beneath the table. "Sure," he finally got out.

Joan stood up, wobbling only slightly as she made her way to the door. Matt followed her and once they were outside, they walked left until they were out of sight from everyone at the table. They stood in a darkened area of the sidewalk, away from the end of the main drag.

She groaned and held her belly with both hands. "Need to puke?" he asked.

Joan thought for a moment. "I can probably hold it till I get back to Lacy."

"Better to go before the Uber arrives. Ares Donovan threw up in one during Initiations last year and *that* was a shitshow."

She considered it. "It's still a minute or so away."

"Then why are we out here now? And why did you say I'd be right back in?"

"Because you will be."

He laughed. "That doesn't answer my question."

Joan sighed and walked over to him, placing both hands on his shoulders. He smiled and put his arms around her waist. "Don't throw up on me again."

She rolled her eyes. "I'm not, just… You need to get back in there and impress Randall." She set about adjusting his bowtie.

He smiled, amused. "It's after one in the morning and I'm drunk and tired. How am I going to do that?"

Joan finished straightening it. "I don't know, but… I saw the way he and Logan talked to each other at the bar. And I've seen them talk before, but this time it just hit me… It was so casual and chill and they're good friends but…Logan gives him a lot of flak and Randall just kind of takes it. He doesn't dish it back at him. And I've heard Logan's been calling him the Pussy Imperator."

Matt raised an eyebrow. "Well, that's just dumb."

"I don't think that's why he's saying it, though. I *saw* the way they interact and…I think it's a strategy. I think Logan is trying to chip away at Randall and get him to bend to his will. And name him his successor."

"Logan Brewster doesn't seem like the manipulative type to me. He just acts like a careless fuckwit."

A sedan came around the bend, the Uber logo glowing on its dashboard. Joan shook her head. "People can be manipulative without even realizing it. It doesn't matter. I want *you* to be Imperator and I sure as shit don't want you to lose it to that asshole." He felt her hot breath on his face as she spoke; she seemed really fired up about this. The car pulled up alongside them. Matt motioned for the driver to wait just a second.

"Look, I really appreciate that, but I'm not putting you alone and drunk in the back of an Uber."

Joan looked past him and waved. He turned around, one of her arms still around his shoulder, and saw Sophia and Val heading toward them, still holding hands. "Hey," Joan said. "Wanna ride with me back to Cliffe?"

"Sure," Val said, and she and Sophia walked past them to climb into the backseat.

Joan wrapped both arms around him again. "See? I'll be fine."

"Are you sure—?"

"Yes." She caressed his cheek. "You'll see me tomorrow. Come wake me up and we can have some fun before brunch." She ran a finger down his side, then gazed at his lips.

Matt's pulse started racing and he gave an awkward laugh. "Right. Um, sure, definitely brunch… But I'm not sure if we should, you know, go *there* yet." He managed another laugh, wanting to smack himself. *What are you waiting for, you idiot?*

Joan looked disappointed for a moment, but then smiled again. "Right, of course. No rush."

"Text me when you're in your room safely, though. If you're still up when I get back, I can swing by and make sure you're alright."

She looked amused. "This isn't the first time I've done this, Matt. But you're very sweet." She kissed him, then pushed him off. "Now *go*." He started heading back to Ni Hao Ma, but glanced back to watch her climb in and shut the door. The sedan did a U-turn and headed back along the main road.

Matt re-entered the restaurant to find everyone at the table still chatting, save for Randall and Gemma, who were standing and putting on their jackets. When the Imperator saw Matt enter, he whispered something to his girlfriend, and made his way over just as Matt headed for his seat.

"Hey, I've gotta talk to you about something real quick."

"Sure. Wanna chat outside, or…?"

A large crowd passed behind them, most with their phones out waiting for rides.

"Actually," Randall said, "I think we'll be better off downstairs by the restrooms." They went through a door to the side and headed down a flight of steps. Roy and Pandora were having a conversation about halfway from the bottom.

"…but how can you keep getting away with it?" Pandora laughed.

He shrugged. "That's the Roy Tash charm, babe." He looked up and saw them. "Oh, hey guys."

"Sup," Randall said.

"You got a little something right here," Pandora teased Matt, pointing to her lips. He rubbed his with a finger, realizing Joan's black lipstick had rubbed off when she kissed him. He wiped his mouth with the back of his hand.

Once they passed Roy and Pandora, the two went back upstairs. Randall looked around the basement corridor, which housed four small restrooms. They waited a moment, but heard no sounds. "Okay, I think we're good." He turned back to Matt.

"Did I get all of it?" he asked.

Randall chuckled. "Yeah… So, anyway…I talked to Rufus yesterday about…you know…"

He nodded.

"…and it's all taken care of. Everything should be good now. He said he doesn't have anything against you; even he's noticed he sometimes writes a lot of jokes about one person and then snaps out of it. That's all."

"But what about the things he told Tanner?"

"Well, I couldn't pretend to have heard that. I just made it seem like this was something I'd noticed myself. But talking to him, it really didn't seem like he has a problem with you. He was quite apologetic."

Matt sighed with relief, but part of him still felt uneasy. "Thank you."

"No worries."

"Is Joan okay? She didn't tell me what happened. At least, she hasn't yet."

Randall gave a dismissive wave. "It's fine. Lambda just went all out this year, which is annoying. I'm gonna have a talk with Geoff and he's just gonna have to get his people in line. It's unacceptable that they still raid us every year. I'd hoped that would've died out by now." He shrugged. "Guess not."

The two of them headed back upstairs. For a moment, the corridor was quiet, then Rufus Danvers exited one of the restrooms, drying his hands with a paper towel. He heard the door close on the upper floor and scoffed to himself.

"So that's how you've been playing it…"

THIRTY-ONE

C RAWLEY KNOCKED on the Provost's office door. She heard his voice say, "Shit, I forgot I had a meeting now. Hold on, hold on, we'll talk about this later." Then, louder, "Come on in!"

She opened the door slowly and entered, feeling like an intruder. John Mustard stood behind his desk in exercise clothes, drenched in sweat and holding his phone to his ear. "I'll call you in the afternoon, Mark. I've gotta go." He hung up and his expression brightened. "Donna! How are you this fine Monday morning?"

Beyond the windows, gray clouds blotted the sky. She shrugged. "Alright, I guess. Business as usual."

"Good, good. Take a seat." She did so and Mustard did the same. She noticed a Jazzercise DVD sitting beside a disk drive plugged into his laptop. Mustard's eyes followed hers and he quickly snatched the case off the desk, shoving it in a drawer. Then he smiled, sighed, and folded his hands on the desk.

"I've reached a decision about the Formals."

Crawley exhaled. "Oh good, I've been telling students Fall Formal should be back on track soon. It'll be nice to make it official for them. Is it still going to be next Friday or should we push it to the 30th?"

"No, Donna. I'm *cancelling* the Fall Formal this year."

She sat up straighter. "Wait, why?"

He held up his hands. "It was a tough decision to make, but I just don't think the students are ready to have a big event like this."

"What about the Winter Formal?"

"Ah," he said, raising a finger. "That one will still happen…*if* the kids behave."

"But the Fall dance is a charity ball. We had a Banff conservation group lined up for this year."

"So we'll make Winter Formal the charity ball instead and they'll get their money then. Beggars can't be choosers. We are fighting to modernize an institution here, Donna. The trees can wait."

"It was an animal conservation group, actually," she said, looking at the desk.

He shrugged. "Whatever. The point is, Fall Formal isn't happening. I'm going to send out an email tonight saying that both myself and the Dean's Office would prefer if we only had one Formal this year, and that student behavior at that event will decide the fate of all future on-campus parties. Then they'll inevitably get too drunk and mess that one up, so next year we can do away with them altogether."

"But those events were held even during both World Wars."

Mustard shrugged. "Then congratulations, we will achieve what the Axis could not." He paused and held up his hands. "I didn't mean it like that."

Crawley nodded. "Of course." She bit her lip. "But…those events were good for students to blow off steam. It gave them something to look forward to."

"Yes Donna, but when students 'let off steam' at this college, they get wildly drunk. Ambulances have to be called. *Six* at last year's Winter Formal alone, and that was just for alcohol poisoning—not to mention the one girl who fought off Réjean when he tried to escort her out. Oh, and property damage. That's a big one. The sign outside the Dales Building was smashed after QuadFest last year, the bathrooms in Winslow regularly get wrecked at just about every res party—the list goes on."

He started speaking faster. "Oh, I know what they say about us, Donna. We're the stuffy, evil admin trying to take away their fun and games. But what they don't see is that they're spoiled brats who cause thousands of dollars of damage every year and create endless legal migraines for those of us who try to run this place. *Sure*, less of them are from private schools than they used to be, and *sure* they're more diverse nowadays. But many of them still adopt all these old traditions. And do you know *why*? Because most of them involve getting wasted. It's much nobler to say you're into traditions than to admit you're a hedonist. They create clubs that exist just to have drinking events! They bastardized one of the oldest debating societies in Canada so they could make stupid speeches and get drunk on free beer!"

His face grew red. "That's all undergrad is to them, Donna—a booze-filled, four-year summer camp. And you and I are the counselors. We have to keep things under control. We have to *maintain* discipline and remind them that this is the most prestigious college in one of the most prestigious post-secondary institutions on *Earth* and that they are not going to tarnish its name any longer. I will *not* have Radcliffe be the problem child of WCU anymore."

Mustard caught his breath. "It's all for the good of the students."

Crawley nodded slowly. "I agree that the traditions are mainly excuses for drinking and that the alcohol culture here is a problem, but they'll become even *more* upset with us after this. They'll just take their parties underground, or go to other events…*dissociated* events."

Mustard inhaled through his teeth. "Right. *Them.*"

THIRTY-TWO

THAT TUESDAY, Matt ended up sitting with Randall and Logan at lunch. He had originally been making his way toward the Imperator, but then saw Logan across from him and froze with doubt. Before he could locate another place to sit, Randall spotted him and called, "Hey Richardson, over here!"

So Matt sat down to his left.

"We were just talking about Mustard's email. Did you read it?" Randall asked.

"No, but I heard about it. It's B.S. that they cancelled Fall Formal. I always liked the free bubbly."

"Yeah, same," Logan said, leaning back in his seat. "But what did we expect, really? Mustard's a fuckin' piece of shit. At least his dumb new alcohol policy will increase Second Sermon attendance."

"Potentially." Randall took a sip of apple juice. "I think the lack of parties lured more people to the First. We had pretty good attendance."

"Yeah, but you were still too soft on the first-years. Some of them came up to me at the Foxhole and were literally like, 'Hey, why didn't you hit us harder?' " He laughed. "I'm telling you; they're *asking* us for it. Literally. They want to be spanked."

Randall laughed. "Look, we didn't know that before the Sermon and just because a few satirical masochists are begging for more doesn't mean that we have to hit everybody harder. It's better to be safe than sorry."

Logan sighed. "There you go again with this safety bullshit. That's all it is with you—safety, safety, safety."

Matt was taken aback. *Is he joking?*

Randall laughed again. "Yeah, well, I'm an Officer. Safety is one of my concerns—both for the students, and for the Anathema."

"You know what I bet you do every night? You curl up in bed and stroke yourself down there moaning, *'Safety, safety, safety.'*" He jerked his body in a mock orgasm, then looked back at Randall with disappointment. "You can't even last seven seconds when you're thinking about *safety.*"

Matt was horrified, but Randall just chuckled along. *Joan was right,* he realized.

"Cut it out," the Imperator said, still laughing. "Anyway, we're done for this semester, so I can finally focus on my non-Anathema shit, i.e. everything else."

Logan shook his head. "So much safety, so little time."

Carl Dunlap sat down beside the Legatus. "Hey guys, what's up? Also, I've just gotta say that was a fire Sermon, Jack. Absolute fire."

Randall nodded. "Glad you took it well, Carl."

"Hey," he said, leaning closer. "So with Fall Formal cancelled, I've been talking to a bunch of people—other Officers, my Winslow boys, the Lacy girls, even a few Saunders guys—"

"Not Blaine, I'm assuming?" Logan raised an eyebrow.

Dunlap forced a laugh. "No, no, not him—anyway, we're getting a bunch of people to pitch in for our own cheap bubbly to make Winslow Christmas the biggest it's ever been. It's still several weeks away, but spread the word. The bubbly's just over $15 a pop. We've already got twenty bottles donated, but we're aiming for forty—or more. If you guys could pitch in too, that'd be great."

"*Forty* bottles?" Matt asked, incredulous.

"You know how fast Cliffe students go through booze," Logan said. "We ran out of wine in like, five minutes at the Sermon. Roy was swinging an empty box at those Lambda idiots."

"Just spread the word," Dunlap reminded them, standing up. "We're gonna make this the most *fire* Christmas party ever."

◆

Weeks went by.

The air grew colder, the remaining leaves fell from the trees, and snow kissed the ground, but never for more than a few days at a time. It was an unusually warm November, at least by Albertan standards. No one was sure if it meant a mild winter was in store for them, or if a brutal one was just around the corner.

As the semester drew to a close, the end-of-term workload sucked Matt and Joan's lives into its vortex. Even full-year classes had midterms and essays due the weeks leading up to Exam Week, so instead of going on dates or outings with friends, much of the time they spent together was in Mackenzie Library.

Joan didn't mind. She enjoyed his company and found that with both of them equally swamped by assignments, they were able to concentrate without distracting each other.

The upside to the grind was that it kept her mind off certain burning questions. Randall, Doug, and Sandrine hadn't wanted to discuss the cloaked marauders' affiliation after that night; Val had said her guess was as good as Joan's. She'd told Matt about what happened the following day, along with her theory, but while he believed her, he hadn't said anything about it since.

And yet, she frequently noticed him looking troubled. She'd watched him staring off, deep in thought, several times in the past few weeks and couldn't help but wonder if the same question was on his mind too. Finally, on the second day of December, the Sunday before the final week of fall classes, she decided to ask him as they sat in a study room on Mackenzie's third floor. They had a northern view looking out across the town and its woodlands, mountain ranges farther in the distance. The highway was visible from here too, curving out of sight as it headed toward Banff National Park.

"You've been thinking about it."

Matt turned to her; he'd been gazing out the window. "Thinking about what?"

"What I said. My theory about the people who raided the Sermon."

He paused. "Yeah, I have."

"And?"

He seemed to debate something internally, then one side won out. "I've been wondering how it connects to some…other stuff that's been going on here."

"Like the missing skull?"

"That, and…" He sighed. "Rich Benson."

A chill shot down her spine, but all she said was, "That's interesting." She looked back down at her Global Macroeconomics textbook and began chewing a nail. Quickly, she noticed what she was doing and pulled it out of her mouth.

"I didn't want to mention it because I know you and him…"

"We never actually dated," she blurted out.

He looked surprised. "Oh, my bad. I'd heard that you did."

"I *thought* we were dating, but…" She let her voice trail off.

Matt took the hint. "Right, sorry."

"Don't be. I want to hear your theory."

He laughed. "My theory?"

"Yes."

He shook his head. "I don't really have one yet about how it connects—"

"Not how it connects, just your theory about *him*. You think somebody killed him?"

Matt nodded. "Roy and I looked into it a little while ago…" He told her about their visit to *The Westerner* and what Dinesh had said, then what Peter Larch had told him, along with some other observations he'd made.

Joan sat back in her seat, glancing around the wood-paneling of the room. There was an interior window to her right. It looked out through the book stacks and she saw some other students quietly studying at a table in the center aisle. The lighting was dim, as it usually was in Mackenzie, but at least their study room seemed to have brighter bulbs.

That Rich had been working on a big article was news to her. She tried to fit it in with everything else she knew.

Matt watched her. "I know it's probably crazy to be looking into this stuff when not even the RCMP suspected anything, but I just got curious and—"

"Really, it's fine." She gave him a warm smile.

He returned it, then leaned back in his seat. "I just don't get how it connects to Serpentine, though. If that's who those people really were."

"The original Serpentine was founded to oppose Anathema. I can't think of any other groups who would attack us wearing snake pendants."

"But they got absorbed into Anathema at the end of the 1920s."

"Somebody must've brought them back recently," she said.

"Wait. You told me you chased a guy with a green sash, like how our

Tetrads wear silver sashes. So do you think this guy is the Vizier, like the History said?"

"Yeah. And I think this new Serpentine is co-ed. It looked like the people surrounding me were both male and female, so I think there's only one Bard and one Vizier. They probably don't have enough members to justify two branches."

"But then if the Vizier was the one calling the shots that night, where was the Bard?"

"Maybe in the crowd, watching. That's what I would've done, just to keep an eye on things. The History said they used to wear veils over their faces to hide their identities, but this person doesn't even need to do *that* anymore. Back in the day they gave competing Sermons, but I think this new Serpentine is more of a militant anti-Anathema organization. The Bard wouldn't have to do anything in person, just relay information to the Vizier and have them oversee the dirty work."

"But then who is the Bard?"

Joan shrugged. "Somebody who knows the History."

"But both branches read that to the frosh every year at the Beckonings."

"Most of them don't pay attention; they're too drunk by then."

"So…you think it's somebody in Anathema?"

"Well, it fits with your theory that Benson was onto one of us. What if Serpentine was the secret they were trying to keep under wraps, so the Bard killed him?"

"Wait, wait, wait. If somebody was willing to kill to keep the existence of a second secret society at Radcliffe hidden, why would they attack us wearing snake pendants? That kind of gives their whole game away."

Joan bit her lip and tapped on the table. She knew she should be studying. "I don't know. Maybe the Bard didn't kill Benson and it's unrelated. Or maybe someone in Serpentine other than the Bard killed him, someone who's also in Anathema. But I bet Serpentine stole your skull, and I want to find out who's behind them."

"I mean, I do too, but…*how?*"

"Somebody at Lambda has to know something. Their guys raided us with Serpentine's help."

"*If* they really are Serpentine."

"Yes, but you told me you saw the Vizier giving the signal for *all* of them to charge down the hill, not just his own people."

Matt sighed. "Yeah, but they're not gonna tell us anything. Nearly everyone in Lambda Phi hates Anathema and they even kept Geoff out of their plans. Supposedly."

"What about Ryan Marshall? You know him, right? He doesn't seem to hate it."

"I've never asked his opinion on Anathema."

"Maybe he heard something."

Matt thought for a moment. "Maybe. But I haven't seen him since the Halloween party and he rarely comes to Galbraith, so I don't know when I'd see him again."

"Well," she said, "the next time you do, would you please ask him? Work it into conversation somehow?"

He sighed. "I'll try."

"Thank you," she said, then opened up her textbook again.

He went back to typing an essay on his laptop. After a minute, she looked up again and watched him for a while. He didn't notice, completely immersed in his screen. She sighed, thinking of everything he'd just told her about his little investigation. It pained her not to tell him more and she felt a familiar sadness coming over her once again.

There are so many things you don't know, Matt. So many things.

As it happened, he got a chance the next evening.

There was Ryan, grabbing a slice of pepperoni pizza from the trattoria. Matt and Joan had just entered the cafeteria after getting swiped in by Doris. She saw him too and nudged Matt on the shoulder.

"Go talk to him."

"I'm not just gonna ask about Serpentine in the middle of the cafeteria," he whispered.

"He'll probably be sitting with other Lambda people. You'll only have a chance in here."

Matt sighed, knowing she was right. Carefully, he made his way over to the trattoria while she watched from behind the salad bar. "Hey, Ryan. The pizza any good tonight?"

Ryan laughed. "Looks like it's as good as it usually is."

"Gotta love the Galbraith Gold Standard," Matt said, grabbing a slice for himself. "How've you been? I haven't seen you since Lambda Halloween."

"Oh, just swamped with IR essays. And exams are coming up."

"Where are you sitting?"

"Uh…nowhere yet, actually."

Perfect, Matt thought.

"Where are *you* sitting?" Ryan asked.

"Uh, just with Joan."

"Joan?"

"Yeah, Joan Keating. She and I are dating."

"Oh, congrats!" He gave Matt a pat on the shoulder. They grabbed some sodas at the fountain, then headed out to the third-year table. Joan had already grabbed seats at the far end near the High Table, well out of earshot from everybody else.

"Hey, have you met Ryan?" he said.

"Yeah, like a million years ago." She laughed. "I think we were in the same frosh group."

"Oh yeah," Ryan chuckled.

Matt sat down across from Joan, Ryan to his right. "Were you at the Sermon?" he asked.

Ryan shook his head and laughed. "Oh no, don't worry. I didn't have anything to do with ah, *that.*"

"Yeah, it was pretty rough this year," Joan said, taking a bite of over-cooked roast beef. "They really went after us."

"I heard. That was probably those other people our guys worked with. I don't know who they were, but my friend Tyler told me they were pretty weird." He hesitated. "Tyler was the one you chased after, by the way."

"Oh." Matt laughed. "Tell him I send my regards."

Ryan chuckled. "Will do. But yeah, he wouldn't tell me who they were, just that they reached out to Lambda Phi and said they had a mutual interest in hating Anathema. Just to clarify, most of us don't hate you. Even our guys who did the raid were just in it for fun. But these people…" He shook his head.

"Any idea who they were at all?" Joan asked, looking at her plate and trying to sound casual.

Ryan thought for a moment, then looked around to make sure no one was listening. "Alright," he said, quieter now, "you didn't hear this from me, but I heard Isaac—another one of our guys who did the raid—

mention Chet Tremblay."

"One of the Saunders guys," Matt said, nodding. *Why doesn't that surprise me?*

"Yeah, but they said some girls were involved with these people too. I don't know, it was super weird and even Tyler and Isaac seemed pretty freaked out by them. And those guys don't get freaked out by much."

"Huh," Joan said, taking another bite. "That's interesting."

And then the conversation moved on to other things.

THIRTY-THREE

"**I** CAN'T believe they're charging $10 for a glass of wine," Joan groaned. "We all know it's gonna be the cheapest stuff they could find, but at least they used to give it out for free."

"Might as well enjoy it," Roy told her. "It's the last licensed booze we'll get here until Winter Formal."

"I'm just glad they're serving wine at this thing at all," Matt said, trying to peer past the people ahead of them.

The line extended from the dining hall entrance down the stairs all the way to Radcliffe's front corridor. Fortunately, they'd gotten here before it became too long, and were currently standing halfway up the steps leading to Galbraith's doors. It was 8:45 in the morning.

"I've gotta get to class soon," Val said, looking at her watch. "When do they start the wristbanding?"

"Not until 9 a.m. sharp," Tanner said. "So we're gonna be stuck on these stairs until then."

Matt appeared to be the most excited out of all of them. Christmas High Table had always been his favorite dinner event of the year. He'd stayed up until 2:30 last night finishing his assignments due Thursday just so he could have tonight off. Joan had a psych paper due later today, so she'd joked she was glad they were still offering wine, only for Matt to tell her about the price.

After what felt like an eternity, the line began moving and he, Joan, Roy, Tanner, and Val eventually reached the front. The kitchen staff had moved the card-swiping machine out here to verify their meal plans. Once swiped through, they shifted to a table on the left where they received a ticket with a reindeer and the words *Galbraith Hall*. Christmas High Table was such a popular event that extra seating was offered in Picard Hall, above the Dean's Office. He was glad they'd gotten here early enough to secure Galbraith seats; it always had the better decorations, toasts were given, and the attendees sang carols.

"They haven't put the tree up yet," Roy noted, looking into the dining hall as Doris swiped his card.

"They're closing Galbraith later to do that and set up the tables. That's why lunch is being served in the Mess Hall," Joan said.

Matt shilled out $10 for a drink ticket and received a green wristband to confirm he was over eighteen, then watched with amusement as his girl-friend begrudgingly paid $20 for two.

As the group exited into the West Quad, Joan held up her tickets and said, "These better be the best glasses of cheap wine I've ever had."

Matt was dressed and ready in his suit and gown just after six. He'd been saving his Christmas tie—white and peppered with evergreen trees—for this occasion, but now grew worried he'd accidentally spill red wine on it. *Oh well.*

He waited for Joan outside Lacy's eastern door, watching other students head toward Galbraith and Picard in their gowns. Though there was no snow on this fifth day of December, it was well below freezing—con-siderably colder than the night of the Sermon. His teeth were starting to chatter by the time she came out the door, her gown draped over a long-sleeved red dress.

"You look gorgeous," he said.

"Not so bad yourself. I like the tie." She gave Matt a kiss, then held him by his shoulders. "You're cold. How long were you standing out here?"

"Not long." Probably longer than he should've been.

"Let's go warm up." She kept her arm around his shoulder as she guid-ed him across the darkened West Quad. Inside, they found students packed by the Galbraith entrance doors, eager to get good seats at their year's re-spective tables.

Tanner stood tall above the rest. Like all DebSoc First-Year Reps, he'd been poored out last year, and wore a sash fashioned from the tatters of his gown. Beneath it was a bright blue Christmas suit adorned with Santa faces, reindeer, and snowmen.

"That's quite the outfit," Joan said as they came closer to him.

Tanner shrugged. "I've been told I have a bland personality, so I'm compensating for it with my clothes."

Matt laughed, then looked around the crowd. "I'm glad Roy invited us to sit with him at the fourth-year table. They always get served first—including the wine."

"Upper-year friends definitely have perks."

Turland and his girlfriend Caitlyn pushed their way through the throng past them, oblivious, and Matt tapped on the DebSoc President's shoulder.

Turland spun around. "Oh, hey! You seen Randall?" He shook his head. Turland sighed. "I'll save him and Gemma seats, then. He got her a guest ticket earlier. I think Patrick got Karen one too."

"We're joining you at the fourth-year table, by the way," Joan said, gesturing to Matt and Tanner. Roy had offered Val to join too, but she'd opted to sit with Sophia at a second-year table instead.

Turland mockingly shook his head. "Tisk, tisk. And here I thought I'd finally escaped the riff-raff."

Their group chatted to pass time, deciding they'd take over a large section at one end of the table and that Patrick and Karen could join them too. When 6:30 rolled around, the fourth-years were let in first but Turland vowed to save them seats. Third-years were called next and, upon getting their tickets checked, Matt and Joan went in, finally viewing the full extent of the decorations.

A twenty-foot-tall Christmas tree bejeweled with ornaments towered at the back, to the right of the High Table. White tablecloths were set all around, atop of which sat pitchers of water, baskets of bread, pastry plates, and pumpkin pies. Matt saw Joan's eyes widen as she spotted the desserts on the first-year tables.

"Stealing from the frosh is always my favorite part," she said, turning back to him. "It's probably my favorite tradition."

"Really? I thought you were more into psychological hazing. Snatching pumpkin pie seems kind of tame for you."

She laughed. "Sometimes it's the simple things that count."

Turland stood at the end of the fourth-year table on the center aisle, gesturing to open seats beside him. Matt sat to his right, Joan taking the seat next to him.

Caitlyn raised her eyebrows. "Nobody wants to sit beside me?"

"Don't worry," Turland said. "I see Patrick coming and his personality will take up the entire row."

Sure enough, Patrick plopped down beside her, Karen joining to his left. "Hello, hello," the Officer said. "Where's Randall?"

"Not here yet," Turland said.

Patrick smiled. "Ha, I beat him at something."

Roy walked in next, spotted them, and strolled over, wearing his riding boots and a blue suit under his gown. He grabbed the seat on the other side of Joan. No sooner than he'd done so, Jennifer appeared at the chair across from him and asked, "Is this one taken?"

"No, as long as Tanner can sit beside you. I promised him I'd save one."

As she sat down, Matt saw Pandora making her way toward them until she noticed that Jennifer was already across from Roy. She turned on her heel, heading for the opposite end of the table. Jennifer observed this too and allowed herself a smile. Tanner showed up a moment later and took the seat beside her.

"Roy," Turland said, "can you save the two seats beside you for Randall and Gemma? He texted me right now; they just got through the front doors."

"Sure." He removed his gown and draped it across the chairs.

Patrick looked around at their group and sighed. "Our table's been invaded by other years, Tom. Roy's a fifth-year clinging on, and then look at these pesky second- and third-years sharing in our privileges." He turned to Karen. "And you don't even go here." She rolled her eyes.

"I know," Turland said, adjusting his cutlery. "It's truly a crime against humanity. We should call the UN."

"Oh shit," Jennifer said, covering her mouth. She held a half-eaten bread roll in her other hand. "Tom, when's the next WCMUN meeting?"

"I'd like us to get together next week either Monday or Tuesday, depending on what works best for people. It is exam week." Turland turned to the others. "Model UN. Pulse-pounding stuff." He looked back at Jennifer. "Remind me to tell Dom Lawrence too."

"Got a number of Cliffe people on your exec, there?" Patrick asked, tearing bread.

"I'm the head of it, so I can appoint who I see fit to my Secretariat. Jennifer and Dom are two of the most dedicated members of our team."

"Sounds like nepotism to me." There was only a half-kidding edge to his voice.

Turland shrugged, undeterred. "Sometimes, nepotism lets you pick the ones others would overlook."

"People would overlook me?" Jennifer said.

Turland froze. "Not really, I just mean…"

Randall and Gemma arrived. "Hey guys, sorry we're late," he said. They took the seats Roy had saved. "It's fucking cold outside. I'm ready for some overpriced wine."

"How many tickets did you get?" Matt asked.

"Just one, but she got two." He stuck his thumb back at Gemma.

"Same!" Joan said, waving to her.

Just then, Carl Dunlap got up further down the table to deliver the grace in Latin, which he butchered, and the waiters began to file out of the cafeteria once he had resumed sitting. Mercifully, wine was brought out first. Matt noticed that his server merely looked at his drink ticket and didn't take it. Joan's glass was filled by a different waiter who was either more informed on protocol or simply not as forgiving, and he snatched it from her hand.

After they'd all been served, she turned to him in disbelief. "That's not fair."

Matt put a finger to his lips.

Patrick looked around the room eagerly. "We should steal the first-years pies in a minute or so; let the first round of waiters pass through. Then one of us needs to get up and lead the charge. It's usually someone from this table who starts it."

"I'll do it," Joan said, placing her glass down. She looked like a kid about to enter her favorite store. Matt saw the eyes of others darting between the tables on this half of the hall, the mass of second-through-fifth-years waiting for a sign, a signal. None of them wanted to be the first to get up.

Another minute passed.

Patrick gave one final sweeping look around the room, then turned to Joan and nodded.

She shot up and began walking sternly, swiftly for the nearest first-year table. Patrick stood next, followed by Caitlyn, Tanner, and Jennifer. Students at other tables saw them, got to their feet, and headed across the room.

Roy turned to Matt. "Not going?"

"Nah, I've never liked it," he said. "Stealing pumpkin pie is a cardinal sin for me." He turned to Turland. "I never forgave your year for stealing my table's dessert when I was a frosh."

Turland laughed, then looked at Roy. "Why aren't *you* going over there?"

He shrugged. "I'm lazy."

The first-years didn't know what hit them. Joan snatched up two pies from the nearest table, returned them to her spot, then darted back for more. Several other upper-years made two trips as well. People laughed all around, save for the mortified frosh.

Matt glanced toward the High Table to see the admin's reaction. Mustard sat in the center along the back wall, his loyal servants Crawley and Porter to his right and left, just as in Randall's Prelude. Vice Provost Sarah Knowles sat at the far end away from them. The rest of the occupants were mostly old men from the Senior Common Room—alumni and professors, some of whom had driven in from Calgary for the occasion. They looked amused, but Mustard had a furious expression on his face.

He called a waitress over to him and whispered something to her. The woman nodded and rushed off, hurriedly telling other waitstaff. They descended on the upper-year tables and began seizing stolen pies. Joan had just gotten back to her seat with her second catch, but Matt was unable to warn her in time. She saw an approaching pair of waiters and attempted to conceal the pie under the table, but a server spotted her and wagged his finger. "That's a no, missy. Come on, put it back up here."

Joan did so, trying to hide the anger burning in her face. Patrick arrived back with another pie, only for the same server to take it from his hands. "Excuse me, sir," he said politely. "This is a tradition. We do it every year."

The waiter gave a smug smile. "Well, Provost Mustard says you're not gonna do it anymore." And he walked off.

Patrick sat down and sighed. "Fucking bullshit." Soon only the pies originally allotted to upper-years sat on their tables. Furious whispers rose in the air.

Mustard made his way to the podium before the Christmas tree, Radcliffe's blue-and-gold griffin crest displayed over the left breast of his gown.

He tapped the microphone and the murmuring died down; all eyes in the room shifted to him.

"Before the staff serves the main course, I was hoping to begin my annual Christmas High Table speech on a more positive note. But," he raised a finger, "first I must take a moment to remind you all that we are an institution of higher learning, a college within a university, a part of a whole that serves a greater purpose. And we cannot succeed in that regard with institutionalized hazing and traditions that make things less inclusive for first-years. I don't care if they'll be able to do the same things to next year's frosh. I don't want us to pay this negativity forward. So stealing from first-years at Christmas High Table is hereby banned."

Geoff Bhajan stood up midway down the fourth-year table, on the other side from Matt and Joan. He looked quite drunk already; he must've started preing before his first glass of wine, which was now empty and held upward in one hand. He shouted "Mustard is the worst condiment!" and began banging on the table with his other fist. "Mustard is the worst condiment!"

The Provost looked baffled. "Stop that," he said quietly into the microphone.

Other fourth-years joined in, then third-years, then second-years, and soon it had spread even to the frosh tables. The whole hall was alive and chanting it.

"MUSTARD IS THE WORST CONDIMENT! MUSTARD IS THE WORST CONDIMENT!"

Almost everyone around Matt shouted it along with them. Joan got to her feet and yelled it toward the High Table, a fist raised above her head, a wicked sneer on her face. Matt reluctantly chanted too, but remained seated. He noticed that Patrick, Randall, and their girlfriends were the only ones not participating, though Karen was doubled over laughing. Both Randall and Gemma seemed amused but Patrick looked immensely disappointed at everyone, softly shaking his head to himself.

"MUSTARD IS THE WORST—!"

"*ENOUGH!*" the Provost screamed, the sound of the microphone distorting. Matt briefly covered his ears.

Slowly, students began to sit down again. Joan lowered herself back into her seat, but her facial expression hadn't changed. Roy, Tanner, and Jennifer still looked quite pissed too.

"Now," Mustard continued, "that you've gotten *that* out of your system, maybe we can all behave like adults." As he stood there gripping the edges of the podium, he looked like a raging bull prepared to charge; his face was red and livid and he appeared to breathe through clenched teeth. He took a moment to compose himself before leaning toward the microphone again. "Might I remind you why I cancelled the Fall Formal. Thank you for proving me right. As of now, the fate of Winter Formal will be reconsidered. The Dean's Office and I will reach a decision regarding it in the new year. Happy holidays to you all."

He left the podium and returned to his seat.

The hall was still and silent. Then, the servers came out of the cafeteria with plates of food.

◆

The rest of dinner passed uneventfully until the fire alarm went off.

There had been no toasts or Christmas carols this year, but once conversation had resumed it had quickly turned pleasant. Everyone seemed to enjoy their food, which was turkey with cranberry sauce, mashed potatoes, stuffing, and green beans. Turland and Caitlyn had the vegetarian option with tofu, which they both said was better than Galbraith's usual meatless offerings. Matt's drink ticket had finally been taken after his second glass and Joan had rolled her eyes while using up her remaining voucher.

They'd split up the two pumpkin pies at their end of the table, and afterward remained chatting, waiting for people to start taking group pictures. Every year people posed with friends in front of the fireplace, or they'd wait until the High Table cleared out to get a snapshot by the Christmas tree.

Suddenly, the alarm started blaring and a disappointed groan made its way around the room.

Patrick sighed. "Here we go with this shit again."

"Let's hope somebody didn't pull it as a prank this time," Randall said, getting up.

Crawley hurried down the center aisle, gesturing to the entrance doors. "Out that way, please!" the Dean shouted. "Head into the Quad and wait for the fire department to arrive!"

Once everyone had risen from their seats, it took several minutes for them all to shuffle their way out the hall, down the short flight of stairs to the left, and then through the double doors into the West Quad.

The air's bite seemed to have grown sharper teeth as they stepped outside. Windows around the Quad glowed orange like embers and clouds sped through the night sky, propelled by a strong wind. Joan pulled her gown tighter around her, wishing she'd brought a jacket. Then again, she'd never expected they would be standing outside this long. It would be at least several minutes before the firefighters arrived.

Their group stood by a tree as disgruntled students filed past, fanning out into the open space. Randall started laughing and they all turned toward him.

He was staring at his phone. "That's priceless."

"What?" Turland looked confused, then pulled out his own phone.

"Did someone pull the fire alarm again?" Patrick sighed.

"No," Randall told them. "It was very much a real fire this time, but don't worry. It's already been dealt with and the fire department won't have much to do. But I think it's pretty funny."

"What happened?" Matt asked.

"Not gonna say." Randall shook his head. "I'm just gonna delight in knowing this before anybody else does."

Turland's screen illuminated his glasses from beneath. "Oh, wow. The female Tetrad was trying to make mulled wine in a kitchenette in Martins and it went horribly wrong."

Randall shot him a look. "You ruin all my fun."

Patrick started laughing. "I thought I didn't see any of them at High Table."

Joan sighed. She wondered if Catherine Winters had been the one to cause the fire, and whether that would affect her Imperator chances, then shook her head. Her gaze wandered the Quad as she tried to ignore how cold she was. At least the dress had long sleeves.

Something caught her eye and she turned, glimpsing Chet Tremblay and Chris Newman pushing their way through the crowd, speaking in hushed tones. Joan looked back at the group; they were all chuckling about the cause of the fire alarm. Quietly, she slipped away and scanned the crowd for the two Saunders men.

She spotted them off to the side, deep in conversation. Nobody seemed to be paying attention to them, but they looked like they were trying to be covert. Joan pulled out her phone as she drew nearer, pretending to be texting someone as she skirted the crowd's edge. She could just make out what they were saying over the chatter around her.

"…don't care how much Prosecco they have. It's just a Winslow party. We'll still be able to go once the meeting is over. We have rituals to uphold."

Chris sighed. "Man, I don't know, this shit just seems kinda crazy."

"We go to Radcliffe College. Everything here is fucking crazy. Just remember, be there by 10 p.m. sharp. I have important information to tell all of you. Something I can't share over text."

"Alright," Chris sighed, then moved off. Joan looked up as he did so and Chet turned toward her. She quickly looked back down at her phone. Out of her peripheral, she could see him still staring at her, feeling his gaze bore into her skin. Finally, he headed off after Chris.

Joan remained put for another minute or so, scrolling through Instagram to look occupied, then started making her way back to Matt and the others. When she reached them, her boyfriend turned to her and said, "There you are. Where'd you go?"

"Just walking around. Motion keeps you warmer."

He nodded, shivering. She leaned against his shoulder and tried to follow along with the conversation. They were discussing the chant against Mustard and whether it was justified, but Joan barely paid attention. She reviewed Chet's words in her mind over and over again. The firefighters came past them and eventually returned from the East Quad, declaring everything safe. They were finally allowed to return to Galbraith.

As they headed back inside, she leaned closer to Matt and whispered, "There's something I need to tell you."

THIRTY-FOUR

"**T**HIS IS a really bad idea."

"It's the best one I've got." Joan's voice came through his earbuds, beneath his parka's hood. "Do you have a better one?"

"No," Matt admitted.

"Then let's just stick with the plan. And if we don't see them or nothing happens, we go to the Winslow party. No big deal."

"The bubbly's gonna run out quickly," he laughed.

"Probably not. I heard Dunlap say he's got sixty bottles."

"*Sixty?!*"

"A Winslow alum from a few years ago, some guy who's off at Oxford now, donated a bunch of money."

Matt sighed and shook his head. He stood alone by the central statue of Griffin Park, bundled in his coat and several underlayers. His earbuds were connected to his cell on the inside of his jacket so no one could see that he was on the phone. Even though there hadn't been snow in over a week, the air was significantly below freezing.

Just over a week, then you're back in Phoenix, he told himself, watching his breath trail away into the air.

"See anything over there yet?" he asked.

"Nothing at the front circle. But I think they're gonna walk, not Uber."

"In this weather?"

She laughed. "This is barely winter for Canadians, Matt."

"You seemed pretty cold on Wednesday in the Quad."

"Yeah, I wasn't wearing a coat then. Once I've got my Canada Goose on, it's fine."

Matt sighed and peered out around the statue's base. A few people were walking toward him, but as they drew closer, he saw they were just random students—probably heading back home from one of WCU's libraries. Study spaces were always packed in exam season, even on a Friday night. And with classes out for the semester, all anyone had left to do was study.

Except for Matt and Joan, who had decided to spy on a secret society meeting.

"Still no sign of them." He glanced at his watch: five to ten. "What if they're already at a bar on the main drag or something and won't pass by us?"

Joan paused, then sighed. "We'll give it another ten minutes, then head to the party."

"I might be an icicle by then."

"If that's the case, I'll thaw you out." He could picture the sly smile on her face. "You know the best way to cure hypothermia, don't you?"

He swallowed. "I…I've heard…something along those lines."

She laughed. "Don't take off your coat and freeze on purpose, then."

Matt tried to get the image of her hypothermia cure out of his mind. They'd been dating since October, but hadn't even seen each other shirtless yet—and he was surprised how much he preferred taking it slow. After all this time waiting, he thought he'd be more eager, and yet the whole thing was still so *new*. Joan was the one who always pushed him toward the next threshold, who always wanted him to go further. It irked him how impatient she was getting with it, but he worried that if he didn't progress things soon, she'd get bored and move on to someone more ready. Still, Rufus' words kept returning to his mind and the longer they waited, the more scared he got that she'd discover his inexperience. And surely she knew what to expect from it. What if he couldn't deliver and she grew tired of waiting for him to catch up, or just grew tired of him like all the others—?

There they were, heading down the hill toward him: Chris, Kevin, and Blaine.

Matt realized he'd wandered out of his cover by the statue base. He started walking in their direction, trying to look natural, hoping his hood and the scarf covering the lower half of his face would prevent them from recognizing him. They didn't seem to even notice him as they strolled past, but he glimpsed something dangling from their necks.

Glints of silver circles hanging from chains.

Matt continued walking back toward Radcliffe, then stopped and looked back. "They just passed me, Joan. They're heading through the park."

"Okay, I'm on my way. Just hang back and don't let them see you."

He sighed. "I wonder if we're getting in over our heads, here."

"You're the one who started investigating a murder."

He had nothing to say to that; he began tailing his targets from a safe distance.

The Saunders men passed the statue and continued into the western corner of the park, toward one end of the nearest row of houses. Matt followed them, his heart beating faster as tree branches formed a barren canopy above. There were fewer lampposts along this path, and his targets were now but vague shapes moving through the dark.

"I'm in the park now, trying to catch up."

"I'll keep you posted," he said.

Chris, Kevin, and Blaine didn't glance back as they crossed the street, coming into a well-lit area again. Matt waited by a tree to see if they went into any residence on this row, but they turned and headed to the end of the street, slipping around the corner. He strolled faster across the road to catch up, cold air stinging his lungs. He'd been outside for over half an hour.

Once he turned the corner, he saw they were still heading along the westernmost road of town. To his left was a thicket of trees, and through it he could faintly hear cars whipping by on the Trans-Canada Highway. Stars shone from a sky devoid of clouds and off in the distance, beyond the road's end, the snow-tipped peak of Mount Rundle crested along a mountain ridge.

The three men didn't look back, but appeared to be chatting about something. He debated taking out the binoculars Joan had given him, but realized if one of them glanced back, they'd be a dead giveaway, even from this distance. His targets made it all the way to the last street and banked right. They were heading into the row of houses behind the Foxhole, the Rancher, and that side of the main drag.

"Hey, they've turned," he said.

There was no reply.

"Joan?"

Nothing.

Then, "I think one of them saw me."

"What? Who's—?"

The line cut out. Matt fumbled to take his phone out of his jacket as he headed for the street corner and turned it. He was just in time to see the Saunders men heading up the front porch of a house on the right side of the street. Someone was letting them in. Matt realized he was holding his breath as he walked closer, pretending to be a passerby as he had in the park.

Chet was the one at the door, gesturing them inside as he wore a green sash and his own pendant over a sweatshirt. He glanced out onto the street and Matt's eyes darted forward again. His heart pounded faster as he came closer to the house. Was Chet staring at him? He could picture him narrowing his eyes at the passing figure, wondering if he'd seen him before. Matt didn't dare look.

He heard the door close as he walked by, but continued several houses down before crouching in front of a parked coupe and looking back.

No one was there.

He sighed in relief, then took out his phone and texted Joan, *Are you okay?* Matt stared up at the night sky and tried to calm down, taking his earbuds out and exhaling again. To think they could've been in Roy's room right now, preing on Prosecco with their friends…

Roy. He hadn't talked to him about any of this Serpentine stuff. They hadn't chatted about Rich Benson in a long while. Matt sighed, deciding to update him on everything depending on how tonight went.

His phone buzzed and he saw a text from Joan. *False alarm. Thought I saw Chet but it was somebody else. Where r u?*

He glanced at a mailbox and texted her the street name. She messaged back: *I'll be there in a minute. Two streets away.*

Matt waited by the car and eventually saw her coming from the northeast down the street. Though she was bundled in her black jacket, her face looked cold. "Which house?" He led her closer and pointed. She stared at it for a moment, then glanced at her watch. "They should be starting the meeting soon. We should see if we can get in through the backyard."

"Wait, wait, wait," he said, walking around in front of her. "We're doing *what*?"

"Well, it's either that, or we go home." She sized him up with a look. "Don't you want to figure out what the hell's going on?"

"And what if they find us?"

"They won't."

He hesitated and looked back at the house. It stood silent, nearly in-distinguishable from every other residence on this block. It didn't have the covert feel of the Chalet, set back into the woods. Instead, Serpentine—if that's who these people really were—was hiding in plain sight.

"Alright," he said. After all, they had already come *this* far…

Without saying another word, Joan took him by the hand and led him down the alley between the house and the one to the left. Both had fenced yards with adjacent gates. There was an open window above them as they approached; Matt heard voices and laughter but saw little light through the opening.

"Sounds like they haven't started yet," he said.

"Good, then we have time." She tore her coat's hood back, then unbuttoned his and pushed it off his head. "We need the peripheral." He nodded, even though his ears were now singed by the cold.

Joan reached over the gate, undid the latch, and slowly pulled it open toward her. It creaked slightly and she motioned for him to move through. Matt kept low and entered the backyard. It was mainly just empty lawn, but as he peered around the corner, he saw an elevated porch extending from a sliding door. To his right was a set of steps leading down to the base-ment. There was a soft creak as Joan closed the gate over behind her, then she put her hand on his back as she came around beside him. He watched her eyes sweep the backyard, then down the steps. Her mouth opened to say something—

The sliding door opened and someone stepped outside.

Matt and Joan retreated into the shadows, pressing their backs against the side of the house. There was the sound of a lighter, a brief silence, and then a long exhale. Carefully, Matt withdrew his phone from his pocket and slowly held it around the corner. The dark screen refracted the moon-light, enabling him to make out Blaine standing on the porch. The end of his cigarette glowed softly as it dangled from his fingers. He stayed there for a minute, just staring out at the grass, lost in thought.

Suddenly, the screen lit up as his phone received a notification. Matt hastily drew it back from the edge and Joan gave a sharp intake of breath, before immediately covering her mouth.

The porch floorboards creaked. One footstep came toward their direc-tion, then another.

Then silence.

Matt and Joan held their breath, huddled behind the corner. He knew Blaine would have to come down the steps from the porch to investigate further; that just might give them enough time to get to their feet, throw open the gate, and escape.

The sliding door opened once more. "Hey, come in. We're starting." It was Kevin's voice.

Blaine's sigh reached their ears. "Just another minute or two, man. I'm hacking a dart."

"Chet wants to start now."

Another sigh. "I'm telling you, Chet's too into this fuckin' cult shit. I'm here to get back at Anathema, not play dress up in the basement."

A pause. "What are you trying to get back at them for?"

"I…" Blaine's voice grew angrier. "Let's just say back in first-year, I was in an open relationship with a girl who didn't *know* we were in an open relationship. And Anathema thought that was real funny. Tom Turland read a whole bunch of jokes about it. Then she broke up with me." Another pause. "Why are you in this thing?"

"Oh," Kevin said. "Well, you guys all seem to hate them and…I don't know, they just seem like weirdos to me." Matt remembered that Kevin was the only first-year in the Saunders clique.

"Whatever floats your boat." The floorboards creaked and he pictured Blaine turning away from him, disinterested.

"Just put a cloak on and come downstairs." The door closed back over.

There was a pause, then another exhale, presumably from the cigarette. "Why is everybody at this college so fuckin' mental…?" The sliding door opened and shut again, followed by silence.

Matt carefully leaned around the corner, then turned back to Joan. "Coast's clear."

"I saw a window on the basement door. Let's see if we can get a look."

He nodded. "You go first."

She crawled around him, making for the basement stairs on all fours. He followed closely behind, his palms pawing across frigid soil. Joan shifted into a crouch when she reached the top of the steps and slowly made her way down, gripping a railing to her right. Matt did the same.

The door's window was mostly obscured by blinds, but whoever had lowered them hadn't done so all the way; about an inch was open at the bottom. Keeping her hands pressed against the door, Joan raised herself until she could peer through.

"What do you see?" Matt asked, keeping low beside her.

"They're not down here yet. Take a look."

He poked his head up. Inside was a darkened room with candles placed around the floor. A skull sat atop a black pillow toward the wall left of them. "Is that…?" She looked at him.

Matt nodded. "Yeah, that's it." Seeing the supposed vessel of the Great Lord Anathema here, stolen, saddened him in an unexpected way.

Just then, a door opened at the back, shining light into the room, and several silhouetted figures entered. Matt and Joan ducked down as voices filled the adjacent space. He tried to listen, but they were just hushed whisperings, unintelligible through the door.

"Seal the chamber," Chet barked. His voice was loud and commanding. They heard someone close the interior door. After a moment, Joan raised her head again. When she didn't immediately duck back down, Matt joined her.

He counted eight people inside, all draped in hooded cloaks. They knelt by the candles, forming an arc in front of the skull and the man who stood behind it. A lantern lay at Chet's feet and cast his face in shadow beneath the hood. The cloak was open at the front, leaving his green sash and pendant visible.

"*Igne purgandum*," he said, his eyes sweeping the seven figures before him.

In unison they uttered, "*Igne purgandum*."

"We shall cleanse ourselves by fire," Chet continued, his voice calm and serious. "In the name of Markham, in the name of Hildreth, the first Bards, we recognize that chastisement is the purifying flame, the necessary evil—but that the fire has been held in the hands of the insolent, the weak, and the unjust. We are first in a new line of the Circle of the Seditious Serpentine. We are making history to accomplish what our forebears could not, even when they joined the ranks of our enemies and attempted reform from within. Our new Bard has decreed that Anathema's time has come, and that chastisement must be democratized among the men and women of this college—not spewed from the lips of two filthy *Imperators*."

The other members said together, "The Bard has decreed it."

"And so we shall carry his will forward. We will not rest until our adversaries have been defeated, at which time this Circle will have served its purpose—and shall be honorably retired."

"The Bard has decreed it."

Joan leaned closer to Matt. "And I thought *we* were in a cult."

"I, as his humble Vizier, am to impart the Bard's will to you and report back your progress. I have informed him of our organization's latest motions and I have received further word from him. He was most impressed with our attack on their disgraceful Sermon, and informs me that both branches of Anathema are equally clueless as to guessing our involvement. They are blaming the whole affair on Lambda Phi."

Snickering around the room.

"Now, for the reason I've called you all here." Chet lowered his head and sighed. "As you know, the RCMP was unable to obtain evidence in the homicide of our brother, Rich Benson."

Matt's hairs stood on end. Joan's fingers tightened their grip on the window's edge.

Whispered murmurings passed around the room. Chet held up a hand. "The Bard assures me that justice will be done one way or another. He has permitted me to inform you, to tide us over in our long wait, that he does in fact have a card to play."

Matt could see his smile even from here. With the lamp light beneath him, Chet looked unsettlingly sinister.

"He *knows* the identity of Rich Benson's killer…and can confirm that they are indeed a member of the Anathema… A rather prominent one, in fact."

THIRTY-FIVE

THEY RETREATED from the window. Matt shook his head, trying to process what he'd just heard. Joan cupped her hand over her mouth, looking horrified and deep in thought. He could practically see the possibilities flying through her mind.

"Can you tell us who?" came a female voice. Matt peered through the glass again.

Chet shook his head. "I'm afraid I cannot. The Bard refused to tell even me, the one he trusted with assembling this Circle."

"If the Bard knows who Benson's killer is, why hasn't he gone to the police?" It was Blaine speaking, but Matt couldn't make out which figure he was. Joan rose up and joined him at the window again.

Chet sighed. "I'm afraid the Bard is in a very delicate position and his personal safety may be compromised if he goes to the authorities. That is why we must ramp up these attacks, to fight the Anathema on all fronts, while the Bard tries to find a way to lead the RCMP to the truth. And once they uncover that a member of Radcliffe's most notorious secret society did the deed, it will all be over. A murder charge is one controversy not even Anathema can survive."

Blaine tore his hood back; he was seated in the center of the arc, directly before Chet and the skull. "Look, we can't be fucking around with this kind of stuff. Somebody is dead and we're here in robes and shit talking about—"

"Blaine, please," Chet said in a soothing tone. "I understand that this is a stressful situation, but know that the Bard is hiding the killer's identity to protect us. Otherwise, everyone in this room—and those of our Circle who could not make it tonight—would be in grave danger. We might start falling into creeks ourselves."

"How does the Bard even know this?" Blaine asked. He looked angered and incredulous. "Is he *in* Anathema?"

"The Bard has…a deep connection to our adversaries. I will neither confirm nor deny whether he's a member."

"So he's in it."

Chet held up his hands. "We are not here to inquire as to the Bard's identity, we are here to do his will, which will serve this college in the long-run greater than any of our own individual efforts."

"Does everyone in Anathema know this person is a murderer?" Blaine asked. "Are they harboring the killer?"

Someone else scoffed, but Matt couldn't see their face. "Definitely not. Those idiots can barely keep secrets as it is." It was another female voice, one he'd heard before. It took him a moment to realize it was Kathy Pickering from the Anamicable executive.

"No, the Anathema is not harboring Benson's murderer," Chet clarified. "Most of its members apparently believe his death was an accident, just like the other unquestioning sheep at this college."

"So did the Bard see someone kill Benson or not?" Blaine asked.

Chet put up his hands again. "I trust that the Bard's information is accurate."

"Why weren't the police able to solve it?" Kevin asked.

"They lacked sufficient evidence to pursue a prosecution on their prime suspect, so they ruled it an accident. At least, that is what the Bard has heard."

"Look," Blaine sighed. "This is not a game, Chet. I hate those assholes as much as everybody else in this room, but if someone's going around killing people—"

"The murderer has only struck once."

"That means they probably won't hesitate a second time."

"I will not allow fearmongering." Chet turned back to the others. "This is obviously confidential information. It is to be shared with *no one* outside this room. I will track down our remaining members and inform them individually and in private."

"So what's the Bard gonna do about it? How are they gonna lead the RCMP to the scent?"

"He did not tell me. He merely said it would likely take time and that we must be patient. But this is a long game we are playing."

"And how does doing stupid shit like stealing skulls and raiding Sermons help us? I mean, yeah, it was funny as fuck taking that thing from Doug's room—and *way* too easy. But if the Bard is sitting on a nuclear bomb, why not just use it and end this bullshit already?"

"Our missions serve to disrupt the Anathema and to create disorder for them. As for why the Bard does not go straight to the RCMP, as I have said before, the situation is delicate and the Bard's life could be at risk. And without the Bard, we would be nowhere in this fight."

"Do you even listen to how you're talking? It's like you put the cloak on and become a different fucking person."

"That's enough, Blaine," Kathy barked.

"I understand that this is a difficult and emotional situation we find ourselves in." Now Chet's voice was so calm it was unnerving. "Some of you might be scared, or even wonder if you have gotten in over your head. But I assure you that we are on the right side of Radcliffe's history, and that tomorrow this college will be a better place for our efforts." He looked around the room. "That is all for tonight. We have drinks upstairs, which I suspect you will all need." He bowed his head. "*Igne purgandum.*"

The others bowed in return, even Blaine. "*Igne purgandum.*"

Then they extinguished the candles, got up, and headed for the door. Chet was the last one out into the light of the stairwell, then he closed the entrance behind him and the basement became pitch black.

Matt and Joan slid down again, breathing heavily. Fuck, it was cold out here; Matt's fingers started to feel numb. Joan looked very pale beside him.

"Are you alr—?"

"We need to get that skull," she blurted.

"What? How are we going to—?"

"Let's make a deal. If that door is unlocked, we run in, grab it, and get the fuck out of here. If not, we just leave."

He paused. It *was* right there, just a few yards past the door. But he was still trying to process everything he'd heard. He just wanted to go sit somewhere and think, somewhere warm. He wasn't even sure if he wanted to go to the Winslow party anymore.

I was right. Somebody did *kill Rich Benson. And they're in the Anathema.*

Holy shit, it was all real. He'd been investigating an actual murder and he'd been on the right track this whole time.

"Matt?"

He looked to her. Joan had her hand on the doorknob. She took a deep breath, then turned it.

The door opened.

"Son of a bitch," he muttered. "They really do leave their doors unlocked in Canada."

She rolled her eyes. "This is Canmore Creek, not Toronto." Cautiously, she pushed it open and stood up. "Can you use your phone's flashlight?"

"Yeah," he said, taking it out and activating the beam. He entered behind her and swung the light around the room.

Joan softly closed the door over behind them, but not all the way. "This is insane," she said, looking around.

"Let's just take the skull and get out." He moved toward it. "Wait, are we just gonna carry it?"

She shrugged. "I don't have anything to put it in."

He sighed and handed her his phone to hold the light, then bent down and carefully picked it up. "Alright Dad, let's take you home." He had to be careful not to let the lower jaw detach from the rest of the skull.

Footsteps came from the exterior stairs. They spun around as Kathy's voice asked, "Hey guys, why is this open?"

Joan fumbled with the phone, but managed to turn off the beam before the door opened, spilling pale moonlight into the room. She and Matt stepped back to the wall, seeking safety in the shadows.

Kathy's cloaked figure paused in the doorframe, silhouetted by the moon. Though Matt couldn't see her eyes, he could feel her stare attempting to pierce the darkness in their direction, trying to make out those two amorphous shapes—

Kathy reached for the wall to her right and flicked a switch. Bright light bathed the room.

Matt and Joan stood there, petrified against the wall, and Kathy gasped in shock. Seconds passed, then she threw her head over her shoulder and shouted, "Hey, they're taking the skull!"

Before she'd finished the sentence, Matt and Joan were sprinting for the interior stairwell door. They threw it open and hurtled up the wooden steps, coming out into a kitchen area where several Serpentine members stood around holding glasses of whiskey. A few more were out on the back porch. They still wore their cloaks, but had their hoods down.

Upon seeing them, they hurriedly put their glasses down and prepared to run. "Stop them!" Chet shouted.

Matt and Joan turned and dashed for the front door. She unlocked it, threw it open, and they rushed down the steps onto the street, freezing at the sidewalk. "This way!" she decided, leading him to the right.

As they ran, she tried to unlock his phone. "What's the passcode?" He told her, trying to keep the skull safe in his hands. She opened the Uber app.

Matt glanced back and saw cloaked figures racing after them. "Over here!" He tugged her shoulder and pulled her to the right. They ran down an alley between two houses. Joan unlocked the gate of one and they went through, then Matt went back, shut it, and reached across the fence to open the gate of the adjacent yard.

Crouching low, they stumbled into the backyard. Here there was an enormous barbeque and some lawn chairs that looked worse for wear. They hid behind the grill and listened as the sounds of footfalls grew nearer.

"They went this way!" Kevin shouted.

Matt heard them entering the other yard. "I don't see them," another yelled.

"Did they go over there?"

"I don't think so, I think they hopped the fence this way."

"Spread out." It was Chet speaking. "They could've gone anywhere around here. Head to the next street. They can't have made it far."

Moments passed. He heard the sound of a party several doors down, and a car driving up the street. Other than that, all was silent.

"What's the Uber's ETA?" he whispered.

She glanced at his phone. "Two minutes."

He sighed, looking out around the barbeque. No one was in sight. "Where did you tell him to meet us?"

"End of the street, to the right."

Matt nodded, thinking.

"We should move," she breathed. "They might come back."

"What if they've got people on the street, on each side of the block just waiting for us to pop out?"

"This side we can run to the main drag. They won't be able to do anything to us there."

"We're gonna walk into a bar holding a skull?"

"Just tell people it's fake. Let's go."

She darted out, keeping low. Matt hesitated, then followed behind. When Joan reached the gate, she quickly peered over it, then nodded back to him and slid the latch. They went through, closed it carefully behind them, and continued forward. No sign of Serpentine.

They almost made it out of the alley when a cloaked figure walked out ahead. He turned and spotted them, then rushed toward Matt. He cradled the skull and turned away, but before he knew it Blaine was on him and they tussled for the artifact. Matt worried it was going to break—

Suddenly Blaine was torn away from him. He turned and watched Joan slam him back against a wall. He gasped and chuckled, looking between the two of them, then back at Joan. "How does *he* handle *you*?"

Anger flashed in her eyes and she lashed out, smashing her elbow against his face. Matt heard the crunch from here. Blaine clutched his nose and stumbled, cursing and bleeding. "You fucking bitch, you broke my…"

Joan covered her mouth, horrified.

"We need to go," Matt said, grabbing her by the arm and pulling her toward the street. When they reached the curb, he saw two more Serpentine members off to their left. They hadn't noticed them yet. Quickly, Matt and Joan took off in the opposite direction, heading to where their driver was supposed to meet them. The end of the street was still empty, no sign of their escape vehicle.

"Hey, there they are!" someone shouted behind them.

Matt and Joan ran faster, her hand in his right, the skull tucked under his left arm like a macabre football. They were quarterbacks, together, dashing for the end zone.

Out the corner of his eye, he saw another shape emerge from an alley as they passed it. Their pursuer panted behind them, struggling to keep up. The cold air burned Matt's lungs, but it somehow felt less painful than at the Sermon. Now that he was the prey, adrenaline filled him with warmth and speed. All other considerations dwindled to nothing.

Just as they reached the end of the block, an old sedan turned onto the street, slowing to a halt. They shifted their course, running toward it across the open asphalt. Joan threw open the back-left door and scrambled in,

Matt right behind her and slamming it shut.

"Lock the doors!" she gasped.

"What…?" The driver was bewildered. The cloaked figures closed in on the car.

"Do it!" Matt shouted.

The locks clicked a split second before a pursuer reached the door beside him, tugging violently at the handle. Soon the car was surrounded by four more.

"Drive! Please!" Joan said.

The driver looked between the figures, one of whom started banging on his window. "The fuck is going on?!"

"Please! Go!" Matt pleaded, still catching his breath.

A Serpentine member slammed their palms down on the trunk just as the car lurched forward. The others dove out of the way and they roared down the street. A figure with a green sash stood in the middle of the road before them, diving out of the way at the last second. The driver swerved at the same time and they nearly hit a parked car before straightening their course again.

Before they reached the other end of the street, Matt and Joan looked through the rear window. The cloaked figures formed a line in the middle of the pavement, watching them go. Chet stood in the center and stared straight after them.

With his right hand, he drew a line across his throat.

THIRTY-SIX

JOAN FORCED herself to take several deep breaths, then looked out the window.

They rode along the south side of Griffin Park, past Caledon College. She watched moonlight shine through dark trees as they passed them by, then handed Matt his phone and drew out her own. She texted Randall, *We got your skull back.*

The reply came as the car swung left, speeding up the road to Radcliffe. *What? How? Bring it to Doug's room ASAP. I'll see you at Winslow Xmas.*

She sighed and closed her eyes, her heartbeat gradually decreasing. She couldn't get Chet's words out of her head. *How is the Bard in danger from—?*

The car came to a stop. Joan's eyes flicked open; they were at Radcliffe's front circle. Exhausted, she climbed out of the car and held the door open for Matt to exit. He came around beside her and they looked back in at the driver. He stared out the windshield, tightly gripping the steering wheel.

"Thank you so much," Joan said. He snapped out of it and turned to them. "You literally saved our lives."

"Uh, sure…don't mention it…" The driver glanced past her. "Wait, is that a real skull?"

"Have a good night!" She shut the door and they began hiking up the steps, the shadowed spires looming high above them beneath the stars. When they got to the top, she looked back and saw the rear lights of the car vanishing down the road.

"Now what?" Matt asked.

"I texted Randall. He said to bring it to Doug."

"We should wrap it in something first."

"Let's swing by my room then."

Matt didn't even bother to conceal the skull as they strolled into the front lobby. The receptionist looked up from her Kindle, her expression confused. "Good evening," he said, waving with his other hand. She reluctantly waved back.

They entered the West Quad and headed to Lacy, then went up to her room on the second floor. She realized he'd never actually been in here before, though she'd hung out in his room a number of times.

He walked around looking at the posters on her walls: a large one of the Toronto skyline above her bed and some travel wallpapers of Europe, Asia, and Oceania. Then there was a large one of a wolf howling toward a castle and the full moon. On her dresser were several framed photographs, one standing with her parents and sister at her high school graduation, one on a family vacation to the Caribbean, and one with her Bernese Mountain Dog in a park.

He picked up the last one. "Aww."

Joan took off her jacket and threw it on the bed, glancing over. "Yeah, that's Adeline and me in Trinity Bellwoods, my favorite Toronto park. If you come in the summer, you can meet her and we'll go there."

"I'd like that," Matt said, still looking at the photo. He turned around just as Joan pulled off her sweater and walked to her desk in only a white bra and jeans. He blinked. "Uh…"

"What?" She said it as if nothing was out of the ordinary, but his discomfort amused her. He'd never seen her shirtless. "If we're going to the party, I might as well change. You should too, you look a little messed up." Now she couldn't hide her smirk.

"Um, sure." He tried to fix his hair, failed, and held up the skull. "Where should I put this?"

"Just leave it on the bed. I'll put it in my backpack and take it over."

"Alright." Out the corner of her eye, she saw Matt steal a glance at her as he put the skull atop her sheets and returned to the door.

She looked back at him and smiled. "See you at the party."

"See ya." He left the room, trying to hide the redness in his cheeks. The door clicked shut behind him.

Joan went to her dresser and picked out a crimson shirt, sighing to herself. He was still nervous; that much was obvious, but she found it interesting that she was always the one to guide things forward. Matt seemed like the type to act more prudish the farther they got, only to secretly wish she'd push them farther still. At first, she'd kind of liked it that way, but now it was getting tiring. It had been over a month and a half since their first date and they *still* hadn't done anything below the waist. While applying lipstick, she wondered when they'd get around to sleeping together. Hopefully sooner rather than later.

After all, time seemed to be running out.

She paused before her desk mirror and took a deep breath, then stood there for a moment trying to stay calm. *You knew you were living on borrowed time.* She wished she could call Matt back here and explain it all to him right now. She'd tell him what she'd gotten into and—

No, that wouldn't work. There was so much about the business she didn't understand herself. Who was the Bard? How did he know who murdered Rich Benson? And why would going to the police jeopardize his safety?

There was something manipulative she sensed in the Vizier's words, a greater game the puppeteer behind him was playing at.

Matt could help, she realized. He'd gotten onto the right trail by himself; tonight had proved that. Together, they could dig deeper and unmask this Bard asshole, even if Matt didn't know the full extent of everything. She chewed a fingernail and winced. If she did that, she'd be blatantly using him to her own end. The thought made her feel awful, but it might be the only way out.

Joan quickly put the shirt on and brushed her hair, then emptied her backpack of its binders and textbooks and carefully fitted the skull inside. Slinging it over her shoulder, she went out into the hall. No one else was around, but she knew Kathy Pickering lived on the floor above her. Were the Serpentine members racing back to Cliffe right now? Were some of them here already?

She hurried down the stairs to the steam tunnels, sliding the other strap on as she went. The basement corridor was silent and empty as she darted along it to the next door. She came up into Sub-Winslow, where the party was booming. Wham's "Last Christmas" blasted from the common room upstairs and people stood around with plastic champagne glasses. Many looked quite drunk already. Joan had almost forgotten about the sixty bottles of bubbly in Dunlap's possession; given that it was over an hour into the party, she wondered how many were left.

A few partygoers threw her odd glances as she hurtled up the stairs wearing a backpack, but she didn't care. Doug lived on Third Winslow, but she wasn't sure if he was in the east or west pod. The second-floor landing was packed with people going in and out of the common room, but she managed to squeeze past the crowd and continued up to the next landing, then around and up to the third floor. Garland had been wrapped around the railings and the walls were adorned with reindeer antler and evergreen tree decals.

When she got to the Third Winslow landing, she paused and looked both ways. Doug stood chatting with that first-year girl, Abby, and one of her friends in the western pod. The res room doors were all covered in Christmas wrapping paper. Brushing past a couple drinking bubbly, she threw open the pod entrance and stormed down the hall.

"…is *that* what you dream about?" Abby teased Doug.

"Oh, I don't see people in my dreams. Just animals and abstract shapes." He looked up and saw her. "Ah, Randall said you'd be coming. You got it with you?"

"Got what with you?" Abby asked.

"Yes. Where can we put it?" Joan said, shooting the first-years glances that shut them up.

Doug turned to his paramour. "We'll just be a moment. Duty calls." He winked, then headed back into his room and let Joan in.

"Ooh, is this *secret* stuff?" Abby's friend called after them.

Doug gave an awkward laugh as he shut the door. Then he spun around. "Okay, so what the fuck is going on? Who took—?"

"Serpentine."

"I fucking *knew it*." He snapped his fingers.

"Someone's brought them back. Matt and I infiltrated their meeting." She set the backpack on his desk and glanced around. It was the tidiest res room she'd ever seen with his course readers and binders organized neatly on one bookshelf, novels and extracurricular non-fiction on the other. A copy of Du Maurier's *My Cousin Rachel* lay on the nightstand, a pair of reading glasses resting on top. His desk was immaculately clean and logs were piled carefully beside his fireplace.

"I'll explain later," she said. "Is Randall coming to take it back to the Chalet? It's not safe here."

"Yeah, I think he said he was taking it back. What, does no one trust me to—?"

She shot him a look.

Doug sighed. "Yeah, fair."

She made for the door. "Don't let anyone in here but Randall. And make sure he doesn't go back alone; they might jump him."

"How crazy are these people?" he asked, but she was already out into the hall.

Joan made her way back to the landing. The stairwell was alive with drunken chatter and Christmas music. People took pictures by the decals along the walls, but she cut past them and headed down to the second floor, keeping an eye out for anyone she'd seen at the Serpentine meeting.

She reached the crowded landing and tried to push her way through, only to find a familiar face before her. Randall looked both baffled and glad to see her. "Hey...," he said.

Joan put a hand on his shoulder. "I need to talk to you. *Now.*"

◆

Matt came out of Bowman's south door under the arch of Napier Tower. He turned right and headed into the West Quad, where he could see that Winslow Christmas was already well underway. There were far fewer people clustered outside the house's door this time, so he guessed Dunlap had exercised more restraint with the guest list than he had back in October.

Matt approached the entrance just as a group of girls stepped out, caught the door once they'd moved past, and swung around inside. The stairs weren't nearly as packed as they had been at the disco party; evidently, order had returned to Winslow events.

He went up to the second-floor landing and looked around for people he knew. He saw Patrick and Karen chatting off in a corner and gave them a wave; they smiled and waved back. Then his eyes scanned the crowd for Joan, but he didn't see her anywhere.

He considered going into the common room to find her, but everything that had just happened started catching up with him again and suddenly he didn't want to be around a crowd. He darted into the bathroom, which was mercifully quieter. He seemed to be the only person in here, but could still hear the hum of conversation from beyond the door, the tune of

"Jingle Bell Rock" coming from the common room's speakers.

Matt went to the sink and turned on the faucet, splashing cold water in his face. The door opened as he turned off the tap. He grabbed paper towels to dry himself off, then turned to see Chet standing there. The Vizier wore the same clothes he had earlier, minus his sash and pendant.

He smirked. "Hey, Matt. You look like you've had an eventful evening."

Matt sighed. "Yeah, I guess I have."

"I have a little question for you. Just one Saunders guy to another."

He forced a laugh. "You've lived there much longer than I did, I'm barely—"

"Oh come on…once a Man of Saunders, always a Man of Saunders. So…where'd you put it?"

"Put what?"

Chet's expression grew serious. "Where is it, Matt?"

"I don't know what you're—"

The Vizier rushed forward, grabbing Matt by the collar of his shirt. "Don't fuck with me. Where's the goddamn skull?!" He thought back to Chet Tremblay in first-year, always sitting around playing *FIFA* or beer pong, even when groups of girls came to Saunders to pre and left after five minutes because the guys were doing nothing. Clearly that Chet was long gone.

Matt was startled but managed to keep his cool. "You know I'm not gonna tell you."

"This is serious shit, not fun and games. Somebody is dead and I'm working to bring a killer to justice."

"You don't know who it is, though. How do you know it isn't me?"

Chet scoffed and let him go. "Oh, please. You've always been way too into it, but you don't have it in you. I remember you back in first-year, always sitting around wanting to be a part of things but never knowing how. If you killed someone, you'd have bungled it so badly the RCMP would've solved it in five minutes."

"I appreciate the sentiment." Matt fixed his collar, glaring at him.

"Your girlfriend, though… I can see her doing it. The Bard didn't tell me who, but she's top of my list." He cracked a smile, watching Matt's reaction. "Yeah, you really scored with her. The one person in this college even crazier about Anathema than you are. Oh, she'd kill for it. Plus, Benson was her ex and it didn't end too well, I hear." He walked closer. "It all fits. But *you* would never let yourself believe it. You're just happy you finally got a girlfriend."

"Shut the fuck up," Matt hissed, clenching his fists.

Chet smiled, the same grin he'd seen on many bullies over the years as they tried to get a rise out of him. "You don't mind that she's weird, just as weird as you are—if not weirder. Honestly, I don't blame you. Even with that scar, she's still pretty hot. Decent tits, I guess, but she definitely keeps herself in shape—"

Matt rushed forward, his fist swinging toward the Vizier's face—

And then freezing in mid-air, hovering, shaking. He lowered it slowly, hating himself for not carrying the punch through, and looked down at his shoes.

Chet laughed. "See, you don't have it in you. Joan Keating does. Blaine's in the hospital with a broken nose right now because of her." Matt looked up. "Oh don't worry, he's not pressing charges. We would have to explain how, um, certain events came to pass. But I don't think that'll be necessary. If she did murder Benson—and I'd bet money that she did—the Bard will make sure she gets her due soon enough."

"But the Bard thinks he's in danger from the killer. Joan wouldn't...she wouldn't...kill..."

Chet raised his eyebrows, a mixture of pity and amusement on his face. "Maybe you should question who you're dating a little more, Matt. I bet you're happy you found somebody, but maybe, just like all those times Anathema made fun of you for, it's too good to be true."

The blood drained from Matt's face. He stood there, staring at the Vizier with his mouth open slightly. His thoughts were unable to materialize into words.

Chet smirked. "I know I used to give you shit in first-year for wanting to join Anathema, but I see why you like it. You have no other friends. So I'm gonna give you a warning." He stepped closer once more. "Enjoy it while it lasts, because by the end of the year Anathema's gonna be where it belongs: *history.*"

He turned and left the bathroom, the door closing after him. The sounds of the party died down once more and Matt was left standing by the sink, breathing slowly and staring off into space.

A few people came in and out to use the urinals or stalls, throwing him the occasional glance but mostly being too inebriated to care. Finally, Matt went out to the landing and decided to catch a breath of air—even if it was below freezing.

After pushing his way past partygoers on the stairs, he came outside. Sandrine and Tony were smoking and he stifled a cough, moving to the left down some steps to avoid the fumes. He walked farther into the Quad, away from everyone, then turned and noticed two familiar figures sitting on the bench before Lacy, silhouetted from behind by the glow of res room windows. He made his way closer to see that it was Joan and Randall.

He watched the Imperator say something and Joan put her hand on his shoulder in response, giving him a warm smile.

◆

Randall turned. "Hey, Matt!"

Joan spun around, her hand retreating. Her cheeks burned as she mustered up a smile. "Hey, everything alright?"

Matt glanced between the two of them with a confused expression. "Yeah," he finally said.

"Great job on the skull rescue, by the way." Randall stood up and walked past him. "Doug, Logan, and I are gonna take it back to the Chalet right now. I really can't thank you enough."

Matt's voice was soft. "No worries. It was really Joan who did most of it, she deserves the credit."

"Well, thanks for helping out." Her boyfriend smiled awkwardly as Randall continued on to Winslow's entrance.

She got up and gave Matt a hug. "You look worried. Did you see Serpentine?"

He hugged her back tightly. "There's a few of them strolling around the party, but they can't do much in plain sight."

"Randall and the others will get it out safely. We're off duty." She gave him a kiss. "Let's go get drunk and dance."

He laughed and she felt some tension leaving his shoulders. "Sounds like a good idea."

They went back inside, up the crowded stairs, and hung a right into the common room. Carl Dunlap saw them and hurried over. "HEY GUYS, WASSUP? HAVE YOU HAD ANY DRINKS YET?"

They shook their heads, too tired to tell him they could hear him just fine without the yelling.

"WE RAN OUT OF BUBBLY, BUT I'VE GOT SOME EVEN

BETTER STUFF!" He went to his Officer's Suite and returned with two red Solo cups filled with a milky concoction. "IT'S EGGNOG AND BAILEY'S! BEST SHIT EVER! YOU GOTTA TRY IT!"

Joan had a sip and had to admit it was very good: creamy but incredibly smooth. She could barely taste the alcohol. In no time, they'd downed theirs and tossed away the cups, making their way to the makeshift dance floor. Drunk college students, some wearing Santa hats, danced badly all around them; the chorus of Paul McCartney's "Wonderful Christmastime" played loudly from Dunlap's speakers.

She hadn't eaten anything since her early dinner, so the booze took effect quickly. She and Matt danced slowly among the crowd, holding each other close. Joan rested her head on his shoulder, thinking of his expression when he'd seen her and Randall.

It's not what you think, she wanted to tell him. *It's not that at all.*
It's just a lot more complicated.

THIRTY-SEVEN

O N MONDAY, the snows came to Radcliffe. They blanketed the Quads and the slate roofs, clung to window sills beneath icy glass, and turned the college into a winter wonderland atop the hill.

Twenty centimeters had fallen before dawn, but few snowflakes drifted down after first light. Maintenance quickly shoveled and salted the paths, making walkways traversable. At noon, some students relieved their Exam Week stress by throwing snowballs in the East Quad. The games continued until Réjean stormed over in his parka and reminded them of campus-wide winter safety rules.

People around Joan in Galbraith were ecstatic, chatting about how the weather amplified a holiday mood. She was unable to sympathize as she flipped through her Econometrics notes at the third-year table. The exam wasn't until Wednesday, but she already felt woefully unprepared. Then she had her Economics and Law final on Friday, which would require considerable studying too. Since he was mostly in full-year courses, Matt's only exam was on Thursday. He was staying at Radcliffe until Saturday morning so they could head to Calgary International together; their flights were only a few hours apart, but in different terminals.

She'd hoped that studying would take her mind off of last Friday's events, but worry continually crept back into her thoughts. She'd been able to focus pretty well on academics this semester, despite everything that had happened, and didn't want to crash and burn in the eleventh hour. For some reason, the WCU Economics Department loved to make final exams worth between forty and fifty percent of total course marks. Her psychology classes tended to be more forgiving in this regard.

After lunch, which she ate by herself to concentrate, she spent the afternoon trying to study in Mackenzie and the evening doing the same in her room. Matt messaged her, offering to get anything if she needed it, but she replied no thank you. She just needed to focus; it felt like she'd barely made progress all day.

Tuesday imbued her with the last-minute drive to concentrate that only the day before a big test could provide. She went through several exams from previous years and re-did some problem sets, then made sure to get a good night's sleep.

Wednesday arrived. Since the exam was in the late afternoon, Joan normally would have spent more of the morning studying, but she tended to do better on math-heavy tests when she didn't practice the day of. It wasn't like psych, where she could solidify her memory of concepts just before walking in.

Instead, she took a long walk around the rest of WCU, wanting to get away from Radcliffe. She strolled around Front Campus Circle, past Royal College, sauntered through the buildings of Forrestal, and swung down past St. Mark's and the recently constructed Engineering building. Upon reaching the university's entrance road, which split in three directions, she followed the leftmost one as it curved back home. After eating lunch, she flipped through her notes one last time and tried to calm herself, pushing dark thoughts away.

Then she walked to the Exam Centre, located in the woods behind Royal College, and sat around with other anxious students waiting to be let into the room. Soon the doors opened and they sat down at desks in a stark, white space. As Joan wrote the test, she became gripped by panic. It was even harder than she'd feared and all her preparations felt insufficient. The one saving grace was that as everyone left, she heard people all around her talking about how brutal it was. Maybe there'd be a generous curve. She didn't have anyone to discuss it with; she'd never made any friends in the class.

Darkness had already fallen as Joan made her way back to Radcliffe, tired and anxious. She wiped a tear away, telling herself to calm down by the time she entered the front lobby. If even one person saw her crying in the hall, no matter what year they were in, the whole college would know by the end of the next day.

She reached the West Quad and stopped, staring blankly at the snow. There were no more tears, but Joan was sure her face was still red. She hadn't put her hood up on the walk back; her ears and cheeks stung from the cold, but at this point, she barely minded.

She saw Matt walking from Bowman toward Galbraith's entrance, dressed in a gray sweater and jeans; he waved to her. She waved back and headed over, finally feeling a smile on her lips.

"Hey," he said. "How'd it go?"

Joan walked right up and hugged him.

"That bad, huh?"

She nodded, looking off at the snow.

"Let's get dinner." He walked her inside, an arm around her waist. She figured she could relax now that the test was over, then remembered the Economics and Law exam Friday. The tension in her neck swiftly returned.

They grabbed the most edible-looking food they could find—mashed potatoes, carrots, and Hawaiian pizza—and sat down by Val, Sophia, and Tanner at one of the second-year tables. Everyone was looking at something on their phones and talking animatedly.

"What's going on?" Joan asked.

Val sighed angrily. "It's the Saunders guys… They shared a YouTube video they made to the Radcliffe Facebook group. It's bad. Also, they must've gotten my pendant from those Lambda guys, and…"

"Here, take a look," Tanner said, handing her his phone. The video was already up on the screen. It was titled "A Message to the Anassema."

Joan tapped the play icon and held the device between herself and Matt. The view of the camera entered a washroom on Second Saunders and there was Chet, standing with a smug look on his face. Judging by the fading daylight out the window behind him, this had been shot earlier in the evening.

"This is for the members of the An*ass*ema." He smirked at his own joke. "For more than a century, you've had your way with this college, treating the rest of us like shit. Not even Dissociation could get rid of you. Well, now we've had enough." He withdrew a square of paper from his pocket and unfolded it. "I have here the names of six current Anathema members, three men and three women. These are only a few of the people who torment Radcliffe College. Since they delight in publicly making jokes about others, I'm sure they won't mind if we put their own names on the Internet.

All's fair in love and war, right? Oh, and if the next Sermon isn't cancelled by the time we come back in January, my friends and I will release a new video every week, naming more members from each branch until we've covered…"—he leaned closer—"every…single…one of you. Now, here are today's lucky winners…"

Joan held her breath, anxiously awaiting his next words. *Don't say me, don't say—*

"Jackson Randall…Logan Brewster…Roy Tash…Kylie Patel…Sandrine Bouchard…Alyssa Lee."

She quietly exhaled. Matt rubbed his forehead in relief.

On the screen, Chet continued. "Now, before we go, I would like to remind our fair college of something…that we have put up with Anathema's shit for too long, and that we should put shit where it's supposed to go."

Now from his other pocket, he withdrew Val's pendant and held it up. Joan saw the same look in his eyes she'd seen through the balaclava that night—that of gleeful malice. The camera followed him as he kicked open a stall, dangling the pendant over the toilet. He let it swing gently there for a good several seconds.

Then he dropped it.

There was an audible plop as it landed in the water. The camera came closer as he bent down to flush the lever, the tiny silver skull and chain swirling around before disappearing down the drain. The view pulled back, showing Chet leaning against the stall wall with his arms across his chest. He looked very pleased with himself.

"This year, we're flushing all your shit away, Anathema. Don't fuck with our college."

The video ended.

"Well," Tanner said. "This isn't good."

"What a bunch of idiots." Sophia rolled her eyes. "As if *they* represent this college."

"A bunch of drunken douchebags who somehow had good enough grades to get in here?" Matt scoffed. "I'd say they're not far off."

Joan was still staring at the phone's blank screen, breathing heavily through her nose. Rage swirled within her. He could've named her. He *might* name her next time. Or the time after that. Everyone here already knew she was in Anathema; so did her parents. But how would she explain it to a future employer if it came up when they searched for her? If they ever

Googled the organization, the first thing they'd see would be all those news articles from the 1990s and 2000s, decrying it as institutionalized bullying. And it would do no favors for a political career, though fortunately that had never interested her much. Still, it certainly interested others in the organization. They would be quaking in their boots when the next names were posted.

She still saw Chet's expression from the video, thought back to the things he'd said last Friday and how, at the Sermon, he'd set Serpentine upon her like hunting dogs after a fox. He'd tried to get her pendant, too. He would've done the same to it as he'd done to Val's. Didn't he realize what he'd become entangled in, how dangerous it was? He wore egotism on his face like a badge of honor and it made her stomach churn.

She glanced up and saw everyone staring at her. Matt looked toward her with empathy; the others just seemed slightly unnerved. She realized she'd been staring angrily at the screen.

"You okay?" Sophia asked.

"Yeah…yeah, I'm fine," she said, handing Tanner back his phone.

They continued chatting, wondering who would be named next and if Chet could be reasoned with, but Matt turned to Joan and held her hand beneath the table. He didn't say anything, but she knew what he wanted to know from the look on his face. *Seriously, are you okay? Is there something you want to talk about?*

Yes, she thought. *But I won't.* She merely smiled, then pulled her hand away and began eating.

For the rest of the meal, all she could think of was her hatred for Chet Tremblay.

THIRTY-EIGHT

STROBE LIGHTS pulsed all around as Chet made his way to the bar. He had to shout over the music to order himself another beer, then let his eyes wander down the server's backside as she filled him a pint from the tap.

When she handed it to him, he slid a ten over and pointed to the number on the bill. "That's you, babe. Keep the change." He winked and strolled off with his drink, taking in the atmosphere.

Grotto sat above the Rancher on the main drag. On one half stood picnic tables where tired clubgoers could rest and refresh; on the other was the dance floor. Chet spotted the boys; they were up on the stage at the back, dancing with girls by the DJ's booth. He watched Blaine, his nose still in a splint, grinding on Melissa. He'd acted so protective around her since October, when he'd accused the two of them of sleeping together. Chet rolled his eyes at the memory. His and Blaine's friendship had always been strained.

He sat down at an empty picnic table, taking a load off; he'd been dancing pretty hard for the past forty-five minutes. Chet put his feet up on the bench and kicked back, leaning against the table-top beside him for support.

As he began sipping his beer, he was tempted to pull out his phone and see how many comments the video had gotten now in the Radcliffe Facebook group. It had been a couple days, but last he'd checked, none of them had been from Anathema members. That was disappointing. They probably had a policy not to respond to shit like that, but legions of others—okay, maybe just the Saunders guys and a few other Serpentine adherents—had commented and teased the secret society, attempting to provoke it into that glorious battle of the modern age: the comment section flame war.

Just as he reached for his phone, he decided against it. It was time to chill. As of this morning, he was officially on Winter Break. Tomorrow, he would return home to Montreal a king. He'd helped stir up some shit this semester and hoped some would settle by January, just so he could stir it back up again. And when the Bard finally lit the fuse on Anathema, he intended to enjoy the fireworks.

Kevin emerged from the dance floor, heading straight for him. Chet sat up as he took a seat. "Sup, man?" he shouted over the music.

"Just taking a break," Kevin said.

"You done your exams?"

"Nah, I got one tomorrow. Afternoon, though. I didn't want to miss partying with the boys." The way he said those last two words sounded forced, like he was trying to mimic the way Chet talked.

He didn't like it but shrugged anyway. "Well, here you are."

Kevin laughed awkwardly. "Man, I still can't get over that video you and Blaine filmed. It was so badass! And that nickname you came up with for them—Anassema—was fucking *gold*."

Chet tried not to roll his eyes. Kevin was the only first-year in the group; the boys had taken him under their wing, but he still had so much to learn. Maybe he'd become less insufferable as time wore on. After all, Chet couldn't deny that he'd come a long way since his own frosh days. Back then he was a couch potato with no game, now he was the Vizier of Serpentine. He was the Bard's trusted assistant, the one bestowed with the green sash. He was a fucking baller.

Chet scratched his chin. Kevin might be sucking up hard, but he was right. *Anassema*. It *was* perfect, so witty and deconstructive. Maybe that's why he'd never been Initiated—Anathema was insecure that he'd have out-shined them all. And who *did* they induct anyway, fucking loser nerds like Matt Richardson?

Chet's phone buzzed. He saw he had a notification from an encrypted messaging app he'd downloaded.

Meet me @ Griffin. ASAP. We need to talk.

He slid the phone away and patted Kevin on the shoulder. "I'm gonna dip, man. I'll see you later."

"Yeah, see you," the first-year nodded, trying to act as if they were best friends. Chet laughed as he walked past the bouncer and down the stairs to the Rancher. *What a fucking idiot.*

His thoughts turned to this clandestine meeting and the thrill it gave him. The Bard always had a flare for the dramatic, which he supposed was fitting given their title. Chet left the building, then headed through an alleyway to the residential street where meetings were held, the lawns festooned with Christmas decorations. It was nice that one of Serpentine's members had the house basically all to herself. She did have a housemate, but she ended up staying with her boyfriend so often she was barely there.

Chet thought back to when the Bard had first come to him, how he had been educated on why Anathema was more than just a nuisance. It was an evil that needed to be purged, the Bard had said, a cancerous tumor on Radcliffe. Chet was the only one trustworthy enough to assemble a new Circle of the Seditious Serpentine, the only one who could successfully carry out the Bard's will. Before long, Chet began seeing the college through the Bard's eyes, seeing the way things really worked here. Finally, he agreed that there was only one thing to do, one thing that must happen. And next semester, it would finally come to fruition.

Next semester, the Anathema would die.

He eventually reached the edge of Griffin Park. The snow had been shoveled from the paths and piled to the side. A lamppost flickered as he made his way to the statue, sleet-covered branches reaching overhead. He drew nearer to the metallic griffin and paused. There was something disturbing about the way the lights cast it in shadow. It looked freakish—alive somehow—and waiting to lurch forward.

Chet shook his head. *Don't be ridiculous.*

A couple passed by, nuzzling together in their coats and laughing about something. Chet stepped out of their way and walked closer, reluctantly, to the statue. Trying not to look at it, he took out his phone and messaged the Bard.

I'm here. Is this really a good spot? It's out in the open.

Ever since last Friday, he'd started to think more about protocol. That bitch Joan Keating must've eavesdropped on him and Chris after High Table. His instinct had told him something was off at the time, but he'd dismissed it as paranoia.

It had cost him the skull.

He'd informed the Bard of what happened in person, apologized and sworn nothing like it would ever befall Serpentine again. The Bard had been disappointed, as expected, but told him it was merely a minor setback. Chet had then imparted his idea to settle the score: naming some Anathema members in a video and threatening to disclose more. The Bard hadn't liked the idea at first, but eventually came around to it. They didn't think the Sermon would be cancelled—at least, not from putting members' names online—but they agreed that it *would* draw attention to Anathema, something the organization always hated. And the more attention it gathered, the more vocal dissenters within the college could become.

Chet sighed, watching his breath rise into the night. He hoped it didn't get much colder than this through the winter. Last year's had been particularly brutal, but at least it was better than Montreal. He didn't even have his hood up right now.

The phone buzzed. He read the new message: *Got held up. Will be there soon. We can go somewhere else if needed.*

He sighed and put the device away, looking at the plaque upon the statue's sloped base, above the steps. It imparted the history of Griffin Park, which was completed in 1924 to commemorate the death of Lord Thaddeus Radcliffe ten years prior. His family crest, and that of the college's, was a roaring griffin.

Something cracked behind him.

He spun to glimpse ice falling off a tree branch, remaining tense and alert for a few seconds after. Chet shook his head, trying to laugh off the discomfort. This place was getting to him the longer he stayed. He'd never been here for long at night; he was always just passing through. The last he'd spent this much time in the area had been at the Beckonings in first-year, when they had him, Matt Richardson, and the other attendees run around trying to find certain types of leaves and other hazing bullshit. They'd said he could leave at any time, but he wasn't going to let a bunch of nerds in fucking Venetian masks get the better of him.

Another few minutes passed, the Bard still nowhere in sight. In fact, he didn't see anyone around at all. Granted, it was after midnight now. Most students had gone home for break earlier in the week, though some still had finals left. The thought of Saturday exams made him shudder, but in two and a half years at WCU he'd been fortunate enough not to have one.

He sighed and sent another message: *Hey, I'm freezing out here.*

Chet turned back to the ominous statue. From where he stood, it appeared the talons of its extended right leg were reaching for him. He shivered and was about to take a step to the right when rapid footsteps thudded behind him.

He spun around just in time to see a black blur sweeping toward him. Then a sharp pain exploded in his chest and drove the breath from his lungs. Struggling to remain upright, he looked down. A knife was embedded in his sternum, its hilt gripped by a gloved hand. The wraith forced him back onto the plaque, grunting as it twisted the blade in. Chet tried to scream, but a hoarse cry was all he could muster as blood spewed from his mouth.

Both the griffin and the cloaked figure towered over him, branches and the night sky farther above. He heard a soft *Shhh* as his assailant brought a finger to their lips. But he couldn't see their lips—or their eyes, or any other feature—for their face was obscured by a black veil.

Part III
The Spider's Web

THIRTY-NINE

I T HAD been a difficult Christmas for Staff Sgt. Linda Wright.

As they did every year, she and her husband had gone to her mother's place in Jasper for the family reunion, but this time she didn't want to share details of her RCMP escapades. She tried to avoid the topic altogether, but of course her mother had heard of it; it had been all over the news. It had been dubbed a bizarre stabbing in Griffin Park, just as she'd worded it in the official statement.

Her sister and brother-in-law had come up from Oregon, and her niece kept asking her questions about being the "Sheriff" of Canmore. Her sister would guide the little girl away, telling her to go have some of Grandma Wright's cookies or to go play outside. Everyone could see something was on Linda's mind. She'd go for long walks in the woods, her boots crunching through the snow while she gazed up at the spruces, lost in thought. She figured the big city cops must just get used to it, that after a while you became desensitized to violent death.

Every time the family sat around the fireplace, drinking eggnog and delighting in each other's company, she couldn't stop picturing the Tremblay family in Montreal. Chet had been one of three boys, the middle child. He'd been majoring in computer science and planned to work in tech in Toronto after graduation. Now they'd spent their first Christmas without him, knowing that whoever ended his life still roamed free.

It had been different with Benson. From the start, she'd never been sure if it was murder; she still wasn't. After the medical examiner found no evidence of foul play and their investigation failed to turn up anything concrete, it had comforted her that the affair was probably a big nothing. Though it was undoubtedly tragic, there had been no identifiable evil.

This time, she'd received a call at 1 a.m. on a Saturday morning. Now the image of Chet Tremblay lying there beneath the statue was seared into her mind. She still saw the blood around his mouth, that ghastly chest wound, his eyes agape and staring at the sky.

His wallet and phone were missing. They'd gotten the phone records, but there were no suspicious texts, no cryptic Facebook messages. Only one of his friends had seen him leave the nightclub; it seemed like he was calling it a night and walking home, only for someone to jump him in the park—a mugging gone wrong.

Then again, nobody had been robbed in that college town for years. And something told Wright two deaths at the same college within a few months of each other wasn't coincidence. The RCMP's Major Crimes Unit was officially running the investigation, but she remained involved. It was the most shockingly violent thing to happen in the region for years.

She sat in her office at the Canmore detachment, looking out the window as cars passed on Elk Run Boulevard. Several feet of snow had fallen over the holidays. Mounds of white were piled beside the roads and sidewalks, but more descended as she gazed off to the nearby mountain.

The case file lay open on her desk, turned to the page with her notes on the only real suspect. A photo of the student was clipped to the top of the sheet, given to her by the Radcliffe admin. It was a flimsy case and Wright didn't believe it. Hell, maybe she didn't *want* to believe it. Maybe she'd grown tired of almost everyone she interviewed talking about how odd the suspect was, how *into* that organization she'd been since first-year. Sure, Anathema didn't seem like the type of thing Wright had ever wanted to be a part of, but she could see the appeal for someone like this girl. When she'd questioned her the first time, she had seemed timid, but in a way Wright found endearing. Maybe it was just that she reminded Wright of her sister when she was younger. Mary always had a tough time fitting in, and she remembered the things people had said about her in high school.

Wright became less enamored of the suspect when information arrived from Toronto, from her private school. It had changed the way Wright looked at Joan Keating. Still, if they discovered she had killed Chet—and Benson—Wright knew she'd be sad. Joan seemed capable of so much more.

She was bright and in good academic standing—not an easy feat at WCU. Maybe she didn't see there was a future beyond where she was now, that the pain would lessen with years away from her tormentors. They might be in university rather than high school, but Wright knew people at that age were still cruelly immature. One of her cousins had attended Radcliffe about twenty years ago and had described it as a hotbed of petty emotions. It didn't sound like much had changed.

Though most people had gone home by that Saturday or were leaving in the afternoon, Wright had gone to Calgary to interview a few Cliffe students over Winter Break. Two days before he died, Chet Tremblay had made a YouTube video naming several Anathema members and threatening to name more next semester unless the spring Sermon was cancelled. Joan had been seen looking particularly angry about this in Galbraith Hall, though she hadn't been named in the video. Wright hadn't learned that from Joan's friends, but rather from some other second-years who'd been sitting at the same table listening in; they'd called the RCMP to offer information.

Normally that wouldn't have been enough to go on, but another student, Blaine Harris, insisted he overheard Joan saying she was going to kill Chet after he posted the video. People said that sort of thing all the time, but given that she had a connection to both of the deceased, it at least warranted looking into. The more she learned about Chet and Benson, the less Wright liked them, but the thought of their families suffering alone over the holidays reminded her justice had to be done.

A knock came on the door. "Come in."

Sgt. Jake Dorval entered. He'd mostly acclimated with the rest of the force by now, except maybe for Beckman, but he didn't like many people anyway. "Afternoon, Linda." He'd dropped the formality of addressing her by rank about a month ago.

"Afternoon, Jake."

He held up a box of doughnut holes. "Got some Timbits. Thought you might want a few."

"Ah, bless you."

Dorval brought the box over and set it on her desk. As she reached for a doughnut hole, he noticed the open file. "You really think it's her?" There was a touch of sadness in his voice.

Wright sighed. "Not sure. We'll have to question her again." She paused. "It's strange that both Tremblay and Benson were outspoken critics of that secret society, Anathema."

Dorval hesitated. "I've actually been doing a little digging into that myself."

Wright raised an eyebrow. "How so?"

"Something bothered me about Benson's death. Maybe he could've tripped, but he had no reason to be out there late at night. It seemed like we were accepting too many coincidences. I've read his old articles and asked around the admin and two school papers, one for Radcliffe called *Cliffe-Hanger* and one for the whole university called *The Westerner*; Benson wrote for both. He really had an axe to grind against those Anathema people. Even wrote a self-styled exposé on the organization."

"What did he expose?"

"Nothing much, really. But he definitely seemed to have it out for them. And according to people at *The Westerner*, he was starting to get worried about his last article, a big one with anonymous sources. Nobody knew what it was about, but the more I've looked into Radcliffe, the more it seems to me that—"

"I bet she and her boyfriend killed Tremblay together," came another voice. She looked up to see Sgt. Phil Beckman standing at the door; Dorval had left it ajar. "People said a bunch of the same things about him that they said about her. They're both fanatics for that freaky cult or whatever it is, they're both quiet, both strange..." He held up his hands. "Sounds like the making of a serial killer couple here, like the next Homolka and Bernardo."

Dorval rolled his eyes.

"If you ask me, the two of them killed Tremblay as part of a weird sex ritual thing. Pagan sacrifice." He chuckled but Wright could tell he was only half-joking.

"We'll bring them both in for questioning," she said. "But they're probably not even back yet. I know Radcliffe residences just re-opened from break today, so they'll probably return by the end of the weekend." She turned to the calendar on her wall, showing a wintery mountain pass for January. "Classes start Monday. Let's give them a day or two to get settled, let their guard down, and then we'll ask them questions."

Dorval nodded. Beckman came over to grab a Timbit.

She sighed and stared at the photo of Joan in the case file. This whole thing bugged her. If she was truly responsible for both Benson's and

Tremblay's deaths, why perform a second killing that was obviously a homicide when she'd gotten away with making the first look like an accident? Had she really believed anyone would buy it as a mugging gone awry—especially with how the knife had been twisted into his chest? They still hadn't found the murder weapon.

Wright chewed on a doughnut hole and looked out the window again, her thoughts lost in the swirling snow.

FORTY

"**H**ow was your holiday, Donna?"

"It was...alright," Crawley said, closing his office door behind her. She'd spent it alone in the Dean's Suite, drinking spiked eggnog and watching TV with her dog. After what happened before the break, she avoided walking Adam through Griffin Park. "How was yours?"

Mustard seemed to be in good spirits. He even appeared to have a bit of a tan. "Excellent. My wife and I went to a resort in Cabo San Lucas. *Feliz Navidad* and all that."

She nodded and took a seat opposite him. "You wanted to see me?"

"Yes," he said, his mood darkening. "I wanted to chat with you... about Chet Tremblay."

"Of course," she said. "Do the police have any suspects for the mugger yet?"

Mustard sighed. "I just got off the phone with them. They do have suspects, but actually...they're both students within this college."

Crawley looked confused. "Why would anyone at this college have wanted to kill Chet Tremblay? What, do they think someone here killed Richard Benson, too?"

"About that..." He took a deep breath. "This is not to be publicly disseminated yet, but they are concerned that the deaths may be linked...and would like our full cooperation."

"Oh." She didn't know what to say to that.

"Yes, it is most definitely concerning. When they ruled Benson's death an accident, I just assumed they were right. But this incident was a little more, shall we say, *clear-cut...*"

"Who are their main suspects?"

"Joan Keating and Matthew Richardson."

Crawley paused. She certainly knew Joan and recalled meeting Matthew one time in Bethune's Walk, while taking Adam for a stroll. "I had Joan in my office last semester for an Anathema Policy violation. She seemed like a nice girl, maybe a little misguided, but...that was before I had read the rest of her file." She looked straight at Mustard. "I must say I'm surprised she was even admitted here given her history of violence."

The Provost sighed. "Yes, that was a...delicate matter. I made the final decision on it myself."

"She was suspended in high school for assaulting another student. The girl had to go to a *hospital*. How was there even any debate?"

"Her mother is a Distance Member of the Radcliffe College Senate. And she heads up the Toronto branch of the Alumni Association."

Crawley looked baffled. "So even though she brutally beat up another student, she was allowed in here because she's a *legacy* kid?"

Mustard considered his words carefully. "Not quite. Her mother gave me the full picture of the situation. Joan was badly bullied at her last school, by one group of girls in particular. One day they tried to snatch something out of her backpack and Joan...retaliated. Maybe a little disproportionately. But the injuries to the other girl weren't too serious—"

"She broke her fucking arm!"

Crawley froze, surprised with herself. She'd never swore in front of Mustard before.

She was about to apologize, but the Provost didn't seem fazed. "Yes, but that was an *accident*. Joan hit her and she fell down a flight of steps."

The Dean paused. "Would a non-legacy student have been given the same treatment?"

"If their parent called me personally and gave me the context, then yes."

Crawley shook her head, disbelieving. "I know this college is the last one at WCU to even consider legacy status for admissions."

"That's true," Mustard said. "But it's also worth noting that the rest of Joan's application was flawless—her marks, her personal statement, her letters of recommendation, her involvement in extracurriculars... She was a stellar student, a perfect fit for Radcliffe. And, as our American counterparts have found, there is a benefit to establishing legacies. Especially for donations. Family patronage makes it possible for us to build new facilities, to establish new programs and initiatives here. Donations are an important part of our funding, Donna."

"I know that," she said. "Believe me, I do. I just question admitting someone who is…such a blatant risk to student safety. What if she *did* kill those two people? What would you say if it came out that you knew about her previous incidents?"

"I'll say I gave her a chance because she was bullied, but that I made a grave mistake in judgment." Mustard looked pale, as if he'd just considered the implications of this for the first time. Crawley wondered how it would impact his chances for WCU President if Joan was arrested.

Suddenly, the Provost shook his head. "The main takeaway for the press would be that she's a member of Anathema. Like you said, she's even violated the policy. If it comes out that an Anathema member killed two people who openly spoke out against it…" He smirked. "Well, we just might be rid of those bastards for good. Legally, they're not our problem, but it would be better if they were gone altogether. This…this could finish them." He gazed off, his mind somewhere past her. "Now wouldn't that be something…?"

FORTY-ONE

R ADCLIFFE LOOKED cold even from here, a fortress of gray stone and white snow. Matt made his way up the road to the college, his parka just barely keeping him warm. Winter Break in Phoenix had spoiled him and he already missed the hotter climate.

He had just finished his first day of classes for the second semester, and something about it filled him with dread. This was the half of the year in which many things would be decided. One would be the answer to a three-year long question: would he become Imperator, or at least make Tetrad? And beyond it, darker and more sinister inquiries loomed. Once he'd learned of the Vizier's demise, the last words Chet told him had haunted Matt for the entire break. He refused to believe that Joan had killed Rich Benson. She wasn't the type, he told himself.

But then that conversation in the Winslow bathroom returned. *You would never let yourself believe it. You're just happy you finally got a girlfriend.*

No, Matt had wanted to say. *You don't understand...*

But he'd thought about Chet's words a lot for the past few weeks. His disorder made him susceptible to premature attachment and what others would term clinginess. He tried to avoid it, to notice it, but it was hard. At first thought, he'd say he cared about Joan more than any other girl he'd ever liked, but the more he considered it, the more Matt realized he'd said that about previous crushes.

Granted, Joan *was* his first girlfriend. That had to count for something. She was the first girl he'd kissed who he really cared about. And she was much more like him than the others. Even when he'd fallen for Claudia and others over the past few years, he'd glanced at Joan after Sermons, writing sessions, and High Table dinners and thought: *Wouldn't it be great if I could be with you?* After all, she'd been his first crush at Radcliffe.

Then Chet's voice came back to him again: *Maybe, just like all those times Anathema made fun of you for, it's too good to be true.*

He didn't want to believe Joan had killed them. The thought haunted his nightmares, even on Christmas Eve. He saw her laughing over Benson's drowned corpse, a vicious look in her eyes as she stabbed the Vizier in Griffin Park. He woke up startled that morning and his younger brother, still in high school, was standing there with a concerned expression. They'd always gotten up early on Christmas, but he'd never seen fear in Matt's eyes as they went to investigate their stockings. Matt had mixed some rum and eggnog to help him snap out of it before their parents woke up.

Matt walked up the steps to Radcliffe's entrance, grateful that Maintenance kept them salted. He headed through the front lobby and out into the West Quad, where a snowman had been made in the center, a carrot nose stuck on its face. In Galbraith, the Dean's Office had installed a hot chocolate maker as part of its Wellness Initiative. It didn't assuage the concerns on his mind, but at least it was something.

He texted Joan as he entered, asking if she wanted to grab some cocoa, and she swiftly replied that she'd be there soon. Matt had just finished filling up his cup when she put a hand on his shoulder and kissed his cheek.

"Hey, you done for the day?"

"Yeah. How about you?"

"Same."

His flight had gotten in the previous afternoon, but she didn't get back to res until after midnight last night. It was the first time he'd seen her since they got to the airport before break. They hadn't known about Chet's death then.

At least, he certainly hadn't.

Joan filled up her own cup, then turned to him. "Wanna stand out in the Quad?"

"In this weather?" He laughed. "Not particularly."

She nudged him. "That's what the hot chocolate is for, dummy."

Just seeing her again after several weeks made him so much happier, but doubt lingered at the edge of his thoughts. He remembered the look on her face after she'd watched Chet's video, the rage plain to see for everyone at the table. He'd disliked the Vizier too, but never anything like what he saw in Joan's eyes.

And then a couple days later, he was dead.

"Sure," Matt said. "Let's go outside."

"You alright?" She looked concerned and put a hand back on his shoulder.

"Yeah. Just tired. I've got a feeling it's going to be a long semester."

Joan's eyes widened. "Yeah…"

They left the hall and went into the West Quad. The area to the left of the door was blocked off for the winter due to a persistent icicle hazard; it sat unsalted, covered in ice and snow. The sky appeared to be one sheet of gray and only by looking closely could Matt make out individual clouds. They walked over to the bench before Lacy, the same place where Joan and Randall had sat the night of Winslow Christmas. He tried to push away the memory of her warm smile as she placed a hand on the Imperator's shoulder. He didn't want to read too much into it. After all, it had been Randall who told him not to overthink things.

They sat down and he nearly spilled some hot chocolate as he did so. She took a sip of hers, then leaned back and folded one leg over the other, looking toward Anathema Tower. Sadness flickered across her face, then she turned to him and smiled, a warm look returning.

"It's really good to see you again. How was the rest of your break?" Joan asked.

They'd last talked on the phone about a week ago, but had sent each other Snapchats of their dogs and amusing things around their hometowns since then. They also sent each other Christmas gifts: he'd gotten her a scarf displaying a werewolf and a full moon, while she'd bought him a Phoenix hoodie with desert artwork. The first time they'd talked was nearly a week after they departed. They hadn't discussed Chet until the end of the conversation; Joan had sounded sad, uncomfortable, and maybe even just a bit nervous. They both agreed it was a disturbing turn of events and had hung up after that. He hadn't found out about the murder until he'd landed in Phoenix, when he opened the Anathema group chat to find it bursting with messages. Everyone had been freaking out.

"It was…alright. I missed you," Matt said.

She gave him a kiss, then took another sip of hot chocolate. "I bet you'll miss the Arizona weather more."

He shrugged. "There's enough hot air in people's heads at this college to keep it warm. Was Toronto this cold?"

"No, it does this annoying thing there where it zig-zags above and below freezing. One day it snows, the next day it melts, and then it freezes again and suddenly there's black ice everywhere." She rolled her eyes. "I should be used to it by now."

They fell silent and glanced around the Quad awkwardly. It felt like they each had things they wanted to say, but couldn't bring themselves to speak.

Finally, she said softly, "Matt...I'm worried that—"

Something caught Joan's eye and her head snapped around. He followed her gaze.

A man and woman in black jackets and dark pants were making their way toward them across the Quad, trudging through the snow.

"Ah, just the two people we're looking for," the woman said, drawing a badge. The man beside her did the same. "I'm Staff Sgt. Wright, and this is Sgt. Dorval with the Canmore RCMP." She nodded to Joan. "Nice to see you again, Ms. Keating."

Matt glanced over to her. She swallowed and looked nervous. "Can we help you, Staff Sgt.?"

"As a matter of fact, both of you can," Wright said, lowering the badge. "We'd like to ask you a couple questions down at the station."

"In Canmore proper?" Matt asked.

Dorval nodded. "We won't be long."

"I want an attorney," Joan said. She looked at Matt. "For both of us."

"There's really no need for that," Dorval said.

Wright shook her head. "If it suits you, that's fine. You're not being placed under arrest, we just want to ask you some questions."

"Can we do it here?" Joan asked.

"It's warmer at the station," Dorval said.

"Okay," Matt said, standing up. There was no point in resisting. That would just make them look guilty. Joan reluctantly got to her feet beside him. He looked between the two officers. "Lead the way."

As they headed back to the front of Radcliffe, his hand ended up in hers and she gripped it tightly.

◆

It took just under half an hour to get back to the RCMP detachment. Wright parked the SUV at the back and led the kids inside, Dorval close behind. Eyes watched them as they headed for the interrogation rooms. It had been quiet lately in Canmore proper; the nearby college town was the source of interesting office talk these days. The Major Crimes Unit investigators were off at a meeting with the WCU President, so no one from out of town would meddle with the questioning. Wright wanted this done her way; she'd show the tapes to the investigators when they got back.

She put the suspects in different rooms. Dorval went to interview the Richardson boy first. As she watched behind the one-way mirror, Beckman entered, stood beside her, and smiled. "Prisoner's dilemma. Nice. They won't know what hit 'em."

She rolled her eyes. "Keating's an econ major, probably knows game theory."

He shrugged. "Worth a shot."

"Honestly, I'm not convinced either of them had anything to do with it. But one of them might tip us off to something."

Beckman smirked. "I'm telling you, she did the first then got him to help her with the second. Radcliffe College is *crazy*."

She couldn't deny that last part. "Let's just listen."

Dorval sat down and flipped through a file, then finally looked up. "So Matt...how long did you know Chet Tremblay?"

"Since first-year, actually. We lived on the same floor."

"Were you ever good friends with him?"

"Not really. I moved to a different part of Radcliffe the next year, but he stayed in Saunders. I didn't see or talk to him much."

"He was an outspoken critic of Anathema, correct?"

Matt paused. "Yes, you could say that."

"Are you a member of Anathema?"

He sat up straighter. "I am."

"Is that how you met Joan?"

"It is."

"Did Anathema discuss how to deal with...dissenters like Chet? And Rich Benson?"

"The policy's always just been to ignore people like that. Not everyone enjoys the Sermons, but I know Benson had wanted to be Initiated. He seemed jealous that he didn't get in, so I think a lot of his criticism came from that."

Dorval nodded and made some notes on a pad beside him. "You never heard anyone say anything about…*hurting* these dissenters?"

"No, I did not."

"Did any members in particular seem to really hate these critics?"

He paused, choosing his words carefully. "I'd say nobody liked them, but nobody outright despised them either."

Dorval glanced back at his file, looking at notes from previous interviews. "Really? Because a few said they saw Joan looking really pissed with Chet's video. And they said you were right there beside her."

"She was just upset that he did that. She cares a lot about Anathema. Plus, that was her friend's pendant he flushed down the toilet. I understand why she was pissed."

"Was she afraid Chet would name her in a future video? Given the organization's history, I can't imagine most members would want to have their name tied to it on the Internet."

"If she was, she didn't tell me," Matt said, seeming slightly anxious.

"Were you afraid that Chet would name *you* eventually?"

He hesitated. "I was more baffled by what he thought he would accomplish. Even putting members' names on YouTube isn't going to stop the Sermons. If anything, it would've just made people more interested in going to the next one. He probably helped our attendance. People love controversy. I think he was just doing it for attention, both from Anathema and from the rest of Radcliffe."

Dorval jotted something down. "Several students said Joan was more noticeably angered by the video than any other member."

"That's because the others are just better at hiding their emotions. Lots of people at Radcliffe are. You have to be, because as soon as people there know you care about something, they'll view you as lesser. If you really want to experience something, they'll taunt you about it and make sure it never happens. All the popular kids manage to keep their true opinions and feelings to themselves. But if you don't conform to their forced nonchalance, they'll single you out."

"So…Joan *isn't* good at controlling her emotions?"

"No, no—*hiding* them. People are usually better at *hiding* them at Radcliffe. That doesn't mean they're in control of their emotions."

"Do you think many people at Radcliffe repress their true thoughts and feelings because they're worried they'll be criticized for them?"

Matt thought for a moment. "I'd say that's fairly accurate."

"Do you feel Anathema contributes to that culture?"

A longer pause. "It can, but it's not supposed to."

Dorval looked confused. "How so?"

"It's supposed to make fun of people for social hypocrisy. It's supposed to keep everybody's inflated egos in check."

"Do a lot of people at Radcliffe have inflated egos?"

He scoffed. "Definitely."

"Was Chet Tremblay one of them?"

Matt paused again. "He was. He struck me as the kind of guy who was popular in high school, then came here to find a different social order where traditions like Anathema and DebSoc—our debate society—are on top. When he didn't get into Anathema, I think he told himself he was too good for it, but was secretly hurt. He wouldn't let it show because people would make fun of him for wanting it but not getting in, so he went out of his way to mock Anathema and to…harm it."

"Harm it how?"

"He helped Lambda Phi raid the First Sermon. They do that every year, but for…some reason Chet and a few other people who don't like Anathema tagged along this time and tried to steal people's pendants. They snatched one from Joan's friend. That's how he got it."

Dorval made more notes. "Where were you and Joan the night of Chet's murder?"

Matt paled a little. "We went to the Rancher in Canmore Creek. Together."

"And when did you get back?"

"Around 10:30 or so. We had to get up pretty early for our flights the next day. We took an Uber together to the airport."

"So once you got back from the Rancher, you went where for the rest of the night?"

"My room, on the ground floor of House Bowman. And she went back to her place in Lacy. And I stayed there the rest of the night."

"But you didn't see Joan after about 10:30?"

He paused. "No."

"Have you ever seen her act violently?"

Matt bit his lip. "Not really, no."

"Has she ever told you about her high school suspension?"

Now he looked genuinely lost. "No...I never heard that she got suspended."

"She broke another girl's arm in grade eleven."

Matt fell silent. Wright recognized the face of someone who didn't want to believe something. He finally said, "I didn't know about that. That doesn't sound like her at all."

"It's on record on her file at Radcliffe. The Provost approved her admission only after deliberation. We reached out to her school in Toronto and they corroborated the story. The girl didn't end up pressing charges."

Matt shook his head. "I've never seen her behave any way like that."

The expression on his face said otherwise.

"She looks nervous," Beckman noted.

"Anyone would be. She's just a kid," Wright said, watching Joan through the glass.

"She's twenty-one. Don't go soft on her, Linda. That *kid* might've murdered two people."

She was tempted to say something, but dismissed it. She'd deal with Beckman later.

"...and so you got back to your room just after 10:30?" Dorval was saying.

"Yes." Wright wasn't sure if it was just the lighting, but Joan looked ghostly pale.

"And you didn't leave again after that?"

"No, not until the morning."

"When was the last time you saw Chet Tremblay?"

Joan tilted her head. "I...I think it was earlier that day. I passed by him in Galbraith at lunch time."

"Did you say anything to him, or him to you?"

"No, just passed by."

"And that was the last time you saw him alive?"

"That's correct."

"Did you ever tell anyone that you wanted to kill Chet?"

She frowned. "No, I never said that at all."

"Really? Because I've got a witness who tells me you said that the day after the video was posted. That would've been…Thursday the 13th."

"No, I never said that. I don't know who told you that, but they're either lying or misheard me." She looked angry.

Dorval glanced back through his notes. "Well Ms. Keating, that's all for now. We'll get someone to take you back to Radcliffe."

The two of them stood up. He'd taken only slightly more time to question her than he had for Matt. They probably could've conducted this on campus, but Wright wanted to see their reactions in the interrogation rooms. There was something about their desolate décor that brought out more from suspects. She'd only investigated a few murders, but this case baffled her by far the most and she felt the need to use every tool in her arsenal. She knew she'd be reviewing the tapes of these interviews for quite a while.

She saw the two of them off in an officer's car, which swung out onto Elk Run and drove off.

Beckman came out to join her with Dorval. "So, when do we make an arrest?"

"We don't."

He shot her a baffled look, but Dorval nodded in approval. "We really don't have enough to go on, even for just her. Richardson seems like the type who'd cover up for her, but wouldn't assist with the wetwork."

"She's obviously guilty," Beckman said, gesturing the way the car took them. "Put what we've got before a jury, especially with her suspension for assault, and we've got a conviction."

"Not without a murder weapon," Wright said. "It's nearly impossible to convict without one. Also, the motive is too weak."

"People kill people for stupid reasons all the time."

"Doesn't matter, Beckman. I want clues, not conjecture. If we turn up something that points to her, we'll put Keating in handcuffs. But until then, I think we should focus on finding the knife."

"It's probably hidden somewhere in her dorm room. Let's get a warrant and turn the place upside-down. Case closed."

"We can try that, but what if it isn't there? I think she's too smart to have kept it in her room and I don't think we have enough for a warrant anyway. No, it's probably buried in the forest somewhere. Even with dogs and metal detectors it would take us forever to find it. And we've already searched all over Griffin Park."

"We might as well start combing the woods."

Dorval turned to her. "That's not a bad idea. It'll be hard with all the snow, but if it's out there, the dogs should find it."

"Alright," she said. "That's our next step."

It would buy her some time, she realized, to look back through the evidence, to see if she was missing anything that would point to someone else. Otherwise, the relationship of the two diffident and devoted Anathema members wasn't going to have a happy ending.

FORTY-TWO

THE SKY was darkening when they got back. The sun had breached the clouds in the west and traces of orange blended with the gray over Radcliffe.

The RCMP car let them off at the front circle and they trudged their way up the steps, not saying a word. They went through the lobby and entered the West Quad, where warm lights within windows were beginning to appear in the gloom.

She grabbed his arm. "I don't want to go to Galbraith tonight. Let's just have an evening in my room. You can bring your stuff and we'll order food."

"Okay," he nodded. "I'll be over in a few minutes."

"Great, see you soon." She kissed him and headed off to Lacy.

Matt returned to his room in Bowman and sat on the bed, staring out his window at the Quad. A few people walked along shoveled pathways, heading to Galbraith for an early supper; it wasn't even 5 p.m. yet. He let out a long sigh and massaged the sides of his neck. He was incredibly tense and tired. Though he loved the thought of hanging out with her, he wasn't looking forward to the conversation that awaited. They had things to discuss.

He sat there bracing himself for another couple minutes. Then he slid his laptop into his backpack with its charger and grabbed some course binders. By third-year, most of his classes didn't use textbooks anymore and all the readings were online. Then he put his boots back on, hefted the bag over his shoulder, and left the room.

The cold wind whipped at Matt's face as he headed to Lacy. When he knocked on her door, she opened it and let him in. Her laptop and some textbooks lay around and she told him to put his stuff down, then sat hugging her knees on the floor. Matt took a seat and leaned against the bed.

Neither of them said anything.

Finally, he sighed. "Wanna know something annoying that happens every time I go back to the States?"

She looked up. "Yeah?"

"So many people down there think Canadians speak French all the time. They keep asking me, 'Oh, have you learned any French?' or 'How do you handle classes with French instructors?' And every time I have to tell them it's only really Quebec—and even then, everyone I know from Montreal speaks perfect, unaccented English." He shook his head. "I mean, do you speak French?"

"*Un petit peu.*"

"What's that mean?"

Joan smiled. "A little bit."

They were quiet again for about a minute, each of their eyes wandering the room. Finally, she said, "This is really bad."

He chuckled grimly. "No shit." He stared at the howling wolf poster on the opposite wall. "So…do they think both of us are in on it now?"

"I guess so." She looked straight at him. "We need to find out who the fucking Bard is. *Fast.*"

Matt nodded. "I spent a lot of time thinking about it over Winter Break. One theory I've got is that the Bard killed Chet since he was the only one who knew who they were. Once he made the member-naming video, it gave them the perfect excuse to off him and make it look like an Anathema member did it."

She nodded. "And your other theory?"

He hesitated. "The person in Anathema who killed Benson murdered Chet to send a message to the Bard…or something…"

"I think he got nervous after we stole the skull back and Chet posted the video. Too much attention was getting drawn to Serpentine and Chet was the only one who knew the Bard's identity, so they killed him. I think the Bard killed Benson too and they're trying to pin this whole thing on us to bring down Anathema."

"They killed Benson just to frame us? How did they get it to look like an accident?"

"I don't know, skill?" she said.

Matt paused, thinking. "There's something more there with Benson. But anyway, the Bard cut off their only way to talk to Serpentine. Unless they've already picked another Vizier."

"What *I* would do," she said, "is message one of the other members. I'd make *them* the new Vizier, but say I'm keeping my identity completely secret after Anathema murdered Chet. Those people seem like they'd fall for that kind of thing."

He nodded. "Maybe. Or the Bard might just have Serpentine lay low while they try to get us arrested. Everybody thinks we're fanatics, so it'll smear the organization forever and then..."

"No more Anathema." She spoke the words into her knees.

"But *why*? In that case, why go to all this just to kill a glorified student club? It's not even *that* secret of a secret society. We write jokes about people and then the leaders put on cloaks and read them. That's it!"

"Our writing sessions and rituals *are* secret," she said. "The rest of the college doesn't get to see all the jokes that weren't funny—or were too harsh. They don't hear how we talk about things that go on inside and outside Anathema. Most of them don't even know we have the Chalet. Anathema needs to be kept secret so the murkier parts of it aren't seen by people who wouldn't understand."

"Oh believe me, I *wish* it was more secretive. I feel like people would criticize us less if we didn't treat it like a glorified frat-sorority hybrid half the time."

Joan smiled at him. "I'm with you." She sighed and her expression grew darker. "I think the Bard is someone in Anathema, someone who works within it and uses it for social status but secretly hates it for God-knows-what reason."

"But this goes beyond normal hatred. Somewhere along the line we must've *really* pissed one of our members off."

"Enough to make them turn traitor."

He scoffed. "Enough to make them a murderer. But *who*?"

Joan hugged her knees tighter. "Who pays attention to the History? Who would be familiar with Serpentine enough to bring it back?"

"It could be anybody, really. I can't see anyone in Anathema secretly hating it, except…" He paled. "It could be Rufus. He dropped his pendant, then came back anyway."

She laughed. "So that means he orchestrated a murder scheme? What did Anathema ever do to him?"

"He mainly got in because he broke his wrist during the Beckonings in his first-year. They were worried Rufus would become a big problem if they didn't Initiate him. Nobody really got along with him once he did, and he left after Madler's First Sermon last year. Then Rufus went around vilifying the shit out of Madler and told people he left because all of us, both branches, were full of awful people."

"And then Randall let him back in anyway."

Matt scratched his chin. "Maybe Rufus joined again just to have eyes on the inside while running Serpentine."

Joan shrugged. "Could be, but I feel like we're definitely missing something if he's the Bard. I don't think he'd do all this just because he didn't feel accepted. And that's coming from me." She laughed.

"But that's the thing," Matt said. "Both of us *are* fairly accepted by Anathema; Rufus isn't. Pretty much all of our friends are in it. And even though they sometimes make mean jokes about us, it's the only thing I feel I'm a part of at Radcliffe. Tell me if I'm wrong, but I think you feel the same way."

She nodded slowly. "I do."

"So I'd put Rufus as my number one suspect."

Joan chewed a nail. "It's possible, but who else could it be? I haven't seen anyone in my branch be particularly treasonous. And believe me, I've looked. I think Sandrine was upset she didn't get Imperator, but not even *I'd* kill anyone over that, so I don't see her behind this."

"Yeah… *That's* coming up this semester."

She laughed. "If we haven't been arrested by then."

Matt shook his head. "And here I was thinking my biggest obstacle would be Logan fucking Brewster."

Joan laughed again, putting a hand to her face. "We are *so* fucked." She looked away and bit her lip; tears formed in her eyes. She wiped them away and sniffled, but more welled up. "If I do get arrested for this, I can imagine what they'd all say about you. That they bet you covered up for me…that you're just as crazy as I am."

"You're not going to get arrested, Joan. We're gonna find this fucker."

She still wasn't looking at him. "Maybe we should take a break for a bit.

It might be better for you."

An electric jolt coursed through him. He stammered, "I…I…understand if you need to be alone—"

"I don't want to be," she said, still averting her gaze. She was trying very hard to hold back tears. "I *really* don't want to be, but—"

He came over beside her. "I don't care what they'd say about me—or what they say about you. I'd much, much, *much* rather be here with you." He hesitated. "This is probably gonna sound cheesy, but there's no place I'd rather be in the world."

Joan laughed and finally turned to him, a warm look in her eyes. "Thank you," she said softly. She hugged her knees tighter. "I didn't do it, Matt. I didn't kill Chet—or Rich."

"I know you didn't," he said, though it was relieving to hear her say it. He rubbed her back and she leaned closer.

"I can see why the police think I did it, though. I've…I've done terrible things before. I've hurt people."

He took a deep breath. "Joan, there's something the cops said. I understand, if it's true, why you didn't want to talk about it, but…"

"They told you what I did to Rita Parsons, didn't they?"

"Rita Parsons?"

"She and her fucking friends bullied me in high school. One day in grade eleven, they tried to steal a short story I'd written out of my backpack. They kept teasing me about how stupid it was."

"The werewolf one?"

Joan nodded. "And Rita grabbed my backpack and started unzipping it and she…and she started pulling it out and I…" She balled her right hand into a fist and bit the knuckle. "I hit her. I punched her right in her *stupid, fucking face* and she, and she…there were some stairs right there—not a big flight, just about five or six steps—but she fell and…she broke her arm. And it was all my fault. They told me if she had landed differently, she could've broken her neck."

She took several deep breaths. "I got suspended. So did all of them, actually, but everyone at school thought I was a monster. Just like the story I wrote." She gave a bitter laugh. "Self-fulfilling prophecy, huh?"

Matt didn't know how to say what he wanted to say. He continued rubbing her back, trying to put it into words.

"And then I still got into Cliffe because my mom went here, because she runs the Toronto Alumni group and sits on the Senate. Can you fucking believe it?"

"I'm sure the rest of your application was—"

"Perfect, that's what my parents told me. They kept saying how smart and talented I was and that they weren't going to let this blemish hold me back. Oh, they were *furious* at me for what I did, of course. I got grounded for months, but I deserved it even though Rita didn't need surgery. She's fine now; she plays lacrosse at Laurier, actually." Joan sniffed. "I felt horrible though. And I knew that if anybody at Cliffe found out *that's* how I got in, they would *end me*. There would be an entire Sermon on it, all written by Alyssa Lee and Katy Coulson. And the girls not in Anathema would still eat it up. The other ones who went to private school don't care for me because I'm not enough like them, and the girls who didn't go to private school hate me because I did."

He hugged her and kissed her forehead. She pulled his arms tighter around her. "I'm a terrible person, Matt." Her voice was calm without a trace of self-pity; it sounded like a detached observation.

"Well, this college is full of terrible people. At least you're not alone."

She managed a smile. "And yet I *still* have a tough time fitting in."

"That's because the rest of them are worse than you." *Tell her*, he thought. *Tell her you have BPD. Come clean. Get it off your chest.* "Trust me, I'm pretty messed up too."

"No, you're not," she laughed. "You're really not. What, have you sent somebody to the hospital?"

"No."

"Beaten anybody up?"

"Does playing *Mortal Kombat* count?"

She rolled her eyes and nuzzled closer.

"There's...something I've been wanting to tell you for a while—"

"That you're a virgin?"

"Well yeah, that too—wait, how did you know?"

She pulled herself up and put an arm around his shoulder, shooting him a look. "It's pretty obvious."

"What, to anybody walking on the street?"

Joan laughed. "No, to *me*. I can tell you've been nervous, but really there's nothing to be afraid of." She stroked his cheek. "Here, I'll show you."

She yanked him closer. She'd always been a passionate kisser, but there was something especially aggressive about the way she went at him this time. He suddenly felt a bit uncomfortable and pulled away. "Hey, maybe… we shouldn't today."

She tilted her head to the side, amused. "Oh, come *on*. You're joking, right? We both need this." She leaned closer again, grabbing the bottom of his shirt and starting to pull it up.

He gently pushed her hand away. "Joan, I'm serious. We just got questioned by the fucking police about a *murder*. I'm still processing everything."

"And this will take your mind off of it." Her amusement had become annoyance. "You've never done this before; *I* have. It helps better than drinking, trust me."

"I'm just not sure I'm ready right now."

She stood up, glaring down at him. "Oh, for fuck's sake, what are you waiting for?! Now's as good a time as any."

He sighed, not meeting her eyes. "I'm just not in the headspace for it, I'm sorry. Maybe later."

"Later *when*? Tonight? Tomorrow? A month from now?"

"I…I really don't know. Just not right now."

"After everything that's happened today, I just think now would be a really good time for a release."

"So that's all I am? A release?" *Careful*, he told himself, *don't let yourself go. Scale this back. Scale this back* now. *You can still salvage this.*

"I have been *very* patient, Matt. This was tiring in November, and it's fucking *January* now. We've basically been dating since mid-October and we've never done anything below the waist."

"I'm sorry I've been taking so long, but I just need more time. Look, I've been anxious about this stuff for years. And to be honest…I've been worried I'll disappoint you. You're more experienced than I am."

"I don't give a shit about that. I'm surprised you'd even *think* that about me." Now she was quite angry; he couldn't believe this had escalated so quickly. They'd never argued before. "You know, I always wondered why you had such a tough time getting laid, but now I think you're just your own worst enemy."

Silence hung over the room.

He paused and opened his mouth to say something, but stopped. That last remark had cut unexpectedly deep and it took his entire willpower not to tear up.

Joan seemed to snap out of her rage, her expression softening. She covered her mouth, horrified with herself. "I'm so sorry. I shouldn't have said that. Any of that. I don't know what I was thinking… If you're not ready, you're not ready. I'm really sorry I pressured you. I…" She moved toward him slowly.

"I think I should go," was all he managed. He got to his feet and made for the door.

"Matt…," Joan called behind him. But then he was out and hurrying along the corridor, trying not to cry. It didn't work.

He took the steam tunnels back to his room so that he wouldn't be seen.

◆

Once he'd gone, she placed both palms on the desk to steady herself and took several deep breaths. She closed her eyes.

What the fuck, Joan? What the actual fuck? *What the hell were you thinking?*

I wasn't, she realized. *It all just came out.* She shook her head. *It's his fault. I've waited long enough. We've waited long enough. How the hell could he just run out like that?*

No, you're being way too hard on him. You just tried to pressure him into losing his virginity, for fuck's sake. You're just as bad as a douchebag high schooler on prom night.

She smacked her forehead. "Stupid, stupid, *stupid…*"

You fuck up everything. Everything.

Joan gripped the edge of the desk until the wood creaked, her knuckles turning white. Breath came violently in and out of her nose. The tension rose within her, higher and higher and—

She slammed her right fist into the wall.

Pain seared through her knuckles. Joan cried out, falling to the floor and clutching her hand. She hissed through clenched teeth and sat there, summoning the courage to inspect the wound. Finally, she glanced down at it. Blood smeared her fingers and everything hurt; in no time, there'd be a horrific bruise.

Great. How are you going to explain that?

She winced and sat there cradling the injury, thankful for the distraction pain afforded her, as the last light vanished beyond the window.

FORTY-THREE

"**W**ELL, THAT concludes the discussion. I'll talk things over with the Tetrad, and then I'll make the final decisions myself. But I think we have some good choices for Initiates this year, and I'll tell 116 to keep an eye on the ones who didn't make it this time. They could still be good candidates as upper-years."

Matt had expected Randall to appear well-rested after the holiday, seeing as he'd looked a bit better after the November long weekend. Instead, the Imperator seemed more exhausted than ever as he stood before the Chalet's fireplace. Heavy bags were pronounced beneath his eyes and his normally firm posture had slackened. The incident in Griffin Park seemed to have consumed his thoughts too.

"We'll have our first writing session for the Second Sermon soon. I want to get on that so we're not rushed like last time."

"Is it true the skull is back?" Hamid asked. "The *real* skull?"

"Yes," Randall said. "See, I told you Dad was just on vacation. Uncle served his purpose, but we've sent him on to the Big Catacombs in the Sky."

"So what happened with Dad?"

"The important thing is that he's back now and I don't need to beg the alumni to buy us a new one."

Geoff shrugged. "We could've just done a grave-digging field trip."

"Anyway, that case is closed. Have a good weekend, everybody. Oh, and remember to start thinking about your Scrapbook photos." At that, Matt smiled. He'd already taken his back in Phoenix—underwater in fact, holding a prop skull he'd ordered just for this purpose beneath the surface of the neighborhood pool. Most members took photos around the college, doing funny things, stupid things, or a combination of the two. He was pretty sure no one had ever taken an underwater one before, so he hoped Randall was impressed.

People stood up from the sofas, chatter among them resuming. Roy walked over to Matt. "Hey, how've the texts been going with Joan?" he asked quietly.

Matt sighed. As soon as he'd gotten back to his room on Monday, he'd immediately messaged Roy about what happened—minus the police interview—and waited for his response, wiping tears away from his eyes. Roy had said that the only thing to do was to wait a couple days. Hopefully Joan would reach out to him first, but if she hadn't sent anything by the weekend, he should send a text saying they needed to talk.

Fortunately, she did message first, on Wednesday.

Hey, I'm really, really, really sorry about those things I said. I don't know why I said them, they just came out, but that's no excuse. I want you to know that I did NOT mean any of them and I'm SO sorry I tried to push you to do something you weren't comfortable with yet. I can't believe I did that and I feel absolutely terrible about it. I'm totally fine with waiting as long as you want and I promise I will never pressure you like that again. You mean a lot to me and I hope we can go back to the way things were.

When he'd first read those words, he wasn't sure how to feel. Part of him was enormously relieved and he certainly wanted to continue the relationship, but the other part was hesitant. He'd never seen that side of her before and it had startled him. He still blamed himself for the whole thing, but Roy had come over to his room and tried to convince him otherwise on Wednesday.

"Matt, she shouldn't have said that. It was completely uncalled for. Not being sexually satisfied is reasonable, but she could've talked about that with you calmly instead of doing what she did."

"It's been an emotional time for both of us," Matt said. Avoiding any mention of the RCMP had proved to be verbal gymnastics. "I think she's just stressed."

Roy nodded. "That's fair. But you should never let anyone pressure you into doing something you don't want to, even your girlfriend." He paused. "If you don't mind me asking, why *haven't* you guys had sex yet?"

Matt shrugged. "I was just nervous about it. It's stupid, I know."

Roy shook his head. "It's not stupid. It's totally valid, *but*...if you're not ready to go that far for a while, it might be a dealbreaker for her. And no offense, but I get why."

"I know, I know. I think I'll be ready soon; it was just that day, in that moment..." He shook his head. It seemed surreal. His first time seeing her in several weeks, then the police, then the fight—all within a few hours.

Roy looked at the message on Matt's phone again. "This is a good sign, though. This kind of fight has killed many relationships, but she seems committed to repairing things. You two just need to take it easy for a while."

Matt had responded to her with a simple *Thank you* and left it at that. The next day she had asked him how his new classes were going and he said they were good so far, then asked about hers, to which she replied that they seemed okay. And that had been where it ended.

Standing in the Chalet's lounge that Friday evening, watching the other members head for the door, Matt turned to Roy and said, "Still nothing after yesterday. It's weird—I haven't seen her around Galbraith all week, even at the times she normally goes. I wonder if she's avoiding me."

Roy shrugged. "I don't know. But if you aren't going to talk to her tonight, I was gonna ask if you wanted to get some drinks at the Royal."

He hesitated. "I would, but I've really gotta work on a paper. It's due Monday." His next assignment actually wasn't due for over a week, but he didn't feel like going out tonight. He just wanted to get away from everything for a bit. "Some other time for sure, though."

"No worries. I'll go ask Tanner, then." Roy paused. "And good luck. I hope things work out between you and her." He smiled. "You two are my favorite Cliffe couple."

"Thanks, Roy. I appreciate that."

He nodded and walked off toward Tanner and Hamid. Matt pulled his backpack on and sighed. He wondered if Roy had wanted to get his thoughts on Chet's murder, to see if he thought it connected with their little investigation last fall. He still hadn't told him about Serpentine. Only Randall and his Tetrad knew; he assumed someone had informed Kylie.

Matt suddenly realized Rufus was looking at him with narrowed eyes. He turned to the fourth-year and raised an eyebrow, but Rufus merely smirked, shook his head, and headed for the door. Matt paused for a moment, then followed the others outside.

Before he got to the gate, he glanced back. Situated among the trees with its snow-covered roof and glowing windows, the Chalet looked like a postcard of a winter cottage. Shadows moved beyond the blinds in the lounge, the Tetrad no doubt discussing recent events.

He followed the others along the edge of Griffin Park back to Radcliffe. As he did so, he thought back to Winter Break. His parents were incredibly concerned about his safety after Chet had been killed, but he couldn't bring himself to tell them about Serpentine and Rich Benson. If they knew there had been *two* murders, they might not have let him come back at all. His brother questioned whether he should still apply to WCU next year; Matt told him he might want to consider some other options.

Sighing, he ascended the college's front stairs, back toward his room and a night spent alone.

◆

She took a deep breath and exhaled. It did little to curb the fluttery feeling in her stomach as she knocked on the door, keeping her bandaged right hand hidden behind her back.

She hadn't planned on talking to him until tomorrow, but while gazing absentmindedly out her window into the West Quad she'd spotted light in his window through a gap in the curtains.

"It's me," Joan said, swallowing.

A moment later, the door opened. He was dressed in a collared shirt and jeans and looked tired. It was nearly midnight and she guessed he'd gotten back from drinking, probably with other Anathema members. She'd heard about the meeting tonight; her branch had already discussed Initiate picks yesterday.

"Hey," Matt said, offering a weak smile. He seemed guarded. It was the first time she'd seen him since the incident.

"I…I just wanted to talk to you. About what happened on Monday. Apologizing over text wasn't enough, and I want to make sure we're still good."

His eyes flicked down, then widened. "Oh my God, what happened to your hand?!"

She'd let it drift to her side without realizing and quickly hid it behind her back again. "We can get to that later. I just wanted to say how sorry I am for how I treated you."

He opened the door wider. "Here, come on in." She did so and made her way to sit on the bed as he closed it behind her. As she rubbed her bandages and thought of what to say next, Matt came over and sat to her right, inspecting her hand.

"Seriously, what happened?"

"It's not important right now."

He gave a weak smile. "If the RCMP saw you, they'd think you'd been beating people up."

She laughed for the first time that day.

"Have you heard from them?"

"No, thankfully not. But…" She rested her injured hand on his shoulder. "Even if they broke down the door and arrested me right this minute, I just wanted to say something. I have…this side of me, and I try to keep it hidden but occasionally it claws its way out, and I say or do horrible things. Sometimes it helps me write Anathema jokes, but it's not good for much else." She forced a laugh, then sighed. "You're the *last* person I wanted to hurt, Matt. Again, I'm so sorry for what I said. You're not driving me off, but I'm worried I nearly pushed *you* away. And I really, really don't want that to happen. I won't ever treat you like that again. I *promise*."

Matt leaned over and kissed her. "I don't want that to happen, either. I'm sorry for being such a prude." He laughed.

"No, no, you weren't! I shouldn't have gotten upset with you. We can take as long as you'd like. I don't want you to feel like you *have* to do anything just to please me."

"Thank you, Joan." He kissed her again. "We'll get to it soon, I promise. I just need…a little bit more time. Though I don't think you'd be down for it tonight anyway with that hand of yours."

Joan pulled it back and looked it over, smiling softly. "Yeah, you're probably right."

"So seriously, tell me what happened!"

She sighed. "It's really dumb, it's nothing."

"No, it's not. Nothing you tell me is dumb. Did you…did you do that to yourself?"

Joan swallowed and nodded. "It was right after you left. I got so angry at myself that I just needed to…*hit* something, and the wall was right there and—"

"Jesus."

She rubbed the bandages. "Val took me to the campus clinic the next morning. I managed to get their last walk-in appointment for the day and they X-rayed me right there. I didn't break anything and the bones aren't even bruised, but it's still all purple and nasty. And sore." She winced.

"What did you tell the doctor?"

"I said I'd just gotten one of my final grades back from last semester."

He put a hand to his head. "And what did you tell Val?"

She sighed. "That I fucked up."

Matt kissed her again, this time for much longer. "You're worth so much more than that and you know it."

"Thank you," she said quietly. "I was avoiding you this week because I didn't want you to see the bandages."

"I'm really sorry." He gave her a peck on the cheek. "I missed seeing you around."

She turned and kissed him on the lips. It lasted longer than she thought it would and he smiled as she pulled away.

"Don't be sorry," she said. "None of it was your fault."

Matt nodded slowly, averting her gaze. "Brunch tomorrow?" he finally said.

Joan kissed him again. "That sounds great." She stood and looked down at him. "I should get going. But I'm really glad we had this talk."

"I am too." He was still smiling.

She headed back into the hallway and sighed with relief, stress flowing out of her shoulders.

At least that's one thing this year that you haven't fucked up yet...

FORTY-FOUR

Pitch black surrounded them on all sides, but they continued walking. Matt feared he'd slip on ice at any second.

Finally, Roy turned on his phone's flashlight beside him and swept it across the ground. The road curved to the right, taking them toward the parking lot of Bethune's Walk. "He's supposed to be by the sign, right?"

"Yeah," Matt said.

"Nobody got sent to the griffin statue this time, I'm assuming?"

"Or to the bridge."

They came into an open space. The parking lot was empty save for a lone figure standing by the entrance to the trail. There were no clouds tonight, but the price of seeing constellations was enduring the bitter cold.

"You got the blindfold?" Roy asked.

"Yep. You got the flask?"

He held it up, brand-new and filled with vodka.

Matt sighed and adjusted his toque. The male branch's meeting to discuss Initiation picks had been two weeks ago today. Neither he nor Joan had heard a word from the RCMP or seen any sign of them around Radcliffe. Part of him hoped their trip to the detachment had been a mutual hallucination. Each day passed with increasing dread and he could picture a meal in Galbraith interrupted by officers, walking toward them with handcuffs. He could see the two of them being arrested in front of the whole college, hearing snickering and whispers of *I knew it* and *Took them long enough* as they were taken away.

Or even just Joan being taken, with him left alone to be stared at by everyone in Galbraith. He wasn't sure which would be worse.

Aside from an impending arrest, things with him and Joan had been steady. She stayed true to her word and didn't pressure him about going farther, but it felt like the two of them were walking on eggshells the first week after their talk, only hanging out casually in Galbraith or studying together. Last weekend they'd finally gone on a proper date and gotten drinks on the main drag, though it had been overshadowed by a discussion of the Bard's identity.

There had only been two writing sessions since the Initiations meeting, and Matt had done his best to keep his eye out for suspicious behavior—especially from Rufus. He recalled the look the fourth-year gave him two weeks ago, how he'd narrowed his gaze and just stared right at him. And when Matt had raised his eyebrows to tell him *I see you, fuckhead*, the bastard just smirked and walked off. He'd tried to visualize Rufus killing Chet since then. He wasn't the fittest Anathema member, but he looked capable.

Randall's words came back to him again: *Don't overthink things.*

Standing there in the cold evening, he turned to Roy and said, "Alright, let's do this."

They strode across the gravel to the sign and the first-year waiting against it. When Brandon Lehane saw them approach, he straightened up and adjusted his tuxedo. His calling card told him to procure one and to stand at this location on this evening, the 25th of January, at 9:42 p.m. precisely. The exact time was bullshit; the supervisors always showed up five to ten minutes late. For his Initiation, Matt had arrived fifteen minutes before his printed time just to be safe.

"Good evening, gentlemen," Brandon said, looking between the two tuxedo-clad, masked upper-years.

"Mr. Lehane," Roy told him, "do you consent to proceed with the Rites of Initiation?"

"I do."

"Do you say this knowing that you may leave at any time you like, but that if you do, you will forfeit your invitation to join the Great Lord's ranks forever?"

"I do."

"Excellent." Roy gestured to Matt. "Give him the blindfold."

Matt did so and helped fit it around Brandon's head. "Don't take this off unless we tell you to."

"Got it."

"Put out your hand," Roy commanded and the first-year did so. "I'm giving you a flask as the first token of your journey. You must keep it on you at all times and drink from it, but you may only keep it if you finish it by the end of the night."

"Twist my arm." Brandon unscrewed the top and took a swig, then coughed. "What is this shit?"

"It's a secret," Matt said, smiling with contempt.

"Ha-ha, very funny," Brandon said.

"I think this one's got a mouth on him, Roy."

"Seems like it." He came around behind Brandon. "You know, Mr. Lehane, a little bird told me you're acting in the Forrestal Dramatic Society's production of *Mamma Mia*. What's your role again?" He tapped his chin. "Pool Boy Number Four?"

"Hey, fuck you, I'm Pool Boy Number *Three*."

"Look out Broadway, here he comes," Matt said.

Roy shook his head. "So what girl are you trying to impress and what role does she play? Or is she on tech?"

"Honestly…I'm just in it for the ABBA music, man."

Matt and Roy exchanged looks, then shrugged. "I really can't argue with that," Matt said.

"Brandon, I think it's time you began your journey into the mysteries of Initiation." Roy grabbed his arm and began leading him forward.

"Are you gonna make me run around town and do some weird fuckin' scavenger hunt or something?"

"You'll find out soon enough," Roy said. "But first, we're gonna escort you to a secret location."

"Well, I do like secrets."

"Then you came to the right club."

They led Brandon back around the gravel bend to the main road, then hung a left and made for the Chalet. Along the way, they said very little to heighten his tension, though they were careful to make sure he didn't step on any ice. An Initiate slipped and sustained a head injury back in the early 2000s and had to drop out of school, which had caused a big scandal. It prompted that *Calgary Herald* article on them with a photo in Griffin Park, painting them as an ancient evil that not even Dissociation could kill. Since then, Initiation protocol had been much stricter on safety.

The sidewalk was fairly well cleared since it hadn't snowed in days, but piles still lined the asphalt and more clung to trees. No moon shone this evening, so the snow refracted light only from lampposts and the bright starscape.

The trio turned up the Chalet's winding drive and soon found themselves at the gate. Matt buzzed the intercom and Logan's voice came through. "Which one do you have?"

"Lehane."

"Come in."

The gate unlocked and Matt pulled it the rest of the way open, enabling Roy to guide Brandon through. As they walked into the clearing before the Chalet, Matt saw it seemed less cozy than it had recently. Instead, there seemed to be something more sinister about it. He chalked it up to there being fewer lights on in the main floor; most activities tonight would be held in the basement.

At the front door, Roy stopped Brandon and said, "We are about to enter the Great Lord's house. You will be absolutely quiet unless directly spoken to. Do you understand?"

The Initiate nodded. Even with the blindfold on, it was easy to see he was nervous.

"Alright," Matt said, opening the door. "Enter."

Roy guided him forward from behind, his hands on Brandon's shoulders. Once inside, Matt closed the door behind him and wiped his boots off. Hamid approached them and took Brandon from Roy. "This way, Mr. Lehane. We're going to be heading down a flight of stairs, so I'll need you to follow me very carefully…"

Logan headed back to the lounge where Randall and Fennell, the Pontifex, sat on a couch discussing something. The fireplace was the only light in the room and the glow flickered across their masked faces as they talked.

"I guess Doug is downstairs," Matt said as they followed Logan. The Magister was usually responsible for reading the First Rites, then the Legatus read the Second and the Imperator the third. The Pontifex didn't read rites since they were written long before the position existed.

Logan turned around as they entered the room. "You guys head downstairs to supervise the First Rites with Doug."

"Actually," Randall said, standing up. "Roy, you go to the basement. I need to have a word with Matt." Roy nodded and headed down the hall toward the stairs. Randall walked past Matt and said, "Follow me."

They entered the Imperator suite; he closed the door as Matt sat down in the desk chair. Randall poured both of them some scotch and handed him a glass, then took a seat on the bed.

Matt had a large sip, nervous.

"How have you been? I haven't really talked to you since before Winter Break."

"It's been…strange being back after what happened."

"I know what you mean." Randall took a sip. "The other Officers look at me like it's my fault. They'd never say it out loud, but I can tell they think there's some fanatic in our ranks killing people. Patrick and Veronica always defend me and Anathema, but I can tell even they're starting to have doubts."

"It *might* have been a mugging," Matt offered. "What happened to Benson and Chet could've been two unrelated things."

A grave look came upon his face. "Not if you know what I know."

The atmosphere in the room had shifted and Matt felt uneasy. Randall set his glass on the nightstand beside him, folding his hands in front of his face.

"I've been thinking about this a lot over Winter Break and the past three weeks, and I've decided I want to bring you into the fold. What I'm about to say does not leave this room, got it?"

Matt nodded.

"Someone in this organization has behaved suspiciously for a while. I denied it for months, but after Chet's murder I've had to come to terms with it. However, I'm not sure this person is guilty, so I need you to help me fill in some blanks."

Matt swallowed. "Okay."

"Can you put aside your feelings for Joan and answer some questions about her behavior? Just a few questions. I need to rule her out—if I can—for my own peace of mind."

Matt was silent for a moment. Then he softly uttered, "Yes," and looked up. "But do you mind me asking why you suspect her?"

Randall took another big sip of scotch, then set it down again.

"Because she was there in Bethune's Walk the night Rich Benson died."

The Imperator put a hand to his forehead. "And so was I."

FORTY-FIVE

IT TOOK effort to keep her teeth from chattering. Joan shivered and withdrew the flask from her coat, taking a long pull. The alcohol burned its way down her throat and warmth bloomed inside her stomach. It made her feel only slightly better, but it would have to do.

She'd been standing outside for over an hour now. She and Val were at the edge of the Pit while their Initiates—five first-years and three second-years—were led blindfolded to the gazebo to have the First Rites read to them by Catherine Winters.

Her hand had healed considerably in the past couple weeks. Bruising was still evident, but she could flex her fingers much better now and she'd managed to ward off questions by saying she'd slipped on black ice. Several people had raised their eyebrows, disbelieving, but questioned her no further. The main thing was that she and Matt seemed to be on solid footing again, like they had been before Winter Break. With every day the RCMP didn't arrest her, she was glad to have him as her ally.

"It sucks that the guys get the Chalet first this year. By the time they make it out here they'll be so drunk they'll barely feel the cold," Val said, staring down into the Pit.

Joan smiled. "Last year, we had it first for *your* Initiation."

She laughed. "Yeah, but I barely remember that night."

"You did well."

"Which by Initiation standards means I didn't puke, right?"

Joan shrugged. "Last year one of the boys' inducts threw up in an Uber, all over the center console."

"How? Wouldn't they have the drunkest person sit by a window?"

"You would think."

Val laughed again and shook her head. "I feel bad for his supervisors. You know, I think it's actually a lot more fun being drunk and going through this thing than it is for us to run it."

"Then let's go fix that." Joan eyed two Initiates standing in the center of the Pit with Kristen Edwards, a third-year member. The others were still back at the gazebo, waiting to be seated before Catherine while the Pontifex, Lexi Choi, supervised. These two must've already finished their First Rites. Kristen just stood there, letting them drunkenly chat and laugh. They didn't look terrified at all, not like she'd been by this point in her Initiation. Then she realized they had their blindfolds off; they were supposed to put them back on after undergoing each Rite.

"Come on." She made her way down into the Pit, striding toward the first-years with a wolfish grin.

Val followed behind her, looking concerned. "Don't take it too far…," she muttered.

"Relax," she said. Then, louder, "Hey worms!" Kristen and the two Initiates turned around. "Why aren't your fucking blindfolds on?"

"Um…," one of the girls began, looking to Kristen for support. "She said we could keep them off for now, said we could take a little break."

"Oh. Did you enjoy your break?"

They looked between each other. Kristen started slowly backing away. "Um, yeah," one of them said. "It was nice."

Joan smirked. "I bet it was. Just *how* nice was it?"

"Pretty nice, I guess," the other said.

"Oh, good, good." She put one hand on her hip and tapped a finger to her chin with the other. "Since it's pretty nice, how would you like to *not* wear blindfolds for the rest of the night?"

All of them were silent. Even Val and Kristen looked confused.

One said, "Um, I'm fine with putting it back on, actually—"

"Oh no, no, no. You just said it was pretty nice having it off, and if anything, the Anathema is pretty nice right? All rainbows and sunshine?"

"Uh…"

"So here's what the two of you are gonna do. You are not to wear blindfolds for the rest of the night unless someone from the Tetrad tells you specifically otherwise."

The girls silently exchanged looks, fear and confusion plain on their faces. "Um, okay…," one said.

"That's it. You're good. Go walk over there and enjoy how nice it feels."

The two girls stood still for a moment, then started shuffling away toward the hillside.

"*Wait.*"

They stopped dead in their tracks. Joan walked around in front and adjusted her mask. She stood there, staring between the two of them, sizing them up. One girl gulped. Off in the gazebo, she heard Catherine reading the Rite and tried not to notice how good her delivery was.

"I think something's missing. Val, Kristen, what do you think?"

"Yeah, something's missing," Kristen said, though she looked uneasy.

Joan clasped her gloved hands behind her back and stood up straight, one side of her smile curling higher than the other. She began walking a circle around the first-years. "You see, the point of the blindfold is so you won't accidentally spoil the surprise. If you saw what was coming next, Initiation wouldn't be very exciting, would it?"

The girls shook their heads.

She stopped in front of them again. "So you need something to cover your eyes—and I can't trust you to keep your eyes closed. To be honest…" She stepped closer and leaned toward the girl on the right, so close her face was inches away. She looked straight into her eyes and held the gaze. "…I don't think you could trust yourself." The girl trembled slightly.

Joan moved to the one on the left and leaned closer. "I don't think either of you could." She straightened her posture again and stepped back, sizing them up once more. "So we have a problem here. You need to have your eyes covered but you said you liked having the blindfolds off…"

"No, no," the one on the right said. "It's okay, really—"

"*Quiet!*" Joan barked. The two girls stood rigid. She stepped a little closer again and offered a warm, but insincere smile. "I hate the thought of you losing a feeling you so eloquently described as '*pretty nice.*' That was fucking poetry, by the way. I think I might cry."

The girls said nothing.

"Hmm…what to do, what to do…? We need to have your eyes covered, but you'd prefer not to wear your blindfolds. *So*...this is what's going to happen." A malicious smile formed on her lips. *"You"*—she pointed to the one on the right—"are going to cup a hand over her eyes, and *you"*—she pointed to the other—"are going to do the same to her. And you're going to do that for the *rest of the night* whether you're standing, sitting, or shitting. Do I make myself clear?"

"Even in the bathroom?" the left one groaned.

"Well, it's a good thing you're going to have your eyes covered. My advice? *Hold it.*"

The girls reluctantly covered each other's eyes and stood there in the cold night air. "And don't you dare let me catch you not like this—or with your blindfolds on again." She came closer, leaning over so her head was directly between the two of them, and breathed, "Otherwise, I'll be really disappointed... And when I'm disappointed, I tend to be the opposite of pretty nice."

Joan turned and walked away. Val and Kristen stood staring at the two girls for a moment, then Val shook her head and sighed softly.

Riverside Park had a small washroom tucked away in the trees. It stood just off the path to the playground, the women's on the left and the men's on the right. A familiar despair settled over Joan as she finished up and she thought she might start crying.

Then she heard someone else enter the stall beside her and pulled herself together. After washing her hands, she went back outside and around the building. Joan placed both hands on the wall and rested her forehead on it, the cement cold against her skin. She wasn't sure how long she stood there, breathing the frosty air, but she had just realized she wasn't going to cry after all when she heard voices approaching around the corner.

"...really think you should get it over Catherine. She's too soft and she's already been Tetrad once. Bad enough we'll have to deal with Logan Brewster again." It was Katy Coulson's voice. Joan had never liked her, but was overruled when they discussed her as an upper-year pick for last year's Initiations. Alyssa had lobbied very hard for her.

Sure enough, her voice came next. "Yeah, but I think she's Kylie's favorite and you know how it goes at this college with favorites..."

"Well, just keep focusing on it. It's either you or her for sure. I mean who else would it be?" Katy laughed. "Joan Keating?"

Alyssa burst into hysterics. "Don't you even fucking joke about that! Oh my god…she's such an *idiot*. Socially, at least—I guess she was smart enough to get into Cliffe. But it sucks she has a boyfriend now; we can't write about her dating life anymore. I loved all those jokes we wrote last year about her Bumble profile."

"Yeah, but Matt's only dating her because he was desperate for a girlfriend. He doesn't care how weird she is; he's just glad a pretty girl wants to fuck him. He doesn't even mind the scar."

They both laughed and Joan's stomach tightened, tears welling for real this time.

"I wish we were allowed to make fun of her for that," Alyssa said. "It's such a waste of good material. She *should* be able to take jokes about it. And everyone would laugh because they'd all get it. I mean, we all see it there on her face. Not even the fucking mask can hide it."

They both laughed again. She heard Katy say, "Yeah, why *can't* we make jokes about it?"

"Why do you think?"

Silence. A third voice had entered the conversation. Someone walked out of the bathroom, boots crunching on the snow.

"Well," the voice said. "I'm waiting. Why do you think we don't make fun of Joan for her scar?" It was Sandrine. The Legatus must've been the one in the stall beside her.

"Because it's…mean?" Alyssa offered.

"It is, but the Anathema has made many *mean* jokes over the years. Why not make this one, or ones like it?"

More silence. Joan pictured Sandrine standing there with her usual stern gaze, dressed in all-black save for the silver sash across her coat.

"Because," Sandrine continued, "our organization is meant to criticize people's *actions*, not things they can't help. Making fun of someone for an old injury is not satire, it is *bullying*. And we are not bullies…although you two appear to be exceptions."

"No, no," Katy stuttered. "We were just joking."

"Good. Keep it that way. Let's head back to the Pit and find the others. The boys are just finishing up at the Chalet, so it's time to leave."

Joan listened as their footfalls faded and wiped away tears. She took out her flask and, tilting it back, downed the rest of the vodka in a few long pulls. Then she slid it back into her jacket, sniffled, and headed after them, grateful her mask would conceal some of the redness around her eyes.

FORTY-SIX

"**I**T STARTED at the end of last year," Randall said. "We were coming up on the big Student Governance Meeting where our...dissenters were trying to amend the Electoral Policy against our favor. So, you remember, I sent a message to our group chat telling all of you to be there and to bring along every pro-Anathema member of college you could find. Kylie sent her branch a similar message.

"Then, the day of the SGM, I got called into the Dean's Office. Crawley said she'd heard reports of 'Anathema collusion' and that we were going to try to rig the vote or something. I told her the truth, that I was just encouraging like-minded individuals to show up and voice their opinions. And I told her I knew people on the other side who were also getting people out to vote.

"Anyway, we got a modified amendment passed, so we basically won that round...but I kept wondering who told the Dean. She wouldn't tell me, just that it was *an* anonymous source. Singular."

"Patrick?" Matt suggested. "He was really going off on his high horse at the end of last year."

"*At the end?*" Randall chuckled. "He was tripping on power the entire goddamn year. Him winning his Officer election was just icing on the cake. Do you remember his whole pendant-dropping ceremony outside Ni Hao?"

Matt nodded. Patrick had made a big show of retiring from the organization last year.

Randall sighed. "He's gotten better since then, but I still suspected him. He told me he would abstain from voting because being both Imperator and Officer was, I quote, 'immoral.' But he had left the group chat by then, and I'd never told him we were mobilizing."

"He could have guessed it."

"Maybe. But it seemed to me that it was someone in either the male or female branch at the time."

Matt thought for a moment. "What about Rufus?"

Randall shook his head. "He didn't rejoin Anathema until the summer. He messaged me, we discussed things, and then I re-added him to the chat in mid-July. I don't even remember seeing him at the SGM."

"Did you tell anybody outside the group chat?"

"Just Tom and Veronica, but they were both Imperators. I'm assuming they wouldn't shoot their legacy in the foot by going to the admin."

Matt nodded. "Right."

"Tom wasn't exactly big on the whole Officer-Imperator thing at first, but he told me I had his support because he trusted me. Patrick still backs me up on the Council, but he's told me many times he hopes I'm the last to hold both positions—at the same time, at least. He doesn't mind that Veronica became an Officer a year later."

Randall took another sip of scotch. "So anyway, that was that. The summer went by, September rolled around. We came back. It was Frosh Week, and we had our first meeting of the year, a joint one. We didn't write anything because there wasn't much to write about yet, but both Kylie and I stressed the importance of paying attention to stupid shit the frosh did. Especially to the second-year members who were frosh leaders. And I joked that if you had to goad these people into saying dumb shit, so be it, because we needed lots of jokes on first-years so they'd know who we were talking about at the Sermon."

He waved a hand. "Next thing I know, Donna Crawley's hauling my ass before her desk again, telling me an *anonymous source* heard that we were purposely trying to get the frosh to say stupid things to write jokes about them. So now I know we've got a fucking problem. Ultimately, this is petty, pissant stuff. The Anathema has faced a lot worse, but it really stings me that we've got a snitch.

"So Kylie and I talked and decided we'd do a little mole hunt. She told me she'd look into it, but mostly kept me out of her stuff. Fair enough. I knew I wouldn't be able to do much snooping myself, because nobody would tell me anything. So I left it to Logan. People talk to him, people tell him stuff. He's Tetrad, but he's a third-year so he's a little more approachable. And, let's face it, he's pretty popular. Doug's also tapped in around Social Cliffe, so I sent him sniffing on a few trails too."

Randall sighed. "Now comes the part I'm not proud of. I had faith in Kylie, but I'm better friends with other people in the female branch. I got really worried about this snitch bullshit—what if this person somehow got me impeached?—and figured it wouldn't hurt if I had a spy in their branch, just keeping an eye out and reporting back to me."

Matt nodded. "And so that's where Joan came in."

"I was actually her frosh leader. Of course, we both weren't Initiated yet. I got in the same night you two did." He took another sip and returned his glass to the nightstand. "But I could tell even then that she was into it, the kind who would make a dedicated member. I was glad to see she got in, but we'd been friends since Frosh Week." Randall held up his hands. "And *just* friends, don't worry. I saw that look on your face at Winslow Christmas and I don't want you to get the wrong idea."

Matt's shoulders relaxed a little. "I figured as much, but it's good to hear it anyway."

Randall smiled. "I've been dating Gemma since high school. There's never been anyone else and, honestly, I hope there never will be." He took a deep breath. "Back to this. I trusted Joan and asked her if she'd help me root out the snitch—and not tell Kylie I was going around behind her back. She was worried it might affect her Imperator chances if she was caught, but agreed this was more important to Anathema as a whole, so she was willing to risk it."

Matt furrowed his brow. "Wow. And Imperator's a really big deal for her."

"Yeah, so she and I started having secret rendezvouses at the Chalet late at night, where she'd update me on her progress. We would arrange meetings in person or over the phone—I didn't even want a text trail. I told no one about this except Gemma, just in case she thought I was meeting another girl at the Chalet for other reasons. But nobody at Cliffe knew, not even Tom. At least, not until later. I talked to him about it after the First Sermon, when Serpentine attacked.

Randall cleared his throat. "Joan was pretty sure Kylie had gotten Catherine to do the snooping, since, like Logan, she's also pretty popular. But by the end of September, nobody had any leads—not her, not Logan, not Catherine, not Kylie, and certainly not me. We were scheduled to have another meeting on the second of October at around 12:30 a.m., but Kylie had a meeting with her Tetrad about something and wanted to use the Chalet. So I called Joan and we planned to meet at another location."

"Bethune's Walk."

The Imperator nodded. "Exactly. So I went out there late at night, wearing my cloak and medallion—" He saw Matt's confused expression. "Yeah I know, that sounds a bit much, right? But it was all to make Joan more comfortable spying on her own branch. She told me she'd feel better if we wore full Anathema attire during our meetings, discussing secrets in the lounge by the light of the fireplace with masks and everything. I was like, okay, if it makes you feel better—I've never really been into the whole dress-up part of this thing, but to each their own."

The candlelight rituals and masks were actually Matt's favorite part, but all he said was, "Yeah, that sounds like Joan. She's always been into the ceremonial aspect of it."

Randall laughed. "Really? I couldn't tell." His expression became more serious again. "We were supposed to meet in an area of the park past the bridge, so I went there and waited for Joan to arrive. A couple minutes passed. Then five, then ten. She still wasn't there, but she'd never been late before. She always arrived on the dot. So I started to get a little worried and broke protocol. I texted her: 'Hey, everything alright?' But Joan didn't respond. I waited another five minutes, then I started walking back along the path and…" He paused. "I'm certain I heard someone walking, just on the other side of a bend. So I hid in the trees and waited but didn't see anybody. Maybe they slipped by, I don't know…"

Randall looked increasingly nervous. He wiped sweat from his brow and finished the last of his scotch, his knuckles going white from how tightly he held the glass. "So I continued walking through the woods—I didn't want to go back to the path, I don't know why… I just had this strange feeling that something was very, very wrong. And so I continued until I reached the creek." He brought his hand to his mouth and sharply inhaled, then slowly breathed out. "And I saw a body, lying there. His face was in the stream and a full moon was out and you could…you could see the blood trailing away from his head. His face was leaning against a rock. And I just stood there, not believing it for a few minutes. It took me a moment to realize I'd seen Benson wearing those clothes in Galbraith at lunch that day. And…"

Matt's hairs stood on end. He could picture it: the corpse in the creek, the moon in the sky—and Randall, standing there in full Imperator regalia off to the side, staring in disbelief through his silver mask.

Randall got up and poured himself some more scotch, then returned to his seat. "I left after that, but I went a different way than I'd come—not out the parking lot. I went back by the Engineering buildings, took off my cloak, bundled it with the mask and medallion inside, then walked back past Front Campus Circle, past Radcliffe, through Griffin—all the way back to Gemma's house. Mercifully, she'd gone to sleep hours earlier. I told her Joan and I ended up cancelling the meeting, but she'd never known where it was. We'd changed our plans that afternoon. Kylie hadn't told me she was using the Chalet until then. I called Joan to let her know and that's when we decided on Bethune's Walk."

"You never told the police this?" Matt said.

"They'd think it was Joan. Or me. And trust me, the last thing I wanted for this organization was more controversy."

"Did *you* think it was Joan?"

Randall paused. "I didn't know—still don't. Benson didn't treat her very well. At first, they went on a couple of dates, then he asked her to Fall Formal. I never liked the guy, but she seemed happy. So they went, and… I'm assuming you know the rest."

"He took her virginity, then stopped talking to her altogether, acted like they'd just gone to Formal casually and hooked up." Joan had never discussed it with him; he'd just put it together over time.

"Yeah, but it got worse. He looked like a dick to people who knew the situation better, but then she got into Anathema. And so he went around telling people the real reason why he didn't continue things with her was that she was super into it and was completely crazy. In his exposé he even referenced her, saying the female inducts were 'depraved wallflowers.' "

"I saw that," Matt said, anger surfacing with the memory.

"Yeah." Randall shook his head in disgust. "Some people called him out for that, and normally he would have been labeled sexist, but he got off because he was saying it about an Anathema member. Suddenly that made it okay, since we're the villains."

"He seemed like a real piece of work."

"You can say that again." Randall drank more scotch. Matt sipped some of his, noticing the Imperator's sad look. "My first thought—before

I'd even considered that he'd tripped or slipped—was that she bumped into him. He must've been out for a late-night stroll or something, and when he saw her with the mask and pendant, he certainly would've said something. Teased her, maybe. And I guess I thought maybe she just snapped and pushed him. An accident, totally unplanned and out of the blue. I didn't even think she would've meant to kill him. But then the more I thought about it, the more ridiculous it seemed. He probably just tripped. Maybe she saw his body, got scared, and ran off.

"She texted me the next day, said she was sorry she couldn't make it. We've never discussed that night, not directly. She continued to update me on her progress, but we eventually gave up. There were a few more leaks here and there, but it was all minor stuff. We had a much bigger problem by then. But as time went on, I realized Rich Benson couldn't have had an accident. Someone *had* to have pushed him. And the only other person in Bethune's Walk that night was Joan Keating. At least, that I know of."

He sipped some more, set it down again. "The RCMP came to me earlier this week. They told me Joan broke a girl's arm in high school and asked if I'd seen her act violently. I told them no. But you spend much more time with her, Matt. I need to know if I've been protecting a killer."

Matt sat in silence for a while, thinking. He recalled that playful punch she'd given him at Lambda Halloween that hurt more than it should've, how she'd smashed Blaine's nose in December, how she'd told him what she did to Rita Parsons. He remembered the words she'd said as they sat on her floor.

I can see why they think I did it... I've done terrible things before. I've hurt people.

He turned back to Randall. "I can tell you with absolute certainty that Joan would *never* have killed anyone, even by accident."

The Imperator leaned back against the wall, closed his eyes, and exhaled. Eventually, he sat up and looked at Matt again. "Thank you. That really puts my mind at ease." He glanced at his watch. "They better be finishing up downstairs. The girls will be here soon."

Matt polished off his scotch as Randall led him out the door, glad the Imperator had bought his words.

He was less sure of them himself.

◆

Afterward, they went to Riverside.

Logan performed the Second Rite by the playground where Serpentine had chased Joan, then they were brought down to the gazebo, one by one, to undergo the Third. Matt stood just off to the side of the gazebo as the last Initiate, a British first-year named Freddie who was good friends with the Legatus, finished his oath.

"…and do you swear," Randall continued, reading from a dusty antique volume, "to use your status among the ranks of His members to chastise only insolence, to abstain from personal vendettas, and to help strike a balance between the Enigma and the Bacchanal, the two core tenets of this organization?"

"I do," Freddie said, kneeling before the Imperator.

"Then on this 25th day of January, in the two-thousand and nineteenth-year anno domini and the one-hundred and fifteenth of the Great Lord, I anoint you, Frederick Evans, as a member of the Anathema." So saying, he drew a skull pendant out of the book's gutter and slowly lowered the necklace over the first-year's head.

Applause erupted from the Tetrad standing in the gazebo and the other members all around—including the other Initiates. Freddie stood up and Randall drew out a Venetian mask next. "Welcome," he said, handing it off.

Then the Imperator turned to the others, slammed the old book shut, and shouted, "Let's go to Ni Hao!"

Somebody whistled. The reverent silence reserved for the ritual now broken, the members began chatting and moving about, removing their masks and checking their phones.

Matt stood still, staring off at the glass-like surface of the frozen stream. Something chilled him, and it wasn't the wind.

FORTY-SEVEN

I T WAS after midnight by the time they got to the restaurant. Joan's eyes had long since dried by then, but she'd been unable to shake the cloud hanging over her. As she removed her mask and walked through the door, she realized she didn't want food, she wanted alcohol. She wanted as much of it as she could drink without throwing up. She wanted to feel light and happy and to laugh at every joke. Her memory of the night would blur come morning and it would only feel like a bad dream.

Except, just like every other time, it wouldn't be. It would always be something that really did happen, only now she would inevitably make herself look like an idiot—and she wouldn't even remember how much of an idiot she'd made herself appear.

Don't do this again, a voice in her head sighed. *You already had to leave early after the First Sermon.*

She shouldn't get blackout drunk again. She really needed to stop do-ing that...but if the RCMP showed up with an arrest warrant tomorrow, what difference would it make?

No.

There had to be another way to alleviate her spirits. And as Matt climbed out of an Uber at the curb with Roy and Tanner, an idea popped into her head.

Yes, that would do. That would definitely do.

Joan bit her lip to hide her sudden smile, thinking how long it had been since the last time. She'd been patient—very, *very* patient. It had been

333

nearly three weeks since she'd pushed him too far, but Joan sensed tonight was the right time to try. She could tell by the look on his face as he walked in that something troubled him, that he would search for a release.

You'd be using him.

The thought made her feel ashamed, but her mind swiftly smothered it. *You've waited long enough,* it said. *So has he. He's been coming around to it. He'd be ready soon enough anyway.*

"Hey." Matt stood right in front of her now and she snapped out of it. "How'd it go?"

"Well, nobody died. So that's something." Joan slid her arm around his waist and pulled him closer. "Let's get a table."

As more members arrived, everyone headed to the rear of the restaurant. She and Matt sat with Kylie, Sandrine, Val, Roy, and a few new Initiates. As people drank and ate and talked, Joan's eyes danced along the dragon imagery of the walls. She smiled and laughed at the right times, but her mind was not sitting here at Ni Hao Ma with the others. It was back in her room in Lacy, thinking how it would go afterward. She saw the scene unfold in her mind as if she were writing it out by pen, her preferred first-draft method. She had to play things carefully, though.

Guilt grew inside her the more vivid the image became.

I'm not going to force him to do anything he doesn't want to. And that was final. But it didn't mean she couldn't be persuasive.

At that moment, Joan realized the internal debate prevented her from thinking back to Alyssa and Katy's conversation. She pushed their words away, focusing on what lay ahead and how to get there.

Members began trickling out after about an hour. Once they'd finished splitting their chicken poppers, she turned to Matt with her phone out and the Uber app on the screen. "Wanna hang out in my room?" She smiled slyly.

"Sure," he said, still looking uneasy. He'd barely touched their food; she'd eaten most of the platter. "We can chat there." The way he said it didn't sound fun and a pang of dread hit her stomach.

"Okay."

They went up to the counter and paid. Joan wanted to cover the whole entree, since she'd had most of it, but he insisted on splitting. She ordered the Uber and they said goodbye to the others, then headed out of Ni Hao Ma to stand on the sidewalk.

A frosty breeze wafted by and she put up the hood of her coat. Matt stood there without his up, looking miserable in the cold while they waited. Frowning, she came closer and pulled the hood over his head, then gave him a kiss.

He smiled weakly. "Thanks." An incredibly torn look resided in his eyes. Before she could say something, their car arrived.

The driver took the highway over to the next exit, its sign labeled Western Canada University. They sped past the school's entrance, swerving onto the leftmost drive as the road split in three directions. Soon the car whipped by Lambda Phi and came around the curve, Radcliffe looming up ahead. A number of lights were still on even at this hour. She glanced at her watch: almost 1:30 a.m.

Joan and Matt made their way up the front stairs, careful to check for ice. When they got to the West Quad, he suddenly stopped and stared off at Lacy's windows, some darkened and others lit.

"What is it?" she asked.

He took the hood off and cupped his hands over his face briefly, then lowered them. "I'm sorry, I've been really out of it."

"Are you drunk?" *Please say no.*

"No, no, I've sobered up. I'll still come up if you want. It's late and I don't want to keep you up."

She laughed. Hadn't he noticed the way she smiled back at the restaurant, that look she'd given him? She wondered whether his lack of romantic success was due to positive signs he'd missed while pursuing the wrong leads.

Pursuing the wrong leads…

Joan shook her head to clear it, then looked back at him. "No, no, it's fine. All I'm missing is sleep." She laughed.

"Okay."

Together, they headed through the western door up to the second floor, her heart beating faster as they climbed the steps. When they reached her door, she turned around, unable to hide her smile. "Put your mask on."

"My mask?" He laughed. "Okay, what's…?"

"And take off your boots. I'll let you in in a sec." And she gave him that sly look again, just to make sure he really got it, then went into her room and closed the door.

◆

Matt stood in the hallway, his mind racing.

He'd been so lost in a trance at the restaurant, thinking about what Randall had told him, that he hadn't noticed her flirtation. It only hit him once he'd reached the Quad what she meant by *hang out in my room*.

And now he was even more torn.

Under any other circumstance, he would've been ecstatic. And he knew he wanted to, *really* wanted to. He finally felt ready, but suspicion gripped him with a tight fist and he found it harder than ever to break free of its grasp.

There's an explanation for it. Someone else was out there that night and killed Benson. She didn't do it. She told *you she didn't do it.*

He put his mask on and removed his boots, setting them beside the door. Why was she taking so long? What was she setting up? What kind of things was she into? He was fine with getting made fun of for "being whipped," but the figure of speech was as far as he would take it. Now he was as intrigued as he was afraid. He stared at the door, wondering what awaited behind it. The longer he stood there, the more comfortable he became staying in the hall, not backing out yet not going in. The perfect purgatory.

"You can come in. It's unlocked."

Matt swallowed, then reached for the doorknob. He turned it and slowly pushed the door open, his heart pounding. The room beyond was dark, and as more of it was revealed he saw candles placed around. He put one foot forward and stepped in, softly shutting the door behind him, the brightness of the hallway snuffed out.

Joan sat facing him in only her mask, pendant, and a black bra and panties; one leg was crossed over the other. She smirked, leaning against the desk and resting her chin on her palm. A candle cast shadows across her face and mask.

"Lock the door."

Matt fumbled for the knob behind him, turning the lock into place with a click.

Then his eyes wandered the room. "This is both better and worse than I expected."

Still smirking, Joan got up and strode toward him. The shyness and awkwardness he saw in her around other people was gone, confidence radiating from her as she approached. He opened his mouth to say something, but in the next moment, she slammed him back against the door and shoved her tongue into his mouth. If her bruised hand still bothered her, she didn't show it.

Rapidly, she began undoing the buttons of his shirt, their lips still locked in a rhythm. He managed to undo his bowtie and let it fall to the ground, shaking off his coat and tuxedo jacket. He ran his hand under her arm, past her bra, and down her side. Her knee came up to his hip and he slid his palm along her bare thigh.

Joan pulled back and tore his shirt off, helping him slide out of his sleeves. He got the undershirt over his head, but the pendant still swung from his neck. He started to take it off, when she grabbed it and forced him back against the door, her face very close to his. "No," she breathed. "Leave it on. And the mask."

He managed a laugh, then said in a hushed voice, "This is the kind of thing people *think* you and I are into."

"Let them."

She drew him away from the door and threw him onto the bed, climbing astride him and bringing her lips back to his. He fumbled with his belt and zipper and kicked his pants away, then managed to get his socks off using only his toes while she gave him a hickey. He reached around and unclasped her bra; she shrugged out of it, the pendant dangling before her breasts.

Joan came back down and kissed him, then slowly pulled away. Behind the mask he saw sadness in her eyes.

"No, this isn't right." She pushed away and sat on the bed's edge, her feet on the floor.

Matt sat up, gently reaching toward her. She let him put his hand against her back and he gently rubbed up and down. "What's wrong?" he asked.

"I'm using you, just like I would've been after the police interviewed us. I'm upset and I'm using you to make myself feel better." She turned around. "I'm sorry, this isn't how your first time should be."

He managed a laugh. "I really don't mind, Joan. I feel ready now and you've certainly waited long enough. I'd just be glad to have my first time with someone I care about."

Joan smiled warmly and stroked his cheek. "You *should* mind. You shouldn't let people treat you like that. Loyalty is only a virtue when it's rewarded; otherwise, you're just letting people take advantage of you."

"You're not taking advantage of me. If you're upset and I can help, I want to. What happened?"

She gripped the edge of the bed. "It was Alyssa and Katy. I heard them talking about how they wished they could make fun of my scar. And they said you were only dating me because you were desperate for a girlfriend."

His mood darkened. "Well, that's not fucking true. The time I told everybody I lost my virginity wasn't a complete lie. I was about to do it with someone, but I realized I'd rather wait for a girl I actually liked. And I've liked you for a very long time." He hesitated, then decided to tell her. "I've had a crush on you since the first day of Frosh Week. *Our* Frosh Week. I was going to ask you to dance at the Fall Formal that year, but I realized you were with Rich Benson."

She stared off and a sad smile came to her lips. "I wish you had asked me."

Matt leaned closer and kissed her bare shoulder. "I've thought about it and I'm ready if you are. I will admit I thought the whole…masks and pendants and candles thing was a bit much, but it's grown on me in the past few minutes. It really has."

She turned back to him, her expression warming. "Are you absolutely sure? You only lose it once."

He took a deep breath. "Yes."

Joan continued staring at him. Her posture became straighter and one corner of her mouth curled higher than the other. "I was hoping you'd say that."

She tackled him to the bed, sinking her teeth into his shoulder. He cried out and gripped her back tightly. She bit his arm next, then the side of his chest. Wincing, he rolled her over and they accidentally butted heads.

"Shit, sorry."

Joan rubbed her forehead and laughed. "It's okay," she said, more amused than anything else.

She kissed him again and pulled him on top of her. He continued past her lower lip, down the side of her neck, taking his time. She moaned as he buried his face in her chest, kissing her breasts and feeling the cold metal of her pendant against his cheek. He moved on, venturing down her belly and, finally, below her waist.

Matt pulled her panties down and hesitated, unsure exactly of how to handle this, but she grabbed his head and guided him in. He quickly stopped thinking about it and let his tongue find its way. She arched her back and whimpered, thrusting her hips to help him as he wrapped his arms around her legs, gripping the inside of her thighs.

Minutes blurred away and he became lost in the motions. It was some time before her entire body shuddered and she held Matt tighter with her hands and legs, her loudest moan yet filling his ears. She arched her back higher, then collapsed atop the sheets, breathing heavily.

He pulled back and exhaled, wiping sweat from his forehead.

Joan propped herself up on the pillow, still catching her breath, and glanced down toward him. She looked impressed, a lustful gleam in her eyes behind the mask.

"You look tired," was all she said.

He laughed, panting. "I'm good, really."

She leaned over to her nightstand and fished out a small blue package with the Trojan emblem. "You *do* know how to use one of these, right?" she teased, dangling it from her fingers.

Matt rolled his eyes. "Give me some credit."

She tossed it toward him and put her hands behind her head. "Whenever you're ready…" He tore off his underwear, finished putting it on, and climbed over her, but hesitated as she spread her legs. She smiled softly and rubbed a hand along his left arm. "Do you want me on top?"

He gave a slow nod.

She smirked. "That's more my forte, anyway."

Joan rolled him over, but her motions were much gentler now. She gave him one last, brief kiss, and then they began.

The whole time she kept her face near his, their arms around each other in a tight embrace, their bodies pressed together. They took things slow and steady, and Matt quickly eased into it. It was different than he'd imagined, but he was immensely grateful she was the one to initiate him. He kissed Joan as she rode him, the two of them drenched in sweat and panting. And when they reached the end, he realized that nothing compared to the real thing.

It was still dark out. He lay awake, unable to get back to sleep. He'd stirred about half an hour ago, but didn't want to lean across her to look at the clock for fear of waking her. They'd removed their masks and pendants and had drifted off in each other's arms. Now he held Joan while she slept, listening to the sounds of her breathing as he stared at the ceiling.

He thought of what she did to Rita Parsons in high school and how she'd broken Blaine's nose. He thought of how much she enjoyed hazing, how she admitted she had this hidden side to her, one full of rage that delighted in torment and perhaps even cruelty. He thought of what Benson had said about her, both behind her back and in print for the whole college to read.

He knew she was capable of harming Benson, even if it was just by accident. But that didn't mean she had. There *was* a reason why she'd fled her meeting with Randall so suddenly. Either she'd done it because she killed Benson or because she'd seen something and ran, but as he cradled her closer, he wasn't sure he wanted to know the answer.

FORTY-EIGHT

W ITH LESS than a week to the event, the caterers paid, the decorations purchased, and the affairs all in order, it appeared that Mustard would not be cancelling the Winter Formal after all.

There was always a certain hurriedness among Radcliffe students the week before a ball. The day of was spent preparing and preing, the day after nursing hangovers and sharing tales of debauchery. As such, Mackenzie Library was always packed leading up to a Formal, students scrambling to accomplish assignments before the weekend.

Matt and Joan bought tickets as soon as they became available the Monday after Initiations. He realized this would be the first time he'd gone to such an event with a girlfriend and Joan agreed it was a special occasion. She even suggested using the event's photo booth for new Facebook profile pictures, as a couple.

As they entered the final days before the dance, Matt grew increasingly worried that they hadn't heard anything from the RCMP. Ever since Randall told him he'd been interviewed, Matt knew they were around and digging for evidence. They were unseen phantoms lurking the college's halls, waiting to leap out and startle him and Joan.

Maybe they'd get lucky. Maybe the police would find clues to the real culprit behind the killings. Matt hadn't gotten much else in his search for the Bard. At writing sessions, Rufus was his usual self and no one else seemed to be acting odd or anxious. Anyone except for Randall, already burdened by his legion of commitments and that ever-present specter of an impeachment inquiry. Not to mention the information he'd withheld from the police about Joan. At the last meeting, he'd mentioned he was DJing the dance, and it appeared to be something he was looking forward to. Back when Radcliffe still had licensed parties year-round, he'd done a fair bit of DJing and always provided good mixes, so it would be nice to see him back in that saddle.

Winter Formal was the first Saturday of February, and that Thursday evening Matt went for a stroll in Bethune's Walk to clear his head before dinner. The woods were different in wintertime. The snow-covered grounds were desolate, and without the leaves one could still see Radcliffe back up the hill. He walked through the parking lot and around the gravel road, strolled past the Chalet, then cut across the eastern section of Griffin Park before reaching the college's front circle.

The Provost's BMW was parked in its spot at the side of the road. This time however, more cars accompanied it than usual. Many alumni came to Winter Formal, even more so than the Fall dance despite its status as a charity ball. This year, Mustard would find himself flanked by both the environmental group the proceeds were going to and important donors he needed to impress. Matt shook his head and continued up the front stairs.

When he entered Galbraith, he didn't see Joan anywhere and texted her. She messaged back as he was grabbing some water to drink.

Ate earlier w/Val. Sorry :(

Also, gotta work on an econ group project with Turland tonight.

It turned out Tom Turland still needed another third-year level econ course to complete his major, and had ended up in Joan's Advanced Microeconomics class. Both of them had vented to Matt about its incomprehensible PowerPoints and bone-dry lectures.

Looking at his phone, Matt nodded and sighed. He looked around the dining hall for anyone he could sit with. The only person he even remotely talked to was Logan Brewster, hunched over a plate at one end of the third-year table.

Bracing himself, he walked over and stood behind the seat across from him. "Anyone sitting here?"

Logan looked up, then shook his head. "No, no," he said, his mouth full. "Have a seat."

Matt did so and began eating. After about a minute had passed, he glanced across the table. The Legatus paid him no attention as he continued his dinner.

"How are your English classes?" he asked.

Logan seemed surprised. "Oh, uh…they're going alright. I'm in a Shakespeare course, which I thought would be cool, but the prof's a total bitch. I turned in a paper on *Macbeth* today, but I'm sure I'll get fucked up the ass by her red pen."

"That sucks. I like *Macbeth*, it's probably my favorite Shakespeare."

"Yeah, I just kinda admire the characters. His wife's a piece of work, but I like how she basically tells Macbeth he's a pussy unless he does all this stuff. Sometimes that's what you gotta do to get things done."

Matt paused. "They both end up dead by the end of the play."

"Oh…yeah…" He shrugged and went back to eating.

They sat in silence for another couple minutes, then Matt said, "When's our next meeting?"

"I don't know. I'll talk to Randall. Probably next Tuesday. We should have at least one more before Reading Week." He continued his meal.

Matt sat there, watching him. There was no *How are your history courses?* or any other attempt to extend the conversation. Logan just sat there, hunched over his plate in a T-shirt and ripped jeans, chewing with his mouth open and, aside from Matt, sitting alone. He couldn't help but think how many times he'd seen Logan like this, just as he often sat unaccompanied himself. He narrowed his eyes, examining his competition. Where was the allure, the charisma? Where was the brilliance everyone saw?

Clearly, he was fucking missing it.

What was so special about him? He'd written some funny jokes, but he'd also written some rather cruel ones. Matt would never forget one time in second-year, before Madler's First Sermon. "Future Causes of Death for men of college," Logan had snarled in the Chalet's lounge. "Matthew Richardson—ah, who the fuck cares? Just get it over with already." Not even many in the room had laughed; it had struck them as random. Madler didn't read it at the Sermon. Matt told himself it was just joshing, but he wasn't sure exactly what he was being chastised for. The joke wasn't about something he'd done or said, it was a dismissal of his entire existence.

And it had been very much on his mind when he nearly committed suicide last year.

Logan still hadn't noticed he was staring at him, hatred in his eyes. *I've tried since first-year*, Matt thought, *since Initiation, to be friends with you. You always brush me aside, you never—*

"Hey, Logan."

Matt snapped out of it, his emotions decelerating. The recently-Initiated Freddie Evans and a friend of his, another first-year, were approaching their seats.

"Sup, guys," Logan said, leaning back in his chair. He gestured beside him. "You got plans tonight?"

"Not currently," Freddie said, sitting down. "You?"

"Me? Nah. Just seeing if you guys wanna do something. How about we chill in Tony's room and play some *FIFA*? I've got beer and I know Tony doesn't have anything due until March."

"Yeah, sure," Freddie said.

He looked to his friend, who nodded and said, "I'm down."

"Dope." Logan wiped his mouth and stood up. "Let's head out." He grabbed his plate and cup and looked back to Matt. "Say...have you fucked Joan yet?"

The two first-years whipped around, watching with amusement as he went scarlet, though Freddie appeared a bit uncomfortable with the question. Matt finally said, "Yeah..."

Logan smirked. "See, I told you you'd be in for some of that. Is she as fun as Vance said?"

He narrowed his eyes. "None of your fucking business."

The Legatus chuckled and walked off, Freddie in tow. The other first-year stayed behind, a smug look on his face. He laughed and shook his head. "I'd hate to be you."

Matt stared at him, unblinking. "One step ahead of you, pal."

The first-year walked off, still laughing, and he was left to finish his dinner alone.

FORTY-NINE

SATURDAY NIGHT arrived and a blizzard along with it, but the festivities were to continue as planned. Snow swirled outside the window as Matt closed his curtains to get dressed. The Formals were the only times he got to wear his tux for non-Anathema purposes, though he'd subconsciously put his pendant and mask out on the bed anyway.

He still had one small task to carry out for the organization tonight, however. On his desk sat a letter addressed to Marko Duric, 111, the Imperator the year before he came to Radcliffe. Second Sermon invitations were sent to all alumni, no matter what part of the world they were in or what rank they had served, though if they were to be at WCU before the event it was to be handed to them personally. Duric was now a research assistant in the Physics Department and had informed Randall that he would be at the Winter Formal this year.

The event officially began at 8:30 with a cocktail reception that went until 10 p.m., when the whole affair turned into a dance party. Galbraith had been closed for half of yesterday and all of today while decorations were set up, with food served in the Mess Hall of the Dales Building.

Matt had gotten out of his other clothes and was putting his pants on when a knock came at the door. He'd asked Roy to bring him a safety pin for one of his shirt buttons; it had accidentally gotten torn that first night in Joan's room.

"Just a second," he said, quickly doing up the zipper. He'd put the shirt on later. Matt went to the door and pulled it open. "Thank you so much for—"

He froze. Joan stood before him in an elegant black dress, her lipstick and eyeshadow the same color; her purse was slung over her shoulder. She looked absolutely gorgeous and it took him a moment to realize he was still shirtless.

Her eyes looked him up and down, a familiar sly smile coming to her face. He ducked behind the door and leaned out. "Oh, hi…"

Joan rolled her eyes and pushed her way in. "I've already seen everything, dumbass," she teased, her hand brushing across his shoulder as he closed the door.

"What's up?"

She sat on the bed and held up a safety pin. "Roy said you needed this."

"I did, thanks." He took it and placed it on the desk, then started putting his undershirt on. "I thought you were preing with Val and Sophia."

She sighed, a sad look falling across her face. "I was, but then Katy Coulson showed up to the party and suddenly I had somewhere else to be." She bit her lip. "I don't know, was that a bad move?"

He sat down beside her and kissed her, then reached around to rub her right shoulder. "I don't think so. I'm glad you're here." He laughed. "Sorry I'm not ready yet."

Joan smiled. "I went to see if you were at Roy's, then thought I'd surprise you."

"You look really fantastic, by the way. I love the dress."

She blushed and drew her Anathema flask out of the purse. "Started preing yet?"

"No, I need to get caught up." Matt stood and went to his dresser, where his own flask stood, already filled with rum. He took a large swig, then set to work putting on his tuxedo shirt and doing up the buttons. He took the safety pin off the desk and used it to help hold the loose one in place. Fortunately, that part of his shirt would be covered by the jacket when done up.

"I took the steam tunnels here from Winslow. It's insane outside."

"I feel bad for the off-res students coming in. Even if they Uber to the front circle, they'll still have to make it up the steps in this weather." Once he tied his bow-tie and got his jacket on, he took some styling paste and a comb to the bathroom to fix up his hair, then returned to the room. "Alright, I'm good to go when you are."

Joan stood at his desk, looking at the calligraphy-labeled envelope. "Ah, you got Duric. Mine's easy, it's Veronica."

"I've talked to Duric a couple of times; he'll recognize me."

"If he's not too drunk by then." She handed him the letter. "I've heard some of the alumni were invited to Fourth-Year Bar."

"That's already over now, isn't it?"

She nodded. "I saw a bunch of fourth-years stumbling down from Picard in the lobby earlier. They all looked pretty sloshed."

He slid his flask into one inside pocket and the letter into the other, and flicked off the lights. They headed down the hallway to the basement stairs, going through a door beside the exit to the Napier archway. When they reached the steam tunnels, they continued south toward the east-west corridor.

"I hope nobody gets too drunk," Matt said. "If they call any ambulances, Mustard will shut down events for good."

She took another swig from her flask. "When I was a frosh leader, I convinced a first-year the Provost's middle name was Dijon."

He laughed and turned to her. "And someone fell for that?"

She nodded, a proud smile on her face. "For the rest of the week. I got a few other leaders to go along with it." She frowned. "You weren't a frosh leader though, right?"

Matt shook his head. "I didn't get accepted."

"Aww." She gave him a kiss on the cheek, then offered him her flask. "If this is the last Winter Formal ever, we might as well enjoy it." He considered, then took a swig and handed it back. "At least if people make complete idiots of themselves," she continued, "we'll have good material for the next Sermon."

Soon they came up the stairs into Sub-Winslow, where they were greeted by a booming voice that echoed through the entire res house.

"…IS THE MOST *FIRE* EVENT IN RADCLIFFE HISTORY! No, no…it's more than that. It is…AN INSTITUTION UNTO ITSELF!"

Matt and Joan exchanged looks, then inched their way up the stairs, past the front door, and then onto the next flight leading to the second-floor landing.

"For those of you just tuning in, I am Carl Dunlap, and I just got back from Fourth-Year Bar." His disembodied speech was slightly slurred. "And you know *what*…? I'm having a really good time right now. I've got my trusty bottle of Smirnoff—I call him Vladimir—and I've had about…eight vodka crans by now? And guess *what*? WE HAVEN'T EVEN GOTTEN TO THE MAIN EVENT!"

They reached the landing as Dunlap stumbled out the door from the common room. He leaned against a wall, his face red and dripping with sweat. Several buttons of his tuxedo shirt were undone, the bowtie nowhere to be seen. He turned and saw them, aiming his phone's front camera toward them. "Hey look, it's Matt Richardson and Joan Keating, two of my favorite people! They wrote a very nice poem about me one time. I really enjoyed it, really." He sounded genuine.

They froze as he turned the camera back around. "And Blaine buddy, I gotta say I'm sorry again for putting pubes on your doorknob. It's really nothing personal, you're just a dick and I thought it would be funny."

Matt and Joan made a move for the stairs, but Dunlap had the camera back on them. "You know something about these two...? They're both members of...*the Anathema!*"

She winced and forced a laugh. "I don't know what you're talking about..."

Dunlap turned the phone back to himself and shouted, "THE SPOOKY SECRET SOCIETY!" He covered his mouth in mock terror, then burst into hysterics.

Joan grabbed Matt's hand and pulled him up the steps, running in her high heels. They swung around the next landing and bolted for the third floor, Dunlap's laughter rising with them. As it did so, it almost seemed to grow sinister.

◆

They knocked on the door to Roy's room and he opened it. Tanner sat at his desk, watching the Instagram livestream on the computer monitor.

"Well," Roy said, looking between them, "if it isn't my two favorite members of the Spooky Secret Society."

Tanner was doubled over in his chair. "It keeps getting better. Come watch."

They walked in and Roy closed the door behind them, then joined the others at the monitor.

"...much I love Radcliffe College. This is truly the best place on Earth, with the best times, and the best people. Even Blaine." He appeared to be seated on one of the common room's sofas. Voices were muffled in the background, likely other Winslow residents preing and enjoying their front-row seats to the show.

"Radcliffe is such a wonderful community. I've been so happy here and I feel so…accepted and appreciated…"

Roy shook his head. "Ignorance is bliss."

"This is actually kind of touching," Tanner said. "He's a nice guy minus the late-night doorknob presents."

"…I just wanted to say, I love you all, and I'm gonna miss this place so much once I graduate. So let's go make this the most *fire* Winter Formal ever and—" He paused, squinting his eyes at the screen. "My mom just texted me. She says: 'Are you okay? Dad and I are concerned.' Don't worry, Mom!" He hefted the vodka bottle. "I FEEL GREAT!"

Dunlap got to his feet. "I feel like I can take on the world. I feel—" He stopped, putting a hand to his mouth and gagging. Then he ran, the camera shaking wildly, out the common room to the second-floor landing, into the washroom. He bent over a sink, his face still in view as he—

"Aw, *fuck!*" Tanner said, looking away.

Matt, Joan, and Roy averted their eyes but the noises filled the room. They all started laughing.

"Holy shit, is he still recording?" Matt asked.

"Turn it off!" Joan managed to say, doubled over.

Trying not to look, Tanner managed to close the browser and the retching noises abruptly ceased. They breathed a collective sigh of relief. Joan wiped away a tear.

"On that note, I think we all need a drink." Roy headed to his liquor cabinet.

Tanner looked at his watch. "I've gotta meet my date in Lacy. See you at the Formal." He ducked back out the door.

Roy pulled out some scotch and three glasses. As he began pouring, Joan said, "I need to use the restroom. I'll be right back."

Matt watched her go wistfully. He hoped it would be a relaxing, uneventful evening for both of them. They'd enjoy hors d'oeuvres at cocktail hour and be drunk enough to dance once Randall began DJing. They'd get photos taken, then retire to one of their rooms and maybe get up to something—if they were sober enough and still had the energy. Otherwise, it could wait until morning.

Suddenly, Roy forced a glass into Matt's hand, his face stern. "We have a problem."

FIFTY

"**O**KAY."

Matt sat down on the edge of the bed, glass in hand. Roy paced the room, looking nervous and taking a big swig of his scotch.

"I lost my letter, the one I was supposed to give to Jacob Eamon. He was Imperator fifteen years ago or something. I think his girlfriend was an Imperator too."

"Any idea where you left it?"

"That's the thing." Roy sat down, placing the glass on his desk. "I know exactly where I left it." He opened his tuxedo jacket, pointing to the interior left pocket. "Right here."

"Okay, so…?"

"The last time I saw it was before I made out with my date, Pandora—and she felt me up. Now it's gone."

The realization darkened on Matt. "Fuck, I knew she was Serpentine. She wasn't there at the meeting, but I fucking knew it."

"Serpentine? You mean the—?"

"Yes." Matt put a hand to his head, took a big sip of scotch, and sighed. "I have a lot to tell you."

Roy gave an exasperated laugh. "Clearly."

"Someone's resurrected Serpentine, calling themselves the Bard just like the old days. They're the raiders who wore cloaks at the Sermon. Joan and I infiltrated a meeting in December and stole the skull back."

"A meeting where?"

"This two-story, red-bricked house just behind the main drag. It was—"

"You mean Pandora's house? I've been there a couple times. She has a roommate, but told me she's barely ever there. It would be the perfect place to host meetings like that."

Matt nodded. "Makes sense. The skull was in her basement the whole time."

Roy sighed. "So *that's* why Randall wouldn't tell us how Dad reappeared…"

"He's trying to keep the people who know about Serpentine to a minimum."

"Ah, so I'm not in his little loop… *Figures*." Roy sounded bitter; he took a big swig and set the glass down again.

"Chet was the Vizier, the second-in-command. Only he knew who the Bard was."

Roy's eyes widened. "And now he's dead…"

Matt nodded. "At the meeting, Chet told the others the Bard knew who killed Rich Benson, that they were a prominent Anathema member. I think the last part is right, but that the member is trying to frame Joan to cover their tracks. She and I believe *the Bard* killed Benson, and that they're someone working within Anathema to bring it down, most likely in our branch."

"Shit…" Roy stared off for a moment, stunned. Then he finished his scotch. "Shit, you and I were onto this bastard last semester."

"Do you think Benson could've been writing an article about Serpentine? All I know is it had something to do with 'wood,' but I still have no idea what that could mean."

Roy paused and closed his eyes. "His article wasn't about Serpentine. I mean, I never knew for sure—but I didn't think…" He put his head in his hands. "Shit, this is a lot more complicated than I thought. I never believed *he* would've actually killed him…"

"He who? What's…?"

Roy looked up, his eyes red and tired. "The article *can't* be related to why Benson got killed. Or if it was, then the Bard had nothing to do with it."

Matt was completely lost.

Roy shook his head and ran a hand through his hair. "I'm afraid I haven't been completely honest with you."

At that moment, the door swung open and Joan stepped back in. Roy froze.

"It's okay," Matt said. "She's in the loop too."

Joan opened her mouth to say something, but another voice spoke behind her. "Discussing Anathema secrets?"

Pandora Lane stepped into the room, wearing a bright green dress. There was something unsettling about her smile. "Don't make me feel left out…" She turned around and glanced between the three of them. No one said a word. Pandora looked to her date. "Roy, I think we should get going. The cocktail hour won't last much longer and it's always my favorite part."

"Sure." He stood slowly, turning to Matt and Joan. "I guess we're going then."

◆

They took the steam tunnels and came out at the washrooms under the dining hall, where people were already streaming in and out, looking inebriated. Once on the upper level, they flashed their wristbands to the guard at Galbraith's entrance. He gave a barely perceptible nod and gestured them through, into the dimly-lit wonderland beyond.

Fractal and snowflake decorations hung along the walls and dangled from the high ceiling. Gone were the dining tables of the day; in their place a single, long row of hors d'oeuvres ran most of the hall's length. There were various breads and pastries, a variety of cheeses and crackers, mini sandwiches and quiches, prosciutto-wrapped mozzarella sticks, various fruits for chocolate fondue, and platters of Galbraith's signature delicacy, pizza. On each side of the hall were tables with water and plastic cups. In the corners immediately to their right and left were bars crowded with students waving drink tickets. Matt and Joan had already purchased a few of their own, but were mostly relying on their flasks to get them through the night.

All around the hall people milled about, drank, ate, and chatted; at least a few hundred were here. Where the High Table normally stood, a band serenaded the crowd with smooth jazz, amplified by speakers around the room. Snow swirled past the high stained-glass windows. Pandora pulled a nervous-looking Roy away from them, smirking as she did so.

As soon as they'd disappeared, he turned to Joan and said, "Did you see the green dress? I bet she's the new Vizier. It was her house we snuck into. And she stole the letter Roy was supposed to deliver."

"*Shit.*" She looked around the crowd. "Keep an eye on yours, then. Do you think they're gonna run around trying to steal them?"

"If that's their goal, I have no clue what the Bard's playing at."

"Trying to keep Anathema on its toes, maybe? Whoever they are, they seem like a super spiteful piece of shit. And calling themselves 'the Bard,' *really*? I know that's what Serpentine dubbed its leaders back in the day, but it just makes you sound like a fucking pretentious asshole."

" 'Fucking pretentious asshole' could describe half the people at this college."

She groaned. "Then it's a wonder they've had trouble fitting in, if that's what all this is to get back for."

He paused as they made their way closer to the nearest water table. "I'm not sure what their motive is, but Roy was about to tell me something about Benson's article."

"Why?"

"I'd just told him about Serpentine. He strongly suspected someone of something, but didn't tell me who or what. Though he *did* say he knows more about the article than he was letting on."

They arrived at the table. Matt filled two cups of water as she stood there thinking, then handed one to her. "We should deliver our letters, get them out of the way. And if either of us can get Roy alone, we should ask him for a full explanation."

"Good plan," she said, pouring some of her flask's vodka into the water. "See you in a bit."

They split and he headed toward the back of the hall, where the band was playing. A glance at his watch revealed there were only a few minutes until 10 p.m., when Randall would take up residence in the DJ booth beside the musicians and the band would depart. The tables would be cleared and everything would become one giant rave, just like every other party. It saddened him that the cocktail portion wasn't longer, or even the whole event.

Around him, friend groups and couples stumbled around, already quite drunk. Logan pulled Lisa by the hand, both of them giddy and heading for the front entrance. His eyes scanned the crowd for Marko Duric and found him chatting by the band with Turland. It must be weird, Matt noted, to have Initiated someone and then have them ascend to the same rank as you the following year. Of course, Duric hadn't picked Turland as his successor, he'd picked Ellis Carmichael, who dropped his medallion in October of Matt's first-year—and no one let Duric forget it.

Making sure nobody he'd seen at the Serpentine meeting was around, Matt slipped the letter out of his jacket and walked toward the two Imperators, gripping it firmly in his hand.

"Excuse me, gentlemen," he said as he approached. "I have a letter for Mr. Duric."

Duric took it and smiled. "Ah, excellent. How are you, Richardson? Turland's been telling me about all the fun that's happened this year. Of course, I've read some of it in the papers."

Matt stood straight, his hands clasped behind his back. "It's…been an interesting time for the organization."

Turland nodded, looking heavily inebriated. "I'll catch up with you later, Matt. We're just discussing some things."

"Of course. Have a good evening." Matt smiled and walked away, exhaling and checking that off his mental to-do list. He looked around for any sign of Roy or Pandora. He wanted to step outside with him so they could continue their conversation.

Rufus stood by the center row of tables, talking to a girl with dark hair. That must be his girlfriend who went to the University of Calgary. He looked happier than he'd ever seen him before, his manner appearing jovial and, if Matt dared say it, pleasant. Maybe she brought out a better side of him. Or maybe he was just nicer to her because he wanted to sleep with her. It was hard to tell.

His foot nearly slid out from under him, and Matt stopped to look at the floor. An envelope lay on the ground, calligraphy written on its front. He picked it up and read the name.

William Favell, 110.

"Holy shit," he muttered, quickly pocketing the letter. He'd met Favell at both Second Sermons he'd attended. The man was a legend within Anathema and Radcliffe writ large. Both his Sermons and his speeches as DebSoc President were still spoken of highly. He was now a film producer splitting his time between LA and Vancouver, though he apparently painted on the side. The posters for his Sermons had been done by his own hand and were incredibly intricate and haunting. Clearly, it had either slipped from his pocket or a Serpentine member had tried to make off with it and lost it themselves.

He kept his eyes peeled for Favell or a Tetrad member who could help him, making his way back to the entrance with the two bars in the corners.

Suddenly, Patrick Mason appeared before him and placed one hand on his shoulder, a drink in his other.

"Do people really think I sold out Anathema?" He looked quite sad.

Matt hesitated, not really wanting to have this conversation right now. "I think people just say that. I don't think that you did, but…"

"Tell me the truth. I helped get you in, you owe me that much."

"I…think you maybe got a little high on yourself toward the end of last year, especially after winning your Officer election, and it rubbed some people the wrong way. Randall included."

Patrick tilted his head back. "I fuckin' knew it." He sighed and looked back at Matt, his hand still on his shoulder. "I don't want to be remembered as *that* guy. I love Anathema, I love this college. And I don't want my friends to hold grudges against me."

"I don't."

"And I appreciate that." He looked around, as if struck by a sudden realization. "I know what I need to do now." He patted him on the shoulder, still staring off. "Have a good night." He moved past him.

"Wait, have you seen Favell or Randall?"

Patrick turned around, confused. "Favell? Is he here?"

"Apparently. His letter was on the ground. I need to give it to him or Randall, so he can get it back to him."

"Sorry, I haven't seen either of them. Good luck!" Patrick continued toward where the band was, and he glimpsed Karen talking to someone over that way.

Matt turned around and headed for the entrance, where Logan Brewster walked in, wide-eyed and glancing over his shoulder. He walked up to the Legatus. "Hey, have you seen Randall?"

"Hey man, how are you?!" Logan grabbed Matt by his shoulders and grinned.

"I'm…alright…"

"Good, good. That's great. I just did some lines off Lisa's tits in the bathroom. *Good* stuff."

"That sounds…um, great…"

"Hey man, I'm sorry for what I said about you and Joan the other day. It's none of my business how or when you fuck. You take care and keep writing those jokes. When I help Randall edit, I see the shit you send in. Keep it up, man. That stuff makes even *me* laugh." He patted him on the back.

"Thanks…Logan," he said, baffled and somehow touched.

The Legatus half-walked, half-stumbled off. Matt turned and suddenly saw Randall. The Imperator was chatting with Mustard, Crawley, and a balding man of average height.

He headed over and Randall noticed him. "Hey Richardson, come join us! Have you ever formally met John and Donna?"

"I've met Dean Crawley." He gave her a nod of recognition and she smiled in return. "But I've actually never met Provost Mustard."

"Ah." Randall turned around. "This is Matt Richardson, he's a friend of mine. Third-year. Majors in history."

"Nice to meet you, Matthew," Mustard said, shaking his hand with a firm grip. "I've heard so much about you."

Matt tensed. What did *that* mean?

The Provost turned to the balding man beside him. "And this is the contractor for the Administration Center and the new expansion of the Dales Building, which we're going to begin work on this summer."

"Hi," the man said, turning to him and extending his hand. "I'm Mark Wood."

FIFTY-ONE

EXHAUSTION CREPT over her once she'd delivered the letter. It weighed on her spirits, the alcohol in her system unable to keep it at bay. She needed more. She needed a real drink, something better than pouring liquid fire down her throat.

Joan sighed and strolled off to one of the bars. She ordered herself a double rye and ginger, only to be told they were no longer serving doubles at on-campus events. It was all she could do to keep anger from flushing through her face.

Mustard and his fucking bullshit.

"Fine, I'll take a single then," she shouted over the chatter.

The bartender nodded and set to mixing the drink. She exhaled and glanced at her watch. The cocktail portion of the event was due to end any minute now. At least Randall would be DJing; he was big into eighties music, so the mix wouldn't sound like every other Cliffe party. Once she got the drink and turned around, she saw Sandrine walking straight toward her in a blue dress.

"I need to talk to you," she said.

"Sure," Joan said weakly, realizing how submissive she sounded. Why did she always cow to the Tetrad? Aside from Kylie, she was taller than each of them. Nobody was ever going to see her as a leader if she was always acting so—

Once they had gotten away from the bar, Sandrine spun around and thrust an envelope into her hands. "I want you to deliver this to Bella Collins. It's her letter."

Joan was stunned. She stared at the name on the envelope in disbelief. "She's here?" she asked, finally looking up.

Sandrine nodded. "I was supposed to give it to her, but I think you need to impress these people more than I do." And for the first time Joan had seen, she smiled at her. Sandrine Bouchard smiled at her.

She swallowed and nodded. "Thank you," she managed to get out.

Sandrine put a hand on her shoulder. "The medallion would suit you." Then she turned and strolled away.

Joan couldn't hide her smile now; anyone passing by would've seen that she was glowing, absolutely glowing.

And it appeared that someone had. She looked up to see Blaine walking over, stern and serious.

"Good evening, Joan. Having a pleasant time?" He smiled, but with a flicker of malice. The formality was forced and unnerving.

She slid the letter into her purse, never taking her eyes off of him. "Yes, as matter of fact I am."

"Glad to hear it. What's that letter for? Or rather, *who*?"

"Have a good night." She stormed off, but he followed close behind. She looked left and right, trying to find Matt, when suddenly Blaine grabbed her arm and turned her around.

"You hit me. You broke my fucking nose and never apologized." He straightened up and smirked. "That wasn't very nice, now was it?"

"I'm sorry," she choked. Her throat was very dry all of a sudden. She was going to say it was an accident, but she couldn't force the lie to her lips. She remembered the heat of that instant, how she'd given in to the impulse and smashed her elbow against his face—and how good it had felt. Even for just a moment.

He leaned closer. "How about you give me that letter?"

"How about you go fuck yourself?" They both turned to see Val standing there, her hands on her hips. She looked to Joan. "You okay?"

She nodded. "We were just chatting."

Val raised an eyebrow. Blaine gave an exasperated sigh and stormed off, much to Joan's relief.

"Seriously," she said, "are you alright?"

"I'm fine now. Thank you."

"Don't mention it. I know his friend died, but he shouldn't be lashing out at Anathema members. We didn't have anything to do with it."

Joan nodded and took a big gulp of her drink. She wished she could tell Val more—wished she could tell her everything, really—but there was no use to it, especially not right now. "I'll see you around," she said, giving her an appreciative nod as she walked away.

She'd only gotten a few feet before she saw Blaine and Pandora standing across the center table row. Pandora stood rigid and listening as he whispered something in her ear, nodding along occasionally. Matt was right, she was certainly the new Vizier, Blaine her underling reporting back.

Then they both noticed her and with horror, she realized she'd stopped to stare at them. Pandora gave a thin smile and waved as Blaine stood beside her, glaring.

Turning, she hurried on and looked for any sign of Bella Collins. She'd been Imperator at the same time as the male branch's William Favell.

Matt bumped into her, looking pale.

"Hey," she said, relieved to see him. She downed the rest of her drink and tossed the cup into a trashcan near the center tables.

"I think I know what Benson's article was about," he gasped. "Larch told me it had something to do with 'wood,' but I had no clue what he meant." He leaned closer. "It's a name, *Mark* Wood. He's the contractor Mustard works with for all the building projects here."

Joan's eyes widened. "You think they're up to something shady?"

"I'd bet money on it. I think it's what Benson was looking into, but Roy seemed to know more about it. I still can't find him." He frowned and his expression softened. "You look shaken up. Is everything alright—?"

"I need to deliver this." She pulled the letter out of her purse. "Bella Collins."

"Well, that's funny," he said, taking an envelope out of his own jacket. "I found Favell's lying on the floor. Randall told me he's over there."

He nodded toward the band, who was no longer playing. Servers began breaking up the row of center tables and wheeling them to the cafeteria, which had been closed off by a sliding door. Now it was open and light spilled into the room, a waiter directing the other staff through.

"Alright, alright, alright...," a voice boomed over the speakers. Carl Dunlap stood by the musicians as they packed up their things. He looked haggard, but had definitely sobered a bit since his livestream. "Who's ready for the party to *really* begin?" He aimed the microphone out at the crowd, which roared with *Whoos* and *Yeahs*.

"Alright," Dunlap said, bringing the mic back to himself. "For the next hour, we've got a core member of the Cliffe community spinning us some beats. He wanted all eighties music, but I convinced him to include some house favorites." Some people laughed. "You all know him as your Off-Residence Affairs Officer, but tonight he dons another persona."

"One-One-Five?!" someone shouted.

Dunlap chuckled and shook his head. "No, no. Jack Randall is a man who wears many hats, but the one he wears tonight is your master of ceremonies. Give it up...FOR DJ JAXX VANDAL!"

Randall stepped out from the door to the Senior Common Room, wearing a black jacket with enormous shoulder pads. On his face were oversized sunglasses that looked like a silver visor, its frame made of neon magenta plastic. Combined with his crew-cut, it was quite the image.

He strode into the DJ booth, where the laptop and gear were already set up beside a microphone. Dunlap walked offstage as the Imperator took his mic and shouted, "Radcliffe College, ARE YOU READY?!"

People whooped and hollered. Having safely stowed their letters, Joan and Matt made their way to the back of the hall, heading in his direction.

Randall's voice reverberated overhead. "I come from the year 1986... to save you from the autotuned B.S. plaguing these dystopian airwaves. I give you...REAL MUSIC!"

He hit something on his computer and the opening cords of A-ha's "Take On Me" began to play. The crowd went wild, quickly settling into the beat. The lights around the room darkened, multicolored strobes flashing across the fractal decorations.

The crowd fanned out as the tables disappeared and people started dancing all around the room. Joan saw Kathy Pickering walk by, watching them with a cold gaze. Kevin cut through the throng a few meters to their left, staring at them as he did so. Up ahead, Blaine and Hank headed their way from different angles. The sharks were closing in.

She grabbed Matt's arm and pointed.

"*Shit.*" She could barely hear him over the music. He took her by the hand and pulled her toward the DJ booth and most of the speakers. It was louder here, but the crowd was denser. He suddenly stopped and pointed to a woman shorter than Joan with strawberry-blonde hair. She'd seen Bella Collins at the past two Second Sermons, but she'd never talked to her before.

Matt leaned very close to her, and even then, it was still difficult to hear him. "Let's deal with these letters, then find Roy."

She nodded, leading the way toward Collins. As they approached, the crowd parted and another man found himself across from the former Imperator. He was tall with dark hair, a goatee, and wore a three-piece, pinstriped suit with a bowtie, which was adorned with skulls. Favell threw his arms wide in recognition and Collins' face lit up. The old friends embraced and began dancing, swirling around each other as the song reached a piano solo.

Joan and Matt looked to each other, their letters suddenly in hand and held close to their chests. They split up and moved forward, narrowing in on their targets.

The two Imperators still danced in the center of the circle. Favell was doing the Sprinkler and somehow making it look cool. Collins swayed her body beside him, making peace signs with her fingers and slowly moving them across her eyes like the dance scene in *Pulp Fiction*. New sounds entered the music, two songs blurring as one while Randall transitioned to "You Spin Me Round" by Dead or Alive. The crowd roared; this was one of the few eighties songs familiar to them.

Pandora appeared at the other side of the circle, an eerie smile on her face. She wasn't dancing at all, but the people around her seemed not to notice. Blaine emerged from the crowd to the left behind Favell and Kathy popped up behind Collins. Circles formed and dissembled around them, but somehow the Imperators managed to stay in the center of it all. They linked up and began dancing together again, taking turns twirling each other around with effortless grace.

An idea popped into her head and she pulled Matt closer, trying to steer them toward Favell and Collins. Before she knew it, they were in the center of the circle with the Imperators and another pair—Pandora and Blaine. Joan brought Matt's hands to her hips and put her arms around his shoulders, still holding the letter. It would be easy for a Serpentine member to snatch either of theirs now. They had to move quickly.

"We're gonna do a swap," she shouted to him. "On three. You to him, me to her."

He looked confused. "Alright, but—"

"*One! Two...!*"

They readied themselves. Pandora and Blaine swung closer as he twirled her, her arm outstretched and reaching for—

"Three!"

It all happened very quickly. Joan reached out her hand to Collins, who saw and seemed to recognize her, just as she and Favell came apart at the next spin. The next thing she knew, she and Matt had split and she found herself holding one of Collins' hands, extending the letter toward her with the other.

The Imperator's eyes widened with delight. "Oh, thank you—!"

Kathy Pickering made a dive for Collins just then, but Joan raised her foot and she tripped, falling between them and crashing to the floor. Everyone stepped back, a circle forming around the Serpentine agent. She staggered as she got up, turning her angry gaze toward Joan and Collins.

"You…" She raised a finger, but suddenly Réjean and a female security guard appeared behind her.

"Excuse me, miss," Réjean said. "Are you okay, or are you too drunk to—?"

"Fuck off!" she snarled, then took a step toward Joan.

The female security guard grabbed her shoulder. "Excuse me, you better come with us."

"Get off!"

Réjean stepped forward, fire in his eyes. "I already dealt with this shit last year. You are coming with us. I am *deadly serious.*"

By the look on her face, Kathy believed it and allowed the two guards to lead her off. Joan couldn't help but smirk, wondering if Kathy would get two Demerit Points just as she had. People around them went back to dancing, but a few feet beyond where it happened, the party had never stopped.

Collins turned to Joan and laughed, then leaned closer. "Gotta love Cliffe events, right?"

Joan laughed along too. "Yeah, nothing like 'em."

"Say, what's your name again? I really should remember it from last year."

"Joan," she said. "Joan Keating."

Collins held up the letter again. "Well thank you, Joan. Have a good night and I'll see you at the Sermon!"

She moved off and Joan stood there, basking in the moment. Strobe lights flashed all around, people danced badly and made out with their partners, and off in the DJ booth Randall was doing the Running Man, looking almost unrecognizable with those ridiculous glasses and shoulder pads. She knew Imperators frequently turned to their predecessors for advice. Maybe if Kylie asked Collins for her favorite picks, she'd speak fondly of Joan. Maybe between her and Sandrine she'd have a chance.

Maybe.

◆

As soon as he and Joan split, Matt found himself being twirled around by Favell—which was difficult given that they were roughly the same height—and he somehow managed to slide the letter into the Imperator's jacket as he came back around. Favell stumbled back, looking confused as he pulled out the envelope.

"You dropped it!" Matt shouted.

Favell gave an appreciative nod, then Kathy Pickering fell to the floor and security came. Favell led Matt toward Galbraith's entrance, where it was quieter. Once they could hear their own thoughts again, he turned to him and said, "Hey, how have you been, Matt?!"

He was surprised Favell even remembered him. Both times they'd met had been brief. "Good, good... How are you?"

Favell put a hand to his forehead. "It's been crazy. I was here doing some location scouting this week. We're going to be shooting in Calgary right around the time the Sermon usually is, so I should be there." He withdrew a pocket watch from his suit and glanced at it. "I've got an early flight back to LA tomorrow morning, so I should probably get going." Favell turned back to him. "But it's nice to see you, Matt. I always take note when a fellow American enters Anathema."

"Good to see you, too. Catch you at the Sermon."

Favell gave him a thumbs up and walked out Galbraith's front doors. Matt turned around to see Jennifer and Roy heading for the exit too. Roy looked very drunk.

"Hey...," he began.

"See you around." Roy gave a salute and he and Jennifer left the hall.

Matt stood there and sighed. He felt a hand on his shoulder, and glanced over to see Joan at his left.

"Was that Roy I just saw leaving?"

"Yeah. I guess we're not gonna be talking to him for the rest of the night."

ABBA's "Mamma Mia" began over the speakers and the crowd roared; it was probably one of the most popular songs at Cliffe, played at every party.

Joan looked off toward the DJ booth. "Oh well. I'm tired and not nearly drunk enough. What do you say we dance a bit more, head to the photo booth in the Mountainview Room, and then"—she grabbed him by the waist and pulled him closer—"we go back to your room and take our minds off of everything?"

Matt looked at her and smiled. "I like the sound of that." He certainly had a few things to take his mind off of.

As they headed back into the crowd, he saw Pandora leaning against a wall. She smirked and shook her head as she watched them go.

FIFTY-TWO

L INDA WRIGHT stood outside the detachment in her parka, watching the auburn sky. She took another drag from her cigarette and exhaled. Without clouds to trap the heat, it had been cold as shit today, though at least it looked beautiful. The sun dipped out of sight as she stared on, orange and red diffusing upward into the pale blue.

Today had been an important turning point in the Tremblay case, at least publicly. She'd held a press conference earlier in the afternoon to give an update on the situation. Wright's shoulders relaxed even as discontent lingered inside her. At least it gave the victim's family something to chew on, even if it was a dissatisfying answer. And it would keep the press away, although she was almost certain it wasn't the truth.

The Alberta Crown Prosecution Service had decided there simply wasn't enough evidence to arrest Joan Keating, and even less to arrest Matthew Richardson. Beckman kept telling them the high school suspension was enough to convince a jury, but there was a big leap between punching someone and stalking a person through a park with the intention of stabbing them to death. Wright had proposed an explanation to feed the press and the prosecutors concurred. It seemed like the most logical way forward at this point.

She heard footsteps behind her and turned around. Sure enough, it was Beckman himself. He didn't wear his hood up even though it was minus twelve Celsius. Wright took another drag as he approached, then pulled the cigarette away from her mouth and exhaled.

"Come to watch the sunset?"

He shrugged. "I don't get it, Linda. We've got this girl. I'm not even sure the boyfriend's in on it anymore, I'll give you and the prosecutors that, but the girl…" He shook his head. "You know these quiet types; they all snap eventually. You gotta keep your distance from 'em. And Radcliffe's a twisted place. Seems like it could bring out the worst in anybody."

"It does seem…tense there." It was no wonder they had so many humor-focused societies and alcohol-infused events, but coping mechanisms only let you hide for so long.

Beckman shook his head again. "It's what happens when you get all these kids into a little bubble, isolated up on that hill away from everybody else. They get cabin fever and then they're all at each other's throats for four years. I'm surprised it's taken this long for people to start getting murdered."

He chuckled and looked to her, but she didn't laugh. Wright opened her mouth to say something, but decided against it. She wished he'd just leave her to watch the twilight in peace.

The sun had now vanished from the sky. The blue above her began to darken, the red-orange in the distance slowly receding beyond the mountains. Cold bit at her face and she hoped spring wouldn't be late this year. Snow hadn't stayed on the ground until December, so it was anyone's guess how long winter would last.

Beckman stood there, still waiting for her to say something, and when she didn't, he sighed. "Have a good evening, Linda."

"See you tomorrow, Phil."

He headed back inside but Wright didn't take her eyes off the dusk. The press had seemingly bought her explanation, but deep down she knew the two deaths *were* connected, somehow. And she couldn't shake the feeling that it wasn't over yet, that by the term's end more blood would be spilled at Radcliffe College.

FIFTY-THREE

FEBRUARY WORE on.
   After the RCMP's announcement had been made public the Monday after Winter Formal, word spread through the college in hushed whisperings. Talk of an Anathema conspiracy to silence dissenters was replaced by a decidedly less interesting explanation: Chet Tremblay was probably killed by a drifter, someone who'd decided to prey on students in the seeming safety of a college town. As for Rich Benson, it appeared he'd really had an accident after all. The intrigue quashed for most students, Radcliffe gossip settled back into its usual cycle of who said what, who slept with who, and who was going to run for what position in the upcoming student elections.

   Matt, however, felt torn between relief and anxiousness. He heard the news after getting back from a class and went straight to Joan's room. They lay there, embracing on her bed and soaking up the respite. It truly did appear that she was no longer the prime suspect, and even if the police doubted her, they clearly didn't have enough evidence to proceed with a case. The noncommittal explanation of a drifter sounded like them throwing their hands up and calling it quits.

   But Matt was also tenser than ever. If the Bard was hellbent on destroying Anathema and saw Joan taking the fall for both killings as the best way to accomplish it, they wouldn't be so easily deterred. They'd view this as merely a setback and go about concocting another way to reach their endgame. He thought about what Joan said at Winter Formal, about how spiteful the Serpentine leader seemed. Maybe they were someone with more of a goal than a plan, lashing out in all directions instead of waiting for one long-gestating seed to sprout. He couldn't think of another explanation for why they'd waste time having Pandora and the others steal invitations.

Roy became conspicuously absent the week after the Formal. Matt wanted to finish their chat, but he wasn't responding to texts and Matt didn't see him around Galbraith—or even at meetings in the Chalet. Matt and Joan were too swamped with essays and midterms to investigate, caught in the grind that always preceded Reading Week. Even though he longed for warmer weather, he decided to stay here so that his family could save the flight money for summer, when he wanted to visit Joan in Toronto several times.

When she found out he was staying, she let her parents know she intended to get caught up on assignments and studying, though she planned to visit a friend in Vancouver that first weekend of the break. She'd be back just in time for his birthday and promised they'd celebrate; her twenty-first had been back on September fifth.

Since most of his essays had been due that week and he didn't have much else until the second half of March, Matt spent most of the weekend in his room, snug and reading a book. That Sunday evening, he sat alone in Galbraith. The hall was mostly empty and the few diners' cutlery echoed as it clattered against their plates.

He checked his phone as he finished his food. It had been two weeks since the Formal and he still hadn't heard anything from Roy. Putting his plate and utensils on the rack in the dishwashing room, he headed out into the West Quad. Without a jacket or winter boots, the chill quickly got to him, but he only intended to stay out for a moment. He realized he'd used the steam tunnels so much these past couple weeks, he hadn't looked for it before.

But there it was.

Snow drifted down from the dark sky. There had been a chinook at the beginning of the week and much of it had melted, only for another blizzard to blow through on Thursday and Friday. It came down much lighter now, but by the faint moonlight he saw mounds of snow beside shoveled paths around the Quad.

And there, at the top of House Winslow, the light in the Fourth East fireplace room glowed through the flurry of white.

Matt went back inside and took the steam tunnels to Winslow. He hurried his way up the four flights of stairs, entered the east pod, and walked to the end of the hall. Then he knocked on the door and waited. For some reason, it made him think of movies where someone claiming to have important information was found dead before they could impart it. Given the bewildering events of these past few months, he started to worry that's exactly what had happened.

Then the door opened.

Roy stood before him in casual clothes, rubbing his eyes. "Hey, what's up?"

"Oh, hey. How've you been?"

"Good, just swamped with Anthro assignments. And I'm going on this archaeological dig in Finland this summer, so all the stuff for that had to be organized. Come on in." He did so and Roy closed the door. "How's Joan?"

"She's in Vancouver, gets back tomorrow evening." Matt sat on the edge of the bed.

Roy returned to his desk chair; a box of takeout from Ni Hao sat open beside the keyboard. "Oh, nice, nice." He looked off through the window. From this angle, Matt could just make out the slate roof of Rickard. Snow drifted by the glass, some piling up on the sill outside. Roy sighed and turned to him. "Sorry I haven't been around. I really should come to more meetings. How's the Second Sermon coming along?"

Matt shrugged. "Okay, I guess... I'm getting kind of tired writing jokes. I barely know the first-years, most of them haven't done anything that interesting or chastisement-worthy, and... I'm just getting tired of the same formats, the same routine of sitting in rooms and then switching and..."

Roy laughed. "Yeah, it gets tedious after a few years. But it should be better next year once you're editing stuff with the Tetrad—whether you're leading it or not."

"I hope." He thought back to what Logan Brewster said to him at Winter Formal. *Maybe he doesn't hate me like Rufus does. Maybe he would still make me his Legatus.*

Roy had some more of his pork fried rice. "It's weird knowing this will be my last Sermon—as a member at least. I can always come back as an alum."

"Gonna miss it?"

He exhaled. "Well, it's been a big part of my time here so... Yeah. I'll mainly miss the people. You and Tanner are my main friends who are still members. All my upper-year pals have graduated or are just no longer in it, like Patrick. And I like Jack Randall, but I've never been close with the guy."

Matt nodded. "Say…"

"I know what you're gonna ask." He stood up and went to the liquor cabinet. "You've been wondering what I was gonna tell you before Pandora came in—and by the way, we're not together anymore. Jennifer and I are exclusive for the time being."

He rolled his eyes. "Why does everybody say that these days? *Exclusive*. It makes it sound like you've got a record label contract or something."

Roy laughed, pouring them some whiskey. "Good point. I've just heard it so often I've started using it. And I'm not as bad as Ares Donovan. I heard him in Galbraith one time talking about how he and Erin aren't dating, they're just in a 'monogamous exclusive partnership.'"

Matt rolled his eyes. "The lawyers of tomorrow."

"Yeah…" He sighed, bringing his drink over. The radiator hummed loudly and the air in the room took on a toasty quality.

"Thanks." Matt had a sip. "So…"

Roy sat back in his chair. "Yeah, that night was kind of a blur, so refresh me where I was again?"

"You said you hadn't been completely honest with me. And you mentioned something about not thinking 'he' would've killed Benson."

"Ah, right…" He sat up straighter. "This is gonna piss you off, but I've actually known—or at least had a good idea—what Benson was writing about this whole time. You see, my dad is the one who tipped him off about it."

Matt frowned, confused.

"He sits on the Radcliffe College Senate. I think Joan's mom does too; they're both Distance Members. He told me he recognized the name Keating when I mentioned it. Anyway." He gave a dismissive wave. "He'd heard rumors that all these building projects Mustard was pushing were more expensive than they should've been. Apparently, the contractor he works with, Mark Wood, has been involved in some shady dealings before. My dad doesn't like Mustard, hates how he's dismantling the traditions and thinks he's just a ponce trying to become WCU President. He tipped off several newspapers about possible embezzlement, but they didn't seem to do anything. So last year, he asked me which student journalist would be bold enough to take on the Radcliffe admin."

"And you said Rich Benson."

Roy nodded. "That was the last I heard of it, until you started asking me if he might've been looking into something. And then I started to wonder myself, which was why I set up that meeting with Dinesh. But once he told us Benson was actually onto something, I got freaked out a little. I mean, what if Mustard really *was* embezzling money? He never struck me as the kind of guy to commit murder, but maybe he let it slip to this Wood guy, who sounds a little more sketch. Maybe *he* had someone take Benson out."

Matt nodded. "How much have these projects cost?"

"Over two million for the Administration Center, and nearly four million for the Dales expansion."

"Shit. And how much *should* they cost?"

"The first, probably not more than a million. The second, probably about a million less than it will cost. At least, that's what my dad was telling me. He works in real estate."

"So Mustard and this Wood guy are both pocketing several hundred grand each time?"

"Sounds like it."

Matt rubbed his forehead. "Why didn't you say anything before?"

"My dad told me not to tell a soul about this. If it comes out that this is what Mustard's been doing, it'll create a shitstorm for the college like nothing we've ever seen."

"Beside the return of Serpentine with a potentially murderous cult leader?"

He shrugged. "Most people don't know about that."

"I don't see how this could be tied to the Bard. Why would Mustard—?"

"I don't think he is the Bard. If Benson died because of the article, it has nothing to do with Serpentine. I can't see why Mustard would kill Chet under any circumstance."

"He doesn't like Anathema."

"None of the admin *likes* Anathema. We're a thorn in their side, but not a big one—at least, not anymore. This college wiped its hands clean of us over twenty years ago. Mustard's main concern is liability, and thanks to Dissociation we're not his legal concern. You've gotta remember he doesn't really care about Radcliffe; everything he does here is just to impress Charlotte Manderley enough to make him the next President."

"I'm sure he wouldn't mind if we were gone."

"No, but he wouldn't resurrect a century-old secret society just to do it. Evidently, he's got enough secrets of his own."

"How would he have known Benson was onto him?" Matt asked.

"I don't know, maybe Benson asked someone in the admin a question, and that person mentioned it to someone, who mentioned it to someone else who mentioned it to Mustard. Something like that."

Matt thought for a moment. "Or maybe he listened in through the landline phones that are in every room, like Patrick said the admin could. Benson lived in Rickard."

Roy shook his head. "I haven't heard that from anyone other than Patrick, though I could imagine *him* listening to see if people think he sold us out to the admin." He chuckled and looked at the landline on his desk. "I've kept mine unplugged anyway, just to be sure. Not really a point to these things anymore when we've all got cell phones."

Matt looked out the window and sighed. "I don't know what to make of it, then."

"Maybe Mustard didn't kill him. Or maybe he did. Who knows?"

I know someone who might. He watched a snowflake swirl past the glass, then disappear out of sight.

FIFTY-FOUR

BEFORE BED that evening, he decided he would talk to Joan about what Randall told him at Initiations. She got back the next evening and they stayed up late talking about their favorite book genres before falling asleep together. He couldn't find a way to broach the subject.

Tuesday was Matt's birthday, and she woke him wearing nothing but her Venetian mask and a sly grin. After they'd worked up an appetite, they ate an early lunch in Galbraith and took an Uber to downtown Canmore proper. The streets were lined with shops and restaurants and the Rockies rose beyond no matter which way they turned. It was too cold to stroll along Main Street, so they entered a cozy place called Café Books and ended up browsing the racks for hours. Joan bought him a John Grisham novel as a gift, along with a couple horror paperbacks for herself. They went to the Drake Pub for dinner and drinks and stayed chatting well into the evening, consuming more beverages as the night wore on. By the time they took another Uber back to Radcliffe, they were both thoroughly inebriated and went to bed early after fooling around in his room.

They'd both forgotten to drink enough water and spent the next morning nursing hangovers over Galbraith's suspiciously-colored scrambled eggs. Several hours and a few Advil later, they went to Mackenzie to study together through the afternoon. He found it hard to concentrate with everything on his mind, the anticipation of how and when to bring it up singeing his nerves.

It wasn't until Thursday evening that he finally mustered up the courage.

"It's nice," he said, "finally having the police off our backs."

Joan lay on her bed reading one of the horror novels she'd bought, Stephen King's *Bag of Bones*, while Matt sat in her desk chair with his feet propped up on the bed, resting across her shins.

She lowered the book and searched for words before answering. "It is." She went back to reading. He could tell she didn't want to have this conversation.

"I'm worried it's not over, though. The Bard might try something else. Something more drastic than stealing invitations."

"Did you ever finish that conversation with Roy?"

"I did." He told her what they'd discussed on Sunday.

Joan nodded thoughtfully, then lay the book open on her stomach and stared at the ceiling. "I don't know why Mustard would be the Bard, or why he'd kill Chet."

"We both know the RCMP's official explanation can't be true. We heard what Chet told Serpentine. There are only two options: One, the Bard themselves is an Anathema member who killed Rich Benson and is trying to frame someone else—most likely you. Or two, the Bard told Chet the truth and there really is someone in our ranks separate from the Bard who murdered Benson."

"In that case, did *that* person kill Chet too or did the Bard kill him separately?"

"I don't know if there's two independent killers or not. Let's start with Benson. Any idea why he might've been out there after midnight?"

"Honestly, no. I've been just as baffled by that as you are." She sounded genuine and there was concern in her eyes as she looked at him. Then she narrowed them, sizing him up.

"Randall told me," he said, "about the snitch."

A pause. "Oh."

"And your meetings." She nodded. "And the last one…from his side of the events."

Joan froze, staring away from him.

He kneeled on the floor beside her bed, placing his book on her nightstand. He held her hand and looked up at her. She still didn't turn her attention to him.

"I don't think it was you."

"Yes, you do. Everybody does. Even Randall. I got a random note from someone in October telling me to confess. Never found out who it was from, but it doesn't matter. They all think I did it." Sadness had crept into her voice and she seemed to be fighting back tears.

"I don't. I *really* don't, but I think whatever you saw holds a major key to all this. And to figuring out who's behind it."

Joan swallowed, her eyes remaining straight ahead. "It's no use."

"Why not?"

"Because I didn't see anything and nobody would believe that's true. I was the last to see him alive."

"No, whoever killed him was. And that's not you. I know it's not you."

"*How* do you know that?" She finally looked at him. "Seriously. How do you know I didn't do it?"

"It's a...hunch." Matt hesitated. "I believe you *could've* hurt him, but I don't think you actually did."

"See? You said *think*. Not *know*."

"I don't even care if you did do it, Joan." He managed a laugh, finding he was holding back tears of his own. "Really. I'd just like to know for peace of mind." He hesitated. "And if you did, so I don't accidentally piss you off."

She smiled even as teardrops rolled down her cheeks. "I didn't. But I *did* see him right before he died."

"Did you see who killed him?"

She wiped some tears away. "No. I ran off. He...he...confronted me."

"What was he doing out there?"

"I don't know. I think he followed me into the woods. I kept looking over my shoulder—there was definitely someone behind me. And then I got near that bridge and turned around and said 'Show yourself.' And there he was, looking all smug. He asked what I was doing out late wearing my pendant and mask and started teasing me for being so into Anathema and I...I just...I let him have it. I said everything I'd ever thought of him. Horrible things, worse than a Sermon. I didn't yell, but I went on for a while and he...he just *laughed*. This awful, awful laugh—and the look in his eyes—that judgmental look people give me here all the time—and I...I..."

She turned to him, her lower lip quivering. "I ran. I didn't even text Randall; the whole thing really shook me up. I felt like an idiot. I don't know why but seeing Rich just brought out all the thoughts I'd pushed down—I'd never actually talked to him after he..." She wiped more tears away and grew angry. "After he slept with me and then acted like I didn't exist. He went around telling everyone I was *delusional* and *weird* and—a 'depraved wallflower,' *that's* what he called me. That's what he put in the—"

Matt touched her arm. "I know. I read it. He was a fucking douchebag and he didn't deserve you. He never did."

Joan bit her lip and began breathing heavily, trying to calm herself. He slid onto the bed beside her and hugged her close.

She pulled his arms tighter around her, then said softly, "And the next day he was dead. Right where I left him—or near it, I guess. Someone came and pushed him down the hill. Or maybe he tripped while laughing. For some reason, I think it would be funny if that's what happened. If he just stood there laughing so hard he slipped, ended up in the creek, and drowned."

As he nuzzled closer and kissed her forehead gently, he had to admit it would be funny.

If only just a little.

FIFTY-FIVE

Elections were all anyone could talk about once classes resumed. The campaign period officially began that Monday and those running were quick to start advertising their platforms. Officer positions were always the most vied for and appeared to be close in five of the six slots this year; only the female Off-Residence candidate ran unopposed.

Since becoming Imperator had always been her main interest, the election cycle held little allure for Joan. Everyone spent countless Galbraith conversations discussing who would win each year, but she knew the platforms were largely a joke. Candidates always said they wanted to make Radcliffe a better, more inclusive place, but those who won always had one of two things in common: name recognition or big promises. Carl Dunlap hadn't exactly been popular, but he swore he'd host the 'most fire ragers' in the college's history and voters had decided to give him a chance. Last year people believed Patrick Mason could walk on water thanks to his Deb-Soc Presidency, so he'd crushed his only opponent—Tony Madruga—in a landslide. Veronica Yang had name recognition from being an Imperator and easily beat her unheard-of competitor, while the other Officers had already been well-known in upper-year social circles. Randall had run unopposed and the announcement that he would remain an Anathema member during his term hadn't dissuaded anyone until he was revealed as 115—but of course, he'd already been elected by then. It was too late to re-open nominations at that point.

It became interesting when people from different cliques ran against each other, the ultimate test of who was more liked and trusted. For the male Student Affairs Officer race, Tony and Zhang were vying to take Patrick's place. Both were Anathema members, but each hung out in different friend groups. They'd also dated last year, and she wasn't sure if competing for a position helped to smooth any lingering tensions. In other news, Alyssa Lee wasn't running for a position, which many took as official confirmation that she was holding out for Imperator—or that she had already been chosen.

Joan tried not to think about the next Sermon while sitting beside Matt at DebSoc that Thursday. Instead, she noted that attendance had declined little this semester—even with a lack of free beer. People merely brought their own booze, sneaking in flasks and bottles beneath their coats. They technically weren't supposed to have alcohol in here under Mustard's new policy, but if the Provost was trying to strike a blow against Radcliffe's drinking culture, he had failed. The thought made her smile and she took a celebratory swig from her flask.

March began that Friday, and as she flipped the page of her calendar a sense of dread came over her. The Second Sermon was toward the end of this month, the one where the 94th female Imperator's identity would finally be revealed, her name forever etched into the Line of Succession. She'd dreamed of this Sermon since first-year, but now the thought of it instilled fear. She hadn't been asked yet—although it was still four weeks away. Most Imperators didn't speak to their successor until two to three weeks before the event, but the whole thing still had her on edge. She didn't want to think about what would happen if she didn't get it—and if Alyssa did.

She worried for Matt too. Logan seemed to get cockier every time she saw him in Galbraith or around the Chalet, and the way he talked about "next year" made it sound like he already had a medallion around his neck. It was getting tiring to watch and she wished he'd have the grace to leave— like members were supposed to after one year on Tetrad. In that case, maybe he could take Catherine along with him.

People submitted their online election ballots by Friday and the results were posted the next afternoon. Tony won his election, while Katy Coulson became the next female Student Events Officer.

Meanwhile, both she and Matt continued to show up to meetings before anyone else and to give it their best. Matt got laryngitis just before the next writing session but went even though he was unable to speak. He spent the entire time typing words on his keyboard and showing them to others so he could still contribute ideas. Joan made sure to read after every other writing session, not wanting to appear too keen. But when she did, she thought back to her theatre training in high school and focused on projection and enunciation.

That was the problem with the two of them, she realized; they had to put in twice as much effort as their competition.

Otherwise, they didn't stand a chance.

◆

On the Thursday two weeks before the Sermon, Joan and Matt visited the college's annual art show in Picard Hall.

It was mid-March and still well below freezing, but the day held blue skies. The sun shone down through Picard's skylight, the rafters casting shadows on the floor. People moved around slowly, speaking in hushed tones, but otherwise the room felt still and delicate as she and Matt entered.

He looked toward the high glass, which was about five feet by five feet. "That's where an Imperator in the nineties rappelled down from." He turned to her. "Shame they probably won't do anything like that for you. You deserve a grand entrance."

She opened her mouth to say something, then closed it. "That would be neat," she said, glancing up and rubbing her arm. "How did they get up there?"

"Apparently they climbed that way." He pointed to the west side, where windows looked out toward the road and Griffin Park. A cabinet stood beside a window, sitting about five feet below a ledge, which ran within reach of a wooden support beam up to the rafters. Even she figured she could climb that, so long as she could get atop the cabinet in the first place.

"Randall told us back in January he wanted to do some other venue than Psi Beta, but on Tuesday he confirmed that's where we are again."

"Yeah, Kylie told us that too." Joan didn't want to think about it. She let her eyes wander across the nature photography and modernist paintings. They were all done by members of college, though she didn't recognize most of the names—those who went here but stayed far from Social Cliffe all four years. Sometimes, she wondered if they hadn't made a better choice.

Matt stopped before a black-and-white photograph. It depicted picnic tables by a creek, and she recognized the area of Bethune's Walk he had shied away from back in November. He stared straight at it, his face a blank canvas, but his skin paled the longer he looked.

She gently shook his shoulder and he snapped out of it. "You okay?"

"Yeah." He moved past her and headed toward a painting a few spaces down.

Joan sighed and examined the photo. It had been taken on a foggy day and mist reached its tendrils across the ground. She swallowed, thinking back to how she had gotten lost running from the bridge that night. She'd spun around trying to make sense of her direction as branches, still thick with autumn leaves, blotted out the full moon's light. When she finally made it back to her room, she'd collapsed on the bed shaking and in tears. She'd probably cried more this school year than she had since she was a little kid. Or at least since high school.

Joan took a deep breath, then went over to join Matt. She needed to tell him. It would work better if he heard it this way, now. She stood beside him, looking at a modernist painting of interconnected squares. A quick sweep of her surroundings revealed no one in Anathema was around. She did a second sweep, just to make sure nobody people in Anathema talked to were around either. You couldn't be too careful at Radcliffe. If you sneezed around here everyone knew about it in a few days.

"Have you heard from Randall?" she said quietly, gazing at the painting again.

"No." There was tension in his voice. Joan glanced at him sideways and saw he looked rigid, uncomfortable. "No, I haven't and I'm really starting to get worried."

"Do you know if he's picked yet?"

"No."

She thought for a moment. "Is there any way you could find out?"

"Not sure how I could ask him. I'd just like to know so I can sleep normally again."

Joan smiled grimly. "I'm glad I'm not the only one whose been having trouble."

"I went to the campus clinic earlier this week because my ears were hurting. Turns out it's really my jawbone, since I've apparently been grinding my teeth in my sleep a lot. Doctor said it was likely due to stress."

"All the assignments around this time aren't helping."

"No. Especially not with this Bard thing hanging over our heads, either. The fact that nothing's happened with Serpentine in almost a month and a half really bothers me. I wonder if they're planning something for the Second Sermon. I doubt they've just given up."

She bit her lip. "I should talk to Randall about that."

"Can you ask him if he's picked yet?"

"I could maybe work it into the conversation."

"What about you? Heard anything yet?"

Joan tensed, then exhaled and began chewing a fingernail. "*Someone* has."

He turned to her. "What do you mean?"

"I overheard Jaya talking with Kylie after our meeting last night. She made a joke asking if members who lost their Officer races were exempt from getting Imperator, since they'd been willing to leave the organization to pad their resumes." She bit down on her finger until it hurt, then pulled it away and looked at him. "And Kylie said…she wouldn't say what affected her choice, but she already made it. She talked to Ninety-Four last weekend. It's over. Our branch's next Imperator has been decided."

Matt looked back to the painting. "Oh…," was all he said.

She glanced around, seeing if anyone had overheard. They were at least ten feet from the nearest person. Not too many were here, especially since it was barely 5 p.m. The sun had been setting later and later, aided by the start of Daylight Savings Time last Sunday, and dusk wouldn't arrive until roughly a quarter to eight. It didn't really matter if anyone was listening in, she realized. Nobody had thought either of them would end up an Imperator, anyway.

"Yeah," she said, turning back to him. She swallowed. "I still have no clue if it's Alyssa or Catherine, though. Or someone else, but let's not kid ourselves."

"Maybe it's Val. She's really good."

"I hope she at least gets it next year, but Kylie was a fourth-year Imperator and they usually pick rising fourth-years. Unless all of them suck or decline the offer. Guess I fall into the first category."

He put his hand on her shoulder and they locked eyes. His empathy was genuine. "I'm really sorry, Joan. I really, really am. You deserved it more than anybody else. I saw the way you read. You think about the future and where Anathema's heading *way* more than Alyssa or Catherine."

She leaned into him and he gave her a hug. They stood there and for a moment, she didn't care if anyone looked.

"Thank you." The words hung in the air, then she pulled back and looked into his eyes. "You have to get it, Matt. I want at least one of us to get it."

Sadness and anxiousness came across his face. He pulled her closer and stared up at the skylight, watching flecks of dust drift through the rays of sun.

"I'll find out soon. One way or another."

FIFTY-SIX

A s MATT walked to the Chalet, his pendant around his neck, worry gripped him tightly. Over the past few years, he'd imagined what would happen if he didn't become Imperator. Roy had assured him that even if he didn't become 116, he would still "100 percent be on the new Tetrad." But if Logan became Imperator, that wouldn't be a guarantee. He'd always looked down at him, always brushed him aside. He wouldn't want Matt editing his Sermons, sitting with the other Tetrad members in the lounge, shaping Anathema's future together.

And even if Logan did put him on Tetrad, he wouldn't be exempted from jokes like he would be as an Imperator. No one could stop Logan from saying he gave school shooter vibes because he was quiet around most people, no one could stop him from reading jokes about how nobody would give a shit if he dropped dead. Imperators had the final say on everything. He would be powerless to stop Logan's brand of humor from taking Anathema back to the nineties. Any reformations in the secret society would be but a dream.

Not to mention he wouldn't be able to write Preludes, wouldn't get to run Anathema the way he thought it should be run, wouldn't get to appoint a successor. He wouldn't develop strong connections with the alumni, a core part of an Imperator's job. He'd still just be taking orders, barked at like he had been his entire life.

Last year, when the shadow in his mind came so close to taking him, he'd thought of things to look forward to, signs and hopes that better days were just around the corner.

If you go through with it, you'll never find out if you become an Imperator or not.

He'd at least wanted to stick around for that, if only to see if he could prove everybody wrong. When Jack Randall was revealed as 115, he saw he had a chance. Nobody but Randall would even consider someone besides Logan. With Randall, there was hope. He hadn't had the kind of jokes read about him that Matt had, but he hadn't exactly been king of popularity before either. Social Cliffe had only turned their heads after his election as Officer and ascension to Imperator coincided. Randall certainly hadn't had an easy year, but at least he *was* somebody. At least he had something to show for his years of effort.

And now that Joan had lost the position, he felt an even greater pressure mounting. What he'd seen of her delivery was far better than either Kylie or Randall, even better than Veronica Yang, Madler, or the female Imperator back in his first year, Rosie Watts.

She'd had both Preludes already planned, the first of which involved her creeping through an old, rickety mansion with a candelabra. She would've come to the top of a landing and found a shrine with the Great Lady's skull and a closed casket. It would open to reveal a staircase, descending into a nightmarish dreamscape, from which twisted images of Radcliffe happenings would appear. Now the college would never hear it and her work would never grace the Archives. Alyssa and Catherine didn't have half her imagination.

The meeting went well.

The rooms Matt ended up in wrote plenty of good jokes and when they all congregated in the lounge, he was sure to give his best delivery.

"Lose yourself in the words," Joan had told him. "Imagine yourself as an Imperator already, and they're your Sermon audience. What would you do?"

Laughter roared around the fireplace as he read, and even Randall seemed impressed. There it was again, the hope spot. But no matter how many times he'd performed this well, no matter how many times he'd made them laugh, they still never mentioned him as a contender.

Shortly after, the meeting was dismissed; members filed out of the Chalet and through the front gate. Matt approached the Imperator as they reached the sidewalk. "Hey, I'm heading to the main drag to get drinks with Joan. You going that way too?"

"Yeah, Gemma's place is two blocks from the strip."

While the others branched off toward Griffin Park and to nearby residential streets, Matt and Randall headed north by themselves.

"How's the Sermon shaping up?"

He sighed. "So far so good. I'm excited for my Prelude. It's been a long year and I think it'll be a pretty cathartic way to put it all behind me."

Matt nodded. "Joan says writing has helped her work through a lot of stuff."

"Yeah, this definitely has. And I've had even more fun with it than I did with my first. As for the rest of the Sermon, I'm really not too worried. It's not until next Friday, so there's still time to get more good jokes in and clean it up a bit. It always comes down to the last minute with these things. Such is the joy of Anathema."

"I'll bet." He hesitated. "So how many members are we going to have next year?"

Randall thought for a moment. "We've got a lot of fourth-years leaving actually, so they'll probably be about twelve or thirteen in our branch... Yeah, that sounds right."

"Ah." He had to tread carefully now. "So Logan and Rufus are staying then?" He'd already run the numbers in his head. There would be eleven if they both left.

"Well, Rufus has told me he's taking a fifth-year, and Logan... I spoke to him a little while ago about that, and he said he intends to kick around next year."

Matt knew exactly who he'd be kicking around. Now came the hard part. He'd come this far; if it was already over, he didn't want to lose sleep for the next week and a half. Might as well rip the bandage off early.

"Ah...so the rumors are true then?"

Randall looked confused. "What rumors?"

"You know, what everybody's been saying all year...about Logan being the next Imperator." He made sure to sound casual, not leaving a trace of bitterness in his voice.

Randall's expression grew angry. "Well, *fuck them.*" He turned to Matt. "I haven't decided yet."

He did his best not to appear surprised. "Oh."

"I've been thinking about it a lot," Randall said, faster now. "I've talked to previous Imperators for advice, asked them about their decision process. It's been really tough and I hate how everyone just *assumes* things at this college. Like, it's not a fucking vote. The only two who know who's in the running—and I can assure you it's more than just one person—are myself and the Great Lord Anathema. And that's *it*."

"Right," Matt said, his heart thumping.

"There's still a week and a half left, so I know I need to decide soon. 116 needs to get prepared for his Baptism, start planning his Tetrad and all that. And I know Kylie's already talked to her successor, so it's only fair for mine to know soon. But I will not be rushed into this decision. The future of Anathema is something I take very seriously." He turned to Matt. "So until then…we'll see."

Matt only nodded.

"This is Gemma's street here." Randall looked over his shoulder to make sure no cars were coming, then stepped out into the road. "Take care, Matt."

"See you," he said, zipping up his jacket tighter. He waited until Randall was out of sight, then doubled back toward Radcliffe. When he got to his room, he took out a shot glass and filled it with the last of his rum. He'd need to go to the liquor store soon, especially for these last few weeks of class. He was crammed with back-to-back twenty- and fifteen-page research papers this Friday and next Monday, and there were three more assignments throughout next week leading up to the Sermon.

Not to mention this.

Randall hadn't decided yet. That was this college for you, always keeping things up in the air until the last possible second.

But, he noted, it meant there was still a chance.

Matt downed the shot of rum, then exhaled and sat in his desk chair. He reminded himself he really should be more concerned about Serpentine. What was the Bard readying for the Sermon?

The Circle may have gone underground, but if he knew one thing, it was that trouble at Radcliffe rarely stayed buried for long.

That Sunday he was back at the Chalet, sitting in a basement room with four others, their faces illuminated by candles and the glow of laptop screens.

"I heard a rumor that Rufus is telling people he's dropping if he doesn't make Tetrad," Zhang said.

"It's not a rumor." Another second-year member adjusted his glasses.

"He told me that himself. We were sitting in Galbraith and he said that after all he's done for the organization, he better get a position or he's out."

Freddie Evans, the sole first-year in the room, scratched his head. "So… what you're saying is…goodbye Rufus?"

Laughter went around.

Good riddance, Matt thought.

"Yeah," Zhang said, "I can't really see anyone picking him."

Ares Donovan, another second-year, sat up straighter. "What you're saying is you can't see *Logan* picking him."

"Well, I guess," Zhang said. "I mean, we don't know for sure it's him yet."

Matt opened his mouth to say something when Ares cut in. "Of course we know. Jack Randall has three choices for Imperator this year." He ticked them off on his fingers. "Logan, Logan…and Logan."

More laughs went around.

Matt toyed with his pendant. "I mean, we don't exactly know that." He realized he'd spoken his thoughts out loud and immediately regretted saying them.

Ares turned to him. "Who else would it be in your year? Tony's leaving to become an Officer."

"It…could be a rising third-year maybe…"

"Why would Randall pick someone in my year over Logan?"

"I don't know…Randall's been pretty concerned with joke content and Logan writes really harsh jokes. There'd be nobody to rein him in if he got the top spot. Imperators don't have checks and balances."

"Look, I'm not saying Logan will be good for the organization. I know he's a dick. But I also know he's going to be the next Imperator. It's just going to happen."

Freddie chimed in, "I think it might be Logan, but we really won't know until next Friday. I might not be able to make it because my family's in town, but I'd like to be there for him."

"For Logan?" Ares asked.

"For whoever it is, whether it's Logan or not. What I've heard of the Baptism is that it can be pretty intense. And it'll be a big deal for 116. A big milestone for him." The way he talked about it, Matt wondered if Freddie dreamed of getting his own medallion one day. He liked the thought of it, actually; he'd written with Freddie several times in the past month and he seemed like a pretty good guy. And very dedicated.

"It's going to be Logan," Ares said, as if it were the most obvious thing in the world, and Matt wished he'd shut the fuck up already.

"Let's get back to writing," he said, looking at his laptop. "What's something funny that's happened recently?"

The rest of the evening, Matt tried not to think about what Ares had said. It didn't work.

◆

The last week before the Sermon, he was swamped with essays and anxiety. He spent the days between lecture halls and his room, punctuated by breaks in Galbraith for meals. Joan was similarly busy, and he saw her infrequently. They tried to line up their schedules when they dined.

Outwardly, she seemed to be taking things well, but sadness flickered in her eyes whenever they discussed Anathema, especially when he mentioned that Randall hadn't talked to him yet. He'd told her last week about how the decision was up in the air, but it seemed less and less likely that he *still* hadn't talked to 116 with each passing day.

As the event drew nearer, he also dreaded what Serpentine could have in store. He refused to believe that the Bard had given up after the RCMP's announcement in February; if anything, they were probably devising a more dangerous scheme than before. Randall told Joan last week that he and Kylie were being extra cautious and had warned the attending alumni there might be troublemakers. This would be new to them—even Lambda Phi usually left the Second Sermon alone.

Wednesday would be the last writing session of the school year. It would also be their second last meeting aside from the Sermon. The End-of-Year social next Friday would close things out and the new Imperators would announce their Tetrads. If this week went as badly as it seemed it was going to, he'd immediately find himself dreading the next. He knew Joan was worried about it already. If it was Catherine, she'd have a chance at Legatus or Magister, she said. She made a joke about not being entrusted with the PR duties of a Pontifex, given her well-known affection for hazing.

Matt wondered how it would happen if Randall told him. Would he wait until after the last writing session, pull him aside and lead him down that sidewalk like they had a week ago? Would he text him at some other time, invite him to the Chalet, sit him down and say that it was tough, but he knew he made the right call? And what would Matt say in return? How would he react, what would it feel like, that glow of accomplishment? The rush of suddenly knowing that it had worked out after all these years, that the others were wrong to doubt him.

Jack Randall has three choices for Imperator this year: Logan, Logan…and Logan. He tried to push the words out of his head. *Who else would it be in your year? Tony's leaving to become an Officer.*

Sitting in his room late Tuesday night, working on an essay, Matt suddenly bit a knuckle on his left hand and breathed out. His right hand was shaking.

Imagine if they saw you like this, the shadow whispered from afar. *Imagine if they saw how weak and fragile and obsessive you really are, how much you cling to things. Joan only likes you because she's just as much of a fuck-up as you are, if not more so.*

Get the hell out of my head, he hissed to it. *How dare you fucking say that about her.*

Matt managed to focus on his essay again, but his tear ducts felt like dams about to burst. He pictured Serpentine and the rest of the college all sneering and snickering at him and Joan. He saw them seated around Galbraith, the Circle in their cloaks and pendants and the members of college in their casual clothes, and yet despite that distinction, the more they laughed the less he could tell the difference between them.

FIFTY-SEVEN

WRITING WENT late on Wednesday, as it often did with these frantic last meetings.

Matt was one of the first ones to arrive in the lounge after Randall messaged the group chat that it was time to read. The girls were reading in the basement this time, since they had gotten the lounge for the final meeting in November. Randall wasn't there yet as he entered, but Logan, Rufus, Doug, and Tanner stood around the fireplace.

"...not sure Randall's gonna read it, though," Doug was saying.

"He'll read it. I'll talk to him," Logan said, staring at a laptop screen. "Patrick won't like it, but he'll take it."

"I think it should be in the Sermon. It's a joke about a former member. He *has* to put up with it," Rufus said, folding his arms across his chest.

"What's going on?" Matt asked.

Logan sighed. "Rufus' room wrote a very funny poem about Patrick being a small-dicked moose with Down's Syndrome, but Tanner and Doug aren't sure if Randall will read it."

"That's...a bit much, don't you think?" Matt said, stepping closer.

"Patrick can take it," he reiterated.

"Yeah, but what are other people gonna think of us if we read that? I'm fine with hitting Patrick, but that just reflects poorly on us. There are better ways to make fun of him."

"Who would give a shit? Who? Honestly."

"The people who come to these things always looking for an excuse to say Anathema's still like it used to be."

"Who? Those Serpentine fuckwits?"

Tanner looked confused. "What's...?"

Logan gave him a dismissive wave. "Not important. Point is, people are gonna say bad shit about us whether we read edgy jokes or not, Matt. At least this way people will laugh. I know people will laugh. You chuckled a bit, just now, when I told you what the joke was about."

He had. "Yeah, but—"

"People have tried to stop us for years. Believe me, I'm aware. This thing is over a fucking century old, okay? You don't make fun of assholes for a hundred years without a few of them pissing back at you. But guess what? They all come and go, while Anathema stays. This thing is gonna be here years from now, even once all of us are just names in the Archives."

"So what, we have carte blanche to say whatever we want?"

"Yes. Randall won't, because he's still worried people will impeach him even though there's two weeks left of the goddamn school year. What, are they gonna host a special SGM during exam season just to get back at him? Of course not, because nobody gives that much of a shit."

"That's the kind of thinking they had in the nineties and they used it to justify everything they did. That attitude is what got us dissociated."

Logan stood up. "Oh, and what are they going to do to us today? Dissociate us *again*?" He laughed. "What *can* anyone do to us, Matt?"

"What's going on here?"

Everyone turned to see Randall standing in the hallway, watching them with military posture and his hands clasped behind his back. The light of the fireplace reflected off his silver medallion.

"We're just debating whether a joke should go in or not," Matt said.

"Well, I'm the final authority on that." The Imperator stepped closer. "What's the joke?"

"Here," Logan said, retrieving the laptop and carrying it to Randall. "Just read it. It's funny."

Randall took the device and read, laughing as he went along. Finally, he handed the computer back to Logan. "I will admit, that's pretty funny, but I'm concerned about how it would come across."

"Oh who the fuck cares? If it's funny, why not? It's genuinely funny, not just mean, right?"

Randall tilted his head. "It's...amusing to a certain audience."

"And what is our audience? Drunk college students who say worse shit about people in Galbraith every day, who gossip with no opt-out policy." For once, Matt found himself agreeing with Logan. "We cater to them and make them laugh and they keep coming back. That's how it's always worked."

"Down Syndrome's not a joke," Matt said.

Logan spun around. "You would know."

Randall grimaced. "Easy, easy. He's got a point. I am concerned how that joke would play out. Maybe we should revise the poem so it's a bit less offensive. Just a bit. Still edgy, but not stepping over the line."

"Where is the line?"

"You don't seem to have one," Matt told him. "Everything's fair game to you."

Logan flushed red with anger. He jabbed his finger toward Matt. "This guy thinks if we don't pussyfoot around every joke somebody's gonna come and fuck us all up. Well maybe that's how things work in America, where people shoot up their schools because they can't take some mean words—but we do things differently up here, okay?"

"What about Benson and Chet?"

The room fell gravely silent, save for Logan, who merely shrugged. "What's your point? Those were two guys who hated Anathema, and now they're dead. Rather conveniently for us, I might add. One douchebag slips down a hill and the other gets murdered in the safest town in Alberta. You'd have to be a dumb fucking *idiot* to get stabbed in Canmore Creek, but I bet Chet pissed off the wrong fuckin' drifter and that was that."

"And what if...?" Matt hesitated. How much had Randall told Logan about the Bard? Did he believe Serpentine was a threat himself?

He looked to the Imperator, who suddenly appeared very sad and tired. "Let's end this right now. I will review that poem and make the final decision. There. End of discussion." He glanced around, then at his watch. "Where the fuck is everybody? It's after 1 a.m. and I've got a paper to finish still. A big one." He rubbed his eyes.

Doug leaned back on a sofa, typing on his phone. "I'm telling them to get their asses over here."

Laughter drifted up from the back stairwell. The female branch was reading downstairs. Matt wondered if Joan was performing jokes still, now that she knew it was pointless.

Once all their branch's members arrived in the lounge, those with laptops began to read. Though dogged by fear, Matt gave it his best effort and managed to avoid slipping up. He read smoothly and loudly, carefully enunciating the right words and deadpanning the right points. It would probably be his last time reading at a writing session, he thought. If he somehow became Imperator still, it would be his turn to stand by the fireplace and nod along with each joke, thinking how it could fit into his vision of the 200th Sermon—that would be a big one next fall. If he made Tetrad, he'd spend time editing with Logan and the others and wouldn't need to read anymore. And if he didn't make Tetrad at all...

Well then, he wouldn't have the heart to read jokes anyway, if it was truly all a waste.

Then Freddie performed for the first time, his delivery marked by a steady cadence. All of the jokes were smooth until: "Historical Parallels. September 1666. The Great Fire of London swept across London—"

Evidently redundancy amused the tired brain, because the entire room burst into hysterics.

Doug wiped tears from his eyes. "The Great Fire of London...swept across *London*...?" He mimicked Freddie's accent. "You alright there, guv'na?"

Rufus was still doubled over laughing. "Why did we Initiate this idiot again?"

Freddie raised an eyebrow. "Say Rufus, what school did you say you went to in England?"

"Eton," the fourth-year said, adjusting his turtleneck.

"That's funny," Freddie said, chuckling. "I went there and I don't remember you."

Rufus grew angry, clenching his fists. "I was several years ahead of you."

"Yeah, but my mate Noah would've been in your year and he knew everybody. I asked him a little while ago if he'd ever heard of you." Freddie smiled and shook his head.

Rufus had gone pale. "It doesn't matter, I was—"

"It's alright," Freddie said. "I won't tell everyone your accent's obviously an affectation. You slip up from time to time, but since I'm the only other Brit in Anathema right now, I'll keep it hush-hush."

Logan sat up, his jaw dropped. "Are you fucking kidding me? Rufus is faking his accent and we find out about it *after* all the jokes are written?" He put a hand to his head, still stunned. "Un-fucking-believable."

Laughter went around the room. Rufus was petrified. "I'm telling you, I don't know what he's talking about. I went to Eton, I swear! This is how I've always spoken!"

"Don't worry, Rufus. We'll be sure to write lots of jokes about it next year."

More laughter.

Rufus fired a death glare around the room, red in the face but pressed into silence by embarrassment. To his own surprise, Matt didn't laugh.

◆

Randall said nothing after the writing session and all hope seemed lost until late the following evening, the night before the Sermon.

Matt sat in his room, sipping from his flask. He'd finally finished his assignments for the week about an hour ago. He'd skipped DebSoc to finish an essay and submit it online, then asked Joan if she wanted to drink with him. She told him she had a test the following morning along with two midterms and a paper due next week, but said she'd be sure to sit with him at the Foxhole and Ni Hao after the Sermon.

So here he was, drinking alone in his room. A new low. He tried not to think about it too much. He also tried not to think about tomorrow. He'd known all along that it would be a long shot against Logan, but the cinephile in him had held out for that magical twist, the one that would reveal the Imperator was just testing his patience, that the unexpected underdog would win out in the end—just as Randall himself had last year.

Then again, if he still hadn't picked yet—which was absurd—he wouldn't choose Logan now, would he? He'd looked sad to see his Legatus pushing a joke about Down Syndrome. Surely he had to have known that's what Logan's Sermons would have in store. The man had mocked him all year, saying he was a pussy for treading carefully, saying he jerked off to *safety* for fuck's sake. How could anyone ever trust that man to lead something already plagued by PR issues?

Then his phone buzzed.

Matt reached for it and sighed. Maybe Joan had changed her mind about drinking.

Instead, it was Randall.

Hey Matt, are you around? The podium got damaged at the last Sermon and we forgot about it until now. Logan and I are sneaking into Galbraith to steal the one there, but we need a third person.

He typed, *Yeah, sure! Where should I meet you?*

The West Quad in 2 minutes, Randall messaged back.

Matt glanced at the time on his phone. That would put it at 12:30 exactly. Lt. Jackson Randall and his military precision.

He threw on a jacket and went out into the West Quad via the door under Napier. A cold breeze blew through his hair as he stood there, hands in his pockets and looking around. Hopefully it would warm up a bit by QuadFest, which was just a couple weeks away.

Soon, two figures emerged from the shadow of Anathema Tower and made their way toward him. "Thanks for coming on short notice," Randall said. Matt could see deep bags beneath his eyes in the moonlight. "I just looked at the podium now and forgot one of those Lambda fuckfaces pushed it down the gazebo steps. It'll hold, but it looks pretty sketchy and won't impress the alumni."

Matt nodded, glancing between him and Logan. The Legatus looked sad. "So how do we get in there? Everything's locked up at this hour."

Randall held up a keychain. "That's where I come in. I've got a Master R3."

Matt raised an eyebrow. "Do they give those to all Officers?"

"Yeah, it gets me pretty much anywhere in the college. Mia Cote was pissed I still got one because she thought I'd use it to let Anathema sneak around."

"And now we're proving her right," Logan said.

Randall shrugged. "Oh well. It'll let us into the Senior Common Room, and from there we can get into Galbraith. My car's parked out on the front loop, but it'll take all three of us to get it down those stairs."

"We should hurry," Logan said. "There's still night guards roaming around. And Réjean hates any student with a pulse."

They made their way into Bowman through the northern door, then hung left and ended up in the corridor running from the back of Galbraith to another door, which led to Bertrand Hall and the stairs to Saunders. The Anamicable meeting he and Joan had swung by before the First Sermon seemed so long ago.

Making sure there was no guard, the trio hung left again toward Galbraith, which was blocked by a heavy sliding door. "My key won't work on this," Randall said, keeping his voice low. "You need a special maintenance one for that, and to get into the boiler room downstairs and stuff. But mine *will* unlock…"

He turned to the door directly left of them labeled *Senior Common Room*, slid the key into the knob, and turned it. A click rang out in the quiet hall.

"…this." Randall led them inside and stealthily shut the door behind them.

Moonlight shone through the windows and Matt could see lights in the Quad beyond. What he saw of the space made him think of a lounge from an old English manor, the kind of room that would appear in an Agatha Christie novel. There were two ornate bookshelves to the right and a large coffee table in the center. Every week before High Table, Mustard schmoozed and boozed with alumni and donors in this room.

"The door's back here," Randall whispered. He walked forward and nearly tripped over the coffee table, swore under his breath, and continued along past a high-backed leather chair toward the window. Matt and Logan stayed close behind.

There was another click as Randall unlocked a door to his right and it creaked open. He looked back at his helpers and beckoned them to follow, then stepped out into the dining hall. Matt took a moment to take it all in once he walked through the frame. Galbraith was dark and eerie by night, pale light filtering through the stained-glass windows. The vaulted ceilings seemed somehow higher than before. All the chairs were put up on the tables and the space felt emptier, filled instead with a frosty draft and an unsettling presence.

"Let's hurry up and get the fuck out of here," Logan said, shivering.

Randall moved toward the podium, then froze.

A beam of light danced its way along the windows at the other end of the hall. The Imperator turned around and brought a finger to his lips. Logan stepped back and accidentally nudged a chair at the edge of the High Table. He turned to catch it, but it was too late.

The seat crashed to the floor.

Outside the entrance, the beam stopped moving. Then it came closer to the door. Matt could faintly hear a jangling of keys.

Randall grabbed them both by the shoulders and pulled them back into the Senior Common Room, closing the door over very carefully as the entrance to Galbraith creaked open. The three of them stepped back from the door. Footsteps echoed in the hall beyond, drawing closer and closer.

"Hide," Matt whispered.

The trio ducked behind the longest sofa. Matt and Logan pressed their backs against it while Randall peered over the edge.

The guard was now walking around the High Table, and judging by the sound of their footsteps, circling it like a shark.

The chair could've just fallen off. Put it back up and go, Matt thought.

A soft ticking emanated somewhere in the room. Glancing up, he saw a clock halfway between the two bookshelves on the wall before him. He hadn't noticed it before. *Tick, tick, tick.* It was the only sound beside soft breathing and the occasional clunk of a boot.

The footfalls stopped—then started up again, coming closer. Matt glanced around the edge of the sofa. The guard's flashlight swept under the door, then disappeared. The footsteps started up again, getting farther and farther away. Finally there was the faint sound of one of the hall's entrance doors opening and closing.

The three of them started breathing louder. Randall stood up and looked at Logan. "Be more careful this time."

They headed back out into Galbraith and all three of them grabbed the podium. It was heavier than he expected; their old one had been lighter. Randall led them back into the Senior Common Room and they put it down so he could close and lock the door to the dining hall, then they carried it back out into the corridor and set it down again, so he could do the same for the room.

"Now what?" Matt asked.

"We go back to the West Quad. But I'll need you to run ahead and see if the coast is clear in the lobby."

"Sure," he said.

They pushed through into Bowman without needing to use keys, then headed back outside, a chill buffeting them as they did so. The wind had picked up.

Over by Winslow, a figure exited and made their way toward Lacy while never noticing the three Anathema members and their stolen catch. Once they reached the center, they set it down and took deep breaths. Matt's arms were getting tired and it seemed Randall's and Logan's were too.

"I'll scope out the lobby," he said, and took off toward the main double doors.

Inside, security guards were nowhere in sight, but the night reception-ist read her Kindle as usual. Matt casually walked over to the nearby water fountain and took a drink, then headed back outside.

"We've got a problem. The receptionist's there."

"Shit, I almost forgot," Randall said, thinking.

"There's another way out," Matt realized aloud. "Through the chapel. I know there's a basement you can get to behind the altar, and there's a door that lets out by the library, right near the edge of Griffin Park."

Randall and Logan exchanged looks. "Okay, let's head there," the Imperator said.

They carried the podium to a side door on the north side of the Quad, coming into a hallway. Stairs winding up to the Crow's Nest res house were directly to their right, the stone steps leading to Galbraith's entrance farther down the corridor. They waited to make sure a security guard wasn't nearby, then hung to the left and Randall unlocked the door into the chapel while Matt and Logan held the podium, their arms trembling.

Then they were inside and none of them said a word. As they carried the heavy object down the center aisle, Matt was calmed by looking up to the high ceilings. It was surprisingly bright in here, moonlight reflecting off the white stone walls. This place was far more serene and majestic by night than Galbraith.

"Feels wrong carrying something for a pagan ritual through here," he muttered.

"Nobody really believes in the Great Lord Anathema anyway," Logan grunted.

Randall forced a laugh, sounding tired. "I still pray to him every time I hand in an assignment."

They made their way up to the altar, then went to a door to its left, carefully heading down a flight of stairs. The basement was dark and musty. Randall turned on his phone's flashlight and guided them to a door where an exit sign glowed, the only modern addition to the chamber.

Then, finally, they were outside on a sidewalk sloping down the hill to-ward Griffin Park. The library rose before them, its gargoyles barely visible through the night.

"This way," Randall panted, helping them carry it again. When they reached the base of the hill, they swung back around to the front loop where a few cars were parked, including the Imperator's Volvo station wagon.

Once they hefted the podium into the trunk, they collectively exhaled and each of them doubled over.

"I really appreciate that, guys. Thanks."

"See you tomorrow," Logan said to Randall. He turned to Matt. "Thanks for helping out. Take care." He headed back up the front stairs of the college.

Matt looked at Randall. "He seemed sad. Is he alright?"

The Imperator sighed. "Lisa broke up with him yesterday. He's still in a bit of a mood."

"Ah." Matt actually felt sorry for him. It seemed like him and Lisa had gotten along. Then again, there was always that stretch between Winter Formal and the end of classes when couples split every year. It was part of why there were so many hookups at QuadFest.

"Yeah…" Randall looked off, watching as Logan vanished past the top of the steps. Then he turned back to Matt. "I just wanted to say, you've been a really big help this year—and the years before that. I know both Turland and Madler really appreciated what you did for them."

"Madler?" He'd always assumed 114 never liked him.

"Yeah, he told me he admired your dedication. And I have too." Randall paused.

Matt tensed.

"The Anathema has had a lot of members pass through it over the years, but only a few impress the Imperators each year. I just want you to know you've been a real asset since your Initiation." He looked up to the tower. "You've done the Great Lord proud."

"Thank you," he said, incredibly nervous.

"I'm excited for tomorrow. My girlfriend made a great poster again. Do you want to hold it at Griffin, like you did last time? Not many members get to hold the poster more than once a year."

"Sure, absolutely."

"Great. Well, thanks again for helping with this." He gestured to the podium. "I know it's late. I'm gonna go and finally get some sleep. I've been awake for about forty-eight hours." He laughed and Matt laughed too. "See you at the Sermon."

"Yeah, see you." He forced a smile.

Randall walked around the car and got in. Matt turned and walked slowly up the steps, feeling suddenly very frail and empty. The engine turned on behind him and he heard the vehicle drive off. When he reached the top, he looked back. Randall's car cruised along the west side of Griffin Park, back toward the residential streets of Canmore Creek.

He turned around and looked up at the tower, not caring as the wind battered his face. Lanterns were snuffed out in his mind and the shadow returned, closer than it had been in a year. It flexed its talons and bared its teeth, its voice like broken glass.

Did you miss me?

FIFTY-EIGHT

G EMMA HAD truly outdone herself.

Matt admired her last one, but this Second Sermon poster was simply breathtaking. It depicted two cloaked figures locked in sword combat while Radcliffe burned behind them, the night sky ablaze with flame. *Now there's some wishful thinking.* He couldn't help but laugh.

He stood beside Tanner in Griffin Park, each of them holding one edge of the frame as the attendees sang. The other members joined them from the statue, black candles wavering in their hands, their mask-wearing faces impassive.

He glanced over. Joan and Kristen Edwards held Kylie's poster, depicting darkened, candle-lit catacombs where rows of skulls stretched off into blackness. His girlfriend turned to him, gave a weak smile as she sang, then faced forward again.

At least he still had her.

No, that was much more than an *at least.* She was far more important than some stupid position in a glorified frat that read jokes. Infinitely more important. He couldn't imagine going through his remaining time at Radcliffe without her. Once his upper-year friends—which was most of his friends—graduated, he'd have nothing left to cling to.

There's that word, the shadow hissed. *That's all you do—cling, cling, and cling.*

"Fuck off," he muttered. Tanner turned to him. "Nothing," he said.

Now that you don't have the medallion and your status as unaccomplished loser is cemented, you're going to cling to her more than ever. And it's going to drive her away. And then you will have nothing.

No, no, no, no, no. He wasn't going back there, to last year. He *refused.* He'd escaped it once, told himself it would all get better.

But now look at him and Joan. They were the two overactive Anathema members who had desperately wanted positions they couldn't achieve. He bet everyone could see it, bet they laughed at how stupid him and Joan were to think they could be important.

At least they had each other.

For now. Happiness always has a price at this college. You know that, Matt. Every time something good happens to you, it never lasts. So how do you know she won't leave you?

Shut up.

Maybe she'll still get arrested. She's innocent but she'll go to jail for something someone else did, probably someone more popular. Someone who already has status and nothing can touch them. You know how it is when Social Cliffe fucks up. They get a slap on the wrist, a few snide comments made in Galbraith, but then it still works out for them. Look at Logan Brewster. His girlfriend dumped him, but he's about to become Imperator. After already being a Legatus. Nothing really bad ever happens to Social Cliffe, and if it does, greener pastures are just around the corner for them. You're in a different game.

Shut *up.*

What a nice reward for all your dedication. You get to hold a fucking poster. High return on investment for three years of bitchwork.

No, he could still make Tetrad. There *was* a chance. Logan had three positions to fill and Matt was the only other person in his year still in Anathema. Geoff Bhajan was sticking around for a fifth-year and everyone liked him, so he'd get a spot even though he didn't always show up.

That left two.

Rufus was also taking a fifth-year, but he'd gone around saying he was leaving if he didn't get Tetrad, which was a sure way to shoot himself in the foot. Clearly, he thought he was more of a value-add than he really was. And Logan didn't seem to care for him anyway.

So who else? It could be two third-years, though Tanner and Hamid seemed to be the only ones Tetrad-ready. If Matt got a spot, he was sure one of them would too. Of course, Logan could put them both on and leave him out. He could do whatever the fuck he liked. He always had, and the college still rewarded him.

The songs were starting to wrap up.

Matt glanced at the poster, noting again how nice it was. He wondered what it would be like to punch through the glass, to tear right through the drawing and rip the whole fucking thing to shreds. Then he'd stand there watching pieces of paper blow in the wind, glass shards protruding from his bloody hand.

What would it feel like for someone else who'd worked hard to get their efforts torn up for once? Of course, Randall hadn't drawn it. Gemma had. He'd only met her a few times, but she seemed very nice.

Not like she'd worked on it for three years anyway.

The songs finally ended and Sandrine led the female branch and attendees toward the residential streets. Then Logan headed up the parade of men, marching them off to his coronation. The four members holding the posters followed up behind. This time, they wouldn't return the artwork to the Chalet. The alumni always liked to see the illustrations and Lambda never attacked the Second Sermon.

Of course, this year, someone else might.

That was what he'd truly been dreading. Now the awful week could cap off with a truly awful disaster, the game of life and death forcing itself back upon the middling drama of his life.

You've got bigger things to worry about than all this bullshit, a small voice said inside of him. *Who cares about this stupid cult? Someone is trying to frame your girlfriend for* murder.

Don't remind me, he thought. The wind swiped at his face and he adjusted his mask, his heart pounding faster the closer they got to the venue.

The Bard had taken their sweet time since February, and that could only mean one thing:

Tonight was the night for something big.

FIFTY-NINE

PSI BETA Omicron stood on a street close to Griffin, so they arrived shortly. It was a larger frat house than Lambda Phi, with three levels instead of two, and newer architecture. Last year he'd heard Doug mention that they'd been hosting Sermons here since 2006, after the male Imperator at the time slept with the Lambda President's girlfriend.

Normally that thought would've made him laugh or shake his head, but he was torn between anxiousness and dejection as he walked through the doors into the foyer. There was a kitchen to the left, a staircase leading up to the right, and a large open room dead ahead through another set of doors. It was all arranged with sofas and wooden chairs, and Matt saw the podium off at the back. Beside the stairs, first-year Initiates manned the kegs and filled foamy cups of beer for everyone.

Members, attendees, and alumni milled about the foyer with their drinks. It was strange seeing people in their thirties and forties in a fraternity with a bunch of undergrad students. The way they dressed in tuxedos or black dresses, pendants and old medallions swinging from their necks, they looked more suited to a cocktail party, yet held red Solo cups in their hands.

Though he'd already consumed half his flask, Matt decided he needed another drink. He made his way to the kegs. Freddie and a female Initiate were filling cups and placing them on a table beside them as fast as they could. He took one and nodded to both of them, then turned around and nearly spilled his drink on Roy.

"Shit, sorry," he said.

"No worries." Roy took a cup, then led him aside. "You alright?"

"I didn't get it," he breathed, looking out at the people talking, chatting, and drinking.

Roy paused, then said, "So it's Logan, then?"

"I guess."

He sighed. "I expected better from Randall. He seemed like he'd be different." He took a sip of beer.

"I respect him," Matt said. "I really do, I have all year." *I just want to know why. Was there ever even a chance?*

"That's the problem with looking up to people. They all disappoint you eventually." He shook his head. "Did Joan at least get it?"

"No, she didn't."

"Great, we might end up with Logan *and* Alyssa. Fuckin' two-for-one special." He had another sip. "Thank God I'm graduating and won't have to see that shitstorm. This whole college has been going down the drain. Now I guess even Anathema's going with it."

"And Joan and I will still be stuck here."

"Yeah, but maybe you'll both make Tetrad. At least that might be fun."

"I don't know. Logan doesn't seem to like me that much."

"Logan doesn't seem to like anybody that much. If anything, Alyssa is the more vindictive one. Logan doesn't hold grudges; he just does as he pleases. But if Alyssa doesn't like Joan, I'd be more worried about her not getting anything."

Matt put a hand to his head. "I hate this fucking college."

Roy laughed. "Aside from the architecture, it is truly ugly. At least you and Joan only have one more year. I wouldn't recommend staying for a fifth. You'll both be dying to leave by the end of next semester."

I want to leave now. And I want her to come with me.

He realized Roy was staring at one of the alumni, an attractive brunette woman in her forties wearing a skull medallion. She looked weary, even as she chatted with an old acquaintance, who appeared to be consoling her.

"Who's that?"

"Pretty sure she's Emma Gagnon, Imperator from the late nineties."

Matt's eyes widened. "Isn't she the one who drove that girl to nearly kill herself?"

Roy winced. "Yeah, she did. Let's not get on her bad side." He sipped, then froze. Pandora walked through in a green shirt and jeans, holding

Blaine's hand. Matt hadn't seen him around with Melissa in a long while; maybe he was shacking up with the Vizier now. Unlike the other non-member attendees, they weren't wearing gowns. "Ah, fuck. I'll catch you around." Roy started to move off, then turned back and came closer. "And I'm really sorry. Fuck Randall and fuck Logan." Then he headed to the larger room, where some attendees were already securing seats.

Matt wandered around the floor, not even bothering to say hello to people he knew, merely looking for Joan. A man in his late forties with a mane of dark hair turned around and smiled. "Ah, nice to meet you." He wore an Imperator medallion.

He snapped out of it. Normally, he was much better around the alumni. It took a lot of effort, but he had approached something orbiting personable in the past few years. "Matt Richardson. I'm a third-year."

"Quentin Caleb, His 88th mouthpiece." He shook his hand with a firm grip. Caleb had a warm smile and Matt decided there was something likable about him.

"Ah, so you're from…"

"Graduated in 1993, but I was a third-year Imperator from '91-'92." He held up a hand. "Yes, I know. The bad era." Caleb sighed and looked off toward the other room, toward the podium. "I was a real asshole back then. A lot of us were, but that doesn't excuse it. I took things too far." He looked back to Matt. "I haven't been back in ten years. It had gotten better last time. Is it still better?"

Not for long. "It has. We've made great strides. Less vitriol, more…"

"Humor." Caleb nodded. "I'm glad to see Dissociation didn't kill it. Must suck for you guys, though, having to kiss up to us for money now."

Matt shrugged. "You gotta do what you gotta do."

"I've heard there's been some strange deaths at Radcliffe recently," he said.

"It's been…a weird year."

Caleb scoffed. "Yeah, I'll bet."

Matt tried to think of something else to say but felt too drained. Besides, it wasn't like he needed to impress these people anymore. His name would never join Caleb's, or Randall's, or Turland's on the Succession. And even if he made Tetrad, he'd be at most a footnote.

The 88th Imperator nodded and said, "Well, enjoy the Sermon." Then he walked off.

Matt stood there, people milling about all around him. He stared past them to some unfixed point on the wall, the shadow creeping closer in his head. He was suddenly exhausted and just being here took effort. Matt made his way through the crowd, trying to find somebody else to talk to.

No, he didn't really talk to *him*. It would be hard to strike up a conversation now. Ah, *she* was nice but already chatting with someone else. There had to be somebody to—

Matt found himself face-to-face with Pandora Lane. She looked him up and down and gave a sly smile. "Though I hate you bastards, I will admit the tux and mask make a great combo. Joan must just love tearing them off of you."

"Here to steal pendants and break things like last time?" he asked, his eyes narrowing. "Or does the Bard have bigger plans this evening?"

She gave a casual shrug. "I don't know. I didn't ask him."

Matt was stunned. "He...didn't give you any instructions?"

"He's never given me instructions. He only spoke to Chet, and since one of you murdered him, the Bard's gone quiet. We haven't heard from him since December." She grinned, enjoying Matt's surprise. "I don't blame him, though. There's a real psycho in your ranks. Probably thought they'd come for him next."

Matt took a step back, thinking. "So, stealing letters at the Winter Formal—?"

"Was my idea, yes. I appointed myself acting Vizier in the Bard's absence, keeping Serpentine together until he returns." She looked around the room. "My guess is that he's waiting to find out who the new Imperators are. Then we'll have something to go on. And if for some reason he hasn't reached out by the end of the year, I'll name one of the younger members the new Bard. And they'll appoint another Vizier, then next year they'll pick up where we left off." She smirked again. "If Anathema is still around."

"And why the hell are you telling me all this?" he asked, his mind scrambling to fit the pieces into the puzzle.

She shrugged. "After half a decade of torture, I'm finally graduating from this shithole. When Chet asked me to join Serpentine, I said yes because I thought it would be fun to fuck with all of you. Then people started dying and, well, that got a little less fun. So I might as well tell you, because this is the only enjoyment I have left. And it's not like you can do anything about it. I have faith in the Bard. I know whatever he's planning will finish you people for good. I can sit back, drink, and watch the fireworks."

"So why are you here tonight, if there's nothing planned for the Sermon?"

Pandora smiled. "To be honest, I'm curious about the new Imperators myself. I've had my guesses, but given how antsy you're acting, I'm guessing you didn't get it."

He swallowed. "You thought it would be me?"

"There hasn't been a pick as obvious as Logan Brewster the entire time I've been here." She looked around and sighed, with just a touch of sadness. "And besides, your whole identity is that you're an Anathema member. They all laugh at how much you cling to it. I figure someone like that would be perfect for a thankless job like Imperator, a true fanatic." She tilted her head. "Speaking of which, did your girlfriend get it?"

"No," he said, looking down. "She didn't either."

"Aww, that's too bad. I hate to see so much effort go to waste." Her eyes swept the frat's foyer. "It's why I felt bad for Roy last year, when we started sleeping together. He'd been screwed out of Tetrad twice by then. It wasn't hard to get secrets out of him when he was drunk. When he told me Randall was planning to mobilize Anathema to vote against that Electoral Policy amendment, I just *had* to go to the admin."

Now she really enjoyed his horror, watching his face go pale. "We kept hooking up this year, and I got a good deal more out of him. I don't know if he remembers what he said or not, but it only took a few drinks and some supportive words to drill down to the bitterness. I mined it for all it was worth each time, then fucked his brains out." She smirked. "Randall never did figure out who his snitch was, did he?"

Matt said nothing. She laughed and walked off, leaving him there alone with his cup.

After a moment, he turned and walked to the stairs. He saw Favell chatting with Tony and Doug, but didn't have the energy to say hello. Instead, he climbed up to the second floor and found himself in a darkened corridor. The bathroom was to the left and seemed to look like less of a nuclear apocalypse than it had in previous years. At the sink, he splashed cold water on his face and stood there, staring at himself in the cracked mirror. Then he began pacing the room, lost in thought.

After a while he heard shouting and realized Kylie must be starting her Prelude. Oh well. He knew there would be jokes about Joan being diffident and Joan being awkward, and Joan doing whatever. And they'd all laugh at her for it, no matter how dedicated she was.

At first, he'd thought he'd try to work out what Pandora had told him, but he was too exhausted and drunk to even think. Instead he mindlessly wandered the bathroom for quite a while, occasionally stepping out to the hallway for a change of scenery.

"CARPE RISUS, CARPE CORONAM!" he heard the girls chanting one time, then the crowd shouting *"THREE TIMES, ASSHOLE!"* another.

He finished his flask, held it upside down above the grody tile and shook it just to make sure he'd gotten the last drop. The next time he stepped into the hall, he heard Kylie bellow: "HERE ENDETH THE 184TH SERMON OF THE GREAT LADY ANATHEMA!"

The four eternal words were shouted again, and Matt found himself drifting back downstairs. He hadn't intended to miss Kylie's Sermon and suddenly felt bad for doing so. He didn't really want to see Randall's now, if only because he already knew how it ended. Granted, the reveal of both Imperators was always saved for last. The Second Sermon hadn't been joint until about twenty years ago, and since then it had followed a complex flip-flop schedule.

And then after, they'd all go to the Foxhole to get drunk. That, at least, was something to look forward to tonight. Although judging by the wobble in his step, he knew he probably should cut back for a bit. He reached the base of the stairs and everyone was milling about again, a brief beer break while the Tetrads switched places. Nobody seemed to have noticed he'd gone.

Tony turned to him with an extra candle and offered it to him. "Here, do you need one?"

"Yeah, thanks."

They walked into the adjacent chamber, where many audience members remained relaxing in their seats, not wanting to forsake them for the next round of chastisement. The male branch began to congregate around the podium, lighting candles as the audience returned to their seats with freshly filled Solo cups. Doug sat before the podium, the real skull in his lap this time. Logan and Fennell stood on either side, but Randall was nowhere to be seen. Then the lights went off and the room was only lit by candles along the row of members. The last few attendees took their seats.

The light in the foyer was still on, and a cloaked figure appeared in the frame, his shadow cast along the wooden floor. He stood there for a moment, until the audience turned and noticed.

Then he strode toward the podium.

SIXTY

HERE IT was, the capstone.

He'd come all this way and so many had tried to stop him, but one by one from Patrick to Serpentine they had failed. He'd made it to the end now. The finish line was in sight. He'd gone through an entire year as both Officer and Imperator and come out unscathed.

How would Anathema remember 115? There was a nickname for each Imperator in the Book of Succession, scrawled in cursive beside their real one. Gordon MacTaggart was predictably the First, but others included the Scotsman, the Loud, the Tall, the Feared, and the Dumbass. Duric had been "The Misjudging" for picking Ellis, and Turland "The Band-Aid" for fixing his mistake. Madler had of course been called "The Mad."

What would his be? What nickname would sit beside *Jackson Claudius Randall* for all eternity? "The Unimpeached," perhaps?

Regardless, it felt good to have their eyes on him. Reverence and respect emanated from the room as he slid around the podium. Everyone from lowly first-years to successful alumni—lawyers, doctors, businessmen and women, even some politicians—had lent him their ears.

It was time to say the words.

Randall reached up and threw back his hood, revealing a silver crown atop his head, its color matching that of his Venetian mask. Gasps and murmured whisperings rose from the crowd. An Imperator had never worn one before during a Sermon, at least not in memory. He smiled with contempt as his eyes scanned their faces; it was dark but he could still make them out. Patrick, sitting with Karen to the right on a battered loveseat, didn't look too impressed. Oh well.

"Ladies…gentlemen…distinguished alumni…let us begin."

He tore the Sermon open to its first page.

"I opened my eyes…and there I saw…a red sky lit by fire. I emerged from the woodland and drew my broadsword, checking my armor. I had come to reclaim my kingdom from the clutches of insolence, only to see it standing there ablaze—that wretched fucksack on the hill…*RRRRRRadcliffe College!*

"The final battle had already begun. I ran up the road to the front gate as panicked residents fled past me, taking the few belongings they could manage. I burst inside, where the Provost's evil Wellness Guard was taking prisoners and forcing them to talk about their feelings. With a few strikes, thrusts, and parries with my blade, I had dispatched them all and freed the residents.

" 'Wait,' one of them said. 'You're 115. You're the one the Provost tried to impeach. The one who fled into exile.'

" 'Yes. Tell the others I have returned—and that I've brought chastisement with me.' "

The crowd cracked up. Randall glimpsed Patrick rolling his eyes. The fucker.

"They turned and ran for the exit while I breached the heavy double doors, emerging into the West Quadrangle. What I saw shook me to my core. Flame and death abounded, guards beheading those who dared worship Alcoholus.

"It was a fucking Inquisition.

"One by one, I slaughtered the Guards and set the pagans free. Then I stood there, drenched in blood and catching my breath. I glanced around the Quad. Flames leaped in every window from Galbraith to old Winslow. Smoke billowed into the night sky.

"I held up my sword and cried, 'Where are you, you coward?! Fight me yourself!'

"And there he appeared atop Napier Tower, John of House Mustard, wearing ceremonial robes and an ornate black crown. He gazed upon his kingdom—no, *my* kingdom—with sinister delight.

"Before I could do anything, he lifted his arms and shouted, 'AND HE SHALL SMITE THE WICKED AND PLUNGE THEM INTO THE FIREY PIT!'

411

"Wait. I knew he had gunpowder, but—

"The windows of Vickers and Picard blew out behind me, the fireball erupting one floor at a time, past the Himalayan Suite on the fifth floor, up to the tower—

" 'Father!' I cried, but it was too late.

"The belfry burst in a ball of fire, the steeple scattering in all directions. A wraith was thrown by the force and tumbled across Picard's roof to the skylight. Glass, stone, and copper rained into the Quad as I bolted for the western wall. I held my shield before me, debris bouncing off the metal as I ran, the evil laugh of the Provost echoing all around.

"When I got to the wall, I unspooled my rope and, summoning all my strength, hurled the metal hook toward the roof. It caught a firm hold and I began my ascent—climbing, climbing, climbing. Beads of sweat rolled down my forehead, but I didn't stop to wipe them away. The Great Lord was hurt. He needed my assistance.

"As I scaled past a shattered Picard window, a figure suddenly lunged out of the frame. I saw the blade too late, and it lanced through the side of my abdomen. In the pain, I nearly lost my grip, but I held firm, turning to face my attacker.

"I recognized that self-righteous smirk at once. It was Sir Patrick the Mason, Radcliffe's self-appointed White Knight. 'Your time has come, 115,' he sneered. 'I finally got you. Now fun is finished, and Mustard shall reign supreme. Forever.'

"Clenching my teeth, I wrenched my sword from its sheath and swung it with a breathless cry. Patrick's severed head tumbled down into the Quad, the rest of his body toppling after it.

"I dropped my sword and pulled Patrick's out of me. He'd gotten me pretty badly, but I wasn't done yet. I still had time."

"With the last of my strength, I reached the roof and crawled toward the skylight, toward the Great Lord. He lay there, staring at the stars, his orange eyes glowing weaker. Feebly, he turned to me and extended a bony hand. '115,' he croaked, 'come closer.'

" 'I'm too late, Father. I have failed you.'

" 'You have not failed me yet, 115. There is only one thing that can save me and help me to save Radcliffe: the power of satirical chastisement. You are growing weaker, but there is still time. With it, deliver one final Sermon, let the college heed my word. And with your dying breath, name a successor, so that he may bear our mission forward into the future.'

" 'Your will is my command.' I crawled to the skylight and smashed it with my grapnel, then secured the hook and began lowering myself by the rope—down, down, into the flames and darkness. When I reached the bottom, I saw them standing there beside me, on both my right and left—my Tetrad and the faithful members in my command. Looking straight ahead, I saw a crowd full of Radcliffe's past, present, and future. They were all here, undeterred by the fire, awaiting the Great Lord's word.

"And standing before them was a podium, where a freshly-bound tome awaited me. I limped toward it, gripped its edges, and began to read—

"THE 199ᵀᴴ SERMON OF THE GREAT LORD...ANATHEMA!"

◆

Randall tore through the Sermon like a tiger. It was, Matt noted, his best delivery in the years he'd known him.

Matt wasn't hit too hard himself, which was a relief. Now that he had a girlfriend, they only made fun of him for being whipped. Anything beyond that ventured into blatantly mean territory, and Randall seemed to steer clear of that. Mostly, anyway. There were more jokes about Patrick sucking up to the admin, sucking off the admin, or just generally sucking. Predictably, Doug was skewered for dating a first-year.

Matt was glad to see a lot of his content had made it in, including a Plot Parallel to *Clue* where Provost Mustard killed the alcohol policy in Mackenzie Library with the wrench. The humor blended well with his drunkenness, but even in this inebriated state he dreaded what was coming. He knew exactly what was going to happen, but it would still hurt to watch. He'd dreamed for years what it would be like to see the looks on people's faces as an Imperator called his name, that moment in which they realized they'd made a grave miscalculation.

There'd be none of that tonight. Tonight, Logan Brewster would be crowned the new king of the Anathema, just as everyone had expected, just as he would've been regardless of who became 115, and no matter what he did Matt would always be a nobody to these people. Suddenly thinking about it again, he wanted to scream; he bit the inside of his lip instead.

Finally, Randall got to his big "Here Endeth" line and concluded the Sermon.

Now came the Scrapbook Break.

Matt hadn't drunk anything in forty-five minutes and went straight to get more beer. He arrived at the table before the first-years did, seeing that Brandon and a first-year girl had taken over this shift. They filled up a new cup for him and he turned around to see Joan talking with Val. His girlfriend looked sad and anxious and as he approached, their conversation became clearer.

"...sure you'll be fine whoever it is. I really don't think Kylie would pick Alyssa, so it's probably Catherine and honestly, she's pretty nice. I'm sure you'll make Tetrad regardless, just trust me." Val noticed him. "Oh hey, Matt. Enjoy the Sermons?"

"Yeah, though I missed most of Kylie's. Did you like them?"

"They were fun. Although ours really hit her a lot." She turned to Joan.

"For what?" he asked.

"Oh, just the usual," Joan sighed. "Can't hold my liquor. Really awkward. That sort of thing. Actually, one joke called me the Diva of Diffidence."

Val beamed. "That was mine." She moved toward the line at the beer table. "See you in a bit."

Joan gave him a weak smile. "Hey."

He put a hand on the small of her back. "You alright?"

"Yeah, I'm just...nervous." She looked back toward the podium.

"Whoever Ninety-Four is, they're an idiot if they don't make you their Legatus. You deserve at least that much."

"Thanks." She tilted her head. "What about you? You never told me if Randall talked to you or not."

Matt took a deep breath. "He didn't."

Joan grew sadder. She looked around, then leaned closer. "Wait, actually?"

He nodded. "It's gonna be Logan."

"Do you know that for sure?"

"Well, in the words of Ares Donovan: 'Randall has three choices for Imperator this year: Logan, Logan...and Logan.' " He said it in a mocking tone, finally realizing how bitter he sounded, though his voice was quiet.

"He said that? Who the fuck does he think he is? His name is *Ares* for fuck's sake."

"Actually, that's his middle name. His real name is—"

"So he *chooses* to be called Ares? That just makes him even more of a dick."

"He's not such a bad guy usually."

"Doesn't matter." She'd grown angry. "I don't know why everyone over-looks you. I've watched how you read. As for dedication, you still showed up when you had goddamn *laryngitis*. Plus Logan has no moral compass and is way too fucking obvious. How was there even a debate?"

"Take it up with Randall. He's the king." He gestured to the other room, where 115 was chatting with Kylie and Quentin Caleb.

"That thing looks really stupid," she said, gesturing to the crown. "I don't know what the fuck he was thinking."

He sighed, too deflated to share her rage. "I've been asking myself the same question for weeks."

"*Logan*," she hissed, staring at Randall. "After all this time, are you fucking kidding me?" She put her hand to her head and sharply exhaled, thinking for a moment. Then she looked back to him, her expression slight-ly softer. "I am so sorry, I really am. I know how much it meant to you." She hugged him.

"I know exactly how you feel now," he said, holding her close. "It's fucking awful and I'm really sorry you didn't get it either."

Then Veronica Yang shouted, "Come look at the Scrapbooks! We're about to start the Litanies. Which means I'm about to start mine. So get the fuck in here."

A crush of people pushed them back into the darkened chamber. They managed to grab the Scrapbooks and brought them to a sofa, where they secured a spot on one end. With both members and attendees crammed into the audience, space was at a premium. Matt and Joan found them-selves pressed together, which he really didn't mind.

While waiting for the Litanies to start, they flipped through the vol-umes. Every Scrapbook began with photos from the End-of-Year Social the year before, which was held jointly at the Chalet. Most attendees looking at it just assumed they were taken at a member's house. After that there were highlights from each event—frosh getting hazed, the History being read, a still or two from each Sermon—and then the Class Photos. Some were taken with multiple members in the frame, but most just had one person.

Joan flipped through Randall's book to find Matt's underwater photo while he looked through Kylie's for hers. In it, Val and Sophia had dressed up in police uniforms labeled Anti-Hazing Task Force and were leading her away in handcuffs. Their names were written in ink at the bottom of the picture, he guessed by Catherine. The Magister usually prepared the Scrapbook since it went into Anathema's Archives. All the ones since Dissociation were stored in the Chalet's basement, but everything before the 1997-98 school year was stored in the Radcliffe Archives.

Standing behind the podium, Veronica cleared her throat loudly. Everyone's attention shifted to her. Then she began.

> "Kylie, Kylie, what did you do?
> Why again, did I choose you?"

She tore into her successor for five minutes, claiming she stole her style of delivery and that her Sermons were mediocre at best. It was all tongue-in-cheek, of course. Even the best Imperators had gotten shredded, especially if their predecessor was insecure about how much better they'd been.

He looked around the crowd and realized Madler wasn't here; he must still be in the UK. Suddenly, he realized that must mean Turland would be performing Randall's Litany. He'd already performed Madler's last year and it was rare that an Imperator got to deliver two.

Sure enough, once Veronica finished, the DebSoc President took the podium, his own medallion slung around his neck.

The room was at attention. 113 was back.

Turland took a deep breath in and out, adjusted his posture, and began.

> "Hello, *Jack,* my dear *Jack,*
> I'm not here to attack
> You adorable, cuddly, pitiful *snack,*
> Oh *Jack,* buddy *Jack,*
> Nicely dressed up in *black,*
> For it'd be punching down if I were to smack
> You upside the skull, my closest friend, *Jack,*
> You miserable, mopey, illiterate sack,
> You sniveling, second-rate, plagiarist *HACK!*"

Turland slammed the podium with each insult, his voice growing louder line after line. Matt glanced over to Randall and saw a forced smile stuck on his face while everyone roared with laughter around him. Patrick leaned forward, giddy with delight.

"JACK! Look in a mirror, and what do we see?
A grey-skinned, pubic-stubbled, disheveled zombie
Who hasn't been laid this decade, I would guess,
Cause with all that you do, who would have time for sex?
Yet they call you a pussy? Spineless? Nay, I opine,
You're so fucking bone-headed, you must have a spine
That you use to blame others—and this is top-shelf—
For the wounds you alone inflict on yourself.
Oh Jack 'Shingles' Randall, we wish you were not
Such a self-righteous, dithering, unwashed cumquat.

"I now turn to your 'Sermons,' as they were so-called,
And just as with you, with them we're appalled
You blabbed about robots…and knights…WE DON'T CARE!
All we wanted were jokes, so we went elsewhere!
All you did was mock Patrick, but we know he's a prick!
Do something else, you brain-dead tick!
If you just had good punchlines, we would have been calmed,
But like your Air Force, they unethically bombed
Oh Jack 'Cockless' Randall, we wish you were not
Such a loser, a whiner, a pussy, a thot."

Here, Turland's voice became softer, soothing almost.

"Oh Jack, tender soul, do not look so downtrodden;
Your lackluster performance will soon be forgotten.
I still call you a friend, if that is becoming…"

He paused and silence fell across the room. Then he took a deep breath
and launched back in.

"Despite all your MYRIAD and CRIPPLING SHORTCOMINGS,
Because JACK **FUCKING** RANDALL, ON TOP OF ALL THAT,
We WISH you were NOT such an uppity, short-sighted,
Overworked, sick, blighted
Masochist, hypocrite,
Self-centered piece of shit!"

The room was in hysterics. Patrick almost fell out of his seat. Randall tugged at his collar and tried to laugh along.

"And THAT'S how it's done, you bootlicking swine!
Copy me better when you do it next time!
Because, after you, I cannot fathom lesser;
I hope you have chosen a better successor."

He immediately moved off from the podium, snatching his document as he went, and returned to the laughing crowd. Matt looked over at Randall and for a moment thought he saw his eye twitch. The Imperator sat farther down the row, Gemma doubled over beside him. He stood up and Turland hugged him as the room began to quiet down. Then Randall took his place at the podium. The male members started standing and making their way back to the front of the room.

Matt's shoulders tensed, his teeth clenching. Joan gave him a kiss on the cheek before he got up. He turned to her and smiled, then walked toward the line of members. Each step felt longer than the last one, time slowing down as he reached a spot beside Roy; the Tetrad stood just two spaces to his right.

Before him, the audience leaned forward in anticipation. This was the moment they'd been waiting for, the Second Sermon's biggest draw. *Come see the new Imperators. Witness their Baptisms and the dawn of Anathema's next chapter.*

And here came the holy water itself.

Favell and Duric walked down the aisle, an enormous bucket of beer carried between them. Farther back, Veronica and Collins brought in the second. They'd spent the Scrapbook Break filling them up from the kegs.

It was as if a knife was slowly being inserted between his ribs, the pain growing with each second. He'd seen this moment before, many times in his head. He'd dreamed of it, done everything he could to work toward it for three years, and now Radcliffe had given him a front row seat to watch it go to someone else.

Enjoy the show, the shadow said.

Randall turned to the last page of the Sermon. "The time has come. Since Gordon MacTaggart handed the reins to Andrew Sinclair, the Line of Succession has been a core tenet of the Anathema. Its sanctity has been broken only twice in our branch, and it is each Imperator's duty to carefully consider who will next receive a medallion. It is perhaps his or her most important task.

"115 men have delivered the Great Lord's chastisement upon Radcliffe College. Tonight, a 116th will join their names, his to be forever written in the Book of Succession. The Office of Imperator holds a special place in our hierarchy. Not even His Tetrads are considered more than members in the eyes of the Great Lord. An Imperator is the beginning and the ending, the defining force that guides Anathema through the year and determines what will succeed us in the future.

"Ladies and gentlemen, distinguished alumni… I call upon the 116th member of His most wretched Succession, the new Sayer of Sedition, the Inquisitor of Impudence… I call upon…"

Not him, Matt thought. *Let it somehow be Tanner or Hamid, or even Tony though he's becoming an Officer. Just please not—*

"LOGAN CALVIN BREWSTER!"

Pain seared inside his cheek and Matt tasted blood, realizing he'd bitten deep. He didn't unclench, just held it there as he watched Doug move aside and Logan kneel before the podium. Matt's eyes swept the crowd; it was as if they'd just watched a predictable plot twist in a movie. There was only one shout in support. Everyone else appeared apathetic.

So much for mystery.

Joan sat fuming in the front row, her arms folded across her chest. Even with her mask, he could tell her eyes burned with fury. Patrick put a hand to his forehead. Turland scratched his chin.

The one reaction he didn't expect was Logan's. As he gazed up to Randall behind the podium, he looked almost humbled as the Oath of the Imperator began.

"I answer the Great Lord's call…," Randall started.

"I answer the Great Lord's call." Favell splashed at the back of Logan's head, beer wetting his hair as Randall led him through the words. They blurred together in Matt's ears but the shadow gripped his head tightly, keeping it transfixed on the Baptism.

It would never have been you.

Matt said nothing. For a moment, it was as if he wasn't here anymore. He was very far away and this was all a dream or a memory, or something happening to someone else. He remembered how happy he felt in first-year, how the days had somehow seemed brighter back then, the winters warmer. Surely that wasn't accurate. It must be all in his head.

Just as Logan reached the last line of the Oath, Favell and Duric lifted the entire bucket and dumped its remaining contents over him. Beer sluiced across the floor and members stepped back to avoid getting splashed. Matt didn't bother, letting the lager lick his shoes. It wasn't until 116 stood, slightly trembling, and shook the hands of his predecessors that he finally snapped back.

This *was* reality. This *was* happening.

It was not a bad dream. It was a Friday evening in March. He was standing in Psi Beta Omicron, watching his dread come to fruition.

Randall produced a new medallion from his tuxedo jacket beneath the cloak and handed it to Doug, who bestowed it onto Logan. The new Imperator stood and walked around, shaking hands with the alumni. The male members drifted back to their seats and the female ones took their places. He realized he was still standing near the podium and people shot him looks, wondering why he hadn't moved yet. Quickly, he headed back to his seat in the front row, passing Joan as he did so.

She looked sick to her stomach. "Good luck," he said. She gave a very brief smile, then took a spot between Kristen and Val.

Matt flopped onto the sofa and Tanner joined him. "I'm sorry, man. I know how much it meant to you," he whispered.

He turned to him. "Thanks."

Logan stood with the other alumni, still soaked with beer and folding his arms across his chest. It looked like he was trying to avoid catching a chill, and Bella Collins seemed to crack a joke about it before joining Veronica at the second bucket.

The female Tetrad had taken up residence around the podium: Kylie behind, Catherine holding their skull in the front chair, with Sandrine and Lexi on each side.

"And here we are," Kylie boomed. "The last thing before you finally get rid of me." Chuckles went around. "I will now read this pre-prepared document, which has only been slightly modified from the previous century of Unveilings." She cleared her throat. "Succession is perhaps the most important part of an Imperator's duty, and—

"'ENOUGH!'"

Kylie mocked surprise at her own interjection. "I looked up, and suddenly saw the Great Lady standing there in her cloak. 'Enough of this bullshit!' she cried. 'Every year I hear the same thing about *duty* and *importance* and *blah, blah, blah.*' She lurched closer, her hooded head very close to mine. I saw her ghostly face, her cold eyes boring into me. 'If it's so damn important, why do we give the same spiel every year? This is the Unveiling of the New Imperator, the last step before her Baptism in the Bacchanal. And an Imperator deserves an *entrance*. So let's give her one.' "

The alumni and audience members looked at each other. A Sermon had never ended like this, at least not to their recollection.

"She pulled me down a darkened corridor, and we burst through a door into the night. A full moon hung above the West Quad, casting light upon the gravestones lining the grass. I saw my predecessors, the Imperators of old, as we walked down the rows. Then we reached the final stone, one inscribed with my own name beneath the number Ninety-Three. An open grave lay before it.

" 'Your time has come,' said the Lady. 'Name your successor so I may release you to the Imperatorial Everafter.'

" 'I swallowed. 'Great Lady, I have something to confess. I'm not…sure who Ninety-Four is.'

" 'It doesn't matter. *I* do. And she's going to be quite something. Look at her, already watching you with pity.'

"I turned and followed her pointing, bony finger. There, standing beside Anathema Tower on Radcliffe's roof, a figure stared down at us. Her cloak blew in the wind and I saw a silver medallion glisten in the moonlight. What I could not see, however, was her face.

" 'Say her name and you are freed.'

" 'But I don't know—'

" '*Think.* Think of the Sermons, think of the future. Think of my legacy, of *yours.* Who must it be? There is only one.'

"And in that instant, I knew. The figure tore back her hood, and there I saw her—*the 94th Imperator of the Great Lady Anathema…* "

Kylie paused and leaned forward with a conspiratorial smile. Matt felt himself tilting too, his heart racing. Up and down the row of members, everyone appeared to be in equivalent suspense. Even Logan and the alumni were frozen in anticipation.

Then the Imperator threw her head back and roared:

"JOAN ALICIA KEATING!"

SIXTY-ONE

IT HAPPENED just as she'd imagined it. First, her gaze swept the audience, watching jaws drop and eyes blink in shock. Some were thrilled, some were confused, and a few even looked a little scared.

Then, as she stepped forward toward the front of the podium, she glanced down the row of members. Alyssa's horrified expression was so priceless she almost burst out laughing. Beside her, the blood had drained from Katy Coulson's face. Nobody seemed to have expected it, but a few appeared happy. Val shook her head, laughing in disbelief, but wore a massive grin on her face.

What she hadn't expected was how *good* it felt, and she knew it wasn't all the alcohol she'd swallowed to calm her nerves. It was the sudden whiplash of vindication, the feeling of everything she'd worked for since first-year streaking past doubt, anxiety, and naysayers to converge on an inconceivable bliss.

She knelt before the podium. Catherine moved out of the way, giving Kylie a direct line of sight to her successor. Beer soaked Joan's tights, but she didn't care. She'd never felt so alive, her entire body tingling with excitement, her heart pounding. She committed every second of it to memory as best she could, savoring what true satisfaction felt like.

The crowd and row of members were alive with chatter. "Quiet!" Kylie shouted, raising a hand. Randall hadn't had to do that with Logan, she noted. Everyone had already known what was coming.

Now she was glad she hadn't been an obvious pick. It felt better this way, a true achievement, not just something passed from one popular figure to another. For years they would remember, *Keating was a major dark horse pick. You can never really tell who it's going to be, so don't act like you already know.*

The voices died down to murmurs, then to silence.

"I answer the Great Lady's call…," Kylie began.

Joan repeated after her, surprised by the confidence of her own voice. It was as if the Unveiling had cracked open her shell and let something new, something deep-seeded, into the world. Her body trembled but her voice never wavered, even as Collins splashed beer from the bucket onto her every few words.

"…to take the Office of Imperator…," Kylie continued.

"To take the Office of Imperator."

"…to bear the responsibility of the Anathema and its members…"

"To bear the responsibility of the Anathema and its members."

"…to deliver two Sermons in Her name…"

"To deliver two Sermons in Her name."

"…to Beckon first-years to the mysteries of the Grand Tradition…"

"To Beckon first-years to the mysteries of the Grand Tradition."

"…to Initiate new members into our ranks…"

"To Initiate new members into our ranks."

"…and, finally, to appoint a successor upon the completion of my tasks."

"And finally, to appoint a successor upon the completion of my tasks."

Kylie stood up even straighter. "By the power vested in me as a member of the Line of Succession, I hereby declare you, Joan Alicia Keating, the 94th Imperator of the Great Lady Anathema on this day, the twenty-ninth of March, two-thousand and nineteen."

Now came the Baptismal finale. Joan had braced herself for it, but the force of the bucket-dumping brought her to her hands and knees. Beer drenched her entire body, making a complete mess of her hair and soaking her to the core.

She didn't care. Joan straightened her posture, still kneeling, and looked to Kylie. Her eyes started to water as she said, *"Thank you."*

And she meant it.

Beside her predecessor, Catherine beamed proudly with the rest of the Tetrad, the skull cradled in her hands. Truly, she had her to thank just as much as Kylie. Joan gave the Magister an appreciative nod and Catherine returned it.

Sandrine came around with the new medallion—*her* medallion. She smiled and said, "Congratulations," as she put it around her neck.

Joan looked down and held it in her hands, candlelight reflecting off the silver skull. She allowed herself a moment to appreciate it, then stood and turned to shake the hands of Veronica, Collins, and several other alumni.

Now the feeling she'd managed to push away during the Baptism had returned, the knot in her stomach tying itself once again. There was only a short time before she and Logan were carried back to Radcliffe for the final part of the ceremony. Already people were standing and getting ready for it.

"Where are the first-years?" Kylie barked. "Let's get this show on the road!"

Joan saw a recent Initiate of her branch making her way toward her, having been informed of the protocol, but Joan held up her hand and pushed through the audience. Matt stood by Tanner, a storm of emotions brewing on his face. She saw happiness, relief, and pride mix with shock, hurt, and a hint of betrayal.

Joan hurried over to him. "Congrats," Tanner nodded, moving aside.

"Thanks," she said briefly, then turned to Matt. He opened his mouth to say something but she gave him a bear hug, even though she was still soaked. Of course, the way she'd planned it they were both supposed to be drenched.

"I'm so glad it's you," he breathed. "Really, it's the one thing that's saved this day for me. This month, really."

"I'm so sorry I couldn't tell you," she said quickly. There wasn't much time. "I thought you were going to get it too. I didn't think Randall would *actually* pick Logan. I thought you were just hiding it from me these past few days. I'm sorry I lied; I just wanted to surprise you. I should've told you."

A shout came behind her and they both turned to see Logan being hoisted into the air by the first-year Initiates. "Away to Radcliffe!" he shouted drunkenly, pointing toward the exit. The crowd parted to make way for them.

The female Initiates made their way toward Joan. She turned back to him and cupped his face in her hands, looking straight into his eyes. "I'll see you at the Foxhole. Don't worry, you'll still make Tetrad. I'm sure of it."

She was about to kiss him when the next thing she knew, her feet were off the ground and five first-year girls were carrying her down the center aisle, applause sounding all around. She saw Randall standing with the alumni, looking relaxed and very pleased with himself, as if a great weight had been lifted from his shoulders. He actually looked less tired.

Randall nodded and offered a smile, one Imperator to another. She didn't return it, instead shooting him a look with a very clear message:

How could you?

He seemed confused, but then she was out into the foyer, through the front door, and out into the brisk night air.

Psi Beta cleared out quickly, as it did every year after the Sermon. Once the last few alumni and students had grabbed their coats and made their way out the door, Matt and Roy were the only two left in the building.

Matt walked back into the room where the main event had occurred, the lights now turned on and the beer-soaked destruction plain to see. His hand was shaking and he abruptly grabbed it to hold it still. "Roy, are you sure everybody's left?"

A moment later he heard, "Yeah. Why?"

He lunged for a wooden chair and threw it across the room. One of its legs snapped as it tumbled but he barely noticed, too occupied kicking over several plastic seats, screaming obscenities. Then he stopped and stood in the center aisle, looking around and panting. Several tears trailed down his face, and he aggressively wiped them away.

A mostly-full beer cup sat on the floor. He picked it up, turning it over in his hand; then he glanced around the room. After a moment, he poured it out on the floor, watching it splash his shoes.

"Was that really necessary?" Roy said behind him. There was no judgment in his voice; it was merely a calm question.

Matt looked around one last time, realizing that though Logan would clean the frat with the first-years tomorrow morning, as all Imperators did after their Baptisms, so would Joan.

You can't do anything right.

He threw the cup away and headed for the foyer.

"It was trashed anyway. It doesn't make a difference," he said, brushing past Roy. "Nothing I do at this college does."

SIXTY-TWO

H E WANTED to be anywhere but the Foxhole, and yet here he was. There was already a sizeable crowd inside. Many attendees had skipped the final ceremony and gone straight to the bar, not that they were missing much.

Each year, the Imperators had to knock on the front door of Radcliffe until they had counted the knocks of their number. If the organization survived another century, Matt figured it would get quite tedious. He wondered if 216 and 194 would resort to knocking with two fists, treating the door like a drum set.

The thought almost brought a smile to his face. Almost.

Once he and Roy walked through the door, he took off his mask and went right to the bar. "I'll have a triple rye and ginger, tall."

"We don't serve triples."

Matt stared at him.

The bartender sighed. "You look like you need one, so I'll make an exception."

Matt slid into a stool and exhaled. Roy sat beside him and ordered a gin and tonic, then turned to him. "So...I'm guessing she didn't tell you?"

"Wanted it to be a surprise." Though part of him wondered if it was more than that. He knew Imperators were sworn to secrecy, told to share their new status with absolutely no one before the Unveiling. Still, most informed their close friends and significant others, and yet for the past couple weeks Joan had been telling him and Val how worried she was that Alyssa

426

wouldn't pick her for Tetrad. Now it was going to be the other way around.

He wondered if Joan had deceived both her best friend and her boyfriend just because she took Anathema's code so seriously.

Don't be ridiculous, he told himself. She had just said she thought it would be him, thought it would be a nice twist for him if he feared who his counterpart would be, only to be relieved at the moment of truth. He now understood why she was so angry at Randall when he told her. She'd had it all planned out and 115 had thrown a spanner in the works. Joan was a writer, and writers hated when people messed with their endings.

But she genuinely thought he'd have been better than Logan and assumed it would naturally be Matt until the very end. Randall's choice had completely baffled her. The realization warmed the ice gripping him, thawing it just enough for him to enjoy his drink.

At least one Imperator believed in him.

Joan's Sermons would also be something to look forward to. They were going to be incredible. She'd give even Bella Collins a run for her money.

He'd just been starting to sober up, but the cocktail pulled him back to the paradise of intoxication. He exhaled and set the glass down, handing the bartender his credit card to start a tab. He already knew it was going to be an expensive one.

Roy patted his shoulder. "Just hang in there. This fuckin' year's almost over anyway."

"Maybe he won't be so bad," Matt said, trying to convince himself. "People thought Madler would be worse than he was. Way worse."

"Yeah, but once you spent enough time with Madler, you realized he was a nice guy. I've been around Logan long enough to know he's a dick and nothing more."

Matt stared at him and recalled what Pandora had said back at Psi Beta. Was Roy aware he'd leaked information to the enemy? At this point, did he care? What she said about the Bard honestly bothered him more. *My guess is that he's waiting to find out who the new Imperators are. Then we'll have something to go on.*

Well, there they were for you: Joan Keating and Logan Brewster. Quite the pair they were going to make.

His girlfriend walked through the door right then, dressed in what had been Kylie's cloak and black attire underneath—jeans and a T-shirt with a skull across her chest, the new medallion worn around her neck. Her sneakers were black too, and as she stepped closer, he realized she'd put on earrings that matched her shirt. The only thing missing was the silver Venetian mask, but it wouldn't do to wear that in a bar.

Judging by the dampness of her hair, it appeared she'd just showered. *She had it all planned and ready to go,* he thought. As soon as she finished knocking on the front door, she must've bolted back to her room, stripped out of her beer-drenched outfit, washed off, and put on these clothes. He bet she'd had them lying ready on the bed the whole evening. It's what he would've done.

Evidently Logan hadn't been as prepared. He was still nowhere to be seen.

Matt watched as she shook hands with some more alumni from both branches. There was something different about the way she carried herself, the way she talked and gestured and laughed to them. In his drunken haze, it took a moment to recognize the easy confidence granted by surmounting the insurmountable.

He turned back to his drink. There was only a little bit left. Roy stood up and patted him on the back. "Gonna take a leak, I'll be right back."

He nodded, feeling very detached again. He was here but wasn't here. It felt like reality one instant and a dream the next. He pinched himself—definitely not dreaming.

Matt drained the rest of his cocktail and held it up to the bartender. "Another please. Just a double this time." *Just a double.* It reminded him of high school, when the concept of getting drunk had been, well, anathema to him.

The bartender nodded and reached for his glass.

"Put that on my tab. And his first one." Joan handed her card across, then kissed Matt on the cheek and tenderly placed a hand on his arm. "Hey, how are you holding up?"

He looked up at her and shrugged. "Not great." He smiled weakly. "I like the skull shirt, by the way."

"Thanks, I ordered it a couple weeks ago." She looked guilty, like there was something she wanted to explain but didn't know how.

Matt sighed. "So Kylie told *you* the weekend before we went to the art show?"

Joan grimaced. "Yes. She did."

"How'd it happen?" The bartender handed him his double and he began sipping it.

She sat down where Roy had been. Logan still hadn't arrived, and Matt was trying to enjoy that while it lasted. More people trickled into the bar, the crowd growing larger. She had to talk a bit louder to be heard now.

"Kylie texted me. It was a Sunday afternoon and she asked if I was around. I said I was free and she asked me to come over to her room in Crow's Nest." Joan smiled at the memory. "I had a feeling right then, but I couldn't believe it. I really thought it was gonna be Alyssa or Catherine. But when I got to her place, she told me to sit down in her desk chair and started asking me how I was, making small talk and all that." She swallowed. "And then she said she'd come to a very important decision about who the 94th Imperator would be. And I froze and nodded, trying not to look too excited. And she explained that—"

"*WHOOO!*"

Every head in the room turned as Logan swung through the entrance. He looked wild and insanely happy. Randall had passed his cloak on to him and he wore it over a white T-shirt and ripped jeans. Logan sniffed and wiped under his nose, then placed an order for a beer farther down the bar.

Joan looked pained to see him and turned back to Matt. "I'm going to kill Jack Randall."

"But I like Jack Randall," he said softly, looking at his drink. For the first time, he realized how hard it was to say those words. *Goddamn it.* He took a big sip.

"Logan likes to control people," she whispered, leaning closer. "If nothing else, I bet he'll put you on Tetrad just to keep me happy. You might get stuck with Magister, which I've always thought is the most thankless of all the positions, but at least it's something."

"I've always thought Magister was underrated, actually. The Archives—both the college's and ours—are pretty cool."

She kissed him on the cheek again. "I thought of a joke, by the way: His mother. His father. Jack Randall. Name three people who can claim Logan Brewster as their worst mistake."

A laugh tore its way out of him. He shook his head and turned to her. "You really do have a mean streak."

She rolled her eyes and smiled. "Just hang in there and try not to look too sad. People might notice."

He shrugged.

"The End-of-Year Social is next Friday, so Logan will talk to you soon enough. I've gotta go schmooze with the alumni, but I'll swing back in a little bit, okay? Order as much as you want, but please don't die." She smiled. "I really need you around."

She turned his head then kissed him, smiled, and walked off. Her fingers trailed down his back, just as they had done at Lambda Halloween when she'd gone off to dance with Val. Fuck, it had been a long year.

The last few attendees had flowed in with Logan and the Foxhole was now packed. Matt sat alone on his stool, sipping his drink. Before long he had finished and stood, the inebriation hitting him like a gut punch. Everything felt a little fuzzy, which was good. It was enjoyable. It made him smile.

Why if anyone glanced at him now, they might not think he was such a wreck at all.

He saw Veronica stroll up to Kylie and Sandrine. "Congrats on picking Joan, by the way," he heard her say. "Very bold choice, I like it. You gotta shake the Anathema up once in a while, otherwise things get stale."

Kylie laughed. "It was a tough decision, but I'm glad I made it."

"I never had any doubts last year. Choosing you was probably the easiest thing I did."

They both laughed and Sandrine went pale, her mouth opening slightly, before she turned and slipped away. Neither Imperator seemed to notice as they continued their conversation.

Still holding his empty glass, Matt pushed through the crowd, looking for someone to talk to. Ares Donovan emerged and came closer.

Matt tensed. He shrugged at him and took a sip from the glass, even though it was only ice. "Guess you were right."

Ares raised an eyebrow. "You're the only one who thought it might not be Logan. Literally the only one." And he walked off.

Matt stood there, the crowd milling around him. If they paid him any attention, they didn't show it. He stared somewhere beyond all of them, then swiftly moved to the bar. He slammed the glass on the counter, made his way past the billiard table, and stormed down the stairs into the basement.

It was mercifully quieter here. He suddenly recalled how Joan had thrown up on him in this very spot. It was an odd way to start a relationship, but then again, they were odd people. *Weird* people, as everyone said.

As he got halfway down the steps, he noticed Roy making out with a girl in the back corner. It was darker over there and from his position he couldn't tell if it was Jennifer or not. Matt hesitated, then turned and hurried back up to the main floor. There had to be somebody else he could talk to, someone less...*occupied*. It didn't even have to be a meaningful conversation, just something to take his mind off of everything else.

Heading back into the bar, he looked left and right. The crowd seemed to be getting louder and rowdier. Patrick and Turland were talking animatedly at a table, both very drunk. Matt slowly edged closer, and as he did so, he realized Turland looked more exasperated than he'd ever seen him.

"I'm tired of hearing this, Patrick," he said, putting a hand to his forehead. "The whole year it's just been you talking about what you either did better or would have done better had you held a different position. Nobody fucking cares." He angrily finished the rest of his drink.

Patrick leaned back and spread his hands. "Look, Jack's been making bad decisions like they're going out of style. It's as if he wakes up every day and thinks, 'Hmm, what questionable choice can I inflict on the world today?' Picking Logan was just icing on the cake." He folded his arms. "I'm just saying *I* would have made better decisions. Much better decisions. I would've..."

Matt turned away, not wanting to hear any more of it. He headed toward where people were dancing in front of the stage. A cover band played badly and students—Anathema members and attendees alike—were getting sloppy with their partners, running their hands all over each other in full view of everyone else. Doug felt up his first-year girlfriend as they grinded front-to-front, then slid a hand up under her skirt. She tossed her head back, howling in delight.

Uncomfortable, Matt turned around and nearly collided with a sweaty Carl Dunlap, hurrying to the dance floor with vodka crans in each hand. He spilled nearly half of each before he made it.

"YO GUYS, WHAT'S UP?!" he heard Dunlap shout behind him, but Matt barely registered it. He'd already turned around, scanning the mob of Radcliffe students and alumni.

He saw Randall, leaning against the bar looking satisfied and relaxed. He saw Logan, leading a posse toward the bathroom, stuffing a Ziploc bag with a white substance into one of his pockets as he went. He saw students pushing their way to the bar, waving colorful cash at the staff.

On stools and at tables, people sat laughing and nearly falling over, discretely pointing at others and whispering in companions' ears.

And there, over by the front door, was Joan.

At first, he was relieved to spot her. Then he saw Alyssa and several other members of the female branch crowding her, laughing and making jokes with her, trying to act like they'd been friends all along. She nodded and laughed with them, but even from here he could see the contempt in her smiles. She had them and she knew it. More than that, she was enjoying it. He didn't want to interrupt that feeling. Talking to her now would just ruin the moment. It was her night, not his.

He'd been standing in the same spot for nearly a minute and he saw some girls throwing him suspicious glances. Two first-year guys looked at him quizzically as they brushed past, one turning to the other to make a joke as they headed for the dance floor.

All the stools were taken now, save for one at the very end. Matt walked to it and sat down, staring at the mirror that ran behind the bar. He saw himself, tired and deflated, sitting amidst a sea of sin.

He'd never felt more alone in his life.

◆

Matt managed to finish one more double before the crowd migrated to Ni Hao Ma. He'd hoped it would make him feel even lighter, but instead reality caught up with him. He felt sick to his stomach as he walked through the door, the dragons on the walls seeming to waver with the lights.

Joan was seated at one of the circular tables near the front, but all the chairs around her were already occupied. Kylie sat to her left, Emma Gagnon to her right. It was strange seeing such a notorious figure look so hollow. As he watched, Sandrine handed her skull lighter across the table to Joan.

"Here, it's yours now," he heard her say.

"Thank you so much," Joan replied, looking it over as she grinned. She didn't notice him as he passed her table, so he continued to the rear.

There was an opening beside Roy and Tanner, but only after he sat down did he realize Logan was seated two chairs to his right, chatting with Jaya Noor. A waiter came around to take orders, but Matt only asked for a glass of water. It soon came and he drank it, but still felt ill.

Excusing himself, he went down to the row of basement bathrooms, locked himself in one, turned to the toilet, and shoved his fingers down his throat. He threw up five times, just to make sure he'd gotten as much of it out as he could. Then he flushed, wiped his mouth, and washed his hands.

He stared at his reflection and knew it was time to leave. He'd only make a bigger fool of himself the longer he stayed here, and that would do nothing but embarrass Joan and dampen his Tetrad chances.

He felt lightheaded as he stumbled out of the bathroom and back up the stairs to the restaurant. When he got back to the table and sat down, Roy covertly showed him the Uber app on his phone beneath the table.

Their eyes met and he gave him a slight nod.

Matt and Roy stood to go, said goodnight to everyone, and congratulated Logan. Matt gave Joan a wave as they passed; he saw her excusing herself out the corner of his eye as they reached the door.

Once they were outside, he made sure to walk to the next store over so they were out of sight. And there was Mountain Ridge Coffee just a few venues down. He smiled at the memory of their first date, realizing it was one of the few times he'd smiled all day.

The door to Ni Hao Ma swung open and Joan hurried outside, looking left and right. She saw them and strode over.

"Heading out already?" she asked, concerned.

Matt nodded. "Congrats again. You really, truly deserve it and I know you're going to do a great job."

She hugged him just as the Uber pulled up to the curb. "I'm so sorry," she said. "You have no idea how badly I wanted it to be both of us."

Roy climbed in and Matt moved after him. "Drink lots of water!" Joan called.

"Will do." He blew her a kiss, then closed the door.

The driver took the highway over one stop to get back to campus. Matt leaned his head against the window, watching lampposts whip by. Roy leaned over and nudged his shoulder.

"Hey... If you want to talk about it more tomorrow, just let me know, okay?"

Matt nodded without looking at him.

Roy thought for a moment. "A friend of mine once gave me some really good advice. He said, whenever people have got you down, just tell yourself *fuck the haters*, and don't let them get to you."

Matt paused, then shrugged. "Easier said than done."

He put a hand on his shoulder. "I know, but things will get better. Trust me on that."

Matt continued staring out the window.

At this point, I don't know who to trust...

SIXTY-THREE

MATT AWOKE with a hangover and found he had no Advil left in his room. He trudged to the washroom to refill his water, drank it, then tried to get back to sleep. He tossed and turned for an hour before finally drifting off.

When he regained consciousness, he felt only slightly better, but his clock read 11:48 a.m. so he figured it was time to get up.

He threw on some clothes, brushed his teeth, and schlepped to Galbraith. He took the outdoor route since the air wasn't unbearably cold today, and arrived to find no one he knew among the tables. Maybe he wasn't the only person hungover from last night.

After getting some scrambled eggs and deliberately avoiding the pizza, he sat down at the third-year table and found himself staring at the wood, lost in thought.

It reminded him of Mark Wood and Benson's article, which may or may not have gotten him killed. Now that he'd lost Imperator, finishing his classes and solving a murder mystery were the only two things left to do this year. Just business as usual.

He drank his water, wishing he had Advil and thinking about what Pandora told him the night before. If the Bard had waited all semester to find out who the new Imperators were, he'd have had a lot of time to get something ready. Whoever this fucker was, Matt doubted he'd go out without one last crack at Anathema—especially after his plan to get Joan arrested had failed.

Though something else Pandora said disturbed him. *There's a real psycho in your ranks. Probably thought they'd come for him next.*

What if the Bard *hadn't* killed Benson or Chet after all? What if the murderer was really just some crazed Anathema member, and they'd slain Chet to scare the Bard off?

He still didn't understand why Benson had been in the woods that night in the first place. It couldn't have been just coincidence that he'd gone for a walk after midnight. Joan had thought he was following her, but why would he do that? And what had happened after she ran away, leaving him laughing by the bridge?

Had someone else watched their conversation, figuring they could pin the killing on her afterward? There was only one other person he knew for sure had been out there that night.

Randall.

The thought was absurd and Matt had never considered that he'd be the Bard, but if the killer and the Bard were two separate people, maybe he'd been viewing this whole thing from the wrong angle the entire time.

Joan had told Randall about the Serpentine meeting—and how Chet said the Bard knew the identity of Benson's killer.

Then a week later, Chet was dead.

Randall had looked so pleased with himself at the Sermon, and Matt had just assumed it was because he'd gone a full year without an impeachment inquiry.

What if it was because he'd gotten away with murder?

Don't overthink things, the Imperator had said. Wasn't that the exact kind of thing a killer would say?

Matt shook his head. His mind was taking things too far. He was upset about Randall giving the medallion to Logan and now he was looking for any way to vilify him, a surprisingly hard thing to do; he'd always found him a likeable guy.

But Randall *had* mentioned hearing footsteps on the path that night. By his account, it was why he'd hidden in the woods and ended up standing by the creek's edge. If he wasn't lying, there could've been a fourth person there that night. Maybe they weren't the Bard, but another Anathema member who had killed Benson for reasons unrelated to his article.

If so, he had no fucking clue why.

Or who.

The chair across from him moved and he looked up to see Patrick Mason taking a seat, a soft look in his eyes. "Hey, how are you holding up?"

Matt sighed. "Honestly…I'm getting tired of this fucking college. It feels like no matter what I do, I'm always just a joke to these people."

Patrick shook his head. "I don't think you're a joke, Matt. And I don't think you're a joke to Randall, either. Logan's had him wrapped around his finger all year. You'll probably still get Tetrad, though, and that counts for something."

"Maybe. But it's not just Anathema. It's this whole place. It's…exhausting." He glanced around. "I'm just glad Joan became an Imperator. She really earned it."

"Did she tell you beforehand?"

He hesitated. "No."

"Oh. Wanted to keep it a surprise then?"

"Yeah."

"There was a lot of…chatter about her last night at the Foxhole, and Ni Hao."

"Well, everyone was surprised. They were all convinced it would be Alyssa or Catherine."

"Yeah, but a bunch of people are worried. They think she's…"

"Let me guess," Matt said. "Too into it?"

"Not even that. You'd hope an Imperator would be really into it. It's a lot of work for something you can't put on a resume. No, they're concerned that given how much she likes hazing, things will get really intense next year. Especially since Logan has no filter when it comes to joke content."

"I've never really been into the hazing stuff, but I've heard what Joan does. It's weird, but she never hurts anybody. She just fucks with their heads, like they fucked with hers in first-year. Even before this place, people have always been fucking with her."

Patrick sighed. "I like Joan, but that doesn't make it right to pay it forward."

Matt shrugged. "Of course not. But it happens all the time: One person hurts somebody, who hurts somebody else. Nobody ever thinks about the chain reaction they start." He gave an angry sigh. "Logan's an asshole to people all the time, but everyone's saying *Joan* is the evil one…?"

Patrick looked down at the table. "Speaking of which, Randall won't be around next year to watch him drag Anathema back to the nineties. I feel bad for whoever his Tetrad will be, having to rein him in. If you're on it, that'll fall to you."

"Logan wouldn't listen to me. Besides, none of us could stop him. He's a force of nature," Matt said.

"No he's not. He's an overhyped douchebag. He's popular at Cliffe, but who knows where he'll be five years from now. By then, maybe people will have matured enough to see through him."

"I'm just hoping he's not too bad. Maybe he'll lighten up over the summer and won't go so hard." Matt didn't want to talk about it anymore. He felt very tired and suddenly disinterested in being here, but he didn't know where he'd rather be instead.

"I'm sorry Randall made the choice he did," Patrick said, empathy in his eyes. "Not just for Anathema, but for you. You really worked hard for it."

"Thank you," he said softly, staring at his plate. He hadn't touched it.

Silence hung between them for a moment. Then Matt said, "How's your Officer stuff? That wraps up at QuadFest, right?"

"Yeah, but we still have a lot to do. It's been tense this year, not just with the strange deaths, but with Randall being an Imperator. It's created a lot of drama on the Officer team. Veronica and I have had to defend him a lot." He sighed. "So it's nice to be rewarded by having your head cut off."

Matt nodded. "I thought it was weird that he killed you in both Preludes."

"It's funny how he says I've sold out to the admin. He got a recommendation letter from Mustard too, but once I got mine, I suddenly became Radcliffe's Judas." Patrick shook his head.

Just then, Joan and Logan strode into Galbraith, first-year Initiates at their heels. They made their way to where Matt and Patrick sat. Logan took the seat to the left of Patrick, Joan across from him to Matt's right. The first-years took seats around them, Freddie to Matt's left.

Joan raised an eyebrow and looked around at all of them, disappointed. "Umm, did any of you *ask* to sit at the third-year table?"

They all stood up. "May we sit here?" Freddie said, amused.

Joan gestured to all of them and smiled. "Go ahead." They did so. "That's more like it." Logan watched her and nodded, impressed.

"How did cleaning go?" Matt asked her.

She sighed. "Psi Beta's spotless now, but it was a real mess. People totally trashed it last night."

Matt felt a pang of guilt.

"Look at this," Freddie said, gesturing between Logan, Matt, and Joan. "We got at least three members of the new Tetrads right here."

Matt tensed, but Logan merely shrugged. "I don't know. I haven't decided yet." He looked to Joan.

She laughed. "*I* decided weeks ago. I'll talk to them soon."

The conversation shifted to other topics, ideas the new Imperators had for next year, and through it all Matt felt something was different. He couldn't exactly place what it was, but the way Joan included him in the conversation, if at all, felt detached, as if he was just another acquaintance. There was usually something warmer in her expression, smile, or words that she reserved for him. He detected no trace of it here.

Don't be ridiculous. You always read too much into little things. It's your BPD. Remember what she said last night, how she came to see you off in the Uber. She looked sad to see you leave so early.

Though he was surrounded by other people, it felt like he was receding away to some place inside himself. Their conversation grew distant.

Soon others—Tony, Katy, Alyssa, Sandrine, Randall, and Kylie—entered Galbraith. Joan and Logan got up to go talk to them in the center of the hall while the first-years grabbed brunch. Patrick went to get food while Matt sat alone, picking at his.

He looked over at the chatting group, just off the end of the table. They stood and talked in a big circle and Joan was angled away from him. He continued eating, occasionally throwing a glance their way.

One time, Joan looked back. She smiled, then turned again to face the others.

SIXTY-FOUR

S HE DIDN'T text him at all that weekend and he only saw her again on Sunday evening, when she was entering Galbraith just as he was leaving after dinner. He'd sat with Roy and Jennifer instead. Joan had waved and said "Hey" very casually as she passed him by, and he had done the same.

It made Matt worried, but he told himself to stop acting clingy. He knew she was busy this week with schoolwork already. Now she had to run around and get her Tetrad in order while helping Logan plan the End-of-Year Social.

It was a lot to manage and he didn't want to be demanding. He didn't want her to think of him as that *other* commitment, another drain on her time and emotions. He didn't want her to look at him, sigh, and think, *I like you, but all you do is take up space in my life.*

She'd never said *I love you.*

Nearly five whole months they'd been dating now, and neither of them had broached those three words. He'd felt it for a long while, long enough to know that he hadn't just fallen for the idea of her. He'd had a crush on her for over two years before they finally went on a date, but now that he had gotten to really know her, to see the hidden sides of her, he felt more strongly about her than he ever had before.

And he was terrified she didn't feel the same way. What if he said those words and she awkwardly froze, or said she loved him too but it sounded forced? He would've overstepped and there'd be no going back.

She doesn't need you anymore, the shadow hissed. *She always could've done better, but now she's starting to realize it. And the more you try to hold onto her, the faster you'll push her away.*

He should've told her about having borderline when he had the chance. Now mentioning it would seem desperate. Or it might even give her an excuse to distance herself. There was so much stigma about it, even if you were still a functional person. People saw you as damaged goods if you had any sort of mental illness, and everyone knew dating the damaged only damages you.

He wondered about texting her the next day, then thought it would seem attention-craving. She was busy and needed space. Surely, she'd reach out once she was free.

In the meantime, he replayed events throughout the year, trying to deduce who could've killed Rich Benson—and why they would've wanted to. It was a tangled spider web he and Joan had gotten into, but Matt was sure *how* Benson died was key. Pushing someone down a hill seemed pretty reckless, so he figured it wasn't premeditated. Chet's death, on the other hand, was clearly murder in the first degree.

He didn't get very far with his leads, but a couple possibilities started to form in his mind. At least it kept his thoughts off when Logan would pick his Tetrad.

On Monday, once all the graduating members had left the group chat, Logan sent his first message as Imperator.

No clue why that pussy Randall chose me, but holy fuck are you boys in for a trip next year. No more bullshit. But first, we're gonna get together on Friday for that year-end thing we always do. For the rookie first-years who don't know what that is, we basically just order pizza and chill. Oh, and there's alcohol. Obviously. I'll have more info about that soon but put it in your goddamn calendars. I'll be announcing my Tetrad then, so don't get your panties in a twist asking me who it's gonna be. Peace out, 116.

Matt tried not to think about the eloquent first messages Madler and Randall had written after their Baptisms, tried not to think about the historical document-themed intro he was going to post. It was too painful.

After class, he spent Monday evening in his room, working on an essay due later in the week. He checked his phone before heading to Galbraith, but there were still no texts from Joan. Sighing, he went alone and ended up sitting by himself. The sun was setting quite late these days, early evening light filtering through the stained-glass windows. It gave the meal a certain dreamlike haze, which only contributed to a feeling of unreality. It had continued to surface now and again every few hours since the Sermon. After last year, Matt knew what it was a sign of and realized he should see a therapist again—and soon.

Pausing, he questioned if this feeling truly stemmed from losing Imperator. And yet the more he thought about it, the more he realized that was but one facet of it.

This whole college had finally gotten to him.

He remembered what it had been like at the Foxhole on Friday and reflected on everything he thought he'd enjoyed about Radcliffe. Had it always been like this and he was just too blind to see it, too fixated on his goals to notice the cesspool he'd been wading through? Just being here, sitting alone in Galbraith, made him feel wretched.

He saw Logan with Freddie and Doug at the fourth-year table, but they didn't seem to notice him and he didn't want to intrude.

However, he overheard something a few spaces down, some other people in his year talking. Apparently, Mia Cote—the female Student Events Officer—had recorded both branches' Second Sermons on her phone.

Great, he thought. *Like we don't already have enough problems.*

After getting a draft of the essay completed just before midnight, he had a tough time getting to sleep. He woke up on Tuesday feeling exhausted, his fatigue compounded by everything from over the weekend.

By the time lunch rolled around, Matt found himself sitting alone at the third-year table again. He was eating fairly early, so there weren't too many others around and he had the far end to himself.

He was eating quietly when Joan suddenly sat down across from him.

"Hi," she said, her voice bright but her face concerned.

Warmth flushed through him and he sat up straighter. "Hey, how are you?"

She sighed. "Super fucking busy, it's crazy." She took one of his hands in hers. "Sorry I haven't seen you much, I've been running around talking to my Tetrad and studying for this massive econ test Friday. We don't have a final, so they crammed everything into this term test and—" She shook her head. "Anyway, sorry I've been so swamped with stuff. I'm busy at the turnover dinner tonight, but we'll definitely hang out more soon."

"The turnover dinner?"

"Yeah, Kylie and Randall are taking me and Logan out to the Royal to discuss the future of Anathema." She shrugged. "It's really just another excuse to get drunk."

"Like those are a rarity around here."

Joan laughed. "Exactly… But I didn't want you to think I'd…forgotten about you." She smiled awkwardly.

"No worries. Really, it's no big deal," he said, wishing he could tell her how much it meant to hear her say that.

You are so pathetic, the shadow hissed.

"Every time I've seen you since Friday, you…haven't looked well."

"I've been better."

"Has Logan talked to you yet?"

"No. Have you heard he's going to?"

She shook her head. "He said yesterday he was going to talk to his Tetrad soon. He hadn't finalized who was going to be on it yet."

"The last time someone in Anathema told me they 'hadn't decided yet,' it didn't end too well for me."

Joan squeezed his hand tighter. "I know, but that was for Imperator. I've heard people discuss you as future Tetrad material for a while, even before we were dating. I think you'd make a great Legatus, personally. And you'd look super cute with the sash." She winked.

It cheered him up a little. "I'm just worried he'll put Geoff and two third-years."

"Yeah, but he risks making an enemy of you if you don't get Tetrad at all. You have put a lot of fucking effort into this thing, Matt. I'm not just saying that to be supportive."

He sighed. "I don't think he cares if he makes an enemy of me or not. He doesn't seem to think much of me at all."

She shook her head. "He's mentioned you positively a couple times when we've talked, both since the Psi Beta clean-up. There are *three* other spots, Matt. Magister has been given out to people who deserve Tetrad, but the Imperator doesn't know what else to do with them. So, worst case scenario, he ships you off to the Archives. But you'll still have a position. And the Archives are cool. I went down there again last weekend. A bunch of the old volumes are really ornate and beautiful, and they had way more drawings and poems in them back then."

He loved how excited she sounded talking about it.

"Anyway," she continued. "I'm sure you'll be fine. I'm more curious who else will get it. Probably Geoff, but I don't know if Tanner or Hamid will get the other spot."

Joan noticed Mia Cote standing with some of her friends farther down the table and shot the Officer a death glare, her expression chilling Matt. Mia noticed, looked startled, and moved for the exit with her friends in tow. They glanced back a few times, talking and laughing, no doubt about Joan.

She still stared after them, her eyes burning.

"Hey," he said softly, putting a hand on top of one of hers.

She snapped out of it. "Sorry, I just really hate her right now."

"I heard about the recording."

Joan shook her head. "I'll deal with it later." She stood up and put a hand to her stomach. "I'm starving, gonna grab lunch. I'll be right back."

When she returned a couple minutes later, he noticed she wore a skull bracelet.

"Ah, very subtle," he said, gesturing to it.

She laughed, then stabbed a bite of lasagna and brought it to her mouth. "That's me for you…"

◆

By Wednesday, the good feeling she'd brought him had vanished, and he sat alone in Galbraith eating a late dinner. He hadn't felt like dressing up for High Table and had waited until the staff opened the dining hall for everyone else after seven o'clock.

Matt knew it was just the disorder with its easily-triggered ups and downs. He wondered if it was worse for people with bipolar. His disorder and theirs had some overlapping symptoms and were sometimes confused for each other, but at least he didn't have to take meds. That was one saving grace.

He sat alone again and felt the shadow creeping closer, the protective lanterns going out slowly, one by one. He told himself he just needed to make it to the end of this week. It would be better once he had a Tetrad position. They'd have never even considered him if he hadn't put so much work into it. If he'd done even a modicum less, he was sure he'd have been overlooked.

Still, the wait made him anxious and he didn't like how long Logan was taking. Like Joan, he would've talked to everyone by now. He would've picked them long ago. Not that any of it mattered. He'd spent three years spinning useless dreams in a horrible place and the realization brought the shadow closer still.

◆

Logan finally texted him Thursday at dinner.

Hey man! Are you around right now? I've got something I want to talk to you about for a few minutes.

Matt stared at his phone, his shoulders relaxing as he exhaled. He turned to Tom Turland, who sat with Caitlyn beside him at the fourth-year table, and showed him the screen.

"Ah," Turland said, giving him a thumbs up. "Good luck."

"Thanks," Matt told him, typing in a reply.

Yeah, sure! I'm just finishing up in Galbraith right now.

Logan typed back, *Ah, perfect. Yeah, just come by my room in Winslow when you're done. Thanks, dude.*

Wow. *Thanks, dude.* That was definitely a step up.

Once he'd finished and returned his plate and cutlery to the dishwashing room, he headed out into the West Quad.

Fading sunlight painted the clouds, orange tinting the evening sky. The air was brisk, but pleasant in his light jacket. It was the fourth day of April and it was finally starting to feel like spring. A warm front was blowing through the region and nearly all the snow had melted in the Quad, but there was no guarantee it would last. They could easily have a blizzard in another week or so.

There were a few people standing about the Quad talking, and Matt saw Doug chatting with Sandrine on the bench in front of Lacy. They all seemed to be enjoying the weather and the whole scene made him relax further. It struck him just how tense he'd been these past few days, but it was finally unwinding now.

He approached Winslow and unlocked the door with his R3. Twilight bathed the stairs as he entered the res house, then swiftly vanished as the door closed behind him. He made his way to Second East and knocked on Logan's door at the end on the left. It was, of course, a Quad-facing fireplace room, one of the most coveted dorms on residence.

116 opened the door, a smile on his face. "Hey man, come on in." It was

as if they were old friends, about to crack open some beers.

Logan's bed stood by the window, but he had his desk chair and another, comfier one facing each other across a low table. He took the desk chair and gestured Matt to the other. He wondered if Joan had done it like this when she told her Tetrad. He wondered who they were.

Matt sat down. "How have you been?" Logan asked.

He hesitated. "I've been alright. Just swamped with school, and all that."

"Yeah, yeah. The end-of-year grind's got me down too." Logan bit his lip and rubbed his hands together. "So, let's get right to it. The reason you're here is…I've finally decided my Tetrad."

Matt nodded, leaning forward.

"My Magister will be Tanner Cho." The Imperator looked down, still rubbing his hands.

Matt nodded again. An excellent pick.

"My Pontifex will be Geoff Bhajan." He'd figured as much. But that left only one spot. The Imperator's right hand, the second-in-command.

"And my Legatus…" Logan sighed and looked up at him. "Will be Rufus Danvers."

SIXTY-FIVE

I T WAS as if a bullet had torn right through his chest, blood draining out all over the floor. He felt woozy and it was all he could do to hold back tears.

"Could you…excuse me for a minute?" he said, his voice strained.

Logan nodded, understanding. "Of course." He gestured to the door.

Matt got up and broke into a sprint once he'd left the room. He dashed down the corridor, threw open the pod door, and swerved into the bathroom. Someone else was washing their hands, but he quickly ducked into a stall and shut the door. The person seemed to hesitate, then left the room.

Once the door closed behind them, Matt began hyperventilating, tears spewing from his eyes.

No, no, no, no, no.

It wasn't happening. He pinched himself until it hurt, then again and again. He wanted it to hurt. He deserved to make it hurt. Even after everything he had done for three whole years, Rufus' words were right.

Outside the Anathema, he is completely worthless.

No, he was worthless inside the Anathema too. There was no escape from social destitution. Why had he even bothered trying? Why pour so much love and effort into something that only hates you back?

It wasn't just the shadow laughing at him now, it was the entire college. He could hear their conversations already.

Hey, did you hear Richardson didn't even make Tetrad? Laughter. *Yeah, and get this—Rufus did. I know, right? He went around telling everyone he was going to leave if they didn't pick him and he* still *got it over Matt. Isn't that fuckin' hilarious? Oh, and they even picked a third-year over him too.*

More laughter, then another voice: *You know, I used to think his girlfriend was weird, but she can do so much better than him.*

Ragged sobs tore their way out, his teardrops spattering the floor.

I hate this college. I hate this college. I. Hate. This. Fucking. College.

He thought of the Facebook and Instagram posts made for Frosh Week every year, showing smiling upper-years in the Quads with fuzzy messages about how Radcliffe was such a warm and welcoming place. He thought of Social Cliffe, seated in their cliques at the Galbraith tables, laughing at other people, saying who did what with who, giving each other positions in the same organizations. All of them, having a grand old time.

Fuck you. Fuck every single one of you.

Wiping his tears with his jacket sleeve, he burst out of the stall and headed to the window, then wound it open with the crank. Dusk was still peaceful and beautiful; cool air brushed across his face. He stood there, trying to calm himself and failing. The tears kept coming.

He didn't know what to do next, though he figured he'd have to go back there, to Logan's room. They'd finish the conversation and he would give his bullshit explanation or whatever it was. Kind of him to at least tell Matt he was fucking him over *before* the big event tomorrow. That was about as much mercy you could ask for at Radcliffe College.

The door opened behind him and he tensed, continuing to stare out the window and hoping the person wouldn't pay him much attention.

"Hey, it's me," Logan said. "Sorry, I've just really gotta piss."

Are. You. Fucking. Kidding. Me?

Sure enough, he heard the sound from the urinal a few seconds later. Couldn't he have used a bathroom on a different floor?

Matt gripped the crank, just for something to hold onto. He squeezed tighter and tighter until his knuckles were snow-white. Logan finished up, flushed, and washed his hands. Matt hoped he'd just leave after that, but wasn't so fortunate.

"Hey…I just want you to know, it's not because I don't respect you or anything."

He said nothing, staring off at the orange sky. It was so serene out there, like a painting. He wished he was far, far away from here, someplace beyond the horizon that way.

"I just wanted to talk this through before tomorrow. I don't want you to hate Anathema, or me…"

"It's a little late for that," he managed to get out.

Logan laughed. "I get it, I really do. And if you want to say anything, get it out now. Vent to me. I don't mind."

"Why then?" he asked, still not looking at him.

"It's not a personal thing, really. It's more…well, it's political, I guess. You see, Rufus went around saying a lot of bad things about us being awful people last year. But if I have him standing by my side at the Sermons next year, it'll give me more credibility. It will…let me say the things I need to say."

"Like what?"

"Well, I want to go harder than Randall. He was way too much of a pussy this year."

"So? He was an Officer, that's why. Even I would've gone harder than him. Joan's gonna go harder than him. You don't have to fear impeachment. You can say whatever you want."

Silence.

Suddenly, Matt realized what he was getting at. He spun around. "You want to go *way* harder, don't you? You really *do* want to take us back to the nineties."

Logan held up his hands. "Now, hold on. The nineties get a bad rap in this organization, but they weren't all bad. The Imperator who went on to become a Le Mans racer, he was pretty chill. He even hosted a Sermon in the Quad and invited the press so they could see he wasn't too bad. Gagnon was way worse. When she bullied that girl so much that she attempted suicide, that was too far. I don't want to do anything like that, but I do want to have edgier jokes. That's always been my style.

"I managed to convince Randall I wouldn't go too hard, but I think he always knew what he was getting into when he picked me. The last hard-hitting Imperator was Favell, and even he wasn't too bad. We've gone soft and people don't respect us. We need to regain our prestige."

"We'd be cooler if we acted more mysterious instead of circle-jerking our way around the college. We're supposed to *criticize* clique culture, not embrace it."

"Rufus and I aren't friends," Logan said. "I only picked him for political reasons, okay? I honestly respect you more and I'd come to you for advice more than I'd go to him. And I'll still give you important tasks next year—"

"If you want my advice and you want me to do all these things for you, you should've given me the title I earned to go with them. I have *had* it with being this organization's bitch. I'm tired of running around helping the Imperators whenever they ask me to do something, showing up on time, submitting more homework jokes than necessary, and defending this thing at every turn only to get made fun of for being worthless—Rufus' words by the way—and told I'm too into it. And all I get for it is a bunch of fucking pats on the back! From you, from Randall, even from Madler and Turland, though at least Turland fucking Initiated me. So which one is it? Either I'm a valuable member who the leadership respects, or I'm a sycophant loser who everyone laughs at for throwing himself into something that likes the work he does for it more than it actually likes him!" He caught his breath.

Logan shook his head. "I don't know what other people say, but I respect you, okay? I might've been crossfaded when I said it, but what I told you at Winter Formal about seeing your jokes make it to the Sermons was real. I helped edit Randall's shit. I saw all the good content you sent in. I don't give compliments out for nothing, Matt. You are one of the Anathema's best writers, and I want to have you continue to write for *my* Sermons next year."

Matt shook his head. "How stupid do you think I am? You can bully Randall but not even *I* would've caved to someone calling me a pussy. I would've made an example of you in front of anyone if you fucking questioned me like that! I would've crucified you!"

Logan shrugged. "Randall's just weak, man. To be honest, I was surprised he gave it to me. But I really wanted it, so I said yes, and here we are."

"Alright. Why couldn't you have given me Pontifex or Magister?"

"Well, Geoff is a fifth-year and so that trumps you—just like with Rufus. I know he left and—"

"He went around saying he'd leave if he didn't get Tetrad, and you gave it to him anyway."

He brushed the comment off. "I *told* you why I picked him. And he told me he would've stayed regardless."

"Of course he fucking said that."

Logan shrugged again. "Whether he would've or not is beside the point. He's Legatus now. Geoff is going to be a fifth-year, so he's Pontifex."

"And Tanner's going to be a third-year."

"Yes, but Magister is really a multi-year position. Doug did it for both Turland and Madler before Randall made it official. Before him, Darius

Kazra did it for Favell unofficially before Duric made him his Magister. Now Tanner will get to hold the position officially for two years."

"Unless he becomes Imperator."

Logan shrugged. "Yeah, maybe, I don't know. But even then, he would still get to continue his duties with the Archives."

"If it's only a multi-year position unofficially, why couldn't Tanner have just shadowed me for next year? Then he could get Magister the year after that if he's not Imperator, and I still would've gotten a spot on Tetrad, which is what I've cared about for three fucking years."

Logan paused, as if he hadn't considered this before. Then he shook his head. "That wouldn't have worked. Anyway, I just wanted to talk to you about this before tomorrow. I hope you're still just as dedicated next year as you were this year. Believe me, I noticed."

You're just not going to do anything about it.

"No more school shooter jokes," Matt said. "No more jokes about me being worthless or awful at dating or whatever. Anything else about me is fair game, but those things really get to me, so please stop."

"Okay," Logan said. "I wasn't going to make more school shooter jokes. And I don't think there would be jokes about your dating life either. You've got a girlfriend."

"For now," he scoffed.

Logan shook his head. "Joan kept asking me if I'd talked to my Tetrad all week. I could tell she really wanted you to get it."

Matt raised an eyebrow.

"Yeah, no one doubts that she likes you, man. I've heard people say you're both weird, but I bet they're probably just jealous of your relationship. You look really happy together, so don't listen to what they say. I never do and it seems to work for me." He laughed, then scratched the stubble on his chin. "Why, do you not like *her* anymore?"

"No, no, I lo—I really like her a lot."

"See? You don't have to be so down. I know this Tetrad thing sucks, but you're still dating the hottest female Imperator in, like, a decade. Maybe more." He laughed. "There'll be photos of the two of you from the End-of-Year Social in the next Scrapbooks. You've earned your place in Anathema history, dude."

Matt turned back to the window and looked off at the sky again, taking a deep breath.

"If you want to talk about it more before tomorrow—or after, just let me know, okay?"

He nodded. "Okay," he said softly. Then he turned and walked past him, out the door, down the stairs and back into the West Quad.

Immediately he realized that had been a mistake. His face was still red from crying and there were people about. Now that he was away from Logan, the emotions swirled back. He realized how good the Imperator was at deflecting anger and easing upsets. For a few minutes, he'd managed to make Matt forget just how much he hated him.

The tears began to pour again as he raced to Lacy, hoping Doug and Sandrine wouldn't see him. They were still seated on the bench up ahead, but he managed to unlock the eastern door and slip inside before their heads turned. He raced up to the second floor, ran over to Joan's room, and banged on the door.

"Hello?" came her voice.

"It's me," he said, trying not to sob. "I need to talk to you about something."

She opened the door and saw his face, concern immediately washing over her. "What's wrong?"

"I didn't make Tetrad."

Joan pulled him inside and shut the door. She led him over to the bed and sat him down, taking a seat in her desk chair and turning it toward him. A large textbook and scores of notes were strewn about behind her, no doubt for her econ midterm tomorrow. She wore sweatpants and a faded Toronto Maple Leafs T-shirt. Her hair was a bit disheveled and she looked exhausted. The Imperator in her natural habitat.

"What happened?" she said, leaning closer and taking his hand.

He told her, starting from Logan's message and going right through to him realizing people would've seen he'd been crying, once he got back into the Quad.

When he finished, Joan stood up and put a hand to her forehead. *"Fuck* him. Rufus Danvers? Are you kidding me?"

Matt shrugged and sniffed. "I don't know what to say anymore."

"And I love Tanner, but he could totally just shadow you until next year. He still has another shot at Tetrad. This was your last."

"Honestly, I don't think he gave it much thought. But he did try to be nice about it—"

"No, no, no, Matt. You *can't* let people do this to you. The part about him hoping you're just as dedicated next year is fucking *bullshit*. It shows what he really thinks of you, that you're just a tool he can use and bash around with no repercussions. He thinks if he just talks to you and says 'Hey, I'm destroying everything you worked toward for three years because I'm a careless asshole,' you'll just take it and go back to writing jokes like you always have. Meanwhile, he just picked three people who suited him and only realized you would be left out afterward. Rewarding you wasn't a priority at all. He should've at least given you Magister. Really, if he doesn't care what people think about him, he shouldn't have picked Rufus and just said whatever he wants to say. That he didn't shows he's just as weak as Randall." She sighed and shook her head. "His Sermons are going to be a shitshow next year, I can already tell."

"He said he wouldn't put the really mean jokes about me back in, even though I'm sure Rufus will push for a lot of them."

Joan sat in her chair again and looked out the window. It was getting dark outside. "And people say *I'm* the problem." She turned to him again. "Apparently Mia Cote thinks I'm going to be terrifying. Granted, I think I scared the shit out of her today, but oh well. I got her to delete that recording off her phone."

"What did you do?"

"I cornered her and said she better delete it or she was going to have problems, and it would be better for both of us if she'd take out her phone and erase it right in front of me."

He rubbed his forehead. "Be careful, you don't want people to think you'll be the next Emma Gagnon."

"It was strange talking to her at Ni Hao," she said, remembering. "Given her reputation, I'm surprised she showed up at all, but she was much different than I expected. Softer, kinder." Joan smiled. "She told me I reminded her of her younger self."

"That's...probably not a good thing." He forced a laugh.

"No, no—her younger self *before* she became Imperator. She was a dark horse like me. Everyone was sure it was going to be this other girl, Susanne Ferguson."

"Wait...isn't that the girl who—?"

"Attempted suicide?" Joan gave a grim nod. "A lot of people don't know the full story. Ferguson was popular and bullied Gagnon for being socially awkward. A lot of people here did. But when Gagnon got Imperator over her, Ferguson was so disgusted with Anathema that she left and started speaking out against it."

"But then Gagnon turned around and bullied *her*. She dumped dog shit on her and read jokes that were so mean that that Ferguson girl tried to *kill herself*. Doesn't that make Gagnon worse?"

Joan sighed. "It does, and that's why she felt sad coming to the Sermon. She hadn't been to one in ages, but as she's gotten older, she says she's started regretting a lot of things she did back then. She went on a warpath at this college, letting off three years of pent-up hatred from how everyone treated her. Now they only remember her as the evil Imperator who got us Dissociated." She hesitated. "And people like Mia Cote think I'm going to be as bad as she was."

Joan chewed on a fingernail, looking much sadder. She turned to him again. "I don't want everybody to think I'm a monster, Matt. I've thought about the words I could say, the things I can do now that I have a medallion—and it scares the shit out of me. This week, Randall told me it doesn't matter too much who gets Imperator since they basically just babysit the members and then get up once in a while to read some jokes. But I don't think it's that simple. This organization is a weapon. And only someone who respects the damage it can do should wield it." She swallowed. "I hope I'm that person."

"I know you are." He smiled.

She gave a weak one in return.

"Gagnon's not the only alum who seems to have matured," Matt said. "Quentin Caleb was there too. Even he admitted he'd taken things too far."

She sighed. "We're all still really young. I mean, even the fourth-years are what, twenty-two? That's the problem with college secret societies. They're mature concepts run by people who haven't fully matured." She turned back to him. "I read this article about something called 'extended adolescence' the other day. Basically, until you're twenty-five, you're still socially a teenager. So many people are doing undergrad in our generation that it's pretty much become the next level of high school. Our generation is having sex later, dating later, getting our first jobs later..."

Matt laughed. "I'm glad I'm not the only one who doesn't feel like an adult yet."

She chuckled too. "I don't either. Not that that's an excuse to make bad decisions. I hope I made the right call with my Tetrad."

"Let me guess, Val is your Legatus?"

She shook her head. "No, she's not on it at all."

"Really? I would've thought you'd want to guarantee her a position."

Joan smiled. "Oh, I will."

He realized what she was getting at and his eyes widened. "Does she know she's—?"

"My first, last, and only pick for the 95th Imperator? Of course not. I've got to keep her working for it. But I've thought a long time, even before Kylie talked to me, about who else it could be, and really it's only her. Plus, most people don't suspect her, but they still like her."

He shook his head. "Randall took until the last minute to decide and you've already got it planned out a year in advance."

She beamed. "I'm a writer. I like to know the ending before I start writing the beginning."

He sighed and rubbed his temple.

"If it makes you feel better," Joan said, "I was actually Kylie's second choice."

He looked up. "Who was her first?"

"Catherine. I was about to tell you at the Foxhole, but Logan burst in before I could finish. Kylie told me it was only ever me or her. She thought Catherine would be more seasoned to it, but when she asked her, Catherine said she'd already been on Tetrad once and that I would do more with it anyway. Originally, I was going to make Val my Legatus, but I didn't want to do what Randall did and be responsible for putting a friend on Tetrad twice. One year is enough. We need fresh blood."

"So luck is half of it?" he asked.

"Well," she said, "even Turland became Imperator only because someone else dropped out."

"Yeah, but he would've gotten it eventually."

"Maybe, but you can't assume that. Also, if Patrick hadn't run for Officer last year, he could've been 115 over Randall. People say of course Randall was going to get it anyway, but everyone likes to pretend they were on the winning side all along. Several in my branch have said they thought it would be me, but I know for a fact they only ever considered Alyssa and Catherine. Val told me."

He nodded and softly said, "You're right."

She sat on the bed and hugged him tightly. After about a minute, he stared toward the window and watched light recede from the sky, leaning his head against hers. "I feel like everything I do here is for nothing."

"Not to me," Joan said, kissing him. "Not to me."

The shadow was very close again, almost as near as it had been last year. Only one light kept it at bay now.

And she bore the torch.

SIXTY-SIX

THE SKY was gray and dreadful the next morning. Coming back from the Athletic Center, Matt stopped to stare up at it as thunder rumbled in the distance. He didn't need to check the weather to know it was going to rain; he could even feel it in the air.

When he glanced down again, he saw Tanner making his way toward him across the West Quad.

"Hey," he said, smiling. "Congrats, by the way. You're going to make a really great Magister. I would've picked you for it myself."

Tanner walked right up to him, put his hand on Matt's shoulder, and said, "I am *so* sorry. Logan told me who the others were. If you need someone to talk to, come by my room. My door is always open and I've got some extra beers."

"Thank you," he replied, genuinely touched.

Tanner nodded and continued along. The encounter gave him something positive to think about as he spent the rest of the day alone, working on another essay. The final slog was coming up next week. Then once classes were over, he only had two finals during the exam period, both scheduled for the last week. As usual, he'd be here till the end.

The rain began with a drizzle, then increased in intensity through the afternoon. Isolated in his room, the shadow hung over Matt. It descended closer and closer, its talons extending right above his head.

He wanted to go for a walk, but the weather told him otherwise. There was nothing to do but try to write the paper. He'd barely gotten a page out by dinner and took the steam tunnels to Galbraith. Patrick sat with him and kept him company, which he greatly appreciated. Joan's midterm went from five to seven, but she'd invited him to walk with her to the Chalet.

It was the only part of the evening he looked forward to.

Finally, eight o'clock rolled around and Matt headed to her room in Lacy, again taking the steam tunnels. He wore a leather jacket over a white collared shirt and his best pair of jeans; he'd just shaved and his pendant dangled from his neck. He knocked on her door and idly combed his fingers through his hair while he waited.

The door swung inward and she poked her head around. "Hey, come in."

He headed to her bed to take a seat, just as he had yesterday, then turned around and nearly did a double take.

Joan wore a black corset tube top, leaving both her midriff and shoulders exposed. Her dark jeans fit tightly and she wore lace-up boots with platform heels. She sported more eye shadow than usual and the only splash of color was her red lipstick.

"Um, hi," he said, searching for words. She looked absolutely stunning, but the style seemed uncharacteristic for her.

"Like the new look?" She retrieved her medallion from the dresser and put it on.

"Emphasis on *new*, but I like it." His heart beat faster and he wasn't sure if he was excited, scared, or both.

Joan shrugged. "Figured I was due for a style update. Time to stop playing the meek little ingénue." She sat down beside him and smiled, sliding her arm around his shoulder. "And to remind people that *you* are *mine*." She planted a firm kiss on his cheek, leaving a red mark from her lipstick. "You might not be on a Tetrad, but you're still an Imperator's boyfriend." She brushed a strand of hair off his forehead.

"That would be my favorite title anyway." He kissed her back.

She glanced at her watch. "We should get going. The pizza's been ordered and should be there in half an hour. Logan was on the booze."

Joan stood up and pulled her leather jacket off the back of her chair, then put it on and straightened it out. "The umbrella's right beside you," she said.

He grabbed it and they headed out. They took the steam tunnels to the front lobby, then deployed the umbrella and stepped through the front doors, rain drumming the canopy over them.

As they made their way down the steps, huddling together to avoid getting soaked, she said, "Didn't you once tell me the End-of-Year Social was your favorite Anathema event?"

Matt nodded. "Yeah, I did."

"You said you liked how it was about bonding within the organization, right?"

"I said that back when I actually wanted to bond with these people, back when I thought they still liked me."

"A bunch of them still do," she said.

"Tanner does, and maybe Hamid. All the others have graduated."

"Val approves of you and you seem to have grown on Sophia." She laughed and glanced over, but when she saw he wasn't smiling, she added, "Freddie seems nice."

"Yeah, I like Freddie."

They reached the bottom of the stairs and headed toward Griffin Park.

"A bunch of people don't like me." Joan lowered her head and sighed. "I know Alyssa doesn't, but I made her Magister so she wouldn't be a problem."

"Logan didn't think that through with me," he said.

"Logan and thinking things through are two separate concepts."

"You're gonna have a time and a half reining him in next year."

Joan's face flushed red. "I hate that everyone keeps telling me to rein him in. They should be criticizing Randall. He was the one stupid enough to pick that asshole in the first place."

"Well, there's nothing he can do about it now. No matter what, this college always fucks you in the end."

She took his hand in hers. "Just take it easy tonight. We can do something fun later. Maybe try something…*new*." They'd been so busy they hadn't done anything in about two weeks.

He laughed awkwardly, starting to feel a bit better. "Alright, but masks and pendants are about as far as I'm willing to go."

"Oh, really?" She leaned closer with a mischievous grin. "So…what about the time I wore the ears and tail from my werewolf costume?"

He paled. "That…that was a one-off…"

She raised an eyebrow. "I somehow doubt that."

Matt tried to ignore her amused smile, his cheeks flushing red. They walked along the edge of Griffin and came to the main road that looped around Canmore Creek.

Wanting to change the subject, he said, "Pandora told me something interesting at the Sermon."

"Really?" she said, surprised.

He filled her in on the Bard's absence and how the leaks had really occurred.

Joan put a hand to her head. "Great. So *that's* what got me into this mess in the first place."

"Yeah." He told her his theory, that maybe the Bard really was in hiding and hadn't killed either Benson or Chet. Then he said Randall was his new chief suspect, as far-fetched as it sounded.

She thought for a moment. "I just don't know why he would've killed Rich."

"Me neither. But it's something to consider."

Joan paused, deep in thought. Finally, she said, "Matt, I've been wondering…"

"Yeah…?"

She looked at him and energy seemed to flow out of her, the tiredness she'd kept at bay laid bare. "Maybe…it's time we let this thing go."

"What do you mean?" he said, stunned.

She sighed, putting a hand to her face. "I *really* thought someone was trying to frame me. It kept me up at night, tossing and turning and trying to think who the hell it could be. But it's been *months* since the police gave up their investigation, and even longer since they said Rich's death was an accident. Now Serpentine seems to be falling apart—Pandora could've told you all that just to fuck with you because she hates Anathema…" Joan shook her head. "Maybe this thing has just been a bunch of coincidences the whole time. And even if it isn't, the more we've gotten tangled up in it, the more stressed and confused we've become. So maybe we should just…leave it be. And hope it does the same with us."

He was baffled. "But there has to be an answer…"

She stopped, turning to him beneath the umbrella. "Life's not like movies and books, Matt. Believe me, I'd greatly prefer it if it was. But not every mystery gets solved. Some things in the world don't make sense and never will." Her expression saddened and she chewed a fingernail. "I'm worried you're throwing yourself into something else that leads nowhere."

Matt paused, looking out at the road. He hadn't considered it that way.

And in truth, what had sleuthing brought him aside from anxiety, paranoia, and dead ends?

The shadow's voice re-entered his mind: *You're running out of things to obsess over.*

He turned back to Joan; her eyes brimmed with concern. "You know what?" he said. "You're right. It's been stupid of me to keep looking into it… I'm done."

She looked even sadder. "I don't think it was stupid. I really admired that you weren't giving up. But it's just gotten to the point where I'm worried it's not healthy for you. I know it wasn't healthy for me, so I tried to stop thinking about Rich after Kylie talked to me. I realized I needed to start looking forward—not just for me, but for Anathema."

Because you have something to look forward to. He crushed the thought and held her hand again. "Let's just try to enjoy the party."

"Okay." She gave his hand a tight squeeze and they continued on in silence, rain hammering the umbrella. When they got to the gate, he almost buzzed the intercom, but she held up a finger. "I've got the code now," she said, punching in 1-9-9-7. The year of Dissociation.

"Of course it was that all along," he grunted.

She gave him an amused smile, then pulled the gate open while he held the umbrella. They made their way across the clearing and he saw Randall's Volvo was no longer parked before the Chalet. That era had truly come to an end. The only light on was an exterior one beside the door, barely visible between the evening and the rain.

Joan had the key to the house. "I'm going to be living here next year," she said, unlocking the door. "I'm tired of Cliffe res. How about you?"

"I haven't submitted my application yet. It's not due for another week, but I'm wondering if I should move off."

"You definitely should."

He hoped she would add *And come live with me*, but instead entered the Chalet and flicked on the lights. He followed her inside; the lounge was quiet and empty.

"The calm before the storm," Joan sighed, only to be answered by a distant clap of thunder.

◆

The pizza arrived before the members did and Joan, who hadn't eaten dinner, wolfed down a couple slices before Logan and Tanner showed up, carrying a box full of liquor. Joan appeared to regain some of her earlier energy, or was at least managing to hide the fatigue.

For a moment, the male Imperator stared at the kiss mark on Matt's cheek. He seemed on the verge of cracking a joke about it, but instead glanced around the room and sighed. "Yeah, I had a feeling the four of us were gonna be the first to show up."

Next came Val. "I love the outfit," she said, looking Joan up and down.

"Thanks!" she said, finishing a slice of pepperoni and shrugging out of her jacket. She folded it and put it on a sofa, and as she did so Matt glimpsed both Tanner and Logan stealing glances at her.

You might not be on a Tetrad, but you're still an Imperator's boyfriend, she had said.

You know, that's really not so bad after all, he thought. Everyone would notice the lipstick on his cheek. He was hers and she wouldn't let anything bad happen to him.

You're nothing but a toy to her. She'll get bored of you, the shadow whispered.

Matt's hand started trembling. He slowly breathed in and out, then made his way to the fireplace, where Tanner was setting bottles of booze along the mantel. "Are you bartending?"

"For now, yeah. What can I get you?"

"Something strong," he said.

◆

Unlike the rain, the rest of both branches trickled in slowly.

It took about forty minutes for everyone coming to arrive, and people spent another twenty minutes talking and eating and drinking before Logan whistled. All the attention in the room turned to him.

"Hey, fuckfaces!" The remaining murmurs quieted down. "Alright, I know we're all here to take a break from studying and get wasted, *but...*" He looked around at all of them. "Joan and I know you're interested to find out who our new Tetrads are, so we'll get that out of the way real quick and then you can get back to doing what you're doing."

He extended a hand toward the makeshift bar. "Tanner is my Magister." He pointed back behind Joan. "Geoff over there is my Pontifex."

Logan gestured straight toward Matt and for a second, he froze. That couldn't possibly be right, it was—

"And Rufus is my Legatus." He realized then that the second-in-command was standing right beside him. Rufus gave Logan an appreciative nod.

A round of applause went around.

Matt's eyes swept the crowd, looking for any sign that people were surprised he hadn't gotten anything. There was none.

Of course there wasn't. Nothing new to see here.

The alcohol was supposed to help, but it only seemed to solidify his mood. If he could even call it one mood. It fluctuated between despair, anger, bitterness, and self-loathing.

All eyes in the room turned to Joan as she stepped forward, extending her hand toward each Tetrad member as she talked. "Alright. My Legatus is Jaya Noor, my Pontifex is Kristen Edwards, and my Magister is Alyssa Lee."

Another round of applause. The new Tetrad members took it in, knowing they would be preserved in Anathema history as people who counted, not just meaningless foot-soldiers doing the bitchwork of the top brass.

Like him.

I hope you're still just as dedicated next year as you were this year.

You won't be if you cut your wrists, the shadow said.

And at that, Matt gave a little laugh.

◆

He spent the evening ping-ponging around between different people, trying to make conversations last so he wouldn't have to find someone else to talk to. Normally he would've hung around Joan, but she was busy with the others.

Just after 10 p.m., he bumped into Turland on the main floor hallway. "Oh, hey," the former Imperator said. "How's it going?"

Matt's inhibitors had been dulled by the alcohol, so he told him, "Honestly, I feel like shit."

Turland nodded, understanding, and looked back toward the lounge. The din of conversation drifted toward them. "I get that."

"We should get drinks soon," Matt said. *Make plans. That's a good way to keep yourself going,* part of him said. It was the counter-shadow, the last lantern, the final torch. He brushed the voice aside. "I need someone to talk to," he continued, surprised by his own frankness.

Turland seemed concerned. "Sure. How about Sunday?"

His thoughts probed the drunken haze, seeing if he had anything that evening or something due the next day. "Sure, that sounds good," he finally said.

"Cool." He looked past him. "Ah, Jack and Gemma just got here. I'm gonna say hello. See you around."

"You too." Matt watched him head over to 115 and his girlfriend. Someone earlier had mentioned he'd moved in with her full-time now. Matt hadn't talked to Randall since before the Sermon and hadn't seen him since after Ni Hao Ma the same night. He didn't know what to say to him and it felt awkward being in the same vicinity.

Not that Randall would know why. He'd probably never even considered him Tetrad material.

What are you so upset about? he imagined him saying. *Don't worry, Logan will still let you hold a poster next year.*

Matt shook his head and took another sip of his drink, a rum and coke. Suddenly he heard someone behind him and glanced over his shoulder. Rufus approached from the basement stairs, appearing quite drunk.

"Congratulations," Matt said.

"Thank you," he replied, but it sounded insincere.

Rufus looked around. It was just the two of them back here in the darkness of the corridor. Everyone else had moved into the lounge. The new Legatus leaned closer, a cruel smile on his lips.

"You know…when he told me who the others were, I waited until he was out of sight and then I couldn't. Stop. Laughing." He almost spat the words into Matt's ear. "Even I was surprised you got nothing, but it's fitting really. Look at them, look over there."

He gestured to the lounge and Matt's eyes followed. Members of both branches stood around, chatting, drinking, and laughing as the fireplace crackled beyond them.

Matt continued staring, leaning against the wall to his left for support as Rufus drew closer to his ear. "When are you going to realize that this place just doesn't like you?"

Matt watched the smiling faces, heard the laughter float down the hall. They all seemed so far away.

"Why do you hate me?" he asked softly, still looking toward the lounge. "I never did anything to you—and if I did somehow, I'm very sorry."

"It's not what *you* did," Rufus said, watching them too. "It's what people with your...*affliction* do to others, what I know you're going to eventually do to Joan, what someone once did to me."

Matt turned to him, baffled. "What are you talking about?"

"I dated a girl with BPD once, Matt. Second-year through the summer afterward. I loved her very much—for a time. But she became quite clingy and desperate. No amount of attention was enough for her. Everyone else I talked to was a threat. She thought everyone around her hated her—when few of them actually even gave a shit. I tried to break up with her, but she said she'd kill herself if I left. Every time I didn't feel up to having sex, she said she'd do it unless I fucked her." He swallowed, growing tense. He was even more inebriated than Matt had first thought, his words slurring out. "Do you have any idea what that's like?"

"No," Matt said, feeling awful. "No, I'm very, very sorry."

"The police got involved, eventually. She's better now, she's gotten help, but I had to threaten her with a restraining order to get her to stop contacting me. It took a lot of therapy for me to move past it. I joined support groups, talked to other people, heard similar stories. Former boyfriends and girlfriends who hurt the ones who cared about them. I suppose it wasn't their fault. They were, after all, mentally ill. But I know you have it too. That's why I don't think any girl should go near you—or anyone else like you."

"I've never done anything like that," Matt said, shocked and horrified. "I can't even dream of doing that to Joan."

"Oh, but you'll give into it eventually. Most of your kind does."

"Did...did Claudia tell you? How did you find out I—?"

"I was there at the party last April, heard Claudia's friend Vicky reading the fucking DSM-5 to you in the middle of the East Quad, listing all of BPD's symptoms. I turned and saw you, saying yes to nearly all of them. Not the best way to find out you had a mental disorder, I'm sure, but it doesn't excuse your little meltdown afterward. Claudia explained the whole story to me later when I asked. You had freaked out in front of her, but imagine how much worse it would have been for her had she actually dated you. I'm surprised Joan and you have remained together this long. Maybe she's deluded herself into thinking she likes you, but it's going to end badly for her, I can tell."

He leaned back, studying Matt's reaction. Then he gave a horrible, drunken grin. "You haven't told her yet, have you?"

"I...I..."

"You better. It'll help her understand why you're calling things off with her."

"What?! I'm not—"

"Oh, but you have to, Matt. If you love her—which I think you've convinced yourself you do—then you *have* to leave her. Joan's so much more than you now. Look at her. She's an *Imperator*. She's the future. You belong in her past, a stepping stone to better things. You're going to cling to her. You're going to hurt her. It's time for her to move on—and for you to move on too. Any other man would be lucky to have her."

"What, like *you?*"

Rufus laughed. "Oh, heavens no. Alyssa and Katy think there's something off about her, and I'm inclined to agree. She tries to be friendly, but she's quite awkward and is way too obsessed with this thing." He gestured around the Chalet. "Plus, she's too thin for my type. But I know even she deserves better than you."

"So what, I'm never supposed to date anybody? I'm just doomed to die alone, is that it?" Matt hissed.

Rufus' expression saddened. "I'm sorry, Matt, but people like you aren't built to love. You're not destined for it. I don't think you should all be locked up, but I do think you should keep the hell away from everyone else. You delude yourself into thinking you care about the ones you love, but really you just crave their attention. And the moment it starts to wane, you lash out."

"No," Matt said, shaking his head slowly. This felt like a horrible nightmare. He couldn't believe Rufus was actually speaking these things out loud. Back when he first researched the disorder, Matt came across many Internet posts with similar thoughts: how it was best to avoid dating people with BPD at all cost, how the afflicted could only hurt you, how running from them was the only viable solution. He never thought anyone would have the gall to say those things to his face. "You've got it all wrong."

"I know I don't, Matt. It's what's best for everyone involved. Now, you better tell her about the disorder and break up with her before the end of the evening." Rufus grinned again and Matt smelled the alcohol on his breath. "Or *I'll* tell her for you."

"You wouldn't fucking dare."

"Watch me." Rufus turned and started for the lounge.

Matt rushed past him, hurrying down the hall and emerging back into the party. Joan stood by the fireplace with several members standing around her. He headed closer, his heart pounding.

"…not very nice to violate the Anathema Policy, so that'll be two Demerit Points." She looked a bit tipsy and appeared to be doing impressions. He guessed that last one was Dean Crawley.

Those around her laughed. "Do me, do me!" Freddie Evans said, clearly taken with her.

Joan threw him a sly smile, then tapped her chin, her other hand on her hip. "Hmm… I've got it." She cleared her throat, then mimicked his British accent and moved her hand across the room. "The Great Fire of London *swept* across London—"

Doug choked on his drink and fell off the nearby sofa laughing, gin spewing from his mouth and nose. Geoff and Kristen moved to help him while Freddie doubled over in tears.

Joan looked up to see Matt and smiled. "Hey! Want me to do an impression of you?"

"I need to talk to you about something." His voice was anxious and he realized his hand was shaking.

"Sure." She led him to another corner of the room, then turned around.

"It's Rufus, he's—"

"Matt, you need to relax. You look like you're about to have a mental breakdown."

He laughed at that. "I…I…"

"What did Rufus do?"

"He said…he said…he…" The words were right on his tongue, he just couldn't get them out coherently. Fuck, he felt like an idiot.

"How about you go to the bathroom and calm down a bit? Splash some water in your face or something, it really helps."

"Okay, but—"

"It's alright, I'm not going anywhere. You can tell me after." Someone called her. She smiled and waved, then turned back to him. "I've gotta go."

Joan walked off. Matt turned to see Rufus standing with Alyssa and Katy, the Officer watching the other two compare their silver sashes.

"Who was my predecessor again?" Rufus said. "Oh right, Logan!" Then he gave the most annoying laugh Matt had ever heard. Alyssa and Katy joined in.

The Legatus' eyes locked with Matt's, and he smirked while raising his glass in toast.

Matt turned and walked down the corridor as fast as he could. He swung down the basement stairs, dove into the bathroom and fumbled for the light switch. He only turned on the lower lights, but they would have to do.

He cranked the cold faucet and splashed frigid water in his face. Joan was right, it really did help. He did it again, and again, and again.

What a fucking idiot he was, making a scene back there and embarrassing her in front of Anathema. She was a dark horse, she needed to gain the respect of the establishment. And here he was: a crying, incoherent wreck.

"Stupid, stupid, stupid…," he hissed to himself, cupping water in his hands from the tap and throwing it upward onto his face.

Suddenly, he became aware of a figure standing to his left.

With horror, he realized he hadn't closed the door. He turned to see who it was and his blood ran to ice.

Jack Randall stood in the doorway.

"Hey," he said, his confusion and concern visible even in the low light.

"I was…just getting something out of my eye."

Randall nodded slowly. "I'm sorry you didn't get Tetrad. Actually, I'm kinda pissed at Logan. I was very clear to him that you deserved it, and he said he agreed. But ultimately Tetrad is the Imperator's choice. He *does* respect you—he told me that—and he knows how close you came to beating him."

He blinked. "Beating him?"

"116 was a very tough decision. I only told him about a week before, but I lost a lot of sleep over it."

So did I, Matt thought. He swallowed. "Can I ask you something?"

"Yeah, of course."

"What did I do wrong?"

Randall's face saddened. He shook his head. "You didn't do anything wrong, Matt. Ultimately, I just felt he would do a better job keeping people in line. I had a real problem with members getting at each other's throats this year. It wasn't just you and Rufus. Someone else refused to write with him, some of Hamid's jokes had people concerned… It was a shitshow. But Logan is good with maintaining order. And he's a bit louder. I'm sorry, I figured he'd make you Legatus, especially with Tony becoming an Officer. But you and Logan were my only choices for Imperator."

Matt laughed bitterly. "Ares told me I was literally the only person who thought it might not be Logan."

Randall grew angry. "That's a really fucked up thing to say. Anyone who was paying attention thought it would be you or him. Kylie, Turland, Doug…"

"This college has been really getting to me," he said softly, "and Imperator was the last thing I was holding out for here."

Randall looked down. "I'm sorry I couldn't give it to you. If you want to talk about it more sometime later, I'm totally cool with that."

Matt nodded. "Okay. Thank you." He moved out of the bathroom. "Here, I'll get out of your way."

"No worries. Have a good evening." Randall went in and closed the door after him.

Slowly, Matt trudged back toward the stairs. Thunder roared above, shaking the Chalet.

All this time, and he wasn't fucking *loud* enough. And Randall trusted Logan to fix his moral compass over the summer, but not Matt enough to work on his *projection*.

Yet strangely, he felt neither angry nor sad as he climbed the spiral steps. He felt hollow, like a knife had scraped out his insides and all that was left was an empty shell, waiting to collapse in on itself.

He reached the top of the stairs and walked slowly down the corridor, emerging back into the lounge. People threw him glances as he looked for Joan, their judgment piercing him from all angles. He hadn't finished cleaning himself up before Randall appeared, and realized he must look like a mess.

Roy and Tanner were chatting by the fireplace, both heavily intoxicated, and Matt walked up to them.

"Hey man, fuck Logan," Roy said, taking another sip of his drink. "At least he made one good choice." He nodded to Tanner.

"Yes, definitely. Have either of you seen Joan?"

"Oh yeah." Roy pointed toward the front door. "She and Rufus just stepped outside a moment ago. Smoke break, I guess." He paused. "Does Joan smoke?"

Matt turned and ran for the door before he could answer. His grip closed on the handle as he slammed into it, the rainy night opening up before him. He slammed the door shut behind him and looked both ways.

They were nowhere in sight.

He put a hand to his head, breathing rapidly. His pulse pounded and his entire body was tense. Glancing to the left, he saw a pathway under the overhang of the roof and crept along it.

As he neared the edge, voices grew louder.

"…borderline personality disorder is a very serious mental illness. And people who have it are quite dangerous, I assure you."

"I know what it is, Rufus. But—"

"He had a mental breakdown in front of Claudia Greene last year, right after finding out he had it. Her friend Vicky's got a couple disorders herself and likes to go around…*diagnosing* people. I don't know why she felt she should do it in the middle of QuadFest, but that's how it happened. He checked off nearly all of the symptoms in the Diagnostic and Statistical Manual of Mental Disorders—"

"I know what the DSM is, Rufus."

He sighed. "*The point is…*they went to Roy's room after, where Matt completely lost it and started bawling and Tanner had to escort him out. Claudia was there too—she was a friend of Roy's—and wouldn't talk to Matt again after that. Fortunately, she went abroad for her final year so she didn't have to see him. But I imagine something worse will happen with you. People like him aren't healthy for you. They're not healthy for anyone to date. He's only going to hurt you. I just think breaking it off soon would be best."

Matt drifted around the corner and there they were, leaning against the side of the Chalet by the chimney. Rufus had his back to him. Joan opened her mouth to say something, then peered around his shoulder, her eyes widening.

"Matt?!"

He didn't say anything. He just turned and ran, his tears mixing with the rain.

SIXTY-SEVEN

MATT BURST through the gate.

By the time he heard it clang shut, he was much farther down the wooded path, almost back to the street. He reached the sidewalk and swung left, the torrential downpour battering his skin.

He didn't stop running until he was past Griffin Park.

When he reached the college's front circle, he stopped to catch his breath, his clothes already soaked. Lightning flashed above Radcliffe, and for a moment he pictured the Great Lord floating beside the tower, his orange eyes glowing down at him.

I'm sorry you wasted a pendant on me.

Matt scaled the steps two at time, nearly slipping about halfway up. He kept going, reaching the top of the hill, and walked the path to the large front doors. He continued straight through the lobby, not even glancing at the receptionist, and continued out into the West Quad.

Part of him thought he should stop and take it all in one last time. It used to be his favorite part of the college, bordered by both Anathema and Napier Towers, the stained-glass windows of Galbraith stretching high. Not that he could see much of anything in the storm.

Instead, he continued forward straight through the middle of the Quad, not caring if lightning struck him. It would make it easier that way, though he wouldn't get to write a letter. He owed certain people that much.

Matt entered Bowman from the door under Napier and walked down the hallway, his clothes dripping wet. The lights flickered as he approached his residence.

With a turn of the key, he was back in his room. He tore his jacket off and threw it on the floor, then dove onto the bed, sobbing into his pillow.

Of course it would never have lasted with Joan.

Nothing good at this college ever lasted. Radcliffe gave only to take away. First-year had been a giant false promise of more good times to come, the prologue of a happier story stitched onto one of pitiable misery.

He realized this had been its game all along, since the end of last year. He'd avoided the irreversible, holding out for better things to come, and one by one Radcliffe had torn them from his fingers. He knew what it wanted.

It wanted him to go through with it this time.

They didn't talk about it much these days. People made social media posts about mental health awareness to pay lip service to the fallen, then swiftly went along with their lives. WCU even had a policy where those who attempted it on school property could be given a forced leave of absence, just so the admin didn't have to clean up any messes on campus. When someone did go through with it, you weren't supposed to talk about it. They said it might inspire copycats, so it was better to just sweep the whole issue under the rug and act like it didn't exist.

He'd figured out the real reason a while ago. It was so people wouldn't have to think about those who'd done it, wonder if there was anything else they could've done to stop them, recall the signs they had missed. Victims of it were an inconvenience to their lives. Once they were forgotten, everyone could go on sitting in Galbraith with their friend groups, laughing, talking about how weird some people were, and circle-jerking each other into oblivion.

How long would they talk about him? Probably not more than a week, if that. Wouldn't want to put a damper on QuadFest.

Oh well. Live a nobody, die a nobody.

He pulled himself up off the bed and sat down at his desk. He took out a sheet of paper, grabbed a pen, and began writing. His hand shook, but it was far too illegible so he tore it up and started anew.

To whom it may concern…

Tears spouted from his eyes. God, it was pathetic to actually write those words. Who would be concerned for him? Not anyone at this college.

They all said one thing and then acted another way. At least Rufus had been honest in his hatred. At least Rufus had been truthful.

He knew he would fuck things up with Joan eventually. She would find someone else. He thought of how everyone had looked at her tonight, all the men and even some of the women. Rufus was right, anyone would be lucky to have her. He would be but a footnote in her life, part of her history. And now he'd free her from him.

He wrote to Joan first, apologizing for not telling her he had borderline. He thanked her for being the best part of his life this year. Then he thanked his friends and family by name for their support. He didn't blame them at all and wished them luck for the future. There was no point going forward for him. He could see the long road of desperation and despair and he wasn't strong enough to face it.

Finally, he thanked the Anathema.

They had been his only home here for the past three years, and though the relationship hadn't ended well, he didn't want the organization to take the rap for his death. The alumni had nothing to do with it and he didn't want to taint Anathema for people Initiated down the line, long after he was gone.

Then he signed the letter carefully, folded it up, and exhaled.

All the lights had been extinguished. The shadow drifted closer and he did not resist as it enveloped him.

It was *its* hand, not his, who pulled the paring knife out of his desk, *its* hand that held the blade beneath the lamp light. It was sharp and long, surprisingly dangerous for something used to cut fruit.

Suddenly doubt gripped him, and he set the knife down beside the letter. He didn't have to do it.

Not now, at least. Maybe he could wait.

Maybe things *would* get better.

They only get better to get worse. Happiness never lasts, the shadow reminded him. Its voice was no longer harsh and evil. It soothed him, caressed him, its talons gesturing to the knife.

You're right, he thought. And he reached for the blade—

As a pounding came from the door.

Sixty-Eight

"**M**ATT, PLEASE open up!"

Joan pulled back, panting and completely drenched. Roy stood beside her, wiping his face. She hadn't grabbed her jacket when they ran after him and now was starting to shiver.

She didn't care if she caught a chill. She had bigger problems. Much, much bigger problems.

She knew from her psych classes that one in every ten people affected by borderline personality disorder committed suicide. Their unstable moods left them especially susceptible to depressive episodes. She berated herself for not seeing the signs throughout the week, the way he seemed to snap out of sadness whenever spoken too, the way he'd looked so down and tired.

Joan banged on the door again, harder this time. "Please Matt, open up. I've got Roy here. I just want to make sure you're alright. What Rufus said was fucking awful and I'm going to make sure he gets kicked out for this, okay? He is fucking *finished*."

No answer.

"Matt, I don't care if you have a disorder. It's nothing to be ashamed of, lots of people have them."

Still nothing.

Oh God, what if they were too late? What if he'd already done it? If that was the case, she was going to kill Rufus Danvers.

She turned to Roy. "Get the receptionist. Tell her we have an emergency and that we need the door unlocked. Tell her a student might be attempting suicide."

"On it," he said, running back toward the door under Napier.

Joan knocked again, gentler this time. Tears streaked from her eyes. "Matt, please. Don't do this. If not to yourself, then don't do it to me. It'll finish me. You have no idea how much you mean to—"

She froze.

Sounds had filled the room, loud and clear. She pressed her head against the wood to make sure she was hearing things correctly. But no, there they were. Curtains blowing in the wind, brutal rain hammering the Quad, the growl of thunder.

It was almost as if...

She turned and sprinted for the Napier door, ran out into the storm, and dashed back along the row of windows to see—

There. The window to Matt's room stood open. Cautiously, she peered in.

No one was in there. There was no sign of him at all.

She looked back toward the front of the college, Roy just reaching the doors and darting inside. Where the hell would Matt have gone? They'd need to get Campus Police to search everywhere, to check every—

Of course.

There might still be time. She ran back under the Napier arch and bolted across the East Quad, trying to stay on the stone patterns; she might've slipped on the muddy grass.

By the time she reached the Althouse Gate, her body was on fire. Her lungs screamed; her muscles ached. She brushed wet hair out of her face and fumbled for her keys to unlock the damn thing. Then she looked up to see another student approaching, their R3 already out. The girl was meandering, taking her sweet time.

"Hurry up!" Joan screamed, startling her.

The student looked young, probably a first-year. She glanced from the medallion to the Imperator's angry face and nodded, frantically sliding the key into the lock. Joan tore the gate open before she could do anything else and rushed past her down the hill.

Before her, Bethune's Walk awaited. *Not this fucking place again.*

She didn't stop pumping her legs until the trees closed over her, providing little cover from the monsoon. The leafless branches shook in the wind, the forest quaking all around. She nearly slipped when she reached the T-junction, but managed to steady herself.

Joan tried to get her bearings, gasping for breath. Lightning cracked above, illuminating the bare trees and sopping ground. Water flowed past her boots into a storm drain; she stood amidst a shallow stream on the pavement.

Though it wasn't raining then, it brought her back to that night. She could still hear Rich's laughter, remembered how tears had rolled down her face as she ran away, just as they rolled down her cheeks now.

She nearly doubled over, everything that had happened this year hitting her at once. She squeezed her eyes shut.

Get moving, she told herself. *The worst disaster can still be prevented.*

Joan hurried along the trail as it wound toward the parking lot, barely hearing her own breathing over the storm. She slowed down once she got to the darkened path beside the *Picnic Area* sign. She could barely make out anything back there—the light of the lampposts didn't pierce that far—but knew there were two tables by the embankment.

"Matt!" she called out. There was no reply but thunder.

Terror gripped her as she made her way forward, afraid of what she would find.

SIXTY-NINE

H E SAT at the table closest to the water's edge, leaning his back against the wood and staring at the stream. The rain didn't dance along the brook's surface, it pounded it, brutalized it. Normally calm, the creek now frothed like a miniature rapid.

"Matt," he heard her say, and for a moment he didn't want to turn around.

"Don't worry," he said. "I already decided I'm not gonna do it."

He turned around and held up the knife. She flinched, startled, then he turned and hurled it into the creek. He imagined the shadow drowning with it, screeching and swirling in the stream until it disappeared beneath the surface forever.

Get the fuck out of my head.

Joan approached cautiously and took a seat beside him, looking more concerned than he'd ever seen her. In the next lightning flash, he saw she was crying, tears streaking mascara down her face, her hair a tangled, sopping mess. She didn't have her jacket on and looked cold in her corset top, hugging herself for warmth. If he had his jacket, he'd have offered it to her. Instead they were both soaked and freezing out here.

"Did you hear what I said at the door?" she shouted over the rain.

"No," he said, ashamed. "As soon as I heard knocking, I climbed out. I should've stayed."

She put a hand on his shoulder. "I would *not* leave you because you have a mental illness. My other major is psych, remember? I know a lot about disorders and…I've dealt with some mental health troubles myself." She swallowed. "But this isn't about me. I'm *really* sorry you have border-line. I don't know why someone tried to diagnose you during QuadFest—"

"I was anxious about mixed signals I was getting from an upper-year girl, Claudia. Her friend Vicky had been trying to help me, so I asked her for advice. She said my behavior reminded her of some of her friends with borderline. I said I didn't know what she was talking about and she tried to convince me I had it right there in the Quad. She got the DSM-5 up on her phone and read through the symptoms. I checked off nearly all of them. I went to a therapist in the summer and got an official diagnosis."

Joan shook her head. "I'm sure she was just trying to help, but it's awful that she did that. She's not a medical professional, she can't diagnose you. And in the middle of a *party*, for fuck's sake!" Matt lowered his head, not say-ing anything. She continued, "Looking back, I can see how you've struggled with it, certainly with relationships. But that's not who *I* see you as, okay?"

He hesitated. "I don't want you to feel like you have to stay *because* I have it. Rufus told me why he hates me." He explained the situation with Rufus' ex-girlfriend. "He feels everyone like me is incapable of being in a relationship."

"Well, *fuck* him and *fuck* anyone who thinks like him. And I don't feel like I have to stay with you because you have a disorder. I mean, how would you react if you found out *I* had borderline and nearly killed myself? Would *you* feel pressured to stay with me?"

"No, but I'd want to. I really, really care about you."

"It's the same with me, Matt."

"But…," he said, searching for the right words, trying to make sure she meant what he thought she meant, that he wasn't misreading things.

Joan gave a tearful laugh. *"I love you*, you dumbass." And she leaned over and kissed him hard on the lips. He pulled her closer, feeling the wet skin of her shoulders. She drew back, suddenly looking sadder. "I've known it for a while. A long while. I wanted to say it sooner, but I couldn't think of the right time. You've been so distant lately, and I understand why, but I didn't want you to think I was saying it just to cheer you up."

"I should've told you sooner, too," he said softly. "I've thought a lot about this, and I really do love you, Joan. I really, *really* do."

She kissed him again, then stayed right near him, their faces very close together.

"I was so worried, Matt. So, *so* worried… You have no idea how much you mean to me."

He hugged her tightly, unable to hold back the tears. "I'm sorry, I never wanted to hurt you. I just *hate* this college. I hate how it treats people like us. I hate how everyone here enables assholes like Logan and Rufus and Alyssa and Katy and we just sit there and take their shit and suck up to them. I didn't like my high school, but at least the people there never made me want to kill myself." He pulled back and looked at her. "But I'm *so* glad you're an Imperator now. You have no idea how happy I am one of us got it. You're going to do such an amazing job next year."

She kissed him, then said, "Becoming Imperator hasn't made everything better. I feel more accomplished. I feel more confident. But people still don't like me. They still think I'm weird."

He ran his hand down her side. "You dressed like this to intimidate them, didn't you?"

Joan swallowed. "I did. I kept hearing everyone talk about me as the 'hot crazy girl' in Anathema, so I figured I might as well put the good half of that to use."

"I love the look, but dress like this because you want to, not because you feel like you have to."

She pulled away and leaned forward, cupping her face in her hands. "It's been a long, awful year and I just want it to be over."

Matt gave a grim laugh. "I'm sure it's been better for you than for me. At least you got Imperator. I didn't even make Tetrad."

"No, but it's been awful in…other ways."

"Like what?" Though he figured he could guess.

She looked on the brink of tears again as she stared toward the stream. "Like how everyone thinks I murdered Rich Benson."

He put a hand on her back and rubbed it, looking around in the rain. "That's bullshit and you know it. Only an idiot would think you killed him, okay?" Matt sighed. "And who knows? Maybe it *was* all just coincidence. Maybe he *did* just slip and have an accident after you ran away. Maybe the Bard lied to Chet just to keep Serpentine motivated. Maybe Chet *did* get murdered by some random guy during a mugging. Maybe Randall had nothing to do with it. Maybe I had just read into everything too much." He sighed. "I almost always do…"

She was still gazing off at the creek. "No," she said, very softly. "You didn't read into everything too much. Rich didn't have an accident."

The branches shook violently in the wind, the rain continuing its ceaseless downpour.

Matt froze, every muscle in his body tensing. The way she'd said it put him on edge.

A long silence hung between them. When she didn't say anything, he asked, "How do you know that?"

Joan turned to him, an incredible sadness in her eyes.

"Because I'm the one who killed him."

PART IV

DISSOCIATION

SEVENTY

Now she'd really done it. By the look in his eyes, Joan knew there was no going back.

But of course there wasn't; it would've been idiotic to think otherwise. The threshold had been crossed and now he knew what she really was—and what she was capable of.

Matt hadn't glanced away since she uttered those words, but he stared at her differently, as if she were another person altogether. She pictured the gears turning in his head, trying to understand how he had missed it, recalling all the times she'd lied to him.

Though she'd been terrified he would find out eventually, part of Joan felt freed. At *last* someone else knew. The truth had festered inside her all year long, her successes only compounding the guilt. She realized both of them were with her now, him and her medallion, and they were not far from where the nightmare had begun.

Matt looked toward the creek, torn between sadness and horror. Above all, dismay reigned across his face. His eyes were like those of a beaten dog as they watched the water. She almost lay a hand on his shoulder, then decided against it. He needed time.

Quietly, she slipped out her phone and saw she had several missed calls from Roy. She sent him a text saying she was with Matt and that they were alright, though she doubted the last part. Even if they did somehow come out of this mess—and she didn't see how—this would be the point at which everything changed.

She put away her phone and stared off at the brook, shivering. "I…just want you to know," she managed. "I would *never* hurt you."

Matt turned. It looked like he wanted to believe her, he really did.

"Why?" he finally asked, tears rolling down his face.

She nodded and looked back to the water, clenching her teeth so they wouldn't chatter. "Do you want the long version or the short version?"

He hesitated. "I want to understand."

Joan nodded again, biting her lip. "I've always been violent. I don't know where it came from; it doesn't run in our family—at least that I know of. My sister, Maggie, was a little rough with me growing up, but before that I was always aggressive, always biting people—my parents, other kids in school. I'd gotten in trouble for it for years. I had to see a specialist to try and control it, after I attacked a girl in kindergarten. She'd stolen a toy I was playing with.

"Most of the time I was fine, but then it would come out—this side of me. Maggie used to joke I was like a werewolf in that way. She'd tease me about it, knew she could get away with bullying me. It was *always* easy to blame me. *'Joan started it,'*" she mocked her sister's voice. "And my mom and dad would always side with her. They didn't realize what a bitch she was to me until I was ten, until she gave me *this*."

Joan turned her head so he could see the scar and pointed. "We were getting our basement remodeled; she and I weren't supposed to go down there. It was a day the workers had off. Maggie chased me into the basement, and I tried to push past her to leave, but she shoved me and I fell. There was a nail sticking out of one of the support beams and…" She clenched her fists at the memory. "I was very lucky it didn't take out my eye, and that it was such a clean cut. But I've had this for over eleven years now."

It felt good to let it out, to tell it all to him. She continued, trying not to wonder what he was thinking. Matt sat in silence and listened.

"My parents had more sympathy for me after that, but the girls at school didn't. They called me *Scarface* and *Scar Girl* and *Scar Chick*. I saw a therapist throughout high school and managed to keep my anger in check. 'Every time you feel like you want to hit them,' she said, 'just breathe and remember you're in control.' And I thought I was, I really did—until Rita Parsons stole that story out of my bag."

Joan swallowed again. "When they told me she could've died falling down those steps, I felt awful. *Awful.* You have no idea what it's like to have everyone think you're a monster. I was lucky I even got into Cliffe, just because my mom was able to talk the admin down. She and my dad told me there could be no more mistakes—the next time I might actually kill someone." She laughed bitterly, a tear rolling down her cheek as she turned to him. "Funny, right?"

Matt said nothing. He looked very, very sad.

"I really liked Rich. At least, I thought I did. I'd never dated anyone in high school. Mine was girls-only, so you had to go beyond campus to find someone if you were straight. Guys hit on me when I went to parties, but I knew I was too weird for them to date me. They just wanted to sleep with me so they could tell their friends 'I fucked Scarface.'

"So I didn't want to lose my virginity to any of them. I figured I'd be more ready for it when I got to Cliffe anyway." She bit her lip. "I've always liked you Matt, even after all the things I heard people say about you in Galbraith. That you were quiet, that you were weird... I always hated them for saying those things, even though I'd never really talked to you. I knew they must be saying the same things about me when I wasn't around. I was really happy when we both got into Anathema, but I never summoned up the courage to hit on you."

He gave her a weak smile, but still said nothing.

Joan continued, "And the guys who did approach me back then seemed like douchebags. Chet and Blaine both made fun of my scar. I guess they thought it would make me want to prove myself to them." She scoffed and wiped away a tear. "Rich was the only one who seemed nice. I knew he hated Anathema and I really wanted to be in it, but dumb first-year-me thought there was something Shakespearean about that. The star-crossed lovers.

"Of course, he never loved me. Once he got to know me, it must've always been his plan to hump and dump me. I might be weird, but I was still a frosh to deflower. A sexual conquest, that's all I was. And so he asked me to coffee and we went and it seemed like it had gone really well. I thought we had great chemistry, laughing at everything the other said. And it seemed really fun. And so we went out a second time, this time for drinks, and that went well too. And when he walked me back to Cliffe, he asked me if I wanted to go to Fall Formal with him."

Joan swallowed. For all the rain around her, her throat was incredibly dry. "The dance itself was perfect. I don't think I'd ever felt happier. And he treated me very well. It was *my* idea to go back to his room. He kept asking me through the whole thing if I was alright, said we could stop at any time—just let him know. The sex wasn't great, but what first-times are?

"And then I texted him the next day, asking when we should hang out again." She took a deep breath. "And he...never responded. I kept wondering what I'd done wrong. It had to be me—it was always me. And then I started hearing what he'd gone around saying about me, how we'd never dated at all, that he'd just taken me to Formal and that I was desperate and delusional. You already know about the article, and how he tried to justify things after I got into Anathema, saying I was a fanatic and the embodiment of everything wrong with this college."

Joan's shoulders were incredibly tense and she tried to relax them, taking another deep breath. It didn't work. "It's funny how sadness turns to hatred. I'd never despised anyone so much other than my sister, and maybe Rita Parsons. When I went back to Toronto at Winter Break and in the summer, I was constantly worried about who else knew. Rich was from there too and for a big city, it feels like a small town. You constantly run into people you recognize on the street, at the grocery store, at a restaurant. Rich knew people who knew me, and I knew they'd be talking about me on the private school circuit. It's one of the reasons I came to WCU—a lot of the Toronto prep school kids just went to Ontario universities, and I wanted to get away from them.

"I didn't go for anybody else at Cliffe after that. When I visited my friend Danielle in Toronto during our November break in second-year, I hooked up with one of her friends. He was thousands of miles from here, so I knew it at least wouldn't get back to Cliffe. That year was a shitshow though. My econ courses really got the better of me and I had a tough time fitting in. I made a lot of bad decisions, most involving alcohol—like getting Demerit Points at Winter Formal."

Joan shook her head. "By the end of the year, I didn't care what jokes were made about my dating life. Vance Simmons was hitting on me at QuadFest and I figured...why not? I know people talked about how we slept together, but then again that's all people talk about here. That, and who's going to get what position."

"For what it's worth, last year was terrible for me too," Matt said. "I wish I'd been with you then, it probably would've been better for both of us."

Joan nodded. "I really wish you'd tried to flirt with me before Rich did, back in first-year. Before Anathema. Even if you were awkward, it would've at least shown you liked me."

He nodded. "We've both made mistakes."

Only mine have been much, much worse. "I don't know why he came after me that night. He must've seen me heading to Bethune's Walk in Anathema attire and just decided to follow me. But after he teased me, after I cursed him out and said everything I thought of him, after he laughed, he looked right at me and said, 'There's my depraved little wallflower.' "

She turned back to Matt. "And that's when I lost it. That's when I just *couldn't* hold it back anymore. I just...I just...pushed..." She mimicked the motion without realizing it, then dropped her hands to her sides. "My mom told me after I hit Rita that I didn't know my own strength. I'd done sports for years—field hockey, water polo, swimming—trying to channel that side of me into something productive. I've never been on a team here, but I've kept up in the gym. And so when I shoved him, it was a lot harder than I was expecting. I really didn't mean to...to knock him down the embankment..."

She chewed a nail, remembering the look in Benson's eyes as they'd turned from smug satisfaction to confusion to fear as he fell back. She remembered how he'd tumbled end over end, down into the creek.

"When I walked to the edge and saw him there, I couldn't believe it. He was lying in the water and his head was next to a large rock. I called his name out—several times—but he never answered. He didn't move. I don't know how long I stood there—it felt like an eternity—and then I just...I just didn't know what to do. So I ran, all the way back to Cliffe. I didn't even text Randall. I just cried until I felt tired and empty, then I brushed my teeth and went to bed like it was any other night. It felt surreal.

"And the next morning I slept in so much I nearly missed my disciplinary meeting with Crawley. I'd carved CRCC into the tunnels a couple weeks before and Réjean caught me. She was going to give me more Demerit Points, but decided against it due to 'recent tragic events.' Then Kylie announced the joint meeting that night and Val messaged me separately, but it was awful knowing what was going on already—and worse, knowing I had caused it. I was *horrified* when I heard the RCMP were involved. And when Randall said 'May God help you' at the meeting, I knew he thought I'd killed Rich. And he was right. They were all right."

She looked back at the stream again. The rain seemed to be easing up.

"I didn't know what I was going to do. I thought about turning myself in, but I didn't want my life to be over. I didn't want to let him and Radcliffe win. I knew I'd taint Anathema forever—probably finish it, really—and my family would be outcasts. My mother had convinced the admin to let a dangerous maniac into Cliffe, and then I went and killed another student. I could see Rita Parsons doing an interview, saying how she knew I was unhinged years ago, how everyone should've seen the signs sooner."

Joan shook her head. "And then, everything started to get better." She turned back to him. "I threw up on you, and it was the best thing that ever happened to me. I normally don't make the first move, but I knew if I didn't ask you to get coffee, I might've never had a chance. I thought the police would come for me any day. The week he died, they asked me some questions. I'm sure they thought it was me, but I got really lucky. There was never enough evidence, so they must've felt they couldn't prosecute me. Plus, without Randall telling them about our meeting, they had no way to prove I was even in Bethune's Walk that night. The case was too thin."

She sat up straighter. "After Chet, I really thought they would get me. But they didn't, and things *kept* getting better. I got what I'd always dreamed of. I had a position I'd desperately wanted and a relationship I was so happy in. But I've had to hide what I did this whole time. *That's* how Radcliffe got me. There's always a catch at this college." She sniffed. "It's been eating away at me and I…I can't take it anymore. I *had* to tell someone. You're the only one I trust."

Joan looked at him, her eyes pleading. "I'm *so sorry* I dragged you into this, Matt. It was really, really selfish of me. You deserve someone better."

He shook his head, tears streaking down his cheeks. "I don't want someone better."

She leaned over and hugged him, Matt embracing her tightly in return. By now, they were both thoroughly soaked. Warmth radiated within her chest and she recognized it as an early stage of hypothermia. They needed to head in soon.

"I'm so sorry," she said, closing her eyes. "I'm so, so sorry."

After a moment, he said, "Why did you have to kill Chet?"

She pulled away and looked him in the eyes. "That's the thing. *I didn't kill Chet.*"

He was baffled. "But…?"

"I *swear* I didn't kill him, Matt. I *thought* about it after seeing the video, but I didn't go near him. I was just as shocked as you were when I found out."

"Then…who the fuck—?"

"The Bard. He *knows* what I did. Chet told the truth at that meeting. *I* was the one he was talking about, the prominent Anathema member who killed Rich Benson. Somehow, the Bard figured it out. Rich was in Serpentine too; he must've sent the Bard a text or something as he was following me. The Bard even tried to scare me into admitting it. I think *he* slipped that note into my pocket at the Winslow party back in October. It just said 'Confess your sins, I am watching'—but nothing more than that. And I never got another one. I think the Bard was hoping I'd get arrested."

Matt put a hand to his forehead. "And when you didn't, he figured he'd off his Vizier and make the RCMP think *you* did it too… But why would he have needed to murder Chet in the first place? And if he knew you killed Rich, why not just tip off the police—or even go to them himself?"

"I don't know," she said. "I've been trying to figure it out all year. Whoever he is, the Bard cares more about bringing down Anathema than justice. All that stuff said about avenging Rich at the meeting was just bullshit. Serpentine was a bunch of tools to this guy. He's willing to kill his right-hand man and withhold information just so he can destroy Anathema—and get out unscathed."

"But *why?*"

She shrugged. "I really don't know. I guess he wants to conceal his identity because he's an Anathema member and doesn't want retribution for bringing us down."

"Could it be something you've done, maybe? A personal vendetta?"

Joan shrugged. "I don't know who or why. And what Pandora told you really worries me. If the Bard went underground this whole semester, he must be planning something big for the end of the year. I think he was just waiting to see if I became Imperator or not, but now that I have, it probably just works toward his endgame. It would look especially bad for us if it came out an Imperator killed somebody. There's only a week left of classes and I'm worried the Bard's gonna do something at QuadFest—if not sooner."

Matt sighed and stared off, lost in thought. Finally, he stood up and she did too, though he was still silent. "What are you thinking?" she asked.

After a moment, he turned and hugged her, squeezing her bare, wet shoulders. "I'm thinking we figure out who this son of a bitch is and pin *both* deaths on him." He kissed her hard on the lips, then pulled back and looked at her.

"You mean the world to me, Joan. This college has destroyed everything else I care about, but I won't let it take you from me too."

Seventy-One

She stood atop the embankment and he ran up it toward her. It seemed much steeper now, the branches curling far above. He finally reached her and she embraced him, wearing her cloak and medallion, the hood pulled up.

"I just want you to know…I would *never* hurt you."

Then she shoved him back and he fell, tumbling head over heels down and down and down and finally—

He hit the water and sank deep to the riverbed.

Frantically, he grasped for the bottom, found it, and pushed back toward the surface. Pale moonlight filtered down from above and he followed the glow until he could breathe again.

It was suddenly raining heavily—it had seemed so calm but a moment ago—and it was hard to stay afloat. He struggled, kicked, and splashed, searching for the shore. Tall trees reached above him in the storm, but he couldn't see the embankment. It was too dark all around.

Then he spotted a figure in a boat, floating toward him.

It was Randall, and he looked very sad and pale.

"Please!" Matt called, reaching toward him.

Randall shook his head. "I'm sorry I couldn't help you. Logan's better at giving orders."

"I was never Tetrad!" he managed to get out, his mouth barely remaining at surface level. "I never *got* to give orders. You never gave me that chance!"

Randall shook his head. "People just like him more than you. But here, you can hold this. It's still a really big honor."

He pulled the poster from his Second Sermon out beside him and shoved it toward Matt. Its weight slammed into him, driving him under the water.

The poster was impossibly heavy and he sank deeper and deeper, bubbles rising to the ever-distant surface. Then he plowed into the bottom. The painting pinned him down, crushing his ribs. He screamed, more bubbles exploding from his mouth as he tried to dislodge it.

A shape emerged farther down the riverbed, a corpse ambling toward him. It was Rich Benson, blood trailing from the side of his head, seeping out into the river.

"I was right about all of you." He spoke slowly and his voice was distorted by the water. "You're not just bullies, you're mentally deranged *wrecks*. One of your leaders killed me. She's depraved. She's a fanatic. She's a *murderer*. She has to be stopped." His skin was gray, his eyes dead and lidless. He stretched his arms toward Matt as he drew closer. "You *all* have to be stopped."

Matt pushed harder, his lungs burning. Almost free...

Benson was just a few steps away, starting to bend down, a horrible grin on his face—

There! Squirming free, he kicked upward, the corpse swiping at his feet as he ascended.

This time when Matt surfaced, it was no longer raining. The sky was red and foreboding, as if in warning. The trees were barren, a cold wind sweeping through Bethune's Walk as he climbed out of the creek.

He shivered, looking around. "Joan?! Randall?!"

No reply came.

Alone, Matt trudged his way back to the path and found his way out of the forest. Up ahead, Radcliffe's windows glowed in the scarlet twilight. He headed up to the Althouse Gate, which swung open of its own accord, and by the time he entered the wind tunnel he realized he was dry.

The East Quad stood empty, but a booming voice came from beyond. It grew louder and louder as he walked under the Napier archway, emerging into the other courtyard.

Clouds swirled above Anathema Tower, tinted red by the fading horizon. And there, set on a platform up by the front doors, was a stake with someone gagged and bound to it.

Joan.

Logan, Rufus, and Alyssa stood beside her. Through the Quad were masses of Radcliffe students, gaping black sockets where their eyes should've been.

Matt felt very light as he drifted toward the platform, as if pulled by a supernatural force.

Logan held up a whimpering terrier with an Air Force cap and barked, "If I wanted a pussy, I would've gotten a *cat*."

He threw the dog away. It hit the ground with a yelp, then scurried off to where Doug sat reading in a plush chair, just outside Galbraith's entrance. The former Magister reached down to pet the animal, then resumed reading as it curled up at his feet.

"Ah, Matthew. So kind of you to join us."

He turned toward the platform and saw Logan beckoning him with a smile, dressed in his Imperator attire. Hesitantly, Matt made his way over and climbed the steps.

"How are you, dude?"

"I'm…I've…" He looked back at the eyeless masses, his unease growing.

"Don't worry about them," Logan said, directing his attention back to him. "They don't matter." The way he said it was somehow soothing. Logan put a hand on his shoulder. "Hey, I've just got a small favor to ask you. Just part of your devotion."

"Yes," Matt nodded, feeling better. "Anything."

The Imperator held up a match. "I need you…to burn your girlfriend." He gestured to where Joan struggled against the wooden stake, also in her cloak, mask, and medallion.

Suddenly Matt snapped out of it. "Have you lost your fucking mind?"

Rufus stepped closer. "How *dare* you speak to an Imperator like that?!" he hissed.

Logan silenced him with a wave, but kept his eyes on Matt. "She's a killer. She's a liability. Worse than that, she'll probably outshine me with her Sermons. And I can't have that." He laid a hand on Matt's shoulder again. "I told you—I *have* to say the things I need to say. I've waited so long to say them, Matt. I don't even know what they are yet, but I've been told for years I would get to say them. And do you know why?"

Matt gave a silent nod.

"Because I am divine. Not by *Him*." He pointed up to Anathema Tower and gave it a dismissive wave. "But by *all* of this." He swept his hand around the Quad. "Radcliffe chose me, not the Great Lord Anathema. Radcliffe likes to hurt people, and I don't mind if I do… We're made for each other, this college and I. So…" He held up the match again. "What do you say?"

Matt looked from him, to the sneering faces of Rufus and Alyssa, to Joan's eyes pleading behind her silver mask.

He turned back to Logan and said, "Fuck you all."

Rufus stepped closer again. "We might as well get rid of him. He wasn't going to be much use to us, anyway. He's too sad and bitter now."

Logan put a hand to his head and sighed. "You're right." He looked back up at Matt. "I'm sorry, but I have to do this." He turned to Rufus and Alyssa. "Bind him."

They were suddenly at his sides, grabbing his arms and hauling him to the stake. He struggled, but it was no use. They pulled his arms around Joan and tied him to her side. He leaned closer and kissed her cheek. "I'm sorry I couldn't stop them."

He smelled gasoline and looked down to realize it had been poured all around them.

Logan struck the match and held it out, Rufus and Alyssa at his sides. "I just want you to know, I really do respect you, and I hope you're just as dedicated next year as you were this year."

Then he dropped it.

Flame roared around them, the heat licking closer and closer.

Matt opened his mouth to scream—

And lurched awake in bed, gasping for breath.

He looked around. Daylight streamed through the gap in his curtains, though even from here he could tell it was pale and gray. Another cloudy day.

Joan stirred beside him, then nuzzled closer, still asleep. Their wet clothes sat on his floor in sopping piles, but they were both warm and naked beneath the sheets. They'd both exhausted themselves before drifting off to sleep last night.

The dream was still seared into his memory. He played it several times again in his head, his anger rising. How had it taken him so long to see Radcliffe for what it really was? Why had he put so much time and energy into trying to impress these people? He'd let them get to him so much it nearly killed him, but that was his mistake, one he wouldn't make again.

Lying there in bed, Matt knew only one thing mattered now.

He stroked Joan's bare arm and nestled in closer to her. He knew that by keeping her secret, he became an accessory to a crime. He believed she hadn't meant to kill Benson, but it was still manslaughter at the least. Joan was guilty, and only the two of them knew the truth.

No, that wasn't right. The Bard knew. Somehow he knew, and was ready to use it to bring down an organization he despised. The bodies were irrelevant to him. Whoever he was, he was a cold-hearted opportunist, willing to bend other people's lives to achieve what he wanted. But if this bastard won, then so would Radcliffe. And no matter what came next, they couldn't let that happen.

Seventy-Two

"I don't know what to tell you, Mark."

Mustard sighed and looked out his office window. Beyond the campus, mountains pierced the gray clouds. It was a bleak Saturday, but then again, April always brought the rains.

"I'm getting worried that Benson twerp tipped them off last fall," Wood said in his earpiece. "They're asking too many questions and I'm starting to get worried."

The Provost hesitated. "I'm going to ask you this again, Mark. You had nothing to do with his little accident, right?"

"For fuck's sake, no I did *not*. I almost thought *you* did, but you never really had the guts for that kinda stuff." Wood chuckled grimly. "I will admit that was fortunate for us, once you found out he was snooping around." A pause. "What would you have done if he hadn't...you know...?"

"I don't know. Probably would've tried to pay him off. I'd rather not think about it." He glanced at his watch. "I've got a meeting in a couple minutes. I need to get going."

"Alright. But we should discuss this in person soon. We need to ensure our tracks stay covered. If they can't trace the money, they don't have shit on us."

Mustard nodded, suddenly realizing how tense he was. "Right. Talk to you later." He hung up, then sat back at his desk. A few minutes later a knock came from the door, and he said, "Come in."

Crawley entered and he put on a pleasant face as she sat down.

496

"Donna, how are you today?"

"I'm fine." She appeared troubled.

He frowned. "Is something bothering you?"

"Well…it's just that there've been a lot of kerosene orders lately. I heard about them from the Maintenance staff first, but when I've looked into it myself, I can't find where they're coming from—or why. Winter is over."

Mustard raised an eyebrow. "Kerosene?"

"Yes, for the boiler room, below Galbraith. But we've had a *lot* come in recently, and whenever I ask people in Maintenance, no one can tell me who's ordered it. I checked with the Bursar and he said it's all been billed to their department, so clearly someone's lying."

"That's…very strange." He scratched his chin. "But it's all under lock and key, right? No one can get to it?"

"It's been stored in the boiler room and in some other Maintenance closets, but only admin and Maintenance workers have access to those. At least, no one else should."

"Alright… Well, at the very least we'll be stocked up for the next winter."

"More like the next several."

"As long as Réjean doesn't take a smoke break down there, we should be fine." Crawley still looked concerned. Mustard sighed again. The last thing he needed was another worry—and administrators digging around in the college's finances.

"Anyway," he continued, "QuadFest is this coming Friday."

Crawley brightened. "Yes. I've always thought it's a nice way to unwind at the end of the year. I think your idea to do things differently this time is a good one. I'm particularly excited for the bouncy castle." She gave a little laugh. "Eric and I have been talking about testing it ourselves."

Mustard did his best not to roll his eyes. "Yes." He put on a plastic smile. "It'll be great fun. A fitting end to the year." He spun his chair around and looked out the window again. "I'm excited for the next one. This was just phase one of my modernization plan. In the fall, I want to ban alcohol from all Radcliffe events. I want to turn DebSoc into a real debating society again. And…" He stared off at the mountains.

"I'd like to, if possible, end the Anathema once and for all."

SEVENTY-THREE

ONCE HE'D gotten over the initial shock, once he'd taken a step back to see how things fit together, Matt realized that what Joan had told him was a major breakthrough.

He'd spent a lot of time wondering why the Bard needed to kill Rich Benson, when they had simply never murdered him in the first place. He'd tried to figure out why and how the Serpentine leader would've been in Bethune's Walk that night, when he most likely never had. If Benson had texted him saying he was following Joan to some kind of late-night rendezvous and he turned up dead, it would've been easy for the Bard to deduce his killer's identity.

Matt couldn't work on assignments that Saturday and Joan couldn't find the will to concentrate either, so instead they spent much of the day in his room mapping out suspects on sheets of paper and drawing lines between circles representing different people and organizations. They used a lot of tape and started putting it together on the corkboard behind his desk. As their work progressed, it started to look like a conspiracy theorist's basement wall.

They only knew a few things about the Bard: he had prior knowledge of Serpentine and was therefore likely an Anathema member. He had an extreme personal vendetta against the organization, but most likely didn't show it in public. Whoever he was, he was cunning and devious, keeping his hurt and anger hidden from the college, a master manipulator.

He was also paranoid, most likely killing Chet so no one would learn his identity. Matt figured that Chet's member-naming video and Joan's public anger over it gave the Bard an opportunity to murder him and make it look like she'd committed both killings—a convenient way to tie up a loose end.

By the end of the day, they had a few names high on their list, though they seemed improbable at first glance.

The next day they really had to do work and went to Mackenzie to take their mind off of everything. Matt found that focusing on his assignments helped ease his nerves. It was nice to avoid the Galbraith gossip, the judgmental stares of Social Cliffe following them wherever they went, the Imperator and her emotional wreck boyfriend. And it was good to avoid even the people he liked, at least for the next few days. He just wanted to spend time with Joan and to think.

And then he remembered his prior engagement.

He was supposed to get drinks with Tom Turland that very evening.

◆

Matt arrived outside the Royal Pub just before 8 p.m. He'd wanted to delay it because of his mood, but Joan felt it would be good for him to go.

Turland was leaning by the entrance, reading something on his phone. He looked up as Matt approached and smiled.

"Hey, feeling better?"

"Uh…sort of," he said, scratching the back of his neck.

Turland put a hand on his shoulder and led him through the entrance. "That's what alcohol is for. Come on, let's get some fucking drinks."

The waitress got them a table by the main floor's rear window, looking out through the parkette at the town's eponymous river. The sun had just disappeared behind the mountains, but orange still ruled the horizon beyond them. There were far fewer clouds than yesterday.

Both Matt and Turland stared off at the sky upon sitting down. "That's one thing I'll miss about this school. The scenery is breathtaking." The former Imperator sighed and looked over the drink menu.

"Yeah," Matt said, still gazing out the window.

The waitress came around with a pitcher of water and filled up their glasses. "Can I get you something to drink?"

Matt said, "I'll take a double rye and ginger, please."

Turland scratched the scruff on his chin and said, "I'll go for one of those too." Once the waitress jotted down their orders and moved off, he said, "I'm sorry you didn't make Tetrad. I always figured you would. No clue why Logan would pick Rufus anyway."

Matt told him about the conversation with Logan on Thursday and his justification for his picks.

Turland shook his head, disappointed. "That's bullshit. I've never heard of multi-year Magisters being a thing. Doug happened to do it unofficially for a couple years, but that was it. At least Tanner's a good choice, but he still could've gotten it fourth-year. I guess he'll probably be Magister twice now… I've always been hesitant about people staying on Tetrad for more than one year. Anathema needs new ideas to keep it fresh." He sighed. "I shouldn't be surprised something like this happened. There's a centripetal force at this college and not even Jack Randall could escape it."

"What…kind of force?" he asked, though he already had an idea. He just didn't expect Turland to say these words.

"Nepotism, favoritism—whatever you want to call it. Anathema was created to criticize it, to tear down the egotistical, incestuous fuckshow that reigns year to year, and yet it *always* ends up getting corrupted by it. It doesn't matter how hard you try to stop it. Even as Imperator and DebSoc President I've been powerless to wound it. I thought at least Anathema was in good hands, but…"

He sighed. "People like Logan come through every few years, no matter how carefully Imperators like Madler and I make our picks. It's Radcliffe, finding its way back into the one organization that opposes it, giving us enough rope to hang ourselves so we'll take things too far and spend another decade trying to regain the strides we made." He looked past the mountains, his expression saddening. "Even with all the power I had here, nothing I did ultimately made a difference."

Matt shook his head. "But…I thought you loved this place…"

Turland turned back to him, looking at Matt as if he'd just said the strangest thing he'd ever heard. "You thought I *loved* Radcliffe? You thought *that?*" He burst out laughing. "I hated it!"

Matt was stunned into silence.

Turland took a deep breath and fiddled with his cutlery. "I've told very few people this and sometimes, when something's been bottled up for too long, it just has to come out. I don't figure you care much for the college anymore…"

He swallowed. "Not particularly."

Turland shook his head. "The way I see it, you've been in an…abusive relationship, let's say, with Radcliffe for the past few years. Correct me if I'm wrong, but it seems like it started out very well. It was romantic, it was wonderful—for first-year. Then it started dangling things in front of you—a Tetrad spot, being an exec member on DebSoc, social validation—and one by one it snatched them away before you could grab them, kicked you while you were down, and laughed in your face. It railed you for being socially awkward and for not having a girlfriend. Then it kept telling you things were going to be alright, that things were going to get better. And then it beat you down again and told you the same thing."

Matt nodded slowly. "That's…that's exactly what it feels like."

Turland sighed. "You're not the only one it's done this to. Radcliffe has a strange way of picking winners and losers. Why does someone like Rufus leave Anathema, badmouth it, come back and say if he doesn't get Tetrad he's leaving, and then get it anyway—when after three years of showing up to every meeting and defending it at each turn, you get *nothing*? Why does Logan call Randall a pussy and doubt his every move, making fun of him for caring about safety and our public perception, only to have Randall, a self-described reformist, grant him unchecked power anyway?"

"It took me a while to realize it, but there are different rules for different people at this college. It doesn't seem to really be based on race or class—at least, not anymore. It's more intrinsic than that these days. It all comes down to friend groups. Rufus isn't too popular, but he has powerful friends like Alyssa and Katy. You don't have to be super popular or well-liked to succeed here. You just need to be in a clique."

Matt nodded. "Social Cliffe."

Turland gave a dismissive wave. "Social Cliffe doesn't exist. At least, not the way most people think it does. There's no singular body of like-minded people governing Radcliffe, passing their batons down from one year to the next. No, it seems there's…an *oligopoly* of cliques here. Several different powerful friend groups jockeying for positions against each other, and once one person in one clique gets power, they give all their other friends appointed exec spots. I was going to secure you a committee on DebSoc, but Alyssa quickly gave them to her friends first. And to Carl Dunlap, but just because she thought that would be funny. And he was an Officer. He had influence."

He sighed. "You see? That's the real Social Cliffe. All that matters is that at least one clique member is popular enough to win a position, or sucks up to an Imperator enough to be named their successor. There are so many appointed spots at Radcliffe, it's actually kind of ridiculous.

"I didn't think much about it in first- or second-year. Once I became Imperator, I just tried to use my power to bring in people I thought would be good. Jack had been overlooked for Initiation in his first-year, so I tapped him knowing he'd be a value-add. Same thing with you, though I didn't know you that well at the time. Patrick believed in you and showed me some jokes you had written. And you'd done well at the Beckonings. But most first-year Initiates don't send in jokes. We just induct them because we think they're cool or popular, or they say funny things. Or maybe they seem like future Officer material. Some members didn't think we should Initiate you, as a first-year at least, because none of them knew you. But I liked your jokes, and I liked that you'd taken the time to write them. And you struck me at the Beckonings like someone who cared about traditions, like someone who'd be dedicated."

The drinks arrived and Turland took a sip of his. "Dedication is something everyone here *says* they appreciate, but that they really take for granted. I've seen it in every major club at this college: People working hard because they care and those in power patting them on the back and treating them like footrests. The traditions, the clubs, the college—they're all kept alive by dedication. And yet I've watched dedicated, hard-working people like yourself get screwed out of positions they objectively deserved just so it could go to someone who was better friends with someone else. With Jennifer Horvat and Dom Lawrence, I was at least able to give them spots on my Model UN exec because I knew they'd be good for it. But you...you've experienced the dark side of nepotism."

He shook his head sadly. "What Logan told you about being just as dedicated next year is complete bullshit. You need to pull back your involvement. Pull it way, way back."

Matt stammered, "But...I..."

"I know it hurts. I know how much you love Anathema. And I'm telling you as an Imperator, that up in his tower the Great Lord will take no offense if you miss meetings from now on. Seriously, don't even go to them unless you have *nothing* else that evening.

"I know it doesn't feel like it when you're in the Cliffe bubble, but there *is* a world beyond this college—and a lot of it is a much better place. Even the other colleges are less cliquey and nepotistic. They assume Anathema is what corrupts Radcliffe, when really, it's the other way around. But despite my efforts—and Madler's, and Jack's—it appears like our branch has been soiled again. Joan is the only thing keeping my faith in Anathema alive. That, and Tanner is Logan's Magister. He'll be good. Geoff is alright, I guess."

Turland took another sip. "That's another thing, Matt. You've got a girlfriend. Go beyond Cliffe and join other WCU clubs, explore the Bow Valley, get out into Canmore proper more often. We're surrounded by so much and yet we're always holed up in our dreary stone fortress, always going to the same bars and doing the same things again and again. For fourth-year, I'd even recommend you move off-res. Go and find better times for yourself. Stop waiting for Radcliffe to give you what you deserve."

Matt was stunned. Slowly, he nodded. "Thank you. That really means a lot coming from you."

Turland raised a hand. "I'll be working in Calgary next year, but I love nature hikes. We should get you and Joan and Caitlyn and our other friends together and explore the mountains next fall. We should organize a ski trip during your Reading Week. We should do something beyond this place." He sighed. "Don't live at the mercy of Radcliffe."

Matt nodded again and took a sip. "I hope Joan and I will able to do that next year."

Turland raised an eyebrow. "Why wouldn't you be?"

He realized that had slipped out. "Oh…well…I hope Joan and I are still together then. We're going through…a bit of a rough patch." *If you could call it that.*

Turland looked down. "I'm sorry to hear that. I hope it works out. She and I had a class together this semester and I've really enjoyed getting to know her. It seems like she cares about you a lot."

"Did she talk about me?"

Turland chuckled. "Oh yeah, all the time. And always very positively. After she found out she was the next female Imperator, I was the only one she told. She asked me if Jack had picked his successor yet and I told her I was staying out of that and letting him have his choice. But I told her that I knew he was torn between you and Logan, and that I felt you were more creative and that hopefully Jack would see that."

Turland shrugged. "That's all I'm gonna say about Jack's choice. I love him and respect him, but part of friendship is being able to recognize that friends are still just people. And people make mistakes." He took another sip of his drink, then set it down. "But Joan *really* wanted it to be you. She broke down and told Randall she'd gotten it the Wednesday before the Sermon, but he just texted her back saying he was keeping 116's identity a secret until the big night."

"She didn't know it wasn't me until the Scrapbook Break."

Turland nodded. "Yeah, she told me this week in our class. She felt really bad about not telling you earlier, thought it would be a happy surprise. Even I only found out it was Logan the day before. But she truly cares about you, Matt. And she seems like a really great girl."

He looked down at his drink. "She is." And despite everything he'd learned about her, he still felt it was true.

"I hope everything works out between both of you."

Dusk was receding beyond the mountains. Matt stared at the darkening sky. "I hope so too."

◆

When he got back, he went straight to Lacy and knocked on her door. For a moment there was no reply, and he wondered if she was studying at Mackenzie.

"Joan? You there?"

The door swung open and she stood staring at him, her eyes watering and her face ashen. "What's wrong?" he asked.

Without a word, she led him inside and shut the door behind him, then sat on the bed and rubbed her arm, shivering even though the room wasn't cold.

"On the desk. Someone slipped it under my door while I was at dinner."

Matt turned and saw an envelope addressed to *Her 94th Imperator* in calligraphy. Joan had already torn the seal, so he slid the letter out again and took a look for himself. It was typed and unsigned, just a few lines of text:

You think you've gotten away with it, don't you? The High Court of the Serpentine begs to differ.

The reckoning is still to come.

SEVENTY-FOUR

THE CROW stared at him, unblinking.

Randall stared back, strangely transfixed by its gaze. It continued watching him from up on the branch, then took flight and soared away, disappearing beyond Anathema Tower into the gray sky. Randall shook his head, snapping out of the daze.

He'd gotten barely two hours of sleep last night because of an essay, one of four due this week, but it was no matter. His Officer duties were almost at an end and come Friday, just three days away, his classes would be finished. He'd get wasted and DJ for QuadFest, then complete three exams over the next two weeks and undergrad would finally release him.

Randall breathed in and out, then told himself, *Just hang in there.*

He tried to think about something positive, like QuadFest. He'd already even decided most of the song list. Some had complained about all the eighties music at Winter Formal, but he was going to play New Order's "Bizarre Love Triangle" and people were going to fucking like it.

"Hey, Jack."

Randall spun around. A fellow Officer made his way toward him. "Hey Patrick, how've you been?"

"Ah, just trying to get through my final assignments. I hate how every class has things due the last week. It happens every year."

Randall shrugged. "At least it's almost over."

Patrick laughed. "Yeah." He glanced around the West Quad. "What a trip it's been. This year especially."

You have no idea. "You decided where you're going next year?"

"Yeah, Allard School of Law, UBC. How about you?"

Randall shrugged. "I'm doing the Air Force full-time for a bit, then I'll apply to some grad programs out east." He paused. "UBC, huh? Guess Mustard's recommendation letter really came in handy."

Patrick stiffened. "As I'm sure yours will, once you apply." He narrowed his eyes. "You know, I never got why you hit me so much this year."

He laughed. "You're joking, right?"

"No, I'm really not. I defended you to the other Officers all year and yet you painted me as a sell-out, then both disintegrated me and decapitated me in your Sermons." He frowned. "It was…weird. Karen doesn't get your obsession with me."

"Obsession?" Randall scoffed. "You're delusional if you think I'm obsessed with you. I offered you not one, but *two* Tetrad spots and you *still* turned down my offer to let you return, then bragged about it anyway. You went off telling everyone how *immoral* I was for being both an Officer and an Imperator, trying to make it sound like Anathema was beneath you once you won your election."

"I know. But that was last March and April. I've spent the last year trying to make up for it, and you *still* have a grudge against me. Meanwhile, Logan Brewster treats you like shit and you seemed to forgive him."

Randall shook his head. "I'm tired of people criticizing me for picking Logan."

"And I'm tired of defending your bad decisions."

"Well, maybe if you cared about Anathema so much *you* should've been Imperator."

"Yeah," Patrick said, glancing off at Galbraith's stained-glass windows. "Maybe I should've."

"Too bad you were off padding your resume and playing the white knight."

Patrick glared at him. "Too bad you were too busy sucking up to your younger, piece-of-shit Legatus who made you feel bad because he called you a vagina." He mock-cried with his hands.

Randall shook his head. "You have no idea why I picked Logan."

"You can convince yourself whatever you want. But I can see through it." Patrick leaned closer. "And so can *He*." He pointed up to the tower.

Randall turned around and for a moment it almost felt as if a presence was watching him behind the belfry's windows. When he looked back, he saw Patrick was almost at the door to Galbraith.

"Wait."

Patrick froze, his back still to Randall.

He sighed. "I'm sorry for going after you so much this year. I had a lot of built up stress and frustrations and I took them out on you because I figured you could take the jokes. This year I've—" He put a hand to his head. "It doesn't matter. What's done is done. But I'm sorry for railing you so much. I should've cut it back a bit."

Patrick turned around and nodded slowly. "Thank you, Jack. I've done a lot more thinking about it recently, and…I've said some really conceited shit over the years. I deserved a lot of the flak you gave me."

Then he continued on inside, leaving Randall alone in the Quad.

He sighed and strolled across the courtyard. He tried not to think of how hollow Matt had looked at the End-of-Year Social, how Joan gave him the cold shoulder these days, how only Turland and Gemma still comforted him, how the other Officers beside Patrick and Veronica looked at him with shame.

The thoughts crushed down on him and all he wanted was to sit down for a moment. He walked over to the bench in front of Lacy and took a seat.

It didn't do much for him. He was too exhausted.

He glanced left and right, making sure no one else was around. Then he gently tipped over and lay on the wood. *Just for a moment,* he told himself.

But it was so nice to lie down. His problems seemed so very far away…

He closed his eyes, intending to open them again at any second—but before he knew it, Jack Randall was sound asleep.

SEVENTY-FIVE

J OAN BLINKED multiple times, just to be sure she wasn't seeing things.
Before her stood a giant inflatable bouncy castle, though it had eyes
and a goofy grin on its central tower. Maintenance workers milled about,
strapping it down and inspecting it while Crawley and Porter supervised
nearby.

She clutched her Microeconomics textbook to her chest, a backpack
slung over one shoulder. Despite everything that had happened this year,
this sight now seemed the most surreal. She'd been walking back to Lacy
when she glimpsed it through the Napier archway, and headed into the East
Quad to take a closer look.

Val walked up beside her and they stared at it together. "This college is
a fucking fever dream."

Joan felt as if she were about to deflate. "Tell me about it," she said
softly.

Val put a hand on her arm. "Hey, are you alright? I haven't talked to you
since the End-of-Year Social. You and Matt left early; was everything…?"

She hesitated. "Yeah, yeah, it's all okay."

"You don't look okay. What's up?"

I wish I could tell you, I really do. Actually no, she realized, that would
just make things worse. She'd already burdened Matt with her secrets, there
was no reason to drag Val into this mess either.

"Nothing. Just end of the year stress…you know…"

Val nodded. "Well, if you want to talk to me about anything, just let me know." She smiled. "You might be an Imperator, but you're still my friend first."

Joan smiled back. "Thank you."

"Take care." Val headed back under the archway.

She sighed and looked back to the inflatable castle. It was Thursday, the day before QuadFest, and she and Matt had made little progress in deducing the Bard's identity. They'd heard no word from him since the message slipped under her door. There was no point going to the RCMP, of course. She'd have to tell them she was guilty.

However, she didn't know what the Bard was waiting for. QuadFest, maybe? Or would he strike before that?

Regardless, the reckoning would be soon.

Crawley headed past her for the Napier arch. Their eyes met and the Dean froze. "Oh, hi Joan." There was a touch of trepidation in her voice. "How have you been?"

"I've been…well," Joan managed. "It's been a long year."

Crawley sighed and wiped her forehead. "That, it has." She laughed awkwardly, clearly wanting to hurry along. Of course, the police would've talked to her and Mustard. And her high school suspension had to be on file somewhere. It would've been discussed. Crawley knew what she'd done to Rita Parsons; Joan saw it in her eyes.

"What do you think of the castle?"

Joan realized she'd been lost in her thoughts. "Oh. It's great. I love it."

Crawley beamed. "I'm glad. I knew the students would. Well, best of luck on your assignments and exams."

"Thank you."

Crawley hurried off under the arch, just a bit too quickly. Joan rubbed her arm and watched her go, wondering if the Dean thought she was guilty despite the RCMP's official statements. Then again, everyone here thought she was guilty. She could feel it.

And they were right. They'd always been right about her. She *was* guilty.

Joan exhaled and looked skyward. It was after six o'clock, but the sun wouldn't set for over two hours. Clear blue stretched above her and she knew from the forecast that rain wasn't expected until the weekend. It should be pleasant weather for the party tomorrow. QuadFest could still be fun—so long as the Bard didn't intervene.

Sadness dragged her spirits down, an emptiness growing inside her.

Glancing at her watch, she remembered that Matt should've been back from class for hours now and headed to Bowman to see if he was around.

She knocked on his door and he appeared a moment later. He smiled at first, but his mood darkened once he saw her expression. "Hey, come in."

He took her textbook and set it on his desk, then joined her as she sat on the bed. She leaned her head against his shoulder and sighed, staring at the papers taped together on the wall. They'd started calling it the "murder board."

"How was your day?" he asked, rubbing her shoulder.

"I just finished my last essay; I turn it in tomorrow morning. Now I don't have anything until my first exam next Thursday, then there's just two more the following week. I'm done on the 25th."

"Nice. I just handed in my last assignment this afternoon. And that was my last class for the year. All my exams are on the final week." He kissed her forehead.

They were both trying to avoid the topic staring at them from across the room. Her eyes swept the familiar names.

"It's weird seeing Doug on there. I just can't picture him doing it."

He looked toward the murder board. "I don't really think it's him, but...he knows the History like the back of his hand, so he'd be the most primed to resurrect Serpentine. Plus, he could've deliberately left his door unlocked for them to steal the skull."

"I guess." She exhaled, staring at the names and the connections. "I still don't see what Anathema's done to any of these people to drive them to murder, let alone to orchestrate Serpentine in the first place."

"That's the key to all of this: the motive. It must be something most members don't know about, but that hurt one of these guys *badly*. Something they've kept hidden. Or maybe it's something staring us in the face and we're just not thinking it would be enough of a motive. That's the thing. People kill people for stupid reasons all the time. It's all about whether or not it's a strong enough motive for the murderer."

"I killed Rich for a stupid reason," she said softly. "He called me a depraved wallflower."

Matt remained silent. He stared ahead for a long time, looking unwell, and she wondered if he would say anything at all. Then, finally, he spoke. "He did a lot more than that, Joan."

She swallowed. "Still...it was very stupid of me." Exhaustion crept over her.

He kissed her. "There's still a way out of this."

Is there? she almost said, but then her stomach growled loudly and she realized she hadn't eaten since breakfast.

"Let's get dinner. We can talk about this more later."

She nodded, then they stood up and headed for the door. They'd spent each night since Friday together, alternating the rooms. Tonight, they'd probably end up in Joan's, so she brought her backpack along with her.

However, she didn't think about tonight as they headed down the Bowman corridor. She thought beyond this evening, beyond tomorrow. Even if they did stop this maniac, she wondered if the Bard would've won anyway. Joan would always know what she'd done and Anathema would forever harbor the truth that one of its Imperators was a murderer. Everything ever said and done in the nineties was child's play compared to the mistake she'd made, and all it had taken was one push.

Maybe, she wondered, it would be better if the Bard killed her. Matt wouldn't have to go on hiding her secret, keeping the truth of what she was from the world. She didn't know what was coming, but something else horrified her more.

After all she'd done, after all the people she'd hurt, she wasn't sure how much longer she could live with herself.

SEVENTY-SIX

His eyes flashed open and he sat up at once. Joan lay beside him, adrift in a deep sleep. The room was dark and silent.

Matt glanced over her to the clock on the nightstand. It was 2:13 a.m.

This couldn't wait until daylight. Careful not to wake her, he climbed out of bed by the footboard and got dressed. Matt grabbed his phone and her room keys so he could get back in, then headed out the door and closed it quietly behind him, blinking his eyes in the light of the hallway.

Soon he was out Lacy's eastern door and walking across the Quad, his way lit by the full moon. The sky was clear and peppered with stars, but he didn't stop to take them in as he hurried back to Bowman. Once inside his room, he flicked on the desk light and stared at the murder board.

Standing here at two in the morning, he suddenly felt ridiculous. *You're reading too much into things. It's an unimportant detail and you know it.*

But what if it wasn't?

He tapped his chin and foot at the same time, going back over the board. Then he drew a new circle. *How do you connect?*

He recalled Randall's words from a long time ago: *Don't overthink things.*

But that didn't mean not to think at all.

This person had the means and the opportunity, but at first, he hadn't seen a motive for them. That's what he always came back to: the motive. For someone to hate Anathema this much, they would have to have been utterly crushed by it, their spirit torn to tatters, but the organization hadn't treated anyone like that for decades. The Bard's motive had to be something new, something hidden.

Unless…

A detail Joan told him last Friday had bothered him all week, but he wasn't sure exactly what it was. Tonight, it had come back to him, and it forced him to reconsider everything. What if he'd been looking at it all wrong?

It was no secret that the college had many legacy students, but what if someone had kept their ties to the past buried? Matt couldn't think of anything from the last several years that would drive a person to mastermind such a scheme, but what if the Bard had come to Radcliffe with a hatred for Anathema *already* bred into them?

Follow the lead.

Matt let the scenario play out. If he was right and this person *was* the Bard, then the whole Serpentine scheme had been far more elaborate than he'd previously thought. This was an intricate revenge, not a petty vendetta taken to the extreme. Even if he had deduced their identity correctly, the Bard's whole plan had yet to reveal itself to him.

Get evidence.

There was only one place he could think to find it, but he worried the Bard may have scrubbed all trace of it there.

He thought for a moment.

No, there was still a chance. But to find out at this hour, he'd need to call in a favor.

◆

Tanner rubbed his eyes. "When I said 'my door is always open,' I didn't mean it *literally*."

"Sorry, but it's really important." Matt stood outside Tanner's door on Third Winslow, his heart thumping with anticipation. "As Magister, you have the keys to the Radcliffe Archives, right?"

Tanner blinked. "Um, yeah…"

"So you can get in there at any time, right?"

"Well, I usually like to clear it with Laura first. She's the college's Archivist, but she's chill with us."

"I won't be there long and I won't take anything out. I just need to see something."

"All of our post-Dissociation stuff is at the Chalet, anyway. Or at a storage locker in Canmore proper."

"I know. I need to see something older. I have a hunch, and if I'm right something very bad is about to go down. I might be able to figure out who's responsible for it."

"Is this related to Benson and Chet?"

Matt nodded.

"I thought the RCMP cleared that up a long time ago."

He hesitated. "Maybe not. I just need peace of mind."

"At 2:30 in the morning?"

"Yes."

Tanner sighed. "One sec." He disappeared and came back with a set of keys. "This one gets you into the Archives, this one gets you access to our stuff. The number on the tag is the code for the keypad. You've been there before, right?"

Matt nodded. "Yeah, at the end of first-year."

"If anybody from security comes, you know about the escape routes?"

"Actually, I don't."

"There are two of them. One comes out near the front doors by the reception desk, the other leads up into Picard Hall. The door kind of opens up out of a wall."

"Wait, we actually have secret passages here?"

Tanner chuckled. "Doug told me just last week, but yeah. Another reason to love the Archives."

"Definitely. I'll have the keys back to you tomorrow."

"Yeah, just make sure to hand me them before QuadFest. I'll be too drunk after that to remember where to put them."

"Will do. And thanks, Tanner."

"No worries." He shut the door and Matt headed back down the stairs, coming out into the West Quad.

As he walked toward the front entrance, his mind registered that the grass was wet, but in the moment, he assumed it was dew and gave it no further thought. He was too preoccupied with other concerns to think about the strange smell, still trying to flesh out his theory.

It was a different receptionist at this hour, one who sat reading a paperback book instead of a Kindle. She didn't even notice Matt as he continued down the hallway past the Administration Center. The elevator stood by the chapel entrance and he pushed the button, looking around anxiously.

The halls were empty but for an icy draft. It brushed past him and he shivered, wondering if he should've worn a jacket over his T-shirt.

The elevator arrived and he stepped inside, taking it down one floor to the basement level. When he exited, he found the refurbished Archives to his right. The renovation had been completed a couple years ago and the new entrance was sleek and modern, with large glass panes displaying Radcliffe artifacts.

He saw a camera inside, but didn't worry. He had bigger problems, and they'd probably only review the footage if something was taken or damaged.

Matt unlocked the door and the click resounded through the quiet floor. He froze momentarily, but when he heard no one coming, he slipped inside and shut it behind him, locking it again. Motion-activated lights turned on and he looked around.

Laura the Archivist's office stood in a corner to his right, closed in by glass walls. There were tables around him with old blueprints being studied on one, a griffin statuette on another.

To the left stood a stone wall with a metal sliding door in the back corner, a keypad beside it. He went over and punched in the code on the tag; the door retracted with a hiss of air.

Before him lay a mix of old and new. The lighting was dimmer in here, given only by iron lanterns hanging along the right wall; lightbulbs glowed fiery yellow from within. To the left were rows of mobile shelving storage, their metallic gray contrasting with the stone all around. The whole thing felt like a modernized dungeon.

He continued to the end of the corridor where another door lay, the word *Restricted* on its golden plaque. This one was ancient and wooden, but with an updated lock. He slid the second key Tanner had given him in and turned it, then pushed his way through. Inside, more electric lanterns cast the room in a yellowish hue and still more shelves stood off to the left.

Everything Anathema had produced or owned from 1905 to 1997 was in this room.

There were two other doors, both wooden. One lay directly ahead and the other stood off to the right between two large, oak chests of drawers. A large leather-bound chest sat atop one of them. The doors must've been the escape passageways. When he'd been here before, he just assumed they were storage closets.

Matt went straight to the last shelf and cranked the wheel on the side, creating an aisle between it and its adjacent twin. Here in boxes and crates were the Sermons, Scrapbooks, and miscellaneous artifacts of the 1980s and 1990s. Everything was organized by year and each branch had their materials side by side.

Opening up the last box, for the 1996-97 school year, he saw that the male branch's Scrapbook was still in there. He flipped to the opening pages, seeing photos of the End-of-Year Social from the preceding school year, in April of '96. Back before they had the Chalet, both branches had held it together in the Senior Common Room, with a High Table dinner afterward. Clearly secrecy hadn't been as big of a concern back then, but this was the peak, the time when Anathema had held the most power and influence. They'd thought they were untouchable.

Matt's eyes scanned each photo, searching for one face in particular. He just needed a glimpse—

There.

He nearly dropped the Scrapbook.

Staring at the smiling figure, he noted how uncanny the resemblance was. *Holy shit, I was right.*

At that moment, all the different threads came together in his mind. He stood there, his fingers clutching the book, his pulse racing, as he saw the events of the year in a new light, each realization hitting him like successive shockwaves.

Minutes went by as he mapped it all out, following the Bard's demented logic. But now it made sense. Now it all fit together, though it would be damned hard to prove. And one facet was just speculation, but without it, he didn't see how it all worked.

He was so startled and excited he barely heard the door swing open. By the time he registered footsteps growing closer, it was already too late.

Matt turned just as the cloaked figure lunged for him. He tried to dart past, but in a moment the assailant had him in a headlock and pulled him back against the shelves.

He tried to shout, only for a gloved hand to force a rag over his mouth just as he breathed in. Fatigue crept over him, blackness closing in. Before he lost consciousness, he heard a familiar voice breathe into his ear.

"Congratulations, you found my secret."

SEVENTY-SEVEN

SHE REGISTERED the explosion but didn't open her eyes until it shook the room, rattling her bedframe and furniture.

Groggily, she peered toward the window. Her curtains weren't entirely closed and orange-red light flooded the room. A quick glance at the clock told her it was 3:04 a.m. *That's not sunrise.*

Joan flew out of bed and tore the draperies open, covering her mouth in shock.

Galbraith's windows had blown out and fire raged inside the dining hall, licking out of the frames as smoke billowed to the sky. She stumbled back and turned to the bed.

"Matt, wake—"

But he was gone, and so were his clothes.

Panic and consternation came from the hallway, feet and voices hurrying every which way. Joan threw on a black tank top and jeans and grabbed her phone. She was about to slide it into her pocket when she saw she had a message from Matt about ten minutes ago. Perplexed, she opened it.

It was a photo of him and Logan, facing each other in two chairs. They were both unconscious and tied to their seats.

The text read: *Come alone or they both die. Tell no one, or I'll kill you all.*

Joan swallowed, her heart in her throat. She recognized that room as the Restricted portion of the Archives. The Bard must've unlocked Matt's phone with his fingerprint. Searching around, she couldn't find her keys and realized he must've taken them when he left.

There was no time to try to figure out what had happened—she had to move fast.

Joan burst out into the hallway, where Mia Cote was leading frantic students in their pajamas toward the western Lacy stairwell, knocking on doors to wake people as she went. Joan followed them, trying to form a plan. She needed to find someone else in Anathema. Val lived on the third floor, but Joan didn't see her as they entered the staircase and raced down to the exit door.

A first-year girl pushed it open and the crowd reeled back. The entire West Quad was ablaze, fire reigning across grass and stone. Smoke snaked in as the door shut, causing many to cough as Mia directed them down to Sub-Lacy.

"Head to the steam tunnels! Let's go, let's go!"

They hit the basement level, then turned and filed down through the other door into the lowest level. Once in the musty passageway, Joan followed everyone to the right as they mixed with fleeing students from the other res houses. It was pandemonium, people pushing and shouting all around.

"EVERYONE REMAIN CALM AND HEAD FOR THE EXIT!" Dunlap shouted somewhere behind her.

They reached the stairwell up to the front corridor and when Joan made it to the first floor, panic gripped her. The students were going to be shepherded outside and down the hill and they wouldn't be let back in. She'd have to make sure security didn't see her heading to the Archives.

Suddenly, she noticed Rufus walking alongside her in a white T-shirt and boxers, looking frantic. He wasn't Val, but he'd have to do.

She grabbed his shoulder and he turned to her, startled. "Joan, what the bloody fuck is going on? How is the Quad on fire?"

"Someone must've poured gasoline or something around," she said, the words tumbling out. "Listen, I need to get to the Archives—"

Rufus' face twisted in disbelief. "Are you *insane*? We need to get the hell out of this building before—"

Joan pulled him aside. "Whoever did this has Matt and Logan hostage and if I don't get there soon, he's going to kill them." People rushed by, oblivious to their conversation. Even the Officers were too focused on their escape to stop.

"How do you know that?" She pulled out her phone and showed him the message. Rufus' eyes widened. "Fuck, what do we—you need to get the police, *I* can't help with this."

He moved to rejoin the flow of students, but she grabbed him roughly and slammed him back against the wall. "I need your help. I outrank you. And you owe me after—"

"After what? Trying to do you a favor? Fine, rescue him or not—it's your fucking funeral."

She dragged him down the corridor toward the front lobby, where Réjean and another security guard were directing people out through the entrance doors. As they approached, Joan dashed out while dragging Rufus in tow, darting toward the other side of the corridor.

Réjean did a double-take as they passed, then turned and hurried after them. "Hey, stop! Where the hell are you going?!"

His footsteps steadily gained on them. Flamelight flickered through the windows, dancing across the floor as they ran.

She and Rufus didn't stop sprinting until they reached the end of the corridor and turned right. Ahead was the way to Galbraith, ablaze with smoke and fire, but to the right was a staircase leading up to the Crow's Nest res house and down to the basement.

Rufus turned to her, nervous and angry. "I hope you know what you're doing."

She looked back around the corner. Réjean's run had faltered into a jog as he neared, panting and out of breath. He was just meters away, his face full of confusion and fury.

Joan turned to Rufus. "I don't have a choice."

Taking his arm, she pulled him down the steps into the darkness.

Seventy-Eight

WHEN MATT came to, the first thing he saw was Logan's face. Blood trailed from a cut on his forehead and he looked like he was just waking back up.

Matt glanced around. They were still in the Restricted room of the Archives, though their attacker had brought in these wood-backed chairs from elsewhere, probably the glass lobby. Matt realized the Bard must've been planning to take Logan here anyway. He'd just been in the wrong place at the wrong time, but now that he knew the truth, they wouldn't let him live.

"I heard an explosion," Logan said, shaking his head and blinking blood out of his eyes. "It sounded like the boiler room, back that way." He jerked his head behind him.

"That's under Galbraith, right?"

"Yeah, I think so."

"Shit. Why don't I hear a fire alarm?"

"I don't know. Do you think this guy disabled the alarms?"

Matt thought for a moment. *This was at least a semester in the making. Everything's been thought out.*

"Yeah, I bet they did."

"Someone knocked on my door, so I got dressed and answered it, then a dude in a cloak fucking chloroformed me. How'd he get you?"

"I was down here investigating."

Logan laughed. "At this hour? On what?"

"Who's behind all this."

The Imperator looked around. "Got any leads?"

Matt opened his mouth to say something when suddenly the door behind Logan opened and a cloaked figure entered, a black veil hiding their face. They poured out a heavy-looking cylindrical canister as they went, dumping a clear liquid across the floor. When he was a kid, his dad showed him how to light lamps with kerosene and as the smell hit him, he recognized it at once. He also recognized it as the odor from the West Quad earlier, and with horror understood what the Bard was trying to do.

It was then that Matt noticed the fire extinguisher behind the door.

The figure continued past the two captives and finished the steel can, then grabbed another they'd placed on a chest of drawers and headed to the storage shelves, pouring kerosene down an aisle. Once the Bard finished, they gripped another turning wheel with a gloved hand, opening a new aisle.

Logan shook his head. "Fuck, we're gonna die down here."

"Probably," Matt realized. He tugged at the rope that bound his hands, but couldn't get it free. Then again, it didn't seem to be tied *too* tightly…

"If we're going out…then there's some stuff I want to say." Logan bit his lip. "Joan talked to me about what Rufus said to you last Friday."

The blood drained from Matt's face. "She did?"

Logan gave a sad nod. "Rufus should've just minded his own fucking business. What he did was completely wrong."

He stopped, realizing the Bard was watching both of them.

"What the fuck are *you* looking at?" Logan barked.

In two quick strides, the cloaked figure reached him and sharply back-handed him across the face. If it weren't for his restraints, Logan would've fallen out of his chair, and it rocked back into place. He shook his head, his cheek red and stinging from the slap.

"Fuckin' asshole," he muttered.

The Bard pulled open their cloak to reveal black clothing, a knife belt, and a large medallion dangling from their neck—which depicted Serpentine's ouroboros. The figure drew the blade and, in a swift motion, plunged it down into Logan's thigh.

He howled in pain, gritting his teeth as the Bard withdrew the hunting knife and wiped the blood off on Logan's shoulder. His breath came quicker as the blade slid near to his neck, the edge caressing his throat—then retreating.

The Bard sheathed the weapon. They picked up another container of kerosene and resumed their work.

"Why hasn't he killed us yet?" Logan said through the pain.

Matt racked his brain for answers, then realized he could feel keys in his right pocket but not his phone in his left. "Where's my...?" he muttered, before looking to the Bard, who held it out for him to see.

The device glowed in the darkened room, a messaging app on the screen. The figure tossed it onto his lap and he looked down, seeing a photo of himself and Logan unconscious and a text to—

"You fucking bastard! You want both Imperators down here, and you're using me to lure her... Then what? You're gonna pin the whole arson on her going mad?"

The figure said nothing, but raised their hands and clapped.

"They won't buy it," he said. "Nobody'd believe Joan would do that." But even as he said the words, he knew they weren't true. That's all Joan would be remembered as—the insane Imperator who killed her ex-boyfriend and burned the college to the ground. People at Radcliffe would believe it; they'd believe anything about her.

And the Bard would get away scot free.

The cloaked figure grabbed the container and moved toward the pair of them, pulling the kerosene back to splash it forward.

"Oh shit—no, no, no," Logan winced, leaning back. Matt braced himself.

Back in the outer Archive chamber came the hiss of a sliding door. *Joan's an Imperator, she must've known the code too,* he realized.

The Bard froze, turning their hooded head in the direction of the sound.

"...photo was back there," said a voice—his girlfriend's.

Matt's pulse quickened. "It's a trap! Don't come in—"

The Bard was on him in a second, striking him across the face. Groaning from the pain, he barely noticed the figure drawing their blade and hiding behind the door out to the Archives.

"Hello?" came Rufus' voice. "Logan? Matt? Are you in there?"

"Don't," Logan said, still wincing from the pain.

Somewhere out there, Joan yelled, "Rufus wait!"

The door opened and he stood there, peering around and coughing. Rufus stared at the two captives and fear flashed across his face. He started to retreat. *"Good God"* was all he managed to get out—before the Bard swung around and plunged the knife into his stomach.

Rufus screamed and the Bard hauled him into the room, throwing him against a chest of drawers. He slammed against the wood and went down, the entire cabinet wobbling. The chest on top shifted near the edge.

The Bard's head snapped up and saw it, then moved to grab it.

"Please no," Rufus whimpered, clutching his wound. "Do whatever you want to them, but don't kill me! Please I—"

Gloved hands gripped the heavy object and shoved, tipping it off the cabinet.

Rufus managed a short scream before it came down on his face. There was an awful crunch and Matt whipped his head away. Then reluctantly, slowly, he glanced back. A crimson pool seeped out from under the chest, which mercifully blocked his view of the damage. Rufus' body lay still, except for one of his legs, which twitched ever so slightly.

The Bard put their knife away and straightened up, then turned around—

As Joan slammed a box of files into their skull. The figure fell, hitting their head again on the cabinet, before falling unconscious on top of Rufus' body.

She stood over the Bard, her hands shaking.

"Thank God you're here," Logan panted. "Can you help untie us?"

"Of course." She moved to Matt first and began undoing the knot behind him.

Logan looked over at the two motionless figures. "Holy shit, is Rufus… is he *dead?*"

Matt swallowed, glancing over. "I think so." Suddenly, one of the bodies started to get up. "Joan!" he shouted.

She glanced up as the Bard put a hand to their head, stumbling back to the door. Turning, she saw the last canister, lunging for it as the Bard drew their knife again.

Joan grunted and swung it at the attacker as they charged. The Bard reeled back, narrowly avoiding another blow to the head, but kerosene splashed across their chest. She screamed, moving closer and swinging again and again, inadvertently dousing them with the liquid. Finally, Joan chucked it at the figure and fell back against the door between the cabinets.

Her eyes looked to Matt and Logan with sorrow, as if she wanted to run back to them.

The Bard lunged for her.

She turned the knob behind her, falling back through the opening. The knife missed her by inches, embedding itself in one of the cabinets.

The cloaked figure grunted and yanked the blade out from the oak. For a second, Matt thought they would dart through the doorway after her, but instead they froze and turned back to their captives. Swiftly setting the knife down atop the chest of drawers, the Bard pulled a matchbox out of their pocket, extracted one, and struck it against the side of the box.

The light of the flame flickered across the snake medallion.

Matt and Logan froze, their mouths hanging open.

The gloved hand dropped the match.

When it hit the ground, fire sparked across the floor.

SEVENTY-NINE

JOAN HURTLED up the pitch-black spiral, blood pounding in her ears.
She groped along the wall for a railing and found one, pulling herself higher and higher. Suddenly she slammed into a wall and nearly tumbled back down the steps. From the stairwell, the sound of the Bard ascending grew louder, their knife scraping along the wall as they climbed.

Joan fumbled in the dark, searching for something—anything. She grasped a door latch.

She turned it and pushed with all her might, bursting into Picard Hall. Unlike the last time she'd been here, it was almost entirely empty. The fire from Galbraith and the West Quad provided the only source of light, spilling in through the tall eastern windows.

She ran forward until she realized the rear exit was blocked by packing crates; the only other was the one behind her, the one that led out through the lobby staircase. She spun around just as the Bard crashed out of the passageway, which had been hidden by a slab of stone on the wall.

The figure turned and brandished the blade, crouching, waiting for her next move.

Joan froze, sizing them up. They were about her height, too short to be Patrick but, just maybe—

"Randall?"

The Bard lunged forward, the knife held high.

There was only one place left to go.

Joan turned and ran for the nearby cabinet and jumped as high as she could, her hands grasping the upper edge. With an agility that surprised even her, she pulled herself up on top of the cabinet and scrambled for a wide stone ledge five feet up.

If they managed this in the nineties, you can too.

Once she hauled her way up, she realized it actually wasn't so bad a climb from here to the thick support beam that ascended to the rafters. Reaching the skylight wouldn't be too hard—if you were careful.

And didn't look down.

Below her, the Bard climbed up onto the cabinet, the knife clutched in one hand.

◆

No sooner had the assailant ducked into the passageway than Matt had finished taking his ropes off. Joan had all but untied them before she'd been forced to flee.

As flames leaped around them, he slid his phone into his back pocket and ran around behind Logan's chair to undo his bonds.

"Shit, shit, shit," the Imperator said, looking around. The flames followed the kerosene trail under the door and they could hear it igniting in the outer Archives. "Wait, there's a fire extinguisher up there!" He gestured with his head behind the door.

Matt quickly jumped over the flame trail and grabbed it off the wall.

"Throw it to me!" Logan shouted, and Matt obliged. The Imperator caught it and began spraying it around, dousing the aisles first. "I'm good here, go after them!"

"What about you?"

"I'll be fine, just go!"

"But your leg! And the smoke out there, from the kerosene and the boiler explosion, it'll—"

They locked eyes. "Matt, I said *go*. And here, take these in case you need them. Randall made a copy for me." He fished his keychain out of his pocket and tossed it to him. Matt saw the R3 was labeled *Master*.

Matt nodded, understanding what he meant. He took one last look at Logan Brewster, putting weight on his good leg as he swept the extinguisher around the blazing Archives.

Then he hurried through the open escape door, and climbed the steps as fast as he could.

The exit at the top was open, light from Picard Hall pouring in. Only once he reached the upper level did he realize that the glow wasn't from within the room, but rather the fire raging outside.

A loud crash resounded to his left. He turned to see the Bard dangling from a ledge about ten feet up, having just kicked over the cabinet that made it accessible by climbing. The cloaked figure pulled themselves up and began pursuing Joan along the ledge.

By now she'd reached the largest support beam and was starting to climb it. His eyes followed the wood to the rafters and the skylight beyond. The full moon shone through it, shedding light on the upper woodwork.

Jesus, is she going for the roof?

Both Joan and the Bard were so focused on the ascent, they didn't appear to notice him. Without the cabinet he had no way to follow them, and it looked too heavy for him to right it by himself.

Unless…

Looking down at the Master R3 in his hand, he realized there *was* another way up to the roof. He'd never taken it and he was pretty sure no one in Anathema had been up there for years, but it was his only shot.

Turning, he ran out the Picard doors.

Joan gripped the beam for dear life, trying not to look down. The floor became farther and farther away as she ascended, her muscles aching and lungs burning. If not for the adrenaline, she'd have never made it up this far.

The upper frame drew nearer, the window marked by moonlight. Against her better instincts, she looked behind her and saw the Bard climbing up the beam, moving like a spider along the bottom, their veiled face locked onto her. Suddenly, she remembered the kerosene she'd splashed on them and recalled putting the lighter Sandrine gave her in her jeans yesterday. But were they this pair? She briefly paused and grabbed at her pockets, trying to feel for it, locating nothing.

The Bard climbed closer. Her stomach tightened and she resumed rising.

Don't look down, don't look down...

Out the corner of her eye, she glimpsed just how high up she was. Gulping, she reached up and grabbed the nearest rafter, hoisting herself onto the next beam. She was over thirty feet above the floor now.

The skylight was almost in reach.

She stretched her arm out over open space, grasping for the crank that opened the window. Her fingers barely brushed it.

The Bard was mere meters below her.

Joan reached out again and lost one of her footings. She just managed to grab onto the rafter with her other hand, one leg still wrapped around the beam. It creaked under the strain.

She dangled several stories above the wooden floor, her grip slackening.

The cloaked figure paused and unsheathed the knife, positioning themselves to slash at her.

Joan's hand shot out and, reaching with all her might, grasped the crank, turning it as she gritted her teeth. The window slowly folded upward and the opening widened, brisk air wafting toward her.

In her peripheral, she saw the knife swipe through the air and lurched her other leg upward. The blade nicked her right calf and she grunted, her hand slipping from the crank.

The rafter creaked.

The Bard repositioned themselves, preparing to strike again.

There was only one thing left to do.

Joan grasped for the ledge the opening had created and, with her left leg still wrapped over the beam, pushed off with her right foot and let go of the rafter entirely.

She grabbed the ledge with both hands as her other leg fell off the beam. Her entire body dangled in the air as the Bard slashed again, this time missing her by a foot.

Not waiting to see their next move, she pulled herself up. She'd managed to open the window about a foot, and squeezed her upper body through, grasping the roof's slate tiles to help drag herself outside.

Then she froze.

Just a few feet below her was the edge—and a steep drop.

Elbowing the window open higher, she grabbed the left corner of the skylight and brought her right leg up through the sill. Then, using the other corner for purchase, she pushed herself onto the sloping roof.

She had to move carefully to avoid tumbling down and over the edge. Knowing the roof's ridge was her best bet for something to hold, she slowly crawled her way up and grabbed it. Then she lashed out with her foot, kicking the skylight until it fell closed again.

Joan took a deep breath—then coughed, smoke getting into her lungs. She hauled herself up to the ridgeline and looked out at the rest of the college, her hair blowing in the breeze. She'd never seen it from this high up before, and now the destruction was laid bare to her.

The West Quad blazed softer now but the fire within Galbraith had swelled in size. Smoke poured out of the shattered, stained-glass windows and rose into the night. Behind her, a crowd had amassed at the base of Radcliffe's front steps and appeared to be waiting for the fire department. There was still no sign of them, but she was sure someone had called 9-1-1 by now.

Suddenly, the skylight began to rise once more, the Bard winding the crank from below.

Joan's heartrate accelerated. She shimmied along the ridge to her right, toward the only place left to flee: Anathema Tower.

It was a few meters before she dared to look back. The skylight was open; one gloved hand grasped the edge, then another, as a shadowy figure pulled themselves up onto the roof.

◆

Matt bolted up the stairs in House Vickers, finally reaching the fourth floor. To get to the fifth, he had to go through another door and take a separate staircase up to the top residence rooms, unofficially known as the Himalayan Suite.

There were only four of them, two facing east and two facing west. In the center was a common room area and on the ceiling was an unlabeled hatch.

Last year, Madler had desired to take a Scrapbook picture from the top of the Great Lord and Lady's tower, but it had never come to fruition. However, Matt specifically recalled him saying that the hatch's locks were changed with the others each year, meaning that the Master R3 should work.

It was his only shot left.

Matt grabbed a loveseat off to the side and dragged it to the center of the room. All was dark save for the distant light of the fire through windows to his right. He climbed atop the loveseat and reached up with the key, sliding it into the lock.

He took a breath, then turned it.

It clicked, unlocked.

He gasped in relief, then let the hatch swing downward, revealing total darkness above.

He took out his phone and activated the flashlight, shining it up into Anathema Tower. He saw CRCC graffitied in multiple spots along the walls. One ladder went up about halfway, then there was a landing and a second ladder continued up to the belfry.

Clenching his phone between his teeth, he leaped upward and grabbed the edges of the hatch, pulling himself into the space above. Once he'd gotten his hips inside, he sat on the edge and grabbed his phone again, shining it around—

Two bats swung down out of the blackness. He ducked as they flew by, screeching.

Quickly, he began ascending the first ladder with his phone in one hand. He rose higher and higher, wood creaking all around him.

He finally reached the first landing, got to his feet, and turned around to scale the next ladder. He got about halfway up it before he heard a sharp crack and a rung snapped. His hand fell away, the phone nearly slipping from his fingers.

Shit.

Matt looked above him. Seven or so feet overhead was an opening into the belfry's floor. He could see the tower's windows above, firelight shining through them.

Steadying himself, he continued up one rung at a time, hoping he wasn't too late.

◆

Free of the skylight, the Bard steadied themselves against the sloping roof. Joan continued making her way to the tower, now just off to her right. Here was the point where two roofs met, the central one rising taller. The front entrance of the college jutted out twenty feet from the rest of the façade; the valley in the corner seemed to offer the best leverage.

She glanced back at the Bard again. The full moon illuminated them as they made their way closer, cloak rustling in the wind. Their speed was more daring now, their movements bolder and swifter.

The space between them closed rapidly.

Joan reached the valley between the intersecting roofs as a scream tore through the air. She turned to glimpse the Bard leaping for her. The impact knocked her down into the valley, slamming her skull against the tiles.

She clutched her head, trying to get her bearings, as the figure straddled her.

"You don't know how long I've waited...to get my hands on an *Imperator*..." The voice sounded guttural, inhuman.

Joan tried to parse through the wrath, to match the sound with someone she knew, but suddenly there were gloved hands around her throat. They squeezed tightly and she gasped for air, finding she couldn't breathe. She pushed at the Bard's arms, but they wouldn't budge. She tried wriggling free, but the assailant's grip was too strong.

Finally, she reached up, grasped the veil, and tore it out from under the hood. The breeze took it from her fingers, carrying it away with ash on the wind. And Joan found herself staring, to her enormous surprise, into the snarling face of Donna Crawley.

EIGHTY

"**S**USANNE, STOP!"

The cloaked figure released Joan and her head snapped up toward him. There was confusion and bafflement in her eyes, but once she recognized him, they narrowed.

"You're Susanne Ferguson," he said, leaning out one of the belfry's windows. He was about ten feet directly above her and Joan. "You were an Anathema member in the nineties, then you left after Gagnon came in. You became a proponent of Dissociation and she bullied you until you tried to kill yourself."

Crawley sat up straighter. "I didn't *leave*," she shouted, breaking into a laugh. "Dearest Emma *kicked* me out and told everyone I'd left. She always hated me, so she turned Anathema against me, then the whole college along with it."

"And why did she hate you, Susanne?" He began climbing out the window, slowly making his way down.

Crawley's voice was loud but strained. "Because I was always more popular. She was so *shy* and *weird*. Everyone thought *I* was going to be Imperator, but Kellerman had a soft spot for Emma. She was completely unexpected and had years of frustration to take out on Radcliffe, starting with me."

She appeared lost in a sad reminiscence and barely paid attention to Joan, who was still pinned beneath Crawley and rubbing her throat. She looked confused and terrified.

Matt let go of a ledge and fell a couple of feet to the roof. He nearly tumbled down the side, then turned and grabbed the ridge, his ribs aching from the impact. Crawley snapped out of her trance, drawing the knife and holding it to Joan's neck.

"Don't come closer or I'll cut her fucking throat," she hissed, her eyes narrowing. Joan swallowed, trying not to look at the blade.

Matt put out a hand as he hauled himself back up to the ridge. The wind had picked up and mercifully kept the smoke at bay. Galbraith remained ablaze behind him. *Where the hell are the fire trucks?*

He looked squarely at the Bard, who still wore her hood up. "You did this all to get back at Gagnon and Anathema, didn't you? You faked an identity as Donna Crawley, claimed you went to Atherton University—not a school people usually fake a degree from, and—"

"Wrong! I *did* go to that shit school, after WCU kicked me out for trying to kill myself. I was a liability to them, so they gave me an 'indefinite leave of absence.' I spent a year sitting huddled back at home before finishing my final semester at Atherton. That diploma in my office is real. I doctored it to hide the ends of my full name: Susanne Donna Crawley Ferguson." She grinned, a horrible, painful smile that failed to dam the years of hurt swirling inside her.

He hesitated. It was a wrinkle, but it actually made more sense. He just had to get her to keep talking. Hopefully the rest of his speculation was more accurate. "Well, the Dean's Office loves Atherton, so they were quick to hire you, and Mustard doesn't care who's running what so long as their background check clears and they don't create liabilities. He's never cared about this place. But you did. You used to care about it a lot."

Crawley appeared intrigued, her eyes locking onto him with predatory intent.

"You spent the first year on the job sizing everything up, determining who was who. Using Mustard's phone taps, you spied on people all over Radcliffe, probably took notes on who the members were. You asked around the student community, people like Pandora Lane giving you details on Anathema and leaking information to you by using Roy. But this year was your master plan. The big revenge. This year you brought back Serpentine to have your own little army. You inducted people like Pandora and Rich and Chet who hated us. You heard about Joan and Randall's meeting by tapping the phone in her room and knew they wouldn't be meeting at the Chalet that night. Randall called her and you must've overheard them discussing it.

So you sent Rich to keep an eye out for her when she left and to follow her where she went."

"And *she* killed him!" Crawley sneered down at her, still holding the knife to her throat.

He shook his head. "No Susanne, *you* did that."

Joan's eyes widened as she looked between the two of them. "But...I..."

Matt turned to her. "You pushed him down the hill, but he was still alive when you ran away. I remember at the beginning of the year, when Randall gave details at the emergency meeting, that the RCMP were confused about the position of the body. It didn't seem like he would've ended up at that angle after just a tumble." He looked back to Crawley. "You followed him to Bethune's Walk once he messaged you, Susanne. You were hidden, but you watched him fall down the hill. You must've been so excited. You'd told Rich to get a rise out of her, to get her to beat him up—that was step one of your big plan, wasn't it?"

Crawley forced a smile again, shaking her head and laughing to herself. Joan stared toward him, her mouth agape in disbelief.

"You had Joan's record," Matt continued. "You're one of the only people at Radcliffe who knew about her history of violence. You knew she was supremely dedicated to Anathema from asking around. Pandora would've told you all the members she knew, never realizing she was talking directly to the Bard herself. And Rich had gone out with Joan. I don't know which one of you came up with the idea, but that's why he started taunting her that night." He turned back to his girlfriend. "Rich was *trying* to get a rise out of you, Joan. It would've created a huge scandal: 'Anathema member assaults dissenter.' He was pulling a false flag on himself because he hated Anathema and he enjoyed being a piece of shit to you. He thought it would make him look like a persecuted journalist, thought it would give him credibility."

He returned his focus to Crawley. "But it worked too well; she nearly ended up killing him. And I bet when you saw him still alive, part of you was sad—sad that you hadn't just witnessed an Anathema member commit murder. So you decided to fix that, didn't you, Susanne? Even *Joan* thought she'd killed him! But you went down into the river—probably slid over the bridge railing so you wouldn't leave footprints—and smashed his head against that rock. It knocked him out cold and he drowned while you escaped farther up the stream, fleeing into the woods on the other side of the bridge. Once you were back on the path, Jack Randall heard you coming and hid in the trees. I thought it was odd when Joan mentioned you still had a disciplinary meeting with her the morning a student had died. That's what first tipped me off to you. You didn't cancel the meeting because you wanted to gauge her mental state, maybe even fuck with her a bit."

"Lies!" she shouted, the smile cracking. She jabbed the knife toward him and Joan tried to move. Crawley grabbed her shoulder and smashed her down against the slate tiles, bringing the blade back to her neck.

Matt froze. Far below, he thought he heard a voice call, "Holy shit, are there *people* up there?" The heat from the fire warmed his back and he wondered how much of the college was burning now.

The only way out of this was to continue. "I knew you had the means to spy on us through the phones and that you had access to Joan's records. You were even there when the Winslow disco party got shut down—you could've easily slipped Joan that note telling her to confess. But I couldn't figure out why you'd have a motive to hate Anathema. In fact, the more I thought about it, the only person in Anathema's history who had a motive to hate it this much would've been Susanne Ferguson, who was bullied into a suicide attempt. And then I realized you'd be about her age, but thought, 'Don't be ridiculous.' Still, I figured Susanne Ferguson would've been in some End-of-Year Social photos in the Scrapbooks. And so I went down to the Archives and there you were, the Dean of Students partaking in an Anathema event over twenty years ago, under a different name."

Crawley laughed. "Think you're clever, huh? Alright then, Mr. Detective, tell me my big fucking plan if you've got it all figured out then, the one I've apparently been readying for two whole decades."

He shook his head. "No. I don't know when you began planning this, but it didn't *start* as a murder scheme. You were just going to use Serpentine to bring down Gagnon's beloved secret society—and get back at it for what it did to you. You wanted Rich to pull his false flag and Joan to get expelled for it, creating controversy for Anathema. You probably would've had Serpentine staging protests, calling for an end to the Sermons, trying to turn Radcliffe against Anathema once and for all. But when you killed Rich, that changed things. I bet it made it a lot easier to murder Chet, right? Other than Rich, he was the only one who knew your identity as the Bard. Even though he never learned what you did to Rich, it still would've been a huge scandal to find out that the *Dean* of Students was fucking one."

"*You—*"

"Blaine thought Chet was sleeping with his girlfriend back in October. A Saunders guy saw a blonde girl running out of his room and he just assumed it was Melissa. But it wasn't—it was *you*. And Chet couldn't tell anybody because it would've gotten him into *massive* trouble. You needed someone to manipulate into being your Vizier, and he was horny enough to oblige. That's how you persuaded him and *he* convinced the others to join Serpentine; they already hated Anathema for their own reasons. You were able to talk to Rich in person because he was our most outspoken critic. You figured you could trust him with your identity too, but killing him made everything so much cleaner, right?"

The Bard shook her head, laughing as tears trailed down her face. She looked completely unhinged and it was all he could do to keep himself from trembling with fear. In her current state, Crawley seemed unpredictable. One wrong move on his part and it would be over in an instant; she could slice Joan's throat with a flick of her wrist. He just needed to keep holding the Bard's attention.

"But you got paranoid that you were going to be found out. You couldn't tip off the police because they might discover that *you* were the guilty party in Benson's death, so once Chet posted that video, you saw the perfect opening. Kill him and make it look like Anathema did it, probably Joan again, because he dared to broadcast members' names on the Internet. Really, you were just tying up loose ends. You knew Serpentine had been a big waste of time once you killed Rich, but you had them run around and do pointless shit like stealing the skull and attacking the Sermon just to keep them busy while you decided on an exit strategy. Then once you found a way to get rid of Chet, you cut Serpentine off and left them to flounder, focusing on more direct revenge by yourself. After the police gave up trying to solve Chet's murder, you figured you'd burn the college and frame an Anathema member. And it worked out perfectly that Joan ended up getting Imperator, didn't it?"

She gave a demented laugh. "You don't know anything!"

No, he thought. *But I can guess, and I seem to be doing pretty well so far. Just confess, Susanne. Make it nice and loud.*

"Joan reminds you of Gagnon, doesn't she?"

Crawley looked down. Joan had tears of her own, her chest rising and falling quickly as she tried to tilt her head away from the blade. "Yes, she does," the Bard said, a touch of sadness in her voice. "She's exactly like

Emma. A pretty little rich, private school girl who's obsessed with tradition, thinking it'll help her belong." She leaned closer. "But I don't hate you." With her free hand, Crawley stroked Joan's cheek and wiped away a tear. "I *pity* you. You're just a sad, violent creature who would do anything to be accepted…" The Bard tilted her head. "That's all you wanted, wasn't it?"

Joan squeezed her eyes shut, trying to stem the flow of tears.

Crawley turned back to Matt. "This college wasn't made for people like you and her. It was made for people like *me*. This place was my fucking playground. I climbed to the top of Social Cliffe. I *was* Social Cliffe! I out-prepped, out-gossiped, and out-ran them all. I was DebSoc President in third-year, but an Imperator medallion would've been my crown jewel."

She laughed again. "And then fucking *Emma*—Emma!—got it and *destroyed* me. She kicked me out, tore me down, and overnight I was *nobody*. I hated Anathema and DebSoc and this whole fucking place! I joined the Anti-Anathema Association and Emma, once that quiet awkward girl, was suddenly dumping dog shit on me out the second Winslow landing. The male Imperator that year did nothing to rein in her little warpath, but then again, he was *madly* in love with her. You should've been there at the last Sermon I ever went to. The things she read about me…they were *unspeakable*. She didn't cross the line, she *obliterated* it. And they all just…laughed." She snickered, shaking her head at the memory. "They all laughed. They had worshipped me and then I was nothing but a joke to them… Anathema did that to me." Crawley swallowed. "Do you know what it's like…to feel that taking your own life is the only way forward?"

He nodded sadly. "I do. It's horrible. I nearly went through with it, but I stopped. I'm sorry you actually attempted it, Susanne. No matter what you did to Emma before she became Imperator, you didn't deserve how she treated you. I wouldn't wish that feeling on anyone."

"They kicked me out," she said, staring off at the night sky. "I couldn't even kill myself properly, and this school punished me further by ruining what was left of my life. The prestigious diploma I'd been promised—gone. The job prospects—gone. Even all this time later, it's haunted me what this place did to me—what she did to me—what *Anathema* did to me… I've lost friends and relationships over the past twenty-one years because of my bitterness and sadness, and it all comes back to this fucking cult. My life is a complete mess. A few years ago, I tracked down Emma on social media and oh, don't worry. She's fine. *She's* a successful lawyer in Montreal while I'm a lonely wreck. The only purpose left in my miserable existence is avenging what was taken from me—the life, career, and friends I should've had."

Her voice grew louder, angrier. "Therapists have said I need to move on, but they don't get it. No one *gets* this place unless you've gone here, unless you've *seen* what it does to people." She held up the knife again. "So yes, I killed them. I killed Rich and Chet and that fuckwit down in the Archives. I ordered the kerosene and made it look like Joan had been breaking into Maintenance to do it. I set the West Quad on fire and blew up the boiler room. And once I'm done, I'm going to find Emma fucking Gagnon, make her beg me for mercy, and give her an opt-out policy from the rest of her life." She forced a smile. *"There.* Are you happy?"

He pulled his phone out of his back pocket and held it toward her, pressing Stop on the recording app. "Very."

Crawley's eyes widened. *"You little—"*

Joan lurched up, grabbing at her. The Bard turned and backhanded her across the face; she fell back. Slipping the phone into his rear pocket, Matt lunged forward as Crawley raised the knife over Joan. "Get off of h—"

She turned the blade at the last second and swung it toward him. He twisted to avoid it, but the knife plunged into the left side of his abdomen. He screamed and fell back, grabbing at his side. His hands came away with blood and pain seared from the stab wound. He wasn't sure how deep she'd gotten him, but it hurt like hell nonetheless.

"Matt...," Joan said feebly, reaching her hand toward him. Crawley grabbed her by the hair and slammed her head against the roof, then turned to him, snarling with rage.

Summoning his strength, Matt crawled higher onto the central ridge. It was the only place to go. Suddenly, the Bard grabbed his arm and hauled him upright, only to throw him farther down the roof to the edge. Matt nearly slipped down the side, but clutched the ridge about a foot away from where it ended. Right here, they were five stories up. Matt was directly over the front doors now; the concrete path of about thirty feet that led to the top of the stairs stretched out before him. Farther below at the base of the hill, the crowd watched, pointed, and shouted.

He turned around. Crawley carefully walked toward him, keeping her center of gravity low as she made her way along the ridge. She held the knife out before her and it wavered slightly. The hood shadowed part of her face from the moon, anxiousness and anger in her expression.

"I realized Emma didn't just try to make me kill myself—she tried to *murder* me, Matthew. Anathema tried to *murder* me. But it didn't finish the job." With both hands, she raised the knife above her head and cast a wicked smile down upon him. "I won't make the same mistake."

Matt reached up his hand, as if it would stop her, but in that moment a voice yelled, "Hey!"

They both turned in time to see Joan throw the skull lighter. It sailed through the air and hit Crawley in the chest, igniting the kerosene on her cloak. The knife slipped from her hands and tumbled down the tiles, disappearing over the edge, as she frantically slapped at her clothing and tried to put it out.

It was no use.

The fire ensnared her like a snake and soon she was a writhing, screaming figure engulfed by flames. She turned, stumbling toward Matt with her gloved hands outstretched, her face torn between pain and rage. He let go of the ridge at the last second, allowing himself to slide down the roof.

He managed to catch the edge just as Crawley went off the front of Radcliffe. She managed to twist around once, her arms reaching upward for a nonexistent ledge. A wail pierced the air, growing fainter with her as she dropped away. Then she smacked against the pavement below and was suddenly, unnervingly still.

Matt stared at the blazing shape in disbelief, his eyes fixated on the flames. Somebody at the base of the hill screamed; figures hurried up the stairs to see who had fallen.

A hand grabbed his arm and started to pull him up. It was Joan, a bloody cut on her forehead. She looked very tired, but muscled past her fatigue to assist him. He scrambled up, then turned over onto his back and stared toward the starry sky.

"That doesn't look good," she muttered, examining his wound.

He glanced sideways and looked down again. A crowd had gathered near the burning body and Réjean was trying to keep them back with the help of another guard. Even from here, Matt could see Mustard covering his mouth in horror.

"Joan," he mumbled, "this time I think you *actually* killed someone."

She grabbed his jaw and turned his head toward her, fear in her eyes. "Hey, stay with me, okay?"

It was a strange sensation, losing blood. Glancing down he saw his shirt was soaked and dark liquid trickled down the roof to the edge. Its color looked so odd in the moonlight...

Sirens grew louder off to his left, but he turned to Joan instead. She stared past him, watching the vehicles arrive, a weak smile coming to her face. "The fire department's finally here. They've got an ambulance. It's gonna be okay, Matt." Then she shouted down, "We've got someone wounded up here!"

Joan looked to him again, caressing his face. "Réjean heard me. He's running to tell the firemen. They'll get you down."

He nodded faintly and mumbled, "I love you."

Smiling through tears, she said, "I love you, too."

Beyond her was Anathema Tower, and he imagined the Great Lord floating beside it like a wraith, his orange eyes filled with concern. Joan leaned in to kiss Matt and suddenly it was as if all the bad things that had transpired were just a dream, or something that happened a long time ago to someone else. As the feeling flowed through him and melted away the pain, he started to wonder.

If this is how I die, there are worse ways to go.

PART V
HERE ENDETH

EPILOGUE

"I'M GONNA miss him."

Logan Brewster looked around the Chalet's lounge, a hand on his chin. They sat on opposite sofas beside the fireplace. The blinds were open and pale sunlight filtered in, a dreary day beyond the windows. It was the last Friday of April.

"He'd always had a tough time fitting in with us. I mean yeah, he had friends and he got positions, but I think he always had a love-hate relationship with Anathema. Even though he dissed us, he *was* a dedicated member after he came back."

She nodded. "I feel bad for leading Rufus down there. I should have gone to the Archives alone."

Logan shook his head. "Don't blame yourself, Joan. It was never your fault. Even the stuff with Rich wasn't your fault. Him and Crawley—err, Ferguson—set you up. He *wanted* you to hit him."

Now that he knew the full details, Logan seemed a bit wary around her. He never made direct eye contact and seemed more eager to please, a hint of self-preservation in his tone. She decided she could get used to it.

Joan looked out the closest window, the sky a slate gray. "Thank you, but… It's just…"

"It's over, is what it is," he said, then shook his head again. "Man, this college is gonna be so different next year. I hope Knowles will make for a better Provost. Apparently, she actually cared about the traditions when she was Dean. And she didn't, you know, murder people. Or even embezzle funds like Mustard."

543

"Do you think he'll get arrested, now that he's resigned?"

"I don't know, but he's finished wherever he goes. The press collected dirt on him for a while, their case was solid. They even got that first-year to admit Mustard threatened him, saying he'd kick him off res if he didn't pull the fire alarm at that Winslow party. I wonder who first tipped them off..."

"No clue," Joan lied. Evidently the papers had taken the heads up from Roy's father seriously after all. One of them had begun quietly investigating Mustard about six months ago.

He shook his head. "I'm not surprised that Mark Wood guy disappeared, though. Probably changed his name and moved to Mexico."

"Yeah... Of course, most outlets are still focusing on the murderous Dean of Students."

Logan shrugged. "Homicide *is* juicier than embezzlement. Between the killings, the arson, and the financial fraud, Radcliffe isn't gonna be out of the news for a while."

"At least Anathema is getting portrayed as the victim this time. They're not trying to make it seem like we asked for it, even with how Ferguson was treated back in the nineties."

"She was a vindictive psychopath who murdered three people, so it's hard to see how they could spin that against us." He scratched his chin. "It's crazy she couldn't get over this place for twenty years, never moved on."

Joan hesitated. "This college has a way of getting to people. It's different with everyone." He nodded, then rubbed his thigh where he'd been stabbed. "How are the stitches holding up?"

"They're alright. Thanks for asking." They sat in silence for a moment. "Are you looking forward to next year?" he asked.

She managed a smile. "Yeah. I think it'll be good to put all of this behind me."

"Are you sure you can't convince Matt to be my new Legatus?"

"I've tried, but I think he's done with this college. He'll still be around next year and he'll definitely come to a few writing sessions, but I think he's kind of burned out."

Logan paused, then nodded. "I get that. I...haven't felt the same since that night, either. The whole thing really shook me up... I've done a lot of thinking and...I know I'm going to be more careful with the jokes I read. We're here to entertain people, not to hurt them."

They both were quiet for a moment. Then, wanting to shift to a brighter topic, Joan asked, "Started planning your Sermons yet? Your next is the 200th for your branch."

He laughed. "Haven't got a clue. We have no idea what people will do, what kind of jokes we can make about what…"

She smirked. "Still, I've already got my Preludes mapped out."

"I always thought Randall was nuts writing his a week early. And Turland would do his several weeks before. But every other Imperator I've talked to did them the night before or, like, the day of." He laughed again. "And here you are getting yours ready *months* in advance."

She shrugged. "What can I say? I'm a writer. I like to plan things out as much as I can."

He chuckled and shook his head. "You're crazy…"

Joan smiled. "Who's to say I'm not?" She glanced at her watch; she didn't feel like staying here any longer. "I should get going. If I don't see you around before I leave, have a good summer." She grabbed her backpack, then stood up and headed for the door.

"You too," Logan called after her. "Tell Matt I said hello."

She looked back. "Will do."

◆

Joan stepped through the gate and took a deep breath, staring upward. On the branches, leaves budded beneath the miserable sky. Sighing, she continued on.

The school had deferred their exams to late August due to her concussion and Matt's surgery. He'd gotten out of the hospital a week ago and was just taking it easy here until the end of the school year. Even though she was free to go, she'd convinced her parents to let her stay until the end of April. They'd flown back earlier in the week, as had Matt's parents. Joan and Matt were flying back to their respective homes tomorrow, which was perfect timing since it was expected to snow on Sunday.

Birds chirped and flew overhead as she walked along the edge of Griffin Park. The temperature was chilly and a light breeze blew past. She wore a denim jacket over her skull T-shirt along with a skirt and tights. Like Sandrine, she'd started to wear all black clothing. Even her lipstick was black. She knew others commented about it behind her back, said she was constantly reminding everyone that she was an Imperator.

Perhaps a few months ago, Joan would've avoided such clothing to deprive them of something to snicker at, but now, she no longer cared. They'd always find something weird about her to talk about. If not even half the college burning down could distract them from indulging in petty comments, nothing could.

But it didn't matter anymore. The year was finally over.

It seemed strange to her, just thinking about it. She was still processing everything that had happened, but the one thought that kept returning, no matter how hard she tried to bury it, was the moment she'd shoved Rich into the creek: The rage searing through her, the catharsis of that push, and finally, the way she'd felt staring down the embankment, thinking he was dead.

It was just an accident, she'd told herself. That very night she'd begun drilling it into her head as she brushed her teeth, repeating it over and over. *You didn't mean to kill him.*

And, as luck would have it, she hadn't. Ferguson confessed that she'd been the one to drown him. Rich probably would've gotten off with only a few bruises and maybe a concussion otherwise. He would've been able to accuse Joan of assault just like he planned. In a way, Ferguson had done her a favor.

But still, she couldn't shake one memory from that night. For just a second—Joan assured herself it couldn't have been more—as she'd gazed down at Rich's body, a gloating smile had come to her lips.

Then the realization of what she'd done finally dawned on her. She'd turned and ran, more horrified with herself than she'd ever been in her life.

All that matters is that you didn't kill him. Joan swallowed. She just had to be more careful. There could be no more mistakes going forward.

Her phone buzzed as she neared the base of the college's hill. Matt had texted her: *Want to go for a walk?*

She replied, *Sure. Where?*

When his next message came, her entire body tensed.

He immediately sent another text: *I understand if you don't want to. I just thought it might help put it all behind you. For good.*

Joan hesitated, chewing a fingernail. Then she typed back, *No, you're right.*

She stared up at the trees, closed her eyes, and exhaled.

It was just an accident...

◆

Bethune's Walk was empty save for the hint of a spring breeze wafting through the trees.

Matt watched her with concern as they approached the bridge. During her visits to him in the hospital in Canmore, he sensed something was still eating away at her. She hid it behind her relief at his recovery, keeping their conversations to lighter topics. But once he was discharged, and they spent several nights taking it easy at the Chalet with Roy and Val, he began to realize something was very wrong. The concussion the Bard had given her wasn't the only problem in her head. He recognized the way she seemed lost in thought only to snap back to happiness all too well. And it wasn't hard to guess what weighed her down.

"You still feel guilty," he said as they walked to the highest point.

She didn't answer him right away. Instead, she went to the railing and looked out, not down into the creek but up toward Radcliffe, visible through the branches. WCU had scrambled to get hotel rooms for Cliffe students in Canmore proper; shuttle buses ferried them back to campus for their exams. The residences had yet to be declared safe and there was easily millions of dollars of damage done to the building. There had been talk of reconstructing it exactly the way it was before, but a proposal for a modernist update to the college—to be seamlessly integrated with the undamaged portions of the structure—had apparently been gaining traction among the alumni. Both Joan's mother and Roy's father, staunch Radcliffe traditionalists, were even starting to warm to the idea. The new Galbraith would feel like a twenty-first century cathedral, with more glass and right angles. The West Quad would be repaved and Bowman would be gutted and refurbished into something more minimalist and modern, while retaining an older look on its exterior.

This proposal had the support of acting Provost Sarah Knowles, who was sure to be confirmed into the official position by the end of the summer. The concept sketches had been put together quickly, with WCU eager to begin construction as soon as possible. Still, work would probably last through most of the next school year and even into next summer, if not longer. In her statement, emailed to current students, alumni, and benefactors, Knowles wrote, "It is time to move Radcliffe forward while respecting its past."

Normally, Matt disliked when historic buildings were destroyed to construct new ones. However, in this case he wouldn't have minded if they bulldozed the entire college and started anew. Part of him was sad more of it hadn't been damaged by the fires.

Though he didn't consider himself superstitious, he wondered if some of the evil had been burned out of Radcliffe. Only time would tell.

Joan finally let her eyes drift down to the creek, the water running gently beneath them. "I still caused all of it," she said softly. "I shouldn't have let him get to me."

He shook his head and put a hand on her shoulder. "The whole thing was a set up—"

"And I played right into it. If Ferguson didn't kill him after I pushed him down there, Rich would've won. He would've gone back to the police and told them I left him for dead. His little false flag would've worked. There would've been the huge Anathema scandal he dreamed of, with himself as the victim." She turned to Matt, holding back tears. "And the first time I realized that, I was *glad* she murdered him. Ferguson cleaned up my own mess. And before she could destroy me, I killed her. Now I have you, I'm an Imperator, and everyone thinks I'm innocent. Not even the RCMP knows the whole truth—I told them Rich tried to grab me and *that's* why I pushed him." A drop rolled down across her scar and she swallowed. "They both tried to ruin my life and now they're dead while I have everything. And I only succeeded because of the blood on my hands."

He hugged her. "You are worth so much more than either of them, Joan. They were horrible people. They put you through something terrible and you never deserved that. You're only letting them win—fuck, you're only letting *Radcliffe* win if you think that. *You* won. *We* won. It's over."

Joan buried her face in his shoulder, digging her fingers into his back; he didn't mind. The breeze had picked up and a chill was in the air, but as Matt closed his eyes and leaned his head against hers, there was no place in the world he'd rather be. They stood there for some time, him rubbing her back as she quietly sobbed. A bewildered student passed them by, but Matt paid him no attention. Eventually the crying stopped, but she kept her face pressed against his jacket, breathing slowly and quietly.

He looked up at the trees. "It was never your fault, Joan. This college always tries to make you think it's your fault, but that's how it gets you. Don't let it."

She pulled back and looked up at him, her eyes red and puffy, mascara trailing down her cheeks. "You helped me even before you thought I was innocent. I believed I'd murdered Rich, and when I told you, you helped me anyway."

"Well, I had been about to kill myself a couple minutes earlier. I figured, what have I got to lose?"

Seeing her horrified expression, he kissed her and said, "I'm joking! I would've defended you anyway and I'm very glad I didn't go through with it. There's a lot of things I would've missed…like reading your novella. I finished it last night."

Joan swallowed. "Oh, what did you…?"

"I loved it! Honestly, I really like your style and I think you should keep writing."

She blushed again. "Thank you… I guess this college has given me a fair bit of source material…" She managed a laugh.

Matt nodded. "Sometimes truth is stranger than fiction."

"Yeah…" Her voice trailed off again. They were silent for a moment, then she remembered something. "Logan says hello, by the way."

Matt raised an eyebrow. "He still afraid of you?"

She laughed again, then sniffed. "Seems to be."

"How's his battle scar holding up?"

"He says it's alright." She looked back toward the college. "I'm glad he managed to save the Archives. There wasn't too much damage. At least to our stuff."

"Yeah." He joined her, staring at the building. When he glanced back to her, she seemed to be on the edge of sadness again. He didn't want her to slip back into it. "Seemed like the RCMP were pretty shocked after they listened to the recording."

The Bard's hunting knife matched the fatal wounds on Chet's corpse. His phone and wallet were found in the Dean's Suite, stashed in the false-bottom of a locked drawer, with texts to her over an encrypted messaging app luring him to his death. Ferguson had kept file after file of meticulous notes on Anathema and its membership on a hard drive, which she'd hidden inside a hollowed-out book on her shelf; it also contained hundreds of audio recordings from Mustard's phone tap system.

Her dog, Adam, had been adopted by the new Provost.

Joan nodded. "Staff Sgt. Wright told me she had a feeling I didn't do it

549

and one of the others—Beckman, I think—actually apologized. He'd been pushing me as the killer of both Rich and Chet for months."

"That guy from Vancouver—Sgt. Dorval—told me that in all the cases he's dealt with, he'd never seen anything like this."

"Radcliffe is...a unique place." She sniffed again.

"Yeah." He sighed. "Turland was right when he told me there's a world outside this college, though." He gestured to the mountain behind them, beyond the forest. "I mean, look at all of this. Next year I think we should get out and explore more of it. We've still got a year left."

"A year left *here*." She leaned closer and kissed him. "I've got a feeling you and I are just getting started."

At this, he was relieved. It seemed like she was finally starting to feel better.

"Are you coming to Phoenix this summer? I'd really love to show you around. And we're both legal in the States now."

"Yeah." She smiled and wiped some of the mascara trails away, her face brightening as she continued to talk. "You should come to Toronto, too. You can meet Adeline, and we'll go to the ROM and the CN Tower and the parks—and oh, I'm a member of a yacht club on the island. We can go there. It's beautiful in the summer."

"I'd love to."

She turned back to the college and her mood faltered. "And then we'll be back here..." She glanced at him. "A lot of our friends are graduating. As if next year wasn't going to be different enough already."

Randall, Patrick, Roy, and Turland all seemed exhausted and ready to put Radcliffe in the rear-view mirror. Randall looked ready to collapse the last time he came to the Chalet, when he'd said goodbye to both him and Joan. Matt doubted he'd see any of them around campus before the Second Sermon next year. He wondered how many of them he would keep in touch with over the years—certainly Roy at the least. But between roping her into the snitch mess and his actions through the rest of the year, Joan seemed rather tired of Randall. Matt wasn't sure what to feel about him anymore either.

"Yeah, but at least Tanner, Val, and Sophia will still be around. And I'm really looking forward to living with you in the Chalet."

She smiled. "I'm officially the tenant now. The alumni trust made it official yesterday. We're all set to move in when we come back." She threw him a glance. "Hopefully, we can christen the bed before then..."

"I didn't have anything else planned for tonight."

She gave him a playful nudge.

He grinned. "And I'm very, very excited for your Sermons. I know they're gonna be great."

Joan laughed. "You're just saying that to cheer me up." One side of her smile rose higher.

"No, I mean it," Matt said. "They're the only things about Anathema I'm looking forward to next year."

That was a little franker than he'd intended. Joan pulled back, a somber look returning. She bit her nail, then said, "Matt, can I ask you a question? You don't have to answer right away."

"Of course."

She put both hands on his shoulders. "Do you hate Anathema?"

He paused, but deep down he knew the answer immediately.

"No. I'll always be grateful for it," he said slowly. "I'll always love it."

Matt turned his head and gazed up the hill, the upper portions of the tower visible even from here. It stood tall above Radcliffe, its spire the highest point for quite some distance. "Anathema made this college worth coming to. It's how I met my friends. It made me feel like I finally belonged to something. But most importantly…"

He looked at her again. The wind blew hair across her face and Matt gently swept the strands away, his fingers brushing across her scar. "It brought me to you."

Joan grabbed his shoulders tightly and froze, her mouth hanging open, her eyes cast down. She was suddenly tense and troubled, as if she had something to confess. Worry lanced through him and for a moment everything seemed to stand still. But, instead of speaking, she looked back up at him and gave the warmest smile he'd ever seen. And when Joan kissed him and pulled him close, Matt hoped she would never tell him what she had been about to say.

AUTHOR'S NOTE

If you are feeling sad, depressed, or are having suicidal thoughts, please contact the National Suicide Prevention Lifeline at 1-800-273-8255.

You are not alone and you will get through this.

ABOUT THE AUTHOR

James Cosgrave grew up in New Mexico but now lives in Vancouver, British Columbia with his fiancé and his dog. *Anathema* is his first novel.